OPERATION ORION

BY

HULTA GERTRUDE

Copyright © HULTA GERTRUDE 2017
This book is sold subject to the condition that it shall not, by way of trade or otherwise, be lent, resold, hired out, or otherwise circulated without the publisher's prior consent in any form of binding or cover other than that in which it is published and without a similar condition including this condition being imposed on the subsequent publisher.
The moral right of HULTA GERTRUDE has been asserted.
ISBN-13: 978-1541012653
ISBN-10: 1541012658

I wish to dedicate this work to my family and friends for their much needed support.

CONTENTS

PART ONE *Enemy Interests* 1
PART TWO *The Sisterhood of the Light* 119
PART THREE *Surplus Distrust* 229
PART FOUR *The Orion Observatory* 341
PART FIVE *Loose Ends* 460

This is a work of fiction. Names, characters, businesses, organizations, places, events and incidents either are the product of the author's imagination or are used fictitiously. Any resemblance to actual persons, living or dead, events, or locales is entirely coincidental.

PART ONE

Enemy Interests

Green against the black. Foreign, new and intriguing. A planet. It had been hidden by the shrouds of distance and acatalepsy but now revealed to all. Information travels faster than light, more: information gives light its direction. Information shows light where to shine and when. Things used to the dark shy away from the light because it is too bright for them to see. Far away in a corner, much like a shell, the new await the response of the others. This planet, although unknown to the rest of the galaxy, did not have a similar ignorance regarding the galaxy. It knew. And it stayed hidden for a reason. As, to some, the most terrifying thing in all sentient creation… is humankind.

***

"Scan complete," Kelvin said. His metallic voice had a grating quality that seemed to make his grey, armoured bodywork seem all the greyer. The cockpit was quiet, lit only by the controls. Kelvin was a machine – part android, part robot – performing the role of pilot. Despite the fact that Kelvin had only been fully functional for three days, he looked decades old. Cannibalised from used parts, assembled without a real plan, Kelvin was a completely unique machine. The cloaked figure, sitting next to him, shifted in her seat. Slowly she pulled her hood away, revealing her long red hair, tanned skin and narrow brown eyes. Her name was Satiah and she was a member of Phantom Squad.

Phantom Squad was a department in the Human Coalition. A secret service, made up of unnamed operatives who did whatever they were ordered to. These beings took on the most dangerous or secret assignments on a daily basis. They spied, murdered and deceived in the name of democracy. These covert agents were the best of the best in the business and were recognisable in public only by their trademark grey cloaks. Sometimes their simple attendance acted as a deterrent for those who wish to break the laws.

She stared out of the viewport at the ancient-looking space station before them. Dark silver against black.

"Well?" she asked, at last. Sometimes she wished her eyes could see things like computers could and she was *still* undecided about referring to Kelvin as a *him* or an *it*. She was not the type who usually bothered to name ships or assign a gender to their weaponry. Robots and computers were... different. For Satiah they embodied and demonstrated true loyalty. Unblemished by emotions or ulterior motives, they made the closest thing to a friend that Satiah could trust. Kelvin was not something she had found, bought or stolen, however... she'd *made* him. And that made him even more special to her. Him, it was.

"There are no life signs," he clarified, as she had expected he would.

"How long until the demolition charges activate?" she asked, standing slowly.

"Nineteen minutes and twenty seconds," Kelvin answered, also rising. Satiah, using a device on her wrist, started a nineteen-minute countdown. She already knew that the place was clear of demolition robots and their supervisors. She had even seen some of them leaving. Her orders meant that having the place to herself was vital. No one else was to know. She and Kelvin took the shuttle in closer. Normally no ships would be allowed to go within the detonation zone. Their small shuttle was cloaked, rendering it completely undetectable.

"All security is offline," Kelvin went on. "Life support systems are still in operation."

"Convenient," she acknowledged, without surprise. As the place was about to be destroyed there seemed no point in keeping anything switched on; on the other hand, as the place was about to be destroyed, why bother to deactivate anything? The question seemed vaguely paradoxical to Satiah but did it matter? Was there something significant in the fact that nothing had been turned off? A lifetime of opportunism told her to take advantage of it. They docked with the space station and were quick to disembark. The ramp lowered and Satiah leapt out. She was eager not to waste time.

The signs of entropy were many and varied. The corrosion of the passing of time was everywhere. Dereliction and negligence, brothers in the acts of degradation. Most of the lights were no longer operating, helping to create an atmosphere of claustrophobic gloom. The musty smell also added an air of abandonment to the place. Kelvin, on the two appendages that could be called arms, activated a light on each. Clicking as they rotated, three barrels on his left arm emerged.

"You won't need your flame thrower," Satiah said, even though she was the one who had programmed him to activate it.

"Precautionary," Kelvin buzzed, at her. She glanced at her countdown. Fifteen minutes.

"Come on," she ordered, running ahead of him. His posture skeletal and untidy, he followed her. His metal limbs were encased in rubber and that deadened the sound of his running feet. Satiah was checking the numbers on the doors they ran past.

Twelve. Thirteen. Fourteen. The numbers were displayed in thick white print. This was partly done because it was cheap and partly because it was effective. Even in the partial darkness, it was clear which room was which. They reached door twenty-seven. Satiah stopped, not even breathless. She was a Phantom agent and as such was incredibly lithe. Indeed, some considered her exceptional among the exceptional. Of one thing she was sure: her past was as dark as her future.

"Get it open," she instructed, motioning to the sealed door with mild frustration. Her voice was both aristocratic and sharp, cutting through the ether like a blade wrought from ice. It was how she wanted to sound, when in control of an operation, strong. Sometimes though her voice could be melodic, rich and smooth. Kelvin, his right appendage clicking as a laser burner slid smoothly out into view, began his work on the door. After losing her last computer on a recent mission, Satiah had really done her best with Kelvin. She was good with robots, often preferring them to people, and had made the effort on Kelvin. A robot for any occasion.

Smoke emerged in time with a pulsing sound as he began to cut through the metal door. As the metal was burned away it became molten and red. Satiah kept watch pointlessly. It was out of habit. She knew they were alone and that no one had been on that station for the best part of half an hour. Nevertheless, many years of covert operations had made her compulsive about monitoring her surroundings as often as possible. Another word would be paranoid. Kelvin was making good progress. She eyed the time. Ten minutes. While he was cutting, she gave some thought as to what this space station had once been. Operational for nearly three hundred years, it had been owned by the government and used as a storage facility officially. Unofficially it had doubled as a prison, laboratory and hospital, whenever needed. There were literally thousands of storage areas. Each was numbered in the pale white, anonymous lettering. And now, its time was over. It was being demolished. The new government no longer needed nor wanted it.

And Satiah knew it was just one of many such facilities being quietly disposed of. Balan Orion's military legacy was one that a lot of people wanted to forget. Kelvin stopped and stepped back. With an echoic clang, the majority of the door slid forwards and landed heavily on the metal floor. Satiah wasted not a second as she stepped into the smoky blackness beyond and Kelvin, lights flashing, followed her in gawkily. It took a few moments for the smoke to clear but when it did it was obvious that only one thing was inside. Something Satiah had not expected to find. When she had been given her orders, she'd been expecting to find *plans*. Schematics. A map, or technical data perhaps. Some kind of documentation did seem the most likely thing she would find. A body on the other hand... seemed an odd thing to come across. Other than that the room was wholly empty. He was wearing a worn bodysuit with a company logo across his back. It read: *Jaylite Industries*.

Six minutes.

"Satiah?" asked Kelvin, awaiting instructions.

She glanced at him. "It seems my previous scan was inaccurate. The reading he presents must have been shielded by the door," Satiah muttered, as she checked the man. He was alive and apparently just insensible. There was nothing else either on him or around him. No computers, no plans... nothing.

"We must be going," she said, making a decision. "Help me with him." Satiah and Kelvin between them carried the unconscious man along the decaying corridor. His feet dragged along behind them making a scuffing sound.

"This find does not seem to be within the parameters we estimated," Kelvin announced. Satiah raised an eyebrow. He almost sounded displeased. The hairs on the back of her neck rose and made her feel... tingly. Where was the danger?

"I hope they don't ask me to bring him back," she deadpanned, imagining Randal dismissing her find like someone presented with food that they didn't order. It would be impossible to return the man to a destroyed space station.

"Don't move!" shouted someone from behind them. There it was! Kelvin and Satiah leapt to opposite sides of the corridor instinctively. Kelvin was still dragging the unconscious man along. This would not only present their attackers with more than one target but it would give them both more room to operate. Four minutes! Satiah had her personalised pistol in her hand in a rapid, well-practised, reflex action. Most people would jump when startled, she would pull her gun. Shots rang out, striking the walls around them. Sparks flew. Laser fire on metal.

"Detecting three life readings," Kelvin said to her. She nodded then pointed to the inert man he was still conveying.

"Get him back to the ship, I'll hold them off!" she ordered, returning fire. Someone else must have been in hiding here, or else they had sneaked in like she and Kelvin had done. She'd felt no changes in air pressure, nor had she heard any sound or noticed typical vibrations. Yet this station was vast. She watched, while crouched, as Kelvin lifted the man over his angular metallic back and hurried away.

Three minutes. Satiah rolled across the floor to get to the other side of the corridor, firing as she went. She could not see her assailants and she didn't want to assume that they couldn't see her. Pressed against the wall she utilised what cover there was to its full. From her belt she unclipped a fist-sized grey cylinder. It was a portable power container. PPC. She flung it in their direction, aimed and closed her eyes as she pulled the trigger. There was a blinding flash and cries of pain and confusion from their direction. The energy had exploded the instant it was hit by the laser bolt, shining as brightly as any laser and much more destructively. Rolling to the original side of the corridor once more, Satiah took aim and concentrated. Breathe, wait for a target. *Wait for a target.* A figure loomed among the shadows. She put them to the floor with two bolts to the head. She knew she only needed one but there was no harm in being sure. As clean as a kill ever could be.

One minute, twenty-three seconds. She began the inevitable sprint towards her ship, making the presumption that blind men would not give chase. No one was following – no one she could see, anyway - although there were a few wild shots. Up the ramp she stumbled, into her ship as Kelvin powered up the engines. She reached the cockpit, breathless, at last. A thump indicated that the ramp was sealed closed.

"Where's the man?" she asked, noting the absence instantly. Escape seemed impossible but madder things had happened.

"Your cabin," he answered. She rolled her eyes but said nothing. It was the location of the only bed in the ship. She rarely used it, preferring to sleep in the pilot or co-pilot's seat. Ten seconds. The ship jolted forwards, picking up speed fast. Part of Satiah ached to pilot herself, she loved going fast, it made her smile.

"Faster," she ordered, through her teeth. She strapped herself in and braced for the inevitable turbulence. Engines roared in response to Kelvin's enforced motivation. Being in space, there was no sound of the explosion but about one second after the detonation, the ship was buffeted violently by billions of tiny particles flying into them from the blast.

The ship shook and Satiah remembered that it was nothing when compared to pod-diving through a planet's atmosphere with delayed retro bursts. Her stomach fluttered at just the memory of that. Fiery dots enveloped them as the shields dissolved the tiny fragments instantaneously. No damage was done. The shields saw to that. Satiah allowed herself to relax and activated the scanners. As expected, the space station was gone. A few larger chunks of debris were still spinning away in three directions. More importantly no one had noticed them. And, most crucially of all, there were no signs of pursuit. Pursuit from *anyone*.

"Any data on our mystery attackers?" she asked, standing.

"Three males, tallest six-two and shortest five-ten. Standard laser rifles, probably procured from pirate operatives," Kelvin answered. "Their timing and presence brings into question both our secrecy and their purpose." She nodded, she'd programmed Kelvin well. He thought exactly like she did.

"Get us back to Earth, Kelvin," she smiled, coldly. "I'll see to our guest."

***

Tabre waited at the restaurant table, watching as all the beings went about their business. Always dressed immaculately, Tabre wore a dark green velvet jacket over a grey silk shirt. His trousers, shiny grey, were pressed and had a knifelike crease down the front of each leg. His boots, polished to the point of mirror-like clarity, were a leathery composite material only the richest wore. They were renowned for the durability and elegance at once. His left hand bore three silver rings, each with an emerald in to match his jacket. His face was nondescript, or it would have been were it not for the golden tooth that shone each time he smiled. His brown eyes watched ceaselessly. At last, the operative had arrived.

A middle-aged woman sat down opposite him dressed for business.

"We know you are currently on leave, apologies," she said, not sounding as if she was. Tabre didn't care. He could already see the folder she had concealed in the pages of a newsreel she had carried with her. He smiled, his golden tooth gleaming as he did. Then he motioned to his own drink. A shot of the finest liquor, *Homely Deputy*, one of the most expensive drinks on the common market. Though not strong in alcoholic terms it was renowned as one of the tastiest brews in the universe. The gesture was an offer to her but she shook her head. He lifted the glass to his lips and took in the sweet scent slowly. It was a drink, in his opinion, that had to be savoured.

"Go on," he said, his voice soft and almost melodic.

She pulled out the folder and he almost winced. She was just an office worker, clearly not used to clandestine measures. What did she really do? File reports? What had happened to Wendy? He'd liked her, she knew how to be inconspicuous. Now who had he got?!

"An assignment?" he asked, eyeing the folder with distain. "Must be urgent."

"We would not have requested you to return if otherwise," she answered, as he had expected. After making sure no one else was paying them an undue amount of attention he flicked open the file. After taking in its contents, during a surreptitious sweep, he closed it again and his eyes rose to make contact with hers. He downed the drink in a swift move.

"Consider it done."

***

Earth, in its third incarnation, stood at the centre, albeit not astronomically, of the Coalition. The Coalition, technically the *Human* Coalition, was one of the three great super powers which governed all modern societies. The Coalition, the Colonial Federation and the Nebula Union. Earth itself, a giant cityscape, where the skyscrapers were more numerous than blades of grass in a field, was where billions called home. Satiah loved the view, especially at night. People meant crowds and crowds were places where she could hide herself. Kelvin was guarding the man they had... rescued? If that was the right word. Satiah was flying the last leg of the journey herself. It was always good to keep one's piloting skills sharp. And... it felt good to make your own way through the stars. Coming through the atmosphere she gave no codes to the automated computers checking arrivals.

Her code, like that of all Phantoms, was unlisted. She weaved between the traffic lanes, speedily making the short journey to Phantom Command. A shot of nostalgia hit her... she'd made this trip so many times. Not so long ago she questioned if she could ever make it again... legally. Satiah's history was not exactly long or complicated but it was a burden. Her boss, Phantom Leader Randal, knew she had been *associated with* the Vourne conspiracy. Vourne had been the previous Phantom Leader and, to put it briefly, he had become a criminal. He had promised Satiah that she could have his position of Phantom Leader when he took command of the whole Coalition. Due to one thing or another, Vourne had failed and she had helped him flee to safety.

In the end, despite successfully faking his own death and getting away relatively unscathed, Vourne had not survived. Satiah herself had killed him, even after going to all the trouble of saving and hiding him. She'd murdered him in cold blood when he had refused to stay hidden. He was smarting from his defeat and anxious to make another bid for power or, failing that, revenge. Satiah had known he would have expected her to lay her life on the line for him again. This second time had proved too much for her. So... to ensure her own involvement remained concealed... she had killed him. Ironically enough she had not regretted it for long. She had presumed all was lost and she would be hiding forever from the Coalition. That was when Randal, unaware of her involvement, had invited her back to Phantom Squad. She had been so happy. No longer was she a traitor... she was a Phantom again.

No one knew the truth about her. And naturally, she could never tell anyone about Vourne. Indeed, he was just one of many secrets she had but he was one of the weightier ones. She could never shake the feeling that someone would discover her role in events eventually and then she would be hounded to the ends of the universe. Until that time though she would work for Randal.

"Phantom Satiah," came a man's voice.

"Reporting in," she answered, her voice low.

"Hatch forty," he replied, and cut off. She spied the opening hatch into a tiny hangar area, built for one ship only, and sped towards it. The area was otherwise bare and empty, suited to containment and threat-control as it was. There had been times when Phantom Headquarters had played host to new and deadly viruses which had been contained, eradicated, or used from time to time. Also an attack was always a contingency that no security facility forgot.

The man, her cargo? Her patient? Her prisoner? Well, whatever he was, he had awoken about an hour away from Earth but seemed unable to talk. Satiah had *tried* to interrogate him. First she had attempted to just talk. To have a conversation with him. They would both surely have many questions for each other but he seemed almost catatonic. He never said a word and just stared at her... unnervingly. Satiah was not a naturally patient woman and so she had quickly resorted to other less civilised methods. First she had tried electrocution, hoping that little shocks would get a response. When that didn't work she'd moved onto chemicals. Chemistry, like robotics, was an interest of hers and she was not afraid of using home-made aids while on a mission. Yet, frustratingly, despite her normally effective endeavours, the man remained creepily zombielike. She'd ran out of time eventually and had just locked him up, making a mental note that she might get another chance later should Randal allow it.

There was something just not right about that man. Brain death was a possibility. This was of course assuming he was a normal man. He would need to be properly medically examined. Just looking into those cold blue eyes made Satiah's skin crawl and she was not easily cowed. Those who took lives could not usually be intimidated by being stared at. Well, Satiah couldn't. Yet *this man*... She put him out of her mind, well, as far away as she could, as she mustered herself for Randal's questioning. Kelvin had hold of one of the man's wrists and was leading him down the entrance ramp. Satiah locked up after them before the three of them made their way through the maze of busy corridors to Randal's office. She shook off the fact that the last time she had been inside the headquarters, Vourne had still been alive and in charge of the whole organisation.

She admonished herself inwardly. Dwelling on the past was psychologically redundant. The door swished open revealing a bearded man at a desk beyond. They entered after receiving a wave of invitation from him. Randal. Phantom Leader Randal. He was a man of average size but great skill. Maintaining the exterior of calm, quiet disinterest, he had been overlooked by his enemies all too often.

"Satiah," he smiled, his eyes focussing on the man she had brought him.

"Randal," she acknowledged. "I found him in area twenty-seven. There was nothing else and the station was demolished shortly afterwards."

"What have you done to him?" Randal asked, a little sternness creeping into his tone. Satiah sighed, she knew he wouldn't like this.

"Nothing permanent," she stated, honestly. He scowled at her, wanting more information. "I had expected to find information in that storage area. Plans, technical documents not... a person. As you would expect I assumed that he must have what you want in his mind. I tried to extract it from him but he doesn't seem able to talk so..."

"You turned to violence?" he growled, presumptuously.

"He is unharmed," she said, between her teeth. "He was unconscious when I found him and hasn't uttered a word since he regained it. The man was probably a vegetable long before I got hold of him." Randal let out a breath as he thought about it.

"Well... *whatever, this* will have to wait, something else has risen to my attention," he said, not exactly mollified. He handed her a file and she took it.

"What's this?" she asked, curious.

"*Your* trainee's file," he answered, with a grin. She cursed inwardly. Randal was assigning her someone new to *mentor*. Since the Vourne conspiracy, when a lot of Phantoms had died, personnel were at an all-time low and they were struggling to teach the recruits. Satiah had made it clear that she didn't want to teach anyone. She preferred the freedoms that she had. A cadet tagalong would only slow her down and... potentially expose her. She had her own rules that might not go down well in a more public forum.

"I work alone," she argued, without much conviction in her tone. If he already had the file it was likely he'd already decided this. Plus, making too much fuss might expose her too. She was trapped into this!

"Not this time and, *this time*, you are being reassigned," Randal informed her. She groaned openly, as any agent would.

"...You said that discovering if this weapon existed was *urgent*," Satiah reminded him.

"Well, this is *more urgent*," he replied, almost like he was being funny.

"*If everything is urgent then nothing is*," she mumbled, under her breath.

He handed her another file just as two other Phantoms entered. They took the mute man's arms as they led him out. Satiah made a gesture, informing Kelvin not to try to stop them.

"Your crew are ready," Randal said, eyeing her.

"*Crew?*" she questioned, almost scared.

"Your cadet and another. Both will accompany you on this mission." What? Was he deliberately trying to make her life a misery? She'd gone from a lone agent to a group operative in less than a second and she didn't like it.

"What mission?" she asked, impatiently. "What could possibly be more urgent than trying to find Balan's secret weapon?"

"A new planet has been discovered and it is populated by an alien race. You are being sent on a diplomatic mission to the world in order to provide protection for our ambassador while he tries to get them to join the Coalition," Randal explained.

"*Randal,*" she groaned, trying to persuade him. "*You know me.* You know where my talents lie and they are *not* in diplomacy."

"Maybe the cadet is not the only one who will learn something then," he remarked, frostily. "You will leave immediately."

"What about my other mission?" she hissed, aggravated.

"I promise that that will still be here when you get back," Randal said, and meant it. "You are *the only agent* I have *available*, Satiah, it's you or no one." Hiding her inner anger and restraining the urge to strangle him, she smiled tightly.

"Fine," she allowed, turning to leave. She wasn't even being given the chance to return home. Not that she wanted to return to the tiny apartment she occasionally graced with her presence. But it would be nice to be given the option! In any case her last assignment was nowhere even close to done! She knew she could trust Randal to leave her prisoner alone but the longer she left him the more time he had to prepare himself. And she had research to do!

As she walked with Kelvin in tow, she read the first message Randal had written her. And now she'd been lumbered with a cadet *and* a diplomat! Technically, although she hated to admit it, it was part of her job and she supposed she couldn't have continued her work alone indefinitely. She reached her ship again to find it being loaded up with luggage. Two figures awaited her. One that, cloaked and fairly short, she guessed was the cadet. And the second was a middle-aged man who clocked her the second she entered with Kelvin.

"Ah, you must be Phantom Satiah, greetings," he said, coming over and going for her hand.

"Who are you?" she growled, rudely. He didn't seem in the least put off by her obvious hostility.

"I represent the Coalition as an embassy ambassador," he announced, with a theatrical flourish. "My name is Reed." Reed? Why did that name sound so familiar to Satiah? She produced a fractured-looking smile in response.

"I understand that there is only *one* cabin aboard the ship…?" he began, tentatively motioning at her craft.

"It's yours," she said, carelessly.

"Ah, *marvellous*," he smiled, pleased. With that he made his way aboard, seeming to talk to himself as he went. Great, an *eccentric*! That was all she needed! She couldn't stop herself from shaking her head as she turned to face the shorter cloaked male.

"Cadet Carlos," he said, from beneath his hood. His voice sounded young, probably mid-teens. She gave him an encouraging smile and removed his hood to see his face. He had short, spiky, dark hair and a face that indicated an original Earth far-eastern ancestry. His brown eyes were quick and intelligent-looking.

"Carlos, I am Satiah," she said, shaking his hand. "I'm your teacher for the foreseeable future. Get to the control room and prep the ship for take-off, run all the safety checks." He hurried away to obey.

She watched him go, Kelvin looming up behind her.

"Let me tell you the difference between a good and a bad feeling, Kelvin," she said, ice in her voice. "Don't you think it's thought-provoking how all Phantoms start out as communitarians but end up being libertarians? They are taught that the organisation is everything, yet they learn that the organisation cannot exist without them therefore it uses them?"

"What are they?" he asked, the concepts were unfamiliar to him. She'd not exactly bothered upgrading him with data on modern philosophy.

"Communitarianism is a viewpoint that highlights the connection between the individual and the community they live in. Libertarianism, on the other hand, is a kind of opposite philosophy. Basically, it is what it says and upholds liberty as its primary objective. Libertarians seek to make the most of self-sufficiency *and* freedom of choice," she explained, in brief. "What I'm saying is… when they are in training they are taught that we are a team. When they get out there they discover it's much more like every man for himself."

Kelvin remained silent, processing the information.

"And they *must* be desperate indeed to make *me* a teacher. *I'm the last person that should teach anyone*. Not only do I not have the skills to *effectively teach* but… the lessons Carlos is going to have to learn are cruel."

She sighed, looked at the floor for a moment and then turned to face him.

"You want an example of *the perfect Phantom*? Mensa wins every time if you ask me." Mensa was a Phantom who had infamously betrayed Vourne and had chased him across the galaxy with a relentlessness that had shaken even Vourne himself. He and Satiah had two things in common. They were both ruthless killers who should no longer be in Phantom Squad. And neither of them played by the rules.

"Get both Reed and Carlos on your files, so we can track them if we need to. And… *Just watch them, okay*?" she whispered, as she patted his thick metallic breastplate. He patted her shoulder softly as he began to move past her.

"I will," he buzzed down at her. Kelvin picked up her single bag containing the documents, with his left appendage, and then plodded up the ramp himself. Satiah remained outside thinking deeply. Did Randal have another reason for suspending her previous mission? Had he found something else? Had he actually found the weapon and was now trying to hide the fact that he had it?

She pushed that aside in her mind for now as she strode up the ramp. Reed was already in her cabin with Kelvin watching him. She went on by to the control room where she found Carlos. He bowed his head to her.

"All checks complete, we're good to go," he stated. She could tell that he was correct with a quick glance. "Do you want me to take us up?" he offered, a little uneasy.

"No, I'll do that," she said, settling herself in the pilot's seat.

"Is that robot *yours*?" he asked, talking about Kelvin.

"Yes," she replied, sending her clearance request to the departures office. "His name is Kelvin."

"If Reed's got *the only cabin*, where do we sleep?" Carlos asked, curious.

"In here," she replied, concentrating on other things.

"How long is...?" He cut himself off as she pulled an irate face at him. "Sorry."

She pulled out into traffic and then accelerated upwards, leaving Phantom Headquarters, Earth... all of it... far behind. There was something about flying that made her feel like a little girl again. Excited. She barrel-rolled the ship unnecessarily as they blasted through the atmosphere because she wanted to. She didn't let her pleasure show on her face though. After setting the course, she faced Carlos again.

"I've never taught anyone anything before so you will have to accept that this is a learning spree for both of us. Did Randal tell you anything about the mission or me before we met?" she asked, interested.

"I've never met the Phantom Leader. My supervisor before was Phantom Finch," he answered. Satiah considered, she didn't know Finch. Was that a good thing?

"Well, the first thing a Phantom usually does is work out their objectives. *Objective dictates action* just as *purpose dictates reaction*. Remember that and it will serve you well in most situations. Oh..." She paused and gave him a wide grin. "And don't forget to breathe."

He laughed, the tension easing a little. She had to build a good rapport with him, if nothing else it would make the time go faster.

"In this case, as you will find in most, objectives are easy to find as we have a mission document to read. I've thought about it and I have decided that the best thing will be for us to work through it *together*. One day you will be doing it alone but today, you've got help," she stated. He nodded, seeming eager enough. She pulled out the file that Randal had given her. Not the one about Carlos but the one about the mission. As she flicked it open, from the corridor the sound of music came from her cabin. It was string music of a swift tempo and Reed began whistling along cheerfully and somewhat tunelessly to it. Satiah rolled her eyes in irritation and closed the door. She had no time for Altstradum at the best of times. Altstradum was a renowned orchestra who famously toured the galaxy every few years, delivering tasteful alternative versions of classical pieces to the masses from their own personalised freighter. Satiah preferred the music of the subterranean variety but she rarely listened to anything for pleasure.

Everything in the written mission briefing pack was standard practice to both Satiah and Carlos. Nothing about it seemed out of place or anomalous. First was a set of coordinates which helpfully gave them their first objective. Go to the planet Yevanicha. Serial number: 95577784166. The second would be to make contact with the planet's leadership. The actual negotiations would be left to their resident diplomat Reed. Apart from that all they had to do was keep Reed safe.

"Sounds simple enough," Carlos noted.

"It does," she agreed, irritated that this had been assigned to *her*. She honestly felt that Carlos could do this on his own with only the smallest amount of supervision.

"What was your last mission like?" he asked, clearly a bit enthralled by her.

"Incomplete," she almost spat. She smiled quickly to prevent him being offended. "I can't really discuss it with you, I'm sorry."

He thought for a moment before asking another question.

"...What about your first ever mission then?" he asked, still interested. She cast her mind back and was shocked at how hard it was for her to remember.

"That was a termination assignment," she said, coldness entering her tone. "A Baron from a world where slavery was legal and he couldn't be touched by anyone else. So it was left to us to dispose of him in a way that would point no fingers."

"Did you free the slaves?" he asked, his question telling her how idealistic he still was. *Give him a few years,* she mused to herself.

"Not exactly," she answered, honestly. She was saved from more questions by the door when it opened.

Reed entered, almost dancing to the music as he approached them with three drinks on a tray.

"Hello there!" he bellowed at them. In a much quieter voice he asked, "Drink, anyone?" Carlos went to accept one but Satiah snatched his wrist adeptly.

"Phantoms don't drink intoxicants," Satiah answered, stony. Carlos hid his disappointment well enough.

"More for me then," Reed grinned, plonking himself down heavily in a chair behind them. A long silence began as Satiah and Carlos faced forwards and Reed downed the first of his three glasses. She began checking their progress and was horrified to discover that they had the best part of two days to go before they reached their destination. Two days of *this*? She already wanted to throw Reed out of the airlock. She jumped when she realised he was peering over her shoulder at the screen in front of her. She nearly pulled her gun on him.

"My apologies for startling you," he said, grinning at her. It was an odd grin, Satiah reasoned. It was not lascivious, sarcastic or mocking. Neither was it born of a natural idiocy nor nervousness nor obligatory etiquette. That only left... genuine. He was smiling because he was happy. Frankly she found that quite disturbing.

"Is there something you wanted?" she asked, crisply.

"Well," he whispered, before clearing his throat meaningfully. "I've read *my* file and I'm assuming *you have read yours* so *I thought* we could compare notes, you know? Make sure they tally with one another."

"We are acting as your security for a diplomatic mission to..." She paused, and then checked the file. "...*Yevanicha*."

"That's *great*," he agreed, in apparent delight. "Do you have any questions?"

"No," Satiah replied, turning her back on him.

"Who discovered it?" Carlos piped up, eyeing Reed. Carlos was referring to the planet.

"Now that is a shrewd question, um...?" Reed smiled, and indicated that he didn't know Carlos's name.

"Carlos," Carlos said, shaking Reed's hand.

"Yes, very shrewd, one could almost say *significant*," Reed went on, sipping at his fruit beer. Satiah could smell it.

"My question?" Carlos asked, not entirely sure what Reed was rambling about.

"Of course *someone* must always be *first* when discovering something, *mustn't they*? Don't you find it interesting how neither my file nor yours notes who exactly discovered this planet? Or even *when* they discovered it?" Reed went on. Satiah wasn't really listening but the question he was asking did, for some reason, make her wonder too. She kept silent though, willing both Reed and Carlos to follow her example. This was going to be a *long* journey!

Later when Reed had gone to rest or work or *whatever* he was doing, Carlos drifted off. He was having trouble sleeping in the co-pilot's chair. Satiah, after many years' experience of doing it, regarded it as an art form. After checking that he was asleep she activated her communicator. She had to get hold of someone back on Earth, there was something she had deliberately left out of her report to Randal and that was Jaylite Industries. They changed the clothes of the man they found, as part of the decontamination process, and Satiah had kept the original clothes they found him in.

"Satiah?" came a sleepy voice, on her communicator.

"Rainbow." She smiled, almost fondly. "How are you?"

"Right now, worried about this call, is it encrypted?" asked the man on the other end.

"Of course not," she lied, with a grin. A heavy sigh was the instant response.

"What do you want?" he asked, knowing she never called just to be sociable.

"I need you to do some research for me, I will be out of contact range for a while, not sure how long, in the meantime I need you to look into something. Namely Jaylite Industries. I want you to find out everything you can about them," she instructed.

"Ok Satiah, I'll start now. Security rating?" he asked, serious.

"Urgent," Satiah replied, without hesitation. Then she gave her Phantom code. "And Rainbow? This stays between us."

***

Ruby turned quickly to get an answer out of Ash only to find that he had mysteriously vanished. She swore! That was the third time he'd wandered off like that while she was talking to him. How rude! She spotted him standing a short distance away, staring at some items that were on a stall for sale. She approached him, annoyed.

"*Hey*!" she yammered up at him. Ash eyed her quickly before refocussing on the items. "I was talking to you back then and you just meandered off! *Again*! I'm starting to think you have no interest in *anything* I'm saying *whatsoever*."

"Wouldn't want you to think that," he answered, still not looking at her. She scowled up at him and then turned to regard what he was looking at.

"What are these things?" he asked her.

"Identity display units," she answered, sulkily.

He gave a grunt of understanding, seeming to lose interest completely, and started heading for the departures area. Ruby, confused and frustrated, scampered to keep up. They were in a vast spaceport, crammed with beings of all kinds travelling the vast reality they called a universe. This particular branch was in the dominion of the Nebula Union. It had been two weeks since Ruby had begged Ash to take her with him. Her fascination with Ash had only grown since then. He was an immortal, one of only a few remaining as far as she knew. He was so mysterious and brooding. Despite agreeing to let her go with him he seemed to not care remotely about her. Yet sometimes she'd catch him watching her. She had been dodging angry calls from her family and employers for two weeks now. They knew she was alive and well but she'd not told them where she was, why she'd gone or who she was with. She knew that her parents were angry and had people searching for her. And her boss was mad at her for deleting ten years' worth of financial details by accident.

Yet this was a great opportunity to see the universe and interact with an immortal. And also, though Ruby never admitted it, she always ran away when she could. It was so much easier than fighting.

"Where are we going *next?*" she called up at him.

"Do you really want to know?" He grinned, playfully. His voice was low, almost a growl.

"If I didn't want to know I wouldn't ask, you duffer!" she protested. She'd taken to calling him that a few days ago and relished the fact that he didn't understand what it meant.

"Magnovastar," he said, pointing to the departures screen. "It's on the edge of the known galaxy and apparently very beautiful."

"The *edge?*" she asked, thinking about it. "That's like, a week away by transporter?" It wasn't from where they were but part of her mind still thought as if she was on Earth.

"A week," he repeated, with amused contempt. "A week is *only* seven of your days."

"But why go and see it when we can see a recording of it?" Ruby asked, mildly remonstrating. He lifted her chin and she stared into those brown eyes, which could make her tremble all over.

"Would you rather use your own eyes or someone else's, human?" he asked, level and weighty.

She tried to answer but couldn't find the words.

"Why is it that for one who never stops talking, answering that question is not possible?" he asked, softly.

Because when you look at me like that, she thought, *it's all I can do not to kiss you.*

"I... I was just thinking," she said, colour rushing to her face. He let her go and eyed her speculatively.

"You humans are unpredictable," he stated, pointing an accusing finger at her. Before she could answer that, he was already moving on. She followed quickly as they went with the rest of the passengers towards the cruiser. Scanned and registered, they entered the craft.

"Did you get us a big room?" she asked, interested.

"I got you one, I don't need one," he reminded her.

"Oh yes, I keep forgetting you don't sleep," she remarked, her eyebrows rising as she sighed. "What's that like, exactly?"

"Exhausting," he remarked, clearly deadpanning. Ruby spotted a dance for that evening being advertised on a revolving holographic projector and nudged him.

"*Hey look*, do you think we could get something for me to wear?" she asked, enthusiastic. He turned and looked her up and down with significance.

"These will *not* do," she stated, guessing what he was about to suggest. With a longsuffering sigh, he handed her a large sum of Essps. They were tiny, about half palm sized, most of the detail was for computer scan only.

"See what you can find," he instructed, dismissively. "You have room seventy-eight."

"Where will you be?" she asked, genuinely curious.

"Over there," he said, motioning to the large wall-long viewport. Ruby watched him go. He spent such a long time staring at things. Out of viewports, at plants, people and planets. What did he *see*? What did he really think about her race?

Ash's gaze flickered between stars. Two weeks ago, with the reluctant permission of everyone else, he'd set off on a journey. Unlike any other journey he had been on before, this one had no clear end in sight. Curiosity was a strange motivation for an immortal, he knew. These humans were so complicated. They were a testament to diversity within diversity. At times they fascinated, bored, irritated and confused him. Dreda, his mother, had told him that if he was to work with humans he had to learn them. Understand them. Respect them. He'd learned much over the last two weeks. Ruby was interesting and clearly had more to her than he'd already discovered. Yet she could also be very... stupid, for want of a better word. And, ironically enough she often accused him of being stupid too. He supposed that that irony was lost on her – stupidly.

This was only the start of his journey and even he could not know what else he would discover. He'd decided, early on, on this journey, that he would probably learn more if didn't use his own ship. He left to chance his physical destination: gambling on learning more during the process of getting there than when he arrived. And, bizarrely, this idea seemed to be working. He'd already learned the whole Spatial Transport Schedule (STS) and identified the areas they did not venture. He'd worked out what humans, and many others, used as currency. The Essp system. He wondered why they had bothered to create such a system as he could clearly see that it was not needed. Even though these ephemerals needed food to survive, such things did not require money to grow nor to be consumed. He understood how and why the money was there, of course, but it still amused him.

Deep in thought, he only just noticed as the ship took off, departing the station and heading out towards Magnovastar. He registered the beings around him although took no real notice. Two hours had passed, even though to him it was a mere blink of the eyes, when Ruby found him again. She'd spent that entire time preparing herself. She'd washed, shopped, dressed up, acquired an information projector and… now she was staring at his profile against the black backdrop of space.

"How do I look?" she asked, twirling in the new clothes before him. Still far away in his mind, he didn't answer properly.

"That could be a science in of itself when you consider that no two people can ever truly see the same thing," he said, clearly distracted. Ruby sighed and looked downcast. It was then that he realised she had been trying to impress him. He looked her up and down.

She'd adjusted her long golden mane of hair into a variant of the Asymmetric cut and placed some flashing pink leaves along the parting. It still kept falling across her face though, from time to time. She was employing a close-fitting light blue bodysuit that looked like it was meant to imitate a more military look than it did. Instead of the thicker clasp belt, as it would have had were it military, she had just a paper-thin white belt. Her boots, also blue, came all the way up to her thighs. Over her shoulders she had a pale yellow cape that seemed to encroach across her left side as well as her back. It put his baggy black garb and black cloak to shame in any case.

"You look very beautiful," he amended, without any trouble. She did. She looked up, smiling.

"You're not so bad yourself, duffer," she answered, softly. She handed him back what was left of the money he'd given her and he couldn't help but notice how little of it remained. She'd only been gone *two hours*!

"What have you been looking at all this time?" Ruby asked, in genuine confusion. She stared out with a little more theatricality than necessary. She looked this way and that exaggeratedly. "They're *just* stars."

"*Perhaps*," he allowed, with an aggrieved smile. "What do you want to do now?"

"Well, the dance starts in a few minutes but we don't have to start then…" she began. Suddenly Ash had forgotten she was there. His attention was solely on a human male. The man, tall and lean, was standing some distance away from them and seemed to be… sweating. Sweating a lot. Then he was gone, down some steps and away into the crowd. There was something different about him. Something physical. The next thing Ash knew, Ruby had clobbered him across the shoulder. She turned her back on him and crossed her arms, hurt. Whoops! He reached out to touch her shoulder, apologising for ignoring her.

"You did it *again*!" she hissed, over her shoulder at him. "Am I *so* boring to you?"

"I'm sorry," he apologised, and meant it. "I…" She whirled on him.

"If you want me to go, just say it," she spat, very offended. He pulled her close abruptly, in a hug. "Steady on…!" she complained, taken aback.

"I'm sorry," he repeated, enjoying the warmth of her flesh. "I will try harder to be more attentive in future. This whole galaxy is new to me, there is a lot to take in and I'm easily distracted at the best of times."

"…Of course," she mused, a crafty gleam in her blue eyes. "I hope you're not just lying to make me feel better?" He ran a hand over her back, interested to see how his touch made her mind react.

"I don't have to lie to make you feel better," he said, gently. She giggled, unsure of what to say in response.

"So… do you want to dance with me?" she chanced, hopefully.

***

"Sorry, I suppose this *must* happen a lot, I am new so I will ask stupid questions from time to time. Does this happen often? Are new planets discovered *every day*?" asked Carlos, frowning. They were less than an hour away from arriving and Satiah realised, without surprise, that Carlos was starting to get nervous.

"It's rare but not unheard of. What makes this so unusual is that it's *a habitable world* by all accounts. Normally desolate rocks get found, if anything. The only real interest is mainly materials," Satiah said. Over the last two days she had realised that she didn't mind Carlos being there. *Reed* on the other hand, well… he would drive even the most accommodating people mad. He constantly asked questions about… seemingly anything that he could think of. He never seemed to sleep.

"And we know *nothing* of this world, nothing at all," Reed said, from behind them. He smiled. "It's completely fresh. Thus, putting us among *the first humans to see it*. We certainly will be the first humans to reach planetside."

"That we know of," added Satiah, quietly.

"There will be many protocols and rituals to be observed, you can leave most of those to me. As this is first official public contact, everyone should be on their best behaviour in theory. So *no weapons…*" Reed went on.

"You *what*?" objected Carlos, instantly even less enamoured with the proposition than he had been before.

"It's not an issue," Satiah said to Carlos. She had expected this. It was a diplomatic mission after all. But she knew, any good Phantom didn't need weapons to present a deadly theat. She gave him a calming smile.

"It will be okay."

Reed clearly had expected her to argue too and let his astonishment show.

"That's very understanding of you," he commended.

"I'm a very understanding person," she remarked, in a tone that said the opposite. Then she turned her smile on him. "We don't want them to get the wrong idea, do we?"

"Absolutely not," agreed Reed, his eyes evaluating her. She wondered what he was thinking. He handed her a data cube. "Here is a pre-prepared message I want you to broadcast when we arrive, so they know who we are."

"Wouldn't want them to shoot us down in fright," Satiah grinned. Carlos shifted in the co-pilot's seat and she found his discomfort amusing.

"I hope they don't, I would have gone to all the trouble of translating it into their own language for them for nothing," Reed complained, casually.

Satiah inserted the cube and eyed Carlos again. Perhaps this would be a good time to help him learn again.

"Why don't you take us in, Carlos?" she offered, motioning to the controls. He glanced across at her, his face partly hidden by his hood.

"Is that an order?" he asked, edgy. He didn't like the idea of being prematurely shot down either.

"It's a request," she shrugged. Then she made stern eye contact and raised her eyebrows commandingly. With great reluctance he nodded and she switched the control of the ship to him. He took the controls softly; clearly he had been trained as a pilot well enough. Naturally he would need to learn a lot more but he was still young and the rest would be all down to the experience he had yet to gain. No trainer could prepare you for anything unexpected.

She leaned over and whispered in his ear.

"Remember, objectives dictate actions just as purposes dictate reactions," she said.

"Yes," he said, in a low voice. She nodded in encouragement before inserting the data cube into the communications unit. Normally she would listen to it herself before she played it, just in case. Doing that, however, would be pointless as she had no idea what the new language was like. She checked to see what Reed was up to and noted Kelvin's familiar shadow behind him. Reed was just staring ahead, probably awaiting their first view of the planet.

"Coordinates reached," Carlos said, cutting the engines back carefully. This was Satiah's ship and he did not want to annoy her by damaging it. He had been thrilled at the chance to get out there, away from the training. Now though, he was starting to have second thoughts. Was he ready? Objective action, purpose reaction. It reminded him of Newton's third rule of motion. A bit. For every action, there is an equal and opposite reaction. Almost like karma or the golden rule.

***

Tabre deactivated the long-distance drives as the new planet zoomed into view. He glanced across at his two associates. A man, short, in his mid-sixties, was the diplomat assigned to the mission on behalf of the Colonial Federation. His name was Conrad Willis and was a veteran ambassador. Tabre was compulsive about checking the records of the people he worked with. It was always good practice to know the people you worked with… and know their secrets. To a man as meticulous as Tabre, knowledge was the only true currency. The other person with them was a young CAS agent, assigned to him by Colonial Alliance Security. Deva was her name and she had only just passed her training courses. In her mid-teens she was excitable and clever, always a dangerous mix. Tabre rarely worked alone, being surrounded by others always made him feel safer even with betrayal on the cards. It was easier to spread the blame after a failure if you had a team, than it was if you worked by yourself.

A small green globe appeared in the view port.

"There it is," Deva said, enthusiastic. "Commencing scan." Tabre waited patiently, as did Conrad. Deva's smooth forehead deepened in what looked like an expression of mild disgust.

"Lot of swamps, sir," she explained, evidently a bit put off.

"Population? Defence capabilities? Shields?" reminded Tabre, with some grit in his tone. She was very easily distracted.

"I'm getting two point three seven nine billion, for its size it's quite sparse," she said, ignoring the anger but responding to the question. "They have shields… I'm getting a signal."

"They want to know who we are," Conrad said, levelly. He pulled himself closer to the controls in front of him.

"This is Colonial Federation Ship Mediator," he said, clearly. "Here on ambassadorial business."

"The signal will take you to the area we wish your ships to be stored in," came a voice. The voice was plainly not human but it was understandable. Somewhere between a whisper and a hiss. Deva tensed in her seat upon hearing the words. Tabre locked onto the signal with ease and leaned back in his chair. Something was wrong.

"Ships?" he echoed, considering.

"What?" asked Conrad, preoccupied with something.

"That creature said ships and we only number one," Tabre elaborated.

"So who else did he mean?" Deva asked, realising what Tabre meant. Tabre eyed her; there may be hope for her yet. "Nothing showed up on the scan." She'd taken his look as an accusation.

"Maybe they are not yet planetside," Tabre shrugged, pointing at her. "Scan the surround." Her fingers were already at the controls. No one needed to ask who else might be there. It was a new planet and it stood to reason that everyone would want to investigate it and... negotiate with it.

"I bet it's the Coalition," growled Conrad, in obvious irritation. "They stick their noses in everywhere." Tabre had to agree. The Coalition were unpopular because of their tendency to try to police everyone.

"I have *two* ships," Deva said, eyeing the computer diagnosis. "They appear to be completely separate from one another though." Turning representations of each one appeared on the big screen in front of them. No obvious weapons.

"And the Nebula Union have decided to turn up as well, as if we didn't have problems enough," Conrad stated, almost snapping. Now Conrad was going to have to out-negotiate both superpowers.

"I guess *you* have to work twice as hard now," Deva noted, a spiteful grin on her face.

Conrad glowered at the teenager, she was right.

"If you run into difficulties, do let me know," Tabre offered, seriously. Conrad sighed, understanding what Tabre meant by that suggestion. He nodded, realising that it may be necessary.

"You are right about the ships, one is clearly someone's personal craft and bears neither identification marks nor legal registration panels but the other was clearly a Nebula Union vessel. So I'm going to make the educated guess that the first must be a Coalition ship," Deva said, eyeing Tabre.

"*Process of elimination,*" murmured Tabre, with significance. Accidents could happen anywhere at any time despite the best efforts of everyone. Deva glanced across at him, picking up on the change in tone but not grasping exactly what it indicated.

***

Carlos discovered quickly that, despite piloting a relatively unfamiliar ship, following someone else's signal was easy. The computer did all the alterations; he only had to maintain the speed which frankly the computer could manage too. He, like Satiah and Reed, was interested in watching as they descended from the turquoise exosphere through to the much lighter green of the troposphere. Most of the terrain seemed to be flat, green and swampy. There was no sign of any cities or habitation at all. Satiah had quickly realised that they were not alone. Two other ships were also incoming.

"Ambassadors from the Union and the Colonial Federation," Reed surmised, just as Satiah reached that conclusion herself. She glanced at him, noting that he was not without intelligence. He gave a reluctant sigh.

"Planets are hard to keep secret," Satiah mused, still seeking a sign of their destination.

"I'm not detecting any habitation at all," Carlos said, not bothering to hide how puzzled he was. Satiah frowned.

"There's a chance that this world may be some kind of diversion or relay point," she theorised. "This species will be cautious when it comes to contact with us. Perhaps they want to take a good look at us before they even make themselves known."

Reed grinned.

"Or…" he mused, as the signal changed and the craft began to decelerate with it, "perhaps they live *in* the swamps." As if on cue, all three ships dived into the water and blackness took over. Satiah reflexively ran a scan. They were going slowly. About twenty metres down they levelled off and halted.

"We are inside a structure, *probably their equivalent of a hangar area*," Satiah explained, eying the diagram on the screen in front of her. Two loud clanging sounds made them all start. Satiah replaced her pistol which she'd wrenched free of its holster. Lights flooded on, and it was clear that the water was draining away.

"No weapons," Reed reminded, patting Satiah's shoulder.

She produced a crisp smile before spinning the pistol on her finger and catching it to present Reed with the handle.

"Of course," she said, as he slowly took it. Carlos handed over his standard issue pistol as well. Satiah made a mental note to get him something better before he left her company. The regulation arms were tacky. Reed eyed Kelvin.

"Is he armed?" he asked, interested. Satiah would never construct a robot that couldn't kill.

"Three armed," Satiah remarked, adeptly. Reed raised an eyebrow. "I have disabled his combat systems," she lied, casually. He didn't seem to take her word for it but he didn't pursuit the matter further.

"Now remember, *no matter what happens*, unless I specifically tell you otherwise, *please* leave the talking to me," Reed requested, for the first time exhibiting signs of stress.

"With pleasure," Satiah answered, with a cooperative shrug. "I have nothing to say yet anyway."

They headed down the ramp, into the hangar area. The smell of the swamps was the first thing that greeted them. Carlos's nose wrinkled in restrained disgust. He was going to get that a lot on his early days. Satiah couldn't remember who had told her that every world had its own taste but it was something she had found to be an absolute truth.

"Breathe through your mouth," Satiah told Carlos, without sympathy. Her gaze was on the people from the other two ships as they too disembarked. One ship had three people, the other had four. She made calculations, assessing their physical strengths and weaknesses. And, if it came to it, how best to kill them. The floor was wet and covered in seaweed-like plants; even her combat boots had difficulties finding a good grip. A crunching noise came from Kelvin's feet. Wisely, Kelvin had activated his gripping spikes that would pin him to the floor.

"Recognise any of them?" Satiah asked Reed. Reed took in the other delegates.

"Conrad Willis," Reed said, nodding at the older man of the group. "Colonial Federation delegate… *filthy* reputation."

"Corrupt?" Satiah guessed, without caring.

"Only as much as *any* politician, I suppose," Reed allowed, trying to make out the Nebula Union representative. "I don't know any of the others." The cynicism towards political individuals was both deserved and rife. No wonder they were such popular targets for assassins and avenging angels alike. Satiah herself had personally dispatched more than a few in her time.

"Does he know you?" asked Satiah, interested. Were there motives lurking in the pinkish tissues of their minds? Always.

"Probably," Reed admitted, without noticeable connotation.

Any further conversation ended as a door the end of the hangar slid up and open. Beyond were nearly twenty beings. Each was only about three feet high, thin to the point of cadaverous and splay limbed. They all wore green, for want of a better term, robes. Their eyes were glowing in a yellowy hue and were very active. They seemed to blink three times instead of once. Short antennae on their heads arched towards the humans, interested. One stepped ahead of its brethren and squeaked feebly. All the others jumped from one clawed foot to the other in perfect unison.

"What are they doing?" Carlos whispered, trying not to laugh.

"Presumably it is their greeting," Reed said. And then he actually did a modest imitation of them as if he were trying to greet them too. Bizarrely this seemed to please them. Satiah was impressed and began to see why they had sent Reed for this job. He seemed very good at improvising.

"I hope the whole negotiation is not conducted like this," Reed said, seriously. "I'll be exhausted before we even get close to an agreement."

A voice, high pitched, sounded.

"We welcome you, all humans, our guards will escort you to the place we have prepared," it said. The small creatures hurried over to them all and began to push gently at their legs.

"They want us to move," Reed said, allowing himself to be pushed along. "Just go with it." Everyone was treated in much the same way and, as they reached the entrance where the creatures had come from, they all intermingled slightly. Satiah bumped shoulders with Tabre. Reed and Conrad studiously ignored one another. Carlos and Deva met. Both eyed one another and Carlos smiled at her, instantly attracted. She gave a mischievous grin in response but neither of them said anything. The three other strangers all exchanged glances with them and each other. The creatures continued to push encouragingly at their human guests in as friendly a way as possible.

Satiah and Tabre eyed one another the way predators do when trying to work out if what they are seeing is prey or not. Tabre was the first to speak.

"Tabre," he said, his voice clipped and free of the Colonial twang. To Satiah that meant he'd either been hired by them or had spent so much time working outside the Federation that he'd gained other accents.

"Satiah," she answered, shaking his hand firmly. Her finely tuned senses felt the minute pulse of something firing out from his wrist. He'd just planted a listening device on her. Crafty. She inwardly debated the possibility of pretending not to know it was there to use as a tool for disinformation against just destroying it. She decided quickly on the destroying it option. That would be a palpable opening gesture to Tabre to up the stakes. She knew he was a professional who'd just thrown down the gauntlet.

***

Human social culture seemed to be limitless. So many flavours, types, categories... Ash was starting to realise that this voyage could turn into a lifework, even for an immortal. The dance was not uniform; each individual had their own specific style which made it harder for Ash to dance himself.

"It's okay, we don't have to keep doing this," Ruby said, obviously a little disappointed. She was still feeling guilty about her outburst earlier. Ash was not human, so it seemed reasonable to presume that he would react differently and see things from different angles.

"Why do humans dance?" he asked, curious. Ruby paused, actually stopped moving completely. She realised… she didn't know.

Instead of just admitting her ignorance, however, she did what she always tried to do. Make something up to hide the gap in her knowledge.

"Well, there are a few reasons," she said, pretending to deliberate. "First, in ancient times it was to help our young learn to coordinate not just their own bodies but in teams. Also at some point in the dim and distant past we realised how such action would frighten animals away. Now we do it purely for the enjoyment of it." He stared down at her, clearly not believing a word. "*What?*"

"I have theorised that it is out of some kind of *assumed responsibility* that you yourself have created in your own head. You feel you *have* to provide answers to my questions *even when you know* that the answers that you are providing might not be accurate?" he said. There was a twinkle in his brown eyes that made the jibe less hurtful.

"All of that *was completely true* and I'm shocked that you would even *think* I would lie about anything," she retorted, not really serious. "And you should not be so distrusting of your most valuable source of information."

"You lied about that data you *accidentally* wiped," he reminded her, the accusation obvious in his tone. She gaped up at him, making it clear to him that she was insulted by his implication.

"I make *one* mistake!" she declared, defensively. "And now I have to hear about it for the rest of my life!"

"You still haven't told me exactly how that happened," he pointed out, still being annoying.

"It's *private*, what about that do you not understand?" she demanded, getting genuinely testy.

"As a guide and representative of and for your entire species I have to say you're far from ideal," he said, going on with the criticism. "You cover up your lack of understanding with random fiction, you hide your past like a criminal and you have about as much talent for hiding your failings as a malfunctioning drive system."

"What?" she asked, pretending not to hear. "It's so noisy in here, isn't it?" He sighed.

"And your resorting to such an infantile deflection tactic is..." he went on. He was interrupted by something in his subconscious. The sounds dimmed, fading away for the most part with only one remaining. A human... a lone human... coughing. It was less a cough and more a death rattle. Then, everything else came back to his ears, hiding the human again.

"Look, I'm not for chatting endlessly about myself," Ruby smiled. This was another lie but Ash was too distracted to challenge it. "Let's talk about you and your culture. You never talk about where you came from or anything about your origins. Why is that?"

"Didn't have time to bring it up," he replied, evasively. He nearly added. *"Not with you constantly droning on."* At least he was getting better at hiding his changes in attention.

"Where and when were you born?" she asked, as they left the dance floor and returned to the bar area. Closer to the man who had grabbed Ash's focus just a few moments before.

"In a place and time that no longer exists and I don't remember much about my progenitors," he replied, almost honestly.

"What?" she asked, baffled. *"Say that again."*

"Due to a time paradox caused by the consequences of three other paradoxes, the place I was born in has ceased to exist. Of course it had to have existed once, at a conjunctive plane which clings only to my mind through memory. As to when and where *that physically was*, that can both always and never be answered..." he explained, being completely truthful.

"Forget I asked," she cut him off, waving her hand at the bartender. "Why can *I* never make stuff like that up?"

"There's an easier question," he said, grinning smugly.

"What about your mum?" Ruby asked, endeavouring to bring the answers down into terms she could comprehend without getting a migraine trying. "Did she have a name or is that also a hopelessly complex thing to explain?"

"Her name was Dreda," he said, unsure whether to add emphasis to her name because he was unsure if it was necessary or not. He didn't want it to sound like a boast or a threat but he didn't wish to sound pleased either. He got the reaction he was expecting.

Enthrallment. Everyone had heard that name, not always for good reasons but most had heard of her more recent self-sacrificing acts.

"Dreda?" she echoed, her eyes wide. "As in…? You know? *The* Dreda?"

"Grand Admiral, Guardian, Queen Dreda," he spelt out, listing just a few of her titles. Ruby was speechless. She fell silent and just stared at him a mixture of fear and excitement on her face.

"…Isn't she dead?" she managed, without sounding too offensive. He smiled.

"Yet another thing humans don't understand," he answered. She was still too shocked to contest the circumvention.

***

Punes. That's what they were called. Punes. A Pune was a single member of this new species of… swampy dwarves. Reed, Conrad and a man called Edmund, who represented the Nebula Union, were each in a corner of a vast hall. Their guards remained behind their ambassadors. Meanwhile the Punes, twelve of them, occupied the last corner. They appeared to be set apart from the other Punes by some sort of class system. These were the highest of the high. They were the Pune Government.

"This planet appears to be easily classifiable," Reed muttered, over his shoulder. "It's the very definition of an oligarchy. A government which is controlled by the wealthiest individuals. They have twelve ministers but of those twelve, only three are the real power. Those are the three I must focus on winning over to our way of thinking."

Satiah, Kelvin and Carlos were sitting protectively behind Reed. It was not clear if the Punes knew that they were merely guarding Reed as opposed to assisting him. Satiah saw a movement to her left and realised Carlos kept stealing glances at the Federation delegate. She smiled, at first believing Carlos to be searching for threats. Then she caught sight of the teenage girl Deva who was among their number, and realised the truth. After she caught them grinning at each other a third time, Satiah cuffed his ear. She didn't do it hard enough to hurt much but with force that wouldn't fail to get his attention.

"Ow, *what?*" he asked, eyeing her.

"Stop ogling and start listening," Satiah ordered, through her teeth. Angry but embarrassed, Carlos did not look at Deva again.

"For a long time we have been invisible to the humans that we know rule most of the universe. But we knew, the moment we were found, you would come," said a Pune.

"Forgive us our curiosity," Conrad said, quick to talk first. Some believed that by speaking first, they would have more chance of persuading. Reed was content to wait until last, clinging to the idea that in being last he would be able to mould his argument more effectively against those of the Federation and the Union. Satiah tried to ignore the dialogue and concentrate on the body language. No one would normally try anything stupid, especially during the actual negotiation, but some people were stupid. Tabre particularly occupied her focus. Not just because he had tried to bug her already but his whole persona was one that screamed *threat*. He was alert, poised; watchful... he was everything a professional killer would be. And he was aware of her.

After fifteen minutes of Edmund and Conrad trying to get the Punes to join them, it was Reed's turn. He began slowly and carefully. Conrad had already perpetuated a few things about the Coalition, some true and some not. Reed countered them. Everyone remained just professional enough not to verbally attack one another but there was always sniping.

"The Coalition is economically stable and always eager to make new friends. I know you have been watching us and I know you have seen the wars and battles fought both recent and distant. They are over, peace is reigning. We can work together with you to help you grow in prosperity," Reed announced, sounding almost nonchalant. "I can guarantee that, should the unlikely event of conflict begin in the future, you would be under no obligation to join in and yet you would still receive our protection."

The Punes referred to the documentation that he had previously prepared for them which, in unyielding clarity, outlined all the pros and cons of becoming a Protectorate Planet of the Coalition. While transporting cargo was arguably much more difficult due to multiple checks, stringent security and never ending streams of paperwork, militarily it was very advantageous to be a Protectorate. You were protected by a space navy many tens of times greater than anything you could muster yourself. While, should that same navy be pulled into a war, you were not expected to send your warships off to join it. Reed was doing the standard thing that most Coalition diplomats did in similar circumstances. Instead of trying to get them to join the Coalition fully, they would extend the Protectorate argument. A sort of political compromise. Then, after they had been a Protectorate for a while, they would gradually be lured into being a fully fledged member of the Coalition. As a tactic it worked well, especially when the planet was unfamiliar with it.

Yet the other diplomats present were more than familiar with it. They too had proffered counter offers. The Punes might get so fed up with all these offers they may end the negotiation without joining anyone. Such an outcome was unlikely but not impossible. They were completely within their rights to do that even if it was considered by some to be discourteous. The Pune leaders, however, seemed remarkably patient. Reed had the impression that they had wisely prepared themselves for this beforehand. He also had the impression that nothing they had heard so far had satisfied or swayed them. It was hard to tell for sure though; as they were completely new he had no way of accurate gauging how they felt about anything. They had expressed some gratitude to him personally though for bothering to try and translate his greeting into their tongue earlier. Albeit incorrectly. He had apparently misplaced the zarephlic, whatever that was.

A zarephlic is an example of Pune grammar. The closest thing humanity has to it is the comma. As the Punes clearly used a lot of gesticulation while communicating, not only to humans but also to one another, their punctuation system is a system of written prompts to indicate certain bodily movements. And the movements always take place *before* the words. The first line of Reed's message to them had read: Salutations, from the Coalition, from me and my party. So, as far as the Pune translation went, the word came before the action which was grammatically wrong. For them, the action always came before the word unless there was some highly unusual specific reason why it shouldn't. So, correctly written in Pune, Reed's greeting should have been phrased: salutations, from Coalition to you, from me to you and, from my party to you. Every zarephlic would indicate the hopping from one foot to another, in this case, as was the traditional Pune physical greeting. Sometimes, however, it could be used to indicate whatever physical response was expected. Reed was thankful that humans just waved and had no grammatical equivalent.

Reed used this grammatical lecture as an opening, indicating that he had interest in Pune culture and implying that it impressed him. Satiah was aware that he was being clever and that in reality he probably couldn't care less about it. He was building bridges, finding common ground, doing everything he could to understand who or what he was talking to. So his blundering had actually helped him… as it might have been meant to? Satiah couldn't shake the feeling that this Reed, whoever he was, pretended to be very foolish just to put people off their guard. It was an act. A very convincing one but an act nonetheless. After about a hundred minutes, the talks were interrupted. With much to deliberate, or maybe to just wake up again, the Pune government departed and the humans were left in the company of the guards. Carlos was restless, indeed he had been for the last half an hour. Satiah felt she had to give him something to do.

Satiah carefully took the listening device from the inside of her sleeve, where Tabre had expertly positioned it. She set her normal communicator to white noise and transmitted the output fully into the listening device. A screech of feedback would be heard on the other end, if anyone was listening. Deva let out a yelp, which she tried to conceal by coughing loudly. Satiah smiled as she then crushed the listening device between her fingers. While Tabre and Deva were distracted, Satiah knew to make another move.

"Carlos," she said, getting his attention. "A good Phantom always knows their way around. Take this." She handed him a small black box. "This is a transmitter going straight to Kelvin here. I want you to just walk around, just take a wander. The computer will fill in the gaps. That should give us a precise layout to plot on and with." Pleased, he obeyed.

Heading out swiftly, his speed attracted the attention of Tabre who then looked at Satiah, guessing that Carlos was on an errand for her. He said something to Deva who, without any further persuasion required, went after Carlos. Satiah rolled her eyes. Tabre had done exactly what she had expected him to. Now he'd lost his plant he had to keep his eyes on them and when they separated that meant he had to do the same.

"Are you getting the signal?" she murmured to Kelvin.

"Yes," he answered.

"Good, expect disruption. You may have to boost it," she advised.

"Yes," he responded.

"What *are* you guys up to?" asked Reed, turning on them curiously. She smiled mysteriously and didn't answer.

***

Carlos turned the first corner, somewhat puzzled as to why the Punes were happy to just let him roam the place without an escort. Perhaps, as clearly the elder humans were in charge, the Punes dismissed the younger ones as unimportant. Big, potentially fatal, mistake. He had the box Satiah had given him in his robe pocket, out of sight.

"Ambassador!" called someone from behind him. He turned to see Deva jogging lightly towards him. He couldn't stop himself from smiling. He knew she was an enemy agent and had probably been sent to spy on him but, even since they had first looked at one another, he had felt a connection with her. The sort of hormonal connection that younger people did not let politics get in the way of. She reached him, pretending to be out of breath.

"Deva," she said, extending her hand. He took it and gave it a casual shake.

"Carlos," he said, continuing to walk.

"This place is weird, isn't it?" she chatted, quickly. "I can't *think* why the Punes are happy with us just wandering around here. They must have very trusting natures."

"Well, we *are* diplomats, what harm could we do?" he responded, cagey. It was hardly likely that the Punes, if they had any, would leave the crown jewels just lying around for them to stumble across.

"True," she agreed, too quickly. "How do *you* think the first leg of talks went?"

"Bad for *you*," he quipped, unable to stop himself from flirting with her. She raised her eyebrows, not expecting that.

"Conrad was *not* our first choice of ambassador," she informed him, in the lower tone of confidentiality. "We had hoped for another but she proved *unavailable*." Was any of that true?

They walked along together in silence for a few moments.

"Was Reed your first choice of ambassador?" she piped up, again. She was probing. He knew she was probing. She was doing it *so* obviously though. It was as if she either had no training at all or, for whatever reason, was not bothered about him recognising what she was doing.

"I wouldn't know, I'm *just* tech support," Carlos lied, easily. She regarded him searchingly.

"*Me too*," she replied, as if this was a revelation.

"Small galaxy."

"Too small, that's why we are here, to make it bigger," she said, and then she bequeathed him a reproachful glare. Only the gleam in her eyes removed the string from it. "The Coalition is big enough *already*, surely? Why would you want this world *too*?" For a moment he thought she was going to argue that the Federation had 'seen it first' and they had more of a claim to it.

"Well, why are you so *anxious* that *you* have it?" he countered, his tone still just playful enough not to offend. That got her to back off.

"No reason," she mumbled, trailing off. Carlos didn't like the silence; he wanted to hear her voice again. She somehow made even the Colonial drawl elegant.

"Now you've been planetside, what do you think of this place?" he asked, genuinely interested.

"It stinks," she replied, after a moment's contemplation. "And these Punes are weird." Her tone had become condemning and dismissive. "I like how their government is so small though... unlike ours."

"What do you mean?" he asked, as they turned yet another corner.

"Do you know *nothing* about the Federation?" she almost squawked, as if offended. "The Federation was formed after the Common Protectorate war from the Colonial Alliance. Instead of keeping it simple, like before with the Colonial council, the rule of the Federation was spread out unevenly among the richest and most powerful. The government itself is run by the administrators and they are so busy lining their own pockets that poverty is starting to become almost as big an issue now as it was back in the days before the war! These Punes have such a small body governing over everything else that it makes decisions easier to reach. Action will be swift. Our democracies seem to suffer from a collective and debilitating atrophy." As political rants went, this was becoming bitter and it made Carlos uncomfortable. If he agreed with her, she might take it like he was insulting the Federation and if he disagreed she might think he was implying that she was wrong or stupid. A lose-lose. Carlos instead relied on something that had not done him any favours while training to be a Phantom. His sense of humour.

"I won one of those once," he joked, nervously. She glanced at him in bewilderment.

"Won what?" she demanded, as if angered.

"A trophy," he chuckled. She paused, while examining his play on words, as if she'd never heard a joke before in her life. Then she laughed. It was a real laugh, high and girly but a laugh that was pleasing to hear. She leaned into him and began to playfully push at him, like she was trying to get away.

"If *that* is an example of your negotiating skills, then this planet is ours already," she mocked, without being serious.

"Which is why I work in tech support," Carlos laughed, patting her shoulder.

"I see," she nodded, as if impressed. "It is good to know one's limitations." *What are yours?* He could not help but wonder.

***

Ruby was inquisitive by nature; Ash had known this from practically the beginning. Even *he* though, was starting to weary of her seemingly never-ending tirade of queries. There was a lot he could learn about her just by analysing the questions she asked. After realising she was going to get nothing more about him personally at that time, about him or his famous mother, she'd started on their destination instead. If she had bothered to read the brochure he had bought for her, he was sure that only a few of these questions would remain necessary.

"Its origins are obscure," he answered, which was a clever way of saying that he didn't know. Its origins no longer mattered to him, it was its future that was the problem.

"But *surely*," she persisted, not put off or seemingly aware of how much she was trying his patience, "*you* must know where it came from? Being an immortal duffer and everything?"

It was at that moment that the man, the same man who'd drawn Ash's earlier attention, collapsed over the bar. People drew away, panicked by the unexpected fall.

"Oh no!" cried someone, backing away in fright. "He's *dead!*" Ruby, whose attention had been drawn unpredictably, didn't panic immediately. Ash was expecting her to freak out.

"Nah!" she insisted, calmly. "He's probably just passed out! He's drunk." She swigged her own drink after she said the words.

"*Drunk? He's the head-steward*," someone argued, levelly. Ruby eyed the body, uncertainty creeping into her expression. While she was distracted, Ash slipped a pill into her drink.

Ruby stood, to get a better view as people surrounded the body. Ash shook his head slowly, starting to comprehend what was going on instantly. He kept it to himself though, the futility of trying to convince everyone and the inclination to study the humans behaving naturally compelled him to not interfere. He did hand Ruby's drink to her though, quickly.

"Better finish that," he advised, without telling her why. Innocently, she didn't even question him, she just downed it in one to help combat her shock. This was a clear demonstration of trust that Ash was both touched and perplexed by. He'd done nothing to earn such reliance from her. Ruby hurried over to get a closer look herself to ascertain if the man really was dead. Ash took the opportunity to return to the viewport. There, keeping one eye on the commotion, he returned to his state of deep thought.

Ruby forced her way through the throng of confused tourists. When she got close she noticed the strange scabs on the dead man's skin. A doctor was there, to confirm the passing and to work out the cause. She and the rest of the passengers were moved back by the crew, even the Captain was there. Ruby, after working out where Ash had gone, rushed over to him.

"*He really is dead*, you know," she explained, a little shaken. "What do you think happened?"

"No idea, wish I could help," he said, unhelpfully. She suddenly looked right into his eyes, as if something had tipped her off to his deception. She said nothing though, just stared up at him. He was torn inwardly, he could feel the stress and fear she was experiencing and he didn't like to see her in discomfort but if he told her… if he explained the truth, he couldn't tell what she would do.

Her gaze remained on him.

"Why aren't you interested?" she asked, thinking hard. "Why are you not scared?" He didn't answer, just stared back, helpless. She took a step closer, so she was right in front of him.

"I've not known you long but I think I know enough about you to know… that you know something and you're not telling me," she stated, accusingly. Ash was impressed and he had found another of her talents. Despite some evidence to the contrary she was a good reader of people. She didn't know, and couldn't know what he knew, but she knew he knew something.

"What makes you think *that*?" he asked, serious.

"Your lack of surprise," she answered, immediately. "You didn't even *look around* when it happened. You just distanced yourself from…"

She froze, in mid-explanation and Ash knew something else had occurred to her. Fear was growing inside her now, he could sense it.

"It's a *disease*," she hissed, afraid. "And *you knew*, you spotted him earlier which is what kept distracting you…"

"I didn't *know*, I theorised," he cut in. "I could not be sure."

"Until *now*!" she snapped, angry. "And you just let me go over to where the body was, probably getting infected in the process." He gripped her shoulders, knowing he had to stop her.

"Why do you think I made you finish your drink *before* you went over to look?" he asked, intensely. She fell silent, her expression worried and uncertain.

She finally shook her head, not knowing.

"I gave you *immunity*," he answered, more normally. "In the shape of a dissolving pill. You are safe, Ruby. *You are safe.*" Relief flashed across her expression briefly but then it was replaced by horror.

"*What about everyone else?*" she asked, not sure if she wanted to know the answer. Ash shrugged.

"I only carry one because you are my only human," he answered, before realising his mistake.

"*Your* human?" she echoed, infuriated.

"I didn't mean it like…" he began. She tore free of his hands.

"Yes you did! Is *that* what I am to you?" she demanded, tears in her eyes. "Like a loyal and devoted pet? *A test subject*? Something to study while you learn all about us like some kind of alien spy?"

"*Ruby*…" he began, seriously. She made a noise of rage and stormed off. He watched her go, feeling peculiarly guilty.

Ruby made her way towards the command area of the ship. She needed to speak to the Captain. They *had* to be told about the disease, or whatever it was, so they could turn back or at least call for help. She didn't know what the standard procedures were regarding something like this but she was sure that there had to be some. She was surprised that no guards tried to stop her as she found the command deck. There she spotted someone in a chair, piloting the ship. It was not the Captain, he was still with the others, that meant it was likely to be the co-pilot. A flight officer of some variety certainly. Close enough, she decided. She hurried up to them and nudged them.

"I'm sorry to disturb you but…" she began, trying to decide how best to word her account. The man lolled away from her and then fell off the chair. He was dead too! She stared in utter disbelief. That was when a group of people entered behind her and stopped in their tracks.

"Don't move!" shouted someone. Oh fudge!

***

"This is *not* going well," Conrad said, as much to himself as to Tabre. "The Punes are clearly leaning towards the Coalition. That diplomat Reed is *good* and seems to have ingratiated himself among them." Tabre nodded slowly.

"And you feel that *you* are unable to break his stranglehold on the negotiations?" Tabre asked, without even bothering to make the question less offensive. Conrad glowered but reluctantly nodded. They were back aboard their ship, the place that the Punes has insisted they remain during breaks from the talks. A security precaution.

"*Just get rid of him,*" Conrad spat, irritated that Tabre seemed to be implying that he was incompetent.

"Fine," Tabre said, noting that Deva was still absent. It was a shame that his listening device had been detected, although he had to admit he would have been disappointed if it hadn't. He'd been wanting to test himself against a worthy enemy for some time. This could be it.

He never went into a fight blind though, such reckless tactics were for those seeking glory or a quick death. He had sent all the information he had on her, which was not much, back to his office. They had been swift in responding. That was not a shock to him as this mission was high profile enough to warrant only the best efficiency. They had failed to identify her but one phrase at the end had been enough for Tabre.

"She is on *no records anywhere*. There are a few references to the name Satiah but are from erroneous sources. Suspect a Phantom." He had smiled; Phantoms were the most elite of agents the Coalition had to offer, something he considered himself to be the Colonial equivalent of. What better type of enemy to fight? She would be protecting Reed, keeping him safe while he did his job, as Tabre himself was protecting Conrad. They were both professional killers. Both on the same job. A match of symmetry, something his mind found pleasing, he liked things that matched. He liked symmetry. May the best operative win…

Deva entered, looking composed. Tabre looked across at her, silently enquiring as to new developments.

"Carlos is an aide. I didn't get much out of him," she admitted, a little ashamed. "I think that he is probably here doing something similar to me."

"Did you at least establish why he was taking the time to explore?" Tabre asked, a little frosty.

"He admitted nothing but I think he was learning the terrain on behalf of his CO. He probably had a device on him somewhere, recording everything, that was why I had to be careful," she went on.

"You kept watching him during the negotiations," Conrad said, listening in.

"I was…" she confessed, a little sheepishly. "I thought he might be up to something and I didn't think he noticed."

"My dear, *everyone* noticed," Tabre sighed, honestly. A little colour emerged in her face but her posture remained disciplined enough.

"*Relax*, he was watching you too. I think he likes you… you can make use of that. Problem is, he will be instructed to do the same regarding you by *his* superior," Tabre explained, ponderous. She didn't let her disappointment show but inwardly she was starting to hate this. She liked Carlos and she knew he liked her but… now they were being used as weapons to…

"When we strike we must do it in a way that cannot be traced to us," Tabre went on. Deva sat down and crossed her arms. She was not happy. Tabre knew it would be best if the rest was done by him alone. Deva was now emotionally invested which compromised her in his opinion. He reached a decision.

"Leave this with me," he instructed, coldly. Deva and Conrad obligingly left Tabre alone in the control room. Tabre gave them twenty seconds to ensure they were out of earshot before activating the communicator. He placed a call and waited.

"Yes," came a heavily accented man's voice. Roach always answered quickly when he answered at all.

"Roach, it's Tabre," he said, by way of greeting. "I've got a job for you."

***

Carlos cringed as he listened to the playback of his chat with Deva. Satiah and Kelvin were replaying it, listening intently. Meanwhile, a holographic projection was steadily mapping the underground complex before their eyes. It was much wider then they had thought and much deeper.

"She was scoping," Satiah said, with conviction.

"I *know*," Carlos agreed, a little annoyed that Satiah seemed to think him too stupid to realise that. Satiah gave him a stern glance.

"I hope you're not thinking about anything *other than the mission* in regards to this girl because if you are…" Satiah began, carefully.

"Their ship is transmitting a signal off-planet," he interrupted, glad of the action.

Satiah was quick to lock on to the signal.

"Encrypted," she murmured, sighing with disappointment.

"They're hardly going to just let us listen in, are they?" Carlos said, taking the opportunity to bite back.

"No," she admitted, in a tone that implied she didn't care at all. She made eye contact with Carlos and then slid the crushed listening device out in front of him. He gaped down at it.

"When Tabre and I shook hands, he tried to plant this on me," she explained, her eyes never leaving him. The implication was easy to pick up on and Carlos sighed in defeat. He then removed his cloak quickly for it to be examined.

"You're clean," she added, seriously. "Kelvin scanned you as you entered." The relief in his face made Satiah smile.

"When Deva gets close to you I understand that at your age things get… *hazy*. Scan yourself regularly please," she instructed.

He nodded in agreement. He didn't like being embarrassed by Satiah but she was right about what happened when he was with Deva. Despite his best efforts he'd been lucky not to give anything away when he was talking with her. The map was still coming together in mid-air and Satiah's gaze slid back to it. Carlos too found himself amazed by its size. One line went away from the spaghetti junction of corridors and rooms that made up the city. It went down further and further in a straight line until it stopped. Satiah pointed at it with her finger, making the projector zoom in. It was a single shaft that went down, away from the city, in a direct line. It just kept going until it fell off the map they had created.

"Any ideas?" she asked, wondering what it was.

"If the city wasn't supported by others I'd have said it might be a structural prong, there to keep it from drifting away into the swamps," Carlos said, thinking about it. "But that is not needed and even if it was, that shaft is nowhere near big enough for structural support purposes."

"Like an anchor for the whole settlement," Satiah murmured, thoughtfully. "…No, that's not it, you're right. It may be worth studying the swamps more closely. They may have current systems that we need to be aware of."

"Cable tunnel?" he offered, shrugging. It did seem very odd. Its purpose was impossible to work out.

"Without understanding their technology we can't be sure of that… not without going to look anyway," she stated.

"I'll get Reed to get them to give us permission," Carlos sighed, standing.

"No," she said, raising a hand to stop him. "We have a map and I've already plotted their guard positions and patrols. We don't need permission, we can do it without them knowing."

"This is a *diplomatic* mission," protested Carlos, mildly. "This planet is neutral, and while that is still no restriction for us we have to weigh in the variable that *we want them to join us*. They won't join us if we're caught spying on them."

"If we ask for permission and they deny it, they will expect us to try and covertly find out and thus be in a better position to prevent us. If they agree, we get to see it. If we just sneak in, we bypass the whole problem. Besides… we won't get caught," she insisted. Reluctantly he sat back down. He reminded himself that Phantoms often had to work, were encouraged to work, *outside* of the laws of all societies. That was part of the whole point of being a Phantom. Neutrality meant nothing. Friend or foe didn't matter either. Legally they were allowed to spy on whom they liked.

"We'll do it tonight," she went on. There was a silence as they stared out of the viewport, avoiding each other's eyes.

"Who will stay here to guard Reed?" he asked, sourly.

"You will," she said, after a moment's consideration.

"And if he asks about your location or purpose?" Carlos asked, although he could guess her answer.

"Lie," she replied, without batting an eyelid.

"I'll tell him that you're out investigating static charge build ups on the internal bulkhead," he responded, sarcastically. Satiah giggled, genuinely amused.

"That was quite inventive Carlos, even though I know you meant it ironically," she mused, eyeing him. "If he asks, just tell him you don't know but that he is not allowed outside until I return." Carlos nodded.

***

Roach looked out across the planet through his viewport and from underneath his untidy-looking cloth hat. His eyes, pale blue, always made him look like he was half asleep as they rarely opened wide. He chewed lazily as he regarded the new world. He had no interest in it other than it was where his new job was to be. Its green glow didn't fill him with any enthusiasm. His cloaking device on, he began a slow descent. While the computer handled that, he opened a case and began to assemble the rifle inside. He'd cleaned and checked every component himself, as a perfectionist; he couldn't afford his equipment to let him down. He glanced up and grimaced in disgust as he took note of the swampy landscape.

***

Ruby did exactly what she was told and lifted her arms in the universal gesture of surrender.

"Now step away from him!" the next instruction was shouted. She knew what they must be thinking, of course. That *she* had murdered the co-pilot while they were all dealing with the death of the head steward. Motive wasn't important: she was the only person there therefore it *had* to be her.

"*I didn't kill him!*" she said, anxious to get her point across.

"Save your words for security," barked someone, at her.

"He was *already dead* when I found him," she explained, honestly.

"Get her out of here!" ordered the Captain, barging past her. He was trying to get to the controls and Ruby was grabbed by her arms. She didn't dare resist but they never made it to the doors.

"*Wait!* What the hell have you done to the controls?" demanded the angry Captain.

She was pulled around to face him but she could only stare dumbly in response.

"...What?" she managed, confused by the question. Everyone was looking at her and she wanted to hide.

"*Look!*" He motioned at them, agitated. She stared but didn't know what he was showing her.

"What?" she repeated, seriously. He tapped a white triangle which seemed to be placed on one of the many control pads. His expression was one that had mixed emotions. Anger, confusion, sarcasm and surprise. He was under a lot of stress and Ruby didn't want to push him any further.

"You have prevented anyone but yourself from touching any of these controls by installing your override-failsafe proxy device," he spelt out.

"...That's not mine," she said, slowly. It sounded feeble but it was the best she could manage. "I swear, I came here to find you to tell you that you have a *viral outbreak* on this ship and that everyone has to be protected as best as you can while we turn back!" This seemed to give him pause, and then he glanced down at the body again. "All I did was touch him to get his attention and I did that because I *thought* he was still alive."

"...*He's been shot,*" stated a woman, kneeling beside him. The Captain gave a nod and Ruby felt searching hands all over her as the guards tried to find a weapon. She squirmed.

"She's clean," said the woman, still holding her right arm.

"I don't feel it after *that* though," Ruby objected. "At least get me a drink first next time." The Captain scowled. Then he waved a hand at the guards and Ruby was released.

"What did you say?" he asked, in a dangerous voice. "*Before* your cocky one-liner."

"The Head Steward died because of a virus which is a killer, I came up here to tell you that we *must* go back and get all these people quarantined..." she explained, again. Inwardly she didn't know how she was being so... compelling and strong. She'd never spoken to anyone like this before. It gave her a bit of a thrill. "If we *don't* a lot of them will die!"

"...But we can't because we no longer have control of this ship," the Captain exploded, seriously. Ruby had to acknowledge this.

"So, *whoever* killed the co-pilot, doesn't want you to have control of the ship," she mused, thinking hard.

"Might that be you?" demanded the woman, to her right. She sounded as angry as the Captain had. "You may not have killed him but that doesn't mean you have nothing to do with the OFP." She was talking about the override-failsafe proxy device that had effectively paralysed the crew.

Ruby faced the woman and noted her name badge. Jenna.

"I assure you that I neither killed your friend nor installed that thing, *Jenna*," Ruby answered, carefully. "I am only here because I wanted to make sure we returned to port."

"Everything is locked up now. We can't use any of the controls," the Captain said.

"Then we must evacuate the vessel," Ruby said, again surprising herself. "This thing *must* have escape pods."

"It does but they have to be activated from here," the Captain argued.

"*What?*" demanded Ruby, confounded by the apparently nonsensical operating system. Where was the logic? The logic was to prevent any accidental or criminal use of the escape pods while the ship was in flight.

"What about the manual override?" asked Jenna, levelly. "The computers may be jammed but *that* system should still work."

"Worth a try," nodded the Captain.

A call was made but, it seemed, *someone else* was already ahead of them.

"The pods have already been launched, presumably with whoever caused all this on board one of them," one of the guards explained.

"*What?*" demanded the Captain, beside himself with fury.

"Captain, the customers are beginning to ask questions," informed Jenna, looking very stressed. He made a noise somewhere between a cry and a huff as he ran his hands through his hair stressfully.

"Are they all… *feeling normal?*" asked Ruby, tentatively. They all looked at her and she realised her mistake.

"What about *any of this* is *normal?*" demanded the Captain.

"I meant, *medically*, if the virus…" she began, deeply concerned.

"*What virus?*" demanded Jenna, incredulous. Ruby sighed. Understandably, in the confusion, they had already forgotten about it.

She hoped memory loss was not one of the symptoms. If it was then she was too late, they'd all already been infected.

"Captain, you *need* to make everyone go back to their cabins, *you must in order to keep them separated*," she insisted, urgently. "It *may* help prevent the spread of the contagion."

"How do *you* know about the virus?" he asked, his eyes narrowing suspiciously. Ruby froze, she'd not thought about that.

"*I*… I've seen it before," she answered, trying to be plausible. "There was an outbreak last year somewhere else."

"Why were we not notified of it before we even made planet fall?" he demanded, not unreasonably. She shrugged unhelpfully. Now she didn't really know what to say for the best.

"How do you know for *sure* that he died of *your virus?*" asked Jenna, seriously.

"It's not *mine!*" argued Ruby, equally seriously. This was not going how Ruby wanted it to.

"Sir, we must do *something*, at least try and prevent the passengers from panicking," Jenna advised, carefully.

"Captain!" called someone else, before he could even consider his response to that.

"What is it?"

"Someone else has just collapsed," reported that someone else again. The sounds of panic were starting to occur now. Anarchy was moments away. Ruby winced with tension.

"*Captain!*" she yelled, over everyone else. "Send them to their rooms and seal them inside!" The Captain, to his credit, paused, and looked around at the others. Jenna looked at Ruby then at the Captain before giving a swift nod of agreement. He began a hurried list of instructions to the guard he was still talking to.

"Protocol seventeen stroke three is enacted," he stated, his voice clear and level. "Get them into their rooms, use aggressive means if necessary."

**

Satiah reflected that while these Punes were small it was likely they used machinery many times their own size when building or maintaining their dwellings. Underneath their ship, Satiah had cut her way into what she presumed was some kind of ventilation tunnel. And, it was more than big enough for her to crawl along. She had done this so that no one would see her leave either her ship or the hangar area. It was a masterful job, she'd cut it so carefully that, when they needed to, they could replace it and only an expert would be able to know that anyone had cut through at all. She scrambled through the tunnel quietly, her earpiece tuning in with Kelvin as she went.

"Locked on," came Kelvin's voice. She had a map with her but she asked him to direct her. Feeling her way along she made quick progress and soon she'd left the hangar area far behind.

The dark had never bothered Satiah, indeed she liked it. She liked to be unseen. The strange noises, both the ones she made herself and the others of indeterminate origin, she ignored.

"Next left," Kelvin articulated. "There will be an incline." She continued on, adjusting to going forwards and down easily. Her hands were quickly dusty and blackened. The air was, as expected, vaguely swampy.

"I take it *this* is where the route becomes more complicated," she breathed, quietly. She had committed *some* of the map to memory.

"Yes, you are nearing the vertical shaft," he warned. She sighed. Getting down wouldn't be the issue, on the return journey, however, getting up could be. Her foot inched forward into black nothingness. She knew she'd made it. She dropped her torch down the shaft and listened. She hoped there was no air resistance as that would affect her calculation.

She had already factored in the planet's gravity which was ever so slightly stronger than that of Earth standard. The clatter came two seconds after she had released it. Roughly four to four and a half metres, or about fourteen feet. She reached out for the other side of the channel. She could just reach it. In a flick/turn move she slipped down and braced her feet against one side, pinning her back against the other. She allowed herself to slide downwards cautiously. As she had thought, it was too high for her to jump back up. When at the bottom she recovered her torch and shone it up the tunnel she had just slid down. Dust was everywhere flowing like clouds in the light. She pulled another device from her belt, aimed and fired. A cord shot out from it and attached itself to the ceiling of the tunnel she had just come down from.

The end of the rope was covered in thousands of tiny suckers, modelled on those you might find on a tentacle, which could support her weight easily enough. In order to detach it, a tiny electric current would be sent along the cord to destabilise the air pressure in each sucker. She left it dangling there for her return journey and then pressed on in darkness once more. Still she went downwards and she felt the change in depth with her ears as the pressure changed ever so slightly.

"It is twenty-three metres ahead of you," Kelvin said, in her ear. She flashed her torch on again and peered forwards. If she listened hard she was aware of a slight rushing noise. Like a tiny breeze. She scrambled closer. There it was, a gaping maw, awaiting her.

She reached it, shone her torch down and didn't bother to drop anything this time. She knew it went on for miles. She examined the edges carefully. There was a thick coating of... something. She coughed as more dust was disturbed.

"It's just filth," she stated, eyeing her find in disappointment.

"Do not forget a sample," Kelvin prompted. From her cloak she pulled a specimen wallet out to collect some. Sometimes, being a Phantom, there were jobs that needed to be done that Satiah would question. Acts and things committed that just seemed plainly nonsensical, even stupid. Collecting samples of crap for a rarely used ventilation shaft was pretty close to the top of her list when it came to pointlessness. "Enough," she growled to herself. She'd had enough; there was nothing to see and only stale air to breathe. Turning and almost putting her hand in something awful she began the long crawl back. Joking to herself, she wished she had sent Carlos after all.

***

Carlos was sitting in the control room, eyeing the hangar area.

About ten minutes ago Deva had emerged on the roof of the Colonial ship and seemed to be carrying out maintenance. She was wearing, annoyingly, a skin-tight bodysuit which did very little to hide her figure. Transfixed by her, he almost failed to spot Tabre sneak off in the direction of the Nebular Union ship. He smiled, Satiah would be impressed that the distraction had not fooled him. Obviously there was no way he could work out *where* Tabre had actually gone but he could keep track of *how long he was gone*. Reflexively, he set a timer. Satiah would want precise information.

Deva spied him watching her, smiled and waved. He waved back casually. Awkward. Maybe he could get her communicator code... *more valuable information*? And it would be nice to hear her voice again. He wrote out his question on the back of one of the maps Satiah had printed out earlier and held it up for Deva to see. She stopped, pulled a haughty face to imply that he had no business asking anything like that of her. He thought initially that she'd rejected him. Then she smiled again and nodded. He smiled back. She pulled a long white marker from her bag and waved it in the air for him to notice, after that, very carefully, she scrawled her code across the bodywork of the ship. In a strange way it looked almost artistic, like graffiti could.

Such white markers were normally used for circling areas that needed repair or adjustment, not for teenage flirting, but it seemed perfectly adept for its new task. After that she put her hands on her hips and stood there, watching him. Her expression spoke of terminal boredom. He debated whether or not to use his communicator, knowing if he did she would know his code too. Well, she *had* given him hers so... He called her. She smiled, as if in triumph, as she answered.

"Can't you see that I'm busy?" she demanded, as if angry. He knew her well enough now to know that this was her way of joking. Colonial humour was an acquired taste and there was never any accounting for taste.

"Busy *defacing a spaceship* with random drawings?" he chuckled back.

"Hey, on *some* worlds *that* would qualify as abstract expressionism," she retorted, still staring at him through the glass.

"I *knew* you weren't from a civilised planet," he said, in a disappointed tone.

"Come out here and say that," she giggled, crossing her arms. They grinned through the glass at one another.

"I can't... I'm working," he said, genuinely awkward.

"Me too," she said, not put off. "Maybe we could meet *later*, after our shifts are over." The irony that they had both been left on guard dog duty did not escape him. It seemed that, because of their liking for one another, both of them had been... not exactly punished but *relegated*? Reduced or confined to menial tasks and probably excluded from planning and new developments.

"I'd like that," he admitted, honestly.

"I know," she allowed, a shyer version of the normal smile on display.

"Shouldn't you check if it is okay with Tabre?" he asked, taking the opportunity to test her allegiance once again. She blushed and looked away for a moment. What she did next surprised him.

"...You saw him sneak away, didn't you?" she asked, not pretending that he was still in the ship as he had thought she would.

"Tell him he's *not* as subtle as he thinks," he chanced, grinning. That made her smile again.

"I'll pass that along."

"No, don't, I was just kidding."

"So was I." After promising they would speak soon, they ended the communication session. She slipped back inside the ship. It was only when Tabre returned, in full view, that Carlos realised what they had really been doing.

She had admitted the truth, or what he had assumed was the truth, to build trust between them. Tabre had left *knowing* Carlos would see him. He'd anticipated that Carlos would challenge Deva about it and had craftily told Deva to *just admit it*. Carlos flushed with alarm and disappointment. Satiah would have seen through that straight away and it had taken him nearly half an hour. When he met Deva later, which he still intended to do, should he act as though he still believed her? Or should he reveal that he had seen through her deception and yet had chosen to meet her anyway? Could he imply that every time they interacted, no matter what she did, *he could tell what she was hiding*?

He wished he could talk to Satiah about it but she would just forbid the meeting and, enemy agent or not, Deva was too attractive for him to ignore.

Could they just be normal? No lies? No politics? Just a man and a woman, enjoying each other's company. No, they were on opposite sides. There was no war but there was an eternal coolness between the superpowers that made any romance between them dangerous. The Commandment Benefactor of the Coalition, Brenda Watt, had managed to prevent a war breaking out. There had been and still was great controversy over a world called Pluto Major. Concentration camps. Life form abuses. All under Balan Orion's regime. After a desperate battle or two, peace had been restored but still… It was like everyone was still holding their breath. And now there was something else for them to fight over, the Coalition and the Federation. A new world.

Both had interests in this world and if they lost it because of a teenager's crush… He sighed heavily. He knew that Satiah would not fall into this kind of pit but if she did… what would she do? He realised he hardly knew anything about her. And what about Deva? Was she having a similar struggle with herself about him? Or was he nothing to her? Nothing had happened, there was no *them*. There was no him and her. He'd never felt this way about anyone before and he honestly believed she did too. While both of them were capable of using the pretence of romance to get information… they didn't mind the rituals. Quite the contrary, they seemed the best part.

***

"So we can't change course, we can't leave this ship and we can't even communicate with anyone outside?" Ruby clarified, concerned. The Captain shook his head, dismally.

The passengers had been forced back into their rooms nearly an hour ago. Ash couldn't be found for some reason and Ruby was getting really scared. So, she couldn't catch the virus! That didn't mean she couldn't be murdered. When she caught up with that duffer she'd really give him a piece of her mind! Had he known this was going to happen? He'd known about the virus certainly but what about the death of the co-pilot? Ruby had come to the frightening conclusion that she had probably only missed the murderer by seconds. If she had been there too she knew she'd probably be dead as well. Where was Ash? She was angry but she was frightened without him. She didn't know what to do.

"We can't even check the security footage to find out who really did kill the co-pilot," the Captain went on.

"We *need* to find Ash," Ruby said, determined. "He will certainly help us."

"He's your friend?" he asked, uncertain.

"*Right now he's everything I need him to be,*" she muttered, with a wry smile. "I hope."

"Is he a doctor?"

"He knows a lot about human anatomy," she said, trusting that she was correct.

"How many are infected?" asked Jenna, anxious.

"Seven people are dead now, eight if you include the murder victim," the Captain answered.

An idea came to Ruby. Murder and a virus both killed people. Was it a coincidence that they had both struck at once? The chances of that had to be exceedingly low, she'd certainly never heard of it happening anywhere before. Where was Ash!? As if in answer to her silent plea, she felt him in her mind. A touch of his consciousness, in a way she could not put into words, it gave her a similar rush like when he physically touched her. It meant he was still around somewhere and that reassured her. Why was he staying hidden? Her eyes scanned the cameras, trying to spy him. There he was! Standing at the viewport like before. Had he been there the whole time and she'd just somehow missed him? Before anyone could stop her she was sprinting madly towards the area. Shouts followed her but no one gave chase as they realised she must have seen something on the screens and everyone watched those instead.

She stumbled into the area he was in. He remained where he was, staring out into space as if nothing at all was wrong. She ran over to him. He turned to face her, his face enigmatic.

"Ash?" she begged, tearful. "*Where have you been?*"

"There is no way I could leave this ship," he answered, as if that somehow explained everything. She rushed forward and hugged him strongly. "Even if there was, I wouldn't leave you behind."

"Ash, we're in *trouble*," she sobbed, into his cloak.

"You are immune to the virus, it cannot harm you," he reminded.

"*There is a murderer*," she explained, earnestly. "You cannot make me immune to murder!"

"Calm," he whispered, in her ear. His voice began soothing her, making her feel softer and warmer inside. And suddenly she was a lot calmer. She felt his arm cradle her shoulders like a protective blanket. "Be calm. You are safe, Ruby."

"Maybe I am… But what about all these people?" she asked, emotionally. "They are scared and some of them are dying. Can you please help them?"

"I could," he answered.

"Will you?"

"*That* would be interfering," he replied, looking conflicted. "If I were to get involved, the balance may change. Can you not help yourselves?"

"For me?" she pleaded, helpless. "Help them for me."

***

Satiah had reached the vertical tunnel she had slid down earlier and this time, she just held onto the cord she'd set up before, attached it to her belt and activated. Silently she flew upwards, reaching the next level in less than a moment. She swung to the side, detached herself then replaced the whole thing into her robe. She sat there for a moment, enjoying the better air when she felt her communicator buzzing. She pulled it out and activated.

"Can you talk?" asked Rainbow, his voice a little distorted. "If you can't, don't say anything." She grinned, despite her dark surroundings.

"I'm unoccupied," she said, smoothly. "What have you got for me?"

"Jaylite Industries," he answered, his tone almost grave. She found herself tensing and forced her muscles to relax.

"I'm listening."

"They folded the day Balan Orion died." Balan Orion had been the Commandment Benefactor, the ruler, of the Coalition until he had been assassinated by one of his fellow conspirators. It was still a matter of debate as to who had actually pulled the trigger. She knew that Vourne himself had specifically led a mission to assassinate Balan but had arrived shortly after his death and just in time to start the witch-hunt. All the suspects were dead now though, Vourne included. "Until then they operated *mainly* in transportation and security business. They did have a side-line in experimental weaponry though."

"*Who doesn't?*" she quipped, cynically.

"They formed shortly after the end of the Common Protectorate War and are mentioned in several military contracts. Also, six months ago, they are a potential target outlined in Operation Burning Bridge."

"…I don't think I'm familiar with that one," she said, even more curious. "Was it a Phantom operation?"

"Yes, authorised by Phantom Leader Vourne," he answered. "I don't have authorisation to go further without a Phantom code."

"Use mine," she said, shrugging.

"Are you sure you want *this* associated with *you*? We're still dealing with the wake of the Vourne Conspiracy here and if your name…" he objected, not without good reason. She thought about it.

"Use Derad Leigh's," she advised, remembering his code. "0056227100."

"Is he a Phantom?" Rainbow asked, interested.

"Until *recently* he was, I'm gambling that he may not have been erased from the system memory yet," she replied, honestly. "If that doesn't work just use mine anyway."

"One more thing, Randal has had *your suspect* moved to a different part of the building," he said. She scowled. Rainbow was talking about the man she and Kelvin had retrieved from the now destroyed space station.

"He didn't say why. I can find out exactly where if you like?"

"Thank you Rainbow, keep digging. *Take care*, stick to *digging up bodies* rather than digging fresh graves," she said, cutting him off.

She sat there in silence for a few minutes, thinking. Kelvin queried her lack of movement and she started off again. So, Vourne had known about Jaylite Industries, and had ordered a Phantom or Phantoms unknown to do something regarding them. What was Operation Burning Bridge? Vourne had been a political enemy of Balan, even though initially they had worked together. Had Vourne been purposely sabotaging Balan's operations in secret? And why had Randal moved her prisoner? Was he trying to make him disappear? Was he trying to steal her thunder? Or was there some other explanation? Something as trivial as simple locational logistics.

And with that all the old questions returned to her as well. Who was that strange man she had recovered from the space station anyway? The place had been about to blow, literally. Had someone been trying to murder that man for some reason? Was it just an accident? Perhaps some kind of elaborate suicide? And who were those people who had come after them? Kelvin had formed the theory that they were pirates and their weaponry had seemed to support this hypothesis but... Somehow, to Satiah, it just didn't ring true. She didn't know what else might have been stored in that station so she couldn't say why pirates would want to investigate. As she journeyed back to the ship, these questions plagued her. She reached the hole in the hangar floor nearly three hours after she had left. With a past as dark as hers would the light be too blinding for her?

***

"You *said* you wanted him *dead*," stated Roach, casually.

"Shooting isn't the best method currently," Tabre replied, his golden tooth gleaming as he smiled cunningly.

"Who and what did you have in mind?" Roach asked, shrugging. The shrug was to indicate indifference but inwardly he was fuming. He was an assassin by trade and normally his client gave him carte blanche in regard to methodology.

"*Two targets*, one primary and the other secondary. Both are diplomats," he replied, seriously. "As a result of the nature of our operation here, violent intervention is not acceptable."

"*Diplomacy*," chuckled Roach, darkly. "Dying art, eh?"

"Mostly everything has a use," he replied, a little sour. Roach nodded slowly as he chewed.

"…Yes, I think I can do something. I might need some help," he requested.

"Name it."

***

"So she left you in charge but failed to tell you *where* she was going, *why* she was going *or how long she would be?*" summed up Reed, his tone surprisingly amiable. Did nothing upset this man?

"Yup," Carlos nodded, glad that Reed was not angry. Satiah had eavesdropped this much of the conversation shortly before she entered. Covered in dust, some slime and other dirt she did not look her usual self.

"*Ah*," Reed said, with a well-mannered flourish. "We were just talking about you." Carlos eyed her, a little astonished at her condition.

"Good for you," she answered, discarding her cloak with relief. She untied her hair and slumped into the pilot's chair as Kelvin removed her cloak from the floor and took it away. She began to unseal her boots.

Everyone was looking at her expectantly, Carlos subtly and Reed obviously. A meaningful silence occurred.

"Who wants to go first?" she asked, with a wry smile. She was glad that they both seemed unruffled.

"After you," Reed said, to Carlos. Carlos was confused by that and then he realised that Reed would learn more by watching his exchange with Satiah than he might with just his own. Clever man.

"Tabre left the hangar area earlier," Carlos stated, having long ago decided to leave it at that.

"Where did he go and how long was he gone?" she asked, as he knew she would.

"Don't know and forty-three minutes. I *think* he went to see the Union representative but I cannot confirm that," he stated, sincerely. "That was the direction he set off in, in any case."

"*I see*," she said, unrevealingly.

"Done?" Reed asked. Carlos waved a hand at him to the affirmative. "Well Satiah, where were you when Tabre was busy?"

"Getting a feel for the layout of this place," she sighed, almost truthfully. She motioned to the condition her boots were in. "Some cleaning wouldn't go amiss but other than that…"

"And what would have happened had we needed to contact you in an emergency?" he asked, almost chiding.

"Kelvin was here the whole time," she answered, casually. She clicked her fingers and the big robot removed the remainder of the clothes she had discarded. Reed made a show of staring after Kelvin in mystification.

"*Where was he hiding?*" asked Reed, raising an eyebrow.

"Now, how could I know *that?*" she asked, grinning. "I was not here." Carlos was struck by Reed's ability to contain himself. Carlos would have put Essps on him exploding with indignation but Reed just stood there, unobtrusively smiling back at her.

"We are on the same side, you know," Reed stated. Or was it a question? A rhetorical point?

Satiah sighed, leaned forward in her chair and situated the fingertips of her hands together thoughtfully. Her brown eyes evaluated Reed for the hundredth occasion since he had boarded her ship back on Earth. For the first time she was thinking about what he was after, rather than what she had to hide from him.

"You're *looking for something*," she said, in a thinking-away tone of voice. "What is it?" Reed sat down slowly and Carlos realised how tense he was compared to them. He was convinced that in any second he might have to get between them should a fight break out. He realised rapidly that the fight had already started but it was a battle of words more than anything else.

"What would you say this planet has about it that makes it unique?" Reed asked, in an amicable voice.

"*Unique?*" she questioned, interested in the significance he had placed behind the term. She crossed her arms suddenly as if she had caught them doing something they shouldn't before shrugging.

"Nothing," she managed, at last. "The life here *is* new but hardly special. The environment is boring at best. The raw materials and technology… possibly. I would have to leave that for more qualified minds to resolve."

"*Can you keep a secret?*" Reed asked, making eye contact with her. She didn't say anything, just allowed herself to nod very slowly. A nonchalant waving of the hand would not have sufficed. If *anyone* knew how to keep a secret, it was Satiah. Her life was built on them. She had to pretend that this was not the case, however. She *had* to maintain her own security. Her eyes swung around to take in Carlos. He almost gulped under her stare but did not look away. He felt that this was most likely the most honest interaction the three of them had become involved in since they had met. They were all in the business of secrecy, the question seemed loosely daft. When she didn't look away, he realised she was waiting for him to agree too.

"Yes," he added, rather uneasily.

"I was not *randomly assigned* to this mission, neither was I *allocated* as part of a criteria cross match," Reed explained, in the tone of voice one would use when conveying bad news.

"*You lose a bet?*" she deadpanned. He smiled.

"I chose to come. More than that, *I insisted.*" Everyone in that room knew what was to come next.

"Why?" asked Carlos, frowning. There was far more to this than a simple *willingness to do one's job* and he felt that he could safely say that *patriotism* was out of the window at that point too.

"I don't know *who* discovered this planet," Reed said, suddenly grim. "But I *know* who first made contact with them." Satiah was now deeply interested and didn't bother to hide it.

"The Federation?" she guessed, in a tone of estimation. She had found, some time ago, that they were always *involved.*

"No, think *smaller,*" he advised, inviting her to sincerely have an estimate. Satiah disliked guessing games.

"The Remnant?" she asked, wondering if terrorism had reared its ugly head again. The Remnant, or the remains of the Kinkarren Confederacy, once a superpower too, had been formed from a terrorist organisation into a legitimate government. It had never really lost its taint, however. Since the end of the Common Protectorate War they had been a thorn in the side of all three remaining superpowers from time to time.

"Smaller," he mouthed, in barely a whisper. Finally she shook her head, admitting that she didn't know. Carlos too, couldn't think of anyone else save the Coalition itself and the Nebula Union, both of which were clearly too large.

"The Sisterhood of the Light," Reed answered, eventually. Carlos frowned. The who?

"I've heard of them," Satiah said, still very engaged. "They are only *one world* though, one single planet, completely independent of *everyone*. They have no political interest, no influence… they don't even encourage inter-planetary trade."

"All true," nodded Reed, allowing his respect of her knowledge to show. As Carlos could testify, not many had even heard of them. "To some, their world has been nicknamed: the hermit world."

"They have… *strange laws*. Odd cultural traditions… and they don't like *outsiders*," Satiah went on. "Although, at a certain point, every couple of years, a few hundred people visit them never to return."

"Now do you see *why* this is so interesting?" Reed asked, levelly.

"You want to use these Punes as a *middleman culture* in order to start negotiations with the Sisterhood of the Light and get *them* to join the Coalition?" asked Carlos, thinking he understood.

Reed turned to face him, incredulity dominating his expression.

"What? *Good lord no!*" Reed said, almost laughing. For a second, he seemed to give some more thought to that idea before shaking his head.

"Even if I did *somehow* get the Sisterhood interested, the Coalition has no desire for them to join as they are too… um… *distant*."

"*Philosophically?*" enquired Satiah, with a chuckle.

"That as well," he nodded.

"So… *what?*" asked Carlos, mystified and curious.

"The Coalition do not have any interest in the Sisterhood of Light joining them. The Sisterhood probably have no interest in joining anyone, least of all the Coalition."

"Does *everyone* hate the Coalition?" Carlos asked, remembering Deva's words on the subject. Reed and Satiah ignored him.

"The Sisterhood showed interest in *this* planet," Satiah said, thinking it through. "They even came here, beating all three superpowers in the race?"

"They did indeed," Reed said, smiling. "One of the Punes confirmed that fact with me earlier today."

"What were they doing?" asked Satiah, saying out loud what Reed's original question must have been. He smiled.

"*Precisely*. New worlds have been discovered before with no reaction from the Sisterhood. Yet Yevanicha, the Pune home world, had got them to come out of their shell and to dash halfway across the cosmos," he continued.

"I'm assuming the Punes didn't tell you *why* they came?" Satiah supposed.

"They ventured nothing and I haven't pressed them on the matter *yet*," Reed admitted. "I wanted to know if you have discovered anything *special* in your wanderings?" Satiah gave a mischievous grin.

"How did you know?" she asked, not a bit ashamed.

"Well, what else would you have been doing?" he asked, a little testy. "Plotting against the Federation? Investigating the building? Testing their security? Come on, it's child's play."

"*You* have worked with Phantoms before," Satiah noted, still amused.

"Where and when the textbooks endorse, yes." Reed confessed. "You have a tendency to make things happen even in the most inactive of scenarios. Why do you think I wanted you here?" She raised her eyebrows and then gesticulated that she had found nothing. *She hadn't!* Not to her knowledge anyway.

"You have found nothing out of the ordinary? Nothing at all?" he clarified.

"Nothing except that shaft," Carlos muttered, yawning.

"*Shaft?*" Reed asked, sitting up. Clearly it seemed significant to him, as it had to them hours before.

"It's nothing, that's where I was earlier by the way. I brought back a sample," she said, dismissively. She recollected the air being an insect-swarm of dust swirling before her eyes. She hoped none of it had made it into her lungs.

"A sample of what?" Reed asked, interested. "So you found *something?*"

"With any luck Kelvin will know within the hour," she said, beckoning to Carlos as she spoke. "Carlos, show him the map."

Unthinkingly, Carlos passed the paper copy over to Reed and the first thing he saw was Deva's communicator details. He couldn't know it was hers, of course, but when Satiah saw it she made the conclusive leap in less than a second. It also helped that the question he'd originally written to Deva was in huge lettering there too. Reed's eyebrows drew together in apparent deep thought.

"Some kind of code?" he guessed, mildly sarcastic. Satiah almost snatched it off of him.

"What's *this?*" Satiah asked, eyeing Carlos.

"Intel," he said, unconsciously standing to attention. "I acquired the communicator details of one of the Federation delegates…"

She cut him off with a rapid-fire question. "Did you let *her* inside this ship?" demanded Satiah, angry.

"No!" Carlos said, completely honestly. He didn't like the way she emphasised the word 'her' either.

"Then how…?" Satiah began, and trailed off. She glanced out of the viewport and saw what Deva had scribbled on the ship's bodywork. She pressed a button on the control pad in front of her. Moments later, Kelvin entered.

"Yes," he said, his voice the same monotone as ever.

"Play back his last communication," Satiah ordered, pointing at Carlos. Carlos gaped. She'd bugged *his* gear! But she'd not even… then he realised it had been Kelvin. Her mechanical henchman. Carlos was then subjected to hearing the whole conversation between him and Deva in front of everyone. To his surprise, however, Satiah became much less angry during the replaying exchange.

"You're in her head," Satiah concluded, almost impressed.

"She was lying about the lie," Carlos said, trying to convince Satiah that he knew what he was doing. "She pretended to give me that information about Tabre as a gesture of trust. In reality, I'm pretty sure he instructed her to tell me from the start. He sent her out purposely *knowing* I would see through her distraction easily."

"To what end?" asked Reed, a little confused. *"Does this matter?"*

"We will talk about *that* later," Satiah sighed, eyeing Carlos. Inside she was trying to remember what it was like to be young. She was in her early fifties despite looking like she was in her early twenties. The legacy of Linctus Lotion. Her youth had been very... painful. Her own mother had tried to murder her once. When she had been only a child. Her own mother had tried to stab her and may have succeeded had her older sister not intervened. Her mother had had a condition that made her temporarily psychotic. The voices in her head had told her to kill the child Satiah and, to get them to shut up, she had tried to do just that.

Satiah could still vividly remember the towering adult coming at her with a blade. It still gave her nightmares when she was unoccupied. That was part of the reason she preferred to never stop working, while she was working it distracted her from the bad dreams. It gave her mind something else to chew on. It had been that day that the darkness had come into her life and had never really left. It was like a stray animal she had made the mistake of feeding just once... now it would never leave.

It was always there, in the back of her mind. Watching. Waiting. Just a cloud of blackness that snuffed out all but the brightest lights. It would never leave. Yet it gave her strength in cynicism. Foresight in predicting treachery. An ability to forget compassion, hope and even love. It was that darkness that could give her the desperate desire to survive. The power she needed to get her through the direst of storms. Satiah pushed through the darkness in her mind, trying to think about men. She had been with men, many times. Yet never for love or friendship, not even for profit. She'd had missions, objectives and they had been part of those.

To her shock she realised... she'd never truly loved another human being since her childhood. Over forty years of coldness... She shook herself, trying to rationalise. She had no business loving anyone. She knew the price of betrayal and it was not worth it. Carlos had yet to learn this lesson so... learn he must. Satiah knew that she both couldn't and wouldn't need to teach him that... Deva would do it for her. The only question was: would he survive the lesson? This was of course assuming that she would betray him.

"Very well then," Reed said, choosing to ignore that. Instead he concentrated on his latest favourite topic. "What is this shaft exactly?" He and Satiah were still locked in confrontational eye contact before Satiah broke it.

"...I don't know," Satiah sighed, shaking her head. "I had hoped that actually *seeing it* might lend more clues but I'm not much better off than I was before." Reed was examining the map carefully.

"This is a good job," he noted, impressed by the detail.

"Carlos provided it," Satiah admitted, honestly. She felt she had been unduly harsh to him and was trying to find a way of making it up to him. She told herself that she didn't care or feel guilty; she just wanted to ensure their working relationship remained workable. He was young and had a lot to learn. It had been inevitable that mistakes would be made. She should have made more allowances. Carlos let his disbelief at the apparent congratulations show.

"It's not structural," muttered Reed, going through the options Satiah and Carlos had already discussed.

"The analysis of the sample is complete," Kelvin interrupted. "The substance appears to be a solidified coolant compound residual."

"Coolant," echoed Satiah, thoughtfully. Reed too was clearly off in the realms of speculation.

"Maybe it's one of those *emergency reactor overload junctions*," Carlos suggested. "When the power or reaction gets too unstable and they have to cool everything down to prevent damage. That would explain why it is not used often but occasionally." It was conceivable.

"It *would* but it offers no hints as to why *the Sisterhood* are interested in it," Reed answered.

"We are of course assuming that it *is* the shaft or *the purpose of the shaft* that they *are* interested in," Satiah qualified.

"Have you tried just *asking* the Sisterhood?" asked Carlos, aware that such a proposal may be considered lunacy. A lengthy pause was all he got in response. "And why exactly are they called Sisterhood *of the Light*? What's the light?"

***

"Of course you will have to poison *everyone's* drink in order to preserve our plausible deniability," Tabre acknowledged.

"Of course," agreed Roach, going through a wide selection of drugs. "You will need something that can be manufactured *here* too, that way, *should it serve our purpose*, the Punes can be blamed."

"I will instruct my team to accept the offered drinks but *not* to drink them under any circumstances," Tabre went on. He knew it was a poor way to kill an enemy like Satiah but he did have other objectives unfortunately.

"Dosage will not be a problem. Administering the drug will be the hardest part," Roach said, considering. "I will need access to it." He was referring to the source of the liquid repast.

"I have a map of the complex here," Tabre said, spreading out a flimsy parchment across the open table area. Both men leaned in to study it. "Any Pune casualties are unacceptable." Tabre knew that they didn't know if the poison would work on Punes but it was a risk that had to be mitigated.

"Our ships are *here*, in the hangar area," Tabre stated, pointing. Roach nodded. A fresh idea came to Roach and he almost laughed as he wondered why they had failed to think of it before.

"Would it not be easier to poison a ship's water supply than a vat guarded by the locals?" he asked, thinking hard.

"…You mean *three* vats?" confirmed Tabre, reminding the other man. All three delegates would need to be poisoned… or at least that was how he wanted it to look. It made the guilty party harder to pinpoint. Roach paused, in his eagerness he had forgotten that.

"I… It would be so much easier to just shoot three targets," Roach stated, objecting once again to the plan.

"The negotiations cannot be violently disturbed," stated Tabre, coldly. "Last resort *only*."

"When people start collapsing…" began Roach, shaking his head.

"Such disruption is tolerable. You start *shooting*, you might hit the Punes which would in turn ruin the negotiation completely," warned Tabre.

"I never miss," Roach claimed, not backing down.

"Precisely, and in that case I would need you to miss *once* at least," Tabre argued, a grin on his lips making his golden tooth shine. Conrad had to survive in order to continue talking.

"…Fine," Roach said, giving up. He clasped a cylinder with a deep red fluid in it. A deeper red, even than blood. He handed it to Tabre.

"Perfect."

***

Satiah and Carlos had been dreading this conversation for similar reasons but it had to happen. Again, Satiah was pushing concepts about parenthood out of her mind.

"I am glad you are seeing her later," Satiah said, starting off in an unexpected direction. "*Deva*, I mean."

"…You are?" he asked, naturally doubtful. "*Why*?"

"She could have valuable information." Satiah smiled sincerely. Carlos had wondered if she would take this approach. Recognising that directly preventing their interaction would be counterproductive, she was now trying to use it to her advantage. Carlos could not object, he was on a mission. He was philandering with the red line as it was.

"She will be doing the same in regards to you, I'm afraid. She *may* like you, possibly even care about you but her first instinct will *always* be her mission," she continued. Carlos had to admit she might have a point there.

"I find the using of our feelings for one another objectionable," he protested, more heatedly than he meant to. "This is a diplomatic mission *and we are not at war*. There is no rational reason to play it like this." Satiah backed down, doing her best to be as gentle as possible. It was hard for her to be gentle.

"What do you suggest?" she asked, genuinely wondering what his counter offer would be.

"Maybe... given time... I could get her to... join us," he stated, deciding to just go for it. The uncertainty in his tone made it almost sound like a question rather than a statement of intent. Satiah crossed her arms and just stared at him.

"So, you plan to *recruit* her into Phantom Squad?" she asked, a little tersely.

"...I don't know," he admitted, at last casting all pretence aside. Satiah tried really hard to behave compassionately. It was tough for her being as she had trouble empathising with anyone. She placed her hand on his back supportively.

"I wish I knew what you were going through," she said, softly. Maybe she could try something different. The truth? For an odd moment she was wondering what it would be like were he her son.

"You are on dangerous ground, Carlos, and you know it," she said, in the same tone. "I... don't know what to teach you here."

"You *did* say you'd never taught anyone before, I think you're doing all right," he said, encouragingly.

"It all depends on whether she is genuine or not about *you*," Satiah concluded. "Her purpose will dictate your reaction. You just need to find her true purpose." He glanced at her, a new respect in his eyes.

"They should include that as part of every Phantom's training," he chuckled.

"But then everyone would know and *be* the same. The main difference between Phantoms and any other operatives is that their training is *never* regimented. Each Phantom will be trained *slightly* differently. It makes us harder to predict," she elaborated.

He nodded, seeing the wisdom in that.

"What do you feel about Deva?" he asked, inquisitive.

"She's *very* Colonial," smiled Satiah, disobligingly. "Long silky black hair, dark eyes and the inflection."

"You *know* what I mean," he pressed, seeking her feelings. She paused, and stepped away from him as she considered her answer. She didn't like to talk about her feelings, believing it to be a waste of time. Her opinions, however…

"She is what most men would find attractive. She's intelligent enough to be an operative. But she is young… still malleable. She is like a female version of you," she responded, in a way being even more unhelpful. She raised a finger and pulled out a small casket from under the control pads. He stared down at it, curious as she passed it to him. As he took it from her, she snatched the pistol from his belt in a swift move. He flinched and gasped in shock. She smiled, pointing it at him jokingly.

"Men can be *so easy*," she warned him, before placing the gun on the console before them. He was still holding the casket. He managed a half laugh in response. She nodded to the casket; it was a present for him. He opened it and his eyes widened in disbelief. Inside rested a new pistol, clearly expensive and a great improvement on the one she had just pilfered from him. It had bodywork of shiny gold and silver, making it appear brand new. That would be a tough one to clean. Satiah gave an almost flirtatious grin and he half expected her to just take that from him as well as it was part of some joke she was having with him.

"Every man needs his gun," she stated, as he picked it up and inspected it. "If nothing else it will impress Deva." He chuckled. It was heavier than it looked and much more formidable than the one he'd been given back at headquarters. He'd known for a long time that Phantoms, who were out on missions, often had their own personalised equipment. Satiah was no exception. Now, neither was he. Clearly this gun could slug a real wallop.

"…*Thanks*," he managed, at a loss for anything to say.

"Welcome," she nodded, turning to leave. "Don't forget to practise with it."

***

Ash entered the command deck, Ruby hurrying along ahead of him. His glance swept across the room, taking everything in. Instantly he recognised what was happening.

"Ash?" guessed Jenna, eyeing him in supposition. Did all humans look like that when terrified? A pained gleam in their eyes. Their minds losing the connection with logic and relying on likelihood instead? Interesting but this had gone far enough.

"How many are still alive?" he asked, instantly.

"As far as we can tell about one hundred and seventy-two. We have *ten* dead now and twenty exhibiting signs of the contagion," answered the Captain. His attention was strained and his expression weary.

"There's nothing I can do, nothing," the doctor was saying. "If I go in there, I'll only die with them."

"The virus was not acquired until the ship left the planet, meaning someone deliberately released it on-board. That someone would be unlikely to do so *unless* they were in possession of a vaccine. All the escape pods are still here, there is no way off of this ship. Logic dictates that that someone *must* still be aboard," he explained. There was a pause as everyone came to terms with this statement. It was true and somewhat disturbing.

"...Why would they *stay* if they *knew* there was a virus here?" asked Jenna, puzzled. Ruby suddenly understood and she stared at Ash's profile as she spoke.

"...Because they want to see what happens. They are studying its effects, *measuring its progress*," she guessed. It was only a guess because she couldn't be sure but as Ash would like it was logical. A smug smile tugged at Ash's lips letting her know that he had noted the similarity with his own activities she was dredging up.

"A *scientist*," the Captain said, thinking hard. He began a swift search for the list of passengers that had been printed out shortly after disembarkation.

"Or a *doctor*," suggest Jenna suddenly, pistol back in her hand. Everyone froze as they took in what she was doing. She was aiming her pistol straight at the doctor's chest. He was staring at her, an expression of dumbfounded outrage on his face.

"*What?*" he uttered, after a fraught second.

"Whoever is doing this wouldn't be so obvious," Ash said, casually.

"If it was *him*, why is he out here with *us*?" Ruby asked, expressively.

"But *where better to watch* as the chaos unfolds?" Jenna snapped, not lowering the gun.

"He *did* refuse to go and help the infected," Ruby noted, seeing the logic once again. Ash, however, did not give her a show of approval this time. He only seemed to watch, silent and ominous.

"We all agreed it would be a futile action to try to help them!" the doctor shouted, tears streaming down his face. He was talking about when they had discussed trying to help the infected and his instant refusal to go near them. "You can't seriously believe her…"

"Why did you do it?" asked the Captain, too shocked to be angry. "Why would you kill all those…?"

"*I didn't!*" he yelled, literally trembling with terror.

"Who else would know *how*?" demanded a guard, joining in. Ash continued to watch, his face unreadable, but he never said a word. A silence descended. The doctor looked at all the condemning faces with the visage of a hunted man.

"End this," the Captain requested, his tone one of pleading. "You *must* or we will all die too."

"Stop the virus or I will kill you now!" Jenna ordered, beside herself with fury.

"I can't…" sobbed the doctor, shaking his head. "*This is nothing to do with me.*"

"Where is the cure?" petitioned the guard, with aggression in his voice. The doctor shook his head and took a step backwards.

Reflexively the guards moved in to surround him but a shot was fired in the commotion. The doctor screamed and pitched over backwards onto the deck. He hit the floor hard and inert. Jenna stared down at him, gun in her hand, contempt in her eyes. *And so the cycle begins,* thought Ash. Just as his mother described. Human fear would swiftly lead to death. He grasped the lesson easily and made a mental note to analyse human fear more closely.

"*Murderer,*" she accused, not seeing the irony. The Captain hung his head, almost in tears himself. Ruby let out a breath she'd forgotten she was holding. Only Ash remained unmoved except… Ruby saw his eyes. They were not wide with shock or sorrow. They were neither sad nor angry. They were analytical and suspicious. Fear crept back into her heart, this was not over.

"Great, *now he's dead*, how are we supposed to find the cure?" asked the Captain. Jenna was quick to answer.

"His cabin… we should search his cabin!"

They all hurried outside, leaving Ash and Ruby alone. Ash slowly approached the body. Ruby followed and crouched next to him to watch.

"The Captain was right, we *needed* him to find the cure," Ruby sighed, seriously. "Now he's dead and… he could have hidden it anywhere." Ash did not respond. "Do you think they will find it?" He didn't answer. "*Ash?*" He looked up so sharply at her that she almost flinched.

"Fear breeds stupidity," he stated, coldly. He slowly held up the dead man's hand. Ruby glanced at it and noticed what Ash had undoubtedly seen some time ago. A weeping sore… a sign of contamination. The doctor had been infected!

"*He* had the virus *too*! That makes *no sense* unless he messed up somehow or his cure doesn't actually work," she said, shocked. "*Oh no, what if it doesn't work?*"

"It's *simpler* than that, Ruby," he said, in her ear. "He had the virus *because* he did not have the cure. That means he was telling the truth and it had nothing to do with him. *Jenna killed the wrong person.* This suggests that the perpetrator is still alive and active amid us."

***

"Where are you planning on going exactly?" Tabre asked, his tone a little mocking. "There are no facilities for human teenagers here. This mission is a one of diplomacy not frivolity."

"I have *often* been praised for my creativity," Deva replied, in a prickly tone.

"*Of course*," he agreed, as he knew that was true. He had studied her file more than once. "Not for *subtlety* though."

"Everyone has limitations," she quoted, with relish. The defensiveness she had amused Tabre more than it riled him and he waved a dismissive hand at her.

"Find out what you can from him and do not compromise us," he instructed. She nodded.

Tabre watched her go, his mind adjusting where necessary. In *no places*, in other words. Conrad was the only really necessary person on this mission. Even Tabre himself could be described as an optional extra. Deva was little more than a child and, just like a child, she was easily distracted. She didn't really know anything that compromised them but she could give Satiah a way into their ship… in theory. Tabre had been surprised that Satiah had not attempted a break-in at some stage. That was the other question: did he report Deva? He considered for only a moment before deciding against it. He was a professional killer, not a teenager's guardian: so long as she stayed out of his way he would give no more thought to her.

Going out into the hangar area, Deva made her way to the Coalition ship and rapped on the hatchway. The ramp slid down and Carlos leapt out, a grin on his face.

"They let you out, then," he surmised.

"No. I'm a hologram," she retorted, in her usual style. They began to walk along together rather stiffly.

"…Are we going somewhere?" he asked, the question serving two topics simultaneously.

"Where do you want to go?" she mirrored, doing the same thing. Satiah may have been right about the "female version of him" comment.

"Where is there to go?" he asked, getting cagey. They were both stretching in their minds, trying to do… something. She surrendered first.

"Are you bugged? I know I am," she said. "This planet stinks but… I heard swampy air is good for you."

"Never heard of marsh gas?" he asked, only half joking. A Pune was watching them, from the entrance.

"Of course but maybe I want you unconscious for a reason," she said. "Are you always this wary?"

"Are you always this forward?" he asked, mirroring her untactfully.

"The Colonial Federation rewards boldness, what does the Coalition reward?" she asked. Ouch!

"Deva... I don't want to talk to you about politics," he admitted, his tone firm. She responded to the tone by glancing across at him.

"Okay, what are we *allowed* to talk about?" she asked, in a softer voice. He liked that voice, it sounded so tender and almost musical in its gentleness.

"Where are you from?" he said, seeking a *neutral* subject. Was there such a thing?

"My parents were from Earth... I was born on a freighter between worlds. I was born in space so... ultimately that is where I am from," she said, in apparent honesty. There would be no need for her to lie about that but that didn't mean she wouldn't. "That's why I'm called Deva. Deva as in *cluster of stars*."

"Not because of your eyes?" The flirt was clumsy and he regretted it the moment it came out of his mouth but she only laughed.

"I hope *all* my enemies will be so complimentary," she said.

"Am I your enemy?"

"Are you my friend?" To say this conversation was difficult would be a titanic understatement. Carlos was starting to tire of this game: *Can we trust each other or not?* That's all he wanted to know! That and... did she like him?

They followed a corridor that inclined upwards. Maybe it would lead up, out and onto the surface. The second they were out of sight of the ships, she spun to face him. For a moment he thought she was going to attack him. She grabbed his hand and pulled it up to the side of her face. At first he thought she wanted him to caress her but when he touched her ear he knew the truth. She really was bugged. She put her finger on his lips, smiled and then removed the bug. She placed it on the floor and then regarded him solemnly. He took the bug Satiah had given him out of the collar of his cloak and placed it next to hers. Then, holding hands, they crept away from the ears that wanted to hear everything they said. The faster and further they got the more they started to giggle and laugh. They were on a mission, they were on opposite sides, they were being watched, tested and evaluated... but that didn't mean they couldn't have fun.

***

"He has removed his transmitter," Kelvin said.

"...Just as well, I was on the verge of *vomiting*," Satiah grinned, amused. "I think he'll be fine now."

"He is no longer a danger?" Kelvin confirmed.

"No," she agreed, pleased. "He knows the dangers and it is up to him how he chooses to confront them and who knows... maybe she really does love him. He certainly tempts her; I could hear it in her voice."

"They have much to learn about flirting," Kelvin noted. She raised an eyebrow.

"And how would *you* know?" she demanded, mock outrage on her face. Kelvin remained silent and she smirked.

"You are correct though." Satiah was on guard duty now, watching the two other ships they had nearby like a hawk.

She activated her communicator. Rainbow answered.

"Nothing new yet, Satiah, eating dinner with the wife," he said, seriously.

"Sisterhood of the Light," Satiah said, bluntly. "What do you know about them?"

"Give me a sec..." he said, clearly busy. Sounds of muffled conversation and cutlery could be heard. Satiah leaned back in her chair, her gaze never leaving the Colonial ship. She expected Tabre to try something anytime now.

"The only thing I'm getting is the official leadership of the planet Erokathorn," he said. She nodded to herself as he couldn't see her. She had forgotten the name of their planet. "There are plenty of sisterhoods but this is the biggest match," he went on.

"They are the ones, I want *everything* you have on them," she stated, seriously.

"*As well as* Jaylite Industries?" he asked, a little incredulous. "Oh, and it turns out Randal moved your man because that floor of the building is being renovated so... nothing creepy in that."

Satiah did feel a little reassured at that. Of course she would never fully trust Randal; in her mind, no one with any sense trusted their immediate superior. The proof that he was not trying to hide anything was a relief, however.

"That's very helpful," she smiled, pleased. "Now, I'll let you get back to your date."

"*It's my wife!*" he protested, almost believably.

"Goodnight Rainbow," she teased, cutting him off.

"What about Reed?" asked Kelvin, to her. He wanted to know if she still wanted him to watch Reed. Satiah thought about it.

"...No, he's clean too," she allowed, after lengthy consideration. "He's strange and clever but I think we can trust him."

A bleeping caught her attention. She leaned forward checking it.

"There is an intruder in the complex," Kelvin stated, noticing too. He kicked a box over to her, anticipating what she would ask for next. Inside was a new cloak and new boots.

"Punctual as ever, Kelvin," she congratulated, pulling the new boots on quickly. "Stay here in case it's a trick."

"Yes," he said, in his usual monotone. She sprang out of the room, heading for the hole in the floor. She was back in the ventilation system within seconds, making her way towards the other person. They were not going towards the ships but were making their way deeper into the complex, not far from where the negotiations were to be continued the next day. Satiah's first thought was that they were going to plant a bomb and that she was going to have to stop them. It was a predictable strategy and she'd expected more from Tabre.

In darkness, as before, she crept along, using directions from Kelvin as her guide. Getting back wouldn't be an issue as she would probably be using the corridors. Her target obviously knew the layout and the patrols as they were adeptly moving between them in a steady direction. They passed the negotiation area, Satiah only ten metres or so behind them. She exited the ventilation system and padded silently along, after the figure. They were taller and broader than she was, dressed in black. A male operative of reasonable training, she had to assume. What was his purpose? He wasn't carrying anything big, nothing she could see. He did have a pistol though. He stopped suddenly and turned. Satiah instinctively crouched and pressed herself against the wall to hide. It was so dark, both of them were dressed in black. A long silence ensued.

In the distance, at the end of the corridor, a group of five Punes moved along in the formation of a patrol. Satiah and the man watched them go. When the sounds had died away, the man started to move again. Satiah continued to follow. Her boots, typically made from snowsnake skin and lined in screed fur, made no sound as she moved. Her eyes were those of a hunter and her body was poised to fight. There was little else she could tell about the man she was tracking. The details were all important. Knowing them could be the difference between life and death. He entered a room to the side and Satiah caught a scent on the air. The drink given out to them all earlier that day by the Punes had a smell similar to that of apples only much stronger. Annoyingly the man made a point of closing the door behind him presumably to give him some warning should anyone else try to enter while he was inside and to prevent attracting attention. This was doubly annoying as not only would it tip him off to Satiah being there, it also meant she could not see what he was doing while it was closed.

"Kelvin," she whispered. "Is there another way into that room which he had just entered?"

"Follow the corridor to the end, turn right, right again and there should be another entrance there," came his dependable reply. Chancing it, she ran as quietly as she could. She knew she may lose track of her quarry in this period, so she intended to be as swift as possible. Kelvin was right, barely a minute later, she had found the other door. It was also closed. She extended her gloved hand and pushed gently. Soundlessly it opened and she quickly slipped inside, closing it behind her while facing into the room. The room was big, full of rows and rows of barrel-like containers. She couldn't see the man now but she had an idea of where he was. The smell of the drink was almost overpowering now. If there was one thing that she would remember this planet for it would be the smells. Did the Punes not have a sense of smell?

A creaking caused her to stop. Crouching, she listened intently. She could see him again now. He'd got one of the barrels loose from the shelving and seemed to be trying to open it. Satiah used this as an opportunity to sneak closer. The tiny flash of faded light betrayed the blade he was using to her eyes. As she edged closer still she spotted a glass tube resting on its side. It looked a little like an old fashioned test tube only it was thinner and far stronger. A golden screw-top lid prevented any contents from leaking out. It was then that she guessed that whatever he was going to do involved dosing the drink in some way or other. She smiled a small knowing smile as she pocketed the tube herself and withdrew a few steps into the obscurity of the room.

She waited, still watching, wondering what would happen when he noticed that it was gone. Would he have another as a backup? If he did, she would have to intervene more directly. At last he got the lid off of the barrel without making much noise and turned to get the tube. A silent but frantic search ensued. She smiled contentedly, he did not have another. There was a moment of silence as he stood up from checking the floor and put his hands on his hips. He was thinking. Satiah began to wonder if he would even report the failure. He may replace the barrel and return to report it had all gone well. When nothing happened he would probably blame the chemical or insist that, for whatever reason, the barrel was changed. He began to replace the barrel where he had acquired it and Satiah continued to watch from the shadows, interested.

He began to leave the area and, curious as to where he thought he was going, Satiah began to shadow him again. Like last time he easily avoided the Pune watch circuits. He remained unaware of Satiah though. He was heading upwards and eventually he departed the complex, Satiah still went after him, even more interested. If he *wasn't* going for one of the ships in the hangar, that indicated someone had *another ship* somewhere else. She had to find out who and where. The next leg of the journey was through the foggy swamps. The moons were bright, brighter than most Satiah had seen but they were masked by the fog. Much like the sun was during the day. On the muddy, boggy ground a layer of rime was visible. Both were wary not to let anything crunch underfoot. The man had a path through them and Satiah had to carefully memorise it for her return trip. A sixth sense made the man turn around a few times but Satiah was quicker, always ducking away in the fog. And then... she spotted it. A square patch of light ahead in the fog. A viewport.

The man she was allowing to lead her pulled out a light and began to flash it in a pattern. On. Off. On. Off. On, turn left and then up. All this was before he began a straight line approach to the craft. It was obviously a coded greeting to let whoever was aboard know that it was *him* coming back. She also approached, confident that no one would be expecting him to be followed if he had given the signal. The ship itself was small and unidentifiable, half submerged in the swamp itself. Satiah decided it was probably an old personal transporter modified and extensively improved. She didn't follow the man inside, she knew doing that would be a step too far. Clearly there was someone else inside and if there were too many for her, she would be killed. Instead she attached a small dome-like contraption to the side of the ship and then headed back. A sentinel device, only the best could get hold of such gadgets.

***

The search of the doctor's room was as unsuccessful as the doctor had been at convincing them he was not the culprit. There was no sign of the cure. Ash and Ruby had known this before the search had even begun and they also knew that someone else had known that it would be a fruitless endeavour too. Ash had gone through the passenger list himself and identified a retired scientist who was travelling on board. Chris.

"So what you are saying is: whoever released the virus *also* killed the co-pilot to ensure that there was no way anyone could leave?" Ruby asked.

"Exactly," he replied, eyeing the device that was still preventing anyone from using the controls. He knew he could probably crack the codes but not in time to save anyone.

The Captain, Jenna and the rest of the guards had gone to get Chris and force him to go to the command deck.

"You don't think it's Chris, do you?" Ruby asked, perceptively.

"I do not," he admitted. "Again, like with the doctor, it is *too obvious*. This has all been meticulously planned and that planner would not have overlooked the possibility that we would seek out scientists or other professionals who may be involved with viruses or even chemicals. *They've been pretty thorough about everything else.*"

"…But that could cover a lot of people," she stated, concerned. "Virtually any job could *in theory* result in exposure to chemicals if you think about it long enough."

"Indeed," he said, and made eye contact. "That is precisely what the real culprit is using to hide behind."

"So how can we smoke them out?" she asked, on the edge of giving up hope.

"What did you just say?" Ash asked, facing her with that suddenness he did sometimes. As usual it froze her for a second.

"I asked how you were planning to…" she began.

"That's not what you said," he stated, his attention on her unnerving her a little. She repeated, word for word, her original question. Ash went silent for a few moments and then the smug smile appeared which instantly made Ruby feel more hopeful and perhaps a little scared.

"I'm an idiot," he stated, shaking his head. "Searching through all that…"

"What?" she asked, confused.

"We have *no control* over anything on board this ship but we know that whoever has done this is still on board," he said. "They must be as the murder of the co-pilot confirms it. Everything else could have been done remotely but *that* murder ties the culprit down…"

"We've been over this," she said, exasperated.

"Correct and we, you and I, are exactly equal to the culprit *unlike* the rest of the crew. You and I and the culprit are immune to the virus but no one else is. Yet there is something that we can do that will force whoever is responsible to intervene," he stated.

"*What?*" she asked, openly fascinated.

"We start figuratively killing the passengers," he replied, as if it were obvious. For a second Ruby thought she'd misheard.

"No, Ash, you don't understand, we are trying to *save* them from dying not speed up the process," she argued, a little sarcastically.

"Whoever is doing this is testing their virus, trying to find out how fast it works. If we start killing the…" he began.

"We mess up their experiment?" she finished, a little angry. "*Ash!* I know you have a different understanding of morality than we humans and I know you are much smarter than me. Please *don't* think

I'm protesting but I *seriously* object to the murder of innocent people. Did you really think...? What do you mean *figuratively*?"

"All we have to do is *be seen to be* killing them. We fake the deaths or the threat of death. The culprit will believe we intend to kill them or that we are all about to die too and may offer to give the cure to us in exchange for their own life," Ash explained, casually.

"*Or they may not*, they may just hide somewhere," she argued. "Ash, it's completely mad."

"That is why it will work, because it is completely unpredictable," he insisted.

"...What about the Captain? *He* will try to stop us regardless," she sighed. "Always assuming that it isn't him."

Ash's mind ran through options. He had originally intended to just start shooting the passengers and crew as they found them but quickly realised this idea was flawed. He glanced at the controls even though he knew they were currently unusable. Ruby watched him uncertainly. She hoped he was not about to do something crazy. Swiftly he stood and instead of going to the controls, crouched and ripped open a panel exposing their workings.

"Ash?" she growled, fearfully. He glanced up at her, giving her a winning smile.

"Trust me," he requested, with unnerving calm.

"If you're going to wheel out *that* old cliché, you'll have to tell me what you are doing if you expect me to go along with it," Ruby stated, stubbornly. "*Duffer.*" His eyes closed momentarily in irritation.

"If someone is testing a virus, in order to see what is happening, one would assume they need the lights on and the doors closed," he replied, casually. "And... if we evacuate the atmosphere, we may even rid ourselves of the virus."

"...You're going to open the airlocks?" she asked, in comprehension. "While the lights are out?"

"It will effectively filter most of the infected air out of the ship," he shrugged. "The passengers are sealed in their rooms and so will not be swept out into space."

"But the controls are locked," she stated.

"That's why I'm going to sabotage the workings instead," he stated, starting to get impatient.

"...Well, it's better than your idea of going around shooting everyone," she admitted, without enthusiasm.

"*Figuratively*," he reminded, with marked annoyance.

***

Satiah climbed back into her ship from the ventilation system almost casually. She had had to be careful on her return journey from the swamp of the Pune patrols. They seemed more numerous than before. Perhaps the Punes had found out that someone had been wandering around in secret. She had planted the sentinel device perfectly. Kelvin should have been recording everything. Kelvin stood, obligingly holding the metal floor plate to make room for her.

"Anything happen here?" she asked, staid.

"No," he said shortly. "The signal is good." He was referring to the device she had planted. He replaced the floor panel.

"Are they talking?" she asked, hopefully.

"A conversation did occur six point three seconds after the sentinel began transmitting," he answered. She smiled in triumph.

"Got you."

They entered the control room to find Reed patiently awaiting their arrival. Satiah would normally have been annoyed at his nosy intrusion but the apparent success of the night so far gave her extra tolerance. He didn't ask, just looked at her enquiringly.

"I've placed a sentinel device on a ship out in the swamps... one I presume no one is meant to know about," she stated, giving him a brief outline of where she had been.

"Well done," he commended, sincerely. He seemed genuinely pleased at the news. She sat in the pilot's chair, picked up the live thread from Kelvin's system and linked it to the ship's speaker system. At first there was nothing other than complete silence. The conversation was clearly over now. She rewound the footage.

She activated playback, listening intently. The initial blare they heard was that of the sentinel device clunking against the hull. It, as programmed, clamped itself where it had landed. She then hurriedly had to cut out various frequencies in sound, to prevent the dull hum of the ships power generation from making the conversation inaudible.

"What happened?" asked a man. He had a strong accent, not quite Colonial though.

"There was a problem," said another, Satiah guessed it was the man she had followed. So, he was going to tell the truth after all. How likely would it be that doing so would result in fatal consequences for him?

"You *weren't* detected," replied the first, obviously confused.

"I lost the poison in the dark somehow," stated the second man. "Just…"

"That's what I told you to do," interrupted the accented man. Satiah leaned in closer. So… he was never meant to administer the substance after all. Satiah placed the vial on the console in front of her to show Reed that she had recovered it.

Reed never said a word, just listened quietly.

"I brought you back a sample of whatever it is that they will be drinking tomorrow," he said, going on. "But, in the dark I misplaced the phial somehow. I don't understand how." So! They had never *intended* to poison anyone, they had just wanted a sample of the fluid the Punes produced, but they still had poison. Why would they leave the poison behind?

"…It is of no importance, as far as Tabre knows the whole vat will have been contaminated," the man with the accent answered.

"Fine."

"What was their security like?" asked the accented man.

"Amateur at best, I was expecting much more." Satiah had to agree with that. "What will happen tomorrow now that we have pretended to poison the drinks?"

"Nothing, nothing at all. Tabre will be expectant but *no one will drop dead* and the negotiations will continue as they would normally."

"Tabre will assume the chemical was filtered out or possibly countered by other chemicals."

"He *could* accuse us of messing up which ironically enough would be quite correct, in that we did not do what he instructed us to do. But if I am to collect my fee from the Nebula Union, their delegates will have to remain alive until the day after tomorrow," said the accented man. Satiah understood instantly, this man was playing the Federation and the Union against one another. She was half inclined to return to the vat and administer the poison herself just to ruin their plans but knew that in doing so she could be overreaching.

"What then?" asked the other man.

"That will depend on when my fee arrives and Tabre's next instructions. As the negotiations are clearly going the Coalition's way, I'm guessing Tabre will decide he has no choice and will request the immediate dispatch on the Coalition delegates. This time, however, it will be by *my* method, not his," said the accented man. Satiah raised a grim eyebrow, starting to wish she'd placed a bomb under their ship or something similar. A silence descended and it was clear that the exchange was at an end. Satiah just deactivated and sat back to think. Reed remained silent, also thinking. After she had formed her own impressions and opinions, she turned to face him. He was already watching her.

"What are you thinking?" he asked, interested.

Satiah was about to tell him when her communicator went off.

"Satiah," came Randal's voice, as she activated. She almost swore in irritation. She did not need this right then.

"I want an update; I've heard nothing from you since your safe arrival. The Commandment Benefactor is *most* irritated by this radio silence and to be honest *so am I...*" Satiah swallowed her fury adeptly.

"Phantom Leader, I was *just* about to call you, she answered, smoothly. Reed gave her a spirited grin. "Things are proceeding well." There was a pause as she tried to leave it at that.

"...*And?*" he demanded, tetchy.

"You said you wanted an update, you didn't say anything about *details*," she said, amused.

"*Satiah...*" he began, getting ready for a harsh screed. She invited Reed over with a tilt of her head.

"Phantom Leader," Reed interjected. He took the communicator from her gently. "Perhaps *I* would be a better choice of enlightenment regarding the specifics of the negotiations."

***

"My uncle and aunt used to take care of me until I was employed by the government," Deva explained. "It was lucky for all of us really. They never had the means to provide for themselves never mind me too."

"And you have no idea about your parents?" Carlos asked, inquisitive.

"Nah… after dropping me to my uncle when I was still a baby, six days old apparently, they just vanished," she said, sounding sad. "I often wonder what happened back then. Why they left me behind. Did they mean to? Didn't they? And where did they go? Did they mean to return?" Carlos was silent with sympathy as he could find no words adequate for a response to that. She turned to face him and backhanded his chest playfully.

"I'm making it up," she giggled, amused. "My parents have a farm as well and are doing *fine*! *Your face*!" She imitated what he looked like to her.

He glared across at her. She was so… tricky. Satiah was wrong; Deva was nothing like him at all.

"Do you tell *everyone* that?" he asked, a little hurt. She continued to laugh.

"No," she said, probably honestly. "Only the gullible." She stared up into his eyes. "You're *so sensitive*!" she chastised. "It was just a joke."

"I see now why you work for the government. No one else is ready for your *brand of comedy* yet," he said, tersely.

"Are all of you in the Coalition like this?" she asked, obviously put out.

"Are all of you in the Federation sub-standard comedians?" he asked. She sighed and stared at the ground.

They were now outside, walking around the perimeter of the building, stone to the left and the foggy swamps to their right. The air was cold and smelly, meaning that they could never forget the swamps even if they wanted to.

"This planet is going to join us," she said, in a small voice. "There's nothing Reed can do about it."

"I highly doubt that, the Punes are clearly leaning towards us," Carlos argued.

"I know but I also know Tabre well enough to know he won't let that matter," she warned, seriously.

"And you're telling me this *because*...?" he asked, distrustfully.

"So you can persuade Reed to give up?" she replied, after the smallest hesitation. "He is leading your party, isn't he?"

"Maybe," he answered.

"I *won't* tell Tabre if *that's* what you're thinking, I'm trying to *help you*," she insisted, her tone frustrated.

"*Of course* you are," he remarked, letting his disbelief fill his voice.

"How can I prove it?" she sighed.

"I'm not sure you can," he replied, sad again. They stared into each other's eyes, warring emotions simmering in them both. It was like they spoke different languages and were both trying to find a place they could understand each other. Culture had more significance in the development of an individual than most realised. The values people are taught first are forever there and even when proved wrong or inaccurate they are hard to put aside. Their bodies wanted in, regardless of anything. Their minds were standing off, trying to analyse and even compromise. Their hearts were sat right in the middle, torn between their bodies and their minds. Were the Coalition and the Federation *so different*? Did they *matter*? They were just two individuals in the cosmos of too many to count, *did they matter*?

Carlos, deciding that someone had to break this and trusting his theory that she cared more about him than her mission, made his move. He knew that if this was the wrong thing to do, she would most likely try to kill him; he ensured he was ready to strike. He brushed his lips softly against hers. She did not resist, she returned the compliment. A loud squeak sounded. Both Carlos and Deva reacted at once, spinning to face the sound, guns ready. A lone Pune was standing a short distance from them, watching them. It leapt backwards in surprise, squeaking and flapping its arms at them. They both relaxed, lowering their guns and exchanging jumpy laughter.

"The Coalition is foreign to me… *Maybe if I saw it for myself,*" Deva said, slipping her pistol away. "I could… maybe visit it?"

"What are you asking?" he asked, seeking simplicity. She was noticeably struggling with a difficult decision. Carlos had remembered to distrust it, *if* he heard what he wanted to hear. Absurdly that almost made him not want to hear it.

"I want to go with you," she admitted, in complete sincerity. "I lost my faith in the Federation the day I discovered that they rigged the last election to ensure that those still in power remain there."

"Ah… I can't say that the Coalition *doesn't* do that," he stated, grinning. "Everyone in power always takes steps to ensure that they stay or those they wish stay there. They would call it *life insurance*."

"I'm a competent operative, Carlos," she said, a little seductively. "I could resign and *sell* my skills… if you fancy hiring me?"

"Could I trust you to *obey orders*?" he asked, greatly tempted by the offer.

"Maybe," she smiled, not giving any indication of a lie. Carlos wondered how many times she had said that word recently. Maybe seemed to be an intrinsic part of her philosophy. He couldn't help but smile: Satiah was not going to like this.

"I'll hire you now, I think," he said, casually. "We can discuss payment later. Consider your first order a test of your new allegiance." He leaned in close to whisper his instruction into her waiting ear.

***

"I don't think *that* would be very astute," came a voice, from the doorway. Ruby spun around, curious and a little startled. Ash made no move, the knowing smile still on his lips. It was Jenna and she had her gun pointing right at them.

"I didn't either at first but he's *right*…!" Ruby began, trying to convince the other woman.

"She's not objecting to our plan because she feels it's dangerously irresponsible, she's objecting to our plan because it ruins hers," Ash interrupted. Jenna gaped at him, the gun remained raised. To her credit she didn't attempt to deny it. Her whole face seemed to change a little, turning from how it was to an entirely new persona. Her eyes seemed to gleam with an psychopathic rage. Her lips curved into a smile, sadistic in appearance.

"How did you know?" she asked, her tone, now more serious was low and dangerous.

"What I don't know is *why*?" asked Ash, ignoring the question. "From the start it was clear there was a point to all this. Care to let it be known?"

"That virus is a perfect copy of a bioweapon developed by the Coalition during the Common Protectorate war. My mission here was twofold. First to ensure that the virus is realised and transmit data recorded in the flight computer. It had more teeth than they warned me but as you have already guessed: I was never in any real danger."

"And second? You said *twofold*," prompted Ash, seeming to be agonisingly blasé about all this. Ruby was so surprised; she'd quite forgotten that her mouth was still gaping.

"The second was to ensure that the finger of this outbreak points *only* at the Coalition. The ensuing political fallout would guarantee war. Then the Federation and the Union could carve up what was once the Coalition between us," she concluded.

"That's not what their governments want," Ash pointed out, apparently on the level with all this.

"True but a significant minority in each *do*," she answered, congenially. The darkness returned to her voice. "*And they pay better.*"

"Why did you kill the doctor?" Ash asked, although he already knew. Just as he knew the Captain had appeared in the corridor behind her and was sneaking closer. He'd not heard everything, there was no way he could have but he'd heard enough to understand what he had to do. So Ash was obligingly playing for time.

"Ah, *poor doctor Harris*," she sighed, as if in regret. "I could say it was because he *refused* to help those dying from the infection."

"But that wouldn't be true," Ash said, a grim smile on his face.

"Besides, we both know there was nothing he could have done but die with them."

"No, I *had* hoped that as everyone believed he was responsible, his death would relieve me of any suspicion. And it would have done had *you* not kept digging. I knew once Chris was dead too, which he would end up one way or another, you would remain unconvinced. All of this brings me to..." she began, making preparations to strike. A gun fired, hitting her in the back. She dropped her weapon and went down with a scream. The Captain, gun still trained on her, entered, breathing hard. Ruby leapt forward and kicked the gun away from Jenna's outstretched arms.

"Did you kill her?" asked Ash, immediately. His tone was angry and Ruby eyed him in confusion. Jenna had literally been about to decorate them with scorch marks and start an intergalactic war. Why would Ash care about her death?

"What do you think?" asked the Captain, scornfully.

"Just checking," Ash remarked, with a shrug. Then he nodded towards the controls. "What's your plan for the override-failsafe proxy device now that the only one who knew the codes is dead?"

***

"So, after *all that*, the drinks are perfectly safe?" Carlos asked. Like the day before, the conference was in full swing. Edmund was taking his turn, trying to tempt the Punes with promises of economic golden ages and technological renovations.

"Yes," Satiah replied, keeping her mouth as still as possible. Tabre's eyes were on her and she was staring him down. He was probably awaiting the arrival of the drinks, expecting them all to be dead in minutes. Satiah intended to take a large gulp and make sure she was staring right at him as she did it. Another gesture that yet another of his schemes was known to her.

"I need to get the leaders alone," Reed sighed, his face thoughtful. "We must find out what the Sisterhood wanted."

"You mean, *you do?*" Satiah stated, reminding him that that was not the mission. He grunted in reluctant agreement.

Carlos and Deva were avoiding each other's gaze. Satiah had not been surprised by the girl's switch in loyalty and had handled it with the cynicism she applied to mostly everything. Of course Deva could be telling the truth *or* she had been instructed to operate as a double. Satiah had a few ideas about how to ensure that she could be rendered a *non-risk*. Carlos really believed she was sincere. The PLC was always recruiting. The PLC, Phantom Labour Force, was a department of mercenaries and ex-criminals, often used as backup for Phantom agents. Satiah had used them a few times before on missions where she had had to storm a fortification. In any case Satiah felt that Deva would fit right in there. Carlos could even keep in contact with her there if he chose.

With Kelvin being there, keeping everyone under observation and Carlos also playing the vigilant guard... Satiah allowed her mind to focus on other things. What was or what had been Operation Burning Bridge? With the millions of operations that were taking place right at that moment and the billions more that had been and gone it was little wonder she'd not heard of it before. Despite popular belief, it was not true that an operation's name bore any semblance to the *nature* of said operation. Operation Powder Panther was as likely to be an espionage mission as it was to be a so-called *deconstruction* assignment. With nothing else to go on, however, Satiah was speculating about the words. Burning Bridge. Demolition? Interfering with someone else's diplomacy? And, what was *Vourne's* connection to this operation?

Her attention returned to the present when her eyes began to follow the Punes as they provided their guests with refreshments. The previous day she had instructed that no one accept anything that was offered on principle. She had amended that instruction for this day. In case someone else had secretly managed to poison anything Kelvin had spent the night updating himself on vaccines and, ensuring they were stocked up. Satiah *wanted* Tabre to see his plan fail; she knew it would puncture his ego and professional pride. If she could get him emotionally invested in this, she would have the upper hand. She took a goblet from one of the trays the Pune waved at her. She smiled and toasted the little creature in thanks. She noticed the interest Tabre was showing in her now she had a drink. She wondered how well he would hide his reaction when it became clear that no one was going to die any time soon.

She tasted the fluid she'd been so close to the previous night, allowing it to rest on her tongue for far longer than normal. It tasted as strong as it smelt. Carlos was not watching her in a very obvious way. She knew it didn't matter, Tabre would know soon enough anyway. She swallowed and made knowing eye contact with Tabre. She got nothing back. No clue as to what he was thinking or feeling. His brown eyes burned into hers with unblinking focus. She downed the rest, breaking the contact pointedly. The glint of Tabre's golden tooth appeared as he smiled. The smirk of a predator.

Tabre had known the drinks were safe. He'd known ever since he'd realised that Satiah had specifically allowed the refreshments to be consumed. She had failed to do so the previous day as a prudent step to ensure the safety of her charge. Yet today, after the night when the brew was supposedly compromised, she made a point of doing the opposite. She was virtually encouraging her people to drink it. She knew and she was showing off. Tabre appreciated the gesture. How she had done it didn't matter but she had successfully fended off the subtle approach. He deserved to have his own failure thrust back at him like that. It looked like Roach was going to get his wish after all. Tabre sent the encrypted prearranged message code and became aware that Deva was watching him. Had she betrayed them?

Deva was seventeen and Tabre considered it wrong to kill someone so young no matter what they had done. And he didn't know she had betrayed them. Satiah was good, a Phantom agent. There were a dozen ways she could have discovered and thwarted his plans thus far. In either case it would no longer matter soon. Roach would be quick, Tabre had worked with him before. He would already have prepared for this eventuality and would take action with the dependability of an efficient machine. Edmund was still going and Tabre nudged Conrad. He had told him the previous evening what would happen should the poison fail to work. Conrad had been nervous. Tabre had reassured him that Roach was a professional and one of the best shots there were but that had not really helped. The second a shot was fired Conrad had to go down as fast and as dramatically as possible.

Satiah, still watching Tabre, felt the hairs on the back of her neck begin to rise. Danger. Her body was all but screaming it at her. She had not lived as long as she had, not done as much has she had without listening to it. Was the drink poisoned after all? No, it would have felt different if it had. She calmed herself making the effort to check through the whole room. Nothing strange. Bomb? No, Kelvin would have detected or should have detected it. The flash of something in the corner of her eye was enough to let her know what was happening and what she had to do next. She launched herself at Reed.

**

"*What?*" stammered the Captain, taken aback by Ash's withering look. Ruby realised, Ash was right! They had needed Jenna *alive* to release the control of the ship back to them. Also she may have been able to help them with the cure. Dead, she was unable to do either.

"How far out from Magnovastar are we?" Ash asked, knowing that there was no real way for the Captain to know that for sure. Ruby worked it out.

"We must be getting close now, won't *someone* realise we are incommunicado and try to investigate?" she asked, hopefully. There must be patrols and stuff that stop idiots from crashing into it, surely?

"Likely but not *soon enough* to stop us crashing into it," Ash replied, urgency in his voice now. He eyed the override-failsafe proxy device disdainfully.

The Captain took aim at it, determined to end its malevolent purpose with a laser bolt. Ash raised a hand.

"No, that will not work," he warned seriously. "We must take care of the virus first." He crouched and went for the wires. Already prepared, Ruby braced herself for depressurisation. She cautioned the Captain on what he was about to do. He activated the communicator - he had to inform everyone what was about to happen.

"Deep breath, Ruby," Ash smiled, and yanked. Alarms bared and a violent wind began to sweep through the room as the air began venting out into space. It was strong enough to drag Jenna's body out with it. Ruby clung onto the safety railing, holding her breath, and watched as her hip cape was ripped off of her and borne away. Ash was clinging to the controls. He aimed the cable and made contact, making a few sparks. The doors began falling once more but they were essentially in a vacuum. The automatic systems on the ship kicked in, deploying fresh air and heat.

As normality returned everyone gasped and gulped in the fresh air.

"That should bring it back under control," Ash mused, considering. "Any further infections will be completely contained now. Only one thing remains."

"Control of the ship," stated Ruby, nodding. "*Any ideas?*"

"We search Jenna's cabin, it's a longshot but she may have made a note of the code somewhere, check her communicator records too. She could have had it sent to once she'd been successful in deploying the virus or even getting aboard," Ash instructed. The Capitan nodded, heading off, already shouting orders into his own communicator. Ruby sighed and leaned against the console next to him.

"She must have had a way off this ship, that human had nothing suicidal about her," Ash muttered, clearly still thinking.

She watched him, knowing he was paying her no attention like normal. She pushed his knee with hers. He glanced up, hardly noticing.

"I really wanted to see Magnovastar," she sighed, disappointed. He grunted, not listening. "The patterns gravity can make. Physics in action." Still he said nothing. "Gravity is a strange thing. It makes life possible and yet holds us all down like prisoners." She began to realise that seeing it up close with her own eyes was preferable to watching a video screen.

"What?" he asked, suddenly focussing on her. She'd done it again, given inspiration to him. She wasn't sure exactly how she'd done it but she'd seen that expression on his face before. So, there were patterns after all. "*What did you say, Ruby?*" Sighing again, almost with an almost derisive unwillingness, before she cooperatively reiterated herself.

He gave her another kind of look. A look that seemed to imply that she actually already knew what she'd done and was just pretending she didn't know. She just gazed back, an almost jaded expression on her face. She wasn't bored, indeed she felt like she scored a point but she wasn't willing to let him know that. It was nice to be the smug one for once even though she didn't know why she was smug.

"What is Magnovastar?" he asked, levelly. She frowned. Slowly she pulled out the brochure he had given her and began to read from it.

"An astronomical wonder of unknown origin," she read aloud, rather lamely. "Join us for a look at a place where imagination and speculation meet."

"It's a black hole," he stated, careless.

"No, it's not," she said, holding up a picture of it.

The picture displayed a spherical lightening ball of rainbows.

"Ruby, the Magnovastar, is an Ataxorial or Secorial black hole," Ash defined, seeing what she meant.

"Sticking extra words in front of it wouldn't convince a child and it does not convince me," she stated, stubborn.

"It's a type of black hole," he reiterated.

"It's not," she argued.

"It is," he sighed, irritated. "Primordial black holes are the oldest kind, some believed to have originated during the reaction that created this cosmos. Others such as normal black holes appeared later due to collapsing stars. While some others still… have yet to make themselves known to you."

"No, it isn't," she retorted, starting to laugh shakily. "I *know* what a black hole looks like! The clue is in the name."

Ash gave up. "Gravity is different when black holes enter the equation," he went on, letting it drop. "Magnovastar may currently seem to be a cosmological curiosity. Soon it will be an astronomical abomination." Ruby went pale.

"What?" she asked, not understanding. "You think it's dangerous?"

"Not yet but it soon will be," he replied, thinking hard. "We *must* prevent it from collapsing. If we don't it will mean the end for this part of the galaxy." Ruby stopped, starting to wonder what exactly it was they were trying to do. Then a new idea came to her.

"Did you *know* all this before we even got on board?" she asked, suspicious. He was ignoring her now, focussing on the workings, probably trying to do something with the engines.

"Hey!"

He stopped, sighed and turned back to face her again. Her expression was that of someone demanding an answer.

"I knew," he admitted, seriously. "I knew all along about the Magnovastar. I deliberately came here to prevent it from collapsing. *What I didn't know* was that these humans were going to start a pathetic squabble which has paralysed this craft."

"Why didn't you tell me?" she whispered, upset. "I thought you protected humans! I thought you cared."

"Ruby, don't get emotional, we have to stay focussed here or we will all die," he stated, grimly. "We have to regain control of this ship." Ruby shook her head and crossed her arms, defiant.

"You want my help, you have to be honest with me," she stated, tenacious.

He whirled on her, making her jump. "We *must* regain control of this ship or we will die. We must prevent the black hole from being created or many will die," he snapped at her.

"You're a duffer!" she declared, shaking her head again. "There are so many ways you could have prevented this…"

"I don't like to interfere!" he argued.

"And yet here you are," she sneered, expressively. "Working to your own agenda, *just like Jenna was*."

"Except that *mine* has the greater interest of *humanity's survival*," he stated, actually engaging in the dispute rather than brushing it aside like normal.

"You're not as different from us as you think," she stated, raising her eyebrows and huffing at him. He paused and, with an effort of will, his anger and all emotion seemed to vanish from him.

"Perhaps you are right," he acknowledged, his voice much softer. She gave a sharp nod of victory.

"You know I am," she said, pleased with the concession.

"Want to do something meaningful? Help me help your species," he offered, seriously.

"No problem," she stated, as if such a thing was as easy as walking. "How long do we have before the *what's-its-name* collapses?" He winced, annoyed that she had already forgotten the correct scientific terminology. He suspected she had deliberately done so just to irritate him.

"About four hundred years," he replied, as if that made it urgent.

"*Four hundred...!*" she exploded, before controlling herself. She had to remember that for an immortal, four hundred years was sooner rather than later. "*That* soon, huh? Right, what would you like me to do?"

***

Reed had been listening intently to the discussion, formulating his counter offers and arguments. The longer this went on the more likely it would become an argument. *Join us! No, join us, we're better than them! No they're not, they failed to do this or are going to do that...* Reed's mental preparations came to an abrupt end when he was unexpectedly flattened by Satiah. She was heavier than she looked and pinned him to the floor as a laser bolt smashed through the glass and burned right through the head of his chair. Kelvin was on his feet, bursts of flame roaring from his arm as he returned fire. Except of course he wasn't returning fire. There was no way a flame thrower of any specifications had the range to possibly hit whoever was shooting at them. What he was really doing, was providing cover as the shooter would not be able to see through the flames to fire again even if he was using head sensors. Quick as they were, another shot did make it through the wall of flames and killed Edmund outright. A third hit Kelvin but was deflected by his armour.

"Kelvin, get these two back to the ship!" yelled Satiah, over the chaos, as she ducked the stray bolt. She was already running, straight towards the open window. She leapt through the flames that Kelvin was still blasting and fell the three storeys down into the swamps below. She hit the water hard, splashing into the green liquid and plunging several metres down. All was cold, quiet and dark suddenly as she began to rise again. She swam forwards as she went, her lungs already making their wish to taste oxygen again known to her. She forced herself through the water with aggressive strokes. She burst onto the surface, gasping and looking all around. The fog obscured her long-range vision but wouldn't affect whoever was shooting. They had struck far faster than she had expected. She staggered out onto the bank, her boots sinking into the mud as she went.

A shot was fired, scarcely missing her. She fell onto her front, taking cover as she crawled the rest of the way. She found some shrubs to hide behind and pulled out her pistol. Reed had allowed her to bring it with them this time, fortunately. Although a pistol wasn't going to do her much good if she couldn't get close enough to use it. The shooter was not firing until he had a target and he couldn't see her. He may be trying to get another shot at the others. Cautiously she began to crawl forwards, knowing the general direction to go in. She would get to that ship they thought was still hidden. There, when they returned, she could ambush them.

A clacking sound came to her, the source was close. A second later a rapid burst of firing began but it was not aimed at her. Clearly having given up the idea of a precision strike, they were now resorting to a carpet blasting strategy. Using the noise to mask that of her own movement, she rose and sprinted. Sprinting through a swamp was essentially impossible even for someone of Satiah's training and experience. The best she could manage was a faltering half run half jump variant. She made quick progress and was careful to avoid injury. Emerging over the top of a ridge she stopped as, startled, a man dressed in black attempted to turn and bring the gun to bear on her. Reflexively she fired, the shot hitting the large rifle in his arms and knocking him onto his backside.

She darted across the space between them directly towards him as he backward rolled onto his feet. As he stood, he regained his full height just in time to receive another blast of lethal accuracy. It caught him between the eyes and threw him to the ground, dead. Satiah hit the ground next to him, flat out, using his body as cover. She searched him by sense of touch as she tried to get an idea of her exact location. It had been night before, when she had last been out there, and as a consequence it all looked different now but she was certain that she was close. The man's presence here confirmed it. The sounds of engines powering up gave her the final clue she needed. On her feet again, gun ready, she charged through the fog recklessly.

Within less than twenty seconds, the shape of the ship appeared in front of her, looming up black and red. It was already starting to move forwards, its momentum building. Leaping to make it, Satiah reached the entrance ramp, presumably left open for the man she'd killed. Her gun clattered away from her grip as she fought to hang on and fell as the ship rose. Gritting her teeth she hauled herself into the ship, rolled to the left and hit the control to close the ramp. Roach appeared at the end of the corridor and, from a wrist launcher, he fired wire netting at her. It expanded in the air as it came at her. She threw herself forwards, the device missed her but sheared her Phantom cloak to pieces. She slipped into a room, turning as she ran. Roach came in after her, aiming for another shot.

She leapt over a table as he fired another expanding metallic net at her. It caught on the table, unable to go under and over at the same time. A physical impossibility that Satiah had counted on. Back first, she crashed against the wall. She kicked out with both feet at the table; the thrust sent the table, rim-first, straight into Roach's middle. He fell back with a grunt as she rolled out of the next door and onto her feet again. Frantically she searched for something she could use, she checked the usual places. Around the neck, between her breasts and around her belt. The answer rested lower still. In her boot she found a blade she kept there for just this sort of emergency. Still trying to catch or keep her on the run, Roach came into the corridor at a dead run. He only just managed to stretch back to avoid getting his throat slit by Satiah as she slashed at him from the doorway.

She advanced, using advanced knife-fighting techniques to keep him retreating. Roach was good though, managing to avoid her strikes and hold his ground. Countering, he intercepted her arm, catching her wrist. He twisted the limb, trying to break her arm. She went with the move, using the corridor wall and ceiling to run up and around. The momentum she gained enabled her to wrench herself free of his grip and whirl, aiming a high kick at his face. He ducked, using the time it took her to get in close again, to punch her in the ribs. He put all his strength into the blow. Satiah felt some of them crack. She groaned and slammed the knife in the gap between his chest padding and his shoulder armour. He roared in pain and staggered back. Although it hurt her to do so, she planted her boot in his chest and sent him flying backwards against the wall. She went to move in but winced and clutched her broken ribs.

She instead retreated back into the room with the table, now in pieces on the floor, and continued running. She made it into the corridor with the entrance ramp and then headed off in the direction Roach had originally come at her from. She knew he would be following and cursed her bad luck. She could end this in a heartbeat if she had a gun. Then she found a room which probably doubled as some kind of laboratory. She recognised the tubes containing chemicals. Knowing them all well enough by sight she took one of the clear ones and then concealed herself. When she had smashed the light, the whole place became much better for hiding. She waited, in the shadows, controlling her breathing. Wait for a target!

Roach entered and tried to activate the light. Satiah waited. She heard the sound of a blade being unsheathed and felt a bead of sweat trickle from her forehead into her eye. It stung and helped take her mind off of her ribs. Chucking a lucky coin in one direction, she moved. The noise of the coin made him instinctively turn in its direction. Satiah unsealed the container and sloshed the nitric acid it contained straight into his face. The chemical hissed as Roach howled in agony. She snatched up the blade he had dropped and plunged it into his gut, twisting it as she pushed. Roach lashed out, punching her in the face. She felt her nose crunch under the impact, and then her head hit the wall. She almost blacked out. She collapsed, dazed by the blow. Still shouting, Roach fell to his knees next to her, blood spilling onto the floor as he pulled the knife out.

In one final exertion to get her, he lunged with it at her prone body. Using the last of her energy, she rolled herself out of reach and in doing so made her head spin painfully. He landed on his front, groaning and breathing. His face disfigured and his blood making a red pool around him, he left the world of the living. Satiah slowly got up, her injured ribs making normally simple moves challenging. She swayed on her feet, her head still swimming from the blow. Blood from her broken nose formed into droplets over her lips, along to her chin where they dropped to the floor noiselessly. She had to find the control room. Forcing herself to walk, she followed the next corridor, pain her only companion. The ship was still moving and she needed to get it to stop and get back to the others. The man may have been on a pre-set course to a rendezvous and she knew she couldn't fight anyone else in her condition.

Painfully she got into the pilot's chair and tried to focus on the controls. The ship was flying about ten metres above the swamps in a north-west direction. She slowed the craft and then tried to get the communications unit working. That was when the ship was hit by a blast from above. The whole ship shook and she cried out at the unexpected jar. She tried to accelerate but was not fast enough. A second shot took out the port stabiliser completely and she began to spin out of control.

"*Cease fire!*" she screamed, on all channels. A third shot made her feel like her entire body was broken. She knew she should just get into the escape pod and ditch but she had no idea where it was. The ship began a dive, one she knew she couldn't pull it out of even if the stabiliser had still been fully functional.

She strapped herself in, preparing for crash-landing. Her hands instinctively dug into the arms of the seat as she fought to calm herself down. Fear would not help her. The fog parted split seconds before she hit the ground. With a bone-shattering cacophony the ship slammed into the swamp. Satiah screamed as her ribs cracked even more due to the jolt. The ship sank quickly. The sound of rushing water came to her and she remembered that there was no way that the ship was still airtight. Wincing as she moved, she unstrapped herself and stood shakily. A spray of water engulfed her and she waded forward stiffly, trying to get out. The corridor was almost completely submerged. She hoped the chemical containers were still intact.

Forced to go under, she took a deep breath and stumbled on a hole large enough for her to exit the ship. Exhaling as she rose and too weary to really move, she floated upwards at a sluggish rate. Her lungs were once more begging for air, she held on and held on. Reaching the surface she bobbed there, breathing in pained wheezes. With the last of her willpower she managed to get to the bank before falling into unconsciousness. Bruised and bloodied, she didn't look like she was even alive. Kelvin, unfazed by most terrain, came hurdling across the sludge and the pools. His metallic ankles did not twist, his spikes never slipped. Homing in on her signal, he reached his mistress. Exhibiting a care that seemed impossible for a machine, he rolled her onto her back. She let out a murmur, weak but still audible.

"Carlos, this is Kelvin," Kelvin said, transmitting a signal. "Bring the ship here."

***

"I probably *could* decrypt it given time but we don't have that time so I'm going to fry it instead," Ash explained, waving the sparking cable around dangerously.

"And the Captain's laser pistol *wouldn't* work?" Ruby asked, a little concerned.

"It may have done, but I prefer the percentage of likelihood this cable has," he replied. A random shot from the Captain was more likely to damage other things and while he couldn't see anything obvious, Ash could not be sure that the device didn't have anything to counter the brute force approach. Instead Ash was opting for the precision strike. The application of extreme voltage in a very localised area. Before Ruby could do anything his hand came up, covering her eyes as he touched the device. It sparked, zapped a few times and then exploded. Bits of burnt circuit flew everywhere and a lot of smoke rose from the remains of their mechanical enemy.

"Flashy," she smiled, sweeping the remains away with her hand. Ash sat in the pilot's seat and everything started working at once.

Above and in front of them the viewport opened with a computer- generated image of the immediate vicinity. They were still just within the safety zone. Any closer to Magnovastar and they would be in danger of falling straight into it, dragged to their destruction by gravity. Much closer now, closer than they ever should have been, Ruby was struck by the beauty of the thing. So many colours, shapes and lights. It seemed to be swirling endlessly, surrounded by the black, cold emptiness of space. It seemed harmless. She believed what Ash said about it being a time bomb, though. Only one thing was troubling her now. They had flooded the new atmosphere of the ship with the cure after locating it on Jenna's body. The body itself had been hard to find as it had been dragged away during the decompression. Ruby's cape, however, remained missing in action. Ash had been able to convert the cure from a serum into a gas somehow and everyone that was still alive had been cured.

The virus was gone. What was Ash going to do with Magnovastar? How was he going to stop it from collapsing in on itself and becoming a new and terrible black hole? If she assumed this correctly, gravity was pulling everything, within a certain radius, into the centre. The pull was gentle, especially from the distance they were at, but unrelenting nonetheless. In space, things with greater mass exert a greater pull on things with lesser mass. Or at least, that was her *laywoman's* understanding of the laws of physics. This meant that the centre of Magnovastar would be more massive than everything else in the area. It also meant that it would continue to get even more massive, the more stuff it drew into itself. So, how could this process be reversed? It was no use, she realised, she was going to have to ask Ash yet another question.

"Ash, how are you going to…? What are you going to do?" she asked, rephrasing her own question as she said it. He didn't answer for a few moments and she awaited his reply whilst shifting nervously on her feet. She felt so helpless.

"As you know, you cannot just shoot or blow up a black hole. In trying any such thing, even on a black hole in the making, we would only be worsening the problem. Black holes naturally get bigger over time. There are various solutions. Black holes do emit radiation," he said to her. She was still awaiting his answer. "Any ideas?" She motioned to herself questioningly and he nodded.

"You won't make fun of them?" she asked, crossing her arms. He grinned. "I'm genuinely curious to see what a human would do," he replied, casually.

"Then you would be better off consulting an astronomer or a scientist *of which I am neither*," she evaded, knowing he was purposely messing with her.

"True but *you* do have ideas, don't you? You don't *need* to be a scientist to have ideas. Indeed without the initial idea, there would be no scientists…" he rambled.

"Oh shut up!" she hissed, shaking her head. "I know nothing can escape black holes and that this is a black hole in the making. And I trust you to sort it out because you know stuff."

"*Stuff?*" he echoed, as if in disgust. She scowled at him.

"Science, physics, *whatever you want to call it*," she stated, getting noticeably irritated. He watched her intensely. "*What?*" she asked, in an accusatory tone.

"Nothing," he said, the smug grin back again.

"You're *unbearable!*" she snapped, allowing her frustration to bubble over. "Have you got some kind of superiority complex or something? It's like you get off on knowing all this secret knowledge and you watch me try to figure these things out purely for you own amusement. I'll have you know that I refuse to play any more of your games! Now if you don't fix that black hole *right now*..." She trailed off, knowing there was nothing she could really threaten him with.

"Many years ago now, thousands possibly, there was a situation that loosely resembled this one. There were two planets, locked in a perpetual orbit around one another, held in place by hundreds of gravitational satellites. Devices that exerted a gravitational pulls of their own," he explained, still watching her.

"I *know* what a gravitational satellite *is*," she retorted, sulky.

"All was... *stable*... until a black hole appeared and began to destabilise the orbit pattern." He fell silent again.

"*And?*" she asked, pointedly.

"The people refused to evacuate their homes, leaving it to the then Earth Empire to solve their problem for them. There were political matters at the time which secured the involvement of the Empire," he said.

"Election year *again*, was it?" she joked, cynically.

"They were forced to confront the problem of a black hole head-on, which is precisely what they did. The whole fleet went there and acted as a counter pull, exerting gravitational pressure in the opposite direction of the pull of the black hole. Naturally the solution only bought time as gradually the planets were being physically torn apart by the competing forces."

"*Naturally*," she echoed, mocking his tone with her own. Then she frowned, considering the implications. "It was like a tug of war, with the planets in the middle."

"Yes. Like I said, they were only postponing the inevitable. In delaying the end result, however, they bought themselves time. Time to try something else altogether. I already told you that the black holes emit radiation. The radiation some believe to be created when matter is crushed into a singularity. A substance that was radioactively magnetic was brought onto the scene. Giant magnets. Their purpose was simple, to gradually dissipate the black hole by progressively dragging the collapsed matter apart and away in different directions, thus ensuring that the hole couldn't reform. *However, the file tells the story* they *were* partially successful. In the end it made better sense to relocate the threatened planets."

"Okay," she said, nodding. "So how does that help us?"

"It doesn't. They were dealing with a *primordial* black hole. We are dealing with one that has not yet become a black hole," he replied, seriously. "I felt it was worth thinking through that scenario where humans, albeit with some help, managed to thwart a black hole from getting some of its prizes."

"Well what was the use of telling me all that?" she asked, trying not to attack him physically out of frustration.

"It's the clue to what *my plan is…*" He sighed, giving up. "This all happened *in the past*. If someone were to reverse the localised time flow around Magnovastar, pushing it and only it *back in time*, and then released it…"

"…It would reset the clock," she gasped, getting it. "That's *brilliant*… but is it legal?" The question surprised Ash.

"*Legal?*" he repeated, as if such a word was unknown to him.

She huffed at him in triumph. "*Ha*, didn't think of *that* did you?" she asked, rhetorically. "As a former Assistant Manager of the Ministry of Economics, Currency and Finance… I feel *duty bound* to inform you of a number of restrictions in regards to time travel and the like." She also almost stood to attention as she spoke. Ash wanted to laugh but didn't feel that would be the right thing to do.

"…So?" he asked, levelly. He stood up, almost nose-to-nose with her. She quavered a little but refused to back down.

"So… *what?*" she asked, unable to look away from his eyes.

"Well, *inform m*e," he requested, grit in his tone. She shrugged.

"I have no idea what any of them *are* but I was just saying there are laws about this kind of thing," she elaborated, not at all put off.

"*Ruby*," he chuckled, shaking his head. "There are times when you *completely* baffle me."

"There *are?*" she asked, distrustfully.

"Even were you able to recall all such restrictions I have the ultimate authority," he said, tapping her nose gently. "As an immortal I am not *bound* by any of your laws." She put her hands on her hips.

"Be that as it may, I *don't* see any time machines nearby that you *could* use," she argued. Her tone then became sarcastic. "I'll just check the cargo bays, I'm *sure* I saw a couple *lying around somewhere...*"

"Yes, I would like to *remind* you that I'm trying to help all humankind here," Ash stated.

"I know but you have four hundred years to think of a better solution, a *legal* solution. We are touring the cosmos, remember? And you are trying to learn about humans. Well, *most humans* obey the laws," she stated, not letting his eyes bewitch her.

He looked over at Jenna's body and raised an eyebrow.

"*Most* humans!" she repeated, understanding the point he was making. "And you told me, *when I first met you*, that you didn't travel with *law breakers*."

"Nor champions of justice," he muttered, amending the earlier statement.

"I have to say this is the most bizarre conversation I have ever had. We are arguing about you breaking laws to save lives from something that will not happen for four hundred years with a tool you don't have," she said, as it occurred to her.

"But I do," he said, producing a bracelet. He waved it under her nose a few times for effect. "Granted it is a very basic model, but it is all I need."

"Duffer," she muttered, giving up.

***

Satiah regained consciousness, forgetting nothing. The angular shape of Kelvin was leaning over her, his medical appendage a short distance away from her face. She was naked waist-up. All her injuries were conspicuous by their absence. Her only garment was a pair of long back shorts that covered her from just below the belly button to just underneath her knees. A feel of constant tiny vibrations told her that they were in flight.

"Status?" she asked, deliberately remaining as still as she could. He might still be operating on her.

"Two fractured ribs, minor skull fracture, concussion, broken nose, skin mole," he listed, his usual monotone reassuring her.

"*A mole?*" she frowned, confused. "Where was *that?*" She still felt exhausted.

"All injuries completely healed," he announced, his tone never changing. She gingerly sat up and rubbed her ribs casually.

"Thank you, Kelvin," she said, in a tone that conveyed much more gratitude than the words.

She leaned forward and kissed his metal bodywork affectionately. His metallic claw gently ran through her long red hair as if in tenderness. She stared up into the red glow of his eyes, the scopes zooming in on the brown of hers. He handed her communicator back to her. There was a message. It was Rainbow. She switched on and listened.

"Satiah, glad to see that *you're* busy *for once*." Rainbow sounded annoyed. Perhaps Satiah had, inadvertently and without any remorse, ruined his date night.

"You wanted everything on Operation Burning Bridge. Well, I'm still digging but here's what I have *so far*. There was a mining planet, probably still there now, and they had unearthed *something new*. Jaylite Industries link in here with this as they had a material disposal contract *with* this planet. The mining, since the discovery, only lasted three days.

"For whatever reason the *Sisterhood of Light*, which you also asked me to check up on, *did something*... something that stopped the mining. *Permanently*. Phantom Leader Vourne and one other are the only ones associated with Operation Burning Bridge that I can find so far. The mission was classified UE." Satiah was familiar with the *unlisted espionage* classification. It, like many other classifications, were all too often used as euphemisms for other more menacing things. "There *is* a report of what was discovered but I haven't been able to access it yet. As for the Sisterhood of Light themselves I've got coordinates and something kind of chilling... *no spy ever sent there made it back*. Well, their bodies did but they seemed... like they were in comas. If you are thinking of visiting them, I wouldn't think about that any more. I have to go now, I will call back later when I have more. Hope you're okay, speak soon."

She switched off and stood there, thinking. It sounded a lot like all these things were interconnected in some horrible and unforeseen way. The Sisterhood, Operation Burning Bridge, Jaylite Industries, Balan's secret weapon (real or imaginary), Vourne and her current mission. Granted it was almost over now, one way or another. Tabre had seen to that. The man she had brought back from the, now demolished, space station could be *described as* being in a coma. Was that the work of the Sisterhood? What was this new material that the miners had found? And did that have anything to do with Vourne or Balan's secret weapon? And who would the other Phantom agent have been? The one who was working on it with Vourne *before* doomsday. Were they still alive? Watching her at the very moment? She smiled and shivered a little before heading off to the control room.

She entered and Carlos and Reed regarded her. Carlos went red and averted his eyes. Reed stared at her as if he was trying to remember something. This was her ship and she'd almost forgotten that she was still sharing it.

"...If I'd known it was *that* kind of party I wouldn't have bothered getting dressed earlier," he joked, casually. Did nothing faze him? "I'm glad to see you are feeling better."

"What happened?" she asked, without even greeting them.

"The negotiations are over; we have yet to hear the Punes' final decision. That attack was... pretty catastrophic really, regarding our *political relations*. Obviously it can't be pinned on any one of us but the Punes were not impressed. I have updated Randal on the situation, hope you don't mind?" Reed went on.

Still a bit awkward, Carlos presented Satiah with his cloak. She took it and put it on without a word. Inwardly she was pleased she didn't have to talk with Randal, she really didn't feel like it.

"I see," she said, more softly. She slumped into her usual chair, checking the controls. Her healed ribs ached a little but it faded quickly. They were in orbit... along with two other ships. The same two as before. It would be so easy to blast Tabre out of the skies if only the ship was armed.

"We were *respectfully* asked to leave," Reed stated, pulling a face. "Edmund was killed and Carlos was winged." Satiah glanced at Carlos.

"You okay?" she asked, trying to sound sensitive.

"Yes," he replied, tense. "Flesh wound. Kelvin took care of it." Why was he so tense?

"So what's the matter?"

"In the confusion, we managed to acquire a new friend," Reed went on. He tapped the arm of his chair loudly and a very anxious-looking Deva entered. Satiah stared at her for a long time but Deva never once tried to make eye contact. Satiah faced Carlos.

"She's *your* responsibility. She causes any trouble and you deal with it yourself," Satiah stated, unwelcomingly. Both teenagers nodded sullenly. They knew they had been lucky to get anything approaching acceptance from Satiah.

"*Who* shot that ship down?" Satiah asked, anger in her voice. She wanted to know *who* had blasted her out of the sky even after she had gained control of the ship. She suspected it was Tabre but it could also have been the Punes.

"That was Tabre," Deva answered, seriously. Again she avoided Satiah's gaze.

"It seems that he and Conrad, *transparent as ever*, tried to gain the favour of the Punes by volunteering to eliminate their attacker," Reed said, grit in his tone. "They did this knowing you were aboard."

"Charming," Satiah sneered, shaking her head irately. "So... we are literally sitting out here until the Punes make up their mind which one of us is the lesser of the evils?"

"An accurate summary of our present circumstances," Reed nodded, sagely. "I'm sorry about not being able to stop them shooting you down but the rules of neutrality…"

"Forget it," Satiah breathed, waving at him indifferently. "*I'm supposed to protect you, not the other way around.*"

"As Edmund is dead the Nebula Union has launched a full investigation into the attack. The Punes have accepted that much, although that is a somewhat moot point."

"*Pointless*," grunted Carlos, contemptuously. "Everyone will *know* it was the Colonial Federation." Deva's eyes narrowed in anger.

"Edmund and his team *also* bought the services of the assassin, remember?" Satiah said, softly. "They are not innocent in this either. *They most likely want to make sure their tracks are hidden.*"

"I find it ironic that the only ones who played straight were the most unpopular ones," Deva said, eyeing Carlos. "You guys."

"We are only unpopular..." began Carlos, defensively.

"*Enough*, I have a headache," growled Satiah, threateningly. That brought the teenage bickering to an end.

"And one other thing," Reed went on, his tone changing. Now he sounded firm and commanding. "Once the outcome of this mission is known, *when they come back to us with their decision, basically*, we will not be returning to Earth." That got a reaction from everyone.

Kelvin looked directly at him. Carlos and Deva were also didn't hide their feelings. He frowned in confusion while she gaped. Satiah faced Reed.

"What?" she asked, levelly.

"Had a little chat with Randal earlier who in turn had a short chinwag with the Commandment Benefactor and they decided that, *while we are here*, we discover the purpose behind the Sisterhood's interest in this world. Interesting, isn't it? To think that their interest has now got us interested? And as I am a representative of the Coalition I take direct command of this assignment," Reed explained. Satiah didn't like being dictated to, even by her lawful superior, but she kept her composure. She'd not survived as long as she had by letting other people know what she was feeling. In a way this turn *could* work to her advantage being as the Sisterhood were in some way related to the mission she was still aching to get back to. She wasn't prepared to let Reed know that, though, and created the mask of a polite yet resentful agent.

"*Where* is the mission file?" she asked, her tone crisp. It was a typical objection that anyone would throw out when confronted with this sort of thing. She'd done plenty of missions without files, of course, but she didn't go around chatting about them. The rule was more a technicality than anything else, much like law itself. It was illegal to start a mission never having seen the mission file. Satiah had always noted the choice of word was 'seen' and not 'read'.

"Being written up now," lied Reed, casually. Satiah nodded slowly. "We have time in any case."

"Fair enough," she allowed.

"So... *what's happening?*" enquired Deva, questioning.

"We wait for the file before we proceed," Satiah replied, casually. "Then, once we have decided how best *to* proceed we proceed. *I do have a few things to attend to back on Earth but they can wait... I suppose.*"

"I'll tell you about that later," Carlos said, in Deva's ear. Deva would know nothing about Phantom operations or how the documentation was handled.

"You are agreeable *to or with* me being in charge?" Reed pressed, eyeing Satiah uncertainly. "Any questions?"

"I have no choice if *Randal* has sanctioned it," she remarked, as if she couldn't care less. Inwardly this was the worst part of it. The Sisterhood were an objective for both Reed and Satiah; she knew that, even though he didn't. But she always did things her own way. Reed may have other ideas and although he'd proved himself trustworthy and a good improviser she didn't appreciate answering to him. She'd managed so far with this break from routine simply by telling herself that it was a short-term, provisional change that would be shortly discontinued. Now, with no clear end in sight, she was twitchy and bristling.

"It's just I was given to understand that you preferred to work alone and I can appreciate how this will be difficult for you," Reed persisted. "I have taken the liberty to compensate you for this continued disruption by requesting a new ship for you."

That got Satiah's attention. She'd wanted a new ship since... *since she'd lost her old one.* Another less noteworthy casualty of Vourne's bid for universal domination. It had been destroyed in the upper atmosphere of the planet Vourne had chosen to hide on. Along with her previous robot. This old tug, the freighter she'd been calling home since, was hardly a ship at all and was oppressive at the best of times. She'd bought it from a merchant in order to prevent anyone tracing it. Now, with three extra people, it was full to bursting. It had no weapons or anything. She could have easily requested a new ship through Randal but she didn't want to attract attention to herself so soon after getting her job back. Reed, it seemed, really did respect her feelings. She didn't have to pretend to be astonished and didn't try to conceal it.

"*Oh*... we'll say no more about it," she stated, almost stammering. "I would like a chance to give my opinion regarding your orders should I feel you have overlooked anything?"

"Understood," he smiled, quickly agreeing. "I'm sure we will make a wonderful team."

Carlos sniggered. He knew that Satiah was faking at least some of this and it amused him. She glared and he quickly stopped.

"Did Randal mention anything regarding these two?" she asked, eyeing the silent youths balefully. Reed hesitated, sensing that she was devising punishments for them or at the very least, arduous tasks.

"No, no," Reed answered, thinking carefully. "I did ask and he said *provided you were still happy with them*, he was." Satiah eyed first Carlos and then Deva in silence. Neither of them met her gaze this time.

"I *would* make you clean the bilge piping but seeing as we are about to change ships I will have to think of something else," Satiah said, with unnecessary clout. Reed chuckled.

"When the new one arrives in a few minutes maybe you could get them to wash the viewports..." Reed suggested.

"*A few minutes?*" Satiah repeated, stunned. "That was *fast!*"

"Well, truth is I ordered it two days ago," Reed admitted, casually. "As a reward for saving my life."

"That was *today!*" Satiah said, almost shouting.

"I had a premonition," Reed shrugged, as if it meant nothing at all. Satiah's mind raced. Had he already known this second mission was coming as early as that? Was he trying to soften her up for something? *Who was he?* She decided to let it go and sighed heavily. She felt so weary.

"Thank you, Reed. As you are no doubt aware, this ship *does* leave a lot to be desired," she allowed, tired. She needed to rest more after that fight.

"I understand how in this line of work: property can be easily mislaid," Reed smiled, diplomatically. She stood slowly and nodded.

"Wake me when it gets here," she requested, fatigued.

"Will do," Carlos promised.

***

Docking at the destination, Ash and Ruby had spent a few hours with the Captain explaining everything to security. Eventually they were released into the sprawl of a city they didn't know. The poor Captain would not be leaving for a long time yet but security had *generously* released mostly everyone else.

"*Well!*" complained Ruby, her face red. "They didn't need us for *any* of that!"

"Cooperation was vital for the Captain to preserve his innocence and account," Ash said. "Jenna *or whatever her real name was*, murdered the officer before take-off and assumed her position as a last-minute replacement. It seems that while the passengers were all pedantically checked by security, the crew on the other hand could just wander in and out at their leisure. *How reassuring.* Still, that lesson has now been learned. The Captain could hardly be faulted in trusting her, the documentation she had were forgeries that would have fooled any computer. Only the man that looked like he'd signed them off, knew and could prove that they were fakes. And *he* wasn't on board."

"I notice you left all that business about the time loop out of it," she said, casually. "Very shrewd. Even if they had believed you, it would only have made the interrogation worse. The way they were carrying on it was like they thought *we* were all in on it."

"Didn't need to go into any of that," he excused, mildly amused. "I think we can forgive them their panicky diligence. They were worried." His forgiving attitude riled her.

"*You are something else, you are,*" she went on, poking his shoulder accusingly. "First you were all, 'No, I can't interfere, it's against the rules.' Next thing I know: you're casually disregarding some of the most *important laws we have!*"

"Adaptability is a good quality," he replied, unmoved.

"And now we've been *dumped* in a city we don't even know the name of! So much for: a voyage of *discovery*! More like: the jumbled wanderings of lost souls! I haven't eaten since *yesterday*! Thanks to this *incident* everyone's going to know where I am in a matter of minutes! This is all your fault, you know!" she ranted, feeling very sorry for herself. She turned only to discover he was about twenty yards away walking in another direction. She sighed and hurried after him. She caught up and he eyed her warily but she didn't do anything.

"I'm sorry I keep yelling at you."

"I was expecting you to hit me," he stated, confused. She linked her arm with his and leaned against him.

"I was... I was being silly," she admitted, quietly. "I *just* want to eat and sleep. Can we do that please?"

"Always."

***

"Where is Deva?" asked Conrad, confused. Aboard Tabre's ship, *Alastor*, all was quiet and dark. Tabre himself, dressed immaculately as usual, was at the controls. An hour ago the Punes had declared that they wished to join the Coalition. It made sense as, from the beginning, it had been obvious that they had developed a liking towards Reed. Despite Tabre's best efforts, Satiah and Reed had won. Oddly, the Punes had not chosen to become a protectorate, as Reed had been initially steering them towards, they had opted for full membership.

Satiah... that name and her face were under his skin now. The one who had bested him. The one he would get even with. He had the perfect scapegoat though – Deva. Having defected or deserted, it didn't matter which, he had someone to put all the blame on. Failure was something that he didn't deal with very well although he knew it was an unavoidable part of life.

"No idea," Tabre replied, casually flicking something from the sleeve of his jacket. A message came through. His communicator activated automatically.

"We have read your report, we had no idea, Deva was a model employee," came a woman's voice.

"Best spies always are, you may want to check if she had any regular contacts. They could be informers," he replied, casually.

"I have people looking into that. The Coalition may have won this battle but they will never win the war. The Nebula Union have begun an investigation into the death of their delegate but, provided you covered your tracks well, that will not help anyone. I have a new assignment for you, one I *know* will be more to your liking," she said. His golden tooth gleamed as he smiled.

"Name it," he answered, as he often did.

"The Coalition Ambassador. The one operating under the name of Reed. He also has various other codenames. Kill him," she instructed, without a shred of emotion in her voice. Inwardly he was a little disappointed; he had hoped they would send him after Satiah.

"It will help incriminate the Coalition in the Union's investigation as *they will believe* that the Coalition had him killed to keep him quiet and to place the blame onto us, the only remaining ambassador being ours," she went on.

"The murky logic that some people stoop to," Tabre replied, frowning. "Everything has to be so disgustingly convoluted. People anticipating anticipations. The best keep it simple."

"That is why we hire you," she said, and he could tell that she was smiling.

"Naturally," he said, also smiling. "It is far less believable that the Coalition is assassinating him out of spite than a sexy conspiracy theory," he agreed, without much sincerity.

"So… Do you want to do this?" she asked, inevitably. He gave it real thought for a moment.

"Consider it done," he replied, as always. He knew, as he knew the woman did too, he was no envoy. He was a warrior and a professional. His true skills were in fighting, not talking. They didn't blame *him* for the failure. How could they when it was Conrad's job to play diplomat and Deva had betrayed them both?

"Your fee has been transferred," she said. "You will be relieved to know I am now firmly reinstated as Director. From now on I will deal with all your assignments personally." He wondered what complications she had been wrestling with recently. Some political nonsense, he supposed. She, like him, liked things neat and tidy. A common trait among operatives but he and she took it to extremes whenever possible. It was why they got on so well.

"Appreciated, *Director*," he replied, glad that he would no longer have to deal with office riffraff. They disconnected. He adjusted the controls to swing around, placing his arms in exactly the same neat position to stay as symmetrical as possible. It was time for the chase to begin.

"You are supposed to return me to…" began Conrad, reminding Tabre that he was meant to be returning Conrad home. He was stunned by the flick of a switch. On Tabre's ship, all the seats but the pilot's seat could stun their occupants. Tabre eyed him as he sat there, unconscious.

"Sorry, no time like the present."

PART TWO

The Sisterhood of the Light

The target moved. Bodies swayed, guns swung, and eyes flickered. Carlos gritted his teeth as, to the best his ability, he gunned down the simulated enemies. To his right Deva was doing the same. Satiah watched the scores as they appeared on the screen in front of her. Deva was hitting closer to the centre of her targets but Carlos was hitting more targets in general. Neither were where Satiah wanted them, no, needed them to be. As ever it was the age-old difference between quality and quantity that was up for debate. The simulation ended and Carlos and Deva lowered the guns.

This had not been their first session and they were both starting to tire a little. This fatigue was beginning to slow their reactions which, in turn, affected their scores too. As the final scores were told to them by the computer, their combined tiredness boiled over into a round of cheap banter.

"Accuracy is everything," Deva sneered, openly angry at his higher score. One she plainly felt he didn't deserve. "All *my* targets would have died, half of yours would still be alive."

"If everyone is *dead*, who is there to answer your questions?" Carlos argued, shrugging defensively. "More to the point, the more of them left *capable of fighting*, the more chance you won't be able to ask any questions." Deva opened her mouth to argue back further.

"Enough!" Satiah interrupted, their competitiveness making *her* feel tired all over. She was still recovering from her wounds though, and, as was her convention, she was hiding the weakness. She approached the firing range, made a show of taking her pistol with her left hand. *Not* her right which was her firing hand. Her holster was on her right hip.

"*Kelvin!*" she instructed, grim. The big robot restarted the simulation. Satiah opened fire. Her speed and accuracy made both Carlos and Deva look like beginners. She hit target after target in the face or the heart, receiving speed kill bonuses. She even hit the sniper in the background although she only got him in the shoulder. Likely a mortal wound but death would not have been immediate. Had she been more energetic or using her right hand she would have nailed him too. By the end she was weary but triumphant. Carlos and Deva stared wordlessly at her score.

"Now," Satiah said, a little smug. "Any comments?"

Deva bit her lip and looked at the floor. Carlos crossed his arms, sneering playfully at Satiah with an almost pouting stance. They'd known each other for a couple of weeks now and they had a good working affiliation. She expected a wisecrack of some kind from the youth.

"I think you're *a bit* above our level, Satiah," he stated, admiringly. "Which of *us* is the best?" Deva scowled up at him and he chuckled. Satiah just smiled.

"You both have such… *innovative* styles. It's difficult to compare you against each other," she replied, being deliberately neutral. The sarcasm in her tone was obvious though. The simulator was one thing, shooting live targets was different.

"Bad luck, Deva," he said, mockingly. "You keep trying though." She booted him in the ankle. "*Ow!*" Satiah left the teens to their fight and headed towards the control room.

This new ship was perfect in almost every way. Satiah had liked the look of it the moment she had seen it. Almost twice as large as the freighter she'd been lumbered with, *Vulture* was one of the very latest Covert-Class Phantom fighters. Straight off the manufacturing line, painted black with white strips, *Vulture* still had the smell of a new ship. With state-of-the-art weaponry, stealth capacities and armour, it was a working testament to the most advanced technology. It was faster, harder and more efficient than anything less than four times its own size. It could hold its own in most combat scenarios. One thing ruined it for Satiah, though. Inside, it was so bright and well lit. She didn't like that. She preferred dim lighting only and darkness wherever possible. It helped her think.

The control room, with its new flight seats – Satiah was always partial to any chair she could sleep in – was all fresh and ostentatious. Reed was there, reading a screen slowly. He *still* had failed to produce their new mission file! Some kind of printing difficulty, apparently. Satiah had the sneaking suspicion that he was lying about something. She approached the little man from behind.

"How are they doing?" he asked, somehow realising she was there.

"Growing pains still," she admitted, unable to hold back a smile. "I still think *you* should sharpen up your shooting skills."

"This mission shouldn't require a single shot to be fired. Besides, guns can really damage your health," he rattled off, still reading. Satiah peered over at it.

Since departing Yevanicha, after successfully getting it to join the Coalition, they had created a database of their own on the Sisterhood of the Light. No one knew much about it. Their only known planet was called Erokathorn. It was the where the Sisterhood had always been over the last two hundred and ninety years, give or take. The timing of their first mention intrigued Reed and he seemed to believe it was significant. Satiah had developed a peculiar faith in this strange little man. Reed seemed to grasp things from out of thin air with his mind and make it all make sense. They were about an hour out from the planet now. The planet that didn't like outsiders and rarely involved themselves with anything else in the universe.

Yet… there were some questions that needed answering. Reed wanted to know why they had shown such immediate and secretive interest in the new planet, Yevanicha. Also he'd admitted to being somewhat curious about their ways and the ways of the people who must live there. Satiah's questions were more specific and complex. Namely, what happened on that mining world that Rainbow had tipped her off about? What was their association, if any, with Jaylite Industries? And did they have knowledge of Balan's secret weapon? She and Reed had had a... *disagreement* about how best to proceed with this mission. Naturally, as a seasoned intelligence gatherer, Satiah was ready to sneak in and find out the truth via skilled espionage. Reed, however, had insisted that they directly contact the Sisterhood leadership and *politely ask*. Randal had put him in charge so Satiah technically had to obey. But Satiah and rules didn't always mix well. Particularly when those rules impeded her.

She and Randal had also discussed a few things. He still had her prisoner under his direct jurisdiction and had left him largely to himself. There had been an initial problem. The prisoner had collapsed due to refusing to eat or drink anything. The refusal was in the form of silence, of course. He still had not uttered a sound since Satiah had found him. So, to prevent him starving to death, they had medical robots keeping him alive by feeding him. Still, they had not asked him any questions as Satiah had instructed.

"*Kind* of Reed to request a brand new vessel for you," Randal noted, as a parting remark. "Most would have taken the best part of a week to get through checks and authorisation but he did it in less than forty minutes. You've made a powerful friend there, Satiah."

"He must have pulled some strings," she answered, evasively.

"Why did you never ask me for an upgrade?" Randal queried, as she suspected he would. It was a good question. "You *knew* you were entitled to one."

"I was going to," she lied, quickly. "But I keep getting *urgent matters* that distract me, though." He had chuckled grimly at that. It wasn't as biting as it could have been but she'd made her point. She wanted to work alone again, on her original assignment. All of this was keeping her from focussing on that.

"Well, about that, it seems it is Reed you need to talk to now, not me," he stated. "You ever heard of the Gushtapar?" Satiah had. They had been an illegal secret army created by one of Balan's henchwomen. A Commander Spenser.

"Hasn't everyone?" she quipped, taking that in stride.

"It seems, since the recent election, the surviving members have been reintegrated into official law enforcement. They are now called

Division Sixteen. They are looking to expand and link with Phantom Squad as a supporting agency. Manpower and so on…" he explained.

"We already have the PLC, we don't need anyone else," Satiah was quick to fire back. The Phantom Labour Force were an internal body of… *bodies*. A place for experienced criminals and mercenaries to work for and with Phantom Squad. Satiah had used them before and had found them to be… useful enough. All that being so, why would they need Division Sixteen?

"I thought you would say that," Randal said, and she could tell he was smiling. "I said much the same, however, it seems your friend Reed has been involved with Division Sixteen. As you are now clearly friendly with each other, I was wondering if you could get him to prevent the link?"

Satiah sighed, as if she didn't have enough to think about.

"I don't know *exactly why* he got me this ship…" she confessed, the timing of it all still bothering her. Reed had claimed that it was a present for saving his life from the assassin; trouble was he'd ordered her new ship *before* the enemy had struck. Clearly Reed had lied about his motivation. She was an attractive woman; he could easily be trying to get her interested in him. Or at least, that's what she presumed *Randal* had thought. This was why he was asking her to get Reed to change his mind. Yet she knew Reed well enough to know that she was not his type. Still, the gift troubled her. She was a firm believer in nothing ever being truly free. Everything costs something.

"Perhaps he did it only to ensure he had reliable transport for his next mission," she said, not believing that either. "My old chug of a freighter wasn't *exactly* first class."

"You have the opportunity to try to change his mind about this merger, Satiah," Randal spelt out, calmly. "I would consider it *a personal favour* if you succeed." Satiah had been pleased at that. It was always good for your boss to be in debt to you. A possible ultimate escape card.

"I will do what I can," she allowed, being honest. She didn't like the idea of the merger either but they *were* low on experienced Phantoms. Reed probably saw the merger as a way of improving that situation. She would have to get him to see it differently. As soon as she had ended *that* call, Rainbow had come through.

"What's going on?" he asked, confused. "Have you been transferred? I thought you were trying to keep a low profile but those ships don't get randomly given out, you know!"

"...What do you have?" she asked, ignoring him completely.

"Jaylite Industries. There's nothing more I can find except for a name. Malcolm Marlin. He was the director of the company at the time of their closure. He will know the details you want or will at least know more than I can find," Rainbow elaborated.

"Where is he?" she asked, eyeing Kelvin.

"That's the thing… *no one knows,*" he answered, his tone somewhere between intrigued and irritated.

"Friends, family, anything?" Satiah responded.

"Still digging," he answered, and she could mentally picture him shaking his head.

"Anything else on the Sisterhood?" she asked, seriously. They were getting close and she found their lack of knowledge unnerving.

"Why don't you start with the easy questions?" he groaned, sarcastically. "I got nothing on them. A few rumours but no evidence or even documents."

"…Fine," she said, disappointed. "Please keep looking."

"Do I get premium shift pay for this?" he asked, hopefully.

"No!" she squealed, mildly annoyed. "You get your reward when I have sorted this mess out."

Back in the control room, she once again tried to broach the subject with Reed.

"I'm not comfortable openly approaching the Sisterhood," Satiah said, seriously. "What if they refuse to answer our questions?"

"Why should they?" Reed asked, turning to face her.

"*Any number of reasons spring to mind.* In my experience, people *rarely* tell you anything unless either they don't realise what you're asking or… you have the gun," she stated, her voice one of inflexibility. She still hadn't told Reed about her personal mission but she was giving it serious consideration. If he was as high up as Randal seemed to think… maybe he could help. Besides, he had been trustworthy enough... so far. He was obviously playing games and had an agenda of his own but Satiah had no problem with any of that. She really didn't believe he was naive enough to assume the Sisterhood would just tell him what he wanted to know and that would be that.

"Diplomatic protocol plays a role here. I don't mean to throw the Coalition's weight around or anything *but*... they are just one world. We are many. They don't want to associate with us. They will understand that the more they cooperate the more quickly we will leave them alone," Reed explained. There was some logic to that but Satiah had realised that Reed was always capable of backing up his ideas with reason. And he was always plausible. It irritated her in a way, and she struggled to counter his arguments with equally well thought-out ones.

"How can we be sure that what they tell us is the truth?" Satiah asked, levelly.

"Why should they lie?" he asked, his tone not changing. His expression, however, seemed to become more serious and he gave her one of his *looks*. Satiah realised he had become suspicious of her.

"I'm not in the business of *trusting* what people tell me. I'm in the business of trusting what I find out by myself," she replied.

"Satiah... trust *me*," he smiled, aware of the irony. He seemed to completely believe that talking to them would work. Satiah smiled tightly and then headed for her new cabin. His mind was made up, she'd done everything she could. If it messed up, he was the responsible party. Despite her controlling nature she knew sometimes it was best to just let things go. She entered, Kelvin was there, standing silently in the semi-darkness. Instead of going to the bed, she sat in a personalised chair and curled up a little. Kelvin recognised what she was doing and carefully covered her body with a blanket.

"Thank you, Kelvin," she murmured, already half asleep. She found the soft whirl of his circuits comforting. She was safe with him watching over her. She drifted off in seconds into a calm dream. Her mind, free from nightmares, gnawed gently on the questions she had. Kelvin stood behind and to the right of her chair, monitoring the room constantly.

***

Foresight was a quality that Tabre had in great abundance. Now, on a new mission on behalf of the Director, he followed the tracking device. He had planted two trackers. First he'd set one up on the hull of the old freighter Reed and Satiah had been using. When the new ship had arrived he'd deployed a second. The contingency, *that he would have to track them*, at the time, had seemed dubious yet he was now glad he'd allowed for it. Conrad was still unconscious next to him. Satiah's new ship was no freighter and was superior even to his. The freighter had been left behind to drift away. Someone would say careless. Tabre had quickly found it and tried to see if anything had been left behind.

Only a bomb. Satiah had left nothing to chance after all, the second he'd tried to board it, it had exploded. Saved only by his caution, Tabre had his shields up which ably deflected the blast. The rubble left behind was useless. He hoped the rigged explosive had not tipped Satiah off that someone was following her. She might know that the freighter had been interfered with and decided to check her new craft for trackers. She may even have cleverly kept the beacon functioning and attached it to another ship entirely, leading him on a fool's errand. Yet, with nothing else to go on he had to follow that signal. Now he concentrated on following the new ship, making guesses at the destination as the journey went on. Soon it became apparent that, for whatever reason, Satiah was going to visit the Sisterhood of the Light. Why?

***

Satiah jumped awake, her gun in her hand before her first blink. Kelvin was still there. A thumping on the door had sounded. It was Deva. Relief flooded through Satiah instantly and she replaced her pistol in its holster swiftly.

"Satiah, *something's happened!*" Deva shouted, she sounded scared. "Reed's *collapsed*." Satiah opened the door, all weariness falling from her as adrenalin kicked in fully.

"Why?" she asked, needing to know more. The three of them together hurried to the control room, only just managing to stay out of each other's way in the narrow corridor.

"We literally just arrived and he screamed and fell over," she said, at a loss. Carlos was there, crouched next to the inert Reed. Kelvin ran a scan as Satiah too inspected him.

"He's alive and... *apparently* unhurt," Satiah surmised, confused. There were no blood stains or burn marks.

"All life readings normal," Kelvin agreed.

"Maybe he's ill," Carlos suggested, unable to think of another explanation.

"I am detecting nothing," Kelvin said.

"Kelvin, take him to his cabin," Satiah said, thinking quickly. They watched as the robot conveyed the unconscious Reed away and then she then faced the two teenagers. "Did he give you any idea what the plan was?"

"No," Carlos shrugged. "I think he was waiting for you."

"Great, I'll have to fill you in," Satiah said, inwardly elated and outwardly exasperated. Now, regardless of Reed, they could do the mission *her way* after all. What had caused his collapse?

Satiah ran a scan of the green world they could see looming up closer. It was not swampy green but the green of a dense forest. A lot of grey was there too, indicating huge storm clouds. All cloaking devices were operating. She smiled.

"I'll take us down," she said, slipping into the pilot's chair.

"What about *Reed*?" asked Carlos, genuinely concerned.

"We have our orders," she insisted, not really listening. "We will get help for him *only* if his condition worsens. For all we know he could be fine." People didn't just collapse, Satiah knew this. As did everyone above infancy. Yet, this was her chance to circumvent Reed's command and she knew, when she got the information, she could justify it.

Down the ship plunged into the clouds and rainfall. She'd identified the largest settlement and intended to land roughly a mile away for concealment purposes. Their presence had to remain unknown for as long as possible. The direction Satiah had chosen to follow was one that would minimise their exposure to any detection systems. Doing a descent like that would have been impossible in the freighter... well, impossible if you intended to land *in one piece*. She angled the ship carefully as she slowed; the viewport was almost useless as the rain overwhelmed everything. She was working solely with the computer readout. Carlos was keeping an eye on the counter balance but with Satiah piloting he needn't have bothered.

Down into the jungle she lowered them. Kelvin returned just as she touched down.

"He is in his cabin," Kelvin stated, referring to Reed. Everyone was staring out at the rain. A tropical rainstorm of freakish proportions hammered on the metal hull noisily. Distant thunder sounded but it was loud enough to make Deva edge just a little closer to Carlos. Satiah rose, eyeing the weather with indifference.

"You two stay here, protect the ship and look after Reed. If he wakes up, tell him he is to do nothing until I return," she instructed, already pacing down the corridor. Kelvin followed along with Carlos and Deva.

"He outranks all of us, *I* can't tell him *that*," Carlos objected, a little feebly. Satiah stopped, sighed and turned to face him.

"Being a Phantom sometimes means you have to operate outside of the command chain as well as the law," she said, carefully. "This is just one of those times."

***

Ash looked up sharply, a flicker of distant emotion breaking through his thoughts like a light breeze might disturb a sheet of paper. Ruby, sitting directly across from him, noticed the sharp move and tried to follow his gaze. She had been much quieter since the events of the previous day. And much more wary of him. Ash couldn't say that he liked the change.

"What?" she asked, nervously.

"…It's nothing," he explained, after careful consideration. In truth he genuinely did not know. It felt like surprise, pain and a defensive counter… all so fast Ash couldn't even be sure who it had been. Someone, somewhere had been attacked.

"You don't sound very sure," she noted, eyeing him cautiously. "Do you want me to go?" She'd been asking that a lot lately.

"No," he said, producing a warm smile.

"Good because I can't leave now that we're in flight," she joked.

The humour was weak, half hearted. She was still upset about the trip to Magnovastar. She was upset with him too, he could sense it.

"Ruby, do you trust me?" he asked, being deliberately blunt.

"Of course..." she began, before noticing his expression. The serious frown and evaluative eyes. She slumped, defeated. "I don't know," she confessed, being honest. "I mean, I know you did the best you could with the virus and everything. I know you were conflicted; it's not *that* that I'm troubled about. You made sure *I* was safe from the virus too, albeit clandestinely, which again *I'm letting go*. It's the fact that *you lied* about it being a normal trip from the start even though you pretty much straight away were planning the black hole thing. The fact that you didn't tell me bothers me. It makes me wonder *what else* you're not telling me. What is coming next?"

"A very great deal," he answered, also telling the truth. She stared expectantly and then her enthusiasm faded.

"Why aren't you telling me?" she demanded, earnestly. "*Do you not trust me? Is that what this is about?*"

"You are a human and you see things the way a human does," he answered, as if that might help. She crossed her arms and the smallest flicker of a smile crossed her lips.

"I know your mum sent you here for a reason and you told me all that stuff about the gateway but... did she leave you a list of things to finish for her?" guessed Ruby, at last the old excitement returning. "Like a will or something?" Ash sighed, staring right into her eyes. She grew a little smaller as if squirming under his intense attention. He reached out and took one of her hands in both of this.

"Ruby, this is very important, have you ever heard of the Orion Observatory?" he asked, his voice barely audible. She didn't answer for a few seconds and he could sense her straining to remember. Then she grinned.

"I have now," she said, shrugging. He rolled his eyes. "Hey, come on. I'm human, remember! What could be more human than making a joke at the wrong moment?" she protested, quietly. She pulled a face at him, an imitation of how he looked to her. He smiled a little. Then she shook her head.

"No, sorry, never heard of it," she said, a little sad that she couldn't help him.

"Not many have... What about its other name: *ITP 6?*" he stated. She blinked.

"I'm sorry?" she asked, thinking she'd misheard. Since she'd met Ash she'd grown increasingly distrusting of everything including her own senses.

"It's a space station and I need to find it," Ash admitted, deadly serious still.

"...Right," she said, snapping out of her thoughtful trance. "Okay, is it big?" He chuckled, again amused by how her mind worked.

"Unfortunately I have never seen it," he stated.

"Okay," she replied, nodding quickly. "Not a problem. Where is it?"

"That's the problem, *no one knows!*" he stated, letting his very real aggravation show. She made a noise of consideration, somewhere between a grunt and a hum. Her fingers tapped on the table as she reflected.

"So, besides its name, *what do you know exactly?*" she asked, astutely.

"It was built, owned and concealed by the late Balan Orion, former Commandment Benefactor. Most likely it was a secret military establishment. Things were done there. *Experiments.* Others would have been involved but it was a secret known to only a few of the highest ranking humans," he explained.

"You're talking about the Vourne Conspiracy," she said, her eyes excited. "Right?"

"That may or may not be relevant. The term *Vourne Conspiracy* seems to have several different definitions. Some use it as a phrase to encompass the entire of Balan's administration. Others use it to mean Vourne's personal grab for power. Still others apply it purely to the atrocities that occurred on Pluto Major. Vourne may or may not have been involved with this but that hardly seems to matter being as he is dead," Ash ranted.

"So is Balan," she mused, casually.

Their drinks arrived and a hush fell over the table until the waiter had departed once more.

"Everyone high enough to know about this is dead," he stated. "Commanders Grey and Spenser, Vourne and Balan himself. Nothing was kept on record, I know because I looked."

"How do you know what you know?" she asked, interested. "See it mentioned in a document or something?"

"I had four things to do when I agreed to come to this cosmos. I've done two of them. Dreda had information about Orion Observatory. Where she got it, I cannot say," he elaborated.

"I see," she said, in a conspiratorial tone. "So where are we going now?"

"Pluto Major."

***

Water. Water was everywhere. It was warm, moreover. All Satiah could hear was rain, running water and the odd rumble of thunder. Dripping. Running. Pelting. Pummelling the matter that stood between it and the ground. The warm rain bounced off of Kelvin who stood right behind her, giving the pattering a metallic twang. The hood of her cloak was buckling under the weight of the rain. She stared through the sheets of precipitation and groups of trees in the direction of the settlement. Another roll of thunder shook her into action.

"This way," she said, just loudly enough for him to hear. They began to pick their way through the trees. She was pleased that the water was so warm. If the rainfall had been freezing this would feel ten times worse. They plodded on for the best part of ten minutes in silence, bathing in the drizzle reluctantly. Kelvin's metal hand clamped down on her shoulder gently but firmly. She turned to face him.

"We are close, I have life readings," he said. Then he waved his right arm at her. "Flame throwing unit will not be efficient in this climate. I will switch to repeating laser."

"It is a bit wet," she agreed, chuckling darkly. "How many life forms?"

"Eighty-four, there will be others," he informed. When Kelvin said *life forms* he usually meant *people* as opposed to animal life. She nodded, they were neighbouring now. They slowed their pace and began to creep along. All her clothes now completely soaked, Satiah began worrying about how much they would slow her down. She felt pretty much back to normal now, physically. Pushing through a thick barrier of big leaved plants, she crouched. Kelvin too lowered himself.

Ahead was a dwelling. A house of some type. They had come out of the rainforest, reaching the end of a domestic garden area. It was set up like a small farm. Clear crop lines. It would make sense, as this planet traded with no one, that they would need to be self-sufficient. The scan had indicated that what wasn't rainforest was mainly agricultural land. Dressed in waterproofed clothing, a child was dropping seeds into the mud. Kelvin thrust a needle into the mud at their feet. Satiah awaited his prognosis.

"Ten count on fertility scale," he said. She raised her eyebrows, surprised. A ten was almost unheard of. "Also, this soil registered as a trace on the coolant sample you brought back from the shaft." She said nothing, both amazed and perplexed. How had soil from this world ended up in that weird shaft to get mixed up with reactor coolant?

"Must have been the merest trace of a trace," she murmured, still running it over in her mind.

"Registered at naught point naught one six," Kelvin summarised. Tiny but enough to register. Once again, Satiah found herself glad of the investments she had made while building him.

"So that shaft remains a question needing an answer. The Sisterhood reach out to the Punes *before* anyone else can get there to...?" She trailed off. Kelvin remained silent. "This would be much easier if we *knew* what that shaft *was*... maybe Reed was right and we should have just asked them. I've crawled right through that thing and I still am none the wiser for it."

"I have two beings approaching," Kelvin warned, changing subjects.

Gun in her hand, Satiah carefully backed off into the foliage. Two men, walking side by side, trudged along the outer garden. A patrol? They wore red and purple clothes with golden headbands and... no noticeable weapons. Satiah and Kelvin watched them intensely as they walked by. Guards or just civilians? There was certainly something... not right about this planet. Satiah could feel it. There was no… chaos. Everything seemed so well ordered. The lines of the seeds were completely equally proportioned, each placed exactly the same distance away from one another with a precision that seemed impossible. Impossible for an organic life form to perform, yet Kelvin had made it clear they *were* organics. Aside from the rain it was very quiet too. So wet, she felt she might as well be submerged, Satiah sat down to think about her next move.

The men were gone in a few minutes and Satiah rose to her feet.

"We'll follow them," she said, to Kelvin. Taking care to stay out of sight from the dwellings they were paralleling, they quickly caught up with the two men. There was a structure coming up ahead. A much larger towering building. It was a huge square construction, white in colour and it was topped off with a large dome.

"Looks like the centre of it all," she remarked to Kelvin, seriously.

"The whole settlement is a mathematically perfect circle. Computer designed, it is possible that the Sisterhood do not exist and this planet is ruled by an artificial intelligence," Kelvin said.

"Perhaps," she mused, again starting to lose count of the questions that they had no answers for.

Still shadowing the two men, they found their first road. It was a pathway but well-constructed. Again with the symmetry. Everything was so well ordered. Too well ordered. Where was the litter? The graffiti? The cordoned off repair/maintenance works? There were no missing stones, no chipped walls nor even puddles anywhere. A feat of engineering? Some strange natural explanation? Did gravity or magnetism have some role to play in this? The two men entered the large building. It was guarded. Two other men, next to each other, were standing casually by the large door. Evidently they were not expecting anything untoward, their casual poses and lack of observation told her that much. Satiah pushed her earpiece in gently.

"Get back to the woods and wait for me there, I'm going to get inside," she said, considering how best to get in.

"Acknowledged," Kelvin said, his voice in her ear. Satiah broke from cover and sprinted across the road. She reached the side of the building and pressed herself against it. Pulling her grapple gun from her belt she fired straight up. It attached itself to the underside of the dome. She slid upwards quickly after fastening it to her belt. There were windows.

Inside there seemed long halls and vast open spaces, split only by circular columns. She reached the top and swung there briefly deciding how to get in. She was about to get her laser cutter when she noticed that the window wasn't locked. Frowning in surprise, she eased it open and slipped inside. She was in a small room, sleeping bunks were against two of the walls, clearly indicating that this room was home to four occupants. No one was there at the moment, however. She took the decision to keep her grapple gun with her. Even if she needed to get back down in a hurry, leaving it there would only invite discovery. She'd seen a lot of people as she had shot past the windows. The door was not automated, it wasn't even mechanical. It was just wooden. Curious, Satiah pushed it open.

The corridor outside was dark but it overlooked the hall she had seen as she ascended the side of the building. Voices could be heard. Satiah wandered across to the edge and subtly peered over. From above she could see many people walking this way and that, some alone, some in pairs. There was no obvious sign of cameras or security anywhere she looked. She had not expected a place with this kind of reputation to be so technologically backward. Their architecture indicated otherwise. She made sure no one was on her level and she realised that the dome itself was completely hollow, this only added to the interesting acoustics of the building.

"Interesting place, this," she said, studying it hard with her eyes. "It reminds me of some sort of ancient religious structure. Now I'm inside it, it's got *that feel.*"

"If you are correct there will be scriptures, books," Kelvin prompted. He was suggesting she take one.

"You are right but I can't see any," she replied. She padded along the corridor and stopped short when she noticed a procession entering the building. Standing by an alcove for concealment, she watched and waited. Maybe a mass of thirty people, some male some female, were following the path in the centre of the building. Robes, revered tones... the thing certainly had religious overtones. Everyone else stopped what they were doing and began to follow but there was no signs of any aggression. A gentle chanting began but it was disorganised. Satiah was fairly sure they were saying the same things, just at different times. One female continued on when the rest of them stopped, and climbed a small set of steps. Once head and shoulders above anyone else, she removed her hood.

She had long whitish hair and strange purple eyes. She raised one hand and all the sounds died away. Somehow her voice was loud enough for Satiah to hear clearly. It was like she was talking in her mind as much as out loud.

"My people, I am *glad* to see you here this day," said the woman, regal and intense. Satiah decided she *must* be a leader if not *the leader*. She would be the one to track next.

"I thank you for your efforts as the land thanks you for tending it," she went on. "The harvest will be soon and then the festivity of nature can begin. I understand that the young ones have already begun work on their clothes." She smiled as a minor bout of laughter made the rounds among the assembled people. A cloaked figure knelt before her, no words were spoken but concentrated eye contact was made.

"…It is time for convergence," she smiled, and waved at the crowd. They all began to leave… well, not all, several cloaked figures remained. They were in purple, pink and red. So, the people who were not wearing robes were just people? Locals? Not part of the Sisterhood? Satiah began to think those in the cloaks must be part of the Sisterhood, possibly all of it. Did the colours indicate rank? There were many more of them than she had initially spotted. At least sixty individuals. Were it not for the flamboyant colours they wore, this would all have been so sinister. Perhaps that was a calculated distraction, a way for them to look less threatening. It took literally about fifteen seconds for everyone not wearing a cloak to vacate the building. A sign of regular practice? Possibly.

The doors were closed and then locked. The sound of the lock echoed loudly through the whole building. After that crash a deep and creepy silence initiated. Then, as one, *all of them* looked up… *right at Satiah*. Satiah frowned in confusion for a moment. Could they *see her*?

"What do you want?" demanded the woman, anger in her voice. Satiah didn't move or say anything. Was she being spoken to or was this all part of some strange ceremony? The woman made a gesture with her hand and two of the sisterhood, both men strangely enough, began running in opposite directions. Still Satiah didn't move, unsure. How could they see her? It was too dark and she had made no sound.

"How did you get here?" asked the woman, her tone unchanged. "Where are you from?" Then Satiah knew, *somehow just knew*, that this woman knew she was there.

Satiah backed away and began to hurriedly pace towards the escape of the window. A man landed in front of her after leaping up and crosswise from another corridor directly below that one. A move that should have been physically impossible. Gun raised, Satiah fired. The shot should have taken him in the head. A shimmer of light occurred instead and the man's hand was somehow there, as if absorbing the hit. Satiah didn't wait to see more and she nosedived out of the window. She fired the grapple gun, it hit the side of the building, and swung her around as she dropped. In doing so this made her fly back up and to the right. Midway she disconnected the grapple and landed on the rooftop of one of the dwellings. Rolling to a halt she glanced back to see the woman, watching her, from the entrance of the building.

Unsure exactly who or how many were chasing her, Satiah just sprinted. Coming down off of the roof she made her way across the open ground towards the edge of the trees. A glance over her shoulder took in four robed figures moving quickly after her. Others were behind them. Into the forest she charged, getting soaked all over again. She never panicked, her mind remained calm. She began a meandering course, designed to confuse any pursuit and knew that Kelvin was moving in on her from another direction. Over a dell she used her grapple gun again, this time on a thick overhanging branch, to swing straight across. She landed in mid-stride. She jumped a fallen tree and kept going. She and Kelvin met in a gap between bushes. Without a word they continued running together. Only after the best part of ten minutes' continual dash did Satiah halt. She was breathless but not quite winded. They crouched together and stared back the way they had come. Only the rainfall could be heard or seen.

"Life forms?" she breathed, her eyes never leaving the area where they had emerged from. She wanted to know if they were still being trailed.

"Two entered the forest but they have now moved out of my detector range," he answered. Translation: they went the wrong way. Satiah slumped back, relieved. For a moment she just breathed and recovered.

"This planet is odd," she said, checking her gun for faults. How had they seen her? How had that man not died? She'd moved perfectly, too fast for him to dodge, to accurate for him not to die. She told Kelvin everything from the logistics to her feelings.

"We should leave, wait in a system nearby and then return and try Reed's idea," Kelvin stated. "It does not seem we will discover more like this now they know we are here." She had to agree.

"*If* he recovers," she nodded, standing.

They trudged back through the warm tropical rain towards the ship. Kelvin monitored their surroundings. Satiah didn't bother keeping her gun handy as apparently she couldn't trust it to work on this planet. It was then that Kelvin turned to her.

"Approaching craft," he warned. She didn't even break stride, instead motioning to the trees above them.

"They will never see us in this, too much heat for heat detection to really work either," she said, unruffled. Then she realised that he was telling her that the Sisterhood had ships. Of course they must have had ships in order to get to the Pune home world, therefore leaving the planet might not be as easy as she had first assumed. Rainbow's words came back to her. *No one comes back.* Those were words that were just never good to hear, much like: *your planet needs you,* necessity has no law, and *work sets you free.* She composed herself inwardly, a bitter rage and an instinctive fear cancelling each other out into calmness.

"I'm starting to wish we had never come here," she admitted, grim. "There was something about that whole place that just didn't sit well with me. It was too orderly, too controlled. Like it was all put on just so I could see it. An act."

"It is unlike you to dwell in speculation," Kelvin observed.

"Yeah well, this planet is unlike any I've ever encountered before," she muttered, extending her stride slightly to avoid a tiny stream.

"Anything on the others?" she asked, changing the subject.

"They have not moved," he answered.

"Should've followed their example," she sighed, irritated.

***

"No wonder the locals don't come here," Ruby said, shivering. She kicked a rock, sending it clattering down into the space below. It rolled to a halt, resting in the dirt.

"*Ruby!*" chastised Ash, irritated at her destructive carelessness. They were standing at the edge of woodland, overlooking a giant crater. Pluto Major, a Colonial Federation world, had been the site of a rather ugly war a month or so previously. Commander Spenser had been orchestrating civil unrest as an excuse to massacre the local people. They were standing on the edge of what had once been a building. A building that had once had a disturbingly despicable purpose.

Morbid curiosity was something that not many could resist. Despite knowing, or at least supposing, what had gone on there, it was difficult not to stare. Not to imagine. Those fences still standing were capped with twirling fibres sharper than knives, an improvement on the primitive barbed wire. Piles of rubble betrayed the remains of buildings designed for the infliction of death. Nature was beginning to lay the claim of entropy on this sad testament to fanatical cruelty. After the clear-up, less than a week ago the place had been abandoned. If only it could so easily be forgotten...

"Sorry," she apologised, shrugging slightly. "This must have been where Spenser burned the bodies." She'd noticed the charred rock and blackened debris.

"No one knows for sure because she didn't exactly *keep notes* but it is estimated as many as fifteen thousand met their end in this area," Ash informed her, watching her closely. He was interested in the human reaction to the death of many strangers.

"Awful," she said, her tone quiet. "She got what she deserved in the end though, right?" Interesting, to humans, did death really justify death? An exchange, a trade of lives to settle the score? How peculiar.

"She was killed," he stated, leaving it at that. He didn't tell her that the people had executed the wrong person as they retook control. He didn't mention that *that* soldier had never been avenged, nor did she receive any form of justice from the angry mob. The poor young woman that Commander Spencer had used as a scapegoat didn't get what she had deserved. Neither did he tell her that it had been Blint Mensa who had murdered Commander Spenser because she failed to tell him where Vourne was. Her death had come to her not as repayment for *this dreadful deed* but because of something else entirely. Such was the way of the universe; sometimes cause and effect changed their names.

He began to climb down into the remains of the structure. With understandable reluctance she followed. A new silence, a special silence, fell when they reached the bottom. Ruby did change a little when she knew she was standing exactly where thousands of humans had died. She went a little paler, and moved closer to him.

"Ash?" she asked, her voice frightened. "I don't like it here." Motivated with a melancholic curiosity of his own, Ash turned to regard her again.

"Why not?" he asked, trying to guess. "Is it because of what happened here or what is happening now?" That brought her out of her gloom.

"What's happening *now*?" she asked, suddenly more vigorous. She looked at all around uneasily.

"Try to find something which hasn't been destroyed, call me if you do," Ash instructed. She grabbed his arm as he began to move away.

"Where are you going?" she asked, a little too forcefully.

"To search over there," he replied, casually pointing. "It *will* be quicker if we split up." She let go and looked down as if summoning her strength.

"Right," she said, her voice still small and sad. He moved away and she went in the opposite direction. It was a horrible place where horrible things had happened. No, *Ruby amended that*; it was a horrible place *because* horrible things had happened there. She didn't believe in ghosts or spirits or even life after death but she felt that this place could start to change her mind. Ash was looking for information, that could be in document form or data form. She spotted a group of skulls piled in a corner and swallowed. Who in their right mind would keep notes around here? Then again, who in their right minds would commit such crimes?

A breeze that had seemed pleasant enough in the forest felt chillier in the ruins and she focussed on her search intensely to distract herself from her own fear. The remains of a side room drew her attention when she saw half of a metal container. A thick layer of dust and dirt covered everything. She peered into the blackened cavity, once used for storage. Inside the remains of official paperwork lay. Gently, unconsciously biting her lip as she did it, she eased the pile of documents out of the container. A few of the upper pages fell apart in her hands but those *underneath* were still complete and legible. She found herself reading what appeared to be a list of names. Troops? Civilians? Targets? Victims? Without context it was useless to her. She found herself in a depressed reverie, imagining what must have been happening when the killings had occurred. The fear, pain and death.

A noise made her shriek, drop the files and turn around all at once. Ash was standing there.

"Ruby, I have been calling you," he stated, a little startled. She had tears in her eyes as hugged him emotionally.

"Sorry I was just thinking," she said, expressively. She felt his protective arm land across her shoulders and instantly her misery receded a little. It had all happened now, it was gone, part of history. She was safe.

"I've found something," he said, not enquiring further. He led her across the ashes and into a tunnel. It was actually a corridor but it looked and felt more like a tunnel. Activating a light he had with him, Ash led her up some partially melted metal steps and into a room.

"I think this must have been where whoever *managed* this place worked," Ash explained. There were plenty of documents and several of them appeared to be undamaged.

One each in the top right of each page, sometimes behind the text but always visible, was the emblem of the Human Coalition. Light green intertwining lines in a shape not unlike a flower, with the distinctive trio of golden strips in a line at the bottom. Ruby saw it and she shook her head.

"I hate this place," she said, with finality. "It's like its negatively tainted or something."

"Echoes," replied Ash, clearly thinking about other things. They searched for the best part of two hours. Every sheet of paper, each file. At last, Ash packed it in.

"There's nothing here," he sighed, in disappointment. "I don't even know what I expected to find."

"Can we go?" she begged, hopeful.

"There is one more place we could try."

***

"She's been gone nearly *four hours!*" Deva stated, laying down her cards. Carlos had been clock-watching too. It was hard not to. Reed was still unconscious. The rain was too heavy for them to see much outside and Satiah's instructions had been adamant. Watch Reed and *do nothing else!* He had been teaching Deva how to play Gairunn. He had found the set of playing cards in among Reed's belongings while searching for any medication he may have. And, as the ship was monitoring the surround automatically, they had sat at the foot of Reed's bed and started playing. If nothing else it had helped to pass the time.

"I know," he said, motioning for her to re-deal.

"When is she ever going to trust us to do more than just keep watch?" Deva complained.

"When we prove ourselves most likely, don't worry, *she's all right,*" replied Carlos, defending his teacher.

Both heard the door open and watched as, drenched and a bit demoralised, Satiah and Kelvin marched towards the doorway. Carlos already knew not to ask what had happened. Satiah had a look on her face that made it all too clear that things had gone badly. She stopped in the doorway, still dripping.

"No change," she said. It was a statement, not a question. Deva shook her head.

"Nothing," she said, wondering what was going on. Satiah said no more and just headed off towards the control room. On the way she allowed her soaked cloak to just fall from her shoulders for Kelvin to take away. The water had been warm but she was tired of being totally sodden. She ran a scan, noting that over twenty ships were patrolling the area now and what looked like two space defence platforms in the orbital zone. Was this all because of *her?* A manhunt of such proportions seemed a bit of an overreaction! Then a contingency that had never occurred to her happened... someone else arrived. And that someone's ship looked *very* familiar.

***

After a long argument with Conrad, silence had finally returned to the control room on board *Alastor*. He'd taken exception to the fact that Tabre had rendered him unconscious instead of taking him home. Tabre though, had needed the ambassador in case of political complications. Once Tabre had discovered that Reed, for whatever strange reason, was going to visit the Sisterhood of the Light, Tabre had decided that they too would pay a visit. If Reed was there, they could kill him. If he was doing something covert, they could expose him. Simple enough plan. When they had arrived, however, within moments, a battle fleet had greeted them.

"Unknown intruder, *surrender!*" ordered a man. A warning shot flew past and Tabre gritted his teeth. Not the most pleasant of welcomes!

"This is Colonial Federation ship *Alastor*," Conrad began, mustering a cutting tone from somewhere. In normal circumstances, were he really on official business, being shot at would be received in such an indignant way. "And I am an ambassador. If you fire on us it *will* be considered an act of war…"

"You were spying on us, we can prove this," snapped back the other voice. "You will cease your movement and prepare to be boarded."

"*Spying?*" mouthed Tabre, confused. They had only just got there! Conrad waved at him to get him to remain silent.

"I can assure you, we have only just arrived," Conrad stated, quite truthfully. No wonder everyone avoided the Sisterhood, he'd never encountered such hostility to strangers. "I wish to speak to your ambassador."

Tabre suddenly noticed that the tracker he was following was getting further away again. Reed was on the move. In a moment, Tabre understood what was going on. *Reed* had been spying on the Sisterhood, had been spotted and was now running. Unfortunately, probably because he was cloaked, *they* couldn't see him. They had seen Tabre instead and believed him to be Reed.

"I say again, surrender *or you will be destroyed!*" raged the voice.

Conrad gave Tabre a frightened look.

"Leave this to me," Tabre growled. Tabre activated the engines, notching them up to full power. They shot forwards, too fast for the large ships to counter. Conrad strapped himself in, hoping that Tabre knew what he was doing. As they were heading straight for the planet, the Sisterhood's larger ships, expecting an attack, opened fire.

Reed was heading out in the opposite direction at a serious pace. If Tabre could get a shot at him he might be able prevent him from escaping. Yet Tabre had to weave around to prevent his ship getting hit which slowed him down considerably. Reed vanished before he had a chance to get the shot in. Preparing to make the jump right after him, Tabre locked onto the tracking device. It was then that the ship shook violently and all speed fell away. Tabre frantically checked the systems and Conrad stared at him helplessly.

"What's happening?" he asked, fearful.

"I don't know," Tabre said, trying to understand why they were no longer moving. No tractor beam, engines still roaring... they *should* be moving.

A new voice crackled.

"This is High Priestess Chalky, First Lady of the Sisterhood of the Light..." she said. "You cannot escape us so easily." Creaking and groaning as if struggling against some invisible force, their ship began to move to the side and down. It was as if something was physically dragging them along towards the planet.

"Talk to her!" snarled Tabre, at Conrad.

"What do you want?" she asked, her tone forbidding. "Why have you come here?" Her voice had the ice of wisdom about it. An unusual accent neither Colonial nor Coalition.

"...How do I address you, Lady?" asked Conrad, tensely.

"Swiftly unless you wish to die in the frozen void," she bit back. The ship jolted viciously.

The engines were overheating, boiling over in their fruitless efforts to give motion to the ship. Tabre deactivated, and they sped up towards the planet, still going sideways. The other ships that had been firing on them were now backing off in silence.

"I don't know *how* they're doing it but they're dragging us in," Tabre sighed, adjusting his jacket. Neat as ever, his blue velvet-like jacket faintly reflected the colours of the controls.

"We have just got here, we mean the Sisterhood *no harm*, we came to speak with you about the possibility of joining the Colonial Federation," Conrad lied.

"So why spy on us?" she demanded, a little more calmly. "One of your agents invaded the sanctity of our *temple, shot at one of our brothers* and then fled into the jungle. Presumably to end up on *your ship*."

"*Satiah*," smiled Tabre, shaking his head slowly. He chuckled softly. "*You naughty girl.*"

"We have just arrived and have no agents…" Conrad stated, still trying to keep up with the conversation.

"There are only two of you, neither are female," Chalky said, as if to herself. They were approaching a settlement, Tabre could see. A large dome-shaped structure. A temple? On the roof, a lone woman stood, her arm outstretched to them. Her white hair was billowing in the breeze. Tabre raised an eyebrow. Was she using telekinesis to drag them in? Her other hand was holding something to her lips. The communicator.

"Well," Chalky said, simply. "You are here now, whatever your purpose." She cut off before Conrad could reply to that and the ship landed heavily on the stone roof. Conrad stared at Tabre, a look that plainly demanded something.

"We have no choice," Tabre said, removing his gun. "Come on, time to talk to the Sisterhood." They left the ship only to discover that more cloaked figures had arrived to back Chalky up. Nineteen by Tabre's count. Conrad smiled falsely as he stepped forward to greet them in person.

"Greetings, I am honoured to finally meet you," Conrad said, launching into the traditional script. "My name is Conrad Willis and this is my consort, Tabre."

"You cannot hide your true purpose from me so easily," Chalky said, her eyes piercing them both. Tabre noted that two of the figures were now between him and his ship. Not that it would be any good to try to take off.

"*True purpose?*" Conrad questioned, uneasily.

"She's talking about the *spying*," Tabre sighed, pushing past him. Tabre had decided that, for once, honesty would serve them best. In any case Conrad's bumbling was only making it worse.

"My name is Tabre," Tabre stated, without bothering to embellish it with any flowery gestures. He didn't even put on a polite tone. "You *were* being spied on but *not by us*. I'm here on a mission to find a man called Reed. He *was* here and I'm pretty sure *he was* spying."

"Reed," breathed Chalky, her eyes half closing. A lengthy silence began. She breathed out the name a second time. Tabre got the distinct impressed she'd heard the name before. He hoped he'd not misread the situation and that Reed was *friends* with the Sisterhood and he had just *really* angered her.

"And he is now gone?" Chalky asked, focussing on him again.

"His ship has left," Tabre answered, carefully. That did not necessarily mean *Reed himself had gone too*.

"...Anyone within my reach can be found. *You* were found. Why wasn't he? How did his associate get so close before I sensed her?" Chalky demanded. Tabre shrugged.

***

Carlos entered the control room, looking puzzled.

"Why have we *left?*" he asked, inevitably. Anyone could have figured out that the ship had moved, Satiah had really been utilising the acceleration. She'd pushed so hard at one point; she'd almost caused a misfire. When she had realised just who it was that was chasing them, her mind had made instant calculations. How had he found them again? Only two answers had made sense. *He'd* placed a homing device on their hull. Or... *Deva* had tipped him off using the same method. With no idea where the device was situated, Satiah had decided to confront Deva *immediately*. As long as the device remained operational, they could be tracked.

"Recognise *that?*" she asked, pointing to a frozen image of Tabre's ship. Satiah headed back out to press Deva while Carlos stared. Suddenly he realised where she was going. He chased after her.

"Satiah!" he shouted, trying to stop her or at least get her to listen to him.

Deva looked up as Satiah entered, pistol in her hand. Deva began to stand, fear in her eyes as Satiah aimed.

"Where is it?" Satiah demanded, her voice dangerously calm. Confusion and fear battled for supremacy on Deva's face.

"Where is what?" she asked, genuinely puzzled.

"Wrong answer," Satiah stated, making a point of moving the pistol around. It would look as if she was trying to decide where best to shoot her. Carlos stumbled in.

"Satiah, what are you doing?" he asked, seriously. "I've been watching her, she's not planted anything or made any calls."

"Then how did he know where to look?" demanded Satiah, angry.

"You don't *know* that he was looking for *us*," Carlos pointed out, refusing to give way.

"*Who?*" asked Deva, still unsure of what she was being accused of.

"She's talking about Tabre," Reed said, startling all of them. He was wide awake, just sitting on the edge of the bed watching the confrontation. Satiah lowered the pistol as she eyed him in shock.

"You seem to be feeling... *better*," she noted, with some disbelief.

"There was never anything wrong with me," Reed stated, irritably. "The moment we entered the range of the Sisterhood I was subjected to a psychic attack." Carlos and Deva looked at one another baffled.

"The Sisterhood are *psychics?*" clarified Satiah, almost sounding relieved. "That explains a lot."

"I was forced to go under, taking you all with me," Reed went on, seriously. "Trouble was that you all wouldn't have known that."

"We *thought* you'd had *some* kind of attack," Deva stated, seriously. "But there was nothing medially wrong with you which stumped us."

"I knew it was a possibility but I underestimated their power," Reed muttered, apologetically. "It explains a lot about why they don't like visitors."

"Reed, *Tabre* has been tracking us," Satiah said. The allegation was clear.

"I *swear...!*" Deva began, defensively. She was struggling not to take this personally. As motivations went she could understand why Satiah had leapt to the conclusion, albeit incorrect, that she must have betrayed them. It was within the realms of plausibility. And Deva knew Satiah was distrusting and didn't much care for her as a person either.

"I don't know *where* you put it. Kelvin and myself have searched the ship twice since acquiring it and found nothing but Tabre's attendance confirms that it is here as well," Satiah stated, her argument backed by logic.

Reed sighed and slowly, from his pocket, pulled out a homing device. Satiah gaped.

"*You?*" she demanded, incredulity on her face and in her tone.

"*What?*" Deva frowned, her anger and fear fading.

"I think it is time I explained," Reed sighed, looking very tired suddenly. "I agree that I should have told you, Satiah. I'm sorry for not doing so. There was a *very* good reason though." Satiah allowed a grin to show. This would be good. Everyone sat down.

"Is that thing still functioning?" asked Carlos, pointing to the device.

"It is," Reed nodded, his tone soft. Satiah and Kelvin waited for Reed to collect his thoughts.

"The Sisterhood of the Light are one of the most powerful forces in the cosmos," Reed began, seriously. "I don't know who rules them exactly but I needed to find out. I need to know, you see. I had heard many rumours about their powers but I had no idea what would happen so... I made a few contingency plans. First I ensured that I did not go in alone. that I had people around me I could trust." Carlos and Deva nodded but Satiah shifted in her seat.

"I didn't follow your instructions," she stated, with no apology in her tone. "I made no attempt to make contact. I carried out a reconnaissance of their settlement. I was spotted, I don't know *how* exactly, but the end result was that I was forced to run."

Reed sighed.

"Yes, I had a feeling you might have done that," he said.

"You said…" Carlos began, pointing to Satiah. She'd pretended that she was working according to Reed's instructions whereas in reality she'd not even been close.

"I lied," she admitted, without shame or guilt. "I was doing what I thought best at the time. Reed may never have recovered besides… That's *why* you let Tabre follow us, *isn't it?*"

"As a distraction for our *potential* escape," Reed smiled, nodding. "Precisely, yes. I didn't tell you because I didn't want to argue with you about setting up an ambush for him near the Sisterhood's planet."

"What?" Deva asked, still confused.

"I was aware that there was a chance that the Sisterhood may attempt to destroy us regardless of who we were or what we wanted," Reed explained, slowly. "Just as I was aware that if Satiah knew he was coming, she would want to confront him. And I couldn't let either happen, not like that."

"So you invite *Tabre* to follow you?" Deva asked, a little uncertain. "How could you be sure he *was* even following you?"

"*This* being here," Reed answered, showing her the homing device.

"It's a reasonable assumption," Satiah nodded, satisfied.

"Question now is… do we keep it operational?" Reed asked, making eye contact with Satiah. Satiah shrugged lightly, as if it meant nothing.

"Up to you, *you're in charge*," she replied, with a droll smile. He chuckled. "Sorry, I have a twisted sense of humour."

"Well, at least you have one," Reed replied, without missing a beat.

"Reed, there are a few matters we need to talk about," she said, deciding to go all in. She eyed Carlos and Deva.

"You *can* trust us," Carlos insisted. Deva nodded. Satiah sighed, knowing she was taking a risk but she felt that she had to let them know what she was really doing. It was clear this mission was not going to end any time soon, regardless of whether the mystery file of Reed's ever showed up or not. So Satiah started from the beginning.

Balan's secret weapon, Operation Burning Bridge, Jaylite Industries, the soil sample and the Sisterhood. Everyone listened, spellbound. When at last she had finished, everyone was silent.

"That is deep," Carlos said, eyeing her with more respect than ever.

"And *very* concerning," Reed nodded, sharpness in his tone. "The Sisterhood *could* have this secret weapon."

"It's a possibility," Satiah said, a little tense.

"Vourne's involvement in all this concerns me too," Reed muttered. Obviously Satiah had not told them about *her and Vourne*. Such a revelation would be irresponsible. Besides… there were always other anxieties.

"And one other thing," Satiah said, rising from her chair. "Division Sixteen? If you have any control over them or where they are going, I would appreciate it if you ensured they remain separate from Phantom Squad. They will do more harm than good."

"They're *just* operatives, not neo-remnantists," Reed smiled, waving an innocent hand.

"Nevertheless," she shrugged, smiling back. "We don't need them." The ship decelerated suddenly and Satiah went back to the control room.

After all that information being exchanged, a long thoughtful slumber descended on the ship. Reed sat awake, thinking deep thoughts. Carlos and Deva talked endlessly about the ramifications. Satiah returned to her cabin. She washed, dressed and then settled down in her chair for a meal. The faint whir of Kelvin was her only company. It was the only company she wanted. She tucked in to the supply tin. The food was best described as *bland meets drab*. She'd developed a taste for it over the years like many operatives did when they spent long periods of time away from the comforts of home. Occasionally, while working undercover, some agents would eat only the finest dishes. Satiah was a woman of simple tastes. If it was efficient and did its job, she generally liked it.

"Do you think I did the right thing telling them all that?" she asked, to Kelvin.

"Yes," he said.

"I don't want a make a habit out of it but I really felt like I was getting nowhere alone," she confided.

"You had too many objectives," he agreed.

Finished, she passed the empty container to Kelvin who disposed of it accordingly. She curled up in her chair slowly. As usual, Kelvin draped the cover over her.

"Thank you, Kelvin," she said, weary. Her encounter with the Sisterhood had shaken her. Still, those psychic abilities explained how they had been able to protect themselves from her shot. They also probably explained how they had realised she was among them in the first place. What would *they* want with a super weapon though? Assuming it, or even the plans for it existed? They didn't seem the type to make use of it. Perhaps, considering themselves saintly or something, they wished only to destroy it to prevent others from using it? As her mind began to bite on the problems, sleep found her.

***

"I hope you know what you're doing," complained Conrad, very nervous. Tabre regarded him with increasing disdain. Conrad was a very irritating little man with nothing at all to make up for it. He wasn't even that fantastic at his job.

"I'm sure you do," Tabre responded, levelly.

"They can't do anything to us, can they? I mean, they do work along the same conventions as us, don't they?" He was gibbering, driving himself round and round in pointless circles of thought. Tabre knew why and he did feel uncertain but not scared. He was certain of one thing: if they were going to be killed it would already have happened. Their release, though, might be tricky to negotiate. Chalky nonetheless seemed reasonable and, with good manners, Tabre was sure he could persuade her to let them go.

A maiden of incredible beauty was escorting them along a corridor. It just went to show how mentally powerful some of these 'sisters' were. If one woman was completely at ease with two men, one of whom was a self-confessed professional killer, then they had to watch themselves around her. Chalky had pulled them out of space with her mind. With her mind! That kind of power demanded respect and fear in equal portions. They entered a separate chamber where Chalky was awaiting them. Their golden-haired guide, stared at

Chalky and Chalky stared back. A telepathic conference? The guide eventually bowed her head and left.

"You have impressive powers," Tabre said, starting with a compliment.

"I do, as do many of the Sisterhood," she replied, her tone one of complete clipped confidence.

Conrad openly cringed as Tabre bluntly went for the heart of the matter.

"Are you going to let us go or not?" Tabre asked, smiling to her.

"We have been thinking about this," Chalky replied, in an indecisive tone. "You have done us no ill and we were the ones who forced you down. Yet... you have seen too much of things here for our comfort."

"You would prefer that we do not gossip about all this when we have left?" confirmed Tabre, understanding. "Naturally you cannot just take our word for it that we won't. How about we trade?"

"Explain?" she asked, interested.

"Our silence can be bought in the same deal that secures our freedom," Tabre went on. "We will keep quiet about everything we have seen here and you will let us go in exchange for removing those who escaped," Tabre offered. Chalky tilted her head to the side as she considered this. Conrad waited, holding his breath with anxiety.

"The intruder tried to *kill* one of your priests..." Tabre prodded.

"*Acolytes*," Chalky corrected.

"Acolytes," repeated Tabre, shrugging with indifference. "Crime is the same no matter the title. She's got away, she's escaped after seeing way more of this place than us two combined." Chalky looked troubled and stared out of the window at the rain.

"How will I know that you will keep your word?" she asked, bringing up her conundrum. "I can see that it is a fair offering and it is reasonable. Yet... how do I know that you are not lying?"

"Their deaths are in my interests *too*," Tabre answered, in complete honesty. That seemed to settle the matter.

"Death is not the only solution," Chalky reminded him. "You

need only return them to us."

"I'll think about it," Tabre said, in a tone that implied he really wouldn't. Chalky seemed to approve of him being completely honest even if the answers he gave were unfavourable.

"Well… whatever you chose to do, you are both welcome to return here at any time," Chalky offered, standing.

"I thought you didn't like visitors?" Tabre replied, as he and Conrad followed her example.

"We dislike… *some new* visitors. Those who shoot at us for instance," she replied, in a mild tone.

"That is very reasonable," Tabre said. "As you probably already know a lot of people say a lot of things about you and your world."

"They *all* talk but so few learn," she remarked.

***

Satiah awoke as Kelvin shook her gently.

"Your communicator is bleeping, it's Rainbow," he said, handing it to her.

"Thanks," she said, taking it. She yawned, shook her head to wake herself up, and then answered. "Yes?"

"*Malcolm Marlin is still alive*, I have footage from the planet Earth a day old of him waiting for a transporter," Rainbow said, excitement in his voice.

"What manner of man is he?" Satiah asked, pleased at the development. It meant she wouldn't have to go on such a long manhunt after all.

"Tall, gaunt, not the type you would marry," he remarked. "He was a casually dressed normal-looking human. He was wearing a union bracelet but that could mean nothing. We were able to trace that… we should have his wife soon enough."

"Good," she nodded, considering the possibility of approaching her rather than him. Satiah preferred to be direct about these things but sometimes it paid to be more lateral in style. "Anything more on the Sisterhood?"

"You're *still* going there?" he asked, as if she was stupid.

"I've been and come back," Satiah said. She grinned as she predicted the effect that news would have occurred.

"*What?*" he demanded, probably thinking he'd somehow misunderstood.

"I spent nearly five hours planetside… it was very wet," she remarked, in complete honesty.

"*Wet?*" he confirmed, deeply interested. Then he cleared his throat and asked another question in an aggravated tone. "*What did you see?*"

"Not telling you," she answered, pretending that the enquiry had hurt her feelings somehow.

"What the hell happened to you to make you so cruel?" he asked, jokingly. For a second her mood darkened. Indeed, it was a very relevant question for someone like her. A sick parent who had tried to murder her? A career of dealing with the worst sides of nature? A chain of betrayals to save her own skin? Or just constantly living under a cloud of deception? Indeed there were many things in her life that would make Satiah cruel. But Rainbow could guess about some of them and it was only a joke. She brightened, pleased that her twisted sense of humour still worked.

"I came second in a beauty contest, never recovered… been bitter ever since," she replied, playing along.

"Well, there does seem to be a lot of conflicting legends about them but nothing here is upheld. There's just no evidence for any of it. Some of it sounds like the ramblings of a drunk and others sound like religious extremists," he explained.

"Sounds like a typical holy text," she muttered, offhandedly.

"How's it going? Randal told me about you and Reed," he chuckled. "When is the pre-unification party?" Satiah laughed more loudly at that. The idea of her marrying anyone was in itself comical.

"Well, despite some initial friction, we've kissed and made up," she allowed. "Randal's got me to try and enlist Reed in his struggle against Division Sixteen."

"Not a recruitment campaign I'd want to do," Rainbow said.

"It's tricky," she admitted, freely. "You're certainly better off out of it. Any news on my prisoner?"

"Still here," he replied, chuckling again.

"That's a good start," she smiled. "No change?"

"Nothing."

The conversation ended shortly after that.

"Kelvin?" she asked, casually. "Regarding that homing device?"

"It is done," he said, dependably. She'd instructed that they attach it to an escape pod, set the pod in orbit around a nearby moon and then wait for Tabre to appear. It was a trap, of course, but it would be a poorly laid one. She wanted to see what he would do when confronted by such a poor trick. She'd narrowed it down to three potentials. First: he'd simply shoot it down. Second: he may attempt to capture it or board it. Third: he would wait. An escape pod orbiting a dead moon was obvious bait. Yet he would know how obvious it was and he would theorise that she would never be silly enough to employ such a tactic. Which might influence him enough to take what he was seeing at face value. There was one flaw in this plan, though. What if he never showed up at all? This possibility seemed to be more and more likely as the hours ticked slowly by.

Reed was anxious to return to the Sisterhood, this time though, he would remain conscious and talk to them. Satiah was still not happy about this plan although now her reasons were different. This time, unlike last time, Carlos and Deva had actually backed her up. Carlos felt that any diplomacy had been ruined the moment Satiah had taken a shot at one of them, an assessment that Satiah strongly agreed with. Deva had agreed, mainly to curry favour with Satiah more than anything but also because their arguments were logical. Reed swept it all away though, by first saying that he could talk them out of it and then by simply pulling rank. As usual he seemed to act like he had something up his sleeve and maybe he did but Satiah didn't believe in shaking hands *after* shooting. It either happened *before* the shooting or not at all.

She ran her hand up Kelvin's long metallic appendage tenderly.

"No water damage?" she asked, softly. She stared up into his red eyes.

"Engineering tolerances were not exceeded," he said, sounding almost disappointed. She smiled lovingly. His scopes zoomed in to examine her face more closely.

"Good," she smiled. "Rust is the worst."

"I calculate that you were similarly unaffected?" he asked, his left appendage brushing against her left shoulder.

"Human skin may be thin and poorly insulated but it isn't bad when it comes to waterproofing," she stated.

***

Ruby liked this place little better than the one they had left behind on Pluto Major. So quiet, cold and desolate. A planet, one that was apparently unnamed. She glanced back over her shoulder at their ship in the distance. Ahead was what looked like a burnt-out bunker. Ash kept going, his long stride making the journey look so effortless to him. Ruby was falling behind. When he got to the blackened entrance he halted as he peered inside. A little breathless, Ruby reached him.

"Where is this?" she asked, seriously.

"This is the place Vourne died," he replied. Her eyes lit up with awareness.

"Didn't he kill himself?" she asked, a little animated. The Vourne Conspiracy was one of the biggest recent scandals and as such often piqued her interest. The enquiry was still ongoing and typically humans were engaging in one of their favourite occupations... self-deception. Rumours were rife. Speculation was typically wild and unfounded. Ash never bothered listening to news broadcasts but some interaction with the media was unavoidable. As more than familiar with at least some of the truth, the things he heard people say had amazed him. Humans openly perjuring themselves, claiming to be involved, pretending to reveal the inside story... he shook his head.

"So the official report goes," he answered, sounding just a little conspiratorial. She glared up at him.

"Why do you *always* do *that?*" she demanded, with false anger. "You're *such* a duffer sometimes! *Did he or didn't he?*"

"How would *I* know?" he chuckled.

"*Right!*" she declared, as if that somehow verified her argument. She took a step forwards but paused on the threshold of darkness.

He regarded her with his arms crossed as she turned back to face him. She was trying so hard to look brave.

"Would you like me to go first?" he asked, knowing she would. She made as noise as if it didn't matter to her and gave a half-hearted shrug. These humans had such bravado! And they certainly didn't like admitting when they were scared. He sighed and walked past her into the shadows. She followed somewhat more noisily.

As they walked through the tunnel she was cursing, swearing and muttering constantly under her breath. Her hand found his in the dark and clung on tightly. Was there a word that described wanting to know the unknown while at the same time not wanting to be the one that found it out? Ruby wondered. Why couldn't he take her to a glorious ocean that she could float on? Maybe a tropical island? No, actually forget it! Knowing *that* duffer it would start out nice and then turn into something dreadful. The noise of their feet crunching and the dust shifting in the wind formed an eerie consensus. Ruby found her mind drifting to avoid the fear she seemed to be constantly running away from. She was no expert in oneirocriticism but she was starting to confuse reality with daydreaming. Ash stopped suddenly and she bumped hard into him, losing track of her thoughts completely and rendering them uniterable.

"Will you *please* calm down?" chastised Ash, sighing heavily. "There's nothing and no one here, it is just dark."

"Sorry," she said, without meaning it. "*Some* people are afraid of the dark, you know."

"...Are you one of those people?" he asked. She didn't answer, just looked away from him. "*It is possible to grow accustomed to the dark, you know.*" He'd echoed her tone of voice precisely and although she loathed him for it, it did make her smile a bit. She didn't let him know that though.

"You're such... *a pain*," she unleashed, unsure of what exactly to call him. Duffer no longer always captured the appropriate degree of emotional investment she needed to convey.

"Your flawless ability to put how you really feel into words is something I studiously admire," he remarked, a smile taking the cutting edge of his words away. "And I'm not a pain."

"I hate you," she stated, clearly without meaning it.

"I'm sure you do," he said, in a tone that said the opposite. "Are you ready to move on?"

"…Fine," she grumbled, not bothering to pretend. On they went, entering what was once a small area for vehicles to park. There were a few there; covered in dust… none of them looked like they would still work. Signs of fighting and damage were obvious now. It looked like there had been quite the shootout.

"Vourne's *last stand* before the champions of justice," Ruby said, trying to visualise it. Ash raised an eyebrow. Blint Mensa could be described as many things but champion of justice was not one of them. "But, before they got him, knowing there was no way out for him, he chose to take his own life to cheat them one final time," she stated. Ash wasn't sure why she insisted on portraying those events with such poetic romanticism. It did fit in well with how she viewed the universe though. Naively.

"Not out of fear, then?" Ash questioned, grimmer. "Fear of reprisal? Fear of punishment? Fear of consequence?"

Ruby looked over at him, his tall form a darker shadow among shadows.

"Did you know him?" she asked, intrigued.

"I never met him," he answered, evasively. Now though, Ruby was used to how he deflected things and pressed on.

"I asked if you knew him?" He smiled.

"I met the man who wanted to kill him and discovered his body," he said, thinking back. "Vourne himself was a power-crazed, ruthless treacherous individual. He cared only about himself and was loyal only to the power he wanted to gain."

"Not nice then?" she asked, without being serious. He guffawed and focussed on the controls in front of him. She wandered over to him. After some fumbling he found the activation switch.

A distant slamming clamour sounded and dim lights flashed on as the console jolted back into operation.

"It still *works!*" Ruby cried, without needing to.

"*For how long?*" he murmured, rhetorically. He wondered how many of the systems still worked correctly. There were no signs of tampering but Ash had been concerned about traps. His main worry was damage caused during the fight. A monitor flickered into life. Ruby cleared the mess off of a chair and perched on it before the controls next to him.

"What are we searching for again?" she asked, after going for the controls and stopping.

"Orion Observatory or ITP 6," he reminded, patiently. Ruby commenced a search, excited again. Her excitement died though, when the computer asked for a password. She stared up at Ash dismally.

"Should I try one two three four?"

***

Tabre's ship flashed into view among the billions of stars. He'd checked the engines over, making sure that the straining earlier had caused no lasting harm. It hadn't. The escape pod and its path were visible.

"*Still* it circles," Tabre growled, as if to himself.

"Great, he's not moved on," Conrad said, pleased that the hunt was almost over. "Just shoot him down and let's get back…"

"*Why* would you spend so long orbiting a dead moon?" Tabre asked, deep in thought. A trap? It had to be, what else could it be? Yet it was *so obvious*… An escape pod orbiting a dead moon. Remembering that when he had tried to board Satiah's freighter it had self-destructed, he chose not to get too close to the pod. He was half tempted to just blast it out of existence like Conrad suggested but two things stopped him. First, it was *Conrad's* reaction and Conrad was clearly an idiot. Secondly it was far too easy.

A sneer of condescension crossed his face before he chose to keep his distance and run a scan. Not just of the pod itself but of the immediate environment. Satiah was slinking around nearby, watching, he was sure of it. She was cunning and… it's what he would do.

"What are you doing?" Conrad asked, tetchy. "They will be cloaked, it's *your* signal that we're following."

"First I want to see what's so special about that moon, second I want to know if that pod has anyone *alive* on it and third…" He trailed off, as the results came through. As he had suspected: the pod was unoccupied. No life signs. Then an alarm blared, proximity lock-on alert. A warhead was approaching them. Tabre reflexively began evasive manoeuvres, spinning and spiralling away, trying to lose the missile. Conrad clung onto the armrests for dear life.

That was when the other ship attacked. Coming in from the same side that the missile had, Satiah's new fighter streaked towards them, opening up with several lasers at once. It was too sudden and close for Tabre to avoid. The attack took out the shield completely and sliced through some of the armour. Pulling up in time to avoid a collision, the Covert-Class fighter looped away from them at lightning speed. Tabre winced as he almost lost control of his ship. Conrad was screaming now, convinced they were finished. The missile was gaining on them and Satiah was coming around for another strafing attempt. With no shields and a missile still homing in on them, they could be considered dead before they actually were. Tabre, however, revealed why the Director always hired him, when she could afford him: he showed his true ingenuity.

Shields were down, so power was no longer needed for them, it could be redirected to the engines. He did, the transition giving them a burst of speed that took them on a new course away from Satiah and towards the pod. The pod, still orbiting, was coming around the moon again on its never-ending circular course. Going straight for it, as if to initiate a head-on collision, Tabre accelerated. The ship jolted as another volley of lasers cut into the hull like knives through skin. Atmosphere began to vent. Tabre gritted his teeth, diverting some of the power to the auto-repair systems. Conrad's eyes never left the viewport though, they were within sight of the pod now, he could see it coming and he thought they were going to ram it. At that speed, were it Tabre's intention or not, such a collision could result only in the lethal destruction of both ships.

At the last conceivable second, the moment when both their ship and the pod were as good as nose to nose, Tabre dipped underneath the pod, narrowly missing it. The missile still chasing them, however, was not able to change course in time. It struck the pod, destroying it utterly. Through the fire, however, Satiah surged, blasting repeatedly at them with all the fury of an avenging angel. Weaving back and forth, Tabre cut the engines suddenly, transferring all power to the regenerated shielding systems. Satiah shot right over the top of them, banked to the right and vanished behind the body of the moon. Conrad, panting like an animal, his eyes wide and frightened, just stared blankly at the empty space she had left behind her. Tabre though, was still working.

Inwardly, despite the peril, maybe even partly because of it, he realised that he'd rarely been so exhilarated before. *Satiah*! Such a sneaky foe. Such opponents were rare indeed and it was *such a pleasure* to fight her. The ultimate test of his own abilities! The symmetry was there! It was there! Tabre noted that Satiah had removed her ship's cloaking device as she'd gone in for the kill, a kill she'd been unfortunate not to achieve, and was therefore visible. He locked onto her, ensuring that the computer would follow her when she ran. This time, however, he knew that if anyone would be running it would be *him*. He performed a quick systems check while keeping an eye on Satiah's ship. She was orbiting the moon fast, already halfway around. She was probably going to dish out another pasting from the stern.

A technical report returned to his screen. *Still* the shields were recovering. He swore and accelerated after Satiah, following her course, determined to keep the whole moon between them. Getting closer to the moon, he realised it was pockmarked with impact craters from space flotsam large and small. Lowering still further he was able to negotiate a way through the maze of rocky canyons and valleys.

"What are you doing?" demanded Conrad, sounding terrified. "We should get out while they are..."

"If we break for freedom now, she's got us," snarled Tabre, through his teeth. That was when he deployed a new weapon. A mine. It clung to the back of his ship, ready for deployment. Gradually he began to decelerate, letting Satiah catch them up even faster than she already was.

Quick to capitalise, perhaps scenting victory, perhaps not even realising he was losing speed, Satiah's ship caught them up rapidly. Looming behind them like a predator on its prey, she kept coming. Tabre released the mine, giving it a three-second countdown. Laser fire erupted as Satiah probably tried to destroy it. Boom! The concussive wave took out the whole rocky canyon and sent both ships spinning away out of control. A large rock glanced off them, making the whole ship shudder and creak. Tabre fought with the controls to regain something resembling control when they hit the surface. The jolt would have thrown both men around the cockpit had they not been strapped down. Nevertheless they felt the impact from their teeth to their feet. The ship continued to screech as it gashed along the rocks at last coming to a stop. Tabre was back at the controls in an instant.

"Get me a spacesuit!" he barked at Conrad, as he worked furiously.

***

It had been such a simple plan and they had been very unlucky. Tabre was no fool as Deva had warned them. Satiah and Kelvin had been waiting in the darkness in the opposite direction from the pod. Tabre had arrived and, while he was debating what to do next, Satiah had struck. First she had launched a homing missile at Tabre and then, after changing her angle of approach had come after him with laser fire too. All the better to be sure. It had gone well... at first. They'd taken out his shields and the missile was gaining on him. Then, cleverly, Tabre had used the pod against them and destroyed the missile, thus forcing Satiah to come after him again. Using the moon as cover, Tabre had been aware that running was futile and had wisely tried to find cover. Also he'd succeeded in luring Satiah in close enough to damage her. The explosion had sent both craft reeling.

Crash landing onto the surface of the moon, it was clear that the ship had taken some damage. Lights were blaring, telling her so.

"Looks like a fissure in our hull," Satiah groaned, cursing her own impatience. The shield had taken the worst of the blast but all those rocks flying around had dealt blows of their own.

"Repair systems are activating," Kelvin assured her.

"I'd better take a look. I don't want us splitting in half on take-off," she muttered, unstrapping herself. "You stay here and make sure none of the others touch the controls." She knew they probably wouldn't. All three of them were in Reed's cabin discussing what they should do upon return to the Sisterhood. They would have realised that things had not gone according to Satiah's plan, though. Twice in two days!

She encountered a nervous-looking Carlos in the corridor. He said nothing, just tapped the wall meaningfully.

"We've had a little ding, yes," she explained, starting to pull on the spacesuit.

"I take it there was a problem?" Carlos enquired, seriously.

"The problem was: *I* underestimated Tabre's piloting skills," she admitted, without shame. "I thought we'd got him but then he deployed a mine. The blast got us both but I *must* check the hull to see how badly."

"It got you *both*?" he asked, confused.

"It was a last resort as moves go but I *bet* he survived," she sighed, pulling on her helmet. It sealed with a click and her voice sounded wispier as she continued. "Deva was correct when she told us about Tabre." Carlos nodded, thinking about it. Satiah took the long-range rifle and slung it over her shoulder crossways. Carlos tapped her shoulder.

"I'll be in the control room," he said. She nodded as the door closed between her and him, sealing the airlock.

It had been a while since Satiah had been in zero gravity. She had a cord attached to her midriff, just in case she somehow lost her grip on the hull of the ship. Being as they were stationary, that was unlikely but a good planner always made allowances even for the most improbable of circumstances. According to the computer, the near breach was towards the starboard bow of the fighter. She crawled/climbed across the hull of the ship like an insect would over the body of a larger animal. Kelvin's voice sounded in her ear.

"You're getting close, five metres ahead of you," he advised. She smiled, remembering scrambling around the pipework of the Pune undercity. Same method, different place. There it was. A blackened rip in the black and white striped hull. She winced, angered at the damage inflicted on the nice new ship that Reed had got for her. She hoped Tabre had taken worse damage. The hole was big enough for her to get her arm in.

It was deep but fairly short. A few inches more and it would indeed have most likely breached the hull completely. She glanced around at the environment, trying to spot Tabre's ship. There was no sign of it. Rocks floating around ruined most of the view though. A flash got her attention. It was in the distance. She tried to make it out and then, in dawning comprehension, threw herself to the right. A shot sheared by, lacerating the edge of her helmet and throwing her backward. She let out an involuntary cry as she lost her grip on the hull and flipped over, because of the momentum, and crashed into it again painfully. Air seeped out from the hole on her helmet.

"Satiah?" Kelvin's voice came. Satiah wasn't the frame of mind to manage words. Instead she produced a sound much like: uurraaghh! Three more shots came, narrowly missing her.

Floundering with the desperation of someone losing their oxygen, Satiah, on the verge of actual real panic, rolled over to the other side of the hull where she could not be hit. Cleverly though, her attacker, most likely Tabre, unable to hit her again, shot at the safety cord which connected her to the ship. The bolt sheered right through it, sending her floating helplessly away from her ship. She clawed at the void uselessly before realising the futility of the action. Then she tried to staunch the leak of air with her hand. If only she'd brought her grapple gun!

"Under fire!" she screamed, trying to apply the sealant she had in her hand over the damaged part of the helmet. If she'd not moved when she had, she had no doubt that that shot would have removed her head. Her other hand was fumbling with her rifle but the strap had managed to tangle itself around her arm. She let out a growl of anger and frustration.

"Help is coming," Kelvin assured. The ship began to turn, flipping over upside-down so that she was once again facing the airlock. Without any way of propelling herself back to the ship she knew she'd just keep drifting until either they picked her up or she ran out of air.

Kelvin had also moved the ship like that to keep it between her and her attacker, thus protecting her. From the airlock, Carlos emerged, with his own safety cord, and dived out towards her with rope in his hands. Satiah couldn't help but smile in relief. Her air was thinner now but Carlos could get to her in time. He actually missed her but that didn't matter as he threw her the rope he was carrying. She caught it easily. She wrapped it about her wrists out of habit while trying to see her shooter. There was no sign of him. Then they were both dragged back by Reed and Deva. Kelvin operated the airlock controls. The airlock sealed and as gravity was restored, both she and Carlos crashed onto the floor haphazardly.

Satiah ripped off her helmet and flung it away angrily as she lay slumped against the wall. More slowly, Carlos removed his and looked down at her as he stood.

"You okay?" he asked, unable to hide a grin. She glared up at him.

"*Fine*, never been *better*," she hissed, sarcastically. "What is so funny?"

"I thought that um… Trained Phantoms *never* panicked?" he enquired, clearly trying to hold in laughter.

"They don't and I didn't," she retorted, frostily. Slowly he held up a communicator and replayed her scream back to her. She eyed him, an approving look on her face.

"*You* bugged *me*," she stated, amused.

"Consider it payback," he replied, extending his hand down to her. She took it and he hauled her onto her feet.

Reed and Deva were waiting outside as they emerged.

"How bad was it?" Reed asked, bracing himself for bad news.

"We're still flyable," she shrugged, completely composed. "It will take a long time but the systems will eventually repair that puncture."

"And *Tabre?*" asked Deva, seriously. Satiah knew Deva was worried about what would happen if Tabre ever caught *her*. That was understandable.

"Still alive *unfortunately*," grumbled Satiah, genuinely angry. She knew that Tabre was lucky to remain alive but alive was still alive.

"*Now* can we return to the Sisterhood *please?*" Reed asked, in a tone that all but demanded it.

"…Fine," Satiah agreed, with reluctance.

***

Conrad had been so worried about fixing the ship he'd just assumed that Tabre had gone outside to affect repairs. He *had*… he just wanted to check on Satiah first. Through the scopes of his rifle he'd been delighted to see Satiah examining the hull of her ship.

Instantly he'd started shooting. His first bolt should have hit her and killed her outright but at the last second *something* had made her move. A 22nd sense perhaps? Tabre knew he had his own so it seemed fair to accept that she had one too. He'd tried again and again but she managed to get behind her ship where he couldn't hit her. He knew he'd damaged her suit. Unable to get at her anymore, he took out her safety line. Asphyxiation would be a good death for her. Not too long, like starvation, but not too short either, like a shot to the head or the deep freeze of space. A symmetrical compromise.

He watched as, judiciously, the pilot tilted the ship around to protect her and he expected they would be trying to get her back. He'd taken the opportunity to fire another homing device onto the hull as the ship rolled. Whether Satiah was dead or not he still had to bring Reed down and the previous device had been destroyed by the missile. He waited just long enough to realise that Satiah had been rescued before returning to his ship. It might not be long before he became a target too. The engines had been badly damaged in the blast from the mine as it had still been dangerously close when it detonated.

"Can we get out of here?" That was Conrad's question. He didn't phrase it quite like that though. Amid the swearing and angry threats he'd uttered the term: *this ship had better still be flyable.*

Tabre ignored him and set up the computer to pick up the new tracking signal before he did anything else. Then he checked the auto-repair systems. Twenty-four percent complete. He sighed. The fact that they were still alive surely indicated a fortune greater than either of them deserved. Satiah's ambush had been well thought out and efficiently performed. Next time, as there was certainly going to *be* a next time, he would have to try different methods. At last Conrad calmed down and just stared at the percentage bar on the screen in front of them. Watching as bit by bit the computers dragged them back from useless to fully functional. Tabre was used to long periods of waiting and uncorked a bottle.

Taking a single gulp he replaced it after offering some to Conrad. Conrad refused and gave him a look that indicated he felt this was entirely the wrong place for such a beverage. Tabre on some level agreed with him. But they had just escaped death. Typically when Tabre escaped that, he allowed himself a small reward when possible.

Life wasn't worth living without some pleasure. Tabre adjusted his jacket, noting with some annoyance that his sleeves were not quite at the same angle. Seventy percent. Not long now. He reflected to himself about Satiah, trying to hide the amusement. There were many kinds of saint and sinner but so few of them were winners. Whichever one of them she was, she was certainly winning so far.

***

Tristram, his red Captain's uniform perfectly pressed, padded down the carpeted steps into the throng of officers. Finally, as a gazetted naval Captain of the Colonial Federation's 1st Fleet, he'd made it to attend the *Nedlessar Rally*. A giant military function with everything from the finest foods to the latest gossip. It was held once every eight weeks. It began in the early afternoon with a parade and band circuiting the complex. Flags were waved, hands were clapped and much cheering all around. Over one million individual soldiers, naval staff and other military personnel formed the parade in its intricate formations and displays. Always neat, always on time. A perfect depiction of idealised military life. Everything was efficient and impressive in equal measure.

Due to shift changes, however, this was the first one he'd been able to attend since he was a junior officer. He remembered that day with more than a little fondness. The nerves beforehand. The exhilaration and bewilderment when he arrived and, most importantly of all, the successful result at the end. He'd been noticed by a Captain at the time who'd offered him a post. Without any hesitation he'd taken it and he'd never regretted it. In fact it was due to the Rally that day that he was who he was at that moment. Now at thirty he was officially a senior. He paused at the bottom of the steps to take in the frivolities. First, two beauties giggling together, scuttled past him. They stopped, did a double take, blushed and then hurried away.

With a Captain's salary, good looks and youth still in the rear viewport: Tristram understood that he was now what the female cadets would call 'a catch'. He allowed them to see his stern, forbidding stare but softened the blow with a deceptively enchanting smile. Music was still playing, tables were being set and a vast amount of drink was being consumed. Tristram, with his tall frame and fair complexion, was instantly recognisable even to people who'd never met him. As procedure dictated, he awaited his junior officer who was meant to accompany him. Mostly every other junior officer had made it to the bottom of the entrance steps *before* their officer. His, however, was conspicuous by their absence. He sighed irritably. He'd been standing for a few hours now and couldn't sit anywhere until he was told *where* to sit. The junior officer was meant to escort him to his place and then stay with him for the rally as an errand runner.

The junior officers normally would actually fight each other for this job. It was a place where they could be noticed, promoted or who knew...? Seven years previously Tristram had been one of them. Young, ambitious and eager to get a ship to fight on or see the universe. Now older and wiser... he just wanted a place to sit. A young man stumbled through the crowd, heading towards him. He reached Tristram and saluted. Normally, as punishment for being late, Tristram would have made the officer wait. His uniform was green and grey, depicting his lower rank. He had long black hair, perfectly styled, and pale skin. A typical Colonial man, probably only recently recruited.

"I'm *sorry* I'm late, sir..." he began, uneasily. Their Colonial accents were strangely similar and he supposed that this man might even be from the same planet that he was. The traditional V sounding W's and deep tones.

"Don't be sorry, be on time," he cut him off. "*Where* are we sitting?"

"Err..." came the shaky response. He watched as the man fished out his communicator and noticed that his hands were shaking. He was terrified. Tristram sighed and rolled his eyes but did not chastise the younger man again. Instead, to try to make things easier for him, he engaged him in polite conversation.

"They were playing symphony eight earlier, one of my favourites. Reminds me of home," Tristram lied, adeptly. "Did you know it's been the best part of eight years since I was last here?"

"No sir, I didn't," he said, at last finding the location. "This way, sir."

"What is your *name*, officer...?" he asked, genuinely interested.

"W-Wester, sir," he answered, still nervous. He seemed to have *dry-throat-syndrome*.

"Wester," he repeated, smiling. "Pleasure to meet you. Have you ever been to the Rally before?" He thought he knew the answer to that. He took his pale shaking hand in his much larger gloved one and gave it a firm shake.

"No sir," he answered. He was looking over her shoulder and around as if expecting someone to ambush him or something. Tristram guessed what was happening at once. Wester was an unpopular individual for whatever reason and was used to being bullied, tricked and abused by other officers. He was not ugly but he did not share the boyish good looks of many of his fellows. Tristram glanced around too and noticed several of the other younger officers staring vengefully and openly at him.

"Out of interest, why were you late?" he asked, again guessing the answer.

"I promise it will not happen again, sir…" he began, uneasily.

"Wester, I *have* accepted your apology, you are not going to be reprimanded any further for that. I asked why it happened," he tried again.

"It seems my cabin door was the subject of a mechanical malfunction…" he began, covering for his bullies. Tristram knew why, of course. It was simply not done to snitch on such pranksters. If you did that, they often got worse.

"You mean; *one of your rivals locked you in*?" he asked, grinning. Flustered, he lowered his face and didn't answer. "Wester? Do you know the history of the Rally?"

"No, sir," he replied. Why would he know that? To him it was a career opportunity, not a political matter. They reached their booth and he, according to procedure waited for Tristram to sit before he did. Wester poured water and glanced out of the viewport at the masses briefly.

"After the Colonial Council collapsed, in order that the many militaries of the Federation could talk to each other, they would hold the rally. At the time it was for talks of peace to prevent civil war from erupting within the Federation," he explained, watching him closely. "So for hundreds of years it's been used to strengthen our Colonial spirit and remind us of our history and traditions."

"Sir," he nodded, sipping his water tentatively.

"Now..." he stopped himself. Truth? "Now it is a place that our government seeks to manipulate us using cleverly worded speeches and unifying smiles," he stated, his tone hardening. Wester paused mid-sip, watching Tristram watching him.

"Will there be a war, sir?" he asked, in a small voice.

"Yes," he answered. "I can't say *when* exactly but it's inevitable. The Coalition... You heard about Pluto Major?" He nodded. Who hadn't?

"I imagine, after the first round of food, we will be toasting the downfall of the Coalition," he said, sadly.

"...*Possibly*," Wester said, straining to remain as neutral as he could.

"Always understand, Wester, people rarely fight because of anything that has been done or said... they fight because they are afraid," he said. "Afraid of what will come *next*. Afraid of each other, *afraid of looking afraid...*"

"Sir..." he began, really trying to make himself say something that would be meaningful. "I am a coward but I... I scored *one hundred and seventy-nine* on the TT." *That* got Tristram's attention. "The others... they all make fun of me because I'm always hiding but... I *love* warships I just..." He smiled and actually laughed.

"You beat me by twenty and I was above average," Tristram stated, letting him know he was impressed. The TT, or tactical test, was infamously difficult and few rarely passed it. It was designed to be unwinnable so no one ever actually won the battle, scores were based on how many enemies you destroyed and how many of your own resources you saved. People were never told that until *after* they had taken the test, though.

"I know every weapon, every code signal and every specification of every craft in the navy," he stated, completely honest. "*But I don't want to die.*"

"Not many people *do*," he said, soothingly. "You've been tormented by the other officers. They have probably called you all manner of names before... I doubt any of them are accurate. But normally, people like you are never given the chance to come here. Someone else would have forced you to give up this chance... how did you manage to secure your role here?"

"I begged for it, sir," he stated, without shame. "I begged my CO until she got so fed up with me that she gave it to me. That's *why* I was locked up... At least *one* of the others was certain that *they* would be chosen. When they found out it was me... they were not happy." Well, who would be?

"I can imagine. Just as I can imagine what will happen to you, should you return there," he sighed, eyeing him. He *did* need a junior officer. His last one had been promoted so he had room but he'd wanted... someone else. He nodded, looking suitably scared.

"They hate me, sir. They hate me because I beat them in the TT. They hate me because I'm open about my fears and my feelings. They hate me because I got this chance that they did not. They have damaged my faith in my own abilities... I just want to be one of the best," he stated, firmness in his tone. *Getting better,* Tristram thought. Already, out of their influence, his ambition and confidence were resurfacing. Maybe he would be suitable after all. Naturally he had his own concerns regarding career to think about. As children, *Captain* was the rank everyone was shooting at. There was nothing like being Captain of your own battleship. Unlike many he'd actually hit it. He'd achieved the rank of Captain. Boyhood dream fulfilled. That made him think about the next step. *Commodore.*

"Wester?" he asked, cutting him off. "I *need* a Lieutenant. Someone with fire, passion and someone I can trust completely. I'm asking you if you want it." There was no hesitation, only a small smile of triumph.

"Sir, I am honoured, yes," he stated, with conviction.

Serving androids arrived with their first round of food and drinks. Seafood of some kind. He saw Wester light up again and realised he'd probably missed breakfast. He had too, of course, but he'd done it intentionally, knowing how much food he would consume later. They ate to the constant noise of the crowds and the marching music only, pausing only to chatter between themselves. They had a lot in common and even a similar sense of humour. He regaled Wester with an account of when he had attacked a pirate base. Wester told him about his life at home and the differences between 6R engines and 5R engines.

The starters were served before the speeches to ensure that everyone was no longer too hungry to listen. Half an hour later, the first siren rang to signify the first speech. Together Tristram and Wester stood, the viewport lowered and... Tristram gaped. The Director: Madam Ro Tammer, emerged as the first speaker. Tristram had presumed she'd been pushed to the side-lines due to her radical warmongering stances. She had no business wielding anything *resembling* authority! Clearly somehow she'd wormed her way back into the government. The fact that she was going first was alarming as that meant she clearly had the President's favour.

A silence fell. Her voice, rich and cutting, sounded.

"My fellow Colonists, I welcome you back." Her smile would look nice and normal to *those who didn't know her*. Those who couldn't see the evil cruelty it masked. A front, a lie and an act. She made Tristram's skin crawl.

"My compliments to all of you who have provided loyal service to the President, from the Admirals to the guards!" she went on. A cheer broke out. Applause. She let it go on for a few seconds before raising her finger for silence.

"For that is the duty that links *us all*. To serve and defend *our* Federation," she said. "Sometimes... even from itself."

The silence continued. Tristram gritted his teeth; he could guess what was coming. Some looks from other higher ranking officers indicated that he wasn't the only one.

"I have a question that someone asked me on my way here tonight," she continued.

Tristram rolled his eyes. They *always* said that. The fact was that rarely had *anyone* even spoken to them all that day! They had invented it as part of the political fiction some of them even believed.

"Shouldn't someone do something?" she shouted, pausing for effect. "I have to say, at the time, I was a little mystified by that so I asked them: *what do you mean by that?* Mean, *they clarified*, what *do you think* I mean? I told them to just tell me." Another calculating recess occurred as she stopped again. "They asked me: how can you let it happen? How can you let our people be hurt and killed by that Human Coalition? That corrupt, hatful excuse for a society! Horrible things happened on Pluto Major recently, crimes were committed...

against us! Against *our* Federation!" More time was allocated to let that sink it, not that it was needed.

Tristram knew she was manipulating or trying to manipulate everyone into thinking a certain way. What made it worse was that it seemed to be working. Especially on the young. Many of the younger officers looked horrified or furious. He noticed that even Wester, an apparent coward, had balled his fists unconsciously in rage. The trouble was that the Director was using the truth. Crimes *had* been committed… but that wasn't the whole story. He'd spoken with an officer, one who was actually there, a Captain Moxin, and he knew the truth about what had happened there.

"Well I for one won't let them escape *justice*!" she yelled, passionate and compelling. She was good, Tristram had to give her that much credit. She knew how to persuade! How to twist things until they all favoured her. She would begin slowly, accelerate and then start a tirade. She was a skilled public speaker. Tristram had the urge to walk out, to just leave. He didn't want to be party to this! But he knew he couldn't. If he did, with the Director back in favour, an *accident* might befall him if he showed any signs of disloyalty. Colossal roars from the crowd, angry and determined, glasses were raised, toasting her words. What was the President *thinking*? They had only recently come to an understanding with the Coalition after what could have been a very humiliating defeat.

"Our Federation is proud and mighty and it will stand!" She was screaming now. Bellowing at the top of her lungs. "They call themselves the *human* Coalition! I ask: what kind of human would do that to innocence? *They* are causing the famine, *they* are trying to sabotage our economy and *they* are devaluing what it means to be human! The Coalition trying to slowly dismantle our Federation, like parasites! The Coalition wants us to fail and die! They are asking it of us! They are asking: do you want to die? And the Federation can only give *a single answer*! The Federation lives and will continue to live! And through life, the Federation will be victorious!" More cheering, so loud now it was all but drowning her out. She looked genuinely breathless for a moment and smiled out at the crowd in open triumph.

"*The Federation*!" she shrieked, with a bestial ferociousness. The crowd reacted with fanatical fever. She saluted the President who was in the stands nearby. Every officer turned and most of them saluted too. Most of them. Tristram didn't move. Wester, noticed him and he stopped saluting. He leaned in close.

"Sir?" he asked, confused.

"I will explain later," Tristram answered, dismissively waving. "Let me leave it like this: I think you and I just saw the beginning of a tragedy." He frowned and then, after looking out across the crowd again and seeing it differently, he realised… war was always tragic.

***

Satiah returned to the control room. Reed was there, watching the countdown until arrival.

"He *will* find us again," Satiah stated, referring to Tabre. "It's clear he means us harm but I wanted to talk to you about what his mission might be."

"Does it matter?" Reed shrugged. Satiah didn't get angry but she was a little annoyed at his disinterest. In her mind, it was *his* life at risk.

"I believe he is after you," she admitted, sounding much more careless than she felt. He nodded.

"Could well be," he agreed, still without concern.

"…You either have too much faith in me or not enough respect for him," Satiah stated, tetchy. "For whatever reason, he's chosen to make this personal."

"You don't know *that*," Reed told her.

"I can tell," she argued, refusing to back down. "I've been doing this for too long not to have developed an instinct."

"*All right*," he sighed, as if this whole subject bored him utterly. "Let's say *you're right*: Let's say that *he's after me*. I still have work to do and I'm not about to let an assassin get in my way." Satiah said nothing to that. "The *real reason* you want to focus on Tabre is because you don't want to face the Sisterhood again after your little *excursion*." Satiah had to admit that that had been on her mind. Reed didn't have to say: you should have done as I told you. Satiah knew she should have.

"Look, I know you have other things you want to focus on and when we're through with the Sisterhood, I will help you track this secret weapon down," Reed said, casually. "The Sisterhood may even have it themselves."

"They seem a pretty irrational lot to me so *why not?*" she agreed, sulky.

"Religious doesn't mean *irrational*," Reed chastised, gently. "Granted religion is often used as an excuse to create conflict but there is evil in *all* walks of life."

"You have an invisible friend *too?*" she grinned, a little mockingly. Reed chuckled.

"No, no, you can see most of mine," he replied, mysteriously.

"Any of them in Division Sixteen?" she asked, pointedly. He chuckled again.

"What is your problem with them? Look, I understand that sometimes departments are not meant to be melded together and if that is your point can you at least tell me *why?*" Reed asked, politely. Again, always so logical and well thought out. Satiah ground her teeth together.

"These people are ex-Gushtapar, Reed! They are a band of political criminals," she stated, inflexibly. "We already have the PLC for that, we don't need more of them. You want something to do with them? Arrest them! Disband them! Break them up and integrate them among every other military branch but don't lumber us with them." Reed blinked to display surprise he clearly didn't really feel.

"I know that, during the Mulac Building incident..." he began, his tone light.

"Which I had *no part in*," Satiah cut in, too quickly. She cursed her own temper.

"I never meant to infer that you did," he replied, his voice becoming lower and more controlled. "During that incident, Phantom agents, under Vourne's command, entered into a prolonged engagement directly against the Gushtapar *and other parties*." Satiah knew those last three words were heavily laden with significance but she didn't know why.

Satiah had never been inside the Mulac Building but she had been part of the incident. She had been Vourne's escape craft pilot. She and Dasss, another Phantom agent, had been called in at the last moment to provide an emergency escape route for Vourne himself. She hoped her instant and rather prematurely biting denial hadn't made Reed suspicious of her.

"So I quite understand why you have doubts about working with a group of people you only recently did battle with, I too, were it me in your position, would have reservations about it," Reed went on, still being annoying reasonable.

"Why do you want this so badly?" she asked, trying another tactic. "Why must they integrate with *us*?"

"They don't *have* to *do* anything," he stated, shrugging defensively. "The truth of the matter is I don't trust them but I *do* trust Phantom Squad." His eyes turned meditative, as if he were looking into the distance. "*And I have right from the start.*"

Satiah made herself take a cleansing breath.

"Can I be honest with you?" she asked, pretending to be reluctant. Reed shrugged again.

"I don't know. Can you?" he asked, his tone once more becoming light. His eyes were also once again alert.

"I am not the only one in Phantom Squad opposed to this merger. You force it through and you risk losing our department completely," she stated, trying not to sound too threatening. Not being threatening while delivering an ultimatum, though, was a skill she did not possess. He took it well enough though.

"I see," he acknowledged, thoughtfully. A bleeping interrupted them. They were getting close to Erokathorn, the Sisterhood planet, again.

"We can discuss this further later," he remarked, as the others entered. Carlos and Deva watched the viewport, their faces grim. Kelvin's dark shadow loomed up behind them, his red eyes focussing on Satiah. She sat back in her chair and waited. They decelerated as they arrived, coming out of top speed. The first thing they saw were what looked like two battle frigates. The designs of the ships were new and advanced. Both bore markings and sported symbols of the Sisterhood. A simple blue circle becoming steadily whiter as you followed the radius into the centre. It made the current Coalition icon look comparatively complicated.

"Unidentified craft, you will surrender *now* or you will be destroyed!" barked someone, at them. Everyone except Reed tensed. The psychic wave was back – only, this time, Reed tolerated instead of fighting it.

"*Ah*," Reed smiled, tightly. "It's obvious they remember us."

***

Commodore Simmons entered his office and halted in astonishment when he found three people waiting for him. After the events of the Rally he had been hoping for a short drink and then a good eight hours' sleep. Evidently those were to continue to elude him. Captain Tristram, Wester and a red-haired woman turned to face him.

"Commodore," Tristram said, saluting. He nodded.

"Captain Tristram, Captain Moxin," he addressed them. He paused when he got to Wester.

"Lieutenant Wester," Wester explained, stiffly. Simmons smiled uneasily at the three of them.

"What can I do for you?" he asked, sitting at his desk. He had a sinking feeling that he knew what this would be about.

"*Ro Tammer*," Erica stated, pointing over her shoulder with her thumb. There was real anger in her voice. "I was under the impression that she had been stripped of her titles, power and influence."

"...She *was*," he agreed, awkwardly. "Recent events, however, have given her the opportunity to return to politics."

"Were you listening to *anything* she said?" asked Tristram, grim.

"It's just sabre rattling," he said, trying to wave it away.

"She's marshalling the fleet," Erica accused, levelly. "She's preparing to make an unprovoked attack against the Coalition."

"Starting a war we cannot possibly win and have no reason to do so," Tristram joined in.

"*Is it unprovoked?*" demanded Simmons, at last summoning up his personality. "Pluto Major..." He began along the lines exactly as Eric and Tristram had predicted. They were quick and ruthless in cutting him off.

"Pluto Major was *not* a Colonial world at the time, and the things that happened there were not committed by the current leadership of the Coalition," Erica stated, honestly. "Besides, you know it's not as simple as that."

"Ro *needs* to be stopped," Tristram insisted, through his teeth. "Before she gets everyone killed."

"By *any means*," Erica agreed. They were both staring down at Simmons, their stare equal parts intimidation and pleading.

"You're talking *treason*, the pair of you!" he blustered, as expected.

"It is not treason to want to protect the Colonial Federation from itself," Wester said, unexpectedly. Tristram turned to face the younger man in approval. He'd even used Ro's own words. Simmons eyed the young man with unhidden contempt.

"And corrupting the beliefs of the young," Simmons growled, with more menace than he felt. "You're drumming up quite the list of charges. Do *any of you* value your careers?"

"Less than our lives," Erica muttered, cynically.

"Ro is an extremist who cares only about herself," Wester went on, provoked by Simmons's dismissive attitude. "If she succeeds in starting a war between us and the Coalition, the Colonial Federation will be finished." Tristram didn't need to add anything to that and was secretly very impressed by the younger man's fervent determination. He was addressing a Commodore the same way he would address a private. Crudely and with an effectiveness born of being completely in the right. Simmons, a competent enough man himself, seemed to wilt a little. He knew the younger man was completely correct and that arguing the point was a waste of time and breath.

"Very well," he grumbled, a new strain to his voice. "Say I agree with you. What do you intend to do? Go on strike?"

Tristram and Eric exchanged glances. *Oh no.* What they had in mind was much more aggressive and much more destructive. It was also highly illegal.

"We have two options..." Tristram said. He pulled out a knife and placed it on the table in front of Simmons. He stared down at it, beads of sweat on his forehead. The implication was as blatant as it was cold-blooded.

"You plan to assassinate her?" he demanded, in a low voice. "*How*? You'd never even get the opportunity surely?"

"It's one option," Erica reminded him, sourly.

"Our second idea is something Wester came up with," Tristram said, motioning for the younger man to take it from there. Wester straightened, perhaps unconsciously, as he collected his thoughts and formulated his explanation.

"We cannot fight a war without our warships, sir," he stated. Fact. Pure, simple and eloquently delivered. "The Director is mustering the navy as we speak. In hours the entire fleet will be assembled *in one place*." Erica smiled tightly.

"An accident could be prepared," Wester continued, seriously. "An accident that would *cripple* the whole navy." Simmons sat back, genuinely considering it. Yes, properly executed... it could be done.

"And what happens to us assuming we succeed?" Simmons asked. It was a valid question and one that didn't really have a good answer.

"Well, as traitors, we will be executed if we allow ourselves to be caught," Erica stated. Simmons grunted in agreement.

"So you plan to run! Go into a self-exile?" he presumed.

"Depends, but that would be one outcome," Tristram nodded. Simmons eyed the knife once again and then Wester.

"You have clearly given this a lot of thought," he replied, seriously. "There is another thing we can do."

"*We?*" questioned Wester, noting that it was the first time Simmons had used the word. Its significance was not lost on any of them. Simmons nodded.

"I think you're right about this accident but... what exactly were you thinking? If you plan to destroy the ships..." he said.

"Only take out the engines... the damage would be extensive and take weeks for the Director to sort the problem," Tristram informed.

"And in those weeks, *anything could happen politically*," Erica said, casually. "President Raykur might finally realise that Ro is dangerous and should be removed from office."

"*Permanently*," added Tristram, levelly.

"There is no guarantee of that, her grip is pretty strong now," Simmons said, sadly.

"What do you mean?" Erica asked, concerned.

"She's in charge of mostly everything. Military, secret services… those in the government who oppose her have already been marginalised," Simmons stated.

"Then *we must act while we still can*," Tristram stated, with conviction.

"We could just be delaying the inevitable," Simmons sighed, uncertain. "We do not *know* that the war would be unwinnable."

"Even if we somehow defeated the Coalition, we would be vastly overextending ourselves… how long do you think it would be before someone took advantage of that?" Erica asked, astutely. That ended the last of Simmons's objections.

***

"Maybe I should stay here," Satiah said, thinking about it. Since arriving, the Sisterhood had forced them to land on the top of the temple. The exact same temple that Satiah had broken into the previous day.

"I wish you could," Reed said, scowling. "*They're not happy*. Can you blame them though? As before, leave the talking to me. Trust me."

"And if I am accused *directly*?" she asked, raising her eyebrows.

"Tell them you were just following *my* orders," Reed dismissed. Satiah found herself touched by his protectiveness. She'd expected him to be completely honest with them.

"*Thanks*," she managed, a little sheepishly.

"Don't bother with your guns, any of you," Reed instructed. They all followed him down the ramp.

Several cloaked figures were awaiting them on the rooftop.

"They are within range of my flame thrower," Kelvin said, in her ear.

"Not this time," Satiah whispered back, seriously. Reed stepped forward.

"I believe we are expected," he smiled, his manner reverential. Without a word, one of the cloaked figures turned and began to walk.

"Follow him," Reed advised. The rest of the Sisterhood fell in around them as they followed the man. Carlos and Deva exchanged nervous glances. Both had been trying to see out across the lush forests. The view was nice but the rain ruined it a bit.

The temple was strange and echoic. Satiah noticed that it was even bigger than she'd first seen. They were escorted to a chamber where Chalky was sitting. Flanking her chair on both sides were two other Sisterhood acolytes. One male and the other female. Satiah recognised the man as the person she'd taken a shot at the last time she was here. That was not good sign. The guards left and the silence quickly grew oppressive.

"Morning," chanced Reed, casually. Chalky glared at him as if he had just uttered the worst kind of blasphemy.

"Why did you come here?" she asked, to him. Then she made eye contact with Satiah. "And *you?*" Satiah said nothing as Reed stepped in front of her as if to shield her from view.

"*I'm* the ambassador," he said, grit in his tone. "Therefore you talk only to me."

"You invaded the blessedness of our Sanctuary without permission and you attempted to murder one of the Sisterhood," Chalky stated, seriously. Satiah wondered how Reed would talk his way out of this.

"We are *sorry*," Reed replied, calmly. "And it is partly to deliver this apology that we chose to return."

"*Why come at all?*" barked Chalky, slamming balled fists on the chairs armrests. She rose to her feet and extended a hand. A glass rose into the air, lifted by her mind and smashed against the wall. "*This is our place and we did not come to you.*"

"Absolutely," Reed quickly agreed, stepping over to the remains of the glass. He began picking up the pieces as he spoke. "Chalky, I know who and *what* you are. You don't know me but we have a mutual friend," he explained, his demeanour still placid and courteous.

A new silence descended as they all watched him. After collecting all the shards, Reed paced back over to the table where it had been originally and put them down there. The shards rose into the air and began to reform the shape of the smashed glass. Carlos and Deva stared, slack-jawed. Chalky just stared at Reed for a long moment uncertain.

"You may go," Chalky said at last, to the two acolytes. Without a word, they left the room. Satiah shifted on her feet, watching the man she'd once tried to kill as he passed her. His eyes connected with hers but no words were exchanged.

"What do you know?" Chalky asked, to Reed. She tried to push into his mind but found herself being gently brushed out again. This human was strange!

"I know you were once called *Freen* and that you are an immortal," Reed shrugged, as if such a revelation had no more importance to him than any public knowledge would have. Chalky's eyes widened.

"How do you know this?" she asked, her tone low and threatening. Satiah tensed, inwardly imploring Reed to tread carefully. Was he trying to blackmail their way out? Was he just endeavouring to keep her off balance? Either way the look Chalky was giving him reminded Satiah of the countenance that an angry tigress would show were it trying to defend its offspring. Eyes wide, teeth almost bared and every muscle tense. The slightest error on Reed's part would result in a quick and painful death. For them all. Satiah edged a little closer to Kelvin.

"Once, a *long* time ago, you and Dreda battled for dominance in a universe that no longer exists," Reed told her. "After you were taken to be cleansed, Dreda found and released you. You vanished without trace for a few years after Venelka tried to trick you. At some stage *between then and now* you changed your identity to Chalky and... I *presume* created the Sisterhood of the Light to hide behind."

"You challenge me?" she demanded, grim.

"Chalky, *Dreda was betrayed by Venelka*," Reed said, softly. That seemed to strike more of a blow than anything he'd said so far. Chalky sat down in her seat again, a sadness coming over her.

"I... I am sorry for your loss. She was my friend too... in this life," she explained, gently.

"Is the friend of my friend *my friend too*?" he asked, levelly.

Chalky sighed, leaning back in her chair.

"I... I don't want *any* enemies," she stated, seriously. "We just want to be left alone here. Dreda would interfere, try to stop the humans from destroying themselves and I can see now that that is why she died. I have no intention of following her example." Reed made no effort to correct anything she had said even though he knew it to be inaccurate.

"There are some questions I must ask you, *if* you are willing?" Reed pressed, composed and alert as ever.

"If you promise *never* to return here *or* encourage others to come here then I will release you," she answered, thinking he was going to ask for them to leave.

"Why did you visit the Pune home world Yevanicha?" Reed enquired, his tone changing to that of a cross-examiner. Chalky glanced at him, the question clearly shocking her.

Satiah held her breath, wondering how she would answer that. Chalky stared at him and Reed stared back. Were they talking in their minds? To her credit Chalky made no attempt to deny it, neither did she ask how they knew.

"The Punes are telepathic," Chalky began, slowly. "Upon discovery, we found each other in our communion. There was a shaft, used to power the engines in the centre of the planet..."

"What are you talking about?" asked Satiah, interrupting. Reed winced. Chalky glared at Satiah.

"What business is it of *yours*?" Chalky demanded, angrily.

"That shaft could have no possible purpose in engines of any sort!" Satiah argued, very correctly. From an engineering perspective she was on firm ground. "Coolant is occasionally pumped through it but I have no idea why."

"...Who is this this *woman*?" Chalky growled, at Reed. "She is an insult to us."

"*Ah yes,*" Reed said, glad to be able to interject. "This is my bodyguard *Satiah* and her team. They take their jobs very seriously and as a result are sometimes *a little overzealous* but they *mean well,* I assure you. Unfortunately when I was last here, your minds caught me by surprise and as I was unconscious, Satiah thought you meant us harm and attempted to learn more about you. You discovered her and… you know the rest." Chalky's eyes never left Satiah and Satiah could feel pressure in her head. Like Chalky was trying to read her mind. Knowing better than to try to fight it, Satiah did her best to ignore it and think about something else. This tactic seemed to work.

"…You were fortunate that you did not *kill* one of us," Chalky cautioned. "Had you done so, we would have destroyed you." Satiah shrugged, trying to look nonchalant.

"You were talking about *engines,*" Reed reminded Chalky. He didn't want to try her patience again. She seemed willing to tell them what they wanted to know and throwing that away would be foolish.

"What I am about to tell you is one of the greatest secrets of the Sisterhood but if you give me your word that you will not intrude or allow others to intrude here," Chalky explained. "Then I will tell you. We are not a secretive people here but we do value our privacy."

"We have many questions," Reed said, not committing himself to anything easily. "*And* I have to tell you that I am bound by certain constraints. *Constraints that are to do with my purpose here.* If you can prove to me that you are *not* in possession of a weapon, or plans of a weapon that you acquired from elsewhere *then* I will make that promise." Chalky stared at him in utter confusion.

"We have *no weapons here* beside our minds and those on our star ships," she stated, a little hurt in her tone. "Surely the Coalition does not feel threatened by *us?*"

"If *this* weapon exists it would give cause for *anyone* to feel threatened," Reed said, sadly. His eyes were earnest and pressing. His posture one of concern and averseness.

"…What is it?" Chalky asked, also grave. Satiah presumed that this enquiry meant that the Sisterhood had neither the weapon itself nor the plans with which to construct it.

"If you don't already know it is better than you don't find out," Reed said, sincerely. Chalky gave him a long, hard, evaluative look.

"...*We have no such thing*," Chalky assured, honestly. "We only want to be left to our own devices. We wish *no involvement* with either you or any of the other superpowers."

"Understood," Reed sighed. The exhalation of was equal parts relief and disappointment.

The relief being that the Sisterhood remained just another mystery with no real threat and the disappointment that the weapon still remained missing. Like brother vultures they loomed on either side of the pathway to truth. Reed always assumed that the weapon had already been constructed. Just as he allowed himself to believe that someone already had it and was prepared to use it. He always assumed the worst unless he acquired definitive proof that it was not the case.

"The Punes were once able to physically move their world using telepathic power to power and run the engines in the planet's core. We are building something similar and I wanted to study the apparatus," Chalky stated. "So I sent some of my acolytes to do so on my behalf."

"You didn't go *yourself?*" Satiah questioned, politely.

"Why bother when I can see through *their* eyes?" Chalky smiled, mysteriously.

"That explains why the shaft had nothing to do with city..." Carlos said, thinking back to the hours of debate.

"*And* why the Punes said nothing about diplomatic relations with the Sisterhood. They said nothing because there never were any," Deva agreed.

"There was *one last thing*," Reed said, smiling amiably. Chalky also smiled but mainly because she felt it was almost over.

"Name it," Chalky prompted. Reed nodded to Satiah and she began talking.

"Earlier *your Sisterhood* is reported to have *attacked* a mining planet. While doing so you wiped the minds of anyone you encountered to hide your presence there..." Satiah said, brusquely.

"It was not an attack, it was *containment*," Chalky correctly, a little bitter.

"Some of us would want you to compensate us in some way for your actions. *I, however,* have *very few requirements*. Can you *reverse* that process?" Satiah asked. She was talking about the mind-wiping.

"For what purpose?" Chalky asked, mistrustful.

"So that I can question him," Satiah said. "He may have information we need."

"I can," Chalky said, sounding reluctant. "Information about *us* or about this weapon?"

"That will entirely depend on what he saw," Satiah shrugged, cagey. "I can't answer that." Chalky's eyes narrowed.

"It will depend entirely on what questions *you ask*," she argued, not liking the idea.

"I *promise* not to ask anything about your *attack strategy* or whichever of *your acolytes* were involved," Satiah offered, trying to be reasonable. Part of her felt that as the Sisterhood had attacked without being provoked, they should be much more apologetic now they were being called to task. Chalky was apparently of a different persuasion.

"We attacked that mining planet for one reason only," Chalky snapped, deciding to admit everything. "The new material discovered there had properties which could *affect human minds*."

"In what way?" Reed ask, interested.

"Did you get all of it?" Satiah pressed.

"We know some of it was removed and shipped away *before* we acted," Chalky confessed, looking ashamed now. "The vast quantity that remained, we destroyed."

"How exactly did this *material* affect the mind?" asked Reed, his previous question still unanswered.

"It limits the mind's capacity to rest effectively. Or, put another way, prolonged exposure to it would cause insomnia and eventually neutralise the chemicals needed for sleep to occur completely," Chalky explained. "And without sleep, humans rarely remain sane for long."

"Or *alive*," Reed murmured, thinking hard. Chalky then eyed Reed.

"Is it possible that *this weapon you are looking for* may work along similar lines?" she asked, astutely. Reed could only shrug. Even if he did know he wasn't going to say.

"Anything is possible," Satiah allowed.

"Do you have any technical data on this material?" Reed enquired, seriously. "I do not wish to *replicate it*, only to try to understand it better." Chalky shook her head, her white hair swaying with the motion.

"No, all knowledge we could find was destroyed too," she stated. Reed nodded.

"I understand," he forgave. "Can you tell us *where* this planet is?"

"…If you *must* know," she answered, obviously a little reluctant. "I must state that, those we killed, we acted in *self-defence*."

"You don't need to excuse that to *me*," Satiah smiled, grimly. She gave a grim smile. "Accidents happen."

"…As you say," Chalky said, in a pleased tone. She had not expected Satiah to be so accepting about that.

"So… you *will* free the man's mind of your influence?" Satiah asked, hopefully.

"…I shall," Chalky said, after a brief intellectual recap. "Think of him for me and I will know who it is you are talking about." Satiah allowed images of the man to appear from her memory. The blank, vacant stare. The cold eyes seemingly empty of humanity. A mind wiped clean of memory was no mind at all. A man that didn't know how to eat or what to eat… they had as good as killed him too.

Chalky found the man in the ether and removed the mental blocks imposed on him by her acolytes.

"It's done," said Chalky, sighing. "He will regain everything when he next sees *you*."

"You have my word that we will encourage no one else to visit this world," Reed told her. "Nor will we tell anyone about it."

"I am grateful, Reed," she smiled, warmly. "Gratitudes." She paused, her conscience nagging her. Reed was a good human, if a little meddlesome. Tabre was going to kill him and Chalky had played a part in making that possible so… she decided to warn Reed. He responded telepathically that he already knew but thanked her for her concern. Summoned by her thoughts, the two acolytes retuned to escort them back to their ship.

Neither Reed nor Satiah had to impose silence on Carlos and Deva, the pair had learned when not to talk which was a valuable lesson. Even when they boarded their ship, took off and left, they said nothing. It was not until Reed confirmed they were out of *mind-shot* distance from Chalky that the conversation began in earnest.

"Well, I *preferred* that place to the Pune home world," Carlos said seriously.

"It did smell better," agreed Deva, nodding. "They *could* have been lying about the weapon. About having it or the plans to build it."

"Do you think she was making that stuff up about the shaft?" asked Carlos, doubt in his voice. "The whole thing seemed a little crazy."

"Some more of it may become known when we get to the mining world," Reed answered cryptically. "Where we are going next. My main worry is that she lied about where to find it although… I think, in the end, she genuinely decided to help us."

"So you *knew* Chalky?" Satiah asked, at last.

"Do we ever *really* know anyone?" he evaded, adeptly.

"You know what I'm asking," Satiah persisted, irritated.

"I knew *of* her," he allowed, mysteriously. "By another name… in a different time."

"I thought you were just *bluffing*," Carlos stated, awestruck. "You knew *Dreda*? How? She died ages ago."

"*Did she?*" he asked, implying through comedy that he wasn't aware of that. Satiah grinned. She could appreciate what hanging onto secrets was like.

"The soil sample is now explained, as is why the Sisterhood visited the Pune home world," Satiah said, crossing her arms. There was an almost triumphant look about her. "If we *had* a mission file I'd *know* if we had completed it or not but as we are still *waiting*…?"

"They seem to be suffering from technical problems," Reed lied quickly, twitching slightly. "I'm sure it will be here soon enough."

"Soon enough *for what*?" Satiah asked. There was no bite in her tone. She'd already discovered that Reed didn't crumble under bullying or artful cajoling.

"You know, we *never asked* why they *call* themselves the Sisterhood of the Light, *did we*?" Reed asked, changing subjects. Satiah grinned and turned away from him.

"Oh *yeah*!" hissed Deva, annoyed at the oversight. "Now we'll *never* know."

"Always remember never to say never or always," Reed muttered.

"*Some things you're better off not knowing*," Satiah warned, grimly.

***

Ash came back to the ruined control room. Ruby was still sitting at the computer, waiting patiently for him to come up with a password for the verification system. He'd made a few calls while she was not earwigging. First he'd called Phantom Leader Randal to ask if he knew. He didn't. He'd tried Reed but he'd not answered. Finally he gave Mensa a call. Mensa had transferred him to Crystal. Crystal was a supercomputer; specifically *the* supercomputer that had been responsible for breaking into Vourne's network before Mensa had begun his attack. She had provided the codes.

"Password is permino63, one word, no capitals," Ash told Ruby. Instantly she was in.

"Wow, *how* did you figure that out?" she asked, thinking he'd somehow deciphered it from some obscure clue. He was tempted to allow her to believe him capable of that but relented.

"I checked with the computer responsible for infiltrating this system before the attack began and hoped no one had changed them since," he explained.

"There a lot here," she said, going through the files. Ash tried to use the controls himself but was batted away by Ruby.

"I've got this," she stated, cross. He smiled at her possessiveness. She was trying so hard to be useful and to impress him. Her fingers paused over the buttons as she tried to remember what Ash had said before.

"Orion Observatory," he prompted. She searched and got a resounding nothing. Ash sighed, what would he do if there was nothing here? He had no idea where else to go.

"ITP6." A single file appeared and they grinned at one another in accomplishment. Ruby opened it. They both quickly read the agonisingly fleeting transcript that the computer conjured.

(UE) OPERATION BURNING BRIDGE (UE) REPORT: Dated at end. Target located. ITP6. Spatial coordinates: 9980-7948. Designation (TS): Top Secret. Status: ACTIVE. Official staff allocation: 1850. Dasss reports: Reconnaissance correct. Scientific facility with several branches of identified ongoing research. Jaylite Industries is currently contracted with waste disposal duties. Background check required. Experimentation currently at critical stage. Testing is achieving mixed results. Balan's next visit in two days. Evacuate immediately.

There was *more* afterwards but it looked like gibberish.

"We can *find it!*" Ruby exclaimed, pleased. She tapped the screen under the spatial coordinates. "We can go *there?*"

"We know where it *was*, that doesn't mean it's still there," he said, unwilling to give into his own excitement.

"*Either way!*" she scoffed, rolling her eyes. "*Aw…* so much left *unsaid!* This asks *way* more questions than it answers! This looks like a *secret agent reporting in* or something."

"That's because that is exactly what it *is*," Ash pointed out, amused. "What were you expecting?"

"Don't know *what* to expect with *you* around," she guffawed.

"It's the date that concerns me," Ash stated, pointing to it. "Best part of three months ago." She shrugged.

"*So?* Ash, this is *all we have*, we *have* to act on it," she stated, slipping off of the chair. "The longer we wait the more chance that it will have moved."

"Must be a code of some sort," Ash murmured, still trying to make sense of the rest of the report. Ruby came back to look at it again.

"...Mainly numbers. It *may* be a primer code," she said, biting her lip. She was trying to be falsely modest and failing.

"What's that?" he asked, interested. He truly didn't know, the ways of the humans were still a work in progress for him. The way she was talking it inferred that it was a commonplace thing that everyone knew.

"Well, traditional codes are symbols, colours or simple alpha-numeric combinations. Those are easily decoded these days. Computers make mincemeat of them. Many people get around that by employing a primer code. It's *usually* easy. You get a textbook or some other large publication that is likely to contain all the words you're intending to use. Then you have a few options as to how you want your code to be. A word in the book can be represented by its page number or its position in a sentence or elsewhere on the page. Most people will use both. Or you can do the reverse of that. You can even alternate your methodology as you go. Use the words to give page numbers that give you the correct letter, word or even term. Then you switch to make decoding even harder by using a different method every tenth word or something."

She stopped noticing he was staring right at her.

"You know a lot about *that*," he stated, accusation in his voice. She shrugged and avoided his gaze.

"... Just saying," she murmured, mildly defensive.

"And, of course, with such a vast array of literacy out there, it would be very difficult to figure out which book they are using?" he asked, dismally.

"Yes. But maybe they left a reference to it, you know? In case someone previously unfamiliar needs to read it?" she offered, trying to be optimistic.

"This is *Vourne*," he stated, simply. No further words were needed to make his point. She lowered her head, solemn.

***

Wester, now a Lieutenant, stood in a brand new blue uniform on the command deck of the Colonial destroyer: *Warrior*. It was Captain Tristram that had given Wester this chance to prove himself and Wester intended to do just that. He'd show everyone he had just what it takes to be a great battleship Captain. Wester could remember how he had imagined being on his first ship would feel. Exhilaration. Stimulation. Now though, it was made darker by his knowledge of the politics of the times. War had to be avoided at all costs. Of *that* he and Tristram and Erica Moxin had been in complete agreement. Simmons… Wester didn't trust the older Commodore but as Eric and Tristram did, Wester had hidden his feelings. Things were fragile enough without his adding surplus distrust to the load.

"Captain is coming, sir," warned a flight officer, as she hurried past him.

"Very good," he said, smiling at her. She had helped him a lot since his arrival, with introductions, explanations and showing him around. Annoyingly he seemed incapable of remembering her name. He had been told at least once but still it proved elusive. She was very appealing which was another problem too. It was all Wester could do not to ogle at her like an idiot. Tristram was marching towards him, all neat and efficient looking. As with procedure, Wester stood rigidly to attention and tipped his hat at Tristram. Tristram returned the gesture as he scrutinised his command deck for anything that was out of place. There was nothing, as it should always be.

"Report?" Tristram asked, his tone casual. No one must guess they were fellow conspirators. Tristram trusted most of his crew but he knew one or two of them to be the fanatics that Director Ro counted on for her support.

"Stores aboard, crew ready for duty, shipshape," Wester answered, in complete honesty. It was, he'd spent the last three hours making sure of that.

"Inform the navigator that we will move out," Tristram said, his expression seeming to darken.

"*Rendezvous point?*" Wester guessed. Tristram nodded.

"Sir… Oh, *one thing*, sir," Wester said awkwardly. "I'd like to commend *that* flight officer on her helping me earlier." He pointed at her. Tristram turned in disinterest.

"You *can* tell her yourself Wester, you don't need my permission to congratulate the crew for anything," Tristram frowned, in confusion. Wester sighed, he'd hoped Tristram might reveal her name without being asked directly.

"Sir."

Director Ro had begun to mass the fleet of the Federation a few hours after the Rally had ended. You didn't need to be a tactical genius to work out why. Coordinates already programmed in, Wester gave the navigator the nod. The man initiated the course and the engines hummed into life.

"I wonder what will be our first target," Tristram said, seriously. To anyone else he would sound like he was pondering over which of the Coalition worlds their ships would first attack. Wester knew him to be talking about their own ships. The fleet of the Federation and which ships they would first target to cripple to prevent or at least delay the war.

"It will take a few hours for the rest of the fleet to assemble," reminded Wester, again concealing the true topic of discussion.

Tristram and Wester stood together now, overseeing the activity of the crew and watching the stars fly past. They began to pace up and down slowly, talking softly. To untrained eyes they were behaving perfectly normally. No one knew they were discussing high treason. No one could know they planned to make all their crew criminals in an attempt to prevent a war that mostly everyone seemed to want. Tristram had been good to his crew in the past and he hoped they would at least hear him out when the truth became apparent. Captain Moxin's ship, the Colonial destroyer *Prevalence*, was to be on their starboard side. It was unclear which ship in the fleet Commodore Simmons would be on or even if he would be there at all. The debate as to when it would be best to attack had not ended yet either. Did they *wait* for the whole fleet to be there?

If the assembly was complete it gave them a chance to damage more ships while it reduced their odds of successful escape. Yet if they attacked *before* the fleet was all there, while it made getting away easier it would do little to ruin the Director's war effort. They had decided to send a coded signal to Erica when the time was best. She would go one way and they would go the other in an attempt to cause further confusion. Two destroyers against over fifty? The odds were long, even for those who routinely gambled. This longshot, though, was all they had as they had all agreed they could not stand by and do nothing. In the past, many had been criticised for not acting to prevent wars from starting when an opportunity had come their way.

What would future historians think of *them*? Would they be traitors or heroes? Both?

***

"No one *knows* who agent 446 is! That *is* sort of *the point*," Deva declared, impatiently.

"This Tabre is pretty good though," Carlos persisted, seriously.

"He got *lucky*!" she insisted.

"*He gets lucky a lot*," remarked Satiah, darkly. "I don't think he is agent 446 though."

"Why not?" asked Carlos, interested.

"Because I don't think agent 446 is real at all, I think it is only *Colonial propaganda* to help keep their secret services in line," Satiah answered, sighing. "There is nothing better than guarding murderers with murderers. Telling a bunch of spies that they're being watched is only an adaption of that. Basically they are a mismatching lash up of barely compatible organisations. How they have managed to stay together as long as they have is a mystery too. *Maybe Division Sixteen is our version of that.*"

"*Trust me*, agent 446 *is real*!" stated Deva, with conviction in her tone. "I might even have seen her once."

"Oh it's a woman, is it?" asked Carlos, unable to hide his surprise. Both Satiah and Deva glared at him. "What?"

"You do know Deva, that rumours about Federation agent 446 have been circulating since *before I was born*?" Satiah said, allowing Carlos's comment to go unpunished. "While it is not *inconceivable* for someone to have been alive all that time, it is *unlikely* in this line of work."

"But according to the legend *they did die*," Carlos said, checking the file. "Nearly one hundred years ago."

"*What?*" Deva asked, disbelievingly. He showed her the information he had just found as he began to explain to Satiah what he had read. He was starting to have mixed feelings about starting this conversation concerning rogue operatives and legends in the field of espionage. It had led to a competitive one-upmanship battle between him and Deva as to who had the best stories.

"She was part of an operation *allegedly* exposing an assassination attempt on the *then* President. She'd infiltrated a group of, *surprise, surprise, Coalition* spies and was leaking information back to the Federation. Someone betrayed her, though. Interestingly it does not say who or how or even why but she was caught only because she was pregnant. If she'd not been in that condition she could easily have got away. She was taken on board a warship of some kind, again unspecified, where she gave birth. After naming the child, *apparently after her own killer*, she was executed without trial," he explained. "All of this is *wildly* speculative though! Especially when you consider the fact that there is no evidence this person ever existed. I think Satiah's right, it's just propaganda."

"Nevertheless it is yet another example of spy *mythology*," Satiah stated, obviously unimpressed. "You think *that* is a good story? You should read about Phantom Alec Varron."

"*Who?*" asked Carlos, instantly interested.

"*Yeah*," she sniggered, cynically. She stared off into the middle-distance briefly. "Obviously that would be one thing your trainers *would never tell you*." He and Deva exchanged looks of intrigue.

"If it's such a big secret, how do *you* know about it?" he asked, a little hurt. It was a reminder that he was still only learning.

"Never you mind *how* I know, just take it from me," she shrugged, being deliberately obstinate.

"So what happened?" Deva asked, inquisitive.

"Alec was a Phantom agent around the time of the Common Protectorate war. I *forget* how it started actually… something to do with a missing time machine. Or part of a time machine that went missing…" she trailed off, thinking about it.

"Sign of *age*," Carlos couldn't resist quipping. Deva winced, expecting a blistering retort in response. Satiah only grinned.

"Alec infiltrates a pirate gang in search of these parts, meets a young woman called Petula Feece and takes the place of her bodyguard after saving her life."

"*I can see where this is going*," Carlos interrupted, smirking. She raised an eyebrow in irritation.

"Petula is leader of one of the pirate gangs, taking the place of her sister who had been arrested not long before. Unlike her sister though, Petula is *very against* the establishment, not *just* the Coalition but the Federation too. She was... a kind of *revolutionary* I suppose."

"*No wonder* he fell for her, *who* can resist a *pirate revolutionary?*" Carlos deadpanned. Deva scowled at him.

"There is a split in the pirate group, some stay loyal to Petula but most fall under some other guy. A man called Lage if I remember correctly. Evading the inevitable assassins Alec and Petula lie low and... according to the records *fall in love.*"

"*I knew it,*" Carlos grunted, rolling his eyes.

"It *happens,*" Deva stated, meaningfully bumping his knee with hers.

"Are you two finished?" Satiah growled.

"*Sorry,* you were saying?" Deva replied, apologetically.

"This is the tricky bit because... when he reports in next for fresh instructions he is ordered to kill Petula. But he can't because he's become emotionally invested in her. According to some sources, he spent all that night *watching her while she slept...* gun in his hand... debating what to do."

"Getting grim," Carlos mused.

"So he decides to kill Lage instead. Petula agrees and *somehow* they convince the other pirates to help. Once Lage is dead Petula is the unchallenged leader of the pirates. But she is caught and imprisoned. Everyone correctly points the finger at Alec for betraying her. Alec, probably because he'd grown a conscience from somewhere, tells her the truth about himself. He went rogue, broke her out of prison and ran away with her."

"*What an idiot,*" Carlos muttered. Deva nodded in agreement with him.

"How long did it take him to die after he told her?" Deva asked, believing him to have been murdered.

"She didn't kill him. Some think she didn't kill him because she loved him too much. Others think it's because he knew where her sister was being held and promised to help her in the rescue attempt.

Maybe it was a combination of both or some other reason but the point is… From *that* moment, he was no longer a Phantom agent. He was a pirate. And… *scariest thing of all*… even *after* they'd freed Petula's sister, *a convicted felon*, no one went after him or Petula," Satiah concluded.

"…They let them go?" Deva asked, outraged disbelief in her face.

"So the *story* goes," Satiah shrugged, indicating that they could not be sure of that.

"I can see why they don't tell *that one* to the recruits," Carlos said, thinking about it. "Not the *greatest* example of loyal dedication. I bet this was on your mind before Deva decided to join us."

"Actually no, I just didn't want you messing up *my* mission," she smiled, casually.

"Well, I'm sure the histories of *every* secret service are littered with such stories and legends," Deva said, shaking her head.

"No life without energy," Satiah said, seriously. "It goes without saying that if you and Carlos decide to run away together I will personally see to it that you don't get far." She grinned and Carlos laughed.

"Okay," Deva said, smiling a small smile.

"Yeah, wouldn't want *yet another* legend about the rewards of desertion," Carlos chuckled.

"What happened to the missing time machine?" That question came from Reed who, until now, had been just silently listening to the conversation. He was talking about the original reason for Phantom Alec's mission.

"*Oh yeah*," Deva nodded, facing Satiah again.

"It is so often the way that what starts a mission ends up being overshadowed, buried or simply forgotten by the events of the mission itself," Satiah answered, in a casual voice. Reed smiled enigmatically. "Our own mission is surely a great example of that."

"If you mean you don't know, just say so," he replied.

"This is coming from the king of prevarication," muttered Carlos. Reed chuckled and Satiah smiled.

"I was not aware that I had been promoted," he joked.

"Thirty minutes before arrival," Kelvin informed.

***

"Why would they go back to the Sisterhood?" Conrad demanded. Tabre had to admit that was a good question. They had been caught spying but had also escaped. Going back seemed *unwise* to say the least.

"I imagine they're going back to complete whatever task it was they were undertaking last time," he replied, unhelpfully. Engines at fifty percent, they had limped clear of the moon the moment Satiah had gone. Thanks to the new tracker Tabre had shot onto the hull of their ship, they could still trace them. Yet it had become apparent that Satiah and Reed had returned to their previous location.

"Whatever it was they were doing, I doubt the Sisterhood know about it. I'm not going back to the Sisterhood, I will wait for them to leave," Tabre stated, sour.

"If they get captured they might never leave," Conrad argued.

"Satiah's too good to get captured," retorted Tabre, irritated. "In any case she'll be on the ball this time because she's been there before and will know what to expect."

"How can you know how good she is?" he muttered, waving his hands in despair.

"Because of how close she came to killing us, because of her actions on the Pune home world and, because no one would return there unless they were certain they had a way of getting out again," Tabre snapped, seriously considering killing Conrad. Did the man do nothing but ask stupid questions or argue nonsensically? He hadn't even been of any real use when dealing with the Sisterhood. Repairs were almost complete. Then they would wait for Satiah's next move… if she didn't get captured or killed. That was when the tracker began to move again.

"Here we go," Tabre growled, pleased to see that he had been correct.

***

The disappointment was obvious. Ruby had been almost

expecting it. They had gone to the coordinates they had found from the mission report only to find... nothing. They arrived just outside the orbit zone of a planet. Ash ran a scan instantly, seeking for the space station in vain.

"It's not here," he stated, pointlessly.

"I'm *sorry*," she said, and meant it. She'd been trying to translate the rest of the report but had had no luck.

"This planet is devoid of life," Ash stated, in a curious tone. She recognised that he had sensed something.

"*Ash?*" she asked, her tone one of mild reproach. "Come on, spit it out."

"There's something down there," he said, eyeing the computer screen.

"You want to look at it, don't you?" she asked, a sort of helpless reluctance in her tone.

"I'll take the shuttle if you want..." he began.

"Are you joking? I'm *not* staying here by myself," she interrupted, scoffing. She took the report with her. She'd acquired a long overcoat, dark green in colour, that went down just below her knees. It was full of pockets. She'd created a little set of equipment for herself. Torch. Spare power pack. Her communicator, with an ever-increasing amount of messages for her to ignore. And her small computer with the mission report on it. It was thick and durable. Ideal for wandering around in when she was with Ash. She really had no idea what to expect next. An icy wilderness? Caves? Forest? Desert? Anything was possible with Ash around.

He had been *pleased?* If pleased was the right word with her change of attire. It was obvious to anyone who took the time to look at him that he was not into fashion but he seemed to like clothes that were efficient. As such he approved of her new coat. It didn't feel very new though. Ash brought them in to land on the landing pad of a darkened facility. It seemed to be etched into the forbidding rock face. A strong squall whipped around them as they descended the ramp. Ash's cloak fluttered rapidly. Ruby scampered along next to Ash, trying to keep him between her and the biting blasts of wind. They reached the side of the building that did nothing whatsoever in regard to shelter.

"Over there!" he bellowed, pointing. A sealed doorway.

They hurried over to it. Ruby pulled up the protective flap of the control pad and pushed at the buttons. Nothing.

"There's no power," she shouted, over the howling winds. Ash tried anyway. Still nothing.

"Maybe we should go back!" she called, already starting to shiver.

"We've only just got here," he protested.

"It's freezing!" she argued, rubbing herself to keep warm. Ash produced a device from his pocket and did something to the control pad. Sparks flew and the door opened. He pulled her inside before she had a chance to ask what he had done. The door closed very quickly behind them.

"That's better," he said, in the darkness beyond.

Ruby turned on her torch so it shone upwards across her face so that he could see her displeasure.

"Don't start moaning," he said, before she began to rant. She flushed.

"…I wasn't going to," she lied, furious.

"Good," he said, activating his own light. They both looked around. A dark, bare corridor complete with peeling paint and every sign of oxidation.

"You've done it again, duffer," she said, mockingly. "Yet another wonderfully depressing place without anyone else in sight."

"I told you not to moan," he smiled, starting to move forward.

"I'm not *moaning*," she responded sarcastically. "I was trying to *congratulate* you! It must be very tricky to find so many ghastly places." He sighed.

"Come on," he said, leading the way. The air was stale, unfiltered. There was only the faintest of whining noises whenever the wind was strongest outside. Their boots on the metal grilles were noisy.

"Do you even have any idea what this place was?" she asked, miserable. "*Ew!*" She flinched to avoid a particularly stubborn cobweb, failed, flailed wildly and then staggered into him.

"It's in my hair!" she cried, her voice muffled by his cloak. "*Get it out, I think it's alive.*" Ash calmly removed the offending silky snare.

He studied it in the torchlight, a scowl on his face.

"It's *nothing*, Ruby," he stated, irritated.

"...Are you *sure*?" she asked, peeping out at it.

"*Ruby*," he breathed, impatient. "Pull yourself together please."

"I'm *sorry*," she said, abashed. "I thought it wanted to bite me or something. I heard that…"

"You have nothing to fear," he insisted, waving his hand around to demonstrate their safety. He grinned as he watched her grudgingly move forwards again. He reached out to gently stroke her ear lobe. As he predicted, she squealed and reeled on him.

"*Don't do that!*" she ordered, pleadingly. "I'll scream the place down!"

"Wouldn't want that so soon after finding it," he murmured, brushing past her to continue.

"You're so horrible to me," she stated, following again. "*What did I do wrong?*" A philosophical question that almost everyone asked at some stage. Even Ash remembered asking it.

"Have you contacted your family yet?" he asked, knowing she hadn't.

"I *will!*" she declared, stressed. "I just… *don't know what to say*."

"How about *the truth*?" he offered, as before.

"Yeah! As if they would believe *that!*" she scoffed. He had to acknowledge she had a point there.

"You will have to confront them eventually," he stated.

"I'm old enough not to *have to do anything*," she muttered.

They entered a much more cavernous area beyond an open doorway. There were some odd things already that Ruby had noticed. The door seals were at least eight inches above the floor. She knew because she'd tripped on at least two of them. They flashed their lights around and realised they were in an area previously used for some sort of heavy industry. Chains dangled silently from the high ceiling and vanished into a dark chasm in the centre. They approached the hole in the ground and peered over the guardrail, curious.

"It's a mine," he said, with certainty.

"…I'll take your word for it," she replied, trying to penetrate the darkness with her eyes.

"*But what were they mining?*" he asked, rhetorically. His tone turned thoughtful, almost concerned, as he turned and twisted to try and see more.

"What's the matter?" she asked, curious.

"Something is…" he began, stopping. He paused and a deep, spooky silence began. She flashed her torch into his face.

"*Ash?*" she asked, uneasy.

"I don't know," he dismissed, serious. Ruby looked all around again, noting the bad condition everything was in. She couldn't know for sure but she began to suspect some kind of fight had taken place there.

"So, *you don't know* what they were mining or why they stopped," she asked, thinking she understood.

"Correct," he agreed.

"*So?* Who's to say it's got anything to do with what we are looking for?" she enquired, although she began to wonder as soon as the question was out of her mouth.

"I wonder what it was they were getting out of there," he stated, motioning to the giant hole that led who knew where.

"My money is on some kind of…" She paused for dramatic effect and got his attention. Then she pulled a fearful face and made her voice an anxious gasp. "*Rock.*" He scowled and she giggled.

"I am aware that rock will have been removed," he stated, annoyed. "I was more interested in what was in the rock."

"*You should have been more specific,*" she grinned, up at him.

"The space station we are looking for was here, why would it be near a mine? To collect materials?" he thought out loud.

"Most probably," she concurred, nodding slowly. "I suppose that means they must have been very *important* materials but where does this get *us*? Without the identity of the material in question or an idea what they were up to…"

"*I know, I know,*" he sighed, waving at her.

She took a deep breath and leaned against the guardrail carefully. She had an idea it might give under her and she'd fall to a painful death in the dark bowels of the mine.

"Have you considered a different approach? Instead of trying to find the weapon by tracking the thing itself, you could think about who is still alive and willing to use it," she offered.

"Without knowing precisely what it is or how it works, that is trickier than it first looks," he replied, looking up. She followed his gaze and could see loading equipment. Cranes, supporting girders and all manner of things.

"It is small… *for a mine,*" she said, solemn. "I mean normally mining worlds… kind of *the whole place* is a mine. Not one little station on a mountainside."

"How much do you know about mining?" he asked, doubt in his tone. She made a noise indicating hurt. "It's a serious question."

***

"I told you she would have a way of escaping the Sisterhood," Tabre said, exasperated. The tracker was moving again, *away* from the Sisterhood. Tabre was following. Where was Reed going *now*? They were moving out further towards the edges of the cosmos. While they had been waiting, Tabre had used the time productively. Knowing that Satiah's new ship was superior to his he decided that taking her on again would be suicidal. He'd called the Director and explained the problem.

"A Phantom agent," she had said, thoughtfully. "I can send you a team of Colonial Commandos. That's fifty, plus their CO. Will that be enough?"

"Hopefully, she's very good," he said, honestly. "Once I've got rid of her, Reed will be easy."

The commandos were already following him. And, while Conrad slept, their officer contacted him.

"My name is Sergeant Oak," came a woman's' voice, with a very distinct Colonial accent. "I understand I have to report to you for orders. What is the situation?"

"The target has yet to get to his location. When he does, *you will move in*," Tabre explained. "In the meantime, stay on this line."

"Sir," she said, disconnecting. He didn't like using others, he preferred to do it himself but he needed extra firepower to bring these two down. He couldn't help but wonder what they were up to. The longer he had followed them the more puzzled he had become. Clearly this was no diplomatic errand.

***

From out of the void, Satiah's ship *Vulture* flashed into sight, approaching the mining world.

"Destination ahead," Kelvin stated. Satiah studied it closely, her brown eyes narrowing.

"*What a dive*," Carlos grunted, eyeing it.

"That's too bad for you," Satiah grinned. "You and Deva are on recon duty."

"*What?*" Deva asked, sitting up.

"That's right. I want you two to go in and investigate... like *I* normally do," Satiah stated. Carlos nudged Deva in a 'told you so' sort of way.

"Are you *sure?*" Reed asked, eyeing them in surprise.

"Got to learn sometime," she shrugged.

"Okay," Carlos said, standing. "We'll set up." He and Deva left the control room.

"*...Ah*," Satiah mused, noticing something on the scan. She and Kelvin looked at each other briefly.

"What is it?" Reed asked, noticing the interaction.

"A *possible* complication," she replied, thoughtfully. "We've found the facility... *or what's left of it*. But there's a ship down there. Undamaged by the look of it... and *another* in orbit. I think the first is a shuttle of the other larger craft."

"No life signs on either ship," Kelvin stated, after performing his own scan.

"This knowledge does not comfort me," Reed sighed, honestly. "Do you have any theories on who it might be?"

"*Your guess is as good as mine.* It's not a battleship or anything, it looks like someone's *personal cruiser.* Saying *that,* it *does* have its own shuttle so... who can tell?" Satiah said. "They can't see us though. Not until we land at any rate. I think it is fair to postulate that, *whoever it is,* as there are *no life signs* on both ships, they are either *in* the mine or wandering the surface of the world." Reed grunted, still looking at the approaching world.

"Well, we'll find out soon enough," he smiled, seeming to lose his initial anxiety. "I was worried it might be Tabre."

"Unlikely," she said. "Even if he somehow knows where we are I doubt he could get here *before* us. He may be good but he can't see into the future."

"Let's hope not," he replied, his voice meaningful of something she didn't know.

***

Satiah sprawled in a chair with three screens in front of her. The one to the left showed the entrance to the mine from the view of the ship. The middle screen showed her exactly what Carlos was seeing and the one on the right covered Deva. Kelvin loomed over her right shoulder, whirring softly. They had landed and, after waiting a few minutes for a reaction that didn't happen, it was time to investigate. Reed appeared over her left shoulder and pulled a seat over to sit next to her.

"Ramp opening..." she said, to the listening teenagers. "*Now!*" Carlos and Deva's screens jolted and swung around madly as both of them ran in opposite directions, rifles at the ready. They could hear the excited heavy breathing of both youths clearly. They had split up to approach the entrance from two directions at once.

Almost together they found cover and stopped. Swinging their rifles around to spot danger, they surveyed the open landing area.

"Okay," Deva said, quietly.

"Good," Carlos replied. Satiah glanced at Reed who eyed her. She raised an eyebrow and tilted her head at the screens. Reed nodded.

"Move in," she initiated. Carlos reached the door slightly ahead of Deva and, while she maintained a view back at their own ship, Carlos focussed on the door. They could now see the whole landing area and Satiah took the time to zoom in on the unoccupied shuttle. Whoever it was that owned it had left the ramp down. The door beyond was closed, however.

"I can't open this door," Carlos stated, seriously. "Controls are screwed." Satiah debated the idea of searching for another way in when Kelvin answered him.

"Door has been opened recently, observe the scorch marks," he said. Satiah zoomed in on what Carlos was looking at. Reed watched as Deva kept looking over her shoulder at Carlos and then back out across the landing area.

"There is no power," persisted Carlos, uncertain. He was shouting to be heard over the wind.

"Rig a bypass on that coding plate," Satiah instructed.

"Won't make a difference if there is no power," Carlos argued, as he went about doing that.

"Are you carrying a power pack?" Satiah asked, meaningfully. A silence.

"Should have thought of that, sorry," he replied. She smiled.

"Learning takes time," Reed grinned.

"But who can argue with the results?" mocked Satiah, matching his grin with one of her own. Carlos sighed heavily and it was all Satiah could do not to laugh.

"Hurry up, I'm freezing here," Deva grumbled. With reasonable skill and speed, Carlos rigged the self-powered bypass and connected it. Sparks flew and the door jolted up. Deva raced in to cover Carlos who was still crouching.

"Leave the bypass there in case you need to get out quickly," Satiah instructed, as she saw Carlos about to disconnect it.

"Ok," he replied, standing and moving in after Deva. Standing next to each other, Carlos and Deva scanned the surround with the rifle sights. The light from outside was poor at best so they switched to the green of night-sight.

Advancing slowly, they reached an open area where several corridors branched off from.

"Okay, Carlos *right*, Deva *left*," Satiah instructed, patiently. She could get used to this.

"The scans are not definitive," Kelvin reported.

"Probably the rock," muttered Satiah, irritated. They watched as, now separated, Carlos and Deva began to follow their respective corridors. There was still no sign of anyone else. Trying to be as quiet as possible, they were breathing more shallowly and quickly. Satiah glanced back at the landing area. No change. That ruled out a few possibilities of ambush.

"It looks very small for a mine," Reed remarked, watching the computer as it plotted out a layout.

"Like I said, it wasn't operational long enough to really thrive properly," Satiah reminded him. "*The Sisterhood didn't hang around.*"

Deva cried out suddenly and fell forward. Carlos's swung back in her direction.

"*Deva?*" Satiah asked, uneasy.

"It's okay," she grunted, standing again. "I just fell over something." Reed let out a sigh of relief. Satiah too relaxed after initially thinking someone had bludgeoned her from behind.

"Lot of stuff lying around here," Carlos explained, rather needlessly. "Whoever was last here didn't clear up after themselves."

"Bodies? Gore?" Satiah enquired, a little impatiently. No, it was no good. Even with the danger she preferred being out there than watching it in safety.

"A few scorch marks on the wall here," Deva answered, and Satiah zoomed in. "Looks like small weapons fire."

"Rainbow," Kelvin said, in Satiah's ear. Her informant was trying to talk to her.

"*Not now*," she growled back. Reed hadn't seemed to notice. She did trust him but her sources were her own.

"Just a second," hissed Carlos. It all went very quiet. Satiah and Reed leaned forward in their seats. Carlos was watching what looked like a chain. It was moving. Swinging back and forth quietly in the darkness. Proof, if any were needed that, if a chain swings but no one is around to see it, it still moves.

"*I didn't touch it*," he whispered, a little spooked.

"Ok Carlos, stay where you are. Deva, go back and catch up to Carlos," she instructed. She herself stood and nodded to Kelvin.

"Reed, take over here."

***

"Mining is something we've always done to get stuff we need, like ore and stones and... a lot of stuff," Ruby said, thinking about it. Ash listened, deciding not to pounce on the word *stuff*.

"These days though, if a world has been designated a mining world, one of the big corporations move in and the whole planet effectively becomes a mine. If it is inhabited, the people are moved away while the materials are... *extracted*. Then, when it's all gone, the appropriate corporation place the people back after reconstruction is completed," she said, trying to recall the standard process. "It's very lucrative."

"*And very destructive*," Ash muttered.

"My point is," she pressed, ignoring the slur pointedly. "This place has only this bit of a facility, therefore I guess they had not been going long before they stopped."

"Or something stopped them," Ash said. She shrugged in concurrence.

"That's about the limit of my understanding when it comes to large scale industrial mining. If you want more technical stuff then I suggest you talk to a miner," she said, crossing her arms. He gesticulated to indicate that there were none to ask. She only shrugged again and smiled.

"What about small scale?" he asked, interested.

"Oh, you mean *precision* mining?" she asked, starting to invent her answers again. "That is a much more specialised business." He cleared his throat, indicating that he wished her to remain sincere. "That's not very common, it only happens with unusual materials. You know, stuff we don't know much about or radioactive waste removal from buried locations or something."

"There's no radiation here so what were they looking for?" Ash asked, more to himself that to her.

"*And?*" she asked, smiling knowingly. He shrugged. "Did they get it all or not before whatever stopped them, stopped them?" He smiled reluctantly. "*See*, I am paying attention," she stated, again with the false injury in her tone.

"I suppose once again we will have to find a computer," he said, hating the idea. She nodded, also starting to become weary of the task. Vourne's computer had been tricky enough and they'd only got anywhere with it at all because of Crystal. Ruby began to move towards the next doorway when he clutched her arm.

"There's someone else here," he said, in her ear. Slowly she turned to face the area behind them, suppressing a shudder.

"I didn't hear anything," she admitted, her voice a whisper.

They stood for several moments listening intently. Still nothing sounded.

"*Maybe it's a member of staff?*" she whispered, hopefully.

"*…Possibly,*" he allowed, although it was a highly unlikely contingency. She flashed her torch at an adjacent wall, noticing the burn marks and the corrosion. She shivered and stepped to go around Ash to the next door. She only just managed to stop herself screaming when her shoulder nudged heavily into something. It was only a chain, suspended from the ceiling and hanging down. Ash didn't see what she had knocked in the dark and followed her along in silence. Someone had gone to all the trouble of removing the helpful arrows that normally directed people around the facility. She could see where they had been ripped free of their holders.

Upon entering the control room, they encountered the first real sign of the fight that must have occurred. The remains of a barricade across the doorway to the room. Tools and papers scattered around the floor. Although, each sheet of paper was upright, displaying the contents. Ash went over to the controls and noticed that someone had removed the databank.

"*Marvellous,*" he grumbled.

"It's not damaged, whoever removed it was *careful*," Ruby said, encouragingly. She glanced around remembering the archives in her old job.

"Doesn't matter how careful they were as we have no idea where it is," Ash argued, annoyed. Ruby flashed her torch around the ruin of a room. She paced towards the walls and started looking for safes.

Then, she spotted a ceiling tile that was… at an odd angle. She grinned up at her find.

"Ash, give me a boost," she requested. Obligingly he did and she almost laughed as she found herself thrust upwards towards the ceiling. He held her waist tightly and didn't seem in the least taxed by the effort. She gently pushed the ceiling panel aside and extended her hand into the darkness beyond. Gingerly she felt about for anything hidden. Nothing. She tried the other direction and was rewarded by her fingertips landing on something rectangular and metal. Carefully she retrieved it and was lowered to the floor again.

"*Tada*," she murmured, waving it under his nose in triumph. "One dusty database."

"I knew I brought you along for something," was his congratulatory remark.

"Stay where you are!" ordered Satiah, from the doorway. "Both of you." Ruby jumped, gulped but had the subtlety to slip the database into her pocket. Neither Ash nor Ruby moved as three others followed Satiah in.

"Identify yourselves," she ordered, stiffly. Ruby edged backwards a little into Ash. Lights were flashed into their faces.

"I'm…" began Ruby, wondering why Ash had not answered the question.

"Wait!" instructed Satiah, holding up her hand. She was clearly listening to a voice in an earpiece. "What do you mean, you know them?" Another silence. "Fine, I'll send Carlos and Deva back for you." Carlos and Deva went out to escort Reed there.

Satiah sighed irritably and went over to the controls. She too seemed to be looking for something. Ruby nudged Ash and nodded her head towards the apparently unguarded doorway. He shook his head and nodded towards Kelvin who was staring straight at them.

Instead they watched as Satiah searched the room methodically.

"Are you *looking for something?*" Ruby asked, wondering. Satiah grunted to the affirmative. "*What?*"

"None of your concern," Satiah answered, as Ruby expected she would. Lastly Satiah turned her focus onto the empty database slot and ran her fingers along the metal grid them softly. Slowly she turned, gun in her hand, towards them. Ruby felt Ash's hands land on her shoulders as if to stop her going anywhere. Satiah didn't say or do anything, just stared coldly at them and waited.

"My name's Ruby," Ruby said, uneasily. Still Satiah said nothing but focussed intently on the younger woman. "We were just looking." Ruby felt Ash sigh heavily behind her to let her know just how inane that sounded.

"Try again," Satiah prompted, smoothly.

"We were wondering w-who owned this place," Ruby went on, her voice faltering now. Satiah took a determined step forward but before anything else could happen an incredulous voice sounded from outside.

"*Ash!* For goodness sake! What are *you* doing here?" Reed demanded, as he stumbled into the room. "I thought you were supposed to be on a voyage of discovery? *It's a big cosmos you know!* You don't have to keep ending up where *I* happen to be!"

"Reed," Ash smiled, pleasantly. "Would you believe me if I pleaded *coincidence?*"

"Is he with you?" Satiah asked, to Reed. Reed let out a breath, scratched his head nervously and waved a hand at Ash and Ruby.

"I don't know who the lady is but... yes. Ash *is loosely connected* with the Coalition," Reed admitted.

"This is my friend Ruby," Ash stated, patting her shoulders softly. "She's been exceptionally helpful in educating me about the way things work." She turned to look up at him, mouth half open and scepticism on her face.

"Being a friend doesn't matter, I have to ask you some *very serious questions,*" Satiah growled, irritated by this interference.

"I think it would be better if I handled this," Reed said, in a small voice. Satiah gestured at him and the pair went over to a corner for a quick conference. Everyone else stood around awkwardly.

"Reed, the database of that computer *is missing*. The only things I haven't searched in the room *are those two*. We *need* to know..." she began, angry.

"Yes, yes, yes *I know all that!*" Reed insisted, more patiently. "But, if I'm right about them, they *may* help us."

"What aren't you telling me?" she demanded, as he knew she would.

"*Ash is Dreda's son*," Reed stated. Satiah was genuinely shocked. She looked over the top of Reed's head at the man.

"He doesn't look anything like her," she argued, still a little shocked.

"Agreed but he is, *trust me*. Now, I think he might be after the same thing we are and may have valuable information," Reed suggested. Satiah sighed and then nodded.

"You're in charge," she mouthed, a little mockingly.

They returned to talk to the others again.

"Your attendance here betrays your purpose to me, Ash," Reed said, grinning at the taller man. "You're looking for Balan's secret weapon, aren't you?"

"What are you t...?" Ruby began, instantly attempted to deny it as credibly as possible.

"*Don't* play dumb with us," Satiah sneered, silencing Ruby effectively.

"Works two ways, that one, Reed," Ash growled, determined. "I'll even go so far as to assume you are going to suggest an alliance being as we seem to be after the same thing?"

"It seems to make sense that we pool our resources," Reed nodded.

"Who else knows about this?" Ash asked, grim.

"Only Phantom Leader Randal," Reed answered. Satiah didn't mention Rainbow. Reed eyed Ruby speculatively. "*Administrator Ruby*, isn't it?" he asked, at last recognising her. Ruby looked sharply at him.

"Assistant *manager*..." she began to correct him.

"You're a missing person," Reed stated, accusingly. "*You* deleted ten years' worth of financial records." Ruby hung her head and didn't bother to deny it.

"What Ruby *may or may not have done* is irrelevant to any of you," Ash said, defensively. "She's *my* friend and I'm allowing her to show me the galaxy."

"Why did you do it?" Reed asked, huffing slightly as he spoke.

"It was *an accident*," she replied, her voice icy.

"Be that as it may," Satiah cut in, trying to keep them on topic. "It seems we are able to help each other. Do you accede?"

"I agree we are indeed able to help each other. Whether we *will* or not is *still* up for debate," Ash argued, hotly. He did not like humans interfering with his business. Reed was one thing but he didn't like the idea of Satiah and who knew how many others piling on too. This was supposed to be secret! Reed flapped his hand at Satiah distractingly to get her to be unobtrusive. Satiah rolled her eyes: this was *why* she didn't do diplomatic missions!

"Ash, *come on*, you know you can trust me," Reed insisted. Ash crossed his arms and looked down at Ruby.

"What do *you* think?" he asked her. She was more shocked than anyone at being asked. She smiled a little, unable to stop herself flushing red. She tilted her head to the corner and they withdrew to it for their own undisclosed conference.

"Did *you* just ask *me* what *I thought we should do*?" she clarified, excited.

"There's a lot at stake here," Ash said, apparently not hearing her. "But without seeing what's on that database we're stymied." She repeated her question and he scowled down at her. "Yes, of course."

"So you value *my human opinion*?" she asked, not letting it go.

"Will you *just* answer the question?" he hissed.

"Certainly," she shrugged. She cleared her throat. "*What was it again?*"

"Do we or don't we join with them?" he spelt out, exasperated.

She leaned in close to whisper in his ear.

"You said yourself we're running out of places to look and as they are looking for the same thing it does make sense to work together but *I know* what you're *really* thinking," she said.

Genuinely impressed by her grasp of the situation he asked her to tell him what he was apparently thinking.

"You're mainly worried about what will happen *when* we find it. If it was just you and me you could easily force me not to steal it from you or even remember anything about it. But with *all of them involved* that could be much more difficult and you risk losing it to them," she explained. To that he said nothing but ran a hand along her face tenderly. She smiled and waited.

"Reed is clever, *very clever*," he murmured. "Be wary of him, okay?" She nodded fervently. "He will not be above messing with you to get to me."

"Aren't you *friends?*" she asked, confused. "I mean he clearly knows you."

"He was my mother's friend, never mine," Ash insisted. "I know he tries his best to do the right thing but… Even so, don't trust him."

"Does this mean we will work with them?" she asked. He gave her a knowing look.

"What do you think will happen if we say no?" he enquired, meaningfully. Ruby peered around to look at Satiah. Satiah was watching them closely. She smiled at Ruby, not a nice smile, and waved a gloved hand in the way a puppet might. Ruby swallowed and looked away again.

"You don't think they would let us go?" she sighed, depressed.

"Not now *she* knows you have the database," he stated.

"Fine," she said. "Let's do this."

Ash and Ruby moved back towards the others. Expectancy was in the air. Satiah watched them carefully, the way a caged predator might watch her prey.

"*Why not?*" Ash smiled, in enforced cordiality. He extended his hand to Reed.

"I *promise* not to ask," Reed replied, as they shook hands. No one knew what Reed meant by that exactly.

"Which one of you took the database?" Satiah asked, trying to make herself sound more polite.

"I did," Ruby said, pulling it out of her pocket and showing it to everyone.

"Well found," Satiah said, restraining herself from simply taking it from Ruby. Kelvin suddenly moved over to Satiah.

"That ship orbiting the planet has been destroyed," he warned. Satiah's eyes widened.

***

"There's nothing on record about this planet," Oak said, to Tabre. "If it was owned by the Coalition, they no longer have a presence there."

"That's one complication we can forget then," he said, not really caring either way.

"There are no life signs in the ship orbiting the world," Oak reported. "It seems the occupants took a shuttle. Are these people relevant?" She wanted to know if they were in any way connected to Reed. A reasonable question and one he could not answer. They could just be innocent people but… *what were they doing there?* There were of course a group of traditionally plausible answers such as the 'damaged engine' reason or the 'we are lost' answer. But… in this case it would be better if no one saw what happened.

"Any witnesses to what happens here could become a potential loose end," Tabre sighed, irked. He didn't like killing bystanders but sometimes it had to be done. He always reasoned: if *he* didn't do it someone else would.

"Take it out once you've scanned the world," he instructed. He and Conrad exchanged looks while they waited for her next response.

"Scan complete. I have two craft on a landing strip in front of a mining facility of some kind. One matches a description of the ship you are tracking. The other is a landing shuttle of civilian class," she explained. "No life signs are coming from either vessel. It seems likely that if the occupants are alive they are inside the mine complex.

We can destroy the ships easily enough but we cannot get at the targets with a bombing run if they are in the mine."

"Take out the ship in orbit, destroy the ships on the landing platform then go into the mine and kill them," Tabre ordered.

"Sir," she agreed, cutting off.

***

"Did you have a ship in orbit?" Satiah asked Ash.

"...We *did*," he answered, picking up on her choice of word.

"Not anymore," she replied, curtly. "Carlos! Deva! With me!" She sprinted from the control room with Kelvin and the others following them.

"What's happened?" asked Ruby, scared.

"Ah yes," Reed rumbled, hanging his head briefly. "Our Colonial friends have found us again?"

"Your petty factions mean nothing to me," Ash retorted, with contempt.

"People who want to kill us have just destroyed your ship," Reed spelt out, angry. "Does that also mean nothing to you?"

Ash groaned at the inconvenience. Now they would be forced to be on the same ship as Reed and his comrades!

"*No, my clothes!*" gasped Ruby, distressed. "Why would they *do that*? There's no way that ship is dangerous..."

"To stop us and you from leaving," Reed answered, quickly.

"Their next target will be the ships on the landing pad," Ash stated, keeping pace with ease. "Always assuming they're not already destroyed."

"That's most likely where Satiah has gone," Reed said.

"Let's hope she doesn't just leave us here," Ash muttered, critically.

"No, no, you'll understand her better when you get to know her," Reed assured. Ruby pressed herself against Ash and he put his arm around her protectively. But this time he could not tell her for sure that she was safe.

***

The blast on the landing pad took out both the landing shuttle and Satiah's ship. The shuttle disintegrated completely. Burning but still relatively intact, Satiah's ship fell from the landing area and rolled down the mountainside dramatically. It left a long trail down the rock face, marked by some debris, flames and scraping marks. Satiah reached the entrance to the mine with Kelvin right beside her. She was just in time to see the assault craft land and understand what had been done. So much for her exquisite new ship! Instantly she recognised her enemy. Colonial commandos. Well trained and ruthless in reputation. She was glad she'd taken a rifle with her now as she couldn't access anything else. The teenagers caught up and had to shout to be heard over the roar of the landing craft.

"What do we do?" Carlos screamed. Deva had gone pale, knowing she was about to fight what was once her own people.

"We fall back in stages!" Satiah screamed back. "Get down!"

The *rattertatatatatat* of machine lasers made everything else inaudible as they pelted the half open door.

"*Back!*" Satiah bellowed. "Six metre spread! Four volleys and *then back off!*" She knew Carlos understood that formation, and she hoped Deva knew too. Carlos had been supposed to tell her. She did as he did. If Satiah had been in the position of having more time she would have mined the door just to be ironic but alas, as was often the case, there wasn't enough time. Besides, mining a mine was rather a poor display of such dark humour. She winked at Kelvin as he stood on the opposite side of the corridor to her. First there was a silence as the ship's engines cut and the enemy approached the doors. A few seconds for the nods, the few words and then the orders.

A smoke device was hurled in. Satiah had to back off but she had expected this tactic. She rolled away as a few shots tried to get her. Kelvin could see them through the smoke as they approached in a thick formation. When they were pretty much on top of him, he loomed out of the shadows. *Whoosh!* A jet of flame shot out from his arm enveloping the first few rows of commandos with ease. The screaming started. Confusion now reigned as the formation was abruptly ruined by the flames. Satiah poked her head out and let loose three shots at around waist height. She couldn't see what she was hitting so waited for the smoke to clear. Kelvin reached her and slipped to the opposing side again.

"How many?" she asked.

"I got twelve, thirty-eight remaining!" he replied. She swore. They would be hard pressed to kill all of them. Then again, they didn't need to kill them. They only needed to get in the enemy ship and they could escape.

Rapid laser fire struck the walls close by. In accordance with the strategy, she and Kelvin backed off, passing Carlos and Deva as they ran. Carlos looked at across sat Deva. She met his gaze. He smiled tightly. She gave the slightest of nods. Four... three... two... Together they aimed and fired down the corridor. One... two... three... four! As instructed, in unison they retreated, passing Satiah and Kelvin in turn. Satiah looked up at Kelvin. His red eyes were on her, focussing on her brown ones. Two... one! Blasts of flame from Kelvin lit up the corridor as Satiah unleashed her volleys. More screams. Again they followed the pattern, slipping back further into the facility. This time rapid fire chased them with more accuracy. Kelvin was hit at least twice but his thick plating deflected the bolts. Satiah was winged once just below her left knee. She gritted her teeth, ignoring the pain, and slipped to the side once again.

Carlos saw something small tumble out of the darkness.

"*Grenade!*" he barked, grabbing Deva and shoving her into a side corridor.

"But the...!" she began. The explosion sent them both flying onto their hands and knees. A high-pitched resonance deafened them both for a few seconds. His back burning, Carlos rolled to the left and to the right, smothering the flames. She covered him and then chucked his rifle back to him when he was done. They were now cut off from Satiah and the others. In the event of this occurring, Satiah had told him to regroup on Reed.

"*Come on,*" Carlos ordered, tilting his head in the direction to run in. The commandos, sensing an advantage, charged forward, opening fire in both directions. Realising what had happened Satiah nodded to Kelvin.

"Plan B!" she shouted.

They retreated still further until they got to the open area. Turning together they fired back the way they had come. Fire and laser together.

"How are we doing?" she shouted.

"Twenty-one remaining," he answered.

"Better!" she smiled, more determined. They slipped to the side and Satiah dumped her empty rifle carefully on the floor. She took her pistol, got down on all fours and began to crawl slowly and carefully towards their pursuers. She didn't have to go far before she found the first body. Several blasts came close to her and she pulled the corpse over her own body to cover her. The coppery smell of fresh blood was off-putting but tolerable. She lay still, playing dead, partially hidden by the body, waiting.

***

Oak followed the last of her men inside the mine entrance. There was still a lot of shouting and sporadic shooting but it was clear they had forced the opposition back. Annoyingly there were no confirmed kills.

"How's it going?" Tabre's voice asked, in her ear. Oak was tall, over six feet and broad across the shoulders too. She looked almost Amazonian with long brown hair and dark eyes. She checked her computer.

"I've lost almost two thirds of my men, Tabre," she snarled back. "So not great. You said there were only five of them?"

"There *were*," Tabre maintained.

"These guys must be the best of the best then," she hissed. She didn't care that people had died. She only cared because it affected her reputation. Someone was going to pay for this!

***

"I take it things are not going as planned?" Conrad enquired, a little mordant amusement in his voice.

"It seems Oak has encountered greater resistance than anticipated," Tabre admitted, without feeling. "I did warn her who she was potentially facing down there."

"Yes but fifty commandos should be able to handle *one* Phantom!"

Conrad cried, incredulous. Very slowly, and unsettlingly, Tabre turned to face Conrad.

"You're forgetting how brilliant Satiah is. She's not alone either and she's probably been planetside long enough to have at least a little home-field-advantage."

"They were outnumbered ten to one," Conrad said, unnerved.

"They *were*," Tabre repeated, this time in agreement.

***

Tentatively, the group of commandos approached the open area, ignoring the pile-up of bodies. As they passed it, one of the corpses rolled over. Satiah emerged and gunned the group down from behind efficiently. She stood and advanced, taking down two more who, thinking the area was already clear, had made the mistake of letting their guards down. Her plan was simple, secure the ship the commandos had arrived in and use it to escape. More laser fire cut across her path and she returned it with controlled bursts. Aware that she was facing the last of them now, Satiah knew they would be the hardest. Sparks flew from just above her head. She crouched and fired at knee level. A grenade was their response. She dived to the side, rolling down a set of metal stairs painfully.

The explosion sent metal shrapnel everywhere and she hit the floor face down. Her rifle was gone. She stood and pulled out her pistol. Screams from the corridor she'd just left sounded along with the familiar *whoosh* noise of Kelvin's flamethrower. She smiled, guessing Kelvin had got the last of them. She turned the corner and bumped hard into Oak, the collision knocked her pistol from her grip. Satiah instinctively grabbed the rifle Oak was holding, attempting to wrench it away. With an angry snarl, Oak let it go and pushed. Satiah stumbled backwards, and almost lost her balance. Oak followed, her large strides meant that she quickly gained on Satiah. Satiah stopped and aimed the rifle, triumph in her smile. She pulled the trigger. Nothing! Oak held the power pack in her hand up, for Satiah to see, a menacing gleam in her eyes.

In the time it took for it to register that she'd been outsmarted, Oak had closed the remaining distance between them. Satiah ducked the powerful swinging punch that came her way as she dropped the rifle. She kicked Oak in the chest, knocking her back a bit. Satiah leapt at her, going for her face. Oak met her head on and defended herself with unimaginative but formidable blocks. She unleashed a haymaker that, despite only making brief contact, sent Satiah flying to the side. Satiah groaned as she rolled back onto her feet, the side of her head throbbing from the glance of Oak's knuckles. Oak and Satiah both paused to study each other as they circled. To avoid being cornered, Satiah backed off until they had returned to the more open area.

Satiah, increasingly desperate, opened with an aggressive sequence of open-palmed strikes and punches, aiming for Oak's eyes. Oak was tall enough to make it difficult. Oak blocked most and those which were too fast she just took with grunts and groans. Starting to tire, Satiah switched tactic and dropped. She swung her legs and successfully floored the larger woman. Satiah leapt in, in an attempt to strangle Oak. Satiah tried to pin her down with her own body weight while employing a tight headlock. But Oak was too strong. She struggled, writhed and managed to get to her feet. Satiah clung on, squeezing with all her might as Oak rose and slammed Satiah against the wall repeatedly. Satiah refused to let go until Oak sandwiched her against the guardrail overlooking the chasm.

The bar dug into the small of Satiah's back, making her think she was about to get her spine snapped. Breathless, Satiah let go and rolled away, thinking frantically what she could try next. Oak pulled a short blade out from somewhere and advanced towards her. Satiah dodged the swipes and stabs but was unable to counter. In an expert move, Satiah kicked upwards, disarming Oak and sending the blade spinning off into the darkness. She leapt in again and punched Oak as hard as she could in the face. Oak shrugged off the blow and aggressively propelled Satiah backwards. Satiah came to an instant and disorientating stop as the back of her head crashed into the metal wall. She fell forward onto her elbows and knees, straightaway trying to rise again to move. As she looked to see where Oak was, Oak's fist descended into the side of her head, flooring Satiah again. Dazed, she was unable to coordinate or struggle effectively.

Oak grabbed Satiah's flailing arm, hauled her up and struck her again. Blood ran down the side of Satiah's face, this time her own. Only semiconscious now, Satiah feebly reached for anything she could use as a weapon. Oak lifted Satiah off the floor entirely, teeth gritted and advanced towards the guardrail with the intention of hurling Satiah down to her death. Satiah couldn't move and suddenly realised she was about to die. In a last ditch effort she clutched hold of the railing in a death grip. She dropped a knee into Oak's nose. There was a crunch and then Satiah crashed onto the floor as Oak screeched in pain. Her nose was broken. The response, the still prone Satiah was unable to prevent, was the boot she got to the stomach. She let go of the railing and curled up, trying to breathe.

Furious, Oak found an old mining tool on the floor and raised it to strike Satiah with. For a moment, for Satiah, everything was in slow motion. This was it. Her skull was about to be smashed in and her brains smeared across the floor. She'd be dead. She could hardly move and even if she could, Oak was too strong. But that was when a metal hand caught Oak's in mid swing. Kelvin! He was there. In a move of blinding speed, he wrenched the arm backwards, relieving Oak of the mining tool and snapping her arm in the process. He had no need to use the tool himself and began a lethal bludgeoning attack. Oak could not stand before it; no human could no matter how big they were. The second hit took her out completely. She collapsed, fatally wounded.

Kelvin did not continue the attack; it was pointless and would not help his mistress. He knelt next to Satiah, his red eyes ascertaining just how badly she was hurt. An investigating needle embedded itself in her skin as he ran scans. She awaited his summary, marvelling that she was still there to be analysed.

"No contusions," he said, at last. She sighed with relief but her body was still a bit useless. "Brain trauma acquired is within accepted human tolerance guidelines. You will recover."

"...How many are left?" she managed to articulate, still trying to fight the dizziness.

"This female was the last," Kelvin said, as he helpfully pulled her into a sitting position. She groaned, as a fresh wave of discomfort spread through her battered body.

"It is possible that more are on the way," he advised, as was correct. That got her up. Using him to lean on, she dragged herself onto her feet and swayed a little before regaining proper equilibrium.

She raised her communicator to her lips.

"Carlos?" she asked, hopefully.

"Here," he said, quickly. "What do you need?"

"It's time for us to leave," she said, wincing as pain stabbed at her again. "We will meet you at the Commandos' ship."

"Right," he responded. Satiah and Kelvin headed back down the corridors towards the entrance.

"I was expecting to encounter Tabre among them," Satiah admitted, a little relieved.

"There is no one else, I am running constant scans," he assured.

"Good, it won't take them long to figure out their task force is dead. *When they do...*" She trailed off. She didn't need to elaborate further.

They met the others halfway there and even Ash did a double take on seeing Satiah.

"Wow, you look like crap," Carlos said, not bothering to hide his reaction. She was covered in blood and at least some of it was her own.

"Believe me, how bad *I look* is but a fraction of how bad *I feel*," Satiah growled, with a pained smile. They reached the landing pad, the wind whipping around them as they dashed across the open space and into the other ship.

Carlos and Deva took the precaution of searching the ship while Satiah led the others to the control room. The ship was pretty basic but that suited them well enough. It was heavily armoured too. That might give any pursuers, Tabre included, pause. Satiah was annoyed at the loss of her new ship *Vulture* so soon after acquiring it. Randal would be sure to have a few cutting remarks in store for her. All that, though, was of secondary concern, first thing was to get away from that place!

"We will need to report in and make a stop somewhere more civilised," Satiah insisted, making a mental list. "While there we can compare notes and decide what to do next."

"While *you* have a rest," Reed said, eyeing her. She thought about pretending that he was mistaken but decided against it and simply nodded.

***

It had been three minutes and no more sound came from the planet. Conrad eyed Tabre speculatively. Tabre was running scans.

"*Fifty* commandos…" he finally said, softly. He shook his head. "She's proving as tenacious as she is brilliant."

"Like you said, she *obviously* had help. The people from that other ship for example," Conrad said, trying to explain the total defeat.

"Oak *was* highly recommended," Tabre acknowledged, with the grim verb. "I cannot find much fault with the strategy."

"Be that as it may, *you* have failed yet again to kill Reed. It seems to me you are becoming increasingly distracted by obsessing over Satiah and her counter measures," Conrad criticised. Tabre took a deep breath, forcing himself to remain calm. "The Director will not be pleased."

"What would you have done differently?" he asked, coolly. He knew Conrad had no answer to that.

***

Carlos was piloting the ship with Deva working as co-pilot. Reed, Ash and Ruby sat in silence behind them.

"Running a scan," Carlos explained, pointlessly. "Can't *see* any more ships."

"They are likely to be cloaked," Reed sighed, his tone light to prevent his words being misinterpreted as a jibe.

"True," he concurred.

"Do you still have the database?" Deva asked, turning to face Ruby. Ruby patted her pocket to make sure before nodding. Ash and Ruby had hardly said a word since take off but they were both paying close attention to everything.

"The nearest *safe place* I can think of is Forlores Alpha," Carlos said, eyeing the screen in front of him.

"It's a *Coalition* world," stated Deva, eyeing him.

"I'm *not* going to a Federation world, we are not *that* desperate!" he argued, seriously.

"My point *is*, we are in a military Federation ship," Deva said, calmly.

Carlos thought about it.

"Ionar 12 *is closer*," she pointed out, casually.

"But it's *Federation*," he replied, shrugging.

"We are in *a Federation ship*," she repeated, starting to get impatient. They both turned to face those behind them.

"*Reed?*"

"Ionar 12 will be fine," he said, smiling knowingly. "Satiah will not be happy about it but I know a few people from there and they do owe me a huge favour."

"Isn't Ionar 12 a bit of a wilderness? I heard it was devastated in the Common Protectorate War?" Ruby asked, sincerely.

"Actually that destruction occurred *before* that war started," Reed answered, mysteriously.

"Ionar 12 it is," Carlos sighed, almost sadly. He caught Deva grinning at him. "*What?*"

"*You know what*," she mewed back at him. Carlos sighed in defeat before eyeing Reed.

"You know they will be following us again," Carlos stated. "They will find us and we're going to need a new ship."

"I know," Reed agreed. "*Don't worry about it*. We need a place where we can sit about for a while, talk it out and then work it out. We can't do that on the run." Even Deva seemed to have obvious cynicism.

"Hey," Carlos whispered, to her. "I'm starting to think this guy is nuts!"

"I agree," she nodded, discreetly. "Why would he be okay with Tabre still following us?"

"Maybe he's got some plan or something," Carlos sighed, letting it go. "Like before with the Sisterhood."

"He'd better have."

***

Satiah closed her eyes as Kelvin continued to spray her wounds. Some healed within seconds. Others took several minutes to graze over. Then he injected her with a combination of infection protection and painkilling agents. Finally his metal hands landed to rest on her shoulders. Her hands landed on top of them and squeezed.

"Thank you, Kelvin," she said, softly. He began to massage her shoulders and upper back. "That's nice," she breathed, her eyes half closing. Her neck relaxed completely and her head slowly lolled forward.

"I have been analysing your mental health since you activated me," he said, in his typical drone. She grunted lazily. "You are exhibiting signs of stress."

"You do too much of that," she smiled, almost flirtatiously. Her hand snaked back onto his metal hand and affectionately stroked it.

"Humans are social animals; you are devoid of common contact. All your interactions are strictly enforced by your occupation," he went on. Her laugh was low and husky.

"Are you saying I'm a workaholic?" she responded.

"I am advising you to interact more with humans to improve your mental health," he answered. She frowned and turned to face him.

"I don't remember installing *all that*. Have you been updating yourself correctly?" she asked, almost accusingly. A communicator bleeped and Kelvin handed it her immediately.

"It's Rainbow."

"Yes, hello," she answered, a little distracted.

"Is everything okay? I tried to call earlier," he asked. Satiah didn't answer immediately. She watched Kelvin speculatively. She began to realise what she had been doing more and more lately. She was treating him like a person, like a friend and, most creepily of all, like a romantic possibility. He was a servant, a tool and a protector but most important of all he was a computer. She knew she had been doing it and she wasn't even sure why but for brief moments she'd been forgetting that he was a metal lump and thinking of him in terms of... sex.

The realisation didn't freak her out so much as it amused her. She ran a hand through her hair and fought back the laughter. She wasn't embarrassed or ashamed; after all *she* was the only one who knew it had even happened. Just a fantasy. And, doing what he did as a protector, he was protecting her from hurting herself. As a computer he could never truly love her as he couldn't feel anything technically. So, out of *concern* for her, he'd *rejected her*? Again the ironies and peculiar double standards tugged at her twisted sense of humour. She supposed that maybe her humour wasn't the only thing that had got a little twisted recently. At sixty-five, with Linctus lotion, she looked, felt and physically was held in her mid-twenties. She still had a good hundred years left...

"Sorry, I was busy," she apologised, seriously. "What is it?" *Concentrate, Satiah, for God's sake or you may not have a hundred* seconds, she chastised herself.

"Malcolm is under surveillance, nothing untoward do far, and have you had any luck with Division Sixteen?" he asked. She sighed. She had, up until then, forgotten all about Division Sixteen.

"That's good and I'm still negotiating," she answered, temporising. "...How is Randal?"

"Frustrated and stressed... so pretty much normal, why?" he asked.

"Just curious," she sighed, her mind on other things again. "I need everything you can get me on *Ruby*, a missing administrator."

"What?" he asked, surprised by the subject change.

"That's right," she smiled. "Is there a reward for bringing her in?"

A silence began while he checked it out. She examined her filthy fingernails self-consciously for a moment. Lordy, she'd really let herself go recently.

"Five hundred thousand," he answered, casually. "Why? Have you seen her? *Have the Sisterhood taken her?*"

"It doesn't matter," she sighed, disappointed. "Someone was asking me about her that was all and I wondered why."

"Oh, I see," he replied, believing her. Five hundred thousand Essps was not worth Satiah's trouble although it may come in useful if she needed to extract anything from their new friends.

"Keep checking this Operation Burning Bridge and..."

"Oh, one more thing... a message for you arrived earlier. I don't know what it means but you seem to have sent it to yourself,"

Rainbow explained. She closed her eyes. She knew what was coming. "It says, *the trial has started.*"

"That's it?" she asked, pretending to be expectant. It was, like she knew it was. She knew exactly what it meant. "Thanks, talk soon."

She disconnected and eyed Kelvin. Did computers understand awkward silences? Probably being as he had worked out what else had been occurring in her mind.

"Bring Carlos in here," she instructed, calmly. He headed out. She stared into the middle-distance, thoughtful. This had just grown a whole new level and she needed to be at her best, especially with Tabre yapping at her heels. Kelvin returned with a confused-looking Carlos.

"Yeah?" he asked, eyeing her. He thought for a moment she was about to tell him her injuries were worse than they looked and she needed help.

"*Ash and Ruby*... they have information we need and until I say, we cannot trust them. I need you and Deva to choose one to keep an eye on," she instructed. Carlos knew better than to ask if Reed was okay with that. Satiah always assumed guilt until innocence was proven and that in itself wasn't always a bad thing. He stared at his battered-looking teacher casually. Something about her had changed... He couldn't figure out what it was.

"Will do," he nodded. "Are you feeling better?"

"Cuts and bruises," she dismissed. He nodded and turned to go. "Carlos?" she asked, in a curious tone. He turned to face her again. "Do you find me in any way attractive?" she asked, bluntly. He paused, caught out by the question.

"...Well... while your classical beauty *does* enthral me, I fear though I *lack* the maturity in years to do you proper justice," he answered, carefully. "*Besides, Deva would kill me.*" She laughed.

"Maybe you are more suited to diplomacy than I thought. Don't panic, I'm not interested in you but..." she paused and eyed Kelvin. "It has recently been pointed out to me that I may be missing certain opportunities." Carlos frowned and followed her gaze. Upon only seeing Kelvin standing there he looked back at her, not getting it.

"Did you get hit in the head again?" he asked, wincing with sympathy.

"Yeah," she sighed, deciding to let it go. She eyed the chair and waved at him to get him to leave. Carlos did, nodding to Kelvin as he passed the big robot. Instead of going for the chair like normal, Satiah eyed the bed speculatively. She was suddenly, painfully aware of Kelvin staring at her. His whirring seemed almost irritating rather than soothing like normal.

"I can take it from here, Kelvin. Thank you and goodnight," she said, hoping he would take the hint. Obligingly he did.

"You have five hours before we arrive," he said, as he departed.

"Thank you, Kelvin," she said, in a similar monotone to his. No, *its*! *Not his*! It was just that kind of personification of all things inanimate that had most likely got her so confused in the first place! The room seemed so soundless suddenly now he was gone. A little uncertainly, she stripped off and then slid between the sheets of the bed. She sat there for a moment considering the implications. Lie down, adjust pillow, and close eyes. Yes, that was how the routine went. She slid her gun under the opposite pillow and closed her eyes. This was going to take some getting used to.

***

Director Ro was in high spirits after the rally. The President, despite his initial concerns had been first mollified and then completely segregated from all other lines of command. The only person who now reported directly to him was Ro herself. Everyone one else was either under her, paid off or dead. All she had to do now was get rid of Raykur himself and then *she* would be the President of the Colonial Federation. There would be no challenge to her in the ballot box, hell there would be no ballot box! She sipped at her wine and gazed out happily as the parades went on. Her communicator went off and she answered.

"Yes," she said, her voice cold and calm in equal measure, much appeased by the wine.

"Ma'am. It seems we have a problem with some officers in the navy. Do you have time to talk now?" She smiled in a sinister way.

"Certainly."

PART THREE

Surplus Distrust

Space. Emmeff Centre was not a planet but it was a place. The name itself was the combination of two letters from an archaic alphabet of a culture long gone but not forgotten. Emmeff. Emm and eff. M and F. Military and Fleet Centre. The spatial rendezvous point of the Colonial navy. Located at a position of relative equidistance between the Colonial capital planet, the Coalition frontier, SS (Space Station) Bastian and the planet Nedlessar, it was a place of perpetual repositioning. It was far from being an undisclosed subject but it was rarely spoken of and so did often get dragged into conspiracy theories. Destroyer *Warrior*, a warship of the Colonial Federation, had been given clearance for its approach. Observing, from the main viewport of the bridge, Captain Tristram and Lieutenant Wester had a great view of the Colonial navy as it massed its forces.

It would have truly been a wondrous sight. All those ships. Such a testament to sustained military investment. But the men had a task to occupy them. There was one specific ship they were on the lookout for. A destroyer like theirs. *Prevalence*. Captain Erica Moxin's ship. If she was not already there, they would have to wait for her to arrive before they began their secret *undertaking*. Before they committed high treason by not only mutinying but turning their guns on their fellow officers. They would do this heinous crime for a greater good. A higher purpose. Wester found himself reflecting on the strange philosophical mechanics of the situation. They would do something *bad* to ensure something else *bad* didn't happen and thus achieve something *good*. Of course it was up to context as to how bad their action would be. It would be down to individual interpretation to dictate the type of morality at work in this curiously foggy area.

As they had predicted, despite the great number of ships present, no one had their shields up or their weapon systems active. There was no logical reason for any ship to do so in this *apparently safe harbour*. As soon as the shooting started, they would all start to employ them but that would take time. Even the most disciplined crews could only go so fast. Forty-three seconds was the record for an inert ship to achieve full battle stations. Every single one of those seconds would count. The attractive flight officer that had so taken Wester's fancy earlier appeared next to them and touched her hat while waiting to speak. Both Tristram and Wester returned the gesture.

"Sirs, I have a priority message for the CO, broadcasted on frequency nineteen," she stated, her voice low and confident. Frequency nineteen was one of the higher ones of the spectrum and typically used for urgent last-minute communications.

Tristram nodded and went over to the communications booth. Wester caught himself staring at the flight officer. Her auburn hair and dark eyes were hard for him to ignore. Her figure was slender, shapely and capable looking. Her dark blue uniform complimented it too. Then she caught him, their eyes connected. Wester reacted quickly, touching his hat again to her.

"Very good, Flight Officer," he said, more stiffly than he had intended to. She returned the gesture, span on her heels and returned to her workstation. What *was* her name? He caught the scent of her perfume and… *Come on, Wester, stay on the level!* he implored himself. Given what they intended to do, he badly needed to stay focussed. Tristram was listening in to something with an earpiece. His face seemed to change and become… harder. He replaced the device without a word and walked over to Wester.

"She's here," he said, his voice so low even Wester hardly heard him. Tristram was talking about Captain Moxin, their only ally out there. The next stage was to position their ships in the best places to do the most damage. Wester issued the instruction as casually as he could but his heartbeat was already twice normal speed. The thing Tristram was going to do next was where it was most dangerous. He was about to tell his crew what they were going to do. He had to let them know eventually, of course, and he needed them to work together. Tristram had a loyal crew but what he was about to ask of them would severely test that loyalty. Wester kept his distance from Tristram as the Captain pulled out a microphone. Tristram took a deep breath and made eye contact with Wester. Wester didn't know why he did it but he touched his hat to him. *Yes sir, it is time.*

"All personnel, this is your Captain speaking. I require your immediate attention as what I have to say next will affect the futures of you all," he began, his voice ominous. The command deck was usually quiet anyway but now a deathly hush descended as everyone stared at him.

"Most of you have served under me for a few years now. A good deal of you have shed blood for me and put your lives on the line. I know you wouldn't all do that out of only duty. I know you did it out of loyalty. Loyalty to your Captain. Today, I... *We* have a chance to change a dangerous trend. Now we are here, we have an opportunity to preclude a war that we all know in our hearts we don't want," Tristram said. He'd spent many hours agonising over these words, a long time switching them around or swapping them for similar ones. The silence continued as one or two people stood to watch him more closely.

"Our duty to the Federation means sometimes we must protect it *even against itself*," he said, echoing Ro's words. "You can't fight a war without ships and ships can't move without engines." Now he was repeating Wester's phrasing. "What I have planned to do will be considered by some to be treason. But if saving lives is treasonous then label me a traitor now and I'll accept it without comment."

"Sir?" asked one of the officers to his left. Tristram turned. The man had a gun trained on him. The insider. Everyone else noticed too and a few gasps sounded. Tristram was sad but not surprised. He'd predicted that such a person would be on board somewhere.

"Officer Soomit," addressed Tristram, his tone turning icy. "You disagree? *Puppet?*" He spat the word to indicate his hatred for the man's true loyalty.

"I was told you had been turned," he growled, threateningly. "I didn't believe it until now. You shame yourself with your words. *You are under arrest.*" He began a cautious approach. Tristram ignored him and carried on talking.

"If you want to be puppets of tyranny forevermore, it's very simple, all you have to do now is *ignore me*," Tristram went on. A bead of sweat inched its way between his shoulders.

"Enough," hissed Soomit, arming the pistol. A few more officers were standing up now, unsure what to do.

"Put that gun down," Tristram ordered, grimly. His gaze was unflinching, wrought from bravery. "You *know* what I'm saying is right. You understand that war with the Coalition is unwinnable. You recognise that by simply *following orders* you will most likely be killing the ones you love."

"*Ignore him!*" barked Soomit. "War has not even been declared and I know my duty, *sir*. You have five seconds to surrender command to me."

"Remember what we have been through together as men and women of the Federation!" shouted Tristram, still talking to everyone. "Remember you are *not just tools*! You are soldiers and so you have a moral obligation to think on your orders and actions!"

"Four!"

"Remember where courage and loyalty are to be found! Remember that we stand together!"

"Three!" Soomit was less than three paces from him now, a furious glare on his face.

"I ask you now, all of you, to join me in *my war* against the dictatorship of *Ro Tammer*!"

"Two."

"She is the *true* enemy of the Federation!"

Without even counting down to one, Soomit fired. Tristram was hit in the chest and remained standing after staggering back from the force of the shot. He just stared blankly ahead, seeming to be dead on his feet.

"*Captain!*" wailed someone. "*No!*" Soomit spun, trying to defend himself but three shots converged on him simultaneously. Wester hit him in the chest. The flight officer hit him in the knee and someone else got him in the face. There was a scramble as several people rushed forward to help Tristram. He was lying on his back, having at last fallen, still just about lucid.

"*Shut up!*" yelled someone. "He's trying to speak." Wester crouched next to Tristram, trying to see if there was any chance the older man might live. There wasn't.

"You see," he gasped, staring into Wester's eyes. "Ro and her followers have no loyalty and you all do. *That makes you better.* Now... I'm dead. I appoint Lieutenant Wester as Acting Captain." Slowly Tristram pulled his rank bar away and handed it to Wester.

Wester's hand shook as he took it.

"You will now serve him as you have served me before..." Tristram continued, now very weak. He was losing his fight against death but battling valiantly until the end.

"You will follow his orders, and he will stand by you," Tristram said next. "*For... the... Federation.*" He slumped, gone. Dying had never been part of the plan at all! A tear ran down Wester's face, shock and rage vying for dominance of his mind.

"Sir?" called the flight officer next to him. It was her. The one whose name he didn't yet know. One look in her eyes snapped him back to reality. They were all looking to him. The microphone was still on, the whole ship was waiting, having heard everything, for his orders.

He swallowed, and removed his hat slowly, placing it on Tristram's chest, concealing the wound, as a sign of respect and gratitude.

"You heard your Captain," Wester said, summoning a strength he hadn't known that he had. "I will stand by you as I stood by him. For the Federation *we will now fight!*" A ragged cheer rose. "*Battle stations!* Activate the battle computer." He handed the rank bar Tristram had given him to the flight officer. Without *that* she couldn't activate it. She didn't hesitate and darted off with a speed that seemed incredible. A thought suddenly struck him: he needed a second-in-command. A Lieutenant.

"Flight Officer!" he shouted, after her. "I'm grading you Lieutenant!"

"Sir!" she screeched back, busy with the computer.

A claxon began. Everywhere, pilots rushed to their fighters. Gunners hurried to their stations. Weapon and shield systems came online. On a giant screen in front of him Wester could see it all. *Now, just like the simulation, don't mess it up.* They were at the correct position now. A concentrated strike across the stern of the ships would cripple maybe twenty ships if they were lucky. Where was Moxin? Her ship had not moved with them as it had been supposed to. A problem? Wester ought to suppose that, like what had just happened on his ship, Erica Moxin may have been assassinated. To think otherwise would be too risky. Tristram did receive a last-minute communication on frequency nineteen before he had died. What had been said? Some last-minute change? Somehow Ro had found out about their plan and had taken steps to stop them? *Simmons!* Had he betrayed them after all? There was no time for that as he observed some of the other ships starting to show signs of alerting to the danger. Targets were allocated, and, as was part of the plan, the destroyer accelerated.

The sudden burst of speed made Wester reflexively clutch at the guardrail but his eyes never left the screen. The other ships were starting to move as well but they were too close together to perform any clever evasions. Despite the situation, the apparent political clash of allegiances, the crew around him seemed as animated at the prospect of *this battle* as he imagined they would be if they were facing the Coalition forces. The surge forward was accompanied by a great shout of spirit from the crew. Wester did nothing to silence them. Part of him still felt like the newbie. A stranger among a group of old comrades already united in blood and purpose. Favoured by their Captain or not, he didn't want to do anything that might upset them.

"Open fire!" he bellowed. The great guns responded instantly. At full power, their bolts cut across and into the backs of the ships neatly lined up. Chewing through the armour like ravenous animals, they took out the engines completely. Explosions occurred as fuel and power cells alike ignited. Wester didn't let anything distract him; his eyes were firmly fixed on the other ships. The ones they could not get at. They were breaking formation, moving in to attack him.

Twenty seconds! Frantic and confused messages were being beamed at them from a dozen different ships. Some demanded explanations, others requesting him to cease fire and still others threatening to fire back unless he desisted. He ignored them all.

"*Navigator*! Fourteen degrees cape storm!" he ordered, giving him a course to follow. He would send them around, down and looping back to use the crippled ships as cover. The move was dangerous as, in theory, it exposed them completely to the paralysed ships' batteries. They couldn't move but they *could* fire. Wester was gambling, however, that they would be so busy trying to get out of the way or control damage that they would fail to act in time.

The ship swooped down and around with speed. Tristram had told him that his crew were good but Wester hadn't really believed that at the time. Unlike many of the newly commissioned crews and ships, Tristram and his troops had seen action before and clearly remembered how to behave while in it.

"Set course to abscond!" Wester instructed, knowing the coordinates had been pre-set by Tristram before… before he died.

"Very good, sir!"

"Sir!" Alarms blared as their shields started taking hits from the approaching ships. Still Captain Moxin had apparently taken no action. She must have been betrayed too. Fighters were coming at them now from at least two directions. The ship lurched after a particularly powerful deflection.

That was when they shot away, escaping the surrounding bombardment and disappearing into the depths of space. A place often used as a metaphor for the unknown, a place marked by the glimmering specs of distant stars. A place where, for many, all this began and a place where it was easy to hide. Wester still remained where he was, not allowing himself to relax or be seen to relax.

"Damage report?" he asked, crisply.

"None and no casualties," replied a flight officer. "The virtue of surprise gifted us that much, sir."

"…Very good," Wester said, sighing with relief. The flight officer was still standing there when the Lieutenant reached them, still breathing hard. She touched her hat to him. As second-in-command now she no doubt had many questions. And... he still didn't know her name! He tipped his hat slowly.

"Sir... what do you want done with *them*?" she asked, pointing to the bodies of Tristram and Soomit. He paused, thinking about it.

"...If you want we can keep Tristram on ice until we have more time to decide, sir," she suggested, her keen eyes evaluating her new Captain. "Soomit can take a walk out of an airlock, *if you so order, sir*."

"Y-yes," he stuttered, trying to make his mind work again. "Good idea, very good." She turned to obey when he caught her arm. "*Sorry*," he apologised quickly. "It may be worth searching his body and cabin too... *just as a precaution*. He may have installed surveillance equipment or homing devices." Her eyes widened in comprehension and a small smile curled her lips making her look even more radiant.

"Very good, sir, I will order a ship-wide sweep. If there are any such devices on board, *we will find them*."

"Very good, please remember to check the individual fighter craft too," he advised. She touched her hat but didn't move, he realised he was still holding her arm. He let go instantly and straightened, hoping that he wasn't blushing.

***

Satiah shifted in her sleep, finding better comfort on her back. The ship was almost silent. The room was still and quiet, only the low distant hum of the engines could be perceived. Rolling out slowly from under the bed silently, Tabre emerged. He stood slowly, looming over the still-sleeping Satiah, gun at the ready. His eyes flickered as he checked the room once again. Nothing, no one was around. He stared down at Satiah and leaned in closer. She didn't wake or even move. He extended a gloved hand to grip her throat. She sighed and shifted a little as he made contact with her skin. Then he leaned in closer and kissed her lips strongly, his tongue forcing its way past her teeth to taste hers.

Satiah sat bolt upright with a shriek. Gun in her hand, arm raised, seeking targets. Nothing! *Breathe! Just a dream! Just a dream. Breathe.* Sweat covered her skin, making the blanket feel clammy. She let out a breath and slumped back down again in the bed as Kelvin entered. He'd heard his mistress from outside and had entered to investigate the apparent disturbance.

"Is everything satisfactory? You seem distressed," he enquired, scanning. *Distressed?* For a moment there, she'd been positively terrified. Worst still was the possibility that the missions may no longer be enough to hold back her nightmares. She might need to seek professional help after all. If the missions were no longer enough to take her mind off...

"*Satiah?*" he persisted, her lack of response concerning him.

She glanced across at him. He knew all about the nightmares she had about her mother trying to kill her and her childhood. But *this!* This was disturbing in a completely new and horrible way. She couldn't resist the temptation to check under her bed as if to catch Tabre laying there. Nothing, there was no one there of course; Kelvin would have detected it if there were. Would she have had the dream if he had been in the room with her while she slept? It was the first time since she had built him that he had not been there monitoring the room. She shook herself, reminding herself of what that had nearly led to.

"*I'm fine,*" she growled, wrapping the blankets around herself almost warily. "How far out are we?"

"Fifty-three minutes," he responded.

"Thank you, Kelvin."

She treated herself to a long shower to try to collect her thoughts. She was in a Colonial ship that she and the others had stolen after being attacked on an abandoned mining world. She'd nearly been killed and now they had two new friends. Ash and Ruby. Ash was apparently, according to Reed, Dreda's son. While Ruby was a low-grade missing person who was on the run after deleting ten years' worth of financial records. She'd claimed it had been an accident but Satiah's naturally suspicious mind doubted that. If it had been intentional, what had she been trying to hide? A record of transaction? Perhaps. Details of investment or shares? Possibly.

None of that had any real bearing on Satiah's purpose, however. She, under Reed's command, was to find out if a secret weapon existed or not. And, if it did, destroy it. She still needed to interview the man she had rescued from a space station the best part of a week previously. Freed from the influence of the Sisterhood of the Light, presumably he would now be able to talk to her. Then she would know more about this mysterious new material that had been discovered on the mining world they had just escaped from. Also, that database Ruby had might contain some answers. Reed wanted to talk it over when they got to someplace safe and Satiah was already preparing the things she would say. Plus... recently she'd discovered that she needed to change. Human contact? Something about that made her shiver.

She came out of the shower and eyed her old clothes disdainfully. They were so... unsuitable now. She began to search the cabin she was in for some more clothes. She found a woman's brown combat suit and decided she would have it. Its previous owner was presumably dead and gone so therefore she would be unlikely to need it again. It was close fitting and snug. Thicker patches were everywhere, thin sheets of armour cleverly added for extra protection. She adjusted the size and slipped her gun into the holster.

She stared at herself in the mirror. Typically she kept her long red hair pinned down to keep it out of the way. Now though, she released it and brushed it briefly to create her own version of the asymmetric cut. She gazed at herself, evaluative. She'd not worn any kind of make-up for years and examined the few types that there were available to her speculatively. She settled for some light shading around her eyes only. Sparkly blue. This was the first time in a long time so she didn't want to overdo it.

Carlos looked up as Satiah entered the control room.

"Nice look," he remarked.

"Fancied a change," she murmured, sitting in the co-pilot's chair. "Where are the others?"

"All sleeping, except for Deva, she's watching the corridor," he replied. Satiah frowned. She'd not seen her. He saw the look. "There's a room to the left with cameras." Satiah grunted in acknowledgment. Carlos looked tired and kept yawning. He'd only been awake constantly since hours before they had arrived on the mining world. Maybe fourteen hours. She was about to ask him why he was so tired but then remembered that he shared his cabin with Deva and didn't bother.

"Have a rest," she instructed, irritated by the constant yawns and fidgeting. He was so tired he only nodded and slipped away.

Satiah took control of the ship and wasn't at all astonished when Reed slid in to join her.

"How are you feeling?" he asked, by way of greeting. "Do you want me to make any comments about how lovely your hair looks or not?" She closed her eyes in restrained frustration. Maybe this had not been the best time to change her guise.

"What do you want?" she sighed, being blunt. He produced one of his best enchanting smiles.

"Well, I wanted to talk to you about a few things. *Just a few things*. Firstly I've made some calls, *called in a few favours*, and accommodation in the main city *has* already been acquired so you don't need to worry about getting us in or finding us a den. I have also taken the liberty, *on your behalf of course*, of coming up with an idea I know you'll like. We must get a new ship. *Naturally* we can't have this one around as it's a beacon for trouble. And I don't just mean Tabre. All of this means, I need you and your little helpers to pop out and find us a new ship," Reed explained. She raised her eyebrows. Reed shifted gears strangely.

"*While...?*" she asked, knowingly. There was no bite in her tone even though hours ago there might have been. She found that she didn't want to bother Reed any more than she could help it.

"While Ash and I sit down, *with Kelvin listening in, of course*, and talk about our mutual problems," he finished.

"...I concur," she nodded, inwardly amazed that she felt no resentment. "We *will* have to move on fairly swiftly, Tabre is still after us and I don't want to be cornered while on a *Colonial world*."

"Ah *yes* but it may take some time deciding where to move on to," Reed said, as usual sounding so reasonable.

"...It may," she allowed, and then she smiled. "I *suppose* we won't be getting that mission file anytime soon?" He gave an obviously fake laugh. His hand landed softly on her shoulder and he squeezed gently.

"I think we both knew that *no such file exists*, Satiah, nor will it, nor should it," he chuckled. "But I'm sure *you're* past the point now where you think we need one?"

She shrugged, not committing. A sneaky smile tugged at her lips but she fought it down.

"As long as *Randal knows* you are still supervising me, I suppose the paperwork is *but a detail*," she said, smoothly. "My manager isn't very patient."

"I'll talk to him when we reach our safe house," Reed promised, dismissively. The term safe house had two main definitions to someone like Satiah. First, a location *with a roof* prepared by your organisation or yourself previously that would be ideal for laying low in for long periods. Second, a place that would be your base but was not safe at all and not somewhere you should linger if you wanted to live. He tilted his head, awaiting her response. She was deep in thought wondering what was awaiting them.

"Yes," she said, finally. "What's our funding situation like?"

"Money isn't a problem," he shrugged. She nodded.

***

Ionar 12 was not a tourist-friendly place. Colonial and, since a long time ago, it was mainly wasteland. Once it had been a thriving place but immortals had attacked the world, massacring virtually everyone. Since then, rebuilding had been slow and hesitant. There were two main settlements. One in the north and the other in the east. A vast memorial to those who had been killed was an icon of the world and well known in anti-war societies. A giant silver cube, its surface made up of billions of squares. In each square was the name of one of the victims. It was over fifty storeys high and several hundred metres wide. Inside was a museum that was apparently free. That was in the northern settlement: *Palter*. Palter was newer, richer and smaller than its eastern counterpart: *Pilter*.

Pilter was larger, poorer but much more accepting of visitors. It was to this settlement that Reed insisted they went. Satiah ran scans. The equipment was not much compared with what *Vulture* had sported but it was good enough for this job. Slum dwellings on the outskirts. Businesses and everything else in the middle. She brought them in to land.

"This is Ionar 12 security patrol," came a voice, over the communicator. "State your name and business here." Satiah put on her best Colonial accent which, due to lots of practice over the years, was very convincing.

"Afternoon," she smiled, into the microphone. "My name is Kim and I'm here to track down my family. Also I heard about the museum, is it true that it is free?"

"Your ship is cleared to land, bay twelve," replied the man, not interested in her small talk. He disconnected.

Following the instructions the flight computer gave her, Satiah began a leisurely landing. The sun was bright and she eyed the desert she was flying over sourly. It stretched in all directions, making her feel thirsty. That settled it, the first chance she got, she was going to taste some of the local drinks. At last, on the horizon, the first signs of Pilter appeared dark grey against the golden yellow of the sands.

"*City incoming*," she warned everyone. "Anyone been here before?" Her tone was doubtful. A chorus of negatives answered her. She sighed. No guides! Perfect! She reset the diodes and, just out of habit, reset the engine fuel count for the automatic refuelling system to start... even though they had no intention of using the ship again.

"I do have some directions," Reed said, with one of his eccentric grins.

"Let me guess the first one. Avoid the desert?" Deva scoffed.

"Close, *avoid the local security*, they are notoriously corrupt," Reed explained, enthusiastic. "So presumably they are not beyond taking advantage of tourists."

She brought them in to land smoothly, the combat ship took up most of the small hangar and thus made the procedure a little more tricky than usual. It was also hard to try not to look like such an accomplished pilot so she deliberately made her moves jerky and awkward. She supposed this planet was a place where they went without comforts instead of borrowing them. From experience she knew that every desert was different and just because you have survived in one, it didn't necessarily bequeath you with the skills you may need in another. She stood and nodded to Reed.

"You can be my weird uncle who is the reason for me being here," Satiah said, to him.

"*Uncle?*" he coughed, frowning deeply with umbrage. Deva giggled. As a couple Satiah and Reed headed outside to confront the dock master or whatever his equivalent might be. Kelvin accompanied them; all weapons had been concealed except for

Satiah's pistol which remained in its holster in plain view. It would look strange if they had nothing at all.

A circular computer floated over to them.

"Welcome to Ionar 12," it buzzed, the colonial twang programmed into its light chirpy tone. "Before you leave the shipyard, you must be processed. Is this your first visit to this world?" Again, using her best accent, Satiah answered.

"Yes, sorry," she answered, smiling. "You mean documents?"

"I just need to see your papers," it said, pleasantly. Reed handed them over. He'd spend a few hours drawing them up earlier. If at any point their true identities were to be discovered, it would be at this point. This was why Reed had seen to the forgeries himself. The computer scanned it, them and then the ship for weapons and illegal substances. It found nothing of course mainly because Kelvin was countering it.

"Well, everything is in order, enjoy your stay. Do you need to rent a vehicle?" it asked.

"No, we're fine," Satiah said, as it floated away.

"That was easy," Reed said, congratulating himself. Ash and the others came out cautiously. Satiah waved them over.

"We're good?" Carlos asked. He had been nervous about the scan of the ship. They still had laser rifles which were technically against regulations.

"I've set up the charge," Deva said. Under Satiah's orders, she had rigged a booby-trap so that should anyone get curious and try to get into their ship, it would blow up. It would not be wasteful in any way as they no longer needed that ship. The plan was to acquire a new one here. Satiah knew Tabre was coming after them again and while he wouldn't be foolish enough to go for the bait, he would learn nothing from it.

***

Wester played back the recording again.

Captain Tristram. My name is Flight Officer Jasper Kay. You don't know me but we had a mutual friend. Just a few minutes ago, Captain Erica Moxin was murdered by a Federation agent. She made me aware of some of the plan you worked on together. The decision to go on is yours. But know that you are on your own and if they got Erica, you crew is likely to have an agent somewhere too. Good luck, Captain.

It was the message on frequency nineteen that Tristram had received shortly before his death. So, he had known that he was marked for death *before* he even started talking. He had even gone so far as to lie to Wester about Erica to ensure the younger man didn't give up. Wester knew that he wouldn't have done anything different regardless. His new Lieutenant entered and touched her hat. Technically she should have knocked before entering but he wasn't going to pull her up on that. He nodded, giving permission for her to talk.

"His body is now stored," she said, after the recording had ended. "We've gone over everything and…"

"Sorry," Wester sighed, giving up. "I've forgotten your name…" He didn't mean to sound as miserable as he did.

"F… Lieutenant Jenjex, sir," she said, apparently not offended. She was still trying to remember her new rank but kept slipping into old habits. Lieutenant, not flight officer.

"Jenjex," he repeated, nodding. He was still floundering with the most difficult question he had. What to do next. With proof of Moxin's death and without Tristram… Wester had to go the rest of the way alone. They had talked about what to do next, him and Tristram. Did they just run, keep going until they were out of charted space altogether? Did they give themselves up? Did they warn the Coalition? He was distracted out of this by Jenjex putting a hot drink in front of him.

"Sorry, carry on," he prompted, clinging onto his sanity.

"We have found both homing devices that were planted," she said, dropping them onto the table in front of him. One had been smashed but she had left the other alone. It was still working. He opened his mouth to point out that unless she *wanted them to be tracked* she should wreck the other one too.

"I have destroyed one but I thought about it and decided keeping this one *may help us*. If they *believe* we searched and found one, we would *not suspect* there being a second. We can get another ship and place *this device* on that one and they would be following the wrong ship," she explained, enthusiastic. He was overwhelmed. She was smart. And he knew deep down that he should have thought of it.

"That's brilliant," he stated, a little stunned. "It might take them a while to discover the ruse too by which time we'd be a long way away."

"If you say so, sir," she replied, pushing her hair back behind her ear self-consciously. "So... *do I have your permission* to do that?" This being in charge was taking Wester a long time to get used to.

"...*Certainly*, very good Jenjex," he said, dismissively.

"In the meantime, do you wish me to...*do anything else?*" she asked, uncomfortably. She didn't like prodding someone who looked so... tired. Generally prodding superior officers was a fine art at the best of times and these were not the best of times.

"What did you have in mind?" he asked, sighing again.

"Many of the crew are asking about their *family's* safety..." she stated, meaningfully. Wester couldn't look at her anymore, he felt ashamed at having put so many people under threat. Only now had he actually even realised the true scope of what he had participated in.

"We are not in the position to help," Wester said, trying not to sound harsh. "They will be expecting us to make contact with loved ones and it will only be so long before those loved ones are used against us."

"...Do you have family, *sir?*" she asked, a little edge to her tone.

"...Not anymore," he replied, making eye contact with her. "They died."

"Then you wouldn't want our men to feel that pain, would you?" she asked, seriously. This was not what he wanted to talk about. One look in her eyes made any resistance on his part melt away.

"...No," he admitted. "I just... don't know what to do for the best." He pulled out the screen he had been looking at. It listed every single member of the crew of *Warrior*. Over five hundred individuals.

"*How can I possibly save them all?*" he whispered, referring to their families.

"So your solution is to do nothing?" she asked, bleakly.

"I don't have a solution!" he exploded, suddenly. She jumped but didn't back down. Standing, he began to pace as he ranted.

"It wasn't meant to work out *like this*!" he insisted, giving vent to his fears. "We are being hunted by our own people because of what we have done and until Ro is stopped, *that will never stop*. We have *one warship* to our disposal." He tossed the screen to her so she too could see the names. "One! One warship *against hundreds*!" he went on. "What would you do?"

Silence. He paused and looked around to face her. She was frowning at the list as if checking for something. Guilt stabbed at him. He shouldn't have shown her his weakness. He shouldn't give into panic and fear. And… he didn't want to speak to her like that.

"I'm sorry," he said, trying to make up for losing control. "I didn't mean to…"

"Sir, this list is wrong," she stated, flatly and with bewilderment. She pointed to the names. Captain Tristram. That was correct. Lieutenant Wester. Also correct. Flight Officer Gene Red. What?

Wester and Jenjex reviewed the next list of officers, all of which were also wrong. Neither of them had heard of any of these people. Then Wester guessed the reason why. He smiled, as if a great weight had been lifted from him. In a way it had never been there. Tristram would never have left his crew in the lurch, even in death.

"*Don't you get it?*" he asked, smiling. She smiled too but with uncertainty.

"Sir?"

"Tristram *replaced* the official files of the ships roster! *None of these are real people at all*. He did it to protect us! *He must have done*. He kept *his* name on there because he knew he couldn't hide. He left mine on there because he knew I had no family. Anyone else who reads this will think these are real," Wester explained.

"And even if they find out that some of them are wrong *or that they are all fakes* there's no way they can find the correct ones," she said, realising.

"I didn't know it was fake until you told me because *I* don't know most of the crew anyway," Wester went on. Yes, it made sense. "*The families are safe*." They both smiled. Wester collapsed into his chair, relaxed at last. Now all they had to do was to figure out how to stay alive. A much simpler goal all-round. Jenjex turned to leave but then stopped and faced him again an oddly crafty smile on her gorgeous face.

"You should tell the crew that *you orchestrated this*, sir," Jenjex suggested, seriously. "It will give everyone a reason to believe in you."

"But... that would be *lying*," Wester stated, concerned. Why was she suggesting this? She shrugged.

"We are at war," she stated, seriously. "Tristram would want *you* to take credit for this as he would know you need it more than he does. I think you should consider it, sir."

"Look, just tell them their families are safe..." he began, dismissively.

"If I don't tell them *why* they will not believe me," she interrupted, guessing his idea. "And it would be much better coming straight from *you*, sir. Morale is a *big* concern right now and..."

"*I know*," hissed, giving up. She was so... persuasive. "Give me the bloody microphone," he ordered. She smiled, more amused by his outburst than anything. She handed it to him.

"Let me know when we're about to arrive," Wester said, trying not to follow her hips with his eyes as she went for the door.

***

Satiah followed the path across the roof of the building, up, down, across. It had great visibility. The heat from the sun bore down on her as she moved swiftly but carefully along. Even at that height it was possible to hear some sounds from the streets below and they were not the tallest building around. There were even one or two examples of the sky-scraping architecture that was so prominent back on Earth. Over her shoulder the long-distance rifle was heavy, balanced out by the holdall she carried in her other hand. Padding along with the feline grace of big cat, she reached the edge of the corner and casually peered down. Ten storeys, one hundred and forty feet to the ground would be to some, dizzying. She crouched, pulling the tripod out of the bag and began assembling it. It was a task she had done countless times before and she'd set up the weapon in less than a minute. Then she left it there and, somewhere between a jog and a fast walk, she headed back across the roof to the hatch that led back into the safe house.

This safe house displeased her for three reasons. Firstly it was on the top floor. Never a great idea, in her opinion. Safe houses should either be ground floor or lower simply for ease of access and escape. Second, they were right in the middle of the city. Granted it did cut travelling time down to a minimum but it also meant that, because of the crowds, people could easily get close to them without them seeing. Lastly, a few of the floors below them were frequented by a few hundred students of infant age. Ruthless as she was, endangering children did not sit well with her. It was from the playing children that the occasional screams came. Screams that made Satiah have to control herself reflexively every time she heard them. Being a trained Phantom, normally when you heard someone scream it meant a problem... and *most definitely not* a missing ball.

Kelvin had scanned the building and his finds were not good. While their floor was empty and in some places derelict, the rest of the building was highly active with nearly a thousand people constantly present. Ideal for masking their own activities maybe but also just as effective at masking their enemies. The blind seeking the blind. She clambered back down into the only room that had anything useful in it. Satiah glanced at Carlos and Deva. When they had arrived, discovered the bunk beds they had and then a small stockpile of new weapons, they had initially been enthusiastic. Now their feelings were more mixed. They were cleaning the dusty weapons sombrely.

"Well, I have more bad news for you," Satiah said, straight faced.

"What?" Carlos groaned, expecting the worst.

"You two are both on guard duty tonight. Reed and Ash are going to sit down and have their little *conference* where Kelvin will monitor them. You two will ensure *no one disturbs them*," Satiah said, inflexibly.

"Fantastic," murmured Deva, sniffing.

"...And where will *you* be?" Carlos asked, suspicious.

"Around," she shrugged, unable to hide a grin.

"What if there is a situation and we need to get hold of you?"

Deva asked, crossing her arms.

"Kelvin will know how to get hold of me," she replied. "Someone has to get us our new ship."

"Reed said not to get anything too fancy," Carlos said, remembering. "Low profile and all that."

"Look at where we are!" Deva argued, pointing out of a narrow window. "If we get anything *flyable* we will be lucky."

Satiah had to agree with that. She exited the house and made her way down the flights of stairs to the street. It was late afternoon and, now the hottest part of the day was almost over, businesses were starting to reopen. The air shimmered in the middle-distance, reminding her of her thirst. She tried to ignore the optical phenomenon, otherwise known as a heat haze, but still found it oddly compelling. In her mind, when she had been an infant, she'd wondered if the air would spontaneously combust or perhaps explode. Satiah walked out into the street, noticing how mostly anyone who saw her instantly noted her. A tourist. A stranger. Interesting. She shoved her hands in her pockets and began to amble along, making a show of looking at everything she saw with a cautious curiosity. She approached a stall selling some kind of food wrapped in thick sheets of paper.

"Hello," she said, once again using her colonial accent. She began to flutter her eyelids a little, and use big enticing smiles. Anything to make her seem as sociable and unthreatening as possible.

"Hello," growled the lizard that served her. "You a tourist?"

"That's *right*," she said, in a tone that implied his deduction had surprised her. Inwardly she knew it was simple observation manipulated by her acting skills. "I guess I do stand out a bit, are there *many* tourists here?"

"A few," he growled, in the same tone. His eyes narrowed. "Did you want some food?"

"You take Essps?" she asked, knowing he already did. Who didn't?

"Of course!" he snarled, a bit offended. "You don't travel much, do yur?" She pretended to be caught out.

She shook her head and rolled her eyes, making herself look a bit embarrassed.

"I'm sorry, no; I've stayed close to home mostly. What kind of food is this?" Ignorance was always easy for her to feign.

"It *is* safe for humans *if that is what you were wondering*," he rumbled, pleased that she seemed to be hungry. "We call them Heffers but they have many other names. They come in two types. Spicy or non-spicy." She made a noise indicating that the food appealed to her. It actually did, she was fed up of rations and eager to try new things. A clawed hand offered her a bit of meat impaled on a stick. A sample.

"Taste that," he grunted. She did. A strong meaty taste was aided by some kind of spice making her mouth burn a little. It was nice though.

She bought one and asked where the nearest bar was. A tavern called *Tainted Oasis* was his answer and she followed his directions while eating the food. He hadn't been joking about the spice. Sweat began to drip down her face as she wolfed the Heffer. Her mind, though, was still on the job. She was learning the layout, gaining valuable intel. Kelvin had already mapped the place out with his usual skill and accuracy but Satiah had wanted more detail and… she'd wanted to get away for a bit. The merest drift of air, which the locals probably thought of as a breeze, was the only cooling force she could feel. Her throat was burning from spice and thirst combined as she dispensed with the wrapper into a litter conveyer. She turned another corner and there it was.

The Tainted Oasis looked rough on the outside. Cracked walls. Sandstorms had made those cracks smoother and curvy. She entered, noting the two android guards on either side of the doorway. Music and smoke were among the first things she took in. It was dimly lit and quite noisy. As she approached the bar she was groped firmly on the behind by some drunk who howled with laughter as she turned to face him. She raised a coy eyebrow at the portly man as she took his drink from the table. Everyone at that table fell silent in anticipation and others nearby turned to watch as she downed the whole thing in one long motion. She finished, rubbed her mouth along her sleeve and looked at him again right in the eyes. He just sat there, astonished. She pushed his knee with hers to get him to move as if she was intending to sit on his lap. His eyes went wide with lust and drunken optimism. Then she smashed the empty glass over his head, decking him instantly.

She was tense, ready to be rushed, but that's not what happened. Several women from behind the bar cheered and the other men at the same table laughed again, one even falling over in hysterics. The androids came over but instead of arresting Satiah for the indiscretion, they simply helped the man get back on his seat and returned to their station. Satiah continued on her way to the bar, trying to look nonchalant. That beer had been delicious.

"What can I get ya, tough girl?" smiled the woman, from behind the bar. Her two assistants, the ones who had cheered earlier, were looking on and listening in intently. They were young and painfully thin but were obviously admiring Satiah. Satiah eyed the golden bottles stacked behind the women, a freezing mist drifting from them.

"One of those please," she said, in a quiet voice. The drink was bought. "Say, do you know any ship markets around here?"

"You want to buy a ship?" asked the woman, her colonial accent strong.

"Or sell my old one," Satiah nodded. The women exchanged mixed looks.

"I have bad news for you, tough girl," she sniggered. "That guy you just brained owns the largest shipyard in the city. You might want to try your luck in Palter." Satiah matched the woman's snigger with one of her own. Colder and more menacing.

"That's not bad news for *me*, that's bad news for *him*," she corrected, her tone determined. She took the beer, slipped its frozen foamy crown and smiled with pleasure. She was starting to like this planet. It wasn't on many worlds that you could clobber someone in public without any real consequence. She turned away from the bar and returned to the table.

Again, a hush fell as she arrived. Expectantly they all stared at her, wondering what she would do or say. She pulled up a stool and sat down at their table as if she was one of them. She met their stares with an air of challenge in her face. The fat man, her prey, still bleeding from the blow, eyed her warily.

"...I'm sorry for squeezing your muscular buns, missy," he said, hiccupping fretfully. She focussed on him, staring intimidatingly into his blue eyes. She swigged her beer. The harder she stared, the more nervous he became. A huntress cornering her prey.

"...I won't touch you again or any of your friends, I swear," he added, swiftly waving a hand at the other women behind the bar. He would be useful to her; if he owned the shipyard, he would know if Tabre had arrived or not.

"They are not my friends, I'm just a tourist," she told him. "*I'm sorry that I bashed your ugly face, mister.*" One of the men to her right let out a giggle. Her target gave a hesitant nervous laugh of his own before clearing his throat.

"...Will you join us? We were just about to begin another round of Gairunn," he offered, still on edge.

"I'd love that," she agreed, inwardly annoyed. She wasn't very good at Gairunn. It wasn't that she didn't know how to play or even that she found it boring. She was just not that lucky. "What variant?"

"*Loopsplit.*"

The game began.

***

Reed and Ash stared at one another. They were on opposite sides of the table. Reed found this positioning symbolic of their cantankerous association and even their moral standings. Ruby was sat on the edge, closer to Ash than Reed but essentially between them. Kelvin was watching them, silently recording everything.

"Well, in your own time and place," Reed prompted, at last.

"We think that if Balan's weapon exists it was once aboard a space station called the Orion Observatory. One of Vourne's agents infiltrated the facility during a mission relating to Operation Burning Bridge. We have a copy of the report although half of it has yet to be decoded. I have a theory that it was either built there and kept there or built there and removed later," Ash said, carefully.

"What was the name of Vourne's agent?" asked Reed, curious.

"Dasss," Ruby replied, softly.

"Good," Reed smiled, tightly. "Randal may be able to help us with that." Ruby eyed Ash, asking for permission to show Reed the mission report on her computer. He nodded. Reed read it quickly.

(UE) OPERATION BURNING BRIDGE (UE) REPORT: Dated at end. Target located. ITP6. Spatial coordinates: 9980-7948. Designation (TS): Top Secret. Status: ACTIVE. Official staff allocation: 1850. Dasss reports: Reconnaissance correct. Scientific facility with several branches of identified ongoing research. Jaylite Industries is currently contracted with waste disposal duties. Background check required. Experimentation currently at critical stage. Testing is achieving mixed results. Balan's next visit in two days. Evacuate immediately.

"*Evacuate immediately*," pondered Reed, slowly and loud enough for them to hear. "I wonder what he meant by that."

"Well, presumably get out," Ruby answered, shrugging.

"Himself *or* everyone on the station?" Reed asked, shrewdly. Ruby tilted her head as she reconsidered, she'd not looked at it that way.

"Perhaps it goes into further detail later," Ash mused, referring to the remainder of the report.

"Ah yes, *the code*," Reed murmured, eyeing it with intrigue. "ITP6 *I'm assuming* is another name for Orion Observatory?" Ash nodded. Reed thought long and hard about that. He was sure he'd heard of it. He remembered Satiah had mentioned a space station that had been demolished. It was from there that she had acquired the former employee of Jaylite Industries who'd had his mind wiped by the Sisterhood. Well, it was certainly all connected. So could *that* station have been the Orion Observatory? *And* it had been near the mining world the Sisterhood had attacked because of the new material.

"Let's see the database you retrieved from the mining world," Reed asked, politely. Ruby's computer accessed it and, after Reed cracked the password, they were in.

"There's a lot of technical data here," Ash sighed, as he read through it. "So you believe, after visiting the Sisterhood, that the weapon needed this new material to perform its function."

"Chalky indicated that the substance affected the human mind in such a way that it prevented anyone near it from sleeping after a certain period of exposure," Reed explained.

"So it's not a conventional weapon?" Ruby clarified. "Like it couldn't blow up a spaceship?"

"No way to know. This new material, KZ15 as they call it... If they are using that then to me it seems unlikely to be conventional. I imagine that it couldn't damage the hypothetical ship but it *could* start a wave of lethal insomnia among the crew," Reed said.

"How is insomnia lethal?" Ruby asked, puzzled. "I know it's bad but I didn't know it was terminal."

"It's not. As disorders go it's more a nuisance in most cases than a death sentence. There are, however, many different types and categories. It can be long-term, or short-term. It can be acute or chronic. Even transient. *I'm no expert* but I remember reading at length about it one night when, for some reason, sleep was eluding me. Normally it affects the elderly or those under stress. In this case though, my concept is that the weapon utilises the KZ15 to deprive the human mind of the chemicals it needs to rest," he went on.

"So KZ15 creates a chemical imbalance in the human mind," Ash stated, nodding slowly. "How?"

"There, you have me," Reed admitted, gesticulating surrender.

"But would it even kill anyone?" Ruby asked, perplexed. "I mean, *say you use it on someone*, they would have ages left to kill you before it killed them?"

"Humans usually can remain alive for about eleven days without sleep, however, it should be noted that mental capacity is severely hampered long before then. In any case, micro-sleeps are unavoidable normally. It's a safety mechanism of the human mind which forces the mind to rest for short durations. The only way around *that* would be protein mutation," Reed went on. "So we can reasonably assume that KZ15 affects the protein in such a way that it mutates and prevents the mind from shutting down *at all* until death. Another thing, it also seems to affect those with mental abilities too, hence the Sisterhood's involvement. Perhaps that indicates that telepaths and so on are more susceptible to it."

"So, you use it and it takes eleven days to work?" Ruby asked, a little incredulous. "Sounds a bit unreliable to me too."

"What makes you say that?" asked Reed, interested.

"Well, how would you even know if it worked?" she asked, seriously. "You hit someone and they leave, just because you never see them again doesn't mean that they are dead."

"You've both overlooked what else happens when humans can't rest," Ash muttered, sighing. "After just two days they will suffer from hallucinations, delirium and confusion. Say, if the weapon was deployed in secret affecting a whole planet without anyone knowing?" Reed considered this new frightening possibility. It would mean anarchy.

"What if you are under sedation when it goes off?" Ruby countered, shrugging. "Or already asleep? Would it *still* affect you?"

"*All right*," Reed said, deciding to let that drop. "We need more information."

"*We've* given you everything *we have*," Ash said, pointedly. He was inferring that Reed was holding back.

"And we *thank you* for this *essential* contribution," Reed answered, carefully. "For a better understanding we need a scientist. We need to know everything there is to know about this new material KZ15."

"A tester would be good," Ruby noted, quietly.

"Yes although it *could* be tricky to handle as a substance. It's a shame the Sisterhood wiped out most of the…" he paused, and stared into the corner.

"*What?*" Ruby asked, concerned.

"No, no I just wondered… Satiah has been gone nearly six hours," he stated, troubled.

***

Satiah slipped out of the bed quietly. The shipyard owner, Carl, was sleeping peacefully and would remain so for several hours thanks to her homemade sedative. After she was sure he was asleep she'd injected him in the neck with it. Dressing quickly, she took his computer and ran a search. While it loaded she glanced over at him casually. He'd been so easy to seduce and *the things that he told her…*

He'd compromised his own security and business in less than ten minutes. Seldom had she had such a willing confessor. If only all of her targets were so cooperative. She retrieved her gun belt and boots, pulling them on rapidly. She sat and waited for his computer to complete its search. A bleep sounded and she peered over. It was Tabre's ship, docking area nineteen. She smiled grimly at the picture before rising.

***

Conrad shifted on his feet uneasily. Tabre had only been gone twenty minutes but Conrad had heard things about Ionar 12. The corruption! The poverty! The desperate populous! Inwardly he couldn't think of a single reason why Reed would come here. Tabre had left the second they had arrived and had gone to touch base with his contacts… whoever they were. Conrad had got bored of sitting in the ship and had started to wander around on the landing platform. A mechanic was giving the ship a thorough clean and check over but, other than him, Conrad was completely alone. He sat down on a convenient crate and began to seriously consider just buying a ship and leaving. Tabre didn't need him anymore and he just wanted to go home. He was roused from his reverie by a loud crash. He peeped over a supply crate and froze in shock.

The mechanic lay sprawled on the floor; Satiah was standing over him, holding a crate opener she'd evidently just bludgeoned him with. Where was the security guard? Dead already, most likely. She dropped the bar onto the mechanics body, grabbed his ankles and capably dragged him away and out of sight. Conrad swallowed and thought frantically about what he could do. He was not even armed. Satiah was back in a few moments, staring up at the Tabre's ship, and hands on her hips. Her stare was one of evaluation. She circled the ship once and then paused, apparently thinking about her next move. Conrad felt about for his communicator but he'd left it inside the ship! Where was Tabre when he needed him? Her expression stony, Satiah yanked a fresh power core off of a shelf and slotted it inside one of the open engine ports. Conrad was no expert but he was certain her intention was to sabotage their ship.

What could he do? If he moved, he was sure she'd see him. Maybe when she left, he could slip over and undo what she had done but… She stepped back out from cover, surveying the area again and he ducked carefully. Praying to a god he did not believe in that she didn't realise he was there, it was several seconds before he chanced another gander. There was no sign of her. He blinked. Was she still there? She might have gone inside Tabre's ship. Uncertain, he waited, holding his breath and listening hard. He heard nothing. He counted out the seconds for about five minutes. No change. *Then...* approaching footsteps. He peered around from behind the crate to see Tabre returning with another man. The other man looked like local law enforcement.

Conrad broke cover and started to run towards Tabre, waving his arms in alarm. He had to warn him about what Satiah had done.

"*Tabre!*" he shouted, fearfully. "She..." A bolt took him in the side of the head and he crashed to the floor dead before he landed. Tabre and the other man dived in opposite directions for cover. Three storeys up and a mere nine feet to the left, Satiah rose from her spot and unleashed a blistering volley at a new target. The power core. Ignition. Tabre's ship went up in a colossal fireball that threw everything aside violently, set off alarms everywhere and smashed every glass window in sight. Tabre had been shielded from the concussive wave by a row of crates but the force of the blast had crushed him painfully against the containment wall. Winded, he slid to the floor, his ears ringing, covered in dust and plaster. Smoke was everywhere as he struggled to his feet. Pistol raised, he fruitlessly tried to find the shooter. This was revenge and he knew it.

Coughing, he fled back into the corridor for shelter. His associate had not been so lucky. When he'd been alive he was an officer in the local security forces. Tabre had successfully bribed the man into helping him find Reed and Satiah. Unfortunately, she'd somehow found him first. She'd be somewhere high up, overlooking the whole site, using sights to find him and finish the job. His only chance was to get out before the smoke cleared and she came in closer. He began to jog lightly along the corridor as robots hurried past him to combat the fire and search for survivors. He stumbled past security and into the street. He then began an erratic course to try and lose her... if she'd seen him. He'd been alone before but now he'd lost his ship he had no escape. That bothered him. An eye for an eye, he supposed, being as he had destroyed her ship on the mining world.

***

Deva, catnapping on the roof, had jolted awake and upright when she'd heard the explosion. An almighty *kablam* from the direction of the shipyards. Using the rifle Satiah had set up, Deva had quickly focussed in that direction. A cloud of smoke was rising and the distant sirens of emergency could be heard wailing clearly. Then, through the scopes, she noticed a figure hurrying along a rooftop maybe a few hundred metres from the shipyard. She was partly hidden at various times because of the structures around her but Deva could see it was Satiah. Was she being followed? Deva kept keeping an eye on what was going on behind her in case she was being chased but there was no one.

Carlos and Kelvin quickly joined Deva, naturally everyone had heard the detonation. Everyone in the city most likely.

"Did you see what happened?" Carlos asked. She shrugged.

"An explosion in the shipyards. Maybe it was the trap I set up in the ship before we left it but she's coming back I think. I saw her running across the roofs a few moments ago," Deva stated, pointing. After surveying the area and situation Kelvin detected his incoming mistress. He approached the edge of the wall and crouched to lower his arm. Satiah grabbed his metal arm and he hauled her up swiftly. She was panting but clearly unhurt. She dumped the rifle she had on the ground and sat down looking completely unscathed.

"I just took out Tabre's ship," Satiah announced, pointing over her shoulder with her thumb. "I don't think I got him though."

Carlos and Deva exchanged looks. "Never mind *him*; did you get us a new ship?" Carlos asked, teasingly.

"Hey, *I've been busy!*" she smirked back. They all glanced back as a second smaller explosion went off back at the shipyard. More smoke billowed up into the night sky. It would probably still be rising at dawn.

"Anything happen here?"

"I will replay everything for you," Kelvin stated.

"Just the highlights please," she grunted, as she stood again. "But I need to get some sleep before I do anything else... it's been a night." She scrambled down the ladder, into the safe house. Carlos and Kelvin followed her. The others were all awake. Reed and Ash had never gone to sleep in the first place and Ruby had been roused by the explosion.

"Sorry about the noise," Satiah said, without meaning it. "Give me a few hours!" After going to bed with the drunk, fat Carl, as useful as he had been, she'd been dying for a wash. In less than twenty minutes she'd fallen asleep on the dusty mattress of the bunk bed she had.

***

"It was dangerous coming here," Jenjex murmured. Wester and Jenjex were standing on the command deck. To Wester it felt just as odd as it had when he was standing with Tristram. They had arrived at the rendezvous point that Tristram and Erica had agreed on. It was already programmed into the computer when they had fled from the Federation. Wester though, had a plan. It seemed fairly obvious that although they had proceeded to the meeting area, no one would join them any time soon. Jenjex was concerned, not unreasonably, that if their intentions had been known then their plan and this location could also be known to Ro and her followers. And a fast pursuit would not be far behind them.

"I've checked and we are kitted out here for a four-month period of service. Before we do anything, I think we should warn the Coalition about Ro Tammer," he explained. "No declaration of official war has been made but there's no guarantee it would happen at all with her around." Jenjex nodded slowly as she thought about it.

"Will they *believe us*?" she asked, shrewdly. It was the one question he knew that she would be smart enough to ask and it was the one question that he had no answer to. But he'd decided that he wasn't going to start lying to *her* some time ago. He'd already lied to himself enough.

"*I don't know*. I *hope* they will. They will probably ask for some kind of proof but *I can't believe* that they don't have spies telling them exactly the same thing," Wester said, smiling weakly.

"Sir... I've been a flight officer for a year and before that I was a gunner... military life seemed so restrictive but, for the last few hours, I've never felt so free," she said, a thoughtful expression on her face.

"I'm sure someone out there would say it is because we are so young. Too young perhaps," he smiled.

"I like the way when they say that, that they seem to think no one else has said it to us before," she joked.

"Old news," he smiled, an idea coming to him. "Earth is two days away... fancy dinner in my cabin?" She glanced right at him but he didn't look away this time.

"Is it an order?" she sniggered.

"No, no, it's sincere invitation that can easily be rejected," he chuckled. If he could find it in himself to commit high treason... then surely he could ask her to dinner.

"Would you believe me if I told you I had to check my schedule first?" she replied.

"Of course," he nodded. They both smiled. For the first time in their lives, lives that had all been planned to the nth degree, they both had no obvious future. They were the highest ranking officers on board and, given the situation, friendship was essential. But Wester wanted more than friendship with Jenjex and he had a sneaking suspicion that she wanted the same thing of him too.

***

Satiah was amazed that Carlos and Deva could fit on the same bunk together. She had awoken shortly after midday and, completely exhausted, the teenage guard dogs had been more than happy to get some rest. They lay crammed in and curled up on the bunk, utterly shattered. Satiah smiled down at them briefly, feeling a touch of envy. They made a good couple, she reflected. Love could be very uncompromising in whom it chooses to draw together but *occasionally* it did get it right. Kelvin was now guarding everything himself while Satiah caught up with Reed and Ash.

"I see, so let me just set out our objectives. One, find the space station. Two, learn more about this material. And three... get a new ship," Satiah concluded. Objective dictates action and Satiah believed in keeping things simple.

"I thought you were meant to be taking care of that last night," Reed noted, with some annoyance. "Not blowing up shipyards."

"Tabre let his guard down," she countered, defensively. "It was an opportunity..."

"Yes but you failed to kill him," Ash stated, also annoyed. "All you've done is provoke him."

"...Let me see that mission report," she requested, changing the subject. Ruby handed it to her. Satiah read it quickly, deeply interested. Operation Burning Bridge was something that had been on her mind a lot lately.

"I'm going to get hold of Randal to ask him if Dasss is still working..." Reed began, throwing his communicator from hand to hand as he spoke.

"Don't bother," Satiah stated, grimly. "*He's dead.*" Reed sighed, irritated.

"How do you *know?*" Ruby asked, curious.

"...Classified," Satiah stated, her conviction failing her briefly.

"How do you know?" Reed asked, significance in his tone. Satiah rolled her eyes, annoyed.

"He died shortly before Vourne, it's in Mensa's report," she answered, still cagey. Satiah knew exactly how Dasss had died because she was the one who'd killed him. She'd shot him in the back as she had pretended to switch sides. Mensa, in his report had claimed to be responsible for his death to cover her but she didn't want the matter to be discussed again. Then she reached the coded section of the report and smiled knowingly. She knew that code.

"There may be no need for any of that, give me twenty minutes," she said, heading up onto the roof where Kelvin was. Kelvin saw her approaching and gave her a status report.

"Quiet," he said, in his normal intonation.

"Great, I need you to translate this," she said, sitting next to him and wincing in the sun. There was still some smoke rising from the shipyard. "Phantom code book 91," she prompted. Kelvin took in the data and then sent it to her on her communicator. He'd not translated it before simply because no one had asked.

"Thanks Kelvin," she said, starting to read it.

(UE) OPERATION BURNING BRIDGE (UE) REPORT:
Dated at end. Target located. ITP6. Spatial coordinates: 9980-

7948. Designation (TS): Top Secret. Status: ACTIVE. Official staff allocation: 1850. Dasss reports: Reconnaissance correct. Scientific facility with several branches of identified ongoing research. Jaylite Industries is currently contracted with waste disposal duties. Background check required. Experimentation currently at critical stage. Testing is achieving mixed results. Balan's next visit in two days. Evacuate immediately.

Threat identified as external possible. VIP removed from positions, data transferred and copied. Backup system to be transferred to Station Denepler. ITP6 relocated to: 0000-0002. All testing now suspended pending result of conference. KZ15 is presenting difficulties. I can't get close enough to get a sample but I have confirmed that only robots can handle the substance. Awaiting your confirmation. I only have 2 hour window before I must pull out. Further instructions are needed. Report ends.

Satiah let out the breath she had forgotten she was holding in. Station Denepler had been another name for the space station she'd seen demolished. It had been the place she'd found the man. So... the information *had* been sent there in data form *as a backup* for the Orion Observatory. Where had it ended up? More important though were the fresh coordinates that Dasss had provided. Proof positive that even the dead could still be useful. 0000-0002. The station could be there *right now. There* being close to the centre of the universe. An odd choice of hiding pace but then, no one ever went there anymore. So far the locations they had been searching or considering were on the edges of known space, not right in the middle of everything.

There was a planet there. It was called Durrith and, despite being habitable, no one lived on it. Satiah realised she didn't know why that was. Dwelling on it consciously, she couldn't even remember who owned it. Coalition? Federation? Someone surely had to own it! Yes... a *very* strange choice of refuge. That was always assuming that it was trying to hide still. Careful not to jump to any conclusions, she read through it all from beginning to end once more to give her mind longer to bite on it. The external threat he had referred to was most likely the Sisterhood. Somehow Dasss, or someone else, had seen them coming. Seen them coming fast enough to move the space station and back up the files. Who?

Doing anything else may have aroused suspicion from the Sisterhood and… by the look of it they had what they needed anyway. A supply of KZ15. As a contingency they had backed up everything which was *why* the demolition of Denepler had occurred. It had nothing to do with it being old and disused… someone very high up was covering their tracks. Or someone else who knew about the demolition had tried to use it to their advantage… *those pirates*… had they been pirates? Whoever they were they had left it very late in the day before acting. Had they been sent to kill the man she rescued or wipe the databanks… or both? She smiled, enjoying the puzzle. It would give her many hours of peaceful sleep.

***

"These people are very well trained and completely ruthless," Tabre said, pretending to be regretful. He was trying to paint a picture with those words in which *he* was the one doing *them* a favour. Them being the government of Ionar 12.

"How can you be sure they are still *on world*?" the First Minster asked.

"The ship they arrived on is still here and, according to departures, since last night's fireworks, no one has left the planet," Tabre explained, persuasively. With no place else to turn, Tabre had gone to the embassy and had asked to see the First Minister who was effectively in charge of the whole planet. Normally such an action would have been impossible but, dropping Ro's name repeatedly, had made it happen.

Tabre had then got the minister to speak to Ro and she had basically laid down the law. The First Minister was to place anything he could provide at Tabre's service. He was bristling at the situation. No doubt it put many of his private dealings under more scrutiny than he would like. The corruption of a politician could always be gambled on.

"…What do you suggest?" the man asked, weary.

"I don't know how or if they had help but they *clearly* have a base here. It *may* be in the city, it may *not* be, but we must find it," Tabre explained, seriously. That was essentially true, they had to be operating or at least waiting *somewhere*.

Tabre gave picture of Satiah and Reed to him.

"Get these circulated on the most wanted lists. Bounty *is* negotiable but we want to know where they are, we do not want people trying to get them for us," he went on.

"I will get the chief of security to talk to you," the First Minister decided. "He has *limited resources* but they *are* the only ones on the planet. You could call Ro again and get her to back you up with a ship." It was not public knowledge and might never be but Ro had made Tabre aware of a recent mutiny in the Federation navy. The day after a big rally all hell had broken loose and basically a quarter of the entire fleet was unable to leave the shipyard. The ship was still at large and Ro was livid. She'd been so angry she'd even thought about pulling him out of his current assignment and getting him to chase after the offending mutineers. Basically, no Federation core military forces would be able to help. He was on his own and would have to rely on whatever the locals could cough up. Not a happy situation.

***

Ash, Ruby and Reed pored over the translated document. Ruby was the only one who expressed any thanks to Satiah for having decoded it though.

"How did you do it?" Ruby asked, astonished.

"State secret," Satiah answered, bluntly.

"Well... *thanks*," Ruby had said, tentatively.

"You're sure this is right?" Ash asked, grim.

"No, I made it up," she growled, irritated. Reed winced. "Trust me, it *is* correct."

"Now we know where it went," Reed smiled, pleased.

"All we have to do is get there," Ash stated, pointedly. As a group they all regarded Satiah.

This would not go down well. While talking with Kelvin she'd learned a few things about what was going on in the city. She and Reed had been identified as suspects and their profiles were advertised as bounties. They were both wanted as a result of the murder and mayhem at the shipyards. She explained this to them.

"That's not the worst part," she continued, ignoring the

condemning expression on Ash's face. "The city is now locked down. Even if we had a ship we'd never get out of the atmosphere."

"How terribly amusing," Ash grumbled. "We now know exactly where to go but we are unable to move."

"I like it no more than you..." she began, sighing.

"Reed! You are aware that if she hadn't attacked Tabre yesterday, we would not be in this predicament," Ash went on. "This is why I dislike working with humans."

"*Hey!*" cried Ruby, hurt. "You can't blame *all human kind* simply because one person made one mistake. *And* she did translate that final part of that report for us which, despite your great immortal brain, you were incapable of doing. It's not like she knew this was going to happen."

"I assume you have some wonderful plan that will enable us to escape?" Reed asked, eyeing Satiah.

"I do," she nodded. "It will be tricky but I was planning on using the black market to purchase a vessel, last night I heard a few names that will be worth looking into. Unfortunately... Tabre has kindly provided their security with images of myself and Reed so... we cannot chance being seen in public..." She stared right back at Ash. "If you want to leave anytime soon maybe instead of yelling at me *you* should get us out of here."

Reed tried to hide his smile but failed. Ruby shrugged.

"She's right, you and me *are* just tourists here... nothing weird about us finding a ride," Ruby added.

"If this city is in lockdown it doesn't matter who wants to leave," Ash pointed out, swiftly. "No one will be allowed out until the lockdown is lifted. I've already lost one ship because of you, Reed, why should I get you one?" Reed sighed, not pleased with the direction this conversation was going in.

"Typical immortal, *always* wanting others to do their work for them," Satiah put in, provocatively.

"Guys, we're supposed to be a *team* even if we're not friends, we should be working this out together..." Ruby began, trying to stop a fight.

"She lost the ship, she caused the lockdown and she should be the one to get a new ship," Ash persisted, undaunted. "It *was* Reed's original instruction to her *if you remember?*"

"I'll do it!" shouted Satiah, glaring at him. "Forgive me for caring about *your* bloody safety! Forgive me for thinking you might want to make a very difficult task a little easier. May I remind you that as you do not represent an official government body *I don't even have to protect you?* I don't have to do anything for *you*! I could even report you for interfering in *my* investigation! *I could have you arrested.* Ruby is already wanted for destruction of property, it would be very easy to add extra charges to that…" Ruby gaped and flushed red. She'd been trying to be friendly to Satiah and apparently this had boomeranged badly.

"*Satiah!*" Reed said, commandingly. "A word?"

Satiah rolled her eyes and followed him to the ladder. As she went past she brushed into Ruby.

"Talk some sense into him *please*," Satiah growled, at her. Ruby nodded, still trying to get on this antagonistic woman's good side. Ash hadn't moved, just remained seated. Despite the anger in his words he'd remained in complete control. Ruby sidled over to him and sighed.

"Oh dear, it's all got a bit fraught hasn't it?" she chanced, hopefully. Ash, for all his secrets, rarely snapped at Ruby. He didn't answer at all, just continued to sit there a ponderous expression on his face.

"I'm *sure* she wasn't serious about arresting us. She's just under a lot of pressure and you didn't even say thanks for her decrypting that coded report," Ruby listed, softly. "But we need to find that weapon and…"

"I feel like taking the air, checking out this planet a little, want to come?" he asked, standing abruptly.

"…Okay."

***

"I'm *not* apologising for *anything I said in there*," Satiah hissed, keeping her voice down now that they were outside. "Just because he's immortal, he seems to think we're all stupid…"

"Satiah, *please*, I wasn't going to ask you to apologise for anything. I knew from the moment I started working with you that you have your ways of doing things and I don't expect you to change them unless you feel you have to. I only wanted to express my gratitude about you decoding the remainder of that report for me and for you actions yesterday," Reed said, calmly. As usual, she found herself on the back foot.

"...*Right*," she said, forcing her temper back into its box. When confronting an enemy she had complete control of herself but when dealing with others' things... "I'm *sorry* for getting nasty, I didn't mean to lay into Ruby either. He just hit the right spot."

"Ash is not particularly fond of humans, I know because I've been at ground zero for some of his most scathing remarks... Please, *don't take it personally*," Reed advised, patting her shoulder gently.

Mollified, Satiah nodded curtly.

"Because of you we now *know* that Tabre has indeed followed us here. *More importantly* we know where to search next. All we need is a ship. Two out of three, you're doing *brilliantly* so far," Reed said, being very complimentary. "Now obviously you're responsible for *some* disruption but I'm of the belief that it was *unavoidable*." She smiled.

"You don't have to say all of that," she said, trying to be kind. "I *was* acting recklessly but it was a great chance to kill him and I was *so close* to succeeding. At the very least, attack is sometimes the best form of defence. He can't kill you if he is busy trying not to be killed himself."

"That's very profound, Satiah," he replied, without sincerity. They shared a laugh.

"Just out of interest," he said, as he seemed to be on the verge of leaving. She sighed, resigned to her fate. "How *do you* intend to get us a new ship in order that we may make the most of that report you so diligently translated for us?"

"I have an idea that I think stands a reasonable chance of working," she smiled, patient. "If it doesn't work I will have to try something more... *extreme*."

"I see," he mused, seeming to add a disproportionally large

helping of salt to her words in his mind. This salt apparently weighed so great it warranted one of his eyebrows to rise as a counterbalance. Her smile grew wider with real amusement.

"I thought we trusted each other now?" she asked, grinning.

"It's Ash's trust we should be trying to earn now, not each other's," he replied, thoughtfully. "But, for argument's sake, were it *my trust* that *was* being earned…?"

"Don't worry," she insisted, mildly defensive.

He returned inside and Satiah saw Kelvin watching her.

"What now?" she demanded, irritated.

"Ash and Ruby have left the building. The tracker you asked me to place on Ruby is functioning," he stated.

"Maybe some fresh air will do them good," she muttered. "Thank you, Kelvin, carry on." She activated her computer and began searching. She quickly found Carl's details. She gave him a call. It was a bit risky but she needed speed.

"Hello, Carl here," he said. He sounded unhappy.

"Hello Carl, *remember me?*" she quipped, unable to stop herself from grinning. A clunk from the other end occurred followed by a scrambling noise. He'd dropped his communicator.

"*Kim?*" he asked, sounding confused. "*What the hell did you do?* You caused thousands of…"

"*One million Essps!*" she cut in, over him. Silence. She smiled, imagining the battle of emotions within him.

"What?" he asked, greed having apparently won.

"I need a ship to leave on… you sell ships," she stated, inflexibility.

"…*Who are you?*" he asked, obviously scared. "I've got security crawling all over me *because of you*. And you may be the hottest girl I've ever known but you're not worth *my whole business!*"

"*Carl…*" she said, in a gentle tone. "Calm down, big boy. Do they know about… *us?*"

"Are you kidding? As far as they know I've never even heard of you before," he retorted. *Sensible enough,* Satiah thought.

"As long as that does not change, you have no reason to worry," she said, persuasively. She let a little tinge of seduction into her voice which was difficult as she was still using her Colonial accent. "I think it's sweet that you lied to protect me but *I still need more...*"

She let that linger for a second.

"You get me a ship and I go away and you can go back to your normal business," she spelt out. "I have one million Essps... surely *that* can get me something."

"...Is *Kim* even your name?" he asked, a little sadly.

"If you want to live I'd leave off that line of questioning," she stated, gravely.

"...I'll be at my office tonight, about eight. If you come back and are willing to talk to me about what the hell this is about I will help you," Carl offered.

She raised an eyebrow. Clearly the drunk had fallen for her. She was pleased at first, it would make him easier to manipulate. Then the guilt slid in. Granted, he'd started it, but her counter measures had been punishing to say the least. She'd used him and got the information she'd needed; now she was doing it again. Not so long ago she wouldn't have felt the guilt and it troubled her. Guilt and conscience were weaknesses she could not afford to have. She steeled herself.

"If I see *any sign* of security..." she began warningly.

"I swear *I won't say anything!*" he insisted, guessing what her threat would be.

"I'll be there."

***

"There have been some sightings of Satiah," the woman said, going through a report. "She's operating under the name of Kim. No sign of Reed." Tabre nodded. It made sense that as she was protecting him, he would be undercover somewhere while she patrolled the place.

"The sightings seem to centre around a bar called the Tainted Oasis but a market stall owner reported seeing her in the street earlier in the afternoon. Apparently she bought a Heffer," the woman continued. Tabre frowned, pretty sure that if they were able to find that out, it wasn't important.

"She will be after a ship. She cannot go back to her old one as she knows that I know about it," replied Tabre, thinking hard. "Without knowing her funding situation I cannot say what her capital is. Transport will be essential though."

"We are in a lockdown situation here, sir. No one will be allowed to take off," she reminded him.

"Satiah is not employed to obey laws," Tabre argued, starting to get irritated. "She's employed because she breaks them."

Ro had sent him a new ship; it would be there by sunrise. He took a copy of Satiah's picture with him as he departed to make a few enquiries of his own. He glanced up at the roof of a nearby building before heading off just in case.

"I'm going to find you," he promised himself, with a determined smile. He reached the Tainted Oasis after half an hour of walking. He entered and ordered a drink. He glanced around trying to understand why she had been there in the first place. She didn't strike him as the kind who celebrated as they worked. He showed the picture to the barmaid. She looked at it for a few moments, the gleam of recognition in her eyes, but she shook her head.

"Nah, I thought I knew her but it's not her," she stated, casually. Why would she lie? Had she been bribed? Tabre smiled, deciding to let it go… who knew? Perhaps Satiah might even return there. One thing troubled him though. She had come here for a reason and he still didn't know what that reason was. Her game may not be escape at all.

***

Breathing heavily from effort of climbing the stairs, Carl got into his office about ten minutes early. He doubted she would turn up. When he entered, the lights, which were automatic, failed to activate as normal. The door slid closed behind him, locking without him doing moving a muscle. From the chilling darkness a voice spoke up.

"You're early," Satiah said, her voice devoid of emotion. "Are you armed?"

"*Kim?*" he clarified, unsure exactly what to feel. Relief? Fear? Anger?

"*I am armed,*" she said. The sound of a movement came to him and then he felt the tip of a gun in his side. "Why don't you sit down?"

"…Are you going to kill me?" he asked, afraid.

"Sit down," she ordered, her voice sharp. He felt his way to his desk and sat down awkwardly.

"Look, I'm here and *no one is with me…*" he began, thinking she thought he'd informed on her.

"I know, I've been watching," she replied, as if it didn't matter.

"Now, I'm a reasonable guy…" he began, trying to shake himself out of his shock. That got a soft guffaw from the darkness.

"…*What?*" he asked, seriously.

"You squeezed my bottom," she sneered, incredulous.

"That's nothing compared with what you did to me. And I'm not just talking about the glass you smashed me with," he argued, hoping that she could take criticism without going mental on him.

"Touché," she replied, finding him as amusing as she had the previous evening.

"Your voice…" he said, noticing that her accent was completely different and… Coalition sounding.

"That's because you're talking to the real me now, Carl," she purred, this time her voice coming from his right and much closer. He looked in that direction but could make nothing out.

"I *knew* you were using me," he said, sadly. "I just couldn't figure out *why*."

"If it's any consolation you weren't bad," she replied. It was and he couldn't remember the last time anyone had said something like that to him.

"…*Really?*" he asked, unable to stop himself grinning.

"I'm *not* in a flirty mood, Carl," she warned, levelly.

"Then you're going to have to stop being so hot," he chanced. The gun tip found him the dark again. "Sorry, sorry," he said, nodding seriously. "You wanted to buy a ship?"

"You have a Kilmister fifteen for sale and…" she began.

"How did you know about *that?*" he demanded, outraged. That ship was not for sale yet, he'd only just got it himself.

"It is my job to know," she replied, quickly. "It's fast and fairly tough for a civilian craft. *I want it.*"

"Oh come on, please, I have plenty of others that would be better," he begged, seriously. "I was saving that for *myself.*" Her lips brushed against his ear, sending a shiver down his back.

"I'm willing to pay you," she said, her voice husky. The tip of the gun dug into the back of his neck. He swallowed.

"With *money* right?" A low giggle came from behind him, making the hairs on the back of his neck rise.

"Don't push it, Carl."

"One million?" he asked, nervously. "You said one million when you called before."

"It's just under twice its value and I'm sure you'd rather *make a killing* than play the central role in one," she said, influentially.

"Well… I'm guessing saying *no to you would be the end for me* so I'm going to go with: *why not?*" he offered, optimistically.

"So we are agreed," she said, turning to leave. Then she stopped and sighed. He tensed in his chair, not daring to move.

"My name is Satiah," she admitted, thinking she probably owed him that much at least. "And if you breathe a word about me to anyone *ever… you remember what I joked about doing to you last night?*"

"Hard to forget that *now,*" he remarked, suitably scared. She smiled in satisfaction. He might be terribly unfit, unpleasing to the eye and more than a little perverted, but he did and could make her laugh.

"*You're a funny man.* Do you have any questions?" she asked, softly.

"Do I mean anything to you?" he asked. She winced in the dark, remembering her prepared answer. She leaned in and kissed his lips strongly before breaking contact and sighing.

"I'd rather not have to kill you…" she offered, fondly running her finger along his face.

"...Fair enough, thanks for that," he said, actually sounding pleased. She smiled and left.

***

Would there ever be peace? Would humanity always be on the knife-edge of total war with itself? Wester didn't know. He'd never seen a fight, never been through a war before. He'd heard a lot about it, most of it bad. When innocent people were hurt in consequence to a situation not of their making it filled him with a bitter rage and a great sadness. Why wouldn't it stop or at least change? He couldn't eat, and just stared down at his plate. Jenjex, sitting opposite him, was watching him keenly. She had been doing her best to eat slowly to try and somehow improve the meal.

"Don't, sir," she warned, grim.

"What?" he asked, seriously.

"Don't think too much about whatever it is you're thinking about," she advised. "No good will come of that."

"I'm sorry, I can't stop thinking about it," he admitted, upset. He rested his face in his hands and sighed heavily.

"Do you want to talk about it?" she asked, concerned.

"I don't want to see people dying and hurting. I don't want there to be fighting, I don't want there to be... *this*," he admitted, freely.

"No, of course not," she said, trying to be as soothing as professionally possible.

"I'm a coward, Jenjex. I'm terrified of what is happening around me," he confessed, emotionally.

"I don't think you are," she stated, honestly. "If you were, surely you would never have continued with Tristram's plan."

"It was just... easier to continue," he stated, clearly in turmoil. Jenjex sighed and patted his hand softly.

"You're under *a lot* of stress, Wester, it's *completely normal* for you to feel afraid and confused about all this. I'd be worried if you had no reaction at all," she said, softly.

"...You seem fine," he pointed out. He wasn't resentful; he was just stating a fact.

"That's because *I'm not in command*," she said, trying to inject a little humour into the conversation. "We are all feeling this strain, believe me. *None of us know what is going to happen*. I can assure you though, that we are all with you. Don't ever forget *that*, okay?" He nodded, holding in tears.

"I'm... *I'm sorry* I'm such lousy company tonight," he apologised, ashamed.

"Sir, I'm relieved that you feel you can talk to me like this. I'm not qualified to evaluate your mind but I know that being able to talk about it does indicate that you're getting through it," she said. "I'm *sure* you've thought of this already but it may be wise not to tell anyone about this?" He chuckled weakly.

"No... Definitely not," he agreed, a little better.

"Earlier you said you were struggling with the decision of what to do next?" He nodded, remembering. "I know you will have considered this already but..." she said, minding her place and her manner well. "If your aim is still to delay the start of all-out war... there may be something else we can do."

"Yes?" he asked, eyeing her.

"Someone as smart as you will, I'm sure, be aware of how close we are to the industrial world of Rymar Delta?" she said. Wester began to realise how much she was trying to please him with all these compliments. She was so brilliant. When his mind was clear from the fog of despair, would he be as sharp as her?

"We *are* close," he replied, indicating he wanted her to carry on.

"There is located one of the biggest factory cities... if it were to be destroyed..." she trailed off.

"It would reduce ship production by about twenty percent! And when it blows there would be no loss of life because it's all automated," he stated, suddenly realising.

"It *is* heavily guarded but... With guile we could talk our way in and then..." she trailed off again.

"They'd never see it coming, they'd think we've run and will be searching deep space for us and we'll be right on their door seal!" he hissed, enthusiastic.

"Sir, that's marvellous, I wish I had thought of that," she said, her acting skills slipping just a little bit. Wester faced her, a knowing look on his face.

"You did," he admitted.

"If you say so, sir," she replied, being annoying subservient. They both stared at one another and it was too much to take. Laughter broke out.

***

That was the sixth security patrol Satiah had spotted. Five soldiers walking the streets in a loose formation. From the rooftop Satiah watched as they turned right at the next intersection. In the darkness she'd be hard to spot where she was but she was taking no chances. She found a gap between two antiquated solar generators and crouched between them. She got hold of Kelvin.

"I have your position, did he agree?" he asked.

"He did. We have not got all the particulars but I *believe* our next ship is secured. *Let Reed know*. Also, it appears the lockdown is not being lifted anytime soon," she reported.

"Understood."

She slipped back out onto the walkway again cautiously. She froze. A woman was standing not far away, having a smoke. She had not been there a split second before and she turned, her peripheral vision detecting movement. For a while both women stared at one another.

"Not a…" Satiah began, trying to get her to stay quiet. The woman screamed and turned to flee before Satiah could stun her. Satiah fired but only caught her leg. Rapid laser fire sounded from below and Satiah lay flat as the edges of the roof was pelted suddenly. Blast! She crawled swiftly along hoping to slip away before more units arrived. That was when the drone descended. It came in fast and let go of a large static flare. Static flares were like stun shots but when they landed they radiated out in all directions.

Satiah had no choice if she wished to remain conscious. Using her grapple gun she swung dramatically across the street and in through the glass of a window. Shouts from the street outside could be heard as she regained her feet and tried to make out where she was in the darkness. An office of some kind. She raced into the next unit knowing she only had seconds before every patrol in the area descended on the place. A loud crashing noise from the opposite end told her that she'd already been found. She crouched and skulked along. She could hear a lot of boots on the floor. The searching team was spreading out, quickly covering the ground between them and her. She stood no chance alone against this many. Staying calm, she reached the windows near the opposite side and peered out. The next street along was deserted.

Gently she pushed the window open and aimed the grapple gun. She fired at the next building across and then slipped out of the window. She fell and activated. In a curving fall she was swept up against the side of the next building. She clung on there, motionless for a few seconds, wondering if her departure had been observed. Apparently not. She searched for cover and spotted a duct on the ground. She knew from Kelvin's maps that it led to the sewers. Slowly she slid down the side of the building. Using a laser cutter she sliced her way through the metal panel and then, just as she was about to go down, a shout came from the window. She glanced up, clocked a rifle barrel and dived forwards. The shot missed and struck the ground where she had been.

She landed with a splash in something cold and disgusting. She ignored the smell and breathed through her mouth only as she flashed her light to see the way. It was waist-high sewage and she could only go so fast through it. The guards reached the open hatch and debated the pros and cons of following her. Tabre came across them then, having been alerted by the main security channel.

"She went down there?" he guessed. They nodded and he jumped down. Satiah heard the splash when she'd got about a tunnel and a half away. She stopped and deactivated her light, plunging the place into darkness. Silence except for the gentle swishing of the gunge. She began to move along more slowly now. Tabre had been waiting for sounds but when he heard nothing he guessed that, if she was still around, she was waiting and listening for him. He pulled a heat seeker from his pocket.

A faint signal came from his left. He began to wade through the slime in its direction. His communicator bleeped loudly and he swore.

"Tabre, is she down there?" It was the chief of security. Before he could answer, rapid splashing ahead of him sounded. Satiah, having heard that someone was indeed down there with her had picked up her pace. Tabre hurried towards the noise. She was too far ahead for him to take her down.

"She is!" he barked back, angry. Satiah, knowing who was after her, was now going as fast as she could. She reached a T-junction and took the right route. Unfortunately she'd not had the foresight to study maps of the sewage system of the city.

Tabre, sensing he would get no closer to her, hatched a vicious plan. The sewers were full of methane. Methane was flammable. Igniting it would kill anyone unfortunate enough to be down there. Turning back reluctantly he used a rusty ladder to scramble his way back to the street. Satiah kept going until she turned to listen. No noise. That didn't by any definition mean that the chase was over. She activated her light again and looked for cables to follow. She had to get out of there. It would only be a few minutes before all the obvious exits were secured and she would be trapped. She had to find a less conventional way of exiting the tunnels. Splashing a little as she went she spotted an alcove high up and a metal door beyond. She hauled herself out to check it more closely. It was where the snaking cables led.

Tabre dropped the firebomb. It fell almost slower than normal in his eyes towards the sewage. The fire started before it hit the surface and a rush of fireballs began, vanishing down every tunnel, consuming the gases voraciously. The first Satiah knew about it was a bright light hurtling towards her, after a strong backdraft. Wincing, she blasted the lock and dived into the room beyond heedless of what might be there. The flames licked at her and her cloak, saturated in sewage, caught fire. She ripped herself free of it and kicked it back into the blaze before forcing the door shut. She couldn't breathe. The fire had not only consumed the methane, hydrogen sulphide and ammonia. It had also eaten up the oxygen too. Gasping and gasping, her lungs dragging in load after load of nothing but monoxide and dioxides. Using the last of her energy she shot open the next door and collapsed, briefly blacking out.

Oxygen starved, Satiah had begun to go through hypoxia but, in the corridor beyond, the air was regulated and clean. Maybe thirty seconds after blacking out she awoke again, breathing normally. She sat up, assessing herself for injury. It would be some time before anyone could confirm that the fire had killed her but most would assume it had. Just as well... she needed that time to recover. She stood and looked around. Where was she? The tidiness and condition of the corridor indicated a business structure. Aware that she stank, she padded along seeking alternative clothes and washing facilities.

She found them and borrowed long grey working overalls. Just another kind of body suit only with no armour and the company logo on the back. *Jaylite Industries*. The name sent a shiver up her spine. The universe could be so creepy sometimes. Her boots, completely ruined after so much strife, she abandoned. She simply took a spare set of safety boots and used them. It had taken her ten minutes but she was clean, dry and in a new disguise. She worked out that she had to be on a lower level and that if she planned on getting out she would have to go up. She did. The lifts required handprints to operate but she just took the stairs. Sloppy security.

She entered the reception area; a bemused-looking receptionist eyed her. As trained, Satiah knew the best thing to do when confronted was to assume the visage of a superior or at least someone in authority.

"Um... Excuse me," she began, standing up from behind her desk.

"*Halt*," ordered Satiah, again employing her accent. Her tone was commanding and the other woman obligingly obeyed, caught out by the abrupt mandate. "Continue with your duties. I have almost completed my safety tour. Code 771." With that she breezed on past and left the building.

Outside Satiah stopped as she took in what was going on. *Apparently* Tabre's plan to cook her alive had *backfired* slightly. Pun intended. The chain reaction of gas explosions at set several buildings on fire and had destroyed a fuel storage depot. The city was in chaos. Fire crews were scrambling around trying to respond to more than they could cope with. Satiah walked briskly along through the madness, an amused grin on her face. Her communicator went off.

"What on Earth have you been up to *now*? I asked you to *get a ship* not *cremate the neighbourhood!*" Reed said, his voice playful. He knew that, if it had been her, it wasn't likely what she had intended to happen.

"That was Tabre," she replied, quickly. "I may have got us a ship but I'm going to need one million Essps."

"*One million?*" he squawked. She stopped, sighing.

"*You said money wasn't a problem,*" she reminded him.

"It wasn't until you asked for it," he retorted, tetchy.

"Okay," she hissed, staying calm. She stopped and slipped into a darkened doorway. "How much do you have?"

"None," he replied.

"*None!*" she almost wailed.

"Well…"

"How am I supposed to get us a ship if I don't have any money?" she demanded, flatly.

"I thought you were just going to steal one, *you usually do,*" he replied.

"*I don't!*" she protested, scoffing. "I *bought* my old freighter out of my own money. You gave me the next one and… okay we *all* stole the troop transport but we had no choice!"

"Well, just steal *this one,*" he ordered. She pouted momentarily. She thought about poor Carl and what she'd already done to him. Stealing the ship was just overkill.

"Reed, I don't want to do that," she replied, stubbornly. He paused, noting her change in tone.

"Then we appear to be stuck again," he replied, patiently. A long silence. She shook her head. He was prodding her, waiting for her to come up with the solution.

"…Leave it to me, *I'll think of something.* There's no actual time that has been chosen for the exchange yet so we have a little interval to sort this problem out," she said.

"That's *wonderful,* I knew you wouldn't let me down," he replied, all smiles again. She smiled too, his mood swings amusing her.

"Tell Kelvin and Carlos to be ready when I get back," she requested.

"Ready for *what?*" he asked, concerned.

"Talking over a few things."

***

Rymar Delta was a rocky planet. Its surface was one huge factory. It built ships for the Colonial Federation. Warships. Destroyer *Warrior* appeared, sliding neatly into orbit.

Jenjex looked up from her station and touched her hat to Wester. He nodded back and opened a channel.

"Rymar Delta control, this is Federation Destroyer *Guardian*," he lied, smoothly. "We have sustained damage to our shielding systems and request repair work to begin."

"*Guardian*, this is Rymar Delta control, we have space at shipyard four. I will send you coordinates," said the woman. "What is your consent code?" Jenjex and Wester made eye contact.

"Red three, Blue sixty, Red eight, green two, and blue nine," he lied.

Code books of the Colonial navy were many and complex. The books were colour coded and numbered. Each number listed a reference and each colour listed the same numbers but with different references. The references, when entered into the code system in the correct order, would spell out a serial number. This number could then be checked on the list of ships which were all there. On that list would be crew, rosters and all other concomitants. The code Wester had given was not for Warrior. It was a complete fake but he was wagering on the infamous lack of efficiency when it came to updating the files.

"...I'm sorry, you do not *seem* to be listed," the woman said, sounding puzzled. Of course they weren't.

"We were commissioned only three days ago," he lied, swiftly. "It's *possible* they have not yet included us in your database." Next came the judgment call, not theirs but *hers*. This poor woman, who would most likely get the blame for letting them in past the shields, simply because it was her bad luck to be on station, would make the call. Wester hoped that she would at least check with her superior first and therefore have a chance at passing the blame back up. Jenjex winked at him to let him know that she felt he sounded convincing.

"Very good," the woman said, at last.

Smiles were everywhere among the crew as they quietly celebrated the success of the ruse. Action did indeed raise spirits and, so long as he remained successful, it increased the crew's faith in their Captain. The coordinates arrived and they set off towards the surface of the planet. During the briefing earlier, it had been decided that their target would be the hollow structural sections which the giant shipyards balanced on. Inside these huge metal tubes were giant lifts used for conveying parts up and down from the working platforms. They were also the weakest part of the constructions. In a well-timed attack run they could cripple half the planet for months. There shouldn't be any loss of life as most of the facilities were operated by androids. The commercial cost, though, would be astronomical.

They accelerated down and battle stations were assumed. Naturally a short burst of acceleration was to be expected from any approaching ship that was leaving orbit. Wester could only imagine the look on the woman's face as she watched the ship continue to accelerate rather than slow down.

"Targets set," a flight officer called.

"Wait for the order!" snapped Jenjex, sounding more excited than angry. Wester too could feel the adrenalin rush as they reached attack speed. The surface of the planet was screaming past at thousands of miles an hour.

"Err, Captain you appear to be..." came the woman's voice from Rymar Delta control.

"*Fire!*" he roared, over her.

Missiles blasted away, thousands of them, all aiming for different structural sections. The lasers also opened up at nothing in particular but just adding to the destruction. Explosions both near and distant shot past as they continued on. Alarms blared, engines howled and debris flew.

"Lieutenant!" he called, eyeing the long-range scopes. Three dreadnaughts, the planet's resident defenders, had appeared and were approaching. "We have enemy ships, point nine seven two."

"Orders, sir?" she replied, tipping her hat. He watched as they formed a triangle formation. In that deployment they could attack and defend themselves without getting in each other's way. When confronting any enemy, it was a sensible enough method.

"We pull up and out," he replied, over the noise.

"Cease fire!"

"Course, sir?" bellowed the navigator. Wester watched the oncoming ships. They couldn't chance splitting up to trap him, as a destroyer could easily outgun a single dreadnaught. Together they were a match but... they had to come at him from one direction or another. And whichever way they chose, he would run the other way. They slowed, reaching the same conclusion he had most likely, and chose left.

"Give me segmentation at forty," Wester replied, after nippy consideration.

"Wedge at forty it is, sir!" he barked back. Slowing slightly as it began a diagonal gradient, the destroyer raced up, away from the surface and into the clouds. The path they were taking would get them back into space while, at the same time, keeping the majority of the planet between them and the approaching dreadnaughts. A message arrived.

"Halt! Captain Wester, we *know* who you are!" shouted an angry voice. Whether they were trying to guess who he was or just trying to keep him talking Wester didn't care.

"That is something we both know," he replied, smugly. Then he cut them off. Jenjex grinned. Guns on the surface were starting to fire at them now but they were quickly out of range.

They were off again. Vanishing in the blink of an eye. Leaving Rymar Delta far behind to burn. As before, they had already decided where they would go next. This time, though, it was no hit-and-run assault. It was a mission of diplomacy. They were headed for Earth itself, the very heart of the Coalition. There, they would hopefully be able to warn them of what was going on. Wester was worried though. Not only was there the chance they may be shot down out of fright or simply not believed, there was also the possibility that the Coalition may detain them. Earth was rumoured to be one of the most heavily defended places in the cosmos so *one destroyer*, he hoped, would not be perceived as much of a threat.

"Damage report?" he asked.

"Nothing, sir," Jenjex replied. She had looked but she hadn't had to. It was fairly obvious that they hadn't taken a single hit.

***

"*What?*"

The scream could be heard everywhere on that floor. Ro had already been fuming about *Warrior's* escape. When she had been told about what had happened at Rymar Delta only that morning, she exploded.

"*How the hell did that happen?*" she demanded, not even listening to the answers she was getting. Her plans were in ruins! With about twenty percent of the fleet out of commission and now the biggest shipyard facility crippled for months, there was no question. The campaign against the Coalition would have to wait. She couldn't fight a war without the ships and now she'd didn't have enough. She slammed her fist down on the armrest, in a frightful rage.

"Execute them!" she ordered, rather confusingly.

"*Who*, ma'am? The ship has gone, *no prisoners were taken…*" began an aide.

"The entire staff of Rymar Delta!" she clarified. "*They will pay for this betrayal!*" The two men looked at one another. Her voice started out soft and smooth. "I can tolerate mistakes, I can tolerate delays, but one thing I will not tolerate is disloyalty. Thanks to *them* our campaign may be delayed indefinitely! People must learn how serious I am about this… they need a strong example of the penalty for failure!" She was screaming again at the end, her eyes gleaming vengefully.

***

"Let me get this straight in my head," Reed sighed, eyeing Satiah. "The city is fighting fires everywhere, there's one right underneath us actually, and *you* want to raid the bank?"

"It's the only quick way I can think of to get the sum we need," she argued. "It's an ideal time to strike as the security forces are already overextended because of the fires."

"It's *brilliant*," he smiled, approvingly. "Just the *four* of you?" That last question displayed his real opinion.

"It should be enough," she replied, shrugging.

"Always assuming they *have* the money in the vault," he murmured.

"Well, if they don't, we're ruined," she muttered. It was possible, on a world such as this, that such large sums were simply not housed there. It was unfortunately their only option.

***

Tabre sighed heavily as he waited for the search team to complete their report. After what seemed like forever, the chief detached himself from the group and approached him. He did not look happy.

"Well?" Tabre asked, without preamble.

"Four bodies were found and examined. All were male. The teams can find no trace of her," he replied. Tabre smiled, shaking his head slowly. The only victims of his plan had mostly likely been the homeless. "*No one* could have survived that, I'm sure," the chief went on, thinking about the damage. "*Assuming she was there in the first place…*"

"She was and she did," Tabre replied, with certainty. "I'm not sure *how* but she did."

"Impossible," the chief argued.

"We'll find out soon enough," Tabre said, grim. "As long as she's stuck here she'll be gunning for us. She's got a few things I haven't. A place to hide. Friendly locals willing to lie on her behalf." He smiled bleakly. "*She's got all that.*" Then he scowled at the chief.

"And all *I* have is *you*," he added, with a good dose of venom. The chief smiled tightly before moving away. Tabre's eyes spotted an incoming ship. It was a military cruiser, normally used for long-distance reconnaissance missions. Either it had arrived by chance for refuelling or… this was the ship Ro had sent him arriving early. At least someone was capable of doing what they said! He marched down the streets towards the shipyard, keeping a sharp lookout for Satiah.

***

"It seems our new friend has been busy," Ash remarked, watching the security teams as they ran hither and thither chaotically. Ruby too noticed the insane amount of activity going on.

"You *know* she's just doing her job," Ruby reminded him, patiently. "I've heard some things about those Phantom agents and they are like… you know? *Really* hardcore. *Very serious people.*"

"You think I should be *impressed?*" he demanded, grit in his tone.

"…As serious as *humans* can be," she amended, for him. "What is it with you and Reed anyway? First you tell me he's all dangerous and then you say I can trust him. Now you and him are just… *fighting.*"

"I don't want them to get involved, this is *my* responsibility," he explained, eyeing her. "*Can you understand that?*"

"You ask another question like that and I'll swing for you, duffer," she muttered, grinning. "Look, if you don't like it, why don't you help them get a ship? We're *wasting time* here."

"*Why* did you delete that information?" he asked, suddenly.

"I told you…" she scoffed, rolling her eyes. "*Stop trying to change the subject.*"

"Satiah might well arrest you," he warned, levelly. "She does have the right and the ability."

"Earlier you *said…*" she began, dismissively.

"Earlier the others were there, now they are not," he interrupted. "*It's time you tell me everything.*" She stopped walking, closed her eyes and held her breath. He waited.

"…I can't," she answered, seriously.

"Don't make me make you," he warned, looming up in front of her. "You are only human after all. I can see into your mind if I choose. I don't want to do it because it would be wrong. But don't think I won't if pushed."

"It's private, *okay*! I *thought* we were friends," she yelled, turning away. His arm shot out, catching her. Normally so protective, the vicelike grip his hands took of her was painful and unyielding. She inhaled sharply in discomfort.

"You're in trouble, Ruby. If you don't tell me everything I cannot protect you from it," he stated, coldly.

"Let go of my arm," she instructed, angry. He released his grip and she began to walk away. Then she was in the air, suspended about a foot off the ground, held there by telekinetic force.

"*Hey!*" Her legs swung madly to try and make contact with the ground.

Slowly she turned in mid-air and floated back over to a grinning Ash.

"Ah, you've returned," he quipped, amused.

"*Put me down!*" she ordered, livid.

"Give it up, Ruby, we can stay like this as long as it takes," he requested, firmly.

"You may well live for all time but I don't have to say *anything!*" she stated, uncooperatively. There was a brief silence before the inevitable outburst occurred.

"It was an accident! How many times do I have to say it…?" Tears formed in her eyes. She swiped ineffectively at him.

"If we *are* friends then you can and should trust me," he said, turning her own words back on her. "Friends help each other, don't they? Just because I can wait forever doesn't mean that I will." He could sense he was nearing the mental barrier she'd created to hide the truth behind.

It would be so easy for him to smash through it and tear the truth out of her but he didn't want to. This was important! Important that she could completely open up before him. Tears were running down her face now and she looked… defeated. He lowered her to the ground and she made no attempt to run this time. She sniffed and her lower lip trembled. He pulled her close for a hug. She resisted at first then relaxed and began sobbing against him. The wall was weakening. She was going to tell him.

"My dad is a businessman," she began, her voice steady but fraught. "He's very successful and wealthy. I know he deals with shares and things." Ash waited, wondering where this was going. "I was just going through the daily reports of sale and exchanges when… I noticed something.

"There are lots of rules about trading but there is one in particular that is most important. The service takes ten percent off of every exchange. It's called the sales tax. It's how we make money while we supervise the market. Well... my dad sold fourteen millions Essps worth of shares... without paying the tax. I don't know why or even how he had managed it. Clearly it had been done before, someone else working there must have been skimming it. Preventing the charge from going through and then hiding or altering the record. Maybe my dad was paying them, maybe not. *Whatever...* I was suddenly confronted with evidence that my dad had just committed fraud," she explained. Her voice was softer now... almost robotic in tone. "I don't know how long I sat there, maybe twenty minutes. I was trying to figure out what was going on. When I realised that it was not a mistake or some kind of system problem... *I had a choice.* Report it... or not."

"You didn't say anything did you?" he asked, guessing. She shook her head and let out a sob.

"How *could* I? *It's my dad!*" she objected, emotionally. "Once I'd taken the decision not to report it, I realised I too was a criminal. *Why?* Because I now had to *hide the evidence*. I had to protect us *both*. So I deleted all traces of it from the system."

"Ten years?" he frowned, confused. She'd deleted not just one thing but ten years' worth of financial records.

"Yeah... that was my *next* mistake. I'm not very coolheaded at the best of times *as you know* and in my panic I... I deleted *everything*, not just the bit I was trying to hide. Of course... when I realised what I had done I panicked all over again. I did what I always do... *I ran,*" she concluded.

"Why did you run to *me?*" he asked, inevitably.

"What I said was before was perfectly true. I'd heard rumours about immortals and I did really want to meet one. Also I needed to get away and I hoped that if I found you, *no one would find me,*" she explained, thinking back.

"You took a huge risk, you only *just* found me in time," he said, awestruck.

"I'd already taken more risks in that last hour than I had for *years*. I was in endgame mode by that stage," she replied, sniffing. Her tears had gone but the paths they had taken remained on her face. "Running on adrenalin, making it up as I went along... Hoping for salvation. *Wishing for it all never to have started.*"

"And of course, you cannot return unless you're willing to not only confess *your* crime but also *expose your father's*," he summarised, thoughtful.

"Who better to run forever with than an immortal?" she murmured, more serious than he'd ever heard her before.

A new silence descended and he still held her. She shifted and looked up at him.

"You hate me now, don't you?" she asked, sorrowfully. "Because I lied to you."

"No," he replied, as if nothing ever mattered. The answer surprised her.

"…I suppose you can't hate someone you've never really cared about," she said, without any bite. She hadn't meant it as a challenge at all. She only implied that he thought of her only as *the human that followed him*. Something to study and test but nothing more than that.

"If I didn't care about you, Ruby, I'd never have bothered saving you from that virus. I'd never have told you why I was here or what I have to do next. If I didn't care, I would not protect you as I do," he replied, solidly. "The only one you ever really lied to was yourself. You've kept telling yourself that something terrible would happen if I knew the truth."

He looked all around suddenly and she tensed. He smiled.

"Have lives been lost because of your secret? Have planets been destroyed? No… silence. *There is no change*," he said, gently. He looked down at her. Tears were in her eyes again but these tears were different in meaning. He leaned in closer, his lips brushed against hers. He pulled back to measure her reaction. She showed no sign of discomfort. He moved in again with more conviction, kissed her again. This time her arms wrapped around his neck as she kissed him back. Heat came from her body and he absorbed it, finding the energy in it.

***

Earth. The blue star. The political centre of the Coalition. Quadrillions of tiny ships flowed in, out and around it. Like a giant nest of insects. It was incredible the difference one extra one could make. The second Federation destroyer *Warrior* showed up, the tiny craft scattered and a message was beamed at them.

"Surrender now!" boomed a voice. Wester oversaw their arrival and was surprised with the speed that Earth security moved at. Granted it had not been long since their last battle but still…

"We have six Coalition destroyers approaching. Also there's a frigate moving in behind us," Jenjex warned, tense.

"This is Captain Wester of the Colonial Federation," Wester stated, formally. "We have no hostile intent. I repeat, *no* hostile intent. I wish to speak to an ambassador or a high-ranking military representative."

"Speaking," stated a man, quickly. Again Wester was taken aback by their efficiency. Did they have one on permanent station there in case this kind of thing happened? Possibly. And Ro had wanted war against these guys?

"Whom do I have the honour of addressing?" he asked, thinking carefully.

"My name is Senator Sython, I represent the Coalition, state your purpose please?" came the calmer, more measured voice.

"Recently the Federation has appointed a new leader. You may already know of her, Ro Tammer…" Wester began, considering wording.

"We're aware of her," a new voice chimed in.

"Who is that?" asked Wester, confused.

"Phantom Leader Randal," he answered. "Your ship is wanted, Captain Wester… for mutiny and illegal attacks… It's a good thing Captain Moxin is here to speak on your behalf."

"*Sorry?*" he asked, starting to think he was hallucinating.

"No, it is *I* who should apologise," Erica answered, her accent was clear. "I was aware that we were betrayed and I had an associate warn Tristram. My double was killed but I survived… I assume that Tristram too is dead."

"…Yes, murdered by the insider you indirectly warned him about," replied Wester, seriously. "He chose to press on regardless of your absence."

"The Coalition is watching the Federation closely. They know all about Ro Tammer. Two Phantom agents were present at the rally, relaying reports of her speeches," Erica explained. "But... we can do all this in person..." Jenjex was speechless but her hand slowly rose to touch her hat.

"Sir... there's a signal for us to follow," she said, staring at him blankly.

***

Satiah peered out of the open window cautiously. The main security station was right across the street from her. She eyed the vehicle parked opposite, loaded with high explosives. She pulled out the controller from her thigh pocket. It had been decided that, just to ensure the security forces didn't interfere with the attack on the bank... Satiah would attack them first. Kelvin, Carlos and Deva would take the bank when she gave the signal. Satiah had spent an hour checking out the security building. It seemed typical enough of most structures on Ionar 12. Cheaply built and not designed for anything strenuous. She activated the autopilot of the vehicle and drove it down a side street. Then she gave one last look around. A lot of them were still out firefighting.

She activated. The vehicle shot forwards, accelerating madly towards the security building's main entrance. It crashed through into the reception area beyond, sending glass and bits of door flying. Satiah dropped the controller, aimed the rifle and fired. The bolt hit the high explosive and it went off. The huge explosion practically ripped the building in half. She tapped her communicator.

"Time for you to move," she advised, as dazed security members began to scramble around. Expertly, she stunned them one at a time. She hurried down the stairs and back out into the street, rifle raised. Smoke was everywhere and she continued to knock out any security she saw.

Then she stopped and looked up, upon realising the building wasn't done moving yet. The left-hand side of the building crashed loudly before falling destructively to one side, knocking into another building as it went. She crouched, covering her eyes. She heard another explosion. Alarms began blaring, people shouting and screaming in multiple tones and directions. She felt a layer of dust and dirt settle over her before standing again and looking around. No one, just smoke and destruction. She lowered the rifle, a tiny bit flabbergasted. Obviously this city didn't have much in the way of security!

The chief was standing there in stunned silence as Tabre waved a hand.

"Told you," he said, simply. "She's not a regular criminal, *she's a Phantom*. You or any of your men get in her way and she will put you down as soon as she sees you." Tabre, guessing that Satiah may make an attack on the security building itself had taken the precaution of moving to a nearby building. Reluctantly the chief had agreed to join him there with a few men but most had remained in the security building. And now, just as Tabre had predicted, Satiah was there remorselessly gunning them down.

"She will be looking for me of course," Tabre went on, amused. "I wonder what she will do when she learns I'm not in there."

"You people are monsters," the chief stated, horrified. The idea that law and order could be so easily overcome or simply ignored had never entered his mind before and he didn't like it. Tabre chuckled grimly.

"Nevertheless, without us, your cosy little societies could not last a day," he replied, without any hint of shame. Inside he was raptured. The hunt was once again on. He was there and she was there too. Bliss. No rules! Nothing else! Just them and their wits! The ultimate test stood there before him... and he was ready to take it. His heart was already racing. He turned and was surprised to see that the chief had his gun trained on him!

"You *knew* this would happen and you just let her..." the man began, furious.

"Oh yes, *you think you could do better*, you and your disgrace of a security force? And what would you have done exactly?" demanded Tabre, coolly. "Politely ask her to *stop or else*?"

"You are under arrest for..." began the chief, enraged.

A burst of air interrupted him and a blade embedded itself in his chest. He stared down at it, despair and surprise on his face. Tabre sighed, displaying the weapon on his wrist that had been concealed under his sleeve.

"*You* have wasted both *this weapon*, which I was saving for her, *and* my time," Tabre stated, as the man fell to his knees. "You are fortunate in a way. For all your failures Ro would never have let you go so quickly or painlessly." Another explosion from outside made him glance around swiftly. A feral smile on his face, he grabbed a rifle and dashed outside.

***

Kelvin burst into the entrance of the bank, Carlos and Deva in tow. Two guards thought about trying to stop them but self-preservation prevailed and they fled. Alarms were blaring but everyone knew no help would be coming anytime soon. Stunning anyone who got in their way, the teenagers, each taking turns to lead the other, snaked their way down to the vaults. Kelvin remained at the entrance to scare anyone else away.

"I thought this job would be boring but it's kind of fun!" Carlos smirked, as they reached the vault door.

"It's all about attitude." Deva grinned back, as she placed the explosive on the door. They retreated. The explosion ripped through everything except the door. They peeped out from behind cover, coughing in the smoke. The door was still intact.

"Shame, I was afraid of this," Carlos muttered. "Nice to see they didn't go cheap on the important doors."

"I've got one more charge," she stated, showing it to him.

"Another one of those things and we risk bringing the whole place down around us," he replied, thinking about it.

"So what then?" she demanded. They exchanged looks and grinned together. Each taking run-ups, they threw themselves at the door. Battered and dented as it was, it might just fall in. Finally they ran at it together and it crunched under them, half falling in. It was by no means completely open but it was enough for them to scramble in. There were the Essps in giant purple bars. Carlos grabbed one marked for a million and started to leave. Deva stared and slowly moved to grab her own. He returned and slapped her hand, making her release her catch.

"We don't *need* any more," he sniggered, amused by her

opportunism. She scowled but nodded.

The familiar whoosh of Kelvin's flamethrower was audible as they sprinted up the steps three at a time.

"What do we have?" Carlos asked, turning Deva around to get to her bag. He shoved the money inside.

"One security vehicle, two female humans using it as cover. Their intention is not to come in and confront but to prevent us from leaving," Kelvin summarised. "But they are only covering the front entrance."

"Only?" Deva confirmed, confused. "Why is that not a problem? That's our way out."

"It *was*," Kelvin correct, starting to run. He literally ran straight through the building wall, smashing through it like a tank and out into another street. Carlos and Deva looked at one another and grinned.

"Time to go," he said, lobbing the remaining charge over his shoulder.

***

Reed was on the roof when Ash and Ruby found him. They were watching; while the sun rose, the city was burning and screaming. Ruby gaped in shock.

"It's a warzone," Ash noted, sourly. Another explosion made Ruby jump and hide her face in her hands. Her fingers parted rather comically so that she could peer out.

"*Yes*," Reed sighed, troubled. "I *suspect* Tabre is behind the worst of it. *No wonder so many sponsor pejorism these days.*" Ash and Ruby exchanged glances of doubt.

"Nothing to do with *Satiah* then?" Ash enquired, meaningfully.

"Do you want to get to this bally space station *or not*?" Reed asked, testily. He was not in the mood for Ash right then. He was having enough trouble with his own conscience as it was.

"Dreda told me you were a lawyer?" Ash asked. Reed slowly turned to look around at them, his eyes narrowed.

"*What have you done?*" he queried, ominously. "I would have thought that someone like you wouldn't consider human justice to be of any relevance to you."

"For an immortal *I don't*, however, it is not I that needs you expertise, it's Ruby," he stated, without getting riled. Reed looked at them both for a few seconds.

"Why should I help her?" Reed demanded, still more than a little annoyed. "It's hardly good timing…"

"Dreda told me you were the best. And I *know* what you did for Elle," Ash went on, in a tone that seemed unconcerned. "I think you owe someone like Ruby more of your time than someone like Elle."

"Elle was different," excused Reed, argumentatively. "She'd been… very unfortunate…"

"Nevertheless, you intervened and saved her from possible execution," Ash reminded him.

"She didn't deserve *that*, in any case you know the whole thing was rigged and I didn't do it alone. Mensa was there and prevented Commander Lewis Grey from simply executing all of us there and then," Reed stated, obstinate.

"I'm trying to appeal to your sense of justice," Ash mused, deliberately using the word 'appeal'.

"First it might be an idea to tell me exactly what she's supposed to have done?" Reed snapped, irritably.

"I did do it…" Ruby began, confused.

"*No!*" yelled Reed, over her. She straightened unconsciously, mildly startled by his interruption. "*Step one*, never *admit your own guilt* until your lawyer says it's in your best interests to do so."

"Sorry…" she replied, a little shocked by his outburst. Another explosion from the city made her cringe.

"Well?" asked Reed, impatiently.

"Tell him what you *think* you'll be accused of," advised Ash, cleverly.

"Malicious damage of company property by way of deleting financial records going back approximately ten years, concealing fraud and fleeing arrest," she replied, after thinking about it.

"First offence?" Reed asked, quickly.

"What?" she asked.

"Have you ever committed a crime before?" he clarified, seriously. She tried to remember, she didn't think so.

"...No," she answered, shaking her head.

"And what is the alleged reason for your actions?" Reed asked, seeming to calm down.

"Huh?"

"What motivated you to destroy the records and then to run?" Ash prompted.

"...Nothing," she said, ponderously.

"Okay... that *is* the correct answer but *I'm the one who needs to know the truth*," Reed stated, patiently. Ruby explained it all to him and he listened intently.

"Does your father know that you discovered his dealings?" Reed asked.

"He may do now," Ash replied, shrugging. Reed sighed.

"Tricky case," he remarked, as if dismissing them. He turned to face the city again. Ash and Ruby exchanged glances.

"*So you'll help me?*" Ruby chanced, hopefully.

"What do I get?" he asked, facing them again. Ash rolled his eyes.

"*Reed*," he growled, warningly.

"I don't see why I should work *for free...*" Reed argued, irascibly.

"*Elle* never paid you..." Ash pointed out.

"Not in money, no," agreed Reed, raising an eyebrow. "She did, however, help me a lot with other things."

"Well... what do you want from me?" Ruby asked, a little puzzled. "How could I help you?"

"*For a start I want Ash to get off of Satiah's back*," Reed muttered, seriously. "She's my employee right now and if anyone has a go at her it should be me."

"Done," Ash smirked, as if it made no difference to him.

Another explosion sounded and they spun to watch a building, not too far away, begin to collapse.

"*And?*" Ruby asked, uneasy.

"And... I think we should get inside," Reed replied, astutely. "I'm sure I'll think of something else you can provide me with."

"Does this mean you will help me?" Ruby asked, hopefully.

"Of course it does, he's just haggling," Ash sighed, as if bored. They retreated back into the safe house where the noises of the explosions were dimmer and faraway sounding.

"All of this won't matter if we never leave this world," Ash smiled, provocatively.

"I thought you weren't going to annoy Satiah anymore," Reed murmured.

"I'm not, I'm annoying you."

***

Through the dust, ash and dirt which now dominated the air, Satiah marched. The place looked like it was experiencing a volcanic eruption. The yellow of flame, the grey of debris and beige of everything else seemed to make the whole world more claustrophobic. Someone else ran out from somewhere to her left. She stunned them too. Surely Carlos must be done by now? A strong wind pummelled her body from the left as a craft skimmed the ground. The craft sprayed water across the front of the burning building. Steam rose, hissing from the volatility of contrasting temperatures. Her lungs would need a good cleaning after this. That dust was dangerous and the levels of monoxide were not worth thinking about.

Tabre emerged from one of the few untouched buildings, firing at her. She rolled to take cover behind the remains of a vehicle, partly crushed by falling rubble. He too was quick to find protection as she returned fire. So he had survived the attack of the security building. He'd probably anticipated the attack and removed himself accordingly. Anxious to end this battle of theirs, Satiah started hammering away at the engine housing of the vehicle he was crouched behind. Before she could cut into anything explosive, something rolled out from under the vehicle. She just recognised it in time to shield her eyes. Flasher charge. A white blinding flash occurred followed by a much paler fog that concealed the vehicle completely.

Tabre charged through the fog, leaping over the remains of the destroyed means of transportation she had been hiding behind to grapple with her *while* she was blinded. But she wasn't there. As he landed he spotted the grenade she'd left behind, timer already counting down. He threw himself backwards, just clearing the metal of the wreckage as it blew. The force flipped the remains, spinning, straight over him and crashing down on the opposite side of the street. Satiah staggered along, partially blinded. Tears and a white haze clouded her vision but she'd guessed his plan and countered it, albeit desperately. She stumbled into darkness, presumably the interior of a building. She collided with something painfully and cried out as she went over. Whatever it was also went down with a clatter.

She lay there in the semi-darkness, blinking away the tears and trying to see again. Her hand fumbled with her belt seeking some field medication she'd had the foresight to carry. Eye clearance drops. Panting in the somewhat cleaner air of the room, she delicately poured some of the pink fluid into each eye and blinked some more. Her sight completely returned and she swung around, checking everything out. It was difficult to say exactly what kind of building this was but it seemed deserted. Her leg throbbed as it seemed she had just blundered right into a metal table. She stood slowly and limped along, deciding that now might be a good time to check in with Carlos.

"Carlos, do you have the money?" she asked, seriously.

"We do," he stated, quickly. "We've escaped the bank area and are just about to re-enter the safe house. Do you need help?"

"I'll be fine," she breathed, patting her injured leg automatically. "See you there." She disconnected and took two paces forward. That was when the wall to her left caved in, sending her reeling through a set of glass doors to her right. She rolled with the momentum, trying to avoid hurting herself even more. Unluckily the set of metal stairs beyond were too close for her to stop herself from falling down them. She lost her rifle as she flipped and crashed her way to the bottom. She encountered the next wall against her back and sat there, stunned.

Tabre, tracking her heat signal, had driven an emergency fire control transporter through the wall. He forced his way out of the control cabin and checked the signal. She was close, scarcely six metres ahead and a few metres below him. She wasn't moving. Setting his pistol to stun, as he still needed her alive to get to Reed, he advanced expecting another trap. Satiah, deducing he would not be far away, fought against the disorientation and kicked the protective grille off a ventilation shaft. She hauled herself inside and began to drag herself along as fast as she could. Tabre crept down the steps cautiously, checking for any mines as he went, towards the now open ventilation shaft. Activating a light he swiftly peeped inside and moved away again, expecting to be shot at. Nothing.

Taking a chance, he peered in more slowly and the light was just in time to illuminate Satiah's boots as she vanished around a corner. He debated inwardly. Follow or find where the shaft emerges and wait there for her to come out? He chose the second option knowing it would be dangerous to follow in such a confined space. Satiah, bleeding and bruised, concentrated on pressing her open palms on the metal and hauling herself along. She had to stay ahead of him. She had to. She couldn't hear him approaching her from behind, that meant he would be moving to where he thought the shaft ended. She stopped, taking a few moments to rest and then activated her own torch. She was lying on her front as there wasn't even enough room to crouch. She had to find a junction and change direction somehow.

She realised she couldn't even turn to go back the way she had come, there was just no room. Rolling her eyes, she continued on. Press down for grip, drag, breathe and repeat. Oddly it was a lot like swimming. She lost herself in the routine for a few minutes and then she happened upon a shaft leading off of the shaft she was in, going up. She began to drag herself up. It was hard going but she was strong enough to do it. Each time she pulled herself up, she wedged herself in place with her legs to prevent herself sliding back down.

She saw the light coming in from a protective grille and that encouraged her on. Nearly there... almost there. There. Breathe, assimilate and act. She reached the grill and peered out, half expecting Tabre to be there already. To her gladness, an elevator shaft lay beyond. Darkness was below and above with just the low red lighting of the powerlines. She used her blade to lever the grille away and then positioned herself so that she was on the edge. She looked up and down the shaft. It was likely, due to this being an emergency situation, that the lifts were immobile. She hoped so as she aimed her grapple gun. She targeted the underside of the lift above her.

Tabre hadn't waited long by the shaft before realising that his quarry was not coming out. He'd tried to access blueprints of the building to determine if there were any alternative routes she could have found. She could have simply doubled back but in the space of that shaft, turning around seemed unlikely to be possible. Without permission he could not access the blueprints so he resorted once again to his heat seeking system. Sure enough, she now seemed to be two floors above him and in what had to be the elevator shaft. Sighing with impatience, he approached the elevator doors and inserted a knife into the seal in an attempt to force them open.

Satiah, just about to allow herself to be pulled upwards, heard the knife in the door and peered across the shaft. It had to be Tabre. She briefly considered trying to electrify the doors or the knife but knew she didn't have time. She pressed the trigger and was dragged upwards. She stopped just beneath the underside of the elevator, swinging back and forth there for a few seconds. Like an acrobat she clung onto it and began to scramble around its body to get to the other side of it where she would be shielded from Tabre. Sweat was pouring off of her and, more than once, she almost lost her grip. She heard the doors screeching as Tabre forced them open and fought to remain as silent as possible. She eventually got onto the roof of the elevator and lay on it, quite drained. She could see a light flashing against the walls as Tabre tried to spot her. Silence. She rolled leisurely onto her front and began to see if there was a way into the lift itself using her fingertips to feel for anything.

Tabre checked the heat seeking device again. She was up there somewhere all right. She had to be in or on top of the elevator. He listened intently. He thought he could hear shuffling but wasn't sure. She didn't seem to be moving. He looked around to see if there was any way he could climb up to see. There was no way that didn't leave him completely exposed. He *could* get the other lift going and use it to rise up and over her. He'd have to be outside on its roof to do that, though, otherwise he'd be trapped in the lift itself. Besides… there was no easy way to restart the lifts. And even if he got it going, she could simply ride hers away. How had she got up there in the first place? The ventilation shaft came out below him!

Satiah was busy with her blade, blinking sweat out of her eyes, trying to force open the maintenance hatch in the ceiling of the lift. It was old and a bit corroded. She slowly and carefully rose into a crouch and began using all her weight as leverage. The metal screeched as it gave way, almost caused her to roll off of the top of the lift altogether. Tabre heard and guessed what she was doing. He sprinted up the stairs, heading for the floor that the lift was on, two above. Satiah lowered herself with care into the darkness of the disabled lift. None of the controls were operating and she knew that Tabre would be heading for the doors. He would force them open and it would be game over, she didn't think she could take him on and win in her current condition, even with a gun.

But escaping via the doors had never been her plan. Her plan was much more foolish. She pulled out her pistol and waited. She would wait for Tabre to begin work on the door and then she would act. She could see the main support pulley above her with her torch. It held the lift where it was. She was about six floors up and part of her had always wanted to try this… Tabre's blade jammed into the gap between the doors, making her jump slightly. The doors were forced open fractionally as he twisted. Satiah fired, snapping the support cable in two. The next thing she knew, she and the lift were plummeting downwards, screeching and sparking as they went. She lay on her back quickly, hoping to reduce injury. Tabre's knife was sliced in two as the lift went down, earning a surprised shout from him. She felt the sensation of falling through her belly and tensed instinctively.

As she had theorised, the failsafe mechanisms of the lift were automatically activated once a certain velocity had been reached. The only question had really been: would she reach that speed *before* she hit the ground? She reached the right speed with only metres to spare. The first jolt made her gasp and the next one, the final one as the lift hit the ground, made her groan. All of her hurt after that. She sat up, checking herself for wounds. Just more bruises. The door was still mostly shut but Tabre had done the hard part for her. Forcing her fingertips into the narrow gap he'd made, she yanked repeatedly. After only a few attempts she successfully ripped one of the doors open. Then she was on the ground floor again. She knew Tabre would be coming down the stairs as fast as he could.

Tabre, trying not to laugh at the recklessness of Satiah's last escape plan, raced down the steps as quickly as he could. She might have just killed herself but that seemed unlikely. If she was unconscious he'd have her. His heat seeker bleeped out a warning and as he pulled it out to check it a shot was fired. Satiah, using the corner of the wall at the stairwell as cover, was waiting for him. The shot burned the edge of his heel on the steps and he jumped backwards, landing on his side. Expecting a quick assault he covered the next line of steps through the gap of the set he'd just descended. Satiah cursed her own impatience. If she'd waited, just a little longer, literally mere seconds, she could have hit his head. Tabre now waited for her to check on him and she waited for his next move.

Satiah was the first to give up. She turned and limped quickly away back out on to the chaos of the street. Despite being a wanted woman, she was able to just walk through the mists and fires without anyone troubling her. Everyone was preoccupied and with all that heat, Tabre couldn't track her. She almost lost her way as the streets now looked very different. She eventually reached the safe house and trudged wearily up the ten flights of steps. As she entered she actually fell through the doorway as she had no energy.

Carlos and Kelvin caught her between them and dragged her, coughing and spluttering, over to the bunks. They lay her down and Kelvin ran his usual checks on her.

"Oh dear," she murmured, managing a weak smile.

"*What happened?*" asked Ruby, deeply concerned. To Ruby, Satiah looked like she was about to die as she was so scruffy, bruised and blood-spattered.

"She will recover," Kelvin stated, and began injecting her with various healing drug cocktails.

"What now?" she croaked, wanting an update. Carlos waved the Essp bar under her noise to show that they still had it.

"Is that *all* you got?" she joked, in between coughing fits.

"We were going to stop off at the bar and get some beers but would you believe that someone had set fire to it?" Carlos replied, grinning.

"...*Some people*," she breathed, wearily staying humorous. Reed came over and stroked her hair caringly.

"Mission accomplished, you must be very proud," he smiled, casually. "We are starting to run out of spare clothes for you though... you may have to steal your own?" She winced as Kelvin injected her leg. Ruby brought water over.

Kelvin handed her a device. She put it in her mouth and breathed deeply through it. Soon all the dust and harmful substances she had inhaled were all contained within it. She sat up slowly and removed the device before downing some of the water. She then proceeded to pour the rest over her face.

"I ran into Tabre again," she explained, seriously. "We *need* to get off this planet."

"All that needs to be done is to liaise with your contact to confirm the purchase," Reed prompted, handing her the communicator.

"In a minute," she said, pushing Ruby and Reed's hands away firmly. "I just *need to recover*." She lay back again and fell asleep almost instantly.

"You're quite sure she's fine?" Reed confirmed, a little anxious.

"No permanent injuries," Kelvin answered. "She will be awake again in an about forty minutes. Lack of activity will help the healing process accelerate." Reed nodded, still watching her. Ruby too stared down, awkwardly.

"I'll take first watch," Deva sighed, heading up onto the roof. Carlos returned to his seat by the main door. Kelvin continued to constantly scan for threats. Reed and Ruby returned to sitting at the table with Ash.

"She orchestrated the gaining of necessary funds," Ash allowed, referring to the inert Satiah. "It's the first thing you've told her to do that she's done." Ruby winced, knowing that Ash was trying to be nice but it may not be received well when phrased like that. Reed though, didn't take it that way.

"She does mostly everything she's told to do... *eventually*," Reed smiled, levelly.

***

Tabre found a room and locked himself in. The burn wound wasn't bad but he treated it meticulously anyway. That had been close, too close. And despite his best efforts she'd got away again! That trick with the lift had been ingenious. Now she'd probably have retreated back to her den again. Her shot had burnt a hole in his boot, if she had held back for a moment she would have potentially killed him. He bandaged the injury skilfully before taking the time to rethink things. He'd had to murder the security chief. Obviously he could blame that on Satiah but it was still an inconvenience. And he still had not discovered what Satiah and Reed were even doing on Ionar 12. He glanced down at the handle of his knife, its blade was gone after being sliced off by the falling elevator. It could so easily have been his hand...

It was time for a new approach. The city centre was largely in ruins now; at least seventy percent was either burnt out or collapsed. That was what happened when poor cities were built. They were not designed efficiently enough to survive such events well. He was starting to realise that he may not be able to handle Satiah himself. He'd tried using others before but they hadn't been successful either... he hissed to himself.

"She bleeds, she's not invincible." He slowly began to walk around the building, quickly finding the lift Satiah had used to escape from him. As he had hoped, some of her blood was there. He collected a sample carefully, wondering what it would tell him about his enemy. He would restart the mission; *pretend* he knew nothing at all about her and *be objective*.

***

Captain Wester and Lieutenant Jenjex were escorted down the corridor to the meeting room. The woman taking them was not armed and that was vaguely reassuring. Instead of actually going to Earth, another ship had docked with *Warrior* and on board everyone was to assemble to... *discuss a few things*. Wester and Jenjex exchanged glances, leaving their mutual questions unspoken.

"This way please," said the woman, as the door opened. Captain Erica Moxin was already inside. She was sat with her back to the door, smoking some kind of strange-looking cigar. She stood upon seeing them.

"Wester," she greeted, not saying his rank mainly because she was unsure how he saw himself.

"*Captain* Moxin," he smiled, shaking her hand. In emphasising the rank in her name, he told her that he considered himself to be a Captain too.

"And who is this?" she asked, eyeing Jenjex. Erica's Colonial accent was stronger than almost anyone Wester had met before. Her deep voice seemed to make it even more gravelly. He had somehow not noticed until now.

"Lieutenant Jenjex," he replied, as the two women shook hands. Erica noted the woman's spotless uniform, reserved but proficient manner and nodded in approval. A promising young officer.

"Who remains to supervise your ship?" asked Erica, interested.

"Who remains on yours?" he couldn't resist asking. She sighed, raised an eyebrow and replaced the cigar in her mouth. She inhaled deeply before blowing out the smoke away from them.

"…I no longer have one," she admitted, a little tersely.

"Flight Officer N…" began Jenjex, about to answer the question.

"*What happened to you?*" Wester asked, cutting Jenjex off. "Why didn't you tip us off earlier? Did Simmons…"

"Simmons told me that Ro was onto us, he didn't know *how* but he knew she was… Apparently he was interrogated but they didn't think he was part of it too. So I used my clone to command my ship that day…"

"*What?*" Jenjex had been so astonished that she'd forgotten to not interrupt. "Sorry, sir."

"For years, *in secret*, I've been creating clones of myself in order to see what kind of tacticians they are… plus I'm getting lazy," she replied, smiling. "Well, I never intended to use one as a double for myself for any longer than a few hours but… when the assassin struck… she killed my clone and not me. That was when I knew Tristram was in trouble too."

"But you didn't warn him yourself?" Wester questioned.

"I couldn't, I wasn't there. Besides, *I was supposed to be dead*," she replied. "I just assumed that he wouldn't go through with our plan because I was not there to help and instead came here to warn the Coalition." She paused, grimly. "*And it turns out I wasn't the only one.*" Wester wasn't sure if she was referring to him or not. Perhaps there were others.

Then she smiled. "Enter a *very brave young man* who then chose to execute the plan anyway... I'm sure it gave Ro indigestion."

"It was *Tristram* who intended to go through with it regardless of..." Wester began, modestly.

"Excuse me, sir, you *know* that was *not the case*," Jenjex stated, politely. "You could easily have turned away from doing it but you are the one who chose to continue."

"...So *my crew* believes," Wester replied, awkwardly. Jenjex gaped but hurriedly straightened her face. She'd made her point. Erica just sat there, staring at them while nodding slowly.

"Sometimes it does not matter who does the deed so long as it is done," Erica said, at last. "And will you two sit down? You're making me want to stand as well." Wester and Jenjex both tried to pull chairs for each other. He lugged one for her as she was female. She drew one for him because he was her superior officer. Erica rolled her eyes.

"So, is it just us or are there others joining us?" Wester asked, facing her.

"I was told to press this button when we were done catching up," Erica said, nodding to a green button on her armrest. "Are we done?"

"You said that they were already aware of Ro and her plans," Wester said, talking about the Coalition. "Are they planning to do anything to counter them?"

"To say this situation is awkward politically is like saying people don't fly," she said, her countenance briefly enveloped in smoke. "The Coalition cannot yet make any sort of pre-emptive strike. Not only does it not sit well with their government but, frankly, it may not be necessary."

"We have only *delayed the inevitable*, as long as Ro is in power, peace is threatened," Wester stated, inflexibly.

Erica rolled her eyes again and pressed the button.

"Tell that to these guys," she said, simply. Phantom Leader Randal, who looked like he'd not slept for a long time entered and with him was, dressed in a white commander's uniform, Commander Sam Igo. Introductions were exchanged.

"We are aware of Ro just as we are aware of everything the Federation do," Randal began, clearly not happy. "Our problem is one of ethics. We are a democracy; we cannot just attack without warning."

"We are also a democracy but that does not mean Ro will do you the same courtesy," Wester argued. "She's quite mad."

"Then who elected her?" demanded Sam, quietly.

"President Raykur has been ill on and off for about a year and, in his weakened state, she's slipped in under the doormat," Erica explained. "Extremists like her are always the flavour of the month, especially when they have a gift for persuasion."

"She's using the war on Pluto Major as a way of stirring up the population. They are already up in arms about the famine," Wester added. "Desperation always increases extremism and crime."

"Can she be removed *by law*?" Sam asked, seeking clarity. As a military commander in the Coalition he understood his own government's ways only as much as he had to. The Federation had a different system that he knew very little about.

"Possibly," Erica answered, although doubt was more than evident in her tone.

"She controls the secret service, the military, and has managed to wipe out all political opposition," Wester admitted.

"If she succeeds in starting a war, it will be the kind of war that lacks victors," Erica said. "Mainly because it would most likely lack survivors."

"Then there is only one option… assassination," Randal said, calmly. Wester had long been afraid it would come to that.

"How would her death be received publicly?" asked Sam, casual. The public, an ever present microcosm in politics, could often be an unpredictable complication.

"Difficult to say without knowing exactly how popular she is," Erica shrugged. "*The vote was rigged.*"

"She does spout out a lot of stuff people like to hear," Wester pointed out. "And she certainly will have her fair share of followers. Plus the media will have their own angle."

"We considered doing away with her *before* but decided against it because she is too heavily guarded," Erica said. "And if the attempt *fails...*" She didn't need to elaborate further on that point. A thoughtful silence commenced.

Ro had clearly done everything she could to secure her powerbase and she would be reluctant, to say the least, to let go of any of it. Who knew, perhaps she really felt she deserved it? Wester often wondered what went on in other people's minds. What were they thinking or feeling? How did they see what he saw? How did Ro see herself? That was of course, assuming she had the strength to look.

"Why does she want war *exactly*?" Wester asked, out of the blue. "She *must know* it's a suicidal bid for supremacy. What does she get out of it?"

"...You *did say* she was mad," Sam reminded him.

"All right, what does she *think* she will get?" he rephrased. It was a good question in that no one seemed to be able to elicit a convincing answer. There were, however, the usual theories that anyone with a brain could apply. Annoyingly, there was no real evidence to support or prove any of them. Another grey area, Wester seemed to be encountering more and more of those of late. Indeed, just weeks previously, he'd no idea there were so many of these areas. The regulations made no mention of them.

"Hatred for the Coalition is strong, especially in the Federation, has been for years," Randal stated. "She may just be blinded by hatred." The way he said it, it made it sound like it happened every day. Maybe in his line of work it did.

"You must help us get rid of her, *one way or another*," Wester appealed.

"Peace is the only vested interest we have in this," Sam assured. "I don't see a way of getting rid of her without starting the war she wants." A long uncomfortable silence began accompanied by a sense of weariness and melancholy. It really did seem that war was unavoidable. Wester wondered if such a silence precluded all wars.

"It's going to have to be us, isn't it?" Wester asked, sadly. "We will have to kill her. If *you* do it the war will start. If we do it ourselves then it will be limited, at least at first, to a civil war."

"That doesn't mean we can't help you," Randal pointed out.

***

The new ship that Ro had supplied was state of the art. Tabre supposed that it was a sign of the faith she had in him. He had successfully removed many of her political opponents in the past. The pilot of the ship, a young woman, was absent, on a supply run. Satiah's blood sample had been analysed and the results were interesting. Type AB-, the rarest type, it was just as remarkably rare as someone with her abilities was. And... it lit a trail of possible acts of violence and fights that spanned the best part of forty years. Wars, assassinations, abductions, spying... she'd done it all most likely. Her blood was also very pure which indicated she underwent regular medical touch-ups. Only to be expected of course, in her line of work. Tabre did that himself. And... most intriguingly of all... she'd been a prisoner of the Colonial Federation once... for a few hours at least. There were pictures of her on file...

Tabre didn't allow her name to be added to the file on the blood sample though. She was a professional like him and he had no intention of making her life more difficult in such a way. He wouldn't want anyone to do that with his identity so he extended that courtesy to her too. So, confirmed, a Phantom agent named Satiah... protecting Reed. Cunning, ruthless and creative, she was indeed a formidable foe. Twice now she'd almost killed him. Granted, he'd returned the favour and she too had survived. A great game of symmetry. Once again she was hiding somewhere nearby but... what did she want? What was she after? He'd gone over information about the planet, trying to see if anything leapt out as something she or Reed would be interested in. There was nothing. The place really was as boring and unimportant as it looked. He leaned back in his chair, his mind in deep thought.

***

Carl knew who had done this to his city even though he didn't know why. Nearly a hundred beings were dead or badly injured. Fires were still raging in at least two places. Someone had raided the bank and someone else had assaulted the main security building. Carl supposed they would be forced to call in help from outside but... why hadn't they already done that? He had spent the afternoon deep underground in a basement polishing the new ship he now was being forced to sell. He was not a mechanic, not officially, *but* he knew his way around ships and he liked making them look good. He wondered if Satiah would notice the fresh layers of paint and polish he'd painstakingly provided. All free for her as well. He checked his communicator. Two messages.

The first was from a foreman working on another ship complaining about a missing safety valve. Carl supposed he had a spare they could use although he'd have to check the model. The second was a call from Satiah... or Kim. Sighing heavily, he debated whether to call her back or not. He didn't want to die but she was like a strong drink. Delicious and deadly at the same time. He'd always been a fan of anything that dulled reality. What the hell, he called her back.

"Hello Kim," he said, straining to sound normal and failing somewhat. It had taken an effort on his part to remember to address her by her fake name. She might go nuts if he called her Satiah on the line, even if it was encrypted.

"Carl," she said, her accent back again. She would most likely use her real voice when they met again in person... if they met again in person. "I have your money," she told him, casually. "You have the goods?"

"Yeah it arrived this morning and I have to say..." he began, about to tell her what a great ship it was.

"That's good," she interrupted. "When will it be ready to use?"

"It's ready now," he shrugged. "I just gave..." He had spent practically all day readying and checking and painting the new ship. While he had been planning to do that anyway, it was no longer *his ship*. Naturally he wanted to extract something akin to appreciation from this scary woman. He went disappointed.

"I will meet you tonight, I know where you live," she stated and cut off. He scowled, so rude! He couldn't help but smile in afterthought though. He didn't often have female company and despite this one being a self-confessed killer he supposed he had to take what he could get. He went back to take pictures of the ship to show her in case she wanted proof.

***

Satiah was mentally comparing how the city had looked when they had first arrived to how it looked now. Smoke still rose from a few of the remaining buildings. Most of the fires had been put out. They had called in extra firefighters from the northern settlement. The bill was going to be huge and would no doubt set back the economy terribly. She was standing on the roof, arms crossed, surveying the devastation morosely. This was going to be all over the news and the Federation would move troops in and then they might never get out. Part of her wondered why the troops had not yet arrived. She believed in Federation inefficiency but still… they were *two days* late. Perhaps something else had prevented them getting there.

Carlos appeared and nodded to her.

"Checking out the scenery?" he asked, grim.

"What's left of it," she replied.

"Turns out Deva was right about Tabre," he said, seriously. "Can you kill him?"

"Yes," she shrugged, indifferently.

"You know what I'm asking," he chuckled.

"I'm doing my best but he's not cooperating," she replied, clinging to the mirth. "I would point out at this point that killing Tabre is not part of our mission."

"Wow, you *really* don't like him do you?" he asked, seriously.

"He's brilliant. Resourceful, intelligent and lethal. I know a kindred spirit when I meet one. He's like me. A killer moulded by the things around him. Searching for something but not really caring if he finds it or not. He enjoys the hunt, seeing it as a competition or a kind of test," she explained. "He and I have no politics. We have no religion. *We don't even have hobbies.* We are a lot like Kelvin. Machines. We just do what we're trained to do… *we survive at all costs.*"

"Nice," Carlos grinned, appreciating the honesty.

"I... *respect* him," she stated, shrugging again. "I appreciate his skills and wonder what he will try next time."

"Does he respect you?" he asked, interested.

"*Of course he does*," she replied, mildly offended.

"What about me?" he asked, digging.

"What about you?" she asked, being deliberately thorny.

"How am I doing?" he asked, seriously. "I think I've made some real progress."

"You're doing fine," she agreed. "Your shooting could still be improved and your tendency to ask lots of questions is irritating but I let those slide." They regarded each other in their peripheral vision and shared a smile. Reed appeared.

"Ah, I'm glad I found you," he said, in his usual way. Satiah didn't say anything about how easy she was to find being as she'd climbed up there in plain view of everyone in the safe house.

"I've made the call, the ship will be secured tonight," she informed.

"Outstanding," he smiled, satisfied. "And the lockdown?" Satiah shrugged.

"The leadership of the city seem to have suffered some casualties and there's a lot of confusion. Several people have already fled to the northern settlement. Some of them used ships and were not shot down," Satiah reasoned. "I think we stand a better than average chance of slipping away without a fight."

"Tabre aside," Carlos added.

"*Tabre aside*," she grinned, in concurrence.

"What will you do when you get the ship?" he asked.

"Haven't decided yet. I will most likely try to come to you but it may be required that you come to me," she replied, considering. "That is likely to be the most dangerous part of the operation." Reed nodded.

"I'm sure we'll manage."

***

Jenjex knocked on the Captain's cabin door. They had been back on *Warrior* for nearly an hour now and Wester had retreated into his cabin, most likely to brood.

"Yes," he said. She entered. He was sat at his desk, staring at the wall, resigned. The discussion had not gone as well as he had hoped. Part of him had wanted someone to just waltz in and solve everything for him but pipe dreams were often flawed. She touched her hat, always perfectly neat and somehow unable to detract anything from her hair's immaculate style and loveliness.

"Are you okay, sir? The crew are awaiting orders," she said, remaining at attention.

"I suppose I should be glad Erica Moxin is still alive..." he murmured, still in a half reverie. "I suppose we should be pleased the Coalition believes us..."

"When we came here we were uncertain about more things," she reminded him. "Sir."

"Ro is going to ruin everything and there's nothing we can do to stop her," he muttered. She sighed. He was clearly in his defeatist stage. In the time she'd been with him she'd discovered this much about Wester. Whenever confronted with a problem he couldn't easily overcome, he would briefly lapse into a depression that could last as long as a day. Yet, he always came out of it with a plan. It was obviously his mind's process and thus was something they needed to endure.

"Sir," she acknowledged, trying to come up with something herself.

"I mean we don't even know *why* she's doing all this," he went on, hardly seeming to notice her.

"Sir," she said, again.

He glared at her briefly and she couldn't hold back a small smile.

"Just to prove you can say still something other than 'sir', status report?" he asked, smirking.

"Our orbit around Earth remains steady, most normal traffic has resumed," she replied. "All crew remain on amber alert but things are quiet." He leaned back in his chair and tried to think about something else.

He activated his holograph projector and a map of the galaxy appeared. Three planets were highlighted.

"To the best of their ability, Coalition intelligence believes Ro to be on one of those three worlds," he explained, to her. "Without knowing precisely where she is, obviously we cannot strike. I did, however, have one idea."

"Sir?" she asked.

"A bomb," he replied. "If one could be placed in a location already searched... close enough to Ro it may be possible to dispatch her without dying in the attempt. Also... a bomb would require an investigation to determine who was responsible. War might not be declared."

"You plan to deploy the bomb *ourselves*?" she guessed, thinking about it.

"*It's just an idea.* You're the only one I've shared it with," he elaborated. Slowly, she walked in a leisurely circle around the holograph.

"How would we even get close enough to her to plant it?" she asked, as expected.

"They would disguise ourselves as cadets, walk in with large standard issue bags each containing spare uniforms. Inside one will be the bomb. They wander around the building as if they are lost and simply ask if they don't know where they are. Through subtlety they ascertain where Ro is and then get as close as possible before setting up the bomb. Then they simply walk out again," he outlined.

"If we are identified..." she began, concerned.

"*I know*," he waved her off. "I never said it would be easy."

He suddenly looked at her.

"*We?*" he questioned.

"...I was just assuming that *this they* you were referring to was us..." she began, shrugging.

"*You're not going*," he stated, with finality. "I will need someone I can trust to stand by here in case we need backup."

"You will need me with you, sir," she argued, stubbornly. "I once talked my way into the Rally without an official invite."

"*What?*" he asked, in shock.

"That was *why* Tristram employed me, sir," she explained. "And…"

"*No!* You can't go with me," he stated, trying not to reveal the real reason.

"…This is our duty, we must do this irrespective of any *personal stakes*," she replied. They stared at each other for a long moment.

Wester couldn't believe it. She knew he liked her and he'd never said a word to her about it. He knew she was clever but now he wondered if he should add clairvoyance to the ever-growing list of her aptitudes.

"How did you know?" he asked, astonished. Denying it now seemed beyond pointless. She smiled and looked away.

"You have *many talents*, sir, but hiding your desire for me is not one of them," she replied, softly. He looked away too, scoffing at his own transparency. How could he have been so stupid?

"*I…* I thought I hid it well," he chuckled, dryly.

"Maybe from *yourself*," she giggled, amused. She stopped laughing, hoping she'd not hurt his feelings. "It's *okay*, I'm flattered to be noticed but it changes nothing. We will still do this together. *I think we're the only people who can.*"

"The Coalition are standing off… but I'm sure they have a bomb we could borrow," he said, smiling.

"Do you want me to remind them that they are not liable to get it returned in the same condition, sir?" she quipped.

***

Phantom Leader Randal looked up as the cloaked figure entered his office.

"Phantom Egill," Randal nodded.

"Randal," replied the big man.

"I have an assignment for you," he replied. Egill removed his hood and stepped forward. He was completely bald, clean shaven and ruddy of complexion. He had over twenty years' field experience making him one of the most seasoned operatives they had remaining. With all the training going on, he had only four out on actual missions.

"Name it, *anything but training*," he grumbled. Randal smiled. A common enough complaint in current times.

"There's a small revolution afoot in the Federation. Ro Tammer has rivals who wish to remove her. We're going to help them," he said, bluntly.

***

Carl did his best not to leap out of his chair in fright. His best wasn't great. Instead of knocking on the door like a regular person, Satiah had infiltrated his house via a window. The first he knew of her presence was a dark figure looming in the corner of his eye.

"…Drink?" he managed, eyeing her.

"That would be sociable," she nodded, slumping into the chair opposite him. He went about making it. "Nice to see you haven't suffered because of the fire."

"Yes," he said, unable to think of anything else to say to that. When he returned, the Essp bar was on the small table in front of her. At once he put two and two together.

"*You* raided the bank? *It was you!*" he accused, somewhat fearfully. "I can't take *that*…"

"Sit down, Carl," she instructed, smiling pleasantly. Mumbling an apology he didn't mean, Carl obeyed. "Where is it?"

"The *ship*?" he clarified.

"No, the monster," she retorted, rolling her eyes. "Yes, the ship!"

"*Wait*, just *listen for a minute*," he began, unhappily. "I can't use *that money*, it would have *been* tagged and the second I spend any of it or put it in storage, *they're gonna know*…"

"I *hope* you're not telling me there is a problem?" she purred. Her eyes narrowed and she casually fished her pistol from its holster.

"*Hey, easy,*" he almost squealed. "You said you didn't want to kill me!"

"I do things I don't want to have to do every day," she shrugged, outwardly nonchalant. She fiddled with the gun meaningfully and eyed him speculatively. His eyes were flashing between her face and the gun rapidly. She stood slowly and advanced over to him. She slid her fingers in his hair and steered his face against her chest softly.

"I'm sure we can work this out," she went on, smiling. She could feel his fearful breathing, warm against her skin, starting to become slower and deeper.

"It is the *only money I have* and you *know* it's not healthy for me to stay around," she mewed, as she backed off a step. She released his hair, replaced her pistol and then returned to the chair. He just stared dumbly at her.

"…Fine," he sighed, half wistfully and half regretfully. He was going to be out of pocket for months now.

"Is there enough blood still in your brain to tell me where it is?" she asked, seductively.

"You're just so…" he trailed off, shaking his head.

"I know I am," she agreed, levelly.

"It's in the lowest workstation of the shipyard," he said, trying to focus on something else. He remembered the pictures and showed her. "No one else knows it's down there."

"…Did you *repaint* it?" she asked, after analysing them. He nodded and shrugged.

"I'm sorry if you don't like it," he mumbled, inwardly impressed she had noticed. "But I can't stand the boring silver and grey style the factories all employ." She cracked up a little at that.

She looked more closely and then pulled a face.

"Is that a little bird on the engine housing?" she asked, seriously. He cringed.

"…Yes," he replied, wishing he'd not painted that as well. He twitched nervously.

"It's a good thing that I like you. If I didn't I'd have to drown you in your own paint for that," she replied. For a second he couldn't tell if she was joking. She laughed at his confusion. *"You're a funny man."*

"Right now I'm trapped with you," he stated, shifting nervously on his feet. "So dead man seems closer to the mark."

She laughed even more. Then she ran at him and tackled him to the floor violently.

"*Wo, wo!*" he cried, as he went down.

She smiled down at him as he tried unsuccessfully to free himself. He was so easy to hold down. His wide eyes gave away the inner struggle between fear and attraction in his mind. Their fingers interlocked and the playful hostility stopped.

"There are worse things than being trapped with me," she sniggered, kissing him.

***

They were all very banal but all utterly necessary. Fuel and food. Spare power cores and other technical equipment.

"We obviously can't go anywhere without a bedrock of supplies," Satiah was saying. "A couple of weeks' worth should be enough."

"*A couple of weeks?*" Ash repeated, clearly annoyed by the delay. "I know these things take time…"

"No, I meant that *we will need supplies for a couple of weeks*, not that it will take a couple of weeks before we can leave," she clarified, as patiently as she could. Satiah and Ash were both working very hard to be civil around each other.

"How long *is* this going to take?" asked Reed. "I ask only because, *ironically*, we're almost out of food here."

"Just hours, eight maybe. *Ten tops*," Satiah answered. She saw Ruby open her mouth with another question. "Yes it *could* be done faster but we need it done clandestinely."

"Who did you get this ship from?" Ash asked, seriously. "*Are they trustworthy?*"

"He knows nothing that could compromise the mission or any of you," she replied, cagey. "He's delivered the ship. I can't think of a logical reason why supplies would be more of a problem. *Can you?*"

"I can but I don't think you will like it," he explained, carefully.

"Please," she encouraged, getting ready to shoot whatever it was down as diplomatically as possible.

"Let's assume that your contact intends to betray us possibly for a reward or simply out of duty. A good way to assist in our capture would be to delay us with something like this," Ash said. "The longer we wait here, the greater our chance of failure."

"Trust me," she smiled. "It's not in his interests to betray me."

"Remind whoever it is to ensure there is ample supply of beer please," Reed requested. Ruby let out a giggle which she quickly stifled. Ash studied the pictures Satiah had brought back to show them their new transport. Satiah nodded, not at all amused or surprised by his request.

"The gold brand is good... *so I've heard*," she added, somewhat guiltily at the end.

"Ship's not bad," Deva stated, peering past Ash at the pictures. "Not worth a million though."

"I'm poor at bargaining," Satiah replied, giving nothing more away. Kelvin was scanning her repeatedly.

"You have attracted a mate," he said, in his usual voice. "Congratulations." She sighed, guessing that despite the wash, he would have detected Carl's DNA. She was glad no one could hear him as it made her feel oddly embarrassed.

"Shut up," she muttered, unsure how to respond to that. "It was *your suggestion*, if you remember?"

What had started out as a simple business liaison or, coercion, had become more to her. She'd realised that it hurt to leave Carl behind. He was crass, unfit, ugly and a total coward. But, despite all that, she liked him. She was fond of his subservience to her and he *could* amuse her. She knew that, when they left, she'd in all probability never see him again and though she was used to such severances of contact... she regretted it ending. Their relationship was one where she had complete control and she liked that too. No... she had to go, she had a job to do. She couldn't take him with her; even if he agreed to go, he'd only end up dead. Sadness crept into her. With her life the way it was, no relationship could last! The secrets! The death! The...

everything! She tried to shrug it off but it refused to leave her be. She was so twisted. She wondered what someone else would do in her position.

"Ship coming in to land," called Carlos, from the roof. "Looks military." Satiah swore and scrambled up and out to look. Kelvin and Reed followed quickly. Deva remained by the door at her station. They were just in time to see the spherical ship circle the area once before moving in to land a short distance outside the city.

"Colonial garrison ship," Satiah noted, recognising the type immediately. They were regular long-distance transporter ships, typically used on worlds where uprisings were occurring. They were fast and could store a whole garrison but they were not heavily armoured and their weapons were only average.

Its presence, though, meant things had to speed up considerably. It wasn't certain what had brought the ship there but Satiah felt that it was highly likely it was a direct request from the Colonial government. She had anticipated the arrival of further enemy forces and had a few contingencies prepared. No decent strategist would have failed to do so.

"Trouble?" asked Reed, considering.

"Yep," she nodded. "Even if *the planet and Tabre* don't chase us out of here when we try to leave… *they will.*"

"Any chance you could hurry those supplies along a little?" Reed asked.

"No choice," she agreed, activating her communicator.

***

"Why are your soldiers arriving *here?*" Tabre demanded, frostily.

"I have a renegade Colonial destroyer roaming our sectors as you know! It's already attacked and destroyed a *very* expensive ship-building facility and crippled a sizable number of my assembled fleet," Ro ranted, levelly. "No one has been able to successfully track it and basically *it could be anywhere*. I have sent troops in to reinforce anywhere that may be lacking in defence facilities. *Ionar 12 fits that bill more than adequately*. They are aware of you and will not interfere in your…"

"Just by *being here* they are interfering," Tabre argued, restraining his temper and sighing.

"...I've received unfavourable reports about you and your mission from the First Minister of the world..." she trailed off, allowing him to defend himself.

"Satiah and I had a difference of opinion. The ensuring violence did have a negative effect on the surroundings," he replied, uncaringly.

"Is she dead?" she asked, inevitably.

"...It's only a matter of time," he stated, unwilling to admit his failure. Everyone's death was only a matter of time.

"Those troops have orders to search the city for apparent terrorists. I suggest you use that to your advantage," Ro said, stubbornly.

"There is *no reason* your missing destroyer will come here," Tabre pointed out. Saying that, he still couldn't think of why Reed would come here either and *he had*. He hoped they were not working together.

"The people commanding *that ship* are *not* reasonable people," she stated, flatly.

***

"...They are searching the city," Kelvin stated, his scanners following the progress of the Federation troopers.

"Tabre would appear to have run out of patience," Reed remarked.

"It's not him," Satiah replied, seriously. "We have to move, if we are discovered up here there is no easy way out."

"But this is the safe house," Ruby said, in a small voice.

"Right now it's just another death-trap," Satiah argued. Reed looked at Kelvin and then Satiah before nodding.

"Can we hide on board our new ship?" he asked.

"I don't know but that's where I'm intending to take you all," she said. "Kelvin, did you find that route I asked for?"

"There is a way but it will be difficult," he replied.

Deva landed in the sewer first. She winced, even though the place wasn't as smelly as before Tabre started the conflagration, it still reminded her a lot of the Pune home world. She flashed her torch around, rifle ready.

"Clear!" she called, softly.

Ash and Ruby slid down next and Ruby let out an aggrieved cry before being shushed by both Ash and Deva.

"This is mental! I'd rather be caught than do this!" she whispered, her tone savage. She stared into the dark fluid around her, disgust and horror on her face. Deva was already wading ahead, slow but steady. Carlos and Reed arrived next. Satiah stood at the top of the ladder and waited for Kelvin to go down but he stood there, motionless.

"Go on," she ordered, seriously.

"You are not joining us?" he asked, his red eyes studying her.

"I *may* get there ahead of you," Satiah said, shrugging.

"Taking the streets is unnecessary," he stated, flatly.

"Not everything humans do is necessary but we still do it," she replied, smiling softly. "I must eliminate *all evidence of us being here*. Once you're at a safe distance I will set off charges to bring this place down. When I do that, all the troops will come running to investigate. When they do, I will infiltrate their ship and ensure it is in no condition to stop us from leaving."

"Tabre may not be fooled by your distraction," Kelvin pointed out.

"Even if he isn't he will not guess my plan, now go," she ordered, starting to get impatient.

"*Good Lord!*" Reed gasped, quietly. "Doesn't half pong down here, doesn't it?"

"Which way?" Deva asked, from the front of the group. They had reached a junction and without Satiah they didn't know the way. Kelvin splashed down, his red eyes flashed to green and then went dark. A quick atmospheric check ruled out the use of his flame thrower so he switched to the repeating laser.

"Deva," he said, in his usual monotone, "go left." She went on, using the rifle sights to see through. In single file, they all waded along slowly. Only Reed paused. He had realised that someone was missing.

"Where's Satiah?" he asked, to Kelvin.

"She will catch up," he answered, unhelpfully.

***

Fifteen minutes should be long enough for them to get clear. Satiah eyed the countdown monitor, ready at thirty. She had scanned the building, to ensure it was empty. One good thing about all the chaos was that no one was working that day. The city was pretty much in ruins, and the populous evacuated for the most part. It was a shame that all this had been done and the only ones to have really suffered were those unlucky enough to live there. Their livelihoods, their property… all of it gone because of a weapon that had nothing to do with any of them. Assuming it existed…

For the ninth time, she checked her rifle, and then glanced at the time again. At last! She started her own countdown and then left. She exited the building without bothering to even close the door behind her and jogged lightly along the street. She kept to one side, using the shadows, in case she encountered anyone but, aside from the soldiers, the streets were mostly deserted. Kelvin had set up a bike for her at a safe distance so that was where she was heading. She turned and watched. The explosions within the building sounded and, section by section, it collapsed in on itself. A vast dust wave swept along in every direction and she picked up her pace, away from the area.

***

Tabre was alerted by his computer that a building had been destroyed. He ran scans quickly, adrenalin kicking in. What was she doing now? He replayed footage of it going down and quickly assessed it had been a controlled explosion. Instantly he knew that had been where Satiah and Reed had been hiding and now… they were on the move. He wanted to rush off and catch them but he forced himself to remain where he was. If she had been ready to blow the building, she would not be easy to find. He would wait for the next sign. The soldiers would rush in for him, no doubt doing precisely what Satiah wanted them to. So *where* would they no longer be…?

***

Satiah lay under the remains of a transporter and watched as armoured vehicles sped past, followed by several troops on foot. They were all going in the direction she had come from. She smiled, pleased. Crawling out from her temporary lair, she again continued outwards towards the desert where the ship had landed. She knew this would be the hardest part. The ship would be guarded and they would be suspicious of anyone coming towards them. She planned to distract them, however, with another remote-controlled vehicle. It would speed towards them and they would be so busy shooting at it that she could sneak in from another direction.

She straddled the hover bike, shoving the rifle in the luggage area behind her, and accelerated away. Her red hair billowed out behind her and the breeze was pleasant even though the air was hot. Kelvin had done his job well in rigging up the alternative control for the other vehicle. She activated it and set it on a passage directly towards the Colonial garrison ship. She went wide, going over the first three or four dunes in the other direction before starting to circle around. The sun was baking everything and she speculated that walking on that sand, with nothing to protect your feet, would result in second-degree burns. The air shimmered in the heat. She poured cold water over her head to stay cool and glanced at the screen which showed her the view the other vehicle had. It was less than a kilometre from its target although she guessed it would never get there.

She slowed as she edged over the top of a sandbank and stopped a few metres down. She shielded her eyes from the munificent sunlight with her hand to see with more clarity. What she would give to be able to see like Kelvin. Anything shiny was almost painful to look at for more than a split second. The ship was there and four guards were outside. They had spotted the remote-controlled vehicle in its approach. Now they were presumably trying to hail the driver. It may be some seconds before they realised that it had none. Holding the rifle with one hand, she began a speedy descent from the dune towards the ship. She too was detected, of course, but now the guards had to split their attention between her and the other vehicle. They began firing warning shots at both her and the remote-controlled transport.

Performing a move that only the best trained Phantoms could pull off, she let go of the controls, leaned forward to maintain balance, aimed her rifle and took out both guards shooting at the remote-controlled vehicle. She swerved violently as she retook control, almost losing it in the process. The troopers still firing at her didn't realise their comrades had fallen until the other transport crashed into them from the side. She slammed on the brakes and leapt off the hover bike, pelting the open ramp into the ship with laser fire. There didn't happen to be anyone there but there could have been. She raced on board, cursing the difference in lighting from bright desert sun to dimly lit red corridors. The ramp began to close but too late. An alarm began.

She sprinted out into an area where soldiers would be briefed. The plans were still on holographic display. Someone fired a shot but she didn't see from where. It missed but hit the wall near her. The sound of a ricochet occurred but she had no idea where it went. She rolled for cover and blinked rapidly to try to speed up her eyes and their adjustment to the new lighting.

"Intruder alert," came a voice, over the speakers. Satiah leaned out and took out the speaker with a single accurate blast.

"*Surrender!*" yelled a man, from somewhere ahead of her. She rolled across the corridor, slamming hard against the wall, and opened fire. A scream told her she'd hit someone. At last she was starting to be able to see properly again. Following the corridors she tuned this way and that, gunning down anyone she saw.

Finally, after starting to fear that the ship didn't have one, she found the storage area. Rows and rows of explosives. She dashed over to them. She could incapacitate the ship in two easy ways. First, most easy, take out the engines. Second, less obvious, was use their own weapons against them by setting off their ammunition pile and wrecking the whole ship. She began rigging up a system to enable this. She wouldn't have long. Any survivors on this ship might happen on her and she was sure that the units in the city would have been at least informed if not ordered back to counter the new situation. Ripping open some secure-tape with her teeth, she strapped the improvised detonator down and started a ten-minute countdown. It was possible that someone could try and interfere with the device once she had gone but the odds were that they would not be able to stop it in that timeframe.

Hurrying carefully back towards the entrance she encountered no one, although the alarm was still wailing. The bright light of the desert almost dazzled her as she carefully exited the ship. The mental countdown in her head had reached four minutes. She sprinted back out into the heat, checking every angle as quickly as she could. No one alive but there were a few extra bodies she didn't remember seeing before. She reached the hover bike and leapt back onto it. She revved the engine, faced the city and froze. There, on the top of the same dune she'd flown down not twenty minutes previously… was another bike. A lone figure was sat on it, long range rifle in his hands. Tabre.

***

"*You what?*" demanded Ruby, fearfully.

"The next section is past three storage vats, the only way to get around them is to swim *under them*. They are thirty metres…" began Carlos, seriously.

"*You're crazy!*" she stated, frightened. "I can't swim and *even if I could*, that's thirty metres *without air!*"

"It's doable," Deva shrugged, not bothered much. "I'll grant you it's really gross but you'll be okay."

"I'll drag you with me," Ash said, also unfazed.

"You'll be fine," Reed assured her. She shot him a doubtful look but quickly realised she had very little choice.

"…*My hair…*" she complained, regretfully.

"Hey, beauty queen, want to go first?" teased Deva, grinning.

"Shut up," Ruby grumbled, without any real malice.

Carlos took a deep breath and went under. With strong, purposeful strokes, he swam along. It was pitch black and occasionally things would brush up against him in the water. He wasn't bothered by sewage particularly but the idea of a tentacled monster of some variety did not fill him with joy. Still thinking deeply about his lungs, he didn't actually realise how far he'd come and bumped hard into something metal. Kelvin grabbed him and dragged him to the surface.

"Clear," Kelvin said, simply. Kelvin had already checked the area.

Carlos grinned sarcastically up at the big robot before getting away from the area to make room. Ash and Ruby came next. Lastly Reed and Deva surfaced.

"...I think I'm going to vomit," Ruby stated, seriously.

"Well, you've come to the right place," Reed joked, merrily. "Come on, worst part is over."

"This new ship had better have baths," Ruby jabbered, fretfully. Ash pulled her along without a word. "Yuck! What was *that*? No, don't tell me, *please*, I take it back, I don't want to know…"

They continued on through the darkness, Kelvin now leading them. Carlos and Deva stayed at the back for defensive purposes. Unimpeded by the water, Kelvin had to stop to allow the others to catch up. They reached the ladder leading up into the hangar area. One by one they climbed up into the small bay and took in their new ship.

"It will do, I suppose," Carlos mused, thinking about *Vulture*. The Covert-Class ship had spoilt them a little bit with all its capabilities. Anything could be seen as inferior after such a ship. Kelvin ran a scan, they were alone. Reed employed a washing hose to help everyone get a little cleaner.

"It would be a shame to ruin a new ship so soon," he declared, before turning the hose on himself.

***

Tabre stared at Satiah through the sights of his rifle. He'd not noticed before how beautiful she looked when her hair was free to catch the wind. She just sat on the bike, watching him, her hands open, empty and away from the controls. She knew it was no good running. Two minutes. He'd not shot her because he wanted something, she knew. She guessed he wanted her to lead him to Reed. That wasn't going to happen. A hasty plan came to her. When the ship blew up, she'd go for it. It was her only chance. Never letting the rifle drop, Tabre drove slowly towards her, stopping only a few metres away. It would be a foolish risk to get close enough for her to try and grapple him. They regarded one another in silence for a moment.

Tabre knew that ahead of him lay one of those 'easy way, hard way' conversations. All the fighting and scheming could be seen as just a preamble, with this being the most difficult part of their battle.

He would try to appeal to her greed and self-preservation. Nevertheless, he wanted her to know that he truly appreciated her.

"I have the *utmost* respect for your skills," he said, bowing his head slightly to her.

"Likewise," she managed, guarded.

"You know what I want?" he asked, knowing she did. Twenty seconds? A flashback of the dream she'd had about him made her lose count.

"...I do," she replied, careful not to make any sudden moves. Inwardly she steadied herself for the blast.

"You give me Reed and I'll let you go," he offered, seriously.

"I need time to consider..." she began.

"*Oh please,*" he smirked at her. It should have gone off by now, maybe somehow someone had stopped it. Had she made a mistake?

"You expect me to believe that you will just let me go?" she argued, as tradition dictated.

"I have no control over what you believe, only whether you live or die," he stated, casually.

"Besides my life, what else do I get?" she asked, trying to keep him talking. He knew what she was doing and the rifle clicked.

"Last..." he began, warningly.

Boom! The ship exploded behind them. Satiah felt the heat from the fire on her back. Her hands slammed down onto the controls and she accelerated away, weaving as she went to make herself harder to target. Tabre reacted quickly, after initially ducking away from the blast, spinning his bike and chasing after her. Engines roared and screeched as they both tore across the sand as fast as they could go. Sand sprayed up behind them, lifted by the speed. Following what could be described as a small canyon between dunes, Satiah leaned forward into the controls, desperate to squeeze every volt of power out of the engine. Dipping over a rise, the bike bounced over another as the flat-out sprint became a ducking and diving contest. Up, over, down, bounce, across, and again.

Satiah tilted right and then banked sharply left, trying to put more distance between them. Burning in the heat, squinting in the light and clinging to the controls she dipped down, almost vertically, into a narrow channel before, breakneck style, she opened up the throttle once more. Shooting between the rocks ahead she turned, staying as close to the sand as she could. She swung around the corner and Tabre's bike slammed into the side of hers. She screamed as she was thrown from the bike. She hit the sand hard with a cry and rapidly flipped over and over down the side of a dune. She did her best to roll and twist to avoid injury but skidded to a halt at the bottom, dazed and in pain. He had to have somehow deduced her course and, instead of directly following, he'd angled off at some point and then intercepted her... *damn*!

Maybe a minute later a shadow fell over her face, mercifully blocking the heat and light from the sun. She opened her eyes, trying to ignore the heat of the sand. Tabre stood over her, shaking his head slowly.

"Nice try," he said, a little breathless. "Where is he?" She stared right into his eyes and said nothing very definitely. He pulled something from his pocket. She recognised it as a jabber. An electrical device originally made for getting dumb animals to move by providing mild electric shocks. Later some inventive genius had discovered how, if you upped the voltage significantly, you had a fantastic way of torturing someone. She let her neck relax and her head fall back onto the sand as she prepared herself. She knew the way it worked having been on both ends of such proceedings numerous times. She felt it as he pressed the end of the device against her thigh. Guessing that someone like her would have heard every kind of threat before, Taber dispensed with any clever formula of words and went straight to a direct appeal.

"You're a very beautiful woman, skilled and deadly. You have something I want. You've now had your *time to consider*. You hand him over and I'll let you go," he stated, seriously.

"Not a chance," she replied, quietly. Inwardly though, she was considering it, anyone would.

"I won't enjoy this," he assured her. A look in his eyes told her that he meant that.

"Tell that to the therapist," she retorted, rudely. She had a job to do, protect Reed. Besides... she wasn't sure anymore that he would kill her. Certainly not immediately. He waved the jabber in her face briefly.

"...I gave you a chance," he reminded her, melancholy in his voice.

"Only a chance we both knew I wouldn't take," she stated. *Brace*, she told herself. *Breathe and let the pain out with a scream.*

"Drop it!" yelled someone, from nearby. Both Tabre and Satiah looked around to see three Federation troopers, guns raised, approaching them. They both quickly glanced around and there were, at least, four others. All were covering them from different angles and distances. The three in a group were approaching slowly and cautiously. The rifle was out of Satiah's immediate reach and, luckily, out of Tabre's. Federation troops were not renowned for their timing; Satiah would have to remember this. An idea came to her, a last-ditch chance of getting away unscathed.

"My name is Tabre!" he announced, commandingly. "I'm capturing this terrorist."

"Don't listen to him, *I'm* Tabre!" Satiah shouted, trying to make this work for her. "He's lying!" He shot her the amused grin of a fellow rebel spirit. She grinned back.

"I said *drop it!*" barked the trooper, and a warning shot hit the sand near to them. He didn't seem remotely interested in who either of them were. Tabre reluctantly dropped the jabber. Satiah forced her knee up, striking his groin solidly. He cried out and doubled over before falling onto his side, taken completely by surprise. Expecting to be shot immediately, Satiah began to rise and was astounded when she only heard some grim chuckling from the soldiers. Taking that as permission to carry on, Satiah snatched up the jabber and stood over Tabre.

He smiled up at her, clearly still in agony but without fear.

"...How can *I* help *you*?" he offered, trying to be funny. She held the button down, letting the energy pulse warningly. He held her eye contact, not even glancing at the jabber. He too, as she knew, was not frightened of pain.

"This is your final warning," she growled, emotions warring inside her. "Next time, I *will* kill you."

"Noted," he replied, still maintaining the eye contact. Two of the troopers came up and restrained Tabre but left Satiah alone.

"Captain Berry," said the soldier, nodding to Satiah. "Division Sixteen." Satiah couldn't believe her ears. "Sorry for the uniforms but they were compulsory. Our orders are to move in and attack the city to give you and Reed enough to time get away. It is *Satiah* right?"

They shook hands briskly.

"How did you find me...?" she began, confused.

"We already had intelligence that you were operating in this area. That big eruption over there tipped us off," he replied, pointing back in the direction of the recently destroyed Federation ship. Then she realised.

"*Reed* called you in, didn't he?" she asked, a little irritated. She couldn't be too upset with them or Reed though, on account of them saving her from being tortured. It may even have been Division Sixteen who had set up the safe house in the first place. Reed had referred to *contacts*. Captain Berry only shrugged.

"With respect, *I think you'd know more about that side of things than me, miss*. You're wasting time, get going," Berry said, giving her a gentle push. "There are only twenty of us and hundreds of them."

"What will you do with him?" she asked, loud enough for Tabre to hear.

"Whatever you tell us to," he replied, careless. Satiah made eye contact with Tabre again. The respectful stare of two crafters lasted only a second. It would be so easy to have him killed and if she didn't the odds were he'd keeping trying to kill them. If he died though, they'd only send someone else and better the devil you knew... She threw him a lifeline.

"Leave him *here*, tied up..." she requested, cruelly. "How long will it take you to get back to the city if we do that?"

"A few hours, maybe longer depending on knot type," Tabre answered, honestly.

"Do it."

***

The city, if it hadn't been before, was now a complete battlefield.

Teams of Division Sixteen, all dressed as Federation troops, were attacking the real Federation troops. As they were all dressed the same way, it was impossible to work out who was who, especially at a distance. Carl had had enough, he wanted out. Satiah was not worth this much trouble. Would she never tell him the truth? A girl like her went around stealing hearts of heroes and anti-heroes alike, if she could find them, not people like *him*! He was *just* a shipyard owner, and her kind of love was just too volatile for him. He was just getting ready to leave when Satiah crept feebly in through the window and the sight of her made him forget all his doubts inexplicably.

"*Kim*... I mean Satiah, *you're hurt*!" he hissed, grabbing her as she collapsed.

"Water," she pleaded, her voice catching in her throat. It had been a protracted journey. Neither of the bikes had been able to move after the collision and she'd been forced to cross the desert on foot. The heat had soon got to her. He grabbed one of the tubes, he usually used for cleaning the ships, and literally sprayed her where she was lying. She gulped some down as she closed her eyes and enjoyed the delightfully cold liquid reviving her. He stared down at her, soaked but radiant and surrendered to his feelings for her. She wasn't that bad after all, and she may be destructive but he was fairly sure she had his best interests at heart.

"*You crazy, crazy lady*," he hissed, helping her onto a chair. "What happened? Listen, I know I'm not supposed to ask but if you don't stop this kind of stuff you will end up dead, you know? Are you hurt? I managed to get the supplies..." Satiah thought she'd never heard anyone talk so quickly. To her it felt like he'd said a million words in about five seconds. She silenced him with a strong kiss on the lips. She stopped only when she felt that his breathing was almost in time with hers.

"I'm okay, Carl," she assured, weakly. "I just... took *the long way back*." He smiled in genuine delight and cupped her face softly and a little hesitantly in his hands. She let him.

"You're still crazy," he stated, devotion in his eyes. She recognised the emotion and shook her head with real sadness.

"And you're still *hopelessly* soppy," she replied, grinning with false spite. "The ship ready to go?"

"Yes," he said. He stood as she draped her arm around his shoulders for support. "It's in the lowest shipyard but there's a shaft it can fly out of. It comes out a few miles out to the south in the wasteland."

"Are you going somewhere?" she asked, noticing the case on the floor.

"*What do you think?*" he demanded, sarcastic. "You know I'm a coward and, since you arrived, this place has become deadly." They entered the lift. "Floor zero," he said, to the lift.

"I suppose the tourist industry here will take a bit of a blow," she admitted, just a small stab of guilt making itself known in her heart.

"All your friends are all ready inside," Carl went on. "Some dude called Carlos nearly shot me. Took me ages to convince him that I knew you."

"What did you tell him?" she asked, interested.

"Only that we were doing business together. I never said anything about you using me as your own personal punching bag," he complained. She grinned.

"You loved every second of it and you know it," she stated. "And you were so sweet just now, *caring about me* and hosing me down."

"...Just shut up," he grumbled, awkwardly. She giggled. The lift reached the lowest station and they entered the area with the ship. Kelvin and Deva were standing by the entrance to the ship, awaiting her. Deva whistled and Carlos came out.

"I see they are all ready to go," she said, a little sad suddenly.

"And so are you," he said, not letting go of her arm. They looked at each other for a long moment.

"You'll be okay," she assured, softly. "No one knows about what you have done."

"I... *I don't know what to say*," he replied, clearly torn. He wanted her gone and he wanted her to stay too. She knew that feeling well enough to recognise it.

"Then don't say anything," she breathed. They kissed, it was long and deep. Quite bedazzled, Carl felt almost dizzy when it was over. "Now go," she ordered, pointing back at the lift. Without a word he obeyed, the doors closed and he was gone.

Satiah walked over to the others. Carlos and Deva both wore expressions Satiah did not care for but didn't care enough about to reprimand them for either.

"*Looks like a change wasn't the only thing she fancied,*" Carlos muttered, to Deva. "What was *that?*" Carlos asked, grinning teasingly. Satiah stopped walking, raised an eyebrow and looked right at him.

"What was what?" she asked, crisply. He shrugged defensively.

"...Nothing," he answered, unsure what kind of mood she was in.

"Are we ready to go?" she asked, commandingly.

"Yes ma'am," he nodded, glad to have got away with it.

"Ship is satisfactory," Kelvin stated.

"Then why are we all standing outside of it?" she smiled, motioning for them to go in ahead of her.

***

The heat of the desert was oppressive and relentless. Tabre had rolled onto his front to shield his eyes from the sun while he gradually worked on the knots holding his hands together. Those men had known what they were doing; he'd been there over fifty minutes. Professional obeisance had saved him that time, although without intervention the tables would have been completely reversed. He vowed to get it right next time. He found it hard to not laugh at it. She'd done a lot of the things he would have. He heard shouting and then people approaching. A woman crouched next to him, a Federation trooper, and helped him onto his side.

"Are you okay?" she asked, rather inanely.

"...Just untie me," he growled, forcing a smile.

***

Mission report. Two words that had haunted her for almost as long as she could remember. Satiah sighed heavily. Once again, they were on the move. Following the trail to the coordinates revealed in the decoded account of Operation Burning Bridge. Where to start? Without a mission file, Satiah didn't even know what classification this mission should be. She quickly settled for UE. Unlisted espionage fitted best as arguably that had been what they had set out to originally do. Designation was easy, top secret. Operation...? Satiah had never had the *privilege* of naming her own mission before and she found it oddly disconcerting. The overwhelming temptation to try to be funny lingered. Operation... *Orion*? Her fingers froze over the buttons as she reconsidered for a moment. It was relevant enough to mean something but commonplace enough not to give anything away. Operation Orion it would be.

The status was easy for her to write too, *active*. She wrote the status in capitals as tradition dictated. Satiah reports... where to begin? Where had it *actually* started? When she'd collected the former employee of Jaylite Industries? When she had taken Reed and Carlos to the Pune home world under Randal's instructions? Their visit to the Sisterhood of Light? That last notion made her remember that she had to keep that part *very* superficial. Not just to cover up her own blunder but also because Chalky had desired them not to spread information about her planet. Satiah chose to use the rescue of the unconscious man from Station Denepher shortly before its demolition as the place to begin. It *had* been a major feature at the time and it remained connected to the... *whatever it wa*s they were doing now.

Space Station Denepher identified at coordinates blah, blah... suggested as possible storage site for information concerning a secret weapon of undisclosed type or classification of the Balan Administration. Site to be demolished at time... blah, blah. Satiah wasn't actually writing the words 'blah, blah' but as she didn't have the details to hand she was just leaving blanks. She would fill those in later when she'd stopped fiddling with the important details. Identity disclosed in file one, she went on, man recovered from space station Denepher. She linked the two files so that Randal could just flick between them at his leisure. Three unidentified beings attempted to prevent extraction. They failed. Who had *they been*? Satiah let that go and moved on. Male returned to Earth for interrogation, there were... medical issues. See file two.

Satiah had struggled over that part. It was difficult to avoid details on that and not reveal more than Chalky would be comfortable with about brain-wiping. In the end, she reflected, it was just easier to simulate ignorance than try to blind *Randal* with science. She had all the technical medical information on the second file already plus a few potential diagnoses provided by the medical robot there at the time of examination. She went into detail on her own attempts to interrogate the man, covering the chemicals she had used, their quantities and just how much pain she'd tried to inflict before giving up. As she knew, they were out of acceptable regulations but she knew Randal would forgive her that.

Then came the part where Reed had got involved... New task assigned, while rescued man recovers, interrogation deferred. Refer to mission file serial number: 95577784166. She linked that file to her own as she had with the previous ones. Satiah let out a groan and pushed the computer away with a combination of overtiredness and impatience. She *hated* writing reports with a passion, especially when they were difficult and this was one of the hardest she'd ever written. Only her involvement in the Vourne conspiracy had been of equal trouble to transcribe. Satiah was someone who much preferred staring down the scope of a rifle, seeking enemies, than she did writing about it later.

"Is everything all right?" Kelvin asked, from behind her. She made a soft sound and rubbed her face with her hands.

"I... I'm tired and... *just tired*," she answered, staring almost blankly ahead.

"...Do you miss the male?" he asked, in his usual monotone. A sob almost burst out of her from somewhere but she managed to contain it.

"...Yes," she admitted, sadly. "It started out as *nothing*. Just a means to an end and..." She trailed off, sombrely.

"And nothing became something," Kelvin replied. It was a statement, not a question and she knew he understood. His metal hand landed on her shoulder and squeezed.

"There will be others," he assured. He didn't mean to imply that it was a simple case of replacing a damaged component in a machine. He was just trying to let her know that, unless she wanted to be, she wouldn't have to stay alone.

"Thank you, Kelvin," she smiled, gently. His hand left her shoulder. She actually felt better, telling him how she felt... a bit. She hoped she was not going soft or, even worse, developing a conscience. Such things would not help her do her job.

"Also… this mission report is a *killer hornet*," she stated, venomously. "I'm *seriously* considering just leaving it all to Reed."

"But you still do not trust him enough to," Kelvin replied.

"It's not that I don't *trust* him, *not exactly*. This is just something *I* have to do… it is *my* mission and I am the most senior Phantom on it," she explained, seriously. She pulled the computer back and began again. "I always watch my own back when I can, no matter who else I'm with. It's… habit. It's why I built you, Kelvin."

She went over the diplomatic endeavour on Yavaicha, the Pune home world, lightly. She referred to Reed's diplomatic report if Randal wanted any further details. Reed's well-written report provided a level of detail that even Satiah had never seen before. He'd even gone to the trouble of translating their language and explaining some of the nuances in simple forms. As they had joined the Coalition, however, it was unlikely Randal would be interested in that. Satiah made no mention of the shaft, its connection to the Sisterhood, the soil sample or the attack on the mining world. Instead she provided a copy of the mission report of Operation Burning Bridge. File four. She didn't make it clear *how* they happened upon the report, however, deciding to keep Ash and Ruby out of it as well. If Randal asked about it she'd say that Dasss had copied her in on the original but she hadn't realised its relevance until… No! *Blast!*

She couldn't say *that*, as it still didn't explain how she knew that the Orion Observatory *was* relevant. There was always the anonymous tip-off argument but Randal would never believe that. Her headache was coming back. She snatched up her communicator and called Reed.

"You do know I'm just down the corridor?" was his answer. She explained her problem. "Ash really won't mind if you include him in your report," Reed said, seriously. "Indeed I was planning on using him extensively in mine."

"I'm protecting *Ruby* mainly," Satiah told him. That wasn't technically as nice as it would sound, in the sense that she wasn't being unselfish. She just didn't want anyone asking Ruby any questions about Operation Burning Bridge. Satiah knew Ash could be relied upon to keep his mouth shut but Ruby was a bit of a loose cannon.

"That's very *altruistic* of you," Reed replied, his voice changing ever so slightly. He knew she was hiding something.

"We're going off topic here," Satiah said, hauling them back onto the original subject. "How do I explain to Randal about the Orion Observatory?"

"Does he *not know* what a space station *is*?" Reed asked, not being serious.

"*Reed!*" she hissed, unable to stop herself from laughing a little. As much as she hated it when he pretended to misunderstand her, it did tickle her.

"Look, frankly you're rather quicker out of the blocks that I thought you would be. I'm assuming, as you have time on your hands, you decided to be efficient and get started on the paperwork?" he asked, knowingly.

"…No harm in an early start," she said, bristling a little. "I trust you weren't going to leave it all to the last minute? This will have to be very carefully compiled from beginning to end and…"

"Satiah, *we've not finished the mission yet,*" he stated, guffawing. "I admire your confidence; *I really do* but just… hold fire. I think we should write it together." She crossed her arms and leaned back in her chair. Mission reports had to be transcribed by *one person in seclusion*. The better to be objective. It made evidence easier to make out for those reading and comparing said reports. What Reed was suggesting was highly frowned upon. Satiah had to admit though, more than once, she *had* done it before. She didn't elect to disclose that to him though.

"*Agreed,*" she grumbled, disconnecting before he could say anything else.

"The portable cloaking device is here," Kelvin stated, after she'd remained still for several moments. Rainbow had come through again then, that was fortunate. In this civilian craft, they were painfully ill-equipped to deal with anything out of the ordinary and so… the cloaking device was essential.

"What about the power?" she asked, remembering their earlier concerns. Such a device ate up energy faster than any other system on the ship could.

"It's doable but life support will have to be minimised," he answered. She nodded, more than a little relieved. Such a device, brilliant in its own way, would be useless if they couldn't breathe while using it.

Satiah went back to writing, focussing on the regular duels with Tabre and the general madness on Ionar 12. She decided to give special mention to the helpers from Division Sixteen. They had been genuinely useful and timely. Plus she knew that her apparent support for them would aggravate Randal and thus distract him from questioning other things. Finally she expanded on details they had theorised about the weapon itself and the new material. KZ15. File six. Then she finished it and leaned back in her chair, relieved. She would re-read it later several times and it had yet to be completed but a lot of laser bolts had been suitably evaded. With this level of detail it was hard to keep things simple. That was fortunate, however, as it gave her plenty of scope to hide things she'd rather not have to discuss.

Then, as before, her thoughts started drifting. Carl. Tabre. Ash, Ruby and Reed. She'd done what she did best... she'd survived. Now, she hoped was the final stage. When this was over she'd be free of Ash and Reed. Even be free of Carlos and Deva, although she'd come to appreciate the teenagers' company. Especially Carlos. He could make her laugh too. But... she knew she had to relearn how to say goodbye. Once it had been so easy, easier still when her own life was at stake. When it wasn't and it was an emotional farewell, it had stung. A foggy sort of ache that came and went with unpredictability she did not care for. She thought back, to all those she had lost and all those she had killed. She knew there would be plenty more to come... that was the real test of survival. Could you live with yourself?

**

Tabre was once again admiring his new ship. The young pilot watched him, her hands behind her back, patient.

"Ro says I am to assist you and provide regular reports back to her," said the woman, with a Colonial accent. Tabre looked right at her critically. She was typical military, no doubt a promising fighter pilot from somewhere.

"I have the supplies ready, sir."

"Well that won't do at all," Tabre said, putting on his best charming grin. "I'm all *for* the assistance part but, I can't have you talking to Ro. Not about *me* leastways." He smiled at her. It was chilling and told her how it was going to be on no uncertain terms. She swallowed but held her ground.

"I *suppose*... if we have *technical difficulties*..." she said, uneasily. "You know? The kind that always plagues *new ships* in their early days. Contact with command may be erratic and sometimes even impossible."

"You're a fast learner," he stated, approvingly.

"I understand you are on a termination mission. A Coalition agent named Reed is your target and he has another protecting him. A ship has left this planet just now, civilian but... *I thought*..." she trailed off. Her silence disclosed her theory. So... she had a brain, he would have to keep an eye on her.

"I think the same," he replied, nodding in approval.

"I have a recording of its departure and the computers are tracking it," she stated. Tabre was impressed. He had genuinely thought he'd at last lost them completely this time.

"Where are they heading?" he asked, curious. He half expected them to be returning to Earth.

"Right now, they're going right for the centre of the universe," she replied, sounding as curious as he felt.

"*Are they?*" he asked, rhetorically.

***

"Do you love me?" Ruby whispered, uncertain.

"Define love?" Ash answered.

"...I'm not sure I can," she replied, grinning.

"How can I answer that?" he smiled.

"I knew this would happen, I feel like I've know you all my life," Ruby sighed, resting her head on him.

"Does it bother you that, unlike you, I won't die?" he asked, curious. She thought about it.

"...Not sure, never considered that," she admitted. Then she grinned playfully. "Maybe it is *you* that have never truly... *lived?*" She squirmed and giggled as he tickled her.

"Stop trying to be clever," he growled, amused.

***

"And this is the bridge," Jenjex said, to Egill. He'd come aboard by shuttle a few minutes previously with a whole supply crate. Wester turned to face the huge man.

"Phantom Egill," Wester smiled, shaking his hand.

"Captain," he replied, his voice quiet and yet strong. "Magnificent ship you have here, you must be very proud."

"I am," Wester agreed, without hesitation. "Has Randal...?"

"You want to blow someone up," Egill interrupted, casually, "in a way that restricts collateral damage and doesn't incriminate you."

"Close enough," Wester nodded. Egill began thinking. He was very experienced with explosives.

"First we need to find the target," Jenjex reminded them. "That's what we're going to do now."

Egill nodded again. "Let me know when you need me."

***

Satiah, at the controls, got ready to activate the cloaking device. The second they decelerated, she hit the button. She and Kelvin had spent a few hours working things out so that they could operate the cloaking device *without* paralysing the ship or making it uninhabitable. It had actually been quite the achievement in engineering terms. Carlos had watched them, trying to learn a few things. The control room and *the way to the entrance ramp* were still safe but the rest of the ship couldn't be supported properly due to limited power output of the generator. They were dangerously close to the safety margin as it was. And this kind of ship was not designed to be adapted like that. Civilian craft rarely had anything good about them. Nevertheless, Satiah and Kelvin had made it work and it was working now.

There was no talking. Satiah frowned and looked at the others, curious. All dressed in fresh clothes, all well rested, they had been in higher spirits than they had been for a while. Satiah couldn't understand the silence. She had been expecting Deva at least to offer up an opinion of their new location, she usually did. They were all staring out of the viewport and she followed their gaze and realised why they had said nothing. There was Durrith, the planet in the centre of the universe. And around it... *hundreds* of space stations were there. She gaped. They had come all this way hoping to find one space station. The Orion Observatory. There had been a chance that it had moved again but they had all hoped it would still be there. Maybe they had been hoping for the wrong favour. Now, with hundreds of stations there, sitting quietly in orbit of the deserted world, Satiah began to realise that their mission was nowhere near done...

PART FOUR

The Orion Observatory

Coordinates 0000-0002. The centre of the universe? While it was a matter for debate as to where the exact centre was, they were close enough to the middle. There were one thousand and eleven space stations orbiting Durrith. Durrith being the deserted planet, *commonly* though *not absolutely,* considered to be located, as near as maybe, to or at the centre of the universe. Of course, according to the *current* standard cosmological view, the expansion of the universe has no actual centre. Yet every map has a core and therefore the cosmos has to have one too otherwise no one would ever be able to find anywhere. Unfortunately, other more *pressing* issues plagued Satiah so she had to momentarily put aside the problem of solving the paradox of the missing core of the universe.

With the cloaking device active, despite its side-effects, no one could have detected their arrival. Satiah and the others glowered out at the vast array of space stations, a mixture of surprise and frustration on their faces. Aside from their ponderous orbits, nothing seemed to be happening. Nothing at all. Deva pushed her hair behind her ear as she ran a scan. If she had been bequeathed an Essp for every scan she'd ran she would be a very rich young woman by now, she reasoned. Their equipment was borderline useless but they had nothing else. She sighed when she saw the disappointingly vague result and began again with the narrowest of parameters.

"I'm assuming *by the silence* that none of you know *which one* is the Orion Observatory or even if it is here?" Ash asked, softness in his tone. He was doing his best to be diplomatic. No one did. The idea that it might not even be there was not a pleasing one either.

"Deva?" Satiah asked, her voice also gentle. Everyone was trying very hard not to explode.

"I can tell you they are there and what their orbits are but I can't tell you anything more about any of them," Deva admitted. "This equipment is older than I am." The computer bleeped as if insulted. Carlos leaned back in his chair wondering how Reed and Satiah planned to counter this unforeseen complication.

Satiah sighed and turned to Reed.

"I have an idea, are you interested?" she asked, imagining that he might have his own.

"Deeply," he responded, tearing his gaze away from outside to look at her.

"Our scanners are not good enough to see with. I think we should infiltrate one of the stations and try and find out more information. At the very least they may have better scanners we can use," Satiah explained. It was logical and practical. There was little else they could do other them literally trying to make contact with one of the stations and that would reveal their presence.

"I'll get suited up…" Carlos began, nudging Deva.

"No," Satiah said, holding up her hand. They stopped, eyeing her. "Kelvin and I will do this."

Remembering what had happened the last time she'd taken a walk in zero gravity, Satiah remained confident that it was the most useful thing they could do. The attendance of *so many stations* was suspicious all on its own. They may even *all be* the Orion Observatory, no one had actually *said* it was just one station. They had *presumed* that it was because it was cogent to do so. Reed followed her along, as did everyone except Carlos who remained at the controls.

"Are you sure there is nothing *we* can do?" Reed asked, seriously.

"No, the fewer of us that go across the better. I will need Kelvin as he can see things I can't. Also... there is the chance that the station may be derelict and unusable. It is possible that all of them are wrecks that have been dumped here over a period of time. We cannot dock with any of them in case they are not wrecks and we are revealed... but Kelvin and I can infiltrate without detection easily enough," she elaborated. "*It's what we will find that worries me.*"

"It may be worth investigating the planet too while we are here," Ash interjected, casually. Reed turned to face him, guarded at once.

"May it? *Why?*" he asked, predictably. "It's rumoured to be uninhabited and while I'm not naive enough to trust *rumours* I'm never a fan of splitting up more than necessary."

"It may explain why all these stations are here, faster than the stations will," Ash answered. Satiah had to admit he could be right; there *were* a lot of stations. One thousand and eleven, to be exact. If they were forced to fully investigate more than a couple of them, they would need to get more supplies.

"Ruby and you?" Reed predicted, eyeing Ash.

"...If you would *prefer*, Deva could accompany and supervise us?" Ash offered, being shadily reasonable.

Ruby glanced up at him, trying to understand what they were all worried about.

"I would have no problem with that," Deva was quick to add. She'd got tired of the ship and wanted to explore somewhere new... even if her beloved Carlos couldn't join her. Reed halted, catching Satiah's arm warily. She raised an eyebrow but said nothing as she made eye contact.

"One moment, *small conference*," he requested, in a tone that all but commanded it. Satiah understood what he was concerned about. Ash looked irritated but he made no protest. Reed and Satiah slipped into a side room, the door closing behind them. Deva gave Ash and Ruby a searching glance and subtly adjusted her pistol to stun.

"I hope that it is still here," Ruby stated, referring to the space station. She swallowed, uneasy, she didn't like silences. Deva smiled, a small knowing smile that succeeded in unnerving Ruby even more. "I mean, with all of those out there it could take quite a while to work out which it is and we only have food for about three weeks..."

***

Bright white lights dazzling. Distant voices, murmuring and steadily becoming clearer. Vision slowly clears as full consciousness returns. The sight is one that would anyone wish cognisance was gone forever. Masked faces staring down… gloved hands touching, moving and holding. A paralysis descends on the one who was unlucky enough to open their eyes. Breathing speeds up, heartbeat races. Impossible to move or to speak. It was like locked-in syndrome but worse. If you cannot tell if you are awake or asleep how can you know what's real and what isn't? One of the masked figures strips off his mask and white protective hood. He had no ears, just two dark holes in the sides of his head! He smiles down, displaying yellowy teeth. The gleam in his eyes betrays an inhuman cruelty. No! Scalpel in hand, he moves in to begin the incision… This was real! No, no, no! *No*!

***

"You think Ash knows more than he says?" Satiah guessed, before Reed had uttered a word.

"…It's *possible*," he allowed, thinking on his answer. "For the entire time on Ionar 12 he never suggested anything. Now we're here he's started trying to plan with us… *why*?" It was no secret that the pair distrusted one another.

"You don't *have* to grant his request," Satiah said, seriously. "Or you could go with him *yourself*."

"There are a few options. It's his interest in *the planet* that made me worry," Reed explained. "If he'd been interested in the stations, *like the rest of us*, I wouldn't have reacted like that."

"Immortals are known to see things that we don't," Satiah shrugged. "Kelvin has been monitoring Ash and Ruby since they became known to us. If they'd said anything…"

"Ash is telepathic," Reed muttered, dismissively. "Ruby isn't but for an immortal that doesn't matter. He could talk to her all day and none of us would hear a word."

"Separate them," Satiah suggested, casually. "Ruby can come with me while Ash and Deva visit the planet's surface."

"*You* would be okay with that?" Reed asked, a little surprised. It was well known that Satiah preferred to work alone and wouldn't willingly accommodate any dead weight. "Won't she slow you down?"

"Of course," Satiah admitted, shrugging. "But..." She trailed off.

"It *would* make things trickier for them," Reed said, nodding slowly. Satiah produced a small hypodermic and held it casually. Reed saw and his eyes widened.

"If you authorise me... *I could interrogate her*," Satiah smiled, seriously. "She would be no trouble and I could ensure that she doesn't even remember it."

"Would you hurt her?" Reed asked, a little grimmer. Satiah shrugged again, thinking it through.

"...*Unlikely*," she replied, after consideration. "Accidents do happen. My biggest worry would be her somehow, *telepathically*, alerting Ash to what I was doing. Kelvin has processed her and given me a detailed physical profile for her. She is healthy if a little puny so there are no chemical restrictions for me to observe. She is soft and innocent... forty minutes tops and she'd have spilt everything I ask for..." Reed reflected, frowning deeply. Satiah could tell he was not particularly enamoured by the idea but they had precious few options if they wanted to understand Ash's purpose. She replaced the syringe in its leather case swiftly.

"Or not, *it's up to you*," Satiah said, crossing her arms. "Ash will reveal nothing and *being an immortal* I doubt either of us could force him to. That being so he may *not* have trusted Ruby with anything useful... assuming that there *is* anything useful."

"Come on, you must understand *why* I..." Reed began, earnestly.

"I do and I agree it does make it seem that he is up to something," she smiled, almost laughing. "I've explained our options as I see them. *You're in charge*, you tell me what you want me to do." Reed sighed, grinned and raised an eyebrow. The stab of responsibility.

"Thank you for the reminder," he hissed, mildly annoyed. She tilted her head to him in mocking thanks. "You're *sure* you won't hurt her? Not only am I not happy with the idea of *you doing that in principle* but Ash would certainly react if he found out."

"I will be as gentle as the caress of the water against the skin, only gentler still," she promised, meaning it.

"...Very well," he agreed, reluctantly. "But *no tidal waves!*"

"Whatever you say, boss," she muttered, not bothered.

Reed came out of the room wondering how best to persuade Ash into agreeing with this.

"We have discussed your idea and you make a shrewd point. We agree it does need to be looked into. We are pressed for resources though, so it has been decided that Deva will accompany you to the surface and Ruby will accompany Satiah," Reed explained. Ash nodded as if he had no issue with this. Ruby, however, piped up.

"What?" she asked, confused. "What possible use could *I* be to Satiah? I've never even *fired a gun before in my life*."

"You *may* be able to assist regarding the computer codes like you did before," Satiah answered, before Reed could think of a clever reply. Ash had never told Reed exactly how they had got past Vourne's computer and they all believed that Ruby had somehow managed it. She couldn't disagree without revealing the deception. Ruby shot a pleading glance at Ash.

"It will be okay," he said, simply. His abruptness told her the exact opposite.

Reed was now even more suspicious because of the complete capitulation. He'd expected a full-blown argument or at least some very intense questions from Ash. Instead Ash seemed to even welcome the notion. That could mean anything! It could indicate that Ruby knew nothing. Or it could denote that whatever Ash was up to, he basically didn't care enough about her to bother to protest. Ruby was now quite pale. Ash sensed her fear and faced her again.

"Satiah will look after you, *won't you?*" he asked, a warning gleam in his eyes. Satiah noticed the gleam and tensed instinctively. Did he know? Had he somehow learned of the plan? Or did he just suspect?

"Kelvin will look after us both, you need fear little with him around," Satiah agreed, wording her answer carefully. Ruby eyed the big robot uncertainly.

"Let's get you kitted up," Satiah smiled, escorting Ruby on. "There are spare suits for everyone. Have you ever...?"

"Shuttle is this way," Deva smiled, taking the hint and pulling Ash along with her. Reed watched both couples departing in opposite directions and frowned. Reed reined himself in, reminding himself that Ash was only a small part of this. The Orion Observatory was one of those stations out there, he was certain of it. How better to hide a tree than place it in a wood? He returned to the control room, Carlos was facing the door, slouching in the seat. He wore an expression of curiosity.

"It's a bit tacky to victimise Ruby, isn't it?" he asked, casually. He had been listening in somehow.

"…If you know about that then you will also know it was *not* my idea," he smiled, tightly.

"You agreed to it and authorised it," Carlos shrugged.

"You know what I asked her not to do," Reed stated, inflexibly.

"Yes, I know," Carlos nodded, still not convinced.

"Do you really think Satiah capable of…?" Reed stooped himself. Satiah was more than capable of hurting anyone and he knew it. She was even the type to enjoy it if she felt her target deserved it.

"You are right though," Carlos went on. "Ash is hiding something and Ruby is nowhere near as hard as he is."

"Despite eavesdropping, have you done anything *useful?*" Reed enquired, irritably.

"Satiah told me to monitor the power fluctuations, just in case the generator packs in," Carlos answered, seriously. "If it does, we are completely screwed." He tapped orange readings on the screen to his left. "We're about seventy below the line but if you were to turn a light on or something we could lose everything." Reed squinted at the screen.

"…*Yes*…" he murmured, thoughtfully.

***

The man with no ears watched as the body was carted away. The experiment was over. Slowly he removed the bloodstained gloves from his hands and deposited them in a waste unit. He smiled. There would be many more and things were starting to form a pattern. He liked patterns, particularly those with wavy lines. He knew that, if the specimen had been able, the patient would have screamed in agony as the dissection progressed. Kept awake by chemicals, the man had to remain conscious throughout as was needed. As far as the man with no ears was concerned, the patient was no longer a man. Just another specimen. Just another walking lump of biochemical mass. He slipped on new gloves, identical but for the blood on his hands. It was time for another…

***

Ruby felt very strange, drifting in the void. Arms and legs outstretched, she just floated there hardly daring to breathe. The view took her breath away too which didn't help.

"Ruby?" said Satiah. Ruby started panting heavily but didn't answer. Her arm was tugged roughly back and she flipped over to face the ship and Satiah again. "*Ruby?*"

"Sorry," she said, awkwardly. "I've never … *this is incredible.*"

"I'm sure it is, now remember, you are in a *completely weightless* environment now. When we reach the first station it is likely, due to disuse, that there will be no gravity or atmosphere inside. Do not do *anything fast*! This is nothing like moving underwater. You kick off of something and you will crash into something else with that *exact force*, understand?" Satiah instructed.

"Yes," Ruby replied, honestly.

"Hold onto my hand," Satiah said, and kicked off of the hull of their ship. Ruby was pulled along in her wake. Slowly but steadily the space station grew before them from the size of her hand to very much bigger in moments. Kelvin overtook them along the way, a thrust unit on his back.

"Your Kelvin really is a brilliant machine," Ruby said, trying to make conversation.

"Scan complete, ship still pressurised," Kelvin stated.

"Any life?" Satiah growled, in a tone that made Ruby shiver.

"None detected," he replied. They reached the space station, Satiah grabbing at the hull and halting them.

"Go to Kelvin," she ordered, pushing Ruby towards the robot. She flailed a little as she floated over to him in a slow but uncontrolled summersault. He caught her and held on.

The idea of just drifting off into space came to Ruby. It spooked her and she gulped. Forever alone in the dark. With only oxygen for so long. If Kelvin simply let go of her...

"Are you *sure* you really need *me*?" she squeaked. Her voice was shrill but still quiet.

"Yes of course." Satiah's voice was smooth and broke no argument. Instinct was telling Ruby that she was in deep trouble even though she wasn't sure why. Reed had told Satiah all about her and the files she had deleted and, after a pause, Satiah had said that she wouldn't arrest her after all. Yet... Ruby just had a feeling that Satiah had plans for her. Bad plans. Ever since she had been little she had a great danger sense. She just knew when trouble was on its way. And right now it was screaming at her that trouble was on its way. And this time Ash was not there to protect her.

Ruby tried again.

"What are you doing?" she asked, clearly agitated.

"Trying to get in without setting the security systems off," Satiah replied. "Do you always talk this much...?" A voice buzzed into the collective ears.

"All okay?" asked Reed, from the ship. Satiah swore in frustration.

"*Yes*, thank you Reed," she replied, exasperated. Ruby had got the message, she was in trouble all right but she still couldn't understand why. Somehow Satiah got the airlock door open and they all entered. Pressure returned and Ruby hit the floor hard in a sprawl, with a groan.

"Get up," Satiah said, raising an eyebrow. Kelvin helped Ruby get back onto her feet.

"Right," Satiah said, drawing her pistol. "Kelvin?"

"Positive atmosphere check," he stated. Satiah unclipped her helmet and sniffed. The air was breathable all right, but also stale. Ruby did the same and winced.

"Find me the control room," Satiah instructed, starting down the corridor briskly. Ruby trotted after her nervously.

"Second left, down two levels and third door on the left," Kelvin said.

"What's the power situation like?" asked Satiah, after several automatic lights failed to activate. Even though Kelvin had picked up nothing alive, she still took the corners as if she was expecting an attack.

"I'm detecting no faults, system should be operating in standby mode," he replied.

"That's probably for a good reason, we must take care not to activate anything we don't need," Satiah cautioned. She said that for Ruby's benefit as she knew Kelvin wouldn't do anything stupid.

Ruby was keeping pace well enough and though she was frightened, she had ended the surplus prattle. She hoped Kelvin was right about there being no one else there. The thought of someone sneaking up behind her was a constant companion. Maybe prison wasn't so bad after all… They reached the control room.

"Sit there," Satiah ordered. She pointed to the chair and Ruby obeyed, wondering why Satiah herself had not taken it. Satiah stood before the controls, studying them. The equipment was old, manufactured by the now defunct company Rush-Systems-Limited. Kelvin joined her, scanning.

"Flight system?" she questioned.

"User preferences appear to favour nonhumanoid form," Kelvin answered. "Possibly Manthor."

"Blues," agreed Satiah. Ruby sighed, resigning herself to the idea that there was just way too much to learn.

Satiah leaned back to stare down at a set of pedals on the floor then returned to face the controls again. A whispered conversation occurred that Ruby didn't quite hear but the tone had changed and she tried to listen in. Silence. Together Kelvin and Satiah turned to regard her. Ruby stared back, confused. Satiah bowed her head briefly as if in thought before facing her properly again.

"Why does Ash want to visit Durrith?" she asked, her tone crisp.

"I don't…" Ruby began.

"*Okay*," cut in Satiah, harshly. "I'm going to ask you that once more and if you tell me *that you don't know*, I'm going to hurt you." Ruby gaped, too shocked to believe what was going on.

"Why?" Ruby frantically tried to think of a way out of this.

"...He said something about *history*!" she blurted, scared. "Erm, I wasn't really listening properly but I... why do you want to know? He's your *friend*." Satiah eyed Kelvin and nodded curtly. He had moved behind the chair to cover the door should she be unwise enough to try to run. Now he came forward and put his metal hands on her shoulders. He applied only regular pressure, nothing more than a heavy pat but it had the desired effect.

"*No, no, please*!" Ruby pleaded, tears in her eyes. "If you don't stop this *right now* I will tell Ash and he will..."

"You won't tell him anything, Ruby, because you won't remember this conversation," Satiah told her, eerily calm.

"No! Stop this! I never did anything to you! I don't know anything..." Ruby ranted. Ruby knew Satiah was not someone to mess with and was inwardly terrified but she had to try something.

Satiah was now ignoring her whilst calmly preparing one of her needles.

"Okay, okay..." Ruby said, desperate. "He wants to go down to Durrith to search for another immortal!" Satiah froze and her eyes focussed on her. Ruby was now making things up but she did that very well and she hoped Satiah couldn't tell that she was lying.

"...He thinks one is there?" Satiah asked, her eyes narrowing. Realising she had stopped preparing whatever drug it was that she planned to pump into her, Ruby persevered.

"He told me that he felt someone reaching out to him from nearby and he was concerned they might have the weapon," Ruby went on.

"*Really*? So *why* didn't he tell Reed that?" demanded Satiah, her tone becoming one of disbelief.

"How do you know he *didn't*?" countered Ruby, changing tactics. Satiah thought about it some more and then a knowing smile played on her lips.

"Ruby, *you silly girl*, do I look like an amateur?" she asked, stepping forward.

"*No*!" screamed Ruby, helpless. She tried to rise but Kelvin held her still. Satiah came in close, aiming the syringe for Ruby's internal carotid artery. It was a traditional place to inject someone when you wished to affect their mind quickly. Ruby wriggled uncooperatively, tears flowing freely now. Kelvin's hand clamped down on her head and tilted it to the right, exposing her neck. Ruby continued to twist and squirm.

"Hold still," hissed Satiah, seriously. "Or it will hurt more. You *wouldn't* want me to hit your jugular by mistake." Ruby surrendered to the injection, knowing that Satiah would not hesitate. She was a trained Phantom agent, not an incompetent administrator. What hope did Ruby have?

The needle slid into her skin fairly painlessly and was then removed. Within seconds, instead of the anguish she was expecting, a wave of euphoria swept through Ruby. Ecstasy, pure and liberating, made her relax completely. Her eyes half closed and Satiah's face seemed to become... nicer.

"How are you feeling now Ruby?" Satiah smiled, pleasantly. Ruby fumbled for words that she couldn't think of.

"Only Ash has made me feel like this before," she said, without meaning to. Satiah grinned in triumph.

"I'm sure he has," she replied. "I have injected you with a drug called Norprenddrox. Its properties are complicated but its effects are simple. You have no inhibitions and you can't control yourself. I could tell you to do or say anything and you would."

"You are so beautiful," Ruby said, in a way not dissimilar to the way someone intoxicated would.

Satiah pressed her fingertip against Ruby's forehead.

"I need to know what's in here and you are going to tell me," Satiah told her, clearly.

"I will tell you," Ruby agreed, a big beam across her face. Kelvin released his grip and she slouched back in the chair.

"Why has Ash gone down to Durrith?" Satiah asked, seriously.

"He told me that the apparent extinction of all sentient life on its surface could be the result of the use of the weapon he is searching for. He wishes to see if it can reveal anything more about the nature of the weapon," Ruby explained. In her mind she was powerless to stop herself but was nonetheless relieved that Satiah no longer intended to tear her to pieces.

"I see... does he intend to take this weapon for himself should we discover it?" Satiah asked, giving voice to an old suspicion she had.

"He sees it as his mission and no one else's to ensure humans do not have such a weapon," Ruby answered, slurring slightly.

"Does he mean humanity harm?" asked Satiah, interested.

"Ash loves me and studies me, I am his now," Ruby answered. "I have no reason to think he would hurt any human."

"Is there anything else you can tell me?" Satiah asked, levelly. "About what Ash plans?"

"He keeps a lot from me, for my own safety," Ruby mouthed. She was struggling to remain lucid. "He speaks of tasks but I... can't explain them. They are too much." She fell silent, the grin still plastered on her face. Satiah prepared another injection and performed it casually. Ruby sank completely into the chair, unconscious.

"She doesn't know much," Satiah said, softly. She patted the younger woman's shoulder. "She's completely under his sway." Kelvin said nothing. Satiah called Reed. "It's done," she said, simply. "Maybe Ash will try to take the weapon if it exists and maybe he won't, she doesn't know."

"Yes, I didn't think Ash would be careless enough to tell Ruby anything important," Reed replied, disappointed. "How is she?"

"Sleeping peacefully, she will awake in a few moments with no memory of the interrogation," Satiah said. She and Kelvin returned to their positions at the controls and began to work on them. They had begun to do that *before* they had turned on Ruby. Her mind would find them approximately in the same place they had been before she had been injected and would not notice any gap in perception. It was a primitive form of brainwashing but when used properly it was still effective.

"I will touch base with Randal," Reed replied, disconnecting.

"*Be as well someone did,*" murmured Satiah, as a yawn came from

Ruby. Ruby's eyes opened slowly at first and then blinked rapidly as she had assumed that she had somehow just fallen asleep. She sat up, rubbing her eyes.

"*Did I just go to sleep?*" Ruby asked, shocked. Satiah glanced around at her, the very picture of bemused innocence.

"Did you?" she asked, casually. "Wow, *that's got to be a record*, one minute you are terrified and the next you're so relaxed that you're dozing off. Wish I could do that." Ruby stood shakily and looked around. "Hold *this*," Satiah said, passing her a component. Ruby took it without thinking. She shook her head slightly, still waking up. Satiah glanced up into Kelvin's red eyes and couldn't resist showing him a conspiratorial grin.

She activated a dim screen which illuminated them all, bathing them in a faint blue light. A progress bar was showing, indicating that the system was loading up. Ruby joined them to watch, her brief nap completely forgotten.

"Anything about the layout?" Satiah asked, to Kelvin.

"A central arena type of zone indicates recreation and sports," he answered.

"A leisure station then?" she guessed.

"Design only, application requires confirmation," he answered, as she knew he would.

"You think this place is where sports tournaments used to be held?" Ruby asked, softly.

"The blueprint gives that impression but, as Kelvin has said, just because it was designed for that sort of thing doesn't mean it was used for it," Satiah explained to her.

"Kelvin, can you tell us *when* Rush-Systems-Limited went out of business?" Satiah asked, curious.

"Seventy-four years, three months and fourteen days ago," he answered, swiftly. "It continued to deal in shares for a few years afterwards but that was the inevitable dispersal of company assets."

"…And this station is at least *that old*," Satiah said, considering. "I don't think we will learn anything more from its history."

"Scanners up and scanning," Kelvin said. A wide screen slid from the back of the controls and a picture began to form. It was all there, stations, orbit paths and the planet. Not much more detail than they had had before.

"Not good enough," Satiah grunted, as she judged it.

"Next station?" Kelvin asked, to her. It was time to move on.

"Next station," she concurred. "See if we can find a more advanced one." Ruby nodded, wholly understanding.

As they moved out, something shiny caught Ruby's eye. She stopped in her tracks and stared right at it. It was partially hidden in a pile of materials, that could have been robes, in the corner. Ruby crouched and, even though she wasn't sure why, approached this strange thing with caution. It looked silver and smooth. She gently pulled the clothing away revealing a silver sphere. It was slightly bigger than her palm and perfectly spherical. It seemed inert and completely harmless yet there was something about it that intrigued Ruby. Slowly she reached out and picked it up. It was lighter than she had expected and she stared at her own reflection on its surface. As she held it, it peeped softly at her.

"Ruby!" shouted Satiah, from some distance away. Ruby scampered after the others, taking the sphere with her.

***

The ship slid back to normal speed adeptly, all stealth equipment was fully functional. Alex, the Colonial pilot who was now helping Tabre, let out a low whistle of awe. One thousand and eleven space stations was a sight to behold, especially when you hadn't expected them. Tabre frowned deeply out at them. Alex began a scan.

"So much here for such a *quiet* backwater," Tabre murmured, adjusting his sleeves automatically.

"I can't find Reed's ship," Alex said, scowling. "And that ship model cannot cloak itself."

Tabre smiled. "Satiah would have found a way," he replied, confidently.

"Are you sure?" Alex asked, not convinced.

"*I* would have," he shrugged.

"This scan is taking a while," she said, sighing. State of the art as it was, there was such a lot of things to scan.

"Time well spent," Tabre murmured. "Do we know whose world that is?"

"Durrith," she stated, telling him its name. "*Human* Coalition." The bitter emphasis on that word did not escape Tabre. Clearly Ro was winning her propaganda war. Tabre did not care what label a society wore, nor what their ideology was or their constitution, just so long as they paid their debts to him. If they didn't, he would not hesitate to employ his talents against his own employers. He'd done it often enough before. He felt a compulsion to help Alex to see things as *he* saw them rather than Ro.

"You've been lied to," he said, his voice low and confidential in tone. She shot a glance at him.

"What?" she asked, not sure what he was talking about.

"The Federation, the Coalition… *all of it*," he elaborated, as if it all didn't matter.

"Are you going to tell me it's *all Ro Tammer? Heard that before*," she shot back, a touch insolent. He forgave her that. Ro could be very persuasive.

"Terrible things happened on Pluto Major but they were not of the current Coalition government's doing. Your beloved Ro Tammer rose to power on wings of blood and a rigged vote. Her greatest rival Kane Viller never killed himself… he was murdered," Tabre said, very slowly.

"And how would *you* know?" she demanded, crossing her arms.

"Because I'm the one that killed him," he replied, bite in his tone. One look at his face told her that he was not lying and it would be greatly unwise to continue to dispute him.

"…So you killed him," she muttered, more uncertainly. "What does that prove?"

"It was on Ro's orders," Tabre answered. "No true vote is ever a landslide. How can it be when people never agree? She had me kill those of her rivals she could not destroy herself and then, just to be sure, she rigged the vote. President Raykur is only still alive because his illness prevents him being a threat to her. But even with such great plans, some still resist her. A man named Captain Wester has taken a political stand against her... well, as close as one warship can stand against a whole battle fleet. Ro wants me to kill him too but this... this job takes priority."

"How is it as important? Wester is a traitor..." she began.

"Wester is a young warrior who cares about the survival of the Federation... *He's no traitor*," corrected Tabre, determined to show her the truth. Alex fell silent, a sulky look on her face.

"Why is *this* more important? *Well, that answer is more complicated.* First, Reed slighted Ro by successfully convincing the Punes to join the Coalition. Not just as protectorate world but as a fully fledged member of the Coalition. Also, from early on it was clear to me that Reed is up to something far more devious. His presence on an apparently unimportant planet such as Ionar 12 I find deeply intriguing. Also he's protected by one of the best I ever fought before. A Phantom agent known as Satiah. Whatever it is that he is up to, I'm convinced it's more important than anything Wester is concerned with," Tabre explained. Curiosity was now in Alex's eyes and he realised she was starting to grow interested too.

"*To the Coalition*," she stated, thinking.

"If it's important *to them* then I think it's safe to assume it's important to the Federation," Tabre replied, nodding.

"Which brings us back to *why would he come here*?" Alex said, still wrestling with the question.

"Durrith has a reputation of being a dead world," replied Tabre, eyeing the database. He brought up the information again and gave it another gander. Alex peered over at it too. There was a short absence of interaction between them as they both read the details. While the validity of general information could *always* be called into question, it was all they had to work with. Much of it was plausible enough for Tabre.

"There are some strange legends about that place," she noted. He raised a discreet eyebrow, astonished by her interest in mythology. She was young, of course, so perhaps it was to be expected. And... who didn't love a good mystery?

The story of the origins of the world was one of the strangest

Tabre had ever come across. Tabre categorised it as a story simply because it couldn't easily be called an account or be seen as mere conjecture. This was the place rumoured to have been the epicentre of *the explosion* that had given birth to the universe, whatever you chose to call it. Yet *before* the explosion, the legend portrayed a previous universe of similar but not identical nature that had collapsed in on itself as part of the process which led to the creation of the current universe he knew. The claim left *wild speculation* in the dirt behind it, Tabre mused.

On the world existed a temple or possibly a tomb, the matter was still being debated, said to be home to strange golden suits of armour which were apparently sentient. It was not explained if these suits were organic beings or cybernetic or both or even something else entirely. Many archaeologists, both prominent and otherwise, had died down there while on investigations. It seemed that the guardians of the temple did not like intruders. Next followed a brief recap of events preceding the collapse of the previous cosmos. An anecdote of kings, crumbling castles and broken morality. Two species locked in battle, the Motarians and the Abars. Two immortal beings were involved. One wanted the universe to end and the other wanted it to survive. The one who wanted it to end had triumphed and end it had.

There they wait proud as gold. Watching time slip by. Just as prodigy are told. Ignoring laws they do not abide by.

Mighty are they who wait. Listening to the passing of time holding the keys to the only gate. Clearing the path clear of grime.

Deadly are those who remain. catching those who are unwary. Watching over the giants that were slain. Through time their duties have varied.

They do not wait through choice. Above all else they desire to be free. They answer to only the one voice. To that which they do decree.

This excerpt of text seemed completely isolated. It was related to the planet but the data did not explain the context. Tabre reread it and then eyed Alex. She noticed he was watching her and sat down again.

"All sounds a bit weird to me," she said, seriously. "Does any of this have any bearing on what we are…?"

"No way to know that yet," he interrupted, dismissively. "Is that scan finished yet?" She checked.

"Two more minutes," she replied. Tabre pulled a face as he thought about his new problem. Where was Reed and why would he come here? The question was even more baffling than the previous one about Ionar 12. He checked his pistol, it was ready as always.

***

"Problems are often prospects in disguise," Egill was saying. The Phantom was trying to cheer Wester and Jenjex up a little. They had been drifting in deep space on the edge of the Federation's territory, awaiting intelligence reports of Ro Tammer's location. These reports were not only slow in coming but also woefully inaccurate or just plain disappointing.

"She's going to have to make a public appearance sooner or later somewhere. When she does, because of numerous reasons, she's going to need a stronghold. Once there we can target her," Egill explained. "You've got her rattled, we just have to wait until she settles."

"She's stirring up a frenzy of hatred," Wester said, shaking his head. "The worst part of it is, mostly she's just using the truth."

"Agreed, it would be so much easier to bring her down if she was lying," Jenjex replied.

"Whatever, we need to do something soon, the crew are restless," Wester stated.

"What did you have in mind exactly?" Egill asked, doubt in his tone. "Nothing *too* extravagant I hope."

"If we *can't* track her down maybe we could lure her out," Wester suggested, seriously. "If we can find something she herself will feel she has to protect and threaten it…"

"We know so little about her as a person, I was researching her and there is virtually no information about her birth, upbringing or previous career. The first detailed information I got begins from about two years ago when she emerges as a radical yet *compassionate* member of the Federation government," Jenjex explained. The disdain and disbelief was more than easy to discern from her tone as she articulated the word 'compassionate'. "Even her age is a matter for debate but I'm confident that she's somewhere between fifty and seventy based on various sources. Didn't you guys ever study her?"

Egill shrugged.

"Very possibly but that would be a question for Randal, not me. In any case the fact that there is so little information about her says to me that she could be an operative and not a politician at all," he answered.

"What about family?" Wester asked, sighing.

"She was an orphan according to the official history. That was why she developed such an understanding and association with the lower classes… another reason why she's so popular… A lot of people see her as one of their own," she went on.

"She was educated in a facility with just generalist skill sets and behavioural parameters with a clean record, and then passed onto higher programmes as with procedure." That was standard practice for every individual child in every one of the societies of man.

"Then I got *this report* from a guy called *Mensa*," Jenjex elaborated, swapping computers. Egill recognised the name but said nothing. "For reasons unknown she was adopted by a family and moved onto her first employment. She worked on a farm for nearly ten years, unremarkably. Up until now everything seems normal. Then, she seems to have had some sort of accident. The circumstances remain unclear but she received a blow to the head that put her in a coma for five years. She wakes up, her family have gone and there is no data as to who they were, where they went or why they abandoned her."

"This is bad, I'm starting to feel sorry for her," Wester admitted, with bitterness.

"That's because you're a good, empathic person," Jenjex smiled, a little annoyingly. He shot her a playful scowl. She continued.

"She seems to have undergone a personality change that may or may not be a result of the accident or her abandonment. She gets involved in community politics, solving their problems with a harshness that is respected and feared equally. Then eventually she makes it into one of the main senates which supports the government. From there she scammed, cheated, lied, blackmailed her way into the government and gradually began to take over. A few months ago she made a blunder and underestimated a rival. He managed to get her suspended but she quickly returned and now has pretty much *everything* under her thumb," she said.

Wester wrestled with the possibilities. Was this all because she had been abandoned? Had her mind been altered or damaged somehow? Was she a mastermind or was she insane? He had recently noted how geniuses and psychotic people had a lot in common. Strange ways, strong views, a certain lack of or a different standard of morality, not forgetting... seemingly unnatural abilities of persuasion. If she *was* an operative, who was she working for? Most disturbingly of all, under a scanner, there was no discernible *physical* difference in the appearance of their brains. A genius or a psychopath. A sinner or a saint. The contrast similarities stretching over a bottomless chasm of conflicting ideologies unsettled him.

"Well, the past, *whatever it was*, is the past. We need to get rid of her *now*," Wester said, sounding as exhausted as he felt.

"You were the one who was questioning her motivations," Jenjex reminded him.

"I know but we're getting no answers, *only more questions*," he stated, seriously.

"Your face and this ship are everywhere on the CNC, we will find it difficult to do any more hit and runs anywhere important," Jenjex sighed, shaking her head.

"We will wait for more information," Egill said, firmly.

***

The second space station, literally the next one along, Satiah repeated her well-practiced process of infiltration. Kelvin scanned, found it once again pressurised but with no life forms. Then she started work on the airlock. This station was about twenty years old, fairly new, certainly one of the newest there that they could see. The scanners would be better than those on the ship they had. As before they entered the space station and after an atmosphere check, Ruby was the first to remove her helmet. She inhaled, wheezed and winced in disgust.

"What is that smell?" she gasped, seriously considering putting her helmet on again. Satiah had smelt that many times before and somehow it never failed to bother her.

"Death," she replied, calmly. She gave Kelvin a meaningful look.

"There are no life readings," he repeated.

Pistol in hand before she even consciously thought about it, Satiah started down the first dimly lit corridor. Kelvin followed her and Ruby, as she had been told, stayed behind them. Satiah reached a half-open door and entered out onto a balcony. She crossed to the guardrail and stared over the edge. Kelvin joined her. Below them, piled unceremoniously, were hundreds of bodies. While the environment was sealed, bacteria still thrived and had enough air to work with. Mostly all of them were in the active or advanced stages of decomposition. While she couldn't be sure, Satiah was sure that insects would not have been able to access the bodies. All of them seemed to be partially skeletonised and at the very least a few weeks old. The temperature being cool would have slowed the process too. Satiah could see her breath in clouds of vapour. Life support was still operating but on the lowest setting, probably due to lack of power. This could mean that there was a problem with the reactor.

"How many?" Satiah asked, still keeping her focus on the shadows of the surrounding walkways.

"Three hundred and forty-six," he answered. A gasp from Ruby sounded behind them and then a splattering noise as she vomited.

"Cause of death?" Satiah questioned, ignoring the retching.

"Machine laser fits the wound patterns," he replied.

"Oh no!" uttered Ruby, at last getting to them. She grasped the railing, clearly fighting to control her stomach. "What happened?" Her skin had taken on the pale green colour of someone rather unwell.

"Someone killed them, come on, the control room is…" she began, turning to move on. Ruby grabbed her forearm rapidly to stop her.

"But they have all been murdered, we *need* to…!" Ruby began, in horror.

"*Ruby*, they have no relevance to our mission. We leave them, *never think of them again*," Satiah responded, coolly.

"We can't just *leave them*!" she protested, disgusted.

"Good luck carrying them back with you," Satiah remarked, pulling her arm free.

"Are you even going to tell Reed?" Ruby demanded, hotly. Satiah turned and sighed. Ruby was… so innocent.

"Ruby," Satiah began, tying to search for the right words. "These people have been dead a while; there is nothing we can do for them. We have a job to do."

"*You* have a job to do," Ruby argued, meekly. "What happened here? Do you know?"

"We will probably find out when we find *the control room*," Satiah replied, thinking about it. She wondered if, as this was clearly illegal dumping of bodies, someone may have done something to ensure that if they were discovered by anyone… A memory came to her.

About seven years ago Vourne had sent her to investigate a criminal organisation called: Ghost. The organisation, aside from drug running and extortion had been in the habit of murdering the smugglers they used in order to cover their tracks. Their traditional move was to kill them while on board their ship and transfer all the bodies to one area. Then, they would ensure the ship be discovered sometime later by rival organisations to send a message. She wondered if this was something like that. It was more likely though, to be a straight forward case of hiding the evidence. How likely was it that these people were on missing personnel lists somewhere? More likely still, they had all been criminals themselves. Satiah smiled coldly at how the leader of the organisation known as Ghost had met his end. Satiah had murdered him and then stowed his corpse under the flight deck of his ship. It had taken days but the smell had eventually given it away as she had planned it would… subsequently the company broke up. Message received.

Speaking of smells, it seemed that the decay had made its presence known everywhere. Tearful but, thankfully silent, Ruby had replaced her helmet, unable to stand the smell any more. Satiah had no liking for the odour but she was used to it and chose to conserve her air supply. They reached the control room. It was much larger than the previous stations and had two levels to it. Satiah glanced at Ruby and couldn't help but feel a little sorry for the younger woman.

"Ruby," she said, getting her attention. "There's a database there, see if you can discover more about this place while Kelvin and I try to get the scanners going." Ruby sighed heavily but nodded. She sat down and tried to get it started.

"This system is more advanced," Kelvin stated. Satiah ran a professional eye over the controls and nodded in approval. Dust covered them but there was no sign of damage; they were far superior to those they had encountered so far.

"I'll check out the reactor," she replied, moving over to an adjacent panel. Everything was off but the standby that was almost always functional was blinking amber. She activated and the unit flashed as all the lights blinked back into life. A hum began. No traps so far… a common one was setting an explosive charge in the engines to blow the station to pieces should anyone try to move it. They didn't need the engines but there were more subtle methods. Setting the reactor core to overload was a less famous one and they did need the reactor.

"Am detecting nitric oxide," Kelvin warned. Satiah hurriedly slid her helmet back on. So, someone *had* set a trap.

"Ruby, keep your helmet on," Satiah instructed, seriously.

"I will," she answered, worriedly.

"As traps go it's a bit hit and miss," Satiah noted, sceptically. "All right I may not have noticed until it was too late but I may never have removed my helmet at all, rendering it useless."

"Perhaps it is a cover for a less obvious strategy," Kelvin suggested. Satiah nodded curtly. He was likely correct as that was the conclusion she had reached herself.

"This has been wiped," Ruby stated, edgy. "…Can we use the scanners?"

"Transferring power now, I'm keeping it on low ebb in case they have tampered with any of the generators," Satiah said. She eyed Kelvin as he set a scan to run. Kelvin though, wasn't moving… his red eyes slid into green and he glanced back towards the door.

"Did anyone hear *that*?" Ruby asked, jumping. Satiah sighed, thinking Ruby's imagination was playing tricks on her.

"You're imagining things Ruby, calm…" Satiah began, trying to sound soothing. Kelvin swung fully around from the scanner, his flame thrower extended. Ruby screamed and dived for cover as a jet of fire erupted powerfully to engulf the doorway in flames. Instinctively Satiah fired two shots in that direction, even though she couldn't see who or what he was shooting at.

"Sentinel robot defence system has activated," Kelvin warned, in his usual monotone. Ruby peeped over the control panel she was hiding behind fearfully.

"How many?" asked Satiah, making decisions.

"Forty," he answered.

She swore and rushed over to Ruby.

"Come on, we're leaving!" she stated, sourly.

"But the scans…" Ruby began, torn between the desire to leave and the duty to get the information for Ash.

"If we are not alive to convey the information there will be no point in awaiting the scans' completion!" Satiah argued, influentially. Kelvin switched to his repeating laser and his second appendage clicked as a small blasting pistol slid out for use.

"Go," he instructed. Literally dragging Ruby along with her Satiah fled down the corridor. Forty was too many for them to cope with. They must have activated the second the power came through, if Ruby and Kelvin hadn't been there Satiah realised she'd be dead by now. She'd never doubt Ruby's hearing again.

Behind them they heard the heavy droning of machine on machine warfare. In a way, Kelvin had a huge advantage. The sentinels would be tracking Satiah and Ruby through heat detection most likely. As a machine, Kelvin would be invisible to them. The flames would also be a useful distraction. Yet there were forty of them. They turned a corner and Satiah yanked Ruby backward so hard she fell and screamed in panic. Pistol drawn, Satiah aimed at the hovering black globe of death that was the sentinel robot. She hit it hard; three well-aimed shots sent it smashing against the wall and reducing it to its components. Ruby rose to her feet again, too scared to cry or scream now. Heavy clunking indicated Kelvin's approach.

Perhaps it had been the sentinels that had killed all those people. Even the gas had been automated in its attack style. Reaching the open airlock, its pressure bubble still in operation preventing depressurisation, Satiah got Ruby out first. Kelvin came around the corner, pursued by no less than three sentinels. Satiah picked them off with ease and they both slipped back out into space. Ruby was waiting, clinging to the side of the ship and panting heavily.

"We should go back and get help," Ruby shrieked. "This is getting dangerous." Satiah sighed and squeezed Ruby's shoulder.

"Ruby, the sentinels will not follow us out here… we are safe. We just need to move on to the next station," Satiah replied.

"And what will we find there?" demanded Ruby, on the verge of hysterics. "A virus? A pirate gang? Some kind of creature that will try to eat us?" Satiah couldn't hold back the grin.

"No reason why all of those can't be on the same station," she answered, smiling pleasantly. Ruby stopped ranting and stared right at her in dawning horror.

"You're *enjoying* this?" she blustered.

"I'm just used to it, that's all," she assured her. Ruby composed herself and, after a long moment of thought, sighed heavily.

"Where next?" she asked, levelly.

"That one."

***

Deva piloted the escape pod through the upper atmosphere of Durrith.

"Anywhere in particular that you wanted to go or are you just wandering?" Deva asked Ash. The immortal regarded her for a moment as he considered his answer.

"See if you can locate any structures," he replied, leaving it at that. Deva frowned, eyeing the results of the scanners.

"Depends what you mean by *structures*," she replied, concentrating. "There's a lot of ruins and wreckage down there. Maybe some of the stations have crash landed in the past."

"Possible," he acknowledged.

"Dense forests… ah, we can try *here*," she said, swinging them down from the upper clouds. Ash didn't tense at all when the teenager began a descent that might have spooked a regular passenger. She came in very quickly and very close to the trees.

Deva snatched up her rifle.

"You stay here," she ordered Ash. "I've scanned the area but, as I said before, these scanners are awful and I need to do a sweep of my own to ensure there are no dangers." Ash said nothing as she departed but slowly rose and began to follow. Deva sprinted down the ramp and, rifle raised, began to circle, seeking dangers. Ash wandered out and began to head in the direction of the building.

"Oy!" she yelled irately, at him.

"There's no danger *out here*," he replied, dismissively. Deva bristled but hurried after him, while maintaining her wary vigilance. Were all immortals so... reckless?

The forest was made up of dense trees, so clustered, it made seeing beyond about five metres almost impossible. There seemed to be an air of expectation, as if a group of collective someones were holding their breath in anticipation of something. The occasional animal calls that Deva didn't recognise didn't sound like anything more innocuous than small rodents or birds. Calling to one another as they foraged in search of food or perhaps a mate. It was easily possible that some of the predators or even plants may represent danger. The pod had detected no mesoscopic dangers. No bacterial or viral threats. While its detectors were hardly top of the range, Deva trusted them to be accurate about that much. On a planet widely regarded to be a home to no one but the dead, it was hard to shake off the feeling that death was not far away.

Ash continued blithely on though, as if he was heading to a tavern after a day at a factory. Deva did not feel as ridiculous as she looked coming after him bit by bit. She could use trees, and bushes to conceal herself behind as she used her rifle sights to seek threats. Within a few minutes Ash stopped. They were in sight of... a construction. Deva paused and eyed the building. It was not that tall, only twice the height of the trees. Its shape was similar to a trapezium. Brown stone with markings and pictographic symbols. Deva wondered what it was. It was odd that the forest hadn't seemed to claim it. It was free of weeds or any other kind of plant contamination.

"What do you think it is?" she asked, her curiosity too much to restrain.

"Not sure, what about you?" he asked, but his tone betrayed a lack of interest in her opinion. She answered anyway.

"A long time ago, people believed in what are known as religions… maybe this is something to do with them," she suggested.

"You think it's a place of worship?" he clarified.

"I've heard of religions but don't understand them," she replied, shrugging. "By the look of it it's *certainly not* an apartment complex." She fished out her communicator from her belt. "Carlos…" she began but Ash covered the device with his hand firmly.

"Why don't we wait until we find something worth reporting before we report it?" he asked, casually. "Come on."

He moved forward, towards the building. Deva remained where she was, thinking about it. She should at least say they had touched down and there were no obvious dangers that had been encountered. Carlos though, would be able to see that with his own scanners… She scampered after him, still checking the angles and distances with her rifle. Ash saw a set of steps leading down into darkness, the entrance? It seemed illogical to presume otherwise. He proceeded down them. Deva followed, rifle still ready. She activated the light on the end of it and rapidly descended after him. Ash produced a torch from his cloak and inhaled the air slowly.

Fetid. Damp. Cold air. Deva said nothing as she evaluated the new surround. Ash took a step forward and something squelched under his boot.

"Ok Ash, why are we here?" Deva asked, grit in her tone.

"Check the walls," he said, his tone conversational. "See if there is anything hidden."

"*Ash?*" she asked again, not moving. Ash began to examine the wall in front of them in silence. "Ash?"

"If I tell you, will you tell Reed?" he asked, levelly.

"Depends on what Carlos choses to do with what I tell *him*. I work for *him* not Reed or Satiah," she reminded him.

"How much do you know about this world?" he asked, not really interested but trying to distract her. Luckily for Ash, Deva had read about the legends and was sufficiently interested in them for them to take precedence in her discussion.

She explained her outlook on the legends and asked several of the rhetorical questions that had been asked before again. Meanwhile Ash continued to search for the way in. He knew it had to be there somewhere, just as he knew who had managed to get in last time. This was assuming that it was the same place, but he trusted Deva enough to know she could read a scan report. It didn't take long for Deva to realise that she didn't quite have all of his attention and suspicion crept back into her tone.

"If you *don't* tell me what you are doing, I'm going to call Reed directly," she threatened, seriously.

"As you know, a long time ago, two immortals battled here," he began, starting to wonder if there still *was* a way in.

"*Yes,*" she replied, pointedly.

"One of those was my mother," he explained.

"*I guessed that much,*" she replied, genuinely unsurprised. "*Dreda was here! So what?* She leave her coat behind or something?" Ash actually laughed at that.

"Not exactly," he replied, smiling. Deva waited. When nothing else seemed to be about to be said she clicked her communicator and Reed answered.

"Yes?" he answered. Ash stopped and raised his hands in a gesture of surrender. Deva smiled in triumph.

"We landed safely, will report in again soon," she said, obligingly.

"Be careful," Carlos replied, as the connection ended.

"You're probably wondering what significance the past has with the present? What possible connection could there be between events before the beginning of this universe and now? Truth is I'm not sure but I have a theory. There was a golden suit of armour that contained a survivor of the previous universe when opened up. The technology seemed able to suspend aging and … *prevented the occupant from sleeping,*" he told her. Deva nodded slowly as the link became apparent.

"This armour may have had the new material in it, to ensure its occupant never slept?" she confirmed.

"KZ15, yes," he supplied.

"Yes... *It could have*," she allowed, and then she frowned. "Even if it does, *what does it prove exactly?*"

"That there is or at least was an alternative supply of the material," he replied, seriously. "We may also learn more about the properties of the material itself and how it works." She crossed her arms, thinking it over. "In any case, none of that will be possible *if we can't get in*, will you help?"

"I thought we *were* in," she mumbled, starting to look around herself. Then she stopped again. "Why wouldn't you want Reed to know about *that?*"

"I don't want him poking his nose into my business, it's bad enough the way things are now," he stated, tetchy.

"Without us you'd never had worked out what that mission report said," Deva argued. He didn't reply to that. She was still not convinced but she felt she'd got about as far as she could.

***

Satiah slipped through into the space station. This one, unlike the others they had visited, wasn't pressurised and was a zero-gravity environment. It was pitch black and silent. Just like space itself.

"I'm not sure about this," Ruby was saying. "If it's got no power we can't use it."

"We don't know that it has no power," Satiah reminded her. "We just know that it's currently inactive." A clatter from ahead, heard through the fabric of the station itself, as a long scraping noise halted them.

"Kelvin?" Satiah asked, seriously.

"No life signs," he repeated.

"*He keeps saying that and there is always something*," Ruby complained. Satiah sighed but didn't bother to argue. There were other explanations as to what could be making that noise.

The slow movement through space may be causing something to

collide with something else. Damage perhaps. Or it could be more *friendly* robots out to kill them. On they went, following Kelvin's directions. Their progress was slower than before due to the fact that they couldn't walk. Ruby had pretty much mastered herself in zero gravity now; nevertheless, she often pushed off of things too hard out of impatience and bashed into things harder than she really should. They reached the control room which looked and felt as dark and dead as the rest of the station. Ruby was now going on about how shocked she was at the waste of all these stations. Space refuse was a big issue apparently, *if one watched the news*, and according to Ruby it caused one in three of all space collisions. How did Ash put up with this constant babble?

"*Ruby!*" Satiah cut in, curtly. "Please could you check that panel over there." Ruby nodded and floated over there. Satiah gently eased herself over to the main control area. The controls seemed completely dead.

"I've got nothing," Ruby said.

"Anything blinking *anywhere?*" Satiah asked, the hope was clear in her tone.

"...No," Ruby replied, after checking again. "Nothing on standby, nothing in low power mode... it's dead." Satiah glowered to herself. This was taking too long! The noise sounded again and Ruby was quick to come closer to Satiah and Kelvin.

"Let's move on to the next one," Satiah said, doing her best to forget the noise.

"*What is that?*" Ruby asked, rhetorically.

They made their way slowly back the way they had come. The noise intermittently sounded but when it was clear that it was getting further away, Satiah relaxed a bit. Back out in space, she checked how much air they had left. They had been doing this for nearly six hours. Ruby seemed fine but Satiah knew it was getting to her.

"One more, then we will call it a day," Satiah announced, glumly. Ruby perked up a little, now that an end was in sight.

"Great," she smiled, not bothering to hide her glee. "Which one?" Satiah looked around and something, a long way past the stations, caught her eye. A distant flicker that reminded her of...

"Kelvin, what's that?" she asked, pointing. His red eyes focussed in and triangulated the approximate area she was referring to.

"I can detect nothing," he replied.

"What did you see?" Ruby asked, nervously.

"A flash... looked like energy leakage or energy fields colliding..." Satiah explained. She'd seen it many times before. Most notably when she had been stalked by a cloaked ship but it had got too close and their energy shields had collided causing a static flash. This time, in theory, the only cloaked ship around should be her own. Yet it was more than likely others were present. She knew that Kelvin wouldn't be able to detect a ship if it was cloaked.

"What would cause that?" Ruby asked, concerned. Deciding not to alarm the younger woman, Satiah smiled.

"Maybe I imagined it," she stated, flatly. "Let's go."

Trusting Ruby to be able to follow her adequately now, Satiah pushed off of the surface of the dead space station and floated swiftly towards her next target.

"Use your grapple gun," urged Kelvin, suddenly slipping past her. "You are close to the planet's gravitational field and risk being dragged down. Grabbing the surprised Ruby, Satiah did as he suggested and fired her grapple gun at the surface of the station. They were drifting to the left, as Kelvin had predicted. While she wasn't sure if she would have made it or not, Satiah was certain that it had been a worthy precaution. They hit the station hard, almost bounced straight off of the hull.

"Sorry about that, Ruby," Satiah said, maintaining her grip with difficulty.

"It's okay... how will we get back?" she asked. Satiah thought about it. Going the other way, they would be too far for the grapple gun and wouldn't be able to counter the pull of the planet no matter how hard kicked off of the surface of the station.

"I'll get Reed to bring the ship in," Satiah stated, hoping that that would be an option. Kelvin clamped himself to the station and grabbed each woman with one of his appendages, holding them down while Satiah worked on the door. Sparks flew and Satiah swore.

"What's wrong?" Ruby asked, worried.

"There was still power in the circuit," she growled. "Kelvin, any life forms?"

"Yes," he replied. "Readings indicate insectoid life forms."

"Insects?" Ruby asked, not sure if that was good or bad.

"Are they dangerous?" Satiah asked, patiently.

"Unknown," he responded.

"Maybe we should try…" Ruby began, about to suggest they find another station instead. The hatch unsealed and Satiah pulled it open. "Never mind." Kelvin released them and they entered. Pressured and with gravity, Satiah removed her helmet and sniffed. The air was… clean. Pistol out and ready, she was scanning the corridor ahead.

"Where are they?" she asked.

"Readings are concentrated in the lowest level, control is in the centre," he responded.

"Good, keep the noise down," she ordered, to Ruby. These corridors were well lit and of a slightly warmer temperature than normal. They crept rapidly along, following Kelvin's directions. Satiah was optimistic that this station would be perfect for what they needed.

Ruby was looking all around, very alert. She didn't like bugs and the thought of them being the only life form on board an abandoned station did not fill her with joy. She wished she was as brave as Satiah. Satiah reached a closed door, pointed at it and looked at Kelvin. He shuffled to indicate a yes. Satiah crouched to examine the lock. She didn't want to shoot it open as that would give away the fact that they were there. Kelvin could maybe burn a hole in it but if there was a way she could get it open then that would be best. Kelvin moved again, this time to face the way they had come. Ruby, having been around Kelvin long enough to recognise some of his signs, tensed. He was scanning… what had made him do that? Satiah began to tamper with the control pad and flipped the cover off quickly.

"Everything okay, Kelvin?" whispered Ruby, as if she was acting in a pantomime.

"Movement detected," he responded. Ruby stared back the way

they had come and swallowed nervously. Satiah continued to fiddle with the exposed circuitry adeptly. The door slid open and she stood to cover it. One by one they all went in, Ruby was still trying to imagine what might have moved. The control room itself, like the rest of the ship was well lit and everything was still working. The controls flashed and hummed almost welcomingly. Satiah did not like it one bit. She examined the controls. Ruby slowly walked around the room and almost tripped over something. She looked down and shrieked involuntarily.

Satiah and Kelvin came over and stared down at the body.

"*Ruby*," hissed Satiah, annoyed. "Noise down, yes?" Hands over her mouth in shock, Ruby yammered wordlessly in protest. The man was lying on his side, eyes still open.

"Kelvin," Satiah ordered, pointing to the corpse. Kelvin examined the body while she returned to the controls. "These scanners are fairly reasonable in quality," she went on, after giving them the once over.

"This dead human has internal wounds and alien matter inside," Kelvin announced. Ruby made a noise somewhere between a yelp and a groan in dismay. Satiah looked up sharply.

"Alien matter?" she questioned. "Would this alien matter be similar in properties to those insects you detected earlier?"

"Yes," he said.

"We need to go, right now..." Ruby began, heading for the door.

"Ruby, stay calm," cautioned Satiah, seriously. "Come on, help me run this scan." Reluctantly Ruby stepped up and assisted. The scan began and, as before, it was going to take a while. The women watched as the computer began an eighteen-minute countdown.

"Reed," Satiah called, into her communicator.

"Still here," he responded, immediately.

"Can you get a fix on us?" she asked, quickly. "I would like you to come and get us. The gravity is too strong for us to escape here."

"Yes," Carlos replied, casually. "We're moving in now."

"Any news from Deva?" Satiah asked, curious.

"Nothing yet," Reed replied, sounding equally curious.

"I am detecting movement," Kelvin stated, seriously. Ruby froze and made sure she didn't annoy Satiah by making a noise.

"Where?" Satiah asked, eyeing the door. She'd heard nothing.

"*In* the corpse," he replied, backing away from the body. Satiah eyed the cadaver, perturbed. She trained her pistol on it. Ruby gulped and also tried to put more distance between herself and it. There was a sickly squelching noise and a motion rippled through the body. It rolled onto its back and its mouth opened. Satiah aimed. From inside the dead man's mouth a pair of beady eyes stared out at her.

"*Oh no, no, no,*" Ruby murmured, terrified. A hissing noise began and a long black tentacle-like thing began to crawl out of the man's mouth.

Satiah fired, and Kelvin too blasted the thing. Smoking and burnt to a crisp, the thing fell and lay inert. Then it too began to shake and then split apart. Thousands of tiny versions of itself emerged from its body and began to slither along in all directions. They resembled circular black pebbles, a little like mini Scarab Beetles. Ruby shrieked and leapt onto the control panel. Kelvin and Satiah did the same. In seconds all three of them were completely surrounded by the insects. Satiah eyed the countdown. Twelve minutes to go before the scan was complete.

"What do we do?" Ruby asked, scared.

"We wait for the scan to end and while we wait we work out an escape plan," Satiah replied, staying composed. "Kelvin, is there another way out of here?"

With one of his powerful arms he reached up and punched through the ceiling. Above was a cable shaft.

"That'll do," she smiled, in triumph. That was when a chiming noise began, like hundreds of prehistoric clocks all going off together. Ruby cried out and clutched her ears. Satiah winced, aiming all around, seeking a target. The chiming fell silent and then a hissing voice began to talk. It sent a shiver up even Satiah's back.

"It is time to feed," it said. "Now there is food."

"Now what?" Ruby asked, her voice fraught. "Don't let them eat me!"

"Ten minutes," Satiah shot back.

"We need to go and find somewhere…" Ruby began. Satiah grabbed her arm to stop her from moving.

"You get down from here and those things *will* eat you alive, I'm sure of it," Satiah insisted. "You will remain here with me and we will leave together *when* we have finished the scan!" Tears were streaming down Ruby's face now, she was petrified.

"I'm sorry, I'm sorry," she kept saying. Satiah clamped her mouth closed strongly.

"Don't be sorry, *be alive*," she retorted. "*Trust me, I will get us out of this.*" Her communicator went off.

"We are orbiting the station, let us know…" began Reed.

"We have a situation here," Satiah interrupted. "Do not dock, repeat do *not* dock. There are hostile life forms!"

"Can we help?" Carlos asked, seriously.

"Wait there… *Kelvin*, get Ruby out," Satiah ordered, pointing up.

"What about you?" Ruby asked, frightened. Satiah was surprised momentarily that she cared enough to ask.

"Do as I say," she responded, coldly. Ruby was going to protest further when Kelvin picked her up and began to shove her into the shaft above. Ruby, adrenalin making her heart race faster than the fear, hauled herself up and made room for him as he dragged himself up after her. He paused, his red eyes looking back into Satiah's.

"…*Go on*," she encouraged, a little more emotionally. He headed off, telling Ruby which way to crawl. The hissing was starting to become irksome. She smiled down as the creatures unsuccessfully tried to climb up to get at her.

"Time for some target practice," she said, and began shooting them indiscriminately. Five minutes.

***

The door wasn't really a door at all and neither was it ajar. It was the whole wall that moved. Ash had found a lever concealed on the floor and used it. The wall began to retreat from them, revealing a set of long thin steps leading down into darkness. Deva quickly covered it with her rifle, swinging left and right to be sure it was clear. Seeming to not mind what might be lurking down there, Ash descended the steps without hesitating. Deva debated the pros and cons of telling him to wait for her to make sure it was safe but gave up on that idea. He was an immortal! He could look after himself; she had to just watch her own back.

The air was musty and cool. Dust was on the floor, making it feel a bit like walking on sand. There were no observable tracks of anyone else that Deva could see. Ash... seemed to know where he was going and she didn't like that.

"Have you been here before?" she asked, seriously.

"Before now, before this point in time? I cannot say as perhaps I will visit in my future, but further back in this place's past, so whether I've been here before..." he began, casually.

"I think you know your way around. You went straight to this place and you..." she argued.

"Why does everyone have to ask so many questions?" he demanded, stopping in his tracks. "Why do you humans have to know everything? Why so curious?"

"Because you are weird," she stated, after a fractional moment of consideration.

"Have you ever considered that *you* may seem weird to *me*?" he asked, instantly. His tone was one of playful accusation and Deva realised he'd had this conversation at least once before.

"No," she replied, being honest. "Why would I have considered that?"

"And therein lies the problem," he replied, moving on. She realised, with amusement, that he'd successfully distracted her from her original query. Well almost...

"So have you been here *or not?*" she persisted, seriously. "I'm an operative. You can't fob *me* off with philosophical dribbling."

"No," he replied, flatly. Was he lying? Deva was starting to understand why Reed had such a hard time trusting Ash.

***

Scan complete. At last! Satiah was relieved. The tiny creatures were using each other to climb up onto the control panel she was standing on. She was shooting still but there seemed to be a never-ending onslaught of them. They were coming in from the main door too now. She transferred the scan results onto a data cube and slipped it into her pocket. Then she hauled herself into the shaft that Ruby and Kelvin had escaped down. Part of the shaft fell out from under her and she grabbed at the support beam above to stop herself falling down into the swarm. She scrambled along quickly. A screeching sounded from her left and she saw that they had infiltrated the shaft and were coming at her from the left. In doing that they had cut her off from her way out, these insects clearly knew their ship at least as well as she did. With no choice but to go right, simply to stay ahead of them, she continued on.

"Did you make it out?" Satiah asked, wondering if she would get an answer. She'd heard nothing so she had presumed that they had successfully evacuated but she didn't know.

"We are back on board the ship," Kelvin answered, in her ear. "You have been cut off; you need to find another escape route." She rolled her eyes, as if she couldn't have thought of that herself!

"Can you still see the insects?" she asked, panting.

"No, there are too many for a detailed reading to be attempted," he replied. She swore.

"Okay... Am I still close to the side of the station?" She checked that she had a mine on her, she had.

"Yes, less than one hundred metres from the edge," he replied.

"Ok, you must move the ship a short distance away," she commanded. "I'm going to blast myself out."

"Did you get the scan?" Reed asked, interested.

"Yes," she answered, through her teeth. "I'm bringing the results back with me." She reached an intersection with a shaft going directly upward. Using her grapple gun she dragged herself up speedily, managing to avoid smacking herself into the sides of the shaft as she went. She then doubled back, going in the direction she had originally been crawling in, only in the higher shaft.

"How far to the edge?" she asked, trying to ignore the screeching.

"Fifty-nine metres," Kelvin answered. "You may wish to abandon the shaft before you explosive charge detonates."

"Yes, that would be sensible," she remarked, trying to figure out how far ahead of the insects she was. It was hard going at that pace, even for her. Knees bruised, hands scratched, filthy and battered.

She reached the edge less than ten minutes later and clamped the mine to the wall of the shaft... the wall facing space. Kicking open the hatch she checked the corridor below her before she set the ten-second fuse. Down she dropped, sealing her helmet as she went. Landing in a deep crouch, she swung left and right, pistol ready. Screeching sounded and more of the insects appeared at the near corner. She opened fire instantly but remained where she was. Five seconds. The insects continued to advance on her. She gave up targeting and started shooting from the hip, splaying them with a deluge of laser fire. One! She dived to the right. The blast shredded the station's hull in the localised area, covering three floors. Depressurisation occurred instantly and Satiah allowed herself to be drawn out into space. The insects were all dying, freezing in the vacuum of space almost instantly.

***

The explosion of the mine was only a distant flash but Tabre still saw it.

"*There*," he said, as Alex fired up the engines. "Approach with caution, there could be more." Alex nodded her eyes wide. "I wonder what she's been up to now." In his mind it had only been a matter of time before Satiah did something.

"You don't *know* it's them," Alex objected, half-heartedly. He glanced at her, raising his eyebrows.

"*Please*," he stated, seriously.

"Localised scanning revealed nothing but debris and... weird alien life forms that are now deceased," she explained. Tabre nodded slowly.

"And the killing has started..."

***

Satiah handed the data cube to Reed. She was covered in sweat and dirt but otherwise relatively uninjured.

"Good day's work," he smiled, satisfied.

"How's Ruby?" she asked, interested.

"She's gone to her cabin and hasn't been seen since," Reed sighed. He gave her a meaningful look. "*Concerned?*"

"*She doesn't remember,*" Satiah insisted, levelly. Her tone lowered to become more private. "I was more worried about *trauma*."

"She's tougher than you give her credit for," he smiled, thinking about it for a second. "I'm still waiting to hear from Ash and Deva." Satiah nodded slowly.

"Wait for me before you review the scan," she requested. He nodded. "I need to change."

***

That sound dominated the nightmares of *every* naval officer. The call to battle stations. Wester opened his eyes. His room was dark but illuminated by a red flashing light. He'd only had about two hours' sleep! Stumbling around as he dressed, he was on his way as quickly as possible. Crew were hurrying in all directions as he too rushed to his station. The bridge.

"Amber alert, we have *two* Federation destroyers approaching," called the flight officer. Wester reached the bridge as, also still dressing as she ran, Jenjex arrived too. "Point three ten."

"Evasive action!" Wester ordered, going for the navigator. "Get the fighters ready for launch. All troops on standby!"

"Sir, they are *hailing* us!" called Jenjex, looking baffled.

Wester thought hard for a few precious moments and nodded after he had composed himself. A man appeared on the screen in front of him. He was gaunt, had short, spiky, black hair and a scar running down from under his left eye to his chin.

"Captain Wester, my name is Captain Keane. We will not fire on you unless you fire on us, we want to talk to you," he stated, his tone official but… there was something else… a bleakness to his face. This was unusual and, as usual Wester only had himself and Jenjex. He couldn't ask her what to do in front of everyone obviously. He went with his gut instinct.

"Who is *we*?" Wester growled, suspicious.

"Captain Clarissa," replied a woman, also appearing. She was small and pretty if you liked that kind of look. Gothic or Celtic... very Colonial. The screen became split so that both Captains could be seen concurrently. Both, like him, were clearly on their bridges. A long silence began and he considered what to ask them first.

"Keep running scans, they could be trying to hold our attention while someone else moves in," Wester instructed, still unsure if this was some kind of trick.

"So talk then," Wester replied, to the Captains.

"...Recently you attacked our factories on Rymar Delta and damaged them very severely with no loss of life to either you or us," Keane said, as if delivering a report. "Our orders, mine and Clarissa's, were to go to Rymar Delta to execute all personnel there... for their failure to stop you." He went quiet to let the horror of those orders sink in for a moment. "After talking... we decided we have no wish to be part of a Federation led by Ro Tammer..." His words, those of treason, reminded Wester of Tristram... and his death. It could all still be bogus. "I will never kill my own men for a failure like that. Treason, yes, but it was quite clear to all of us that no one on the planet had done anything treasonous."

"I have similar concerns about Ro Tammer but how do I know I can trust you?" Wester asked, his voice low and confident.

"...You don't," Clarissa answered, after a pause. "We have discussed this at length and can think of no way of proving to you that we want to join you. But we do... our crews are loyal only to us... now they know what Ro Tammer is really like."

Wester's mind raced. If they were telling the truth then... he would have three destroyers under him rather than just his own. But how could he find out if they were genuine? This could all be some strategy of Ro's to entice him back for destruction.

"Surround is clear," Jenjex stated, thinking he was hesitating because he was awaiting her report. He eyed her and, just through looking at him, she guessed the real reason why he had fallen silent. She leaned in to whisper in his ear.

"Tell them to attack the Federation and see what their reaction is," she suggested.

"The fact that we've not opened fire on you should surely go in our favour, right?" Clarissa asked, breaking the silence. "We could easily bring you down if we wanted it."

"It *does*," he allowed. "If you are sincere then you must prove your new allegiance to me. My crew have proved themselves to me, so you must do the same."

"Yes, Admiral," Keane nodded. Wester's heart skipped a beat. *Admiral?* He liked the sound of that. "What do you want us to do?"

"I'm going to ask you to ambush a Federation destroyer. Lure it here... then you both destroy it while I act as bait," he replied. Jenjex went pale but said nothing. It was a big risk but Wester could see in Keane's eyes that he was serious.

"Admiral," Clarissa saluted. "We will do this and let you know the details... we will ensure you see everything we do and hear everything we say. Our crews are good."

"I'm sure they are," he replied, smiling tightly. After the talking ended, Wester leaned on the guardrail, deep in thought. Egill and Jenjex joined him.

"You're sure we can trust them? Their story is very plausible," Jenjex wanted to know. Typically lies were often very plausible sounding; the truth could often be completely unbelievable by contrast, and unfortunately there was no absolute rule that could be applied to be sure which was which.

"I suppose now that our actions are well known, it was inevitable that someone would eventually seek us out with the express purpose of joining us," Wester said, although his tone lacked faith. He'd been on his own too long to simply rely on anything. "I'm not sure I trust them yet but if they *are* sincere..." He didn't need to elaborate. A couple of defections could lead to more. All of which would further hamper Ro's war effort. And all of that was to the good.

"Ro would not be able to trust anyone around her then," Jenjex said, smiling at the idea. "She'd be *expecting betrayals* and her behaviour would no doubt become more erratic and thus alienate more potential allies."

"We must make sure before we get any ideas," Egill reminded

them. He was concerned that, as they were both still young, enthusiasm was running away with them.

"It is even possible that a revolution may occur eventually," Wester stated, serious. "If that does happen we won't need to take *any* action ourselves."

"Why don't we deal with this *first?*" Egill suggested, firmly. Wester nodded, he was right. A weapon untested may not be a weapon at all. Keane appeared again.

"We have made contact with a destroyer nearby called *Vantage*, it's close," he said. "Its crew and Captain are known friends of Tammer's administration. Are they a suitable target for you, Admiral?"

"They will do. There's a moon nearby. Activate your cloaking devices and use it to hide behind. I will await *Vantage* here and deactivate our engine systems to indicate we have suffered some sort of damage. We will attempt to talk first but… in the likely event of them attacking… you both come out and kill them," Wester said, seriously. Keane nodded.

"I will tell them that you are attacking us so that when they arrive your damage will be more believable," Keane stated. *Smart,* thought Wester. The message was sent, Wester could see it down to the exact wording. If this was a trick they were playing along with him so far and if it wasn't… Ro Tammer had made a grave blunder. Wester began to imagine ships by the dozen just switching sides and a full-scale civil war destroying his beloved Federation. Inevitably some would use the ensuing chaos to settle old scores, grab power or just cut and run. Yet if this didn't happen Ro would destroy them all by starting an unwinnable war against the Coalition. If she was to fall, he had to see to it that it was as much because of political reasons as it was military, if not more so. Better a civil war than a war with the Coalition but he'd rather there not be a war at all.

Wester would have to sit down with Keane and Clarissa and learn what the morale of the navy was like and if more people were likely to join them. He decided to do what Tristram would have done… invite them to dinner. He remembered Tristram telling him that adaptability was one of the greatest skills *anyone* could possess. No matter what life confronted you with, you had to be prepared to change everything in order to defeat it. He would play diplomat,

Admiral and conspirator all at once. He called Jenjex over and she touched her hat to him.

"Lieutenant, please extend invitations to dinner to Captains Keane and Carissa. *You* might want to attend also," he ordered. She flushed.

"Very good, sir."

***

Alex eased the ship into a tight orbit around the space station. Fragments of debris were still tumbling around and Tabre had told her to take care not to crash into any of it no matter how small as it could compromise the cloaking device.

"Now," he mused, eyeing a device in front of him. He activated it and a series of rapid ticking sounds began.

"What's that?" Alex asked, concerned. She wondered if it was some kind of explosive.

"This one of the most advanced listening devices in existence. It operates by measuring sound vibration alongside lip-reading applications and special mapping. Latest model apparently," he said. He fiddled with the dial and gradually the ticking became less erratic and more like that of a conversation. The ticking them became a tone, replicating almost musical notes. Then… it started to sound like voices. Finally, coherent words could be heard and clearly understood.

"We are close enough," grinned Tabre, impressed. They listened.

"There do seem to be rather a lot of them," Reed was saying.

"Presumably we can ignore anything that doesn't have enough power to be the Observatory," Carlos replied.

"That still leaves three," Satiah said, sounding disappointed.

"It could have been a lot worse," Reed reminded her.

"Agreed, three out of one thousand and eleven is not bad," Satiah said. "I guarantee though, that we get the wrong one first." Reed laughed. Kelvin pointed his appendage at one of the stations.

"They have more advanced defences than the rest," Kelvin put in. "Infiltration will not be as easy."

"No," Satiah agreed, seriously. "Did you get any matches on the material?"

"The stations that are our best bets are shielded... their power signatures are too large to disguise but substance traces found nothing," Carlos explained. He pointed to the nearest one. "This one here, you'll notice its orbit is degrading faster than any other station, yet its direction will take it *away* from the planet rather than towards it. My guess is, it's trying to sneak away."

"Perhaps we have been detected," Satiah growled, annoyed. "We know they couldn't see this ship but it's possibly that the explosion tipped them off to someone being around. Or Ash could have been noticed planetside." She glanced at Reed.

"Still quiet and Deva isn't answering," Reed said. Carlos gave no sign of the worry he was feeling inside. He'd not tried to call her himself as Satiah was wisely trying to discourage any unsexy chatter.

"I'm going to assume that that is the Orion Observatory," Satiah stated, pointing to it. "Keep watching the others though, it may be being used as a decoy."

"In theory," Ruby said, from the doorway, "as this station *is* Coalition, couldn't we just make contact and ask about the weapon? Reed, you must have the authority?"

"I had considered that but disregarded it ultimately on the grounds that they may simply lie," Reed smiled at her. He hadn't sounded patronising in the least but Ruby's shoulders slumped as if insulted.

"Just a suggestion," she muttered, affronted. "Anything from Ash yet...?" It was then that Reed noticed what Ruby was carrying. A silver sphere. He leapt out of his chair with surprising speed and Satiah instinctively drew her pistol, a reaction to the sudden action. Ruby jumped at the move but just stared at him.

"*What?*" she asked, trying to understand why everyone was so twitchy.

"Where did you get *that?*" Reed asked, pointing to the sphere. She looked down at it briefly then shrugged.

"On one of the stations," she replied, waving dismissively.

"I thought I told you not to touch..." Satiah began, also unsure as to the reason for Reed's overreaction.

"Put it down, *quickly*," Reed insisted, unusual anxiety in his tone.

"*Reed*," Satiah growled, realising there was yet more he wasn't telling her.

"Why?" Ruby asked, confused. "I found it, it's mine. It's not dangerous…"

"Do you know what it is?" he demanded, levelly.

"It's *just* a silvery bauble thing," she argued, getting angry.

"As I thought," he interrupted, also heated. Evidently she had no idea what she had found. "Put it down please."

"Not until you tell me why," Ruby objected.

"*Do it Ruby*, please," Satiah ordered, pistol in hand. Ruby saw the gun, sighed and placed it on the chair.

"Has it done anything *weird* at all since you found it? *Anything at all?*" Reed asked, staring at it rather than Ruby.

"No," she replied, shaking her head. She pushed her hair behind her ear, a little nervous.

"What is it?" Satiah asked. Ruby went to answer when she saw that Satiah was now pointing her gun at Reed. Reed turned, eyeing her. She stared coldly back.

"…It's a device of immortal manufacture," he told her. Slowly she lowered the gun. "A very specific immortal."

"Dreda?" guessed Ruby.

"Try again," Reed growled, looking very uneasy.

"*Ash?*"

Satiah leaned in close to whisper in Reed's ear.

"That's the one," he replied, seriously. "I'm surprised you *know*."

"I've read a lot." Satiah stared down at the sphere, caution in her vibe. Then she relaxed.

"Reed, I don't *think* it is dangerous but if you want we can lock it up?"

"That might be best," he agreed, clearly unsure what to do with it himself.

"*Ruby*... give it to Kelvin..." Satiah began.

"*No*, don't let it near *any other machines*, it may be able to affect them," Reed advised, his tone tense.

"It's close enough to affect the controls of this ship already and it's done nothing at all," Satiah argued, starting to get irritated by this paranoia.

"...It may not need to yet," he said, quietly. He made eye contact with Satiah. *"Don't let Ash near it either."*

"Fine, *Ruby pick it up and come with me*," Satiah sighed. The women left the room and Carlos stared at Reed.

Tabre leaned back in his chair and Alex stared at him, quite pale with excitement.

"So... Reed's looking for a weapon," Tabre mused, thoughtfully. "And he thinks it's on one of the stations here."

"*This is crazy*," Alex whispered, unsure what else to say.

"Get me Ro, I need to discuss this with her, she may have need of a weapon like that," Tabre stated.

"Like what? We don't even know..." Alex began.

"Just do it," he hissed, impatient. So... this was what Reed had been doing that whole time. Searching for a weapon. He must have been trying to work out where to search next, possibly finding more clues on Ionar 12. Any reasonable strategist could conclude that when he had the weapon he'd give it to the Coalition and they could use it on the Federation. Tabre knew that would be what Ro Tammer would think and he knew what she would want him to do. Get the weapon first. And what was all that other stuff about?

The strange sphere the other unnamed female had found. Why had it scared Reed so much? Was it part of the weapon? Something else even more powerful? Tabre was smart enough to stay focussed on the job in hand and not be lured off into the fields of wild speculation.

"She's busy," Alex said, awkwardly.

"Mention my name," he instructed, without thinking. She did. In moments they'd got an answer.

"What is it, Tabre?" barked Ro's familiar voice. Instantly he picked up on the strain in her tone. She was feeling the pressure. Wester was obviously proving more than a little difficult for her to get rid of. That made no difference to him, though. He explained what they had heard and his opinions as to what it meant. She fired a series of questions at him about the nature of the weapon, none of which could he answer.

"...Very well, you orders are now changed. Get that weapon or at least the designs of it and bring it back here. If you can't get the weapon or the designs, *destroy it*," she responded, and cut off abruptly. Alex winced at the blunt and rude instructions.

"Yes, predictable as ever," Tabre muttered to himself. It was pretty typical of Ro to destroy what she couldn't use. And without knowing the details of the weapon itself, he was surprised she was so willing to use it.

"Those are her orders... *but what are we going to do?*" Alex asked, seriously. He smiled.

"*That*, my dear, is the correct way of thinking," he said, praising her new attitude.

***

"I don't understand!" protested Ruby, feebly. She didn't want to get into a fight with Satiah, such a prospect would get her killed faster than opening the airlock without putting on a spacesuit. "What did *I* do?"

"Reed has his reasons," Satiah said, making the effort to at least try and be polite. It wasn't Ruby that bothered her... it was Ash.

"It's *harmless*, surely if it *were* dangerous something would have happened by now," she replied.

"Would you apply that logic to *accommodation on the slopes of a volcano?*" Satiah asked.

"*Well...*" she paused.

"I will talk to Reed," Satiah said, deciding to take pity on her. She felt that, even though she didn't remember all of it, Ruby had been subjected to enough insanity for one day.

They locked the sphere in a box which Satiah then slid under her bed. Ruby told her what had drawn her attention and where she had found it. None of that gave Satiah any clue as to exactly why Reed had blown a power cell when he'd seen it. So it was immortal technology that allegedly belonged to someone who had not been seen for well over four hundred years. So what? Satiah wished she could dismiss that as the seemingly irrelevant conjecture that it could be framed as. But she had been a Phantom for too long to be able to disregard anything. She glanced at Ruby again.

"You wouldn't be stupid enough to try to half inch your sphere back, would you?" Satiah asked, curtly. "If this disappears, *at any point*, I will naturally assume that *you* have taken it." Ruby's shoulders slumped and Satiah knew she had correctly judged Ruby. She had been considering doing exactly that.

"How can you steal something that's yours?" Ruby demanded, putting her hands on her hips.

"The methodology is similar no matter who owns what," Satiah replied, smoothly. She edged closer to Ruby and Ruby went a bit paler.

"Don't do it," Satiah ordered, in her ear.

"...Fine," Ruby mumbled, reluctantly.

"That sphere may have the power to affect machinery around it... imagine if it had the power to affect your mind too," Satiah said, using fear to discourage her further. Not fear of Satiah herself, simply the fear of the device itself. The two women left the room and Satiah encrypted the lock on the door. She returned to the control room and got Reed's attention. They both went over to a corner.

"Something similar happened before, *many years ago now*," Reed began, without even waiting for the questions. "A man called John Constantine was trying to *replace* politicians and high-ranking military personnel with *life-like androids*. I was talking with one of these duplicates when I was tipped off by their *response time* to questions I was asking. It was taking longer to react than a human would or it would react too quickly, *it was never quite right*. But *also*... the important bit was when its eyes flashed *red*."

"Reed... I'm not sure what point you're *trying* to make. *I* want to discuss what the hell is going on with that sphere Ruby found... what are *you* talking about?" Satiah asked, crossing her arms. She studied the little man as it appeared he'd not even heard her.

"At the time I didn't know, well, couldn't be sure that it *was* an android, and the red flash could have been a sign of *someone else entirely*." He paused, and made strong eye contact with her. Satiah wasn't sure why but that look he was giving her made the hair on the back of her neck rise. She went to ask him for further information, stopped herself and then thought of something else.

"Can the sphere affect a human mind?" she asked, clearly. He seemed to snap out of the intense stare and his face became more normal again.

"I don't know, *possibly*," he answered, as she had expected. "It's not worth taking that chance."

"I've spoken with Ruby about it and I'm fairly sure she won't try to steal it back. *Ash, however*, is another matter, as I'm sure she will tell him. Speaking of him, have you heard anything more from the planet?"

"No… he's been very quiet," Reed murmured, apparently thinking deeply on the new subject. "And, without the pod, we have no way of escaping this ship."

"Then we must proceed onward," Satiah said, deciding to move forward. "Kelvin and I will infiltrate the first station now. You and Carlos will have to look after Ruby."

"…*Yes, I agree*. It will be dangerous enough for you without having to supervise her too," Reed concurred. "It's a great pity that Division Sixteen cannot help us."

"*This has nothing to do with them*," Satiah said, remembering their fortunate intervention back on Ionar 12. She nodded to Kelvin and he began to follow her out. Reed smiled after her in mild amusement.

***

They were too deep to contact Reed now. Ash continued on down the labyrinth of tunnels undaunted with Deva becoming increasingly agitated. She'd lost her bearings a long time ago and was deeply concerned that they may never get out again. The system of caves, warrens and caverns was titanic in size and they seemed to be nowhere near the end of it. Deva knew it was most probably her own imagination but she was starting to suspect that someone was following them. The occasional scuffing noise that didn't seem to be her or Ash. Also... she was starting to get hungry. She had some rations with her of course, but she'd not got much water. At last she realised she had to take action.

She gripped Ash's arm and halted, making him turn toward her as he tried to go on.

"Right, that's far enough for today," she growled, seriously. "If we are to get back to the ship before nightfall..."

"We're almost there," Ash interrupted, calmly.

"Almost *where*?" she nearly screamed. "Look, the situation is simple. We need to get out of these caves so that I can call in to Reed and let him know what we have found. A big fat nothing!"

"Just a minute or two more," Ash pleaded, in a deceptively reasonable tone.

"No!" Deva stated, through her teeth. "Unless you give me a reason, *a good reason*, *why* we should continue... I'm pulling the battery out!"

Ash sighed and, for the first time, something in him seemed to give.

"In the core of this plant there is a geothermal power generator. It's been there since the start of this universe. We need to make sure it's not been discovered," he argued, levelly. She shouldered her gun and crossed her arms.

"I'm listening," she said, although her posture inferred the opposite. She didn't trust him enough to believe any explanation. Yet, as it remained a possibility that he *could* tell the truth...

"The power it could generate would be enough to fuel *any* weapon," Ash went on. Deva made a show of trying to examine her nails.

"If you want to go back then go back," he sighed, losing patience. He turned to go.

"Reed wouldn't like to think that an immortal abandoned a child..." Deva smiled, manipulatively. Ash halted.

"Either you tell me everything or we *are* going back, even if I have to drag you every step of the way," Deva announced, out of patience herself.

"It's technology humans cannot be allowed to access," Ash stated, inflexibly. "I'm here to ensure that never happens."

"You're going to destroy it?" she guessed, her surprise too much to conceal.

"If necessary," he replied, firmly.

"And that's it? That's the only reason you are here?" she questioned, disbelievingly.

"The golden armour is still a possibility *but* if they were still in the area, I'm fairly sure we would have encountered them by now," Ash replied.

Deva thought about those noises she'd been telling herself that she had imagined earlier.

"So this generator is what they are protecting?" she confirmed.

"Amongst other things, yes," Ash replied, turning to move on. Deva began to follow when she felt something touch the underside of her chin. Something cold and sharp.

"No further," said a voice. It was metallic and scratchy in sound. Like an android with a malfunctioning voice system. Ash spun around. Deva glanced to her right and saw the golden-suited warrior. It was holding a blade to her.

"Let her go," Ash ordered, pointing at them. Deva planted a side kick and threw herself against the wall. The robot didn't budge an inch but she used the thrust gained to escape the blade. Rolling with the impact, Deva came up on her feet between Ash and the robot.

She aimed and fired a stun blast at it. Next thing she knew, she was falling backwards onto the ground. The bolt had bounced straight back at her. As she lost consciousness, Ash leapt over her, a sword in his hand. Ash had known for some time that *someone* was shadowing them but he had not expected them to move in so quickly. The robot came at him, wielding a blade with each arm. He parried the blows perfectly and planted a boot in its chest. It flew backwards, rolling over and returning to its feet in a slick move. Ash situated himself between the unconscious Deva and the robot considering his next move.

***

Satiah and Kelvin reached the outer hull of the next space station. It was very dark as now the planet was between them and the sun... and the station had no lights visible at all. It reminded Satiah of working miles underwater... complete blackness... everything floating around. Cold death only inches from her skin in every direction. She glanced around for the best place to try to gain access.

"Right," Kelvin prompted. She crawled carefully along to her right and found the edge of the hatch. She clamped the neutraliser down on the door. It was a simple device used to prevent any interior security systems from noticing that an airlock was being used. All well and good in principle but it still made no allowance for anyone stood on the other side. Kelvin opened the hatch, illuminating them both with bright light.

Wincing as her eyes grew accustomed to the light again, Satiah dragged herself inside. Kelvin followed, sealing the airlock behind them. Air flooded in, as did heat. She removed her helmet, her long red hair tumbling out haphazardly. Her gun slid out of its holster and into her hand, with the well-practised motion. She clipped the helmet to her belt.

"Any life?" she asked, to Kelvin.

"Immediate vicinity is clear but I am detecting 1,224 humans here," he replied. She nodded. A fully manned station would often have a crew of that size. She pulled out a small metal strip from her custom-made cummerbund and looked for the nearest security camera. She spotted it at the end of the corridor.

Calmly she approached it and placed the strip of metal onto its side. It would now freeze every camera view on the ship until she either removed the strip or the system was rebooted.

"Let me know if anyone gets close," she said, patting him as she headed away. He crept along behind her. The low hum, an almost constant presence in any habitation, was the only sound. The place was well lit, clean and had fresh air. You noticed things like that more readily after you'd been visiting the kinds of places she had recently. Satiah knew to avoid the control area of a fully operational station. Going there would only invite discovery. The best find that she could hope for would be an unguarded small computer room where she could tap into the system and extract the information she needed.

What was this place? Was there a weapon? What kind of weapon? Where was it? The list was long enough.

It was difficult to determine exactly what surrounded them. Storage seemed most likely. Vast warehouse-like rooms were at the ends of the long corridors. They entered one and began to head down one of the aisles. Satiah pulled out a crate and opened it. Inside the multiple layers of protective packaging that was pretty commonplace, lay a container of liquid oxygen. This made Satiah immediately think of propulsion system fuel. Liquid oxygen, when mixed with ethanol, would react strongly. This reaction, when directed adeptly, would produce immense thrust. Strong enough to escape gravity in any case. Yet this was more of a *conventional* sort of weaponry... not the kind she felt she was looking for. In a sense that didn't matter though. It could be weaponry therefore it increased the likelihood that they were getting close.

Of course she was making two assumptions about this type of fuel. First, that it was for the weapon itself and not the transport for the weapon. And second, that it was indeed being used as fuel. It may even be an ingredient for the weapon. They replaced the crate and opened another to discover identical contents. Then, at the end of the last aisle, they found a computer. While Kelvin kept watch, Satiah focussed on it. It was a log of all the crates, displaying serial numbers, locations and innards. Liquid oxygen seemed a minor thing compared to some of the things on that list. Ammonium nitrate, another oxidising agent, typically used to increase explosive power. Chloride, uranium-700, hydrogen... It was a long list. And then... right at the end... KZ15.

It was labelled differently to all the others. A red outline, presumably to indicate an additional unknown danger. The traditional chemical warning symbols were everywhere. The other, more dangerous items, were outlined in orange. The least dangerous were yellow. Satiah selected the KZ15 and found its location. She got Kelvin's attention with a wave of her hand.

"I think we've struck gold," she stated, pointing.

"It may not be safe to approach," he cautioned.

"According to this is stored in an add-on structure... separated from this station by lead shielding, the vacuum of space and three layers of Grilith."

Grilith was an expensive absorbent material. Normally used to absorb radiation, in order to make environments safe, the substance itself would absorb anything it its immediate environment. Eventually it would absorb itself, leaving not a microscopic trace of its existence. Lower temperatures would *suspend the biodegrading* but *not* the absorption... which was why the Grilith was exposed to space.

"Given the nature of KZ15, external storage is a sensible precaution," Kelvin concluded.

"They have *fifty-six tonnes of it*," Satiah stated, a little incredulous. "That mine must have been more efficient than it looked."

"Or it was in operation longer than we theorised," Kelvin added. "The Sisterhood may not have been completely honest with us."

"I'm not going back to argue the point," she smirked.

Satiah then went on to access the main station database but was halted instantly when a password was required by the computer. Kelvin moved in to take over. He inserted a connecting device and entered the system himself. He then suggested that he download everything to the ship for Reed to check through while they continued. She agreed, it would save time. In the meantime she vigilantly, but without really needing to, kept watch. The station was immense, so it was reasonable that they had got so far without encountering anyone. Nevertheless habit and experience made her attentive.

"Someone is rebooting the camera system," Kelvin warned. Satiah nodded, having expected such an action to occur sooner or later. She had another few strips but they would remain hidden for an hour before they reapplied it to avoid tipping anyone off to their sabotage.

They found a gap between four crates and waited, completely out of view of any cameras.

"You know what bothers me the most about all this?" Satiah asked, keeping her voice low.

"No."

With a sigh, she slid to the floor to sit while he stood on guard. She tried to get comfortable.

"Why they haven't used the weapon yet," she murmured, her mind restless. "Makes me wonder what they're waiting for."

"Assuming it exists," he answered.

"It's looking increasingly as if it does," Satiah stated, seriously.

"There may be a technical difficulty that is not easily overcome," he said, providing a possible reason.

"Or a political one," she whispered, sourly.

***

Reed and Carlos were avidly reading through the data that Kelvin was sending them.

"Looks like we have found it," Carlos stated, pleased.

"Well, we have found the KZ15, that's for sure," Reed mused. Of course, the weapon itself was still missing.

"Who is *Lara Clement?*" Carlos asked, enquiringly.

"Lara Clement?" Reed echoed, confused. Carlos nodded. Reed turned to Ruby. "Who's Lara Clement?"

"*I don't know,*" Ruby answered, also puzzled. Reed faced Carlos again.

"What *are* you talking about?" Reed asked, his eyebrows raised. Carlos tapped the screen.

"It's the name of *someone on the station*. It's in a message sent eight days ago, look," he stated.

Ruby, trying to make herself useful, tried to learn who the message had been sent to by tracking the signal. Reed read it out loud.

"Your consultant, Lara Clement, has made some unusual recommendations that call into question her loyalty to us," Reed read. "After visiting the specimens she insisted that the results of the project were unsatisfactory and due to this failure and other mysterious financial concerns she intends to close down the project. I await your reply. Director Sam."

"*Specimens?*" Carlos asked, frowning.

"Unsatisfactory results," repeated Reed, intensely interested. He thought back to the mission report from Operation Burning Bridge.

There were references to experiments in that but no details. Just like here… ironically.

(UE) OPERATION BURNING BRIDGE (UE) REPORT: Dated at end. Target located. ITP6. Spatial coordinates: 9980-7948. Designation (TS): Top Secret. Status: ACTIVE. Official staff allocation: 1850. Dasss reports: Reconnaissance correct. Scientific facility with several branches of identified ongoing research. Jaylite Industries is currently contracted with waste disposal duties. Background check required. Experimentation currently at critical stage. Testing is achieving mixed results. Balan's next visit in two days. Evacuate immediately.

Threat identified as external possible. VIP removed from positions, data transferred and copied. Backup system to be transferred to Station Denepler. ITP6 relocated to: 0000-0002. All testing now suspended pending result of conference. KZ15 is presenting difficulties. I can't get close enough to get a sample but I have confirmed that only robots can handle the substance. Awaiting your confirmation. I only have 2 hour window before I must pull out. Further instructions are needed. Report ends.

"There's a reply here, just *two hours* later," Carlos replied, opening the file.

Again Reed provided the vocal honours regarding the analysis.

"Director Sam, I have sent you no consultants. This woman is obviously an imposter. Apprehend and find out who she is working for. Once you have learned all you can… marginalise her," Reed said. Now they all frowned. What was going on? Was someone else *also* investigating this? And if they were, had they been caught and killed? Ruby's results came in and she let out a gasp of shock. That *had* to be wrong. Reed heard and glanced around to see what she was up to and froze in his seat. Carlos, upon noticing their reactions also stared at the result in a combination of disbelief and amazement.

"I must have made a mistake," Ruby stated, at last rediscovering her voice.

"No," Reed said, quietly. "You did everything correctly... it seems that this message came from *Earth* less than eight days ago."

"That would only have been a couple of days after *we left*," Carlos pointed out. Reed leaned back in his chair, thinking through all the potentials.

"So, what does this mean exactly?" Ruby asked, a little unnerved.

"Too early to say for sure but I'll bet it's important," Reed answered. "Any news from Deva?"

"No," Carlos answered. "Shall I go down after them?"

"*How?*" Reed asked, interested. "They took our *only* pod." Carlos motioned to the vast array of stations out there.

"I'll have to borrow my own," he stated, seriously. Reed nodded.

"Very well," he said. "I'm seriously considering involving the Coalition navy in this."

As Carlos headed out, Ruby stood.

"Can I come too?" she asked, tentatively. "I don't think I'm of any real use here." Carlos eyed Reed, seeking permission. Reed considered.

"Yes," Reed said, simply. He had a few calls to make and he'd prefer that no one overheard any of them. Carlos and Ruby departed, leaving him alone. He grabbed his communicator.

"Captain Berry," answered the Division Sixteen man.

"Captain, this is Reed, I need a favour," he answered.

***

Sam stared as the figure of the woman in the bed convulsed. He was watching keenly, his eyes gleaming with a kind of lust. Her eyes were wide, her breathing erratic and shallow. She didn't scream even though it looked like she was trying to. Her voice box had failed her nearly six hours previously. It had been nearly seventy hours since her exposure to KZ15 and she'd been awake ever since. She had been exposed for fifty seconds. Over the months it had become apparent that the longer the subjects were exposed to KZ15 the quicker they died. Mathematically it was simple enough, according to his theory. Every seven seconds of exposure, took about twelve hours off the lifespan. The life span was typically eight days after seven seconds' exposure.

He was a tall, gaunt man. He had a pale face, wiry build and thick curly grey hair. His dark-eyed smile often unsettled those who saw it. What added to the effect was that he had no ears. Just two holes in the sides of his head, revealing only darkness beyond and giving the impression that his head was hollow and empty. He could hear nothing, hadn't heard anything for decades. Maybe that was why his eyesight was so accurate. As she tried to scream, he found it oddly arousing as, even if she could still have made a noise, he wouldn't have been able to hear it. He began typing information into a computer next to him. While he was director of this project he thought of himself only as professor. His long yellowy nails clipped against the keys noisily but that didn't matter to him.

She didn't have long left... only seconds. He leaned in as close as he could to the screen to capture the look in her eyes as life left her. He found it fascinating how oddly similar so many people were looking at that moment. After several more moments he resumed his writing. He was certain now that one hundred and fifty-four seconds of exposure to KZ15 would result in instant death in ninety-nine percent of individuals. So approximately two and a half minutes... They would also have to be within two hundred metres of it for it and be unprotected too, for it to work at all. Yet as few knew of its existence... Sam was sure that that could be made to work.

A light flashed, getting his attention. It was the computer officially confirming the female's death. He watched as two medical technicians moved in to remove the body. He pressed a button and spoke. His voice was high-pitched and squawk-like... and his words were barely understandable.

"Leave it," he snarled. Although it sounded to anyone else more like *lyeeev it*. He wanted it for his personal collection. The two men were clearly uncomfortable and obeyed by withdrawing from the camera's range. He concluded his report and began to encrypt it. The process took several minutes and while he waited he returned to work on his glass sculpture. The example of glassblowing resembled a butterfly of some sort. Only one of the wings was in the process of shattering.

He leaned in close and concentrated on controlling his breathing. To truly create something, in his mind, one had to be as still as possible. Otherwise you were not creating; you were simply altering what someone else had created. The idea was to slow his heartbeat down, to prevent the minutest of movements of his body as he applied the next pattern. A subtle looping sweep that ran back and forth in complex waves was what it looked like. Only *his* eyes and those of microscopic detail designed for the task could see with enough detail to do it successfully. And gradually he continued the job. It had taken him nearly six years of work and he'd almost finished the last wing. Three hours a day... He called it *Neo-chrysalis*. The meaning behind it was simple. A new birth in the form of death.

Butterflies came out of chrysalis as they were reborn from their previous caterpillar state. Much art had gone into displaying this form of rebirth yet no one had ever covered the next stage. The butterfly should have its own chrysalis. As death took it, it would return in the cycle back into the cocoon. Only it would never re-emerge as either a butterfly or a caterpillar. It would be in a forever dormant state. Change was the only universal constant. Therefore even death had to change and as he was showing here... in Neo-chrysalis... it was doing just that.

***

Deva opened her eyes and looked around. She was lying on her back, in darkness. Silence. She felt around for her rifle, found it and activated the light. She was still in the tunnel only now she was alone. Ash and the thing that had attacked them were nowhere in sight. She rose cautiously to her feet, testing her legs to ensure she could walk. She listened hard. Only the natural sounds one would expect of being in an underground tunnel. She didn't know what had happened to Ash and she did not know the way back. She debated her options. Stay, go back, or go forward? If she stayed, she wasn't sure how long it would be before someone found her. Carlos would certainly look, she knew, but... this was a very large system.

She felt sure that if she tried to go back she would become even more lost. Wait, she chastised herself, *lost was lost*; it was a state that did not have conditional values. Lastly, she could continue on in the direction they had been going before they had been attacked. She deduced that, if Ash was still alive, he would have gone that way. Taking a deep shaky breath she pressed on quietly. Now she was alone the tunnels were much creepier but she was trained to have confidence and be able to keep her imagination under control. She realised that she had been stunned by her own blast, rather than the thing stunning her. That meant it was likely that she would be dead had she attempted to kill it. In essence that rendered her rifle almost useless. She wondered how much longer her torch would last…

***

Tabre entered the space station discreetly and then found a maintenance hatch. It led into the maintenance foundation. A maze of cable tunnels and pipe routes that paralleled or twisted under or over the corridors. Once inside, he activated his light.

"Alex, can you hear me?" he growled.

"Yes Tabre," she replied, in his earpiece.

"I'm going to deploy the mole here," he said, pulling a contraption from his bag. The robotic device resembled a rat and its tiny metal legs thrashed as it tried to run. It would run along the tunnels, using ultrasound to map out the whole interior of the station. He released it and it darted away into the darkness.

"Could take maybe half an hour," Alex said.

"It's a big station, probably at least that long," he responded.

"Any sign of Satiah?" asked Alex, anxious. He smiled. Satiah didn't leave signs; she, like him, only left what she wanted to.

"No," he confined himself to saying.

"I spotted a man floating about nearby but heading away," Alex went on. "Took no action like you said."

"Could be Reed or Carlos," Tabre theorised. "Any idea what they were doing?"

"Well, I don't think they are moving to back Satiah up if she's still on board *that* station," Alex replied, considering.

"Let me know if anything out there changes," he instructed.

***

It had been an hour exactly since they had hidden and Kelvin nudged the sleeping Satiah awake. She'd made use of the opportunity to catnap and save energy. She blinked away the sleep from her eyes and nodded grimly. They had not been disturbed by anyone, as Satiah had thought would be the case.

"You handle the neutraliser," she whispered, handing the strip to him. "I'm going to see if Reed has anything important to say." She activated. "Reed?"

"Yes, thanks for all that information Satiah, good work. Carlos has gone down to see what's happening with Ash and Ruby's gone with him. Does the name Director Sam mean anything to you?" he asked, quickly.

"No," she answered, instantly.

"Thought not," he replied, sighing. "Was wondering if you might have heard the name before. What about Lara Clement?"

"Wish I could help," she replied, in a tone that really made it clear she didn't. He chuckled.

"What's it like in there?" he questioned.

"It's active, *no doubts there*. Once Kelvin has taken down the cameras we will be moving on. As you can tell the stuff is here…" She was referring to KZ15 but was wary enough not to mention the name if she could avoid it.

"Indeed, along with many dangerous bedfellows," Reed agreed. "Very impressed with what you have uncovered so far by the way. Be careful in there."

"Will do," she replied, cutting off.

"Cameras disabled," Kelvin stated. They returned to the long corridor outside and crept along again. Kelvin stopped. "Audio sensors scope seven, sound detected," he warned. Satiah nodded, wishing her ears were as good.

"What is it?" she murmured.

"Repetitive mechanical noises… a manufacturing line perhaps," he stated. She thought about it. Manufacturing? They moved on, and soon she too began to hear the crisp clicking and punching sounds made by heavy machinery. A door opened ahead of them and they were on a walkway high above a large hall. Cautiously they peered over the edge. It looked to be an assembly line of a sort. Kelvin would have warned her if any of the harmful substances represented an immediate threat to them.

"Any idea what they are building?" she asked, quietly.

"No," he answered, shortly.

"Keep an eye out," she advised, taking her grapple gun in hand. She fired at the ceiling before diving off of the walkway. She lowered herself onto the top of one of the larger machines efficiently and leaned forwards to stare more closely. Kelvin maintained his scans. Satiah frowned as she stared down at the rhombus-shaped black boxes that the machine spat out regularly. What were they? Containers? She decided to get one and take it back to the walkway. It was just a question of determining the best place to swipe it from the machines. She slipped down onto the floor silently in a crouch before advancing towards the line.

Crunch, pulse, pulse, crunch, blam, hiss. Again and again. She snatched one with all her strength and nearly fell over backwards as she yanked it free. It was far lighter than she had expected. Once again she used her grapple gun to drag her back up to where Kelvin was waiting on the walkway. She handed the strange product to him as she scissor kicked her way over the railing adeptly. Kelvin scanned it thoroughly before removing the lid and exposing the emptiness inside.

"It's a specialised container," he told her. "Judging by the gaps, it's purpose built. Judging by the material… at least some of the contents are likely to be explosives." She nodded, at last this place was starting to make sense.

"A bomb then," she concluded.

"It seems likely," he concurred. "According to my readings, the KZ15 is placed around the exterior while the explosive would be installed in the centre."

"Sounds about right," Satiah nodded. "I'm going to be a pain and put this back where I found it." She chucked it off of the walkway. It landed with a crash onto the assembly line and soon fell into the workings and jammed the whole line.

"Whoops," she smirked, as they left. A siren went off but it was not a general alarm, simply the computer highlighting the malfunction.

"I have two life signs approaching," Kelvin said.

"That will be the maintainers, *quicker than I thought*," she replied, thinking about it. "Let's watch them for now… I had hoped for one but we will just have to take both of them."

***

"This place is indeed vast," Tabre said, as he reviewed the results. "It's got everything from a factory to a hospital."

"...Is that helpful to you?" Alex asked, awkward.

"Information is power, even vague stuff like this can still be used," he replied, adjusting his pistol. "Direct me to the main power generator. I will create a fault there and while everyone is distracted I shall attempt to learn where the weapon is."

"Okay... first right," she began, reading the map herself. Tabre began to make his way along the dusty cable run. Where was Satiah? Did she have the weapon already? He suspected she knew where to look if nothing else. She had picked this station for a reason certainly.

***

"Yes Reed," came Crystal's ever-dependable reply.

"Crystal," Reed replied, seriously. He was not comfortable with this but he felt it had to be done even with Ash around. "Deep inside your memory is a locked-off area. The password is twenty-two. Open it."

"It is open," she responded. "Data loaded... is there anything else?"

"Yes... I need a breakdown of Lara Clement please," he requested.

"Lara Clement was an operative and former travelling companion of Dreda's predecessor. She died thousands of years ago in a space station explosion," Crystal told him. He sat up straight.

"*Where?*" he asked, in a growl. As he asked his eyes rose to regard the hundreds of space stations in front of him.

"There are no further details on her death. She had a brother called Drake Clement, perhaps he would know."

"But he will be long dead too," Reed said, thoughtfully.

"Correct, Reed," she said.

"All right... we've found a silver sphere... is it dangerous?" Reed asked, wariness in his voice. Part of him was wondering if the sphere itself was somehow listening in to the conversation.

"Only when employed as a weapon," she responded. "I designed them myself on behalf of Dreda's predecessor. They have hundreds of independent functions and are designed to be self-aware but are restricted on functions while unsupervised."

"Could a human work as a supervisor?" Reed asked.

"Yes," she replied. He sighed, annoyed.

"If you remove the human contact, will it return to something resembling dormancy?" he asked.

"After a twelve-hour period of inactivity, yes," she answered.

"All right," he said, a little relieved. "You may lock that up again; include this call's record as well."

"It is done. Anything else?"

"I need you to track a transmission for me," he requested, seriously. "I'm sending you the details now. It's old so it may not be easy to pin down if possible at all. See what you can do."

"I'd be happy to."

***

Wester watched as the Colonial destroyer *Vantage* appeared with his escorting frigate *Adjudicator*. They had been quick off of the mark to respond to the fake call for assistance. Response time was less than thirty seconds. In case of a last-minute betrayal from their new *friends*, Jenjex was manning the gun coordination controls herself. Wester waited for the inevitable ultimatum to be beamed at him. Bizarrely he found that what would have terrified him just days before now to be rather tedious. All power systems were at lowest ebb and they were drifting… as if they were damaged. For one destroyer to be able to destroy two was not inconceivable. If it had apparently done so without being damaged, that was a step *too far* into the realms of fantasy. Therefore, getting to battle stations would take them longer even though they were all ready.

"Acting Captain Wester…" began an authoritative voice. Wester tuned out the next few lines of balderdash and kept his eyes fixed on the moon nearby. The one his *friends* were hiding behind. No one appeared and radio silence was maintained.

"It's *Admiral* Wester," Wester corrected, curtly. He'd cut right into the middle of a spiel about treason, dereliction and shame to deliver his counter offer. "The government you serve is unlawful… it is *you* that will surrender to me." The low confidence and bluntness of his reply clearly caught the other Captain completely off-guard. It was evidenced by the eight-second-long silence.

"If you do not surrender we will open fire, do you want to murder the remainder of your crew?" asked the man.

"They are close enough," Jenjex said, seeing that the ships had crossed the line. Wester gave the nod. Power levels rose, gunners swung out into open view, fighters launched. And, from the dark side of the moon, his two destroyers accelerated. They made straight for the hostile, one flanking to the back to cut off his retreat. The frigate had been making for the fighters to intercept them and hold them off from the destroyer. It halted though upon seeing the true strength of its enemy. An explosion of noise of the communications unit occurred as his two Captains reported their battle readiness and began bellowing out instructions to their fighters and gunners. As the frigate changed direction to counter the new threats it made the mistake of exposing its side to Wester.

"Fire!" Wester ordered. The ship began rocking slightly as all its guns converged on the frigate. Its shields held for a few moments and then collapsed. Next they were slicing through the hull which was cut away swiftly. The fighter strike did the rest and the frigate became two halves of a ship after a catastrophic explosion that tore it in two. Meanwhile a steady barrage had begun between the other three destroyers. It was two on one… now three on one. The Captain was clearly a fool as there was no possible way he could overcome all three of them. Not now he had lost the frigate's support. Not now he was surrounded.

He remained where he was and made no further attempt to talk to the enemy Captain. He regretted the loss of a crew who, given the choice, would most likely have never started this fight. It proved that his new friends, Keane and Clarissa, were sincere in their desire to bring about Ro Tammer's downfall. He still wouldn't trust them completely, of course, but they were proving their ability in a fight and had given him no reason to disapprove of them. Keane was a clever man, having come up with half the plan himself. Clarissa clearly had her fighters well trained. They never broke formation once, not even when charged head-on by enemy fighters. A few collisions occurred but no deaths thankfully. Injuries were sustained but nothing the doctors couldn't handle.

Three hours later, the four of them were sat at dinner. Keane was tall and well mannered... a little standoffish but that was to be expected. Clarissa was the opposite. Blunt, full of questions and seemed bewildered when Wester explained to her the origins of the food she was eating. Jenjex remained silent, watching the other two like a hawk. She did not yet trust them and Wester more than respected her opinion.

"These are bred carefully," Keane stated, talking about steak. "The population purity and stock is a matter of great delicacy, so I hear. Much like the meat itself."

Keane was obviously used to social occasions where much meaningless twaddle had to be endured before the real talking began, making him a Captain of some standing and reasonable length of service. Wester had been taught a little about this type of talking by Tristram but not enough to match Keane. The idea was to exchange opinions, exchange ideas and above all else, learn the arts of civilised culture. An area in which Wester was painfully fresh. There was much he could learn from this man. And Keane seemed more than obliging to facilitate this. Wester knew that Jenjex would appreciate him more if he could learn to relax and talk normally without freezing every few minutes. Clarissa, on the other hand, kept trying to steer the conversation to the politics that they all secretly wanted to talk about. Ro Tammer's latest actions. Their future plans... and all that.

Keane though, continued to dwell on meaningless trivialities until the food was eaten. Then, as if a switch had been thrown, he switched gears and drove straight at the subject that concerned them all.

"With every victory we have, the higher on Ro's list we get," Keane stated, his tone almost hard. "Others may join us along the way but I think all three of us are aware of the double-edged sword that can be. I wanted to know what we will do next."

"So you can talk now that you have *finished your steak*?" demanded

Clarissa, a little irately.

"*Etiquette*," he excused, as if it didn't matter. To him maybe it didn't. Frankly Wester had been pleased that Keane had waited until now before addressing the subject. It had given him more time to think of a plan and it had provided the opportunity for him to study his *new friends*.

"The revolution has already started. Us being here is the evidence of it," Wester said. He, unlike them, had not taken wine. He hoped it would not set a precedence as he liked wine. He would like to be able to feel at ease with his men but… that day was not here.

"Ro Tammer remains in power for now," Wester continued, "but each day her influence is increasingly limited. The more people she alienates, the more she uses and discards… in a way her fall is inevitable."

"She will not go quietly," growled Clarissa, not swayed by his words. "She's been kicked into the turf before only to re-emerge stronger than before."

"I agree," Wester nodded. "We are trying to track her down… find out where she is. Then we can strike directly at her. If we fail, however, it is unlikely that such an opportunity would come around again."

"My *concern*…" Jenjex stated, a little harshly, "…is the loyalty of your *crews*. We understand and believe that *you* are genuine but… how do you know there are not agents among your men?"

"And *you* are…?" Clarissa began, a little offended at being spoken to like that by a mere Lieutenant.

"*It is a reasonable enquiry*," Keane soothed, taking it in stride as he interjected. Diplomatic as well as charismatic, Keane was impressing Wester more and more. "There is of course no way we can be sure although I have discussed it with them and, despite some initial uncertainty, they have remained loyal so far." A realist too, apparently.

"My men *always* do what I tell them," Clarissa insisted, a little less aggressively. "They *know* why we are doing this and are in full agreement." Clarissa seemed more bolshy and impatient as a person but she was not stupid.

"Good to hear," Wester smiled, politely.

He liked what he heard but not enough to share with them his plans for Ro's assassination. That would remain a secret until the last conceivable second. Egill was listening in, using some fancy gadget, in the next room along. Jenjex was armed, as was Wester himself but the Phantom had insisted that not only could he not physically be there but he had to know what went on. Wester was important to the Coalition and therefore could not be allowed to die. How touching. Wester had wondered about the possibility of the Coalition and the Federation becoming one many times before, as no doubt most did. Yet he felt that *now* it might be the only way to prevent future wars.

"We *need* supplies," Clarissa was saying. "Even revolutionaries need food. And a starved crew is not an efficient one... Or *loyal*." Her point was a shrewd one. In literature little detail is usually given about things such as food, sanitation or clothing but all were very necessary in real life. It wasn't all battles to the death or scheming in the dark... mostly it was about cleaning and staying healthy.

"This is true," Keane agreed, nodding. They were both looking at Wester, expecting him to have the solution. Fortunately he'd been prepared for this as he had had to consider such things himself back when they had originally gone on the run.

"I have a target in mind for that, we can hit it tomorrow. It's a Colonial world but the target itself *is* military. This way we do not injure civilians and continue to reduce Ro's power. I'm hoping to persuade them to simply give us the food.

"We must get in and out as quickly as possible and any sort of battle, however brief, may delay us enough for Ro to make a move. Evidently now there are *three destroyers* instead of one. I'm hoping this will make it easier for those with the stores to see reason. We will need a lot more food than before, obviously, but I'm confident that they will possess it," Wester answered. Clarissa nodded slowly.

"It would be silly to resist in any case," she added, contempt in her tone.

"Naturally," Keane said, appeased easily enough. "A more long-term solution would, I feel be a good thing."

"We have options," Wester said, keeping it quiet. He wasn't sure if they were ready to hear about his dealings with the Coalition yet either. Egill had stated that Phantom Squad were more than prepared to keep him supplied if they got desperate.

***

Carlos had already located the escape pod Deva and Ash had used, which had been easy enough. After landing though it quickly became apparent that it was unoccupied. Ruby stood there nervously, her arms crossed as she looked around.

"Where could they be?" she asked, forlornly. Carlos also took in the surround, going through likely possibilities.

"They must have gone to the ruin," he answered, seriously. "It's the only thing around here." He headed off, at a brisk pace. Ruby had to jog to keep up. It took them a while to cover the distance in any case but when they got there, Carlos halted. He did not like the look of it, especially now that they were close. Ruby, however, seemed impervious or, more likely, *oblivious* to any of the potential dangers.

"Come on," she said, entering. Carlos followed and they quickly found the entrance to the underground area.

"If they went down there, they could be lost," Carlos sighed, thinking about it. Going after them had its own set of problems.

"Ash will find us if we go down," Ruby stated, with certainty. Carlos wondered if there was something that she wasn't telling him. He knew of the telepathic element, as he had overheard Reed and Satiah discussing it, but he had told himself that she would know more by now if she had conversed with Ash.

"How?" he asked, eyeing her in suspicion.

"He's immortal and he can probably find me," Ruby shrugged. Carlos weighed this new variable in his mind. What would Satiah do? He switched on the light on the end of his rifle and tried to pierce the darkness beyond with it. Dust… and silence. His gut was telling him that going down there would not be a good idea. He pulled a tracker from his pocket and fixed it to the wall before locking onto it with his communicator. It was not fool proof but it might help them find their way out again. Ruby was watching him with pleading eyes. Deva might be hurt or in trouble…

"Fine but don't make a sound unless I say," he instructed, heading down.

***

Satiah had waited for the men to complete their repair work before she had sprung on them. Striking with the fury of a coiled viper, she sent her target straight into unconsciousness. A balding man of middle years with a thick beard. Kelvin, however, being stronger, had held the second younger man down and clamped his mouth tightly shut. The man's eyes were wide with panic and confusion. In Kelvin's grip he couldn't move much at all. Satiah dragged the body away and injected him with a sedative that would last about twenty-four hours. She quickly returned and crouched next to the remaining man.

"What is this place?" she asked, her tone low and dangerous. Kelvin loosened his grip a fraction on the man's jaw. His voice trembled as he answered.

"The manufacturing line..." he answered, fearfully. She scowled.

"I meant the station, what is it called?" she clarified.

"Um... ITP6," he answered, scared. So... they had found it after all. How long had it been there? How long had it been in operation? Probably well over six months. And where was the money coming from to keep it going now that Balan and his conspirators were dead?

"Who's in command here?" she asked next, not letting up for a moment.

"Prof...err Director Sam," he answered, staring at the barrel of her pistol. The thin metal rim and the darkness within was symbolic of the delicate balance between life and death. The trigger was fine-tuned to the point at which a feather's touch would be all that was needed to shoot. One look in her eyes told him that she wouldn't even hesitate.

"Where's the weapon?" she growled, forcing him to face her. A flicker of uncertainly crossed his eyes in the face of her hard stare. A twitch of his left eye, minute but still there, gave away the rapidity of the speed of thought.

"*What weapon?*" he asked. She pushed the pistol into his mouth and smiled viciously.

"Don't be stupid," she told him. "Tell me or I blow your face off."

"I swear…" he began, terrified.

"Oh you *swear* do you?" she scoffed. "Why is it that the people who lie also swear the most?" She'd heard such oaths uttered so many times by so many beings that these days they just made her even more impatient.

"Please, *I don't know what you're talking about*, please *don't…*" he began, unsure what to say next. She stunned him and he slid the rest of the way to the floor. Despite what she had said, she had realised that he had told her all he knew. Kelvin dragged his body over to where she had hidden the other one. Satiah thought about where she would keep such a weapon if she had it. Somewhere safe, somewhere hidden, somewhere where it would be unlikely to self-ignite or do whatever it did. She took the precaution of installing a beacon under a floor panel. If they had to leave and the station was moved, it would be much easier to track with their own beacon aboard. Kelvin returned to her.

"Location confirmed," he stated. She nodded.

"They will be out for about a day but we have to assume their absence will be noticed long before then," she replied. "It's time we found out once and for all if this blasted thing exists or not."

***

Ash positioned himself between the golden robot and Deva's unconscious body defensively. He had to get this thing to talk. It had two blades, each one seeming to have slipped out from the wrist of each arm. They were saw-toothed and angry looking, matching their owner's aggressive posture.

"Can you understand me?" Ash asked, his voice strong and palpable. It halted in its tracks, seeming to re-evaluate him. "*Can you understand me?*" he asked again. "What is it like to never sleep? To never be allowed to escape the endless wakefulness to which you have been sentenced?" It remained where it was, giving him no sign of what it was thinking… if it was thinking or even listening.

This creature was a guardian and a relic of a long-lost civilisation. It had probably been driven mad by its years of darkness and silence. As it could never sleep, did that also mean that it couldn't dream or imagine? Did it see him as he saw it? Could it see in the sense of sight? It could undoubtedly sense him but its cognitive intricacies were invisible to him. A garbled sound was articulated from it sounding like many voices talking at once and saying different things. Was that its language, the only way it knew to communicate? No... it had spoken clearly enough when it had ambushed Deva.

"I know what you are and where you came from," Ash went on, after thinking through what to say. "I know what this place is just as I know what you are trying to protect."

The non-responsiveness continued. Ash took the time to quickly assess Deva's condition. Fortunately she was just unconscious; the blast from her own rifle had done that.

"If you destroy the generator, you will destroy the planet," it said, abruptly. Ash lowered his sword.

"If the humans..." he began, warningly.

"They won't," it cut him off. There was a composed finality to its tone as if it had thought of everything. Ash did realise that the possibility was an unlikely one but nonetheless it had to be countered.

"How can you be sure?" Ash asked, seeking an alternative method of influence. "Can you prove that there is no chance that the...?"

"If you claim to know what this place is then you must know what would happen should you destroy the generator," said another voice. This voice, a man's, came from behind the suit of armour.

"There is a weapon up there," Ash answered, tilting his face up as he spoke. "With the power of that generator behind it, it is a threat to all life."

"They do not know about the generator," came the reply. Ash sighed, this was going nowhere.

"Who are you?" Ash enquired, addressing the other voice.

"Who I am is no longer important," he said, with no clue in his tone as to what *that* really meant.

"Then what *is* important to you?" Ash asked, rudely. An idea came to him... "You're a computer, aren't you?"

"And you are an immortal, what of it?" he responded, coolly. Ash was not enjoying the direction of this conversation and for the first time in a long time he didn't feel like he had control of the situation.

An artificial intelligence, guarding the geothermal generator, which had been there since around the beginning of recorded time.

"Who programmed you?" Ash asked, interested.

"I was programmed by a computer called Raz on a world called Ferrengale," it answered. Ash knew the names and instantly grinned.

"*Curious*," he remarked, in a tone that concealed much.

Raz had once been Dreda's computer just as Ferrengale had once been her world. It no longer existed, although there was a planet called Ferrengale Beta that did still remain. So Dreda had programmed this computer to defend or hide the generator. And now... she wanted him to destroy it before the humans could find it. She had not explained *why* though... Nor had she told him the best way to do it. She had also failed to mention her own security system. He chuckled grimly.

"Yet another test, Mother," he said, to himself. "*Very droll.*" The idea that she was once again testing him was not the only possibility though. She may not have explained further because she no longer remembered or there was some kind of 'power of suggestion' complication at work.

The Ferrengale business was centuries old. The original planet had been located in another dimension but had been destroyed completely before the conclusion of the war between Dreda and Freen. A war that had reduced the whole dimension to a dry husk of desolation. Ferrengale Beta was in the same dimension as Earth but it was a long way out and, to his knowledge, neither world was linked directly with Durrith. Durrith was the place where the old spatial universe ended and this one began. Ferrengale had been located in a different temporal dimension and so Durrith couldn't possibly exist within it. One nexus point among many. The generator itself surely had to have been made after this universe came into existence unless it had somehow survived the collapse of the older one. That was possible as the guardians had survived.

"Did you see the end of the last cosmos?" Ash asked, trying to pin its origins down.

"No, but I have detailed records of life before the implosion," it replied.

"Can you show me?" Ash asked.

"That is permissible," it agreed. The guardian's blades slid away, up the arms and into hiding. It began to walk and Ash began to follow. It was conceivable that if Dreda had programmed the guardian's supervisory system, she may even have built the generator itself. And even if she hadn't, what was it for? If no one now used it, why had it been built originally? He hoped Deva would remain unconscious until he returned but he didn't know how long he was going to be.

***

Padding down the passageway softly, Satiah was running out of ideas and time. It would only be so long before someone realised that the camera system was jammed again and she still was none the wiser regarding the location of the weapon. They had searched the whole storage zone of the station and found nothing other than the KZ15. Kelvin followed gamely along behind her, constantly running scans and ensuring that no one happened upon them unexpectedly. They were close to the centre of the station now and guards, actual people, were becoming more and more commonplace. They had glimpsed what seemed to be scientists of some kind or other, most likely technicians, roaming the corridors. She'd taken an image of one of them and sent it to Rainbow so he could find out who it was.

Her communicator chimed and they slipped into the darkness of a side room.

"Who is he?" Satiah asked, without bothering to say hello.

"Doctor Jack Innis," Rainbow told her, his tone formal. "Professor of phycology and neurology at the Rembrannic Facility on the planet Corcoom." Satiah knew that world to be an urban metropolis with a good current living state. "Rose to prominence after he wrote a paper on sleep disorders and their long-term effects on the mind. Is Vice President of the UCS and often operates as a consultant." The Universal Condition Service was the most well-known health organisation in the cosmos, covering almost every inhabited world. "A highly regarded specialist, one hundred and twenty-three years old, six children, currently single and he likes chocolate. Where did you see him again?"

Satiah had been initially surprised that his background was in medicine. She had been hoping for either a military background or one in chemistry. As she thought it through, however, she realised it actually made sense if they were correct about how the weapon worked. Sleep disorders…

"Is he on vacation right now?" she asked, a knowing gleam in her eyes.

"How did you *know*?" asked Rainbow, not quite sincerely. They both knew he could guess.

"I'm gifted," she muttered, sourly.

"Oh… one more thing… you told me to tell you when the trial starts?" he said, his tone changing to one of secrecy. Satiah froze in mid-step.

"Yes," she answered, her face unreadable.

"It starts next week," he said. "I'll send you the details." Satiah took a deep breath to calm herself down. This had been a long time coming. "Is this related?"

"No…" she said, her voice a little unsteady. She steeled herself. "No, it's a completely separate matter. Thank you for telling me and I will have a look when I get a moment."

"Very good," he said. "Was there anything else?"

"Isn't there always?" she managed, with a shaky grin. "I was wondering if you had any updates for me in regard to the merger between Phantom Squad and Division Sixteen?"

"Um… *No!* Actually, it's all gone *very quiet*," he answered, sounding puzzled. Like her, he'd clearly had other things on his mind.

After terminating the call she eyed Kelvin. He stared back, his red eyes focussing on hers. She looked away and as she did she realised they were passing through some sort of changing area. The white uniforms of the station personnel were easy to make out even in the low light. Silent and still, they could almost be shrunken skins of the dead. She began to change quickly out of her clothes.

"Is that advisable?" Kelvin asked, understanding her new strategy.

"I'm going to have to get in close," she stated, seriously. "You will have to stay in here and operate as a backup." She put on a set of silver glasses and an earpiece. They were standard medical equipment but Kelvin was able to use them too. He could now see exactly what she was seeing. They could still talk too. She pulled the white hood over her head. Only her nose was easily visible, encased in an opaque mask.

"Let me know if anything happens and... if I get into trouble, come get me," she instructed, her voice muffled.

"Yes," he agreed, retreating further into the shadows. Satiah walked brazenly out of the room and then continued on down the corridor. She passed two guards, careful to ensure she maintained a normal look. She entered a room and glanced around as she took in multiple people dressed as she was. It was a hive of hushed activity. Everyone was busily working on something. One or two of them were no longer wearing their hoods and Satiah was able to subtly take pictures of them. More targets for Rainbow to investigate.

Without hesitating she made her way over to the computer, eager to emulate everyone around her. She had to get close to someone in authority and then follow them. As she turned, she bumped shoulders with a thin man. He was a scientist of some kind, possibly an engineer and he was physically small. As a comparative wall of muscle, she nearly floored him.

"Sorry," she said, her voice still stifled by the breath mask.

"...It's fine," he grunted, returning his attention to his work. No one had noticed, they were all preoccupied with whatever they were doing. The cameras were still offline. She slipped closer to the scientist.

She scrutinised over his shoulder to observe what he was doing. Rows of data... eight sets of numbers in each box. Hundreds of boxes going down. Coordinates? Times? They couldn't be coordinates as the symbols that separated the numbers into pairs were the wrong kind. They had to be times. Recorded measurements of duration. Hundreds of them. The man seemed to be matching them up with other times... these of much shorter durations. Satiah waited patiently for more clues. Gradually she began to see a pattern of a sort. Seven seconds... and twelve hours... She couldn't understand what this was about. She backed away, cautious of accidentally walking into someone else as she searched for another person to examine.

"Security system has been rebooted again," Kelvin's voice said, in her ear. That had happened faster than the previous time. In disguise, that was no longer a problem for her unless she was somehow unmasked. It did mean, however, that Kelvin would have to remain where he was.

"Do *you* understand what I'm seeing?" she whispered back.

"Time comparison logs, seven-second increases resulting in twelve-hour decreases. He was searching for abnormalities," Kelvin explained. That would be a likely reason for the analysis of the data, Satiah knew. Patterns and inconsistencies or *abnormalities* were often the main things that data analysts looked for. She suspected they would use more technical terms for them but the meanings would be the same. In this case the apparent trend between seconds and hours remained mysterious to her.

A few years ago she had had to perform a lot of data analysis herself. A refinery, a place where an intense smuggling operation was taking place, had had years of records to go through. Under the name of someone else, Satiah had gone through them thoroughly seeking certain references that were used as aliases for the suspected smugglers. It had become apparent that two codes were used for the concealment of the shipments. *Frog and Heretic* if she remembered correctly. She doubted this was similar though, it was more likely that all of this data was genuine.

"*Why?*" she asked, seriously.

"That, I cannot answer," he replied. She found another person, this one an older woman. On her screen was yet more statistics. Satiah peered over her shoulder silently.

Names. Hundreds of names... Names *and* places. The woman was archiving what appeared to be *medical histories*. In order not to be noticed, Satiah moved on quickly. Someone watching someone else would look suspicious after a few moments no matter how good their disguise. That was one of the few lessons that even the best spies often failed to learn: always move on and never stay where you are for too long. Although no one could see her face she was frowning with bewildered concentration. What *was* this place? Then, with a flash of grim intuition she realised... *they were testing people.* Testing... the weapon? Or just KZ15? This was illegal experimentation! It had to be! She doubted anyone would have willingly volunteered for this. A door opened at the opposite end of the room and sounds came through that gave her another clue. Groans, cries and whimpers that betrayed only suffering of a terrible kind. Drawn not only by the desire to learn more but also a certain morbid curiosity, Satiah took the chance and slipped in as the door was closing.

Beyond were tens of cubicles… going on and on. Each had digital countdowns over each entry arch and other serial numbers. The noises continued, louder than before. Observing robots patrolled the corridor, like walking talking dead men, looking into the cubicles. Satiah paced along, trying to look like she had a purpose. Halting or looking around might attract attention to her. She made way for two men carrying a body bag on a stretcher. They passed her without a word and as they did, she noticed something. A pale arm was dangling freely from inside the bag, blood on its inert fingertips. Satiah was now breathing hard, adrenalin was tensing her up. She forced herself to remain detached from her anxieties. She could feel her gun now, in the small of her back, and it gave her reassurance. She swallowed and decided to take the plunge. She entered a cubicle.

***

The guard heard the noise again. A strange tapping noise, like keys jangling, followed by someone whistling noisily. Tabre strolled around the corner, tunelessly whistling as he moved. The guard turned fully to face him, confusion on his face.

"Halt, who…?" he began. Tabre reacted with the speed and agility of a professional killer. His hand jabbed the guard in the neck, ending the question before it had truly begun. The guard's hands instinctively raised to his throat and his eyes went wide as he tried to breathe. Tabre followed this up with a punch to the gut, doubling the other man over. And, less than three seconds after the initial attack, he karate chopped the man in the back on the neck, killing him. Now the main power system was completely unguarded.

"I'm there," Tabre stated, eyeing the body and wondering where best to stash it.

"Can you get in?" Alex asked, in his ear. Tabre was about to answer to the negative when he took in the entry system. It required an access card and Tabre eyed the body again. On the man's belt he had some access cards attached to an extendable cord. It was not hard to imagine the man using them to allow others to pass through regularly. Tabre relieved him of them; he wouldn't be needing them again in any case.

"I can," he said, confidently. "Are the cameras still out?" He guessed that they must be or else someone would have noticed the murder by now. He'd been trying to find a less obvious way in for nearly half an hour and in the end had opted to simply force his way in.

"As far as I can tell," she answered. Tabre used the card and the door swished open.

Written across the metallic structure Tabre now faced were the words: *Danger Radiation Keep Out*. It was displayed in no less than six languages and its meaning to anyone but the dimmest simpleton was obvious. Tabre gave the room a sweeping glance. The apparatus, the power system towered over him, rising through metal rings which served not only as extra support for the system itself but also as metal walkways. He was alone with the reactor. The door closed softly behind him as he advanced over to the controls that were on the wall. Main power allocation display panels, fluctuation adjusters and output monitors. The lot. He had all he needed to destroy the whole place there and then if he wanted. He tilted his head to the side as he considered what particular disruption would serve him best.

Overflow with potential chain reaction? Always fun. He patted the controls almost fondly before raising the output level by twenty percent and adding additional fuel. The dull hum of the reactor core rose in pitch ever so slightly and he grinned maliciously. It would take hours to fix that. And the resulting panic would likely tie up scores of personnel depending on how far the reaction got. Turning, he then departed once again into the corridor outside and rubbed his hands together as he thought about where to go next. Assuming that the weapon would be in storage somewhere, storage was next destination. Cautiously he made his way there under Alex's direction.

***

Carlos had noticed the occasional sign of recent activity in the dust on the floor, revealed to him by the light on the end of his rifle.

Ruby was once again proving how difficult she found it to remain silent.

"Are you *sure* there's no one behind us?" she whispered, anxiously.

"No," he growled, unhappily. Personally he was more worried about what might be *ahead* of them but what harm could a counter-worry be?

"...It could be them," she said next, her voice hopeful.

"Yes and it *could be* no one at all," he stated, rather harshly. "Stay quiet!" Ruby flushed but managed to contain her objections at having been ticked off so completely by a teenager.

A noise ahead, the slightest shuffle, froze Carlos in his tracks. He turned off the light and instantly felt Ruby's hand grab his arm reflexively. For once she remained silent. Nothing. Not a sound could be heard now but there unquestionably had been something. He patted her shoulder softly and pulled her down with him as he crouched. She followed him down without a word. She was shocked as he placed the handle of a pistol in her hand. He slid out from the backpack adeptly. Without warning suddenly he leapt forwards, leaving her alone in the dark.

A collision occurred and there were shouts and cries. Ruby cringed, unable to see a thing. Then she heard Carlos grunt as he hit the floor hard. Ruby, not knowing what else to do, flashed her torch on. Carlos was on his back and Deva was on top of him, blade to his throat. His hands were on hers and the two of them were clearly wrestling over the weapon. Upon realising who they were they both were, they both stopped in instant relief.

"*You idiot!*" Deva grumbled, massaging her bruised temple. He'd got in a hit early on in their fight and nearly rendered her unconscious. In the dark though he'd been off by a fraction of an inch and the main force of the blow had glanced away from her.

"I could have killed you," she hissed, as she helped him onto his feet. He shuffled awkwardly, more than a little put out that she had got the better of him. On the other hand, if she hadn't been so tough he might have accidentally hurt her badly.

"Sorry," Carlos replied, embarrassed. "I didn't..."

"Yeah well now you *know* it's me, *so what do you say?*" she muttered, her tone chiding.

"*Sorry!*" he repeated, trying to stop himself grinning. She saw and couldn't hide her own smile either. She was too relieved at finding someone else at last to be angry for long.

"Where's Ash?" Ruby demanded, glad that they had not inadvertently killed one another.

"I wish I knew," Deva growled, an angry look returning to her face. "We were attacked, back that way. When I came round I was alone." Ruby went pale.

"What attacked you?" Carlos asked, as he pointed with his thumb over his shoulder. "Ruby thinks we are being followed."

"*I don't know that either.* I think it might have been some kind of robot but I really don't know," Deva admitted. "Let's just go." She started to move in the direction that they had come from.

"What about *Ash*?" Ruby asked again, a little horrified that Deva would just abandon him. Deva saw the look.

"Hey, *he* left *me first*," she complained, a little bitter. Everyone knew that it might not have gone down like that, Ash may have had no choice in the matter. He may even be dead.

"He wouldn't have intentionally left you behind," Ruby argued, unwilling to back down.

"Be that as it may," Deva said, waving her hand at the tunnel. "This maze is vast! I've been wandering around in it for hours and I would very much like to leave before I die down here."

"Why don't we sit down, *rest a bit* and discuss our options," Carlos suggested, diplomatically.

"You have water?" Deva asked, noticing the bag for the first time.

"Help yourself," he smiled. They all sat in the dust and began to make inroads into the supplies. "You're not that far from the way out actually... maybe an hour or so in that direction."

"Anything happening with the space station?" Deva asked, curious. Carlos explained what they knew.

"Right back to Earth, huh," Deva repeated to herself, as she chewed. "I want to visit that place."

"You've not missed a thing," he muttered, remembering the cityscape without fondness. Ruby looked out into the darkness and tried not to think about things sneaking up on them. She tried to think about Ash, hoping that his mind would find hers as she had no idea how to search for his.

"Why did Ash come down here?" Carlos asked. Deva explained her *futile* attempts to get Ash to tell her. She had decided they were futile as she had no way of knowing if they were true or not.

"He really *does* have human interests at heart," Ruby insisted, earnestly. Carlos and Deva exchanged doubtful looks. Brought up to be cynical, unforgiving and distrusting, Ruby knew that the teenagers were a hard crowd to work with.

"Ruby, don't take this the wrong way, but do immortals even *have* hearts?" Deva asked, polite scepticism in her tone. Ruby realised she didn't actually know.

"You two can go if you like…" she chanced, hoping they wouldn't leave her. "I will find him myself." Carlos and Deva made eye contact and Carlos shook his head slightly. It was only the minutest of gestures but Deva understood what he was saying. Ruby was their only connection to Ash, without her, they had no leverage on him. Besides, Ruby was an untrained civilian. Leaving her behind in this place would be too unkind.

"No, no," Carlos stated, feigning casualness. "He *could* be in trouble and *might* need our help." Deva had to hide her mouth with her hand to prevent anyone seeing her amused smirk. Carlos could not act when Deva was around, she saw straight through him. Ruby though did not seem to recognise his insincerity… or she simply chose to ignore it.

***

"Turns out that Earth might be a relay point for the signal," Captain Berry was saying. Reed sighed almost wearily.

"Are you telling me you have no idea where it came from?" he asked, without any bite in his tone. It wasn't the Captain's fault.

"At the moment, no, I'm still awaiting the long-range stuff to come in. There was a security alert on a transmission at the time and everything was frozen mid-link for about ten seconds," he answered.

"I will let you know what we find when we've sifted through all that."

"Have you tried an encryption criteria search?" Reed suggested. "Now we know the code they use, you may be able to dredge up more."

"On it now, sir." They disconnected.

"*Let's hope no one used a mondegreen,*" murmured Reed, staring ahead at the space stations.

***

The walls showed signs of damage from time distortion, Ash noted. He was in a circular chamber, maybe four metres across with a hole in the floor in the centre. He couldn't be sure but he suspected he was in the deepest part of the complex now. Hundreds of metres down most likely. He could sense the residual power from the temporal nexus point coming from the crevasse itself. This had been where it had happened. The epicentre of the implosion that had ended one universe to create the current one. The place where Dreda had fought to prevent its destruction… and lost. At the time, Dreda had been trying to destroy humanity by preventing its creation, as it had been several thousand years before she had been cleansed.

But where was the generator? He knew it must be close by… he could hear the drone it made. He could sense the energy within it. Even while not being fully used, it still had a presence. As promised, the computer was showing him records of events before the implosion. Ash was, in more than one way, playing for time. If he destroyed the generator and the planet was destroyed too… Of course the computer *could be lying*, even if it didn't know that it was. Was the generator a secret ingredient to the hypothetical weapon that everyone was searching for? Mostly everything needed power of a kind, it was true. And if the generator only powered its guardians, what was the point in leaving it on? It had to have another function even if it was not currently performing it.

"Do you know *why* the generator was made?" Ash asked, again.

"The generator was made to supply power," it answered, almost misleadingly. What generator wasn't? Yet that was the only answer it would give him.

***

"It's got enough punch to level a city block," Egill was explaining. He'd created a bomb for them to use. "I know you're aiming to prevent collateral damage but... you've got to be sure you hit the target too. You will not get a second chance." Wester regarded the Phantom, resignation in his eyes.

"I'm aware of that," he replied, crisply. "What are your thoughts on our new friends?"

"I think they are genuine enough," Egill said, his answer coming a little too quickly for Wester's comfort. "They certainly have gone along with everything you have wanted so far. In the end though, you *do* understand there is no way to be absolutely sure?" Wester nodded.

"Have they found Ro yet?" he asked, seriously.

"We have informants everywhere, it is only a matter of time," Egill assured him. They fell silent and stared out into the blackness of space. Wester found himself in intense reverie. Thinking about his childhood expectations of his adult life. The things he had wanted and valued. All changed now. He supposed everyone knew the feeling but it was rare that they got to go this far into the wilderness. Jenjex had fashioned him an Admiral's epaulette. Taking into account what she had to work with, she'd done a commendable job. He just wished he could live up to it. She was asleep now, exhausted by nearly thirty-six hours of constant work. She'd be awake again in six hours. Wester found himself wondering just how many lost hours of sleep a naval officer would accumulate over a career. Too many, was the obvious answer.

If you ever had the chance to see into your future, what would you change now? Wester couldn't see into the future and thought little of predictions, however scientific. The moment had surprises that no one could see coming. No war could last forever... No pain could be felt forever. In the grand scheme of things, no matter what that might be, you can only ever be a tiny part of it. Almost insignificant yet still have a part to play. Wester felt like a man on the cusp of enlightenment for a second, as if some last thought had escaped him. Cheated him of a great wisdom. Human understanding had its limits and Wester realised he was drawing closer and closer to them. He turned away and headed for his cabin slowly, still in a world of his own, various people touching their hats to him as he past them.

***

Brushing the curtain aside, Satiah entered the cubicle. She had experienced much savagery and viciousness in her life yet what she saw in that cubicle made her feel instantly sick. Physically restrained by the neck, wrists and ankles... a man was secured to the bed in front of her. Wires were running from him in various places. She quickly turned to examine the monitors to the right that were presumably all about him. She picked up the clipboard too, mainly to look normal. She could feel him watching, his eyes burning with hostility and fear. His name was listed as Neo but that didn't automatically mean that it was his real name. He was in his mid-forties, six foot two... She went over the medical history of the dying man in front of her.

"Am I dying on schedule?" he croaked at her. She glanced at him, making eye contact. Recognition flickered in him and she realised that he instantly knew she was *not* his regular attendant. She decided to take advantage of his impaired judgement; a desperate dying man that could not be saved could still be useful. It was a harsh cruelty as he had no doubt already been as good as murdered but she had to know what was going on. She moved over to the side of the bed, noting the camera watching the room and her. She leaned in close to whisper, pretending to check the cable connections.

"I cannot save you but you could help me save others if you answer my questions," she stated, her voice low. She could have lied, she could have pretended that she had it in her power to rescue him but she knew that that was too unbelievable.

His attention was strained; as if he was trying so hard to concentrate it was actually distracting him from concentrating.

"Questions..." he repeated, his voice tense.

"I think you have been exposed to a substance that is killing you by preventing you from sleeping... am I right?" she asked, clearly. He managed a pained nod and a tear fell from his eye.

"KZ15," he confirmed, after an agonised breath. She nodded, pleased. "They... lied to me..."

"Who lied?" she asked, grim.

"Professor Sam and that man..." He gasped for air. He seemed to have some kind of problem processing oxygen. This might make sense, as the nitrogen in his body seemed abnormally high.

"*What man?*" she replied, knowing she was close now. So close to identifying the next level of suspects and finally getting to the truth.

"Before I tell you, you *have* to promise me something..." he stated, his eyes bulging at her.

"I can't get you out of here," she growled, getting ready to silence him if he lost control.

"No..." he stated, his eyes leaving her. She followed his gaze. He was staring at a medicine cabinet and then... she understood. He wanted her to kill him, he wanted her to put him out of his misery. A *mercy killing*... putting your hand in hot water some called it. She knew how of course. Chemicals were something she knew a good deal about.

"You have to promise to kill me," he insisted, his hands struggling against the clamps. "*Promise!*" She glanced up at the camera warily. She'd been in there maybe five minutes. Was that too long? Her heartbeat was starting to pick up again as she glanced back at the cabinet again. It was closed but didn't seem to have a lock of any sort.

She checked the cabinet and inside were some chemicals used for termination of life... a precaution no doubt to use on someone who was escaping. The chemical in question would not provide a painless death but then, she supposed he was already beyond his tolerance of pain in any case. His drawn-out, grey face spoke of days of hellish torment. She began to prepare him a syringe. She'd done it so many times she didn't even have to think to do it. Killing him would be a sensible precaution to protect herself, she rationalised. A win-win. She moved back over to him with it.

"Give me the name and I will end the suffering," she made herself tell him.

"Professor Sam and Sethryn Ring," he uttered, his eyes never leaving the injection she had just prepared.

"Who is Sethryn Ring?" she asked, almost breathless.

"He is the one who is responsible for all this... it is funded by him..." he explained, falteringly.

"How do you know this?" she asked, seeking verification. It wasn't that she thought he was deliberately lying... although he was desperate enough to say anything to get what he wanted. Her main concern though, was his mental stability. The desire for his own death ironically displayed a semblance of sanity *to her* as she imagined most would want the same. But she didn't know how long he had been awake or what other *procedures* would have been carried out on him.

"I used to work for Sethryn Ring, I was his head of security... until he decided I knew too much," he stated, his hand extending pleadingly for the injection.

"And who is Sethryn Ring working for?" she asked, wondering who Sethryn Ring was. She'd never heard the name before.

"*Please...*" he began, tearing up.

"Come on, *help me help you,*" she growled, through her teeth.

"Sethryn Ring... works for no one... that I know of," he answered, writhing where he lay. Pitiful didn't really come close to describing how he looked now. She was starting to actually want to end his life.

"Can you tell me why he is doing this?" she asked, levelly.

"*Professor Sam...* He will know... please, please kill me!" he screeched, starting to lose control. She clamped her hand across his mouth, a bandage there to stop him from biting her.

"Silence or you will give us away!" she hissed, at him. He stopped struggling and slowly she released his mouth.

"*One more question,*" she told him, and meant it. She'd spent too long in there already; someone must have noticed her by now.

"Where is the weapon?" she asked, hopefully. He stared at her, as if wondering if he had heard the question correctly. "Is it here?"

"What weapon?" he asked, and her heart sank. She knew he was not hiding anything and he'd done all he could. Now it was his time.

"Thank you for your help," she smiled, even though he couldn't see the expression. She injected him and threw the needle to the side. She paused just long enough to see his relieved and grateful smile before the alarms started wailing. She knew what must have happened, of course. The computers would have detected the chemical and had accordingly alerted all the medical personnel... but, thanks to her, they would be too late to prevent his death.

She started running, knowing that if no one had noticed her yet they would now. She dashed from the cubicle, nearly knocking over an observing robot that had already made it to the scene first. She rounded the next corner, a combination of claxon and cries of terror from the patients pursuing her.

"You have guards surrounding you," Kelvin warned, in her ear. "They know you are there."

"Stay where you are!" she ordered him. She then removed the earpiece and flattened it between her fingers. She wrenched her gun free of its hiding place and fired at a woman running towards her. She'd not been a guard, most likely a nurse of some type. Then, methodically, Satiah began to shoot the occupants of the cubicles. If she couldn't get away herself she'd make sure that the experiment, of whatever it was, was ruined!

A screechy voice, somehow reaching her over the brouhaha, made itself known to her.

"Youuuu!" it screeched. "Surrindarrr!" Satiah continued to gun down anyone she encountered before blasting open a side door. She pulled out a mine from her pocket and slammed it onto the wall above the door. Its strong magnets instantly fixed it in place and prevented to from falling. In the chaos she hoped that it would be missed. Crossfire between two sets of security guards nearly caught her as she rolled out. Hitting the wall hard, she began to fire back. All the lights flickered suddenly as the power seemed to increase. She turned to flee and something slammed into her head. She collapsed, down for the count.

***

Tabre initially thought it had been him who had set off the alarm somehow. He checked for any detectors he may have missed only to find nothing. In a few moments though, it was clear that someone else had caused the ruckus. Satiah had clearly chosen to make her move. That meant she must have already acquired the weapon. Racing down the corridors Tabre only stopped when he too heard the eerie voice screaming on the speakers. Then he heard the all clear with a brief computer summary. Prisoner captured, clean-up operation has begun. Satiah captured? Was that just a part of her plan? Or even a trick simply for his benefit? No, *that couldn't be right*; she couldn't know he was even *there*! Unless... Alex had betrayed him. As he stood there frantically going through the possibilities and trying to decide what to do next, two groups of guards happened on him. Tabre glanced around at them, momentarily furious at his own incompetence.

"Drop it!" barked one, as they all trained their weapons on him. He did as he was told, sighing grimly. He crushed his earpiece under his boot subtly. They led him down the corridors. There was a conversation taking place between the guard and his superior but Tabre couldn't hear much of it. He knew he was in no real danger yet and there was a strong chance he could escape. Nonetheless, Satiah would more than likely realise he was there if she hadn't already. Then... the danger would come.

"Put him with the other two," he finally ordered. Tabre was taken to a room, white and well-lit like the rest of the station. Inside were two women, held against the wall. Satiah, her head lolling forward, seemed to be unconscious and was bleeding onto the floor from a head wound. The other woman he had never seen before. She had short ginger hair and strange eyes. They seemed to have more than two colours in the irises. She stared at him, curiosity on her face. Tabre was forced against the wall and secured there. He wondered what Alex would be doing... nothing, he hoped.

The guards trooped out noisily and the door closed behind them. It was locked. A pregnant pause began. Tabre glanced around searching for cameras or other obvious bugs. He had about forty minutes left before the reactor started to get dangerous. The cell was not a purpose-built one, not designed to house inmates. He guessed it was most likely a storage area that had been adapted in a makeshift way to act as a brig.

"Who are you?" asked the woman, her voice weak but lucid. Tabre knew she could be a fake prisoner, someone placed there to get him to talk. He stared grimly at her and said nothing in a very definite way. He would talk to Satiah... indeed he had to find out what she had done with the weapon, assuming she had successfully stolen it. The woman never stopped staring.

"My name is Lara Clement," she told him. "I know you don't trust me but *you should*."

"Do better next time," he growled at her, disbelievingly.

Satiah suddenly came to, jerking against the restraints and straightening. Her glance swung around, taking everything in including... Tabre. She gaped at him, even more confused by the fact that he seemed to be a prisoner too.

"Morning beautiful," he nodded, to her.

Her mouth opened but no words came out as she was unsure what to ask first.

"This is *our new friend*, Lara Clement," he told her, letting her know what *he believed* through his tone. Satiah, recognising the name, faced her again.

"The *consultant*?" Satiah stated, calmly. Lara eyed her evenly and nodded tentative.

"You know me?" she asked, confused.

"I know *of* you," Satiah growled, trying to get comfortable and failing.

"Okay..." Tabre said, nodding slowly as he watched them. Maybe Lara was trustworthy, at least as much as Satiah could be... this meant there was the possibility of collaboration. Even if it was only for a few minutes. "*Truce?*"

"With *you?*" snarled Satiah, scowling at him. "I told you I would kill you if I saw you again!"

"You did," he agreed, levelly. "Circumstance demands a degree of cooperation though, especially in the short-term. We need to agree on a story. Make sure we all lie the same way about the same things."

"There is nothing that we can say that will be believed," Satiah argued, although deep down she knew he was right. Tabre, annoying as he was, actually had precious little to do with this. The door hissed open and Tabre glowered at her.

"Too late now."

Professor Sam entered, his filthy look and lack of ears instantly making an impression. With him was another man, this one dressed in an expensive suit. He was tall. His hair was dark and curly, like his manicured beard.

"So... Miss Clement, *your team finally* came to rescue you," he said, eyeing Lara. "Too bad they failed... And, as you don't want to talk, perhaps *they will*." Lara said nothing, she only dropped her eyes. Tabre and Satiah followed her example. Professor Sam approached Satiah and made eye contact with her. Not liking his stare, she spat at him. Instead of hitting her, as she had expected, he just continued to stare. Satiah still remained silent. He was trying to intimidate her into talking first, a technique older than time itself. After nearly five minutes, he turned and tried the same thing on Tabre. Tabre just ignored him, not even bothering to express his displeasure.

"Two more hard cases," sighed the other man, as if disappointed. He focussed on Lara. "Perhaps their suffering will change your mind about talking. We know how much you *care* about the plight of strangers." Lara made eye contact with Satiah. Satiah gave the slightest of shrugs. She didn't want to be tortured but it seemed inevitable so it might as well be for nothing. Tabre badly need to know what the women were trying to do, he knew they had to have a plan; Satiah at least would have a plan. They had maybe half an hour before the reactor started *sputtering*. Satiah would detonate her mine when things got too much to stand... to at least buy time. Not forgetting that Kelvin too would most likely strike in addition at some point... she just had to stall. Tabre decided to make his gesture.

"Show that you are chivalrous," Tabre spoke up. "Start on *me*. Leave them alone!" Ploy or not, Satiah chose to work with him.

"You sexist scum!" she scoffed, almost playfully. "You think that being a man entitles you to be tortured first? Just being locked up *with you* offends me!"

They made eye contact and the merest flicker of an agreeing smile touched his lips. Lara was looked from one to the other of them, unsure what to do herself.

"*Really?*" he replied, without missing a beat. "If you're not too hormonal to see straight, perhaps you're just too stupid to realise I'm doing you a favour." Professor Sam, uncertain what was going on, was reading their lips in confusion. He of course doubted their sincerity but he couldn't see what any of them had to gain by this seemingly pointless display. The other man too seemed a little puzzled.

"You can't *feel*!" she shouted, at him.

"You can't *think*!" he countered. Each was now taking on the opinions and characteristics of the age-old sexist arguments. Satiah found herself enjoying the argument.

"*Enough!*" shouted the man. Energy surged through them both and they jolted painfully where they stood. After the shocking was over, both of them only grinned at one another. Professor Sam began to wonder if they were deranged.

"*You* did the most damage," the man said, indicating Satiah. "You killed *twenty-nine people*, some of which were patients!"

"They were dead anyway just like you will be," she hissed and then shrieked, as she was shocked again.

"You *may* have cost me dearly so I will ensure I do the same to you," he snapped. She started to laugh; a low chuckle that was hair-raising to hear. The laughter of a professional killer. Control was what they all wanted and with Satiah and Tabre being strong in matters like self-belief, there was little that would sway them. It seemed to further unsettle the man.

"Bad luck," Tabre sighed, watching.

"It's not over until it's over," Lara said.

"Who are you?" the man demanded, at Satiah.

"Go and die," she growled, in response. Energy surged through her again, making her arch reflexively. Tabre gritted his teeth. Lara looked on, her eyes watery. Satiah let out a wail, slumping forward when it was over. She breathed heavily and tried to control herself.

"Who are you?" he asked again.

"Go and die," she repeated. The same thing happened again. Lara seemed to find the suffering hard to witness and Tabre didn't like it much either. Torture was for animals.... Killing was for the civilised.

"Give me a turn on that thing!" he shouted, over her. "Looks like fun!"

"We will get to *you* in due time, *when she is broken*," growled the other man. A long wait then, Tabre reasoned.

"She'll die before she breaks," Tabre warned, knowing it was true. He'd seen her defiance first-hand and compared to him, these were amateurs. "As will I."

"We will see."

"*Leave her alone!*" screamed Lara, unable to remain silent. "You cowards!"

"Go and die!" Satiah shouted again. Then she slammed herself forwards, crushing her belt against her restraints and triggering the mine. An explosion occurred somewhere and alarms began. Sam and the other man looked at one another before leaving hurriedly. The door closed behind them. A short silence descended as Satiah recovered herself and smiled grimly across at Tabre.

"Can you walk?" Tabre asked, immediately. Satiah managed a feeble nod.

"Yes... I think so," she replied, weakly.

"You two are something," Lara muttered. "I know you didn't come here to get me, why are you here?"

"He's here to kill Reed..." Satiah began, tilting her head in Tabre's direction.

"*Not anymore*," he interjected, being honest. "Neither you or Reed are my targets anymore..." Satiah tilted her head again as she processed that and then... *she knew*.

"You found out about the weapon and now *Ro Tammer wants it*," Satiah stated, putting it together. He smiled, shaking his head impressed.

"She's right, *you* certainly are something," he replied, envying her speed of deduction.

"The weapon isn't here," Lara said, bleakness in her tone. "I thought it was but it's been moved."

"To *where?*" Satiah asked, before she could stop herself.

"*I can't tell you!*" yelled Lara, angry. "I tried to stop them building it but they unmasked me..."

"Who are you working for?" Tabre asked, seriously.

"I can't say!" Lara replied, imploringly.

"I know but I shouldn't say either, we *are* on the same side!" Satiah insisted, persuasively.

"No, *we're not!*" Lara argued, shaking her head.

"*Right now we are!*" yelled Tabre, over her.

"You refuse to help us and I *will* tell them everything!" Satiah threatened, hoping that Lara wouldn't know she was bluffing.

A cracking noise sounded and suddenly Tabre's right arm was free. He had been slowly cutting his way out with a concealed laser since the torture session began. It had been his distraction. Satiah had known he had needed one even though she hadn't known what for. He freed himself completely in less than five seconds. He approached Satiah and then paused.

"...*Come on*!" she hissed, at him. "I can't help you if you don't release me."

"So... I just want to get this settled *before* you have my throat in your hands, *we are working together?*" he asked, seriously. She paused and he smiled knowingly. "*I thought not*... and now that I know you don't know where the weapon is... I don't even need that from you." She stared helplessly up at him as he turned to focus on the door. He was going to leave her there! Part of her hated herself for what she was about to do...

"*I let you live!*" she stated, referring to what she had not done on Ionar 12. He halted as he reconsidered. "Or was all that talk about chivalry just for show?" He turned and slowly came back to stand before her again.

"You could have killed me and you chose not to," he concluded. He ran a hand down her face gently. "Why was that?"

"...It would not have been very *fair*," she answered, after length consideration. He was looking for something and she was sure she knew what it was. Not the weapon... that was merely a detail... he wanted something from *her*.

"You had me beaten, you should have won," she detailed, finding it more than a little difficult to admit it. "But things outside of our control saved me..."

"*Come on!*" Lara implored, not liking how long this discussion was taking.

The restraints snapped and Satiah fell forward unexpectedly into his arms. They stared into each other's eyes.

"Free her, I'll get the door," he ordered, with a softness to his tone that made her feel intimidated. She bridled a little but obeyed, it was the right thing to do. How long would it be before he tried to kill her again? How long would it be before their usefulness to each other expired? Satiah began to release Lara, her mind racing as Tabre focussed his laser on the door control. Distracting her further, Tabre went on talking in his usual voice.

"We've got about twenty minutes before the reactor blows!" Tabre was saying, over his shoulder at them.

"Was that *your* doing?" Satiah grunted, her tone one of blame. Lara fell forward too. Unlike Satiah and Tabre she had been held there for much longer and was badly weakened.

"If *you* hadn't got trigger happy, I'm sure they would have *noticed and reversed* what I did by now but they may not have noticed," he argued.

"Yeah it's *totally* my fault that *you* decided to sabotage the...!" Satiah began.

"Are you two matrimonial partners?" demanded Lara, impatiently. "How is this banter helping?"

"It's not," growled Satiah, as she supported the other woman.

"I do hate it when circumstances come between us," Tabre grinned, a tiny wave of white smoke rolling up as the lock disintegrated.

"Where's the weapon?" Satiah asked again, to Lara.

"*I can't tell you!*" she repeated. Satiah thumped her hard in the chest, doubling her over and winding her. Tabre glanced around at the kerfuffle.

"You're going to have to," Satiah pressed, starting to lose patience. She had a strong hold on the back of Lara's neck and her other hand was in a fist, ready to deploy another blow. Lara seemed too badly weakened to put up any sort of fight.

"*Ladies!*" Tabre scolded, as the door slid open. "Don't make me turn the water cannon on you."

***

"What?" Reed asked, as Kelvin reported in.

"Satiah was captured... she is now escaping... I will rendezvous with her soon," Kelvin told him. Reed ran a hand through his hair, stressed.

"Very well, is there anything *I* can do other than sit here and grow old?" he asked, a little techy.

"No," Kelvin replied, in his usual monotone. Reed rolled his eyes; no, of course there wasn't! And he'd still heard nothing from Carlos or Deva. This was starting to unravel, he could sense it. He was starting to feel a bit exposed where he was, just drifting there, albeit cloaked. He forced himself to relax and trust that Satiah would get the job done.

***

"It was here," Deva said, her voice low. She'd led Carlos and Ruby back to where she and Ash had been attacked. Unfortunately no fresh clues were available.

"He must have gone on or we would mostly likely have seen him," Carlos suggested. Ruby thought about it and nodded.

"I think you are right," she concurred. Deva let out a nervous breath. Continuing on made her worry that they would be lost again, or worse, attacked again. Ruby shivered. It was almost like some invisible force was reaching out and trying to push them back or at least discourage them from continuing on. An invisible force that seemed somehow greater than the normal trepidation anyone might feel. Was it palpable or was it in their minds?

Carlos was the first to move forward, shrugging off the unease like a bear would shrug off an insect bite. He was a Phantom in training and he had Deva with him. He was pretty sure they could handle most things. Ruby followed them along, her neck starting to ache from all the times she glanced over her shoulder. She felt cornered, like there was a danger in both directions and they trapped her in the middle. For the first time since this whole thing had started, Deva was seriously wishing she was somewhere else. She did feel a lot braver now she was not by herself though. She clutched the rifle more strongly than she needed to.

Something glittered in the darkness ahead of them and Carlos tensed. Deva too saw it. A golden shine.

"Don't shoot!" she warned, fear in her voice. "It will redirect it straight back at you." Carlos raised his eyebrows, remembering her account of what had happened before. Yet nothing approached them and the tunnel widened out into a hall. Inside, somewhere around fifty suits of golden armour stood in a square formation. They stood motionless, giving the appearance of statues. Ruby, her eyes wide, stared at them in expectation. Carlos, despite wanting to investigate them more closely, decided to keep going. They kept to the edge of the room, skirting around the formation of silent figures. All of them at some stage had the idea that one or more of the things moved but... no attack came.

"They would appear to be sleeping," Carlos whispered, to Deva.

"They are watching us and waiting," Deva stated, with certainty. "I don't know why but I'm sure that's what they are doing."

"Let's see how far we get before they move on us," Carlos answered. More slowly than before they continued on towards the opposite end of the hall where another tunnel began. While they were moving, Carlos and Deva spoke about the origins of the place and Deva once again repeated what Ash had told her.

"Question is, can we trust anything that duffer said?" Ruby grumbled. They both turned to look at her in surprise.

"We thought *you* trusted him?" Deva asked, a little taken aback.

"I do and I love him but that doesn't mean I believe everything he tells me," Ruby admitted. "He's an immortal and they all have their secret ways."

"Much like this place does," Carlos agreed, mordantly. Ruby suddenly shrieked and leapt against the wall in a panic. Both teenagers spun on her and surveyed the area with their rifles. Nothing, just Ruby sprawled on the floor panting.

"Something touched me!" she explained, her words rapid and scared. Carlos and Deva exchanged looks.

"*Did it leave a note?*" Carlos enquired, a little irritated. "You *imagined it*, Ruby, take it easy. Make us jump like that and you might get shot." Deva extended a hand and hauled Ruby back onto her feet.

"I don't think I…" Ruby began, trying to control herself.

"Ask yourself, why would anything touch you *like that?* What would be the point when it could very easily have done much more?" Deva asked, rhetorically.

Ruby turned in a slow circle as everything seemed to obfuscate itself. Had she imagined it?

"Maybe just to mess with us," Ruby offered, fearfully.

"…Let's go," Carlos said, not wanting that debate to continue. Speculation was almost always pointless and in this case it was not exactly helping their confidence.

"*She's starting to freak*," Deva warned, in his ear.

"*She will be all right so long as we keep moving*," Carlos insisted. Deva did not look convinced but didn't argue further. Carlos glanced once more over at the golden suits of armour… still inert. He began to wonder if it wasn't Ruby's mind that was imagining things… maybe it was Deva's.

The next thing they saw was a light. The flickering, flashes of flame. So… there was something down here after all. Deva had always had the sensation that they were going downwards in slow circles and lines. They could turn off their torches and use the fire torches on the walls to guide them from now on. Ruby was relieved, that darkness had been really getting to her. That was when they heard running feet. Deva and Carlos split, each taking a wall and aiming their guns ahead. Ruby, like a small animal caught in headlights just froze in the middle. Ash came sprinting with amazing speed around the corner. He was carrying something and he almost fell over when he saw them. He concealed whatever it was he was holding in his cloak.

"*Run!*" he thundered at them, reaching for Ruby's hand.

Made from something unknown, the tomb or temple, whichever it was, was not in a state of perpetual temporal duration. Rather it was existing in a form that simply was not subject to the limitations of time. The planet, Durrith, was another matter though. Watched over by the mysterious cryptarchy it was the place where it had all happened before and would do so again. After a short trip into another dimension, Ash had reprogrammed the computer left there by his mother. More by accident than design, Ash had found the generator and, as a kind of compromise, had activated it. In doing so, by the time he had returned, the power core was almost exhausted. He'd done this to ensure that the humans never detected it while not actually destroying the apparatus as he had earlier planned. The computer had taken exception to this anyway and had attempted to entomb him inside the generator housing.

Having already predicted that it would try something, Ash had broken free and was now intent on just escaping. He had intended to go back for Deva but he'd not expected to find Ruby and Carlos there too. Ruby squinted, trying to see what he was concealing in the folds of his cloak. The movement was too quick and shadowy for her to identify anything.

"What's happening?" Deva demanded, following. "What have you done?"

"What I planned to do earlier but with slight amendments," he responded, over his shoulder. They returned to the cavernous space where the golden suits of armour were. They were moving now, or at least trying to. Yet they were now slow and sluggish, mainly because they did not have so much power to fuel them. Ash and the humans easily evaded them and continued on down the tunnel beyond, going up.

***

Overpowering the guards had been easy. The door of the cell had opened and, helpfully, the two men were facing away to watch the corridor. Tabre had taken down one and Satiah had floored them other. Each took a laser rifle from the fallen men.

"I must get to the generator to try and cool it down," Lara insisted.

"You're going nowhere *by yourself*," Satiah insisted, aiming the rifle at her.

"You kill me and you will *never* find it," Lara warned, composed.

"*Satiah!*" barked Tabre, angry. He opened fire at the guards coming around the corner. Satiah turned and gave supporting fire too.

More and more of them came and neither Satiah nor Tabre was able to stop Lara as she ran away. The last set of guards vanished in a wall of fire as Kelvin attacked them from behind. Tabre almost fired on Kelvin but Satiah stepped between them.

"No!" she instructed. "We have a truce."

"This is Kelvin?" Tabre smiled, calmly. "Did you make him yourself?"

"So what if I did? We are wasting time! We must get her back before she gets herself killed," she argued.

"No," Tabre said, clutching at her shoulder to stop her. "Just stop and think for a second! You only have *her word* that the weapon is not here and, one way or the other; she is not the only thing on board that can explain further." Satiah paused... Perhaps he was right. She'd already checked the computers but... Professor Sam would know.

At the very least he would be able to tell her more about this shadowy Sethryn Ring that the dying man had told her about. Then she made eye contact with Tabre. This was not a union she wanted or even needed.

"Why should I trust you? You're probably only using me to help you find it," she accused. He gave her an evil grin. "When and if I get it, you will kill me to take it from me."

"You know trust is a word I hardly recognise," he evaded. "Why don't *we get* the weapon before *we argue* over what to do with it?"

"*Why do you think*?" she countered. More shooting interrupted them and Kelvin adeptly eliminated another guard.

"Professor Sam's office is this way," Kelvin stated, starting to lumber away from them. They followed.

Chaos was everywhere now. The mine Satiah had detonated had damaged a power unit running inside the wall. It had freed all the patients from their bonds. They were now running around and attacking their doctors and their guards violently. Days of anguish were at last being paid for. The guards, now outnumbered were starting to panic. The medical personnel were just trying to get away. Professor Sam, having realised it was time to escape himself had returned to his office. He had a crate prepared for just such an eventuality. Emergency food, clothes and other basic equipment needed to ensure survival. His personal escape pod was ready. He tenderly took the still unfinished masterpiece Neo-chrysalis from its supporting frame and began to pack it into a case.

Outside the guards that had escorted him there were being beaten to death by enraged patients who were after the man they saw as responsible for all this. They did not get their revenge. They had overcome the guards but were annihilated by Kelvin, Satiah and Tabre as they reached the corridor outside Sam's office. Tabre got to work on the door as Satiah and Kelvin stood guard, each covering a different direction. In moments, Tabre got the door to open. In his panic, Sam had forgotten to lock it.

The door opened and though Sam didn't hear it, couldn't hear it, he felt the gentle change in air pressure. He began to turn, expecting… Satiah, Tabre and Kelvin stood before him, guns all trained on him. He gasped in fear and shock. How had they got out?

"You tell us where the weapon is and I will let you live," Satiah offered, taking care to speak clearly. He couldn't hear her words but he could read her lips. One look in her eyes, steely and predatory like those of a furious feline, told him that she wouldn't hesitate to kill him if he refused. Tabre moved over to the controls while Kelvin covered the door.

Sam paused, wondering how best to proceed. He'd not expected anyone to get past his guards. Finch had been right about Lara having a team. Satiah was impatient, too angry to wait. She considered kneecapping him but paused when she noticed what he was trying to pack away. Something of great sentimental value, she supposed. Satiah didn't have one artistic bone in her body and loathed galleries but she remembered that those who did often coveted the art within them. Now she knew how to hurt him! She blasted the Neo-chrysalis into tiny fragments with one single shot to illustrate her feelings.

Sam stared down at the remains of his creation, mortified. He let out an involuntary wail. Six years gone in less than six seconds!

"Next time it will be you, you have *five* seconds," Satiah went on, ready for anything. He didn't answer, just continued to gaze at the shattered remains. She put another bolt to the floor, just by his foot to get his attention. He jumped and whirled to face her, terror ruling his expression.

"The weapon, where is it?" she asked again, her tone dangerous.

"Sethryn Ring has it!" he screeched, his voice strange and almost childlike. His inability to hear himself meant that, over the years, his ability to talk normally had diminished without him knowing. Tears fell from his eyes and he could not bring himself to face the frazzled remains of his Neo-chrysalis again. He cowered.

"Where is he?" she asked, feeling that she was getting closer. Tabre watched, taking everything in, admiring her focus and efficient technique. Sam didn't answer, just stared blankly at her. She walked over to him and pistol whipped him to the floor. Blood dripped down his face and he yelled in fright and pain. Her free hand tore at his hair.

"Tell me or you die," she screamed, forcing him to look at her.

"*He's on Earth! He's on Earth!*" he replied, out of his mind with fear.

"What's he going to do with it?" Satiah demanded, savagely. She had to know what Sethryn Ring had planned for the weapon. In her experience people with such things usually did one of three things. They might sell it, sometimes to bidders already chosen and sometimes to official governments. They could bury it somewhere for later. Or they would simply use it. The last option was the most likely and she had to know.

"I don't know…" he began, raising a pleading hand. "I don't know! Finch knows, he can tell you…"

"*Who?*" she demanded, relentlessly.

"*Finch!* The man who was interrogating you," he told her. "He's Sethryn's new security director. He's very clever, he knew about you and Lara, he thinks of everything…!"

"Thank you," she spat, and shot him dead. With Tabre there, Satiah didn't want him revealing anything else. Tabre raised an eyebrow as he regarded first the corpse and then her. He remembered his father telling him: *revenge never gets old.*

"Are you *sure* that *was* all he could tell you?" he asked, turning off the alarms. The constant siren was getting on his nerves.

"He had it coming, I don't know how many he murdered here but I've never cared for amoral scientists... always thinking up new ways to kill and inflict pain," Satiah explained, preoccupied.

Finch had seen her, he knew her face. Even if he mistakenly believed that she and Lara were working together it was likely that he had told Sethryn about her. That meant he would know she was coming after him. He might go into hiding, he already had the weapon. Finch would most likely have already left and there was no way she could think of to get to Earth before him or prevent him from getting there. Yet... Sethryn was an unknown quantity. Who knew what he would decide to try? Desperate pursuit was never a good tactic, she had to think. She had to get out of there!

"I didn't know you *cared*," Tabre stated, sounding impressed. She paused and eyed him, suddenly realising that she had exposed what she had instead of a conscience to him.

"I don't," she replied, rudely. "Is the generator still on overload?"

"According to this computer it's going critical... we have maybe ten minutes, fifteen if we are lucky," he replied, seeming completely unruffled. "*Seems everyone has been too busy to do anything about it.*"

"I don't trust in luck *either*," she responded coldly before turning to Kelvin. "Where's the quickest way out of here?"

"This way," he replied, in his usual intonation. He led them back the way they had come a little way before they discovered the pod that Sam had intended to use.

"You're not looking for Lara?" Tabre asked, his tone not accusing, just curious. Satiah had given some thought to that but subsequent to weighing the matter carefully, she had decided that they no longer had the time. Not if they wanted to leave the observatory at all.

"I've got what I need... whoever or whatever she was, she is no longer important," Satiah replied, motioning for him to move ahead of her. She knew much more about who she was than Tabre did but... frankly she'd had enough of that station and just wanted to leave. Trouble was... Tabre was still with them.

"*Whatever?*" he repeated, puzzled. In a switch snatch, she relieved him of his rifle and poked her own into his chest.

"Move," she growled, dangerously. He obeyed and Kelvin closed the door behind them.

***

Lara reached the reactor area, panting heavily from the exertions. Someone had turned off the alarm but that was only replaced by sporadic screaming or gunfire. She had given Tabre and Satiah the impression that she was going to close down the reactor or at least prevent it exploding. In reality, however, she was going to do the opposite. The Orion Observatory had to be destroyed and all knowledge of the place expunged. The stored KZ15 had to be wiped from existence. Tabre had already set the reactor in motion; it was as good as any self-destruction system. Lara had only to prevent anyone from tampering with it. As if just the thought had triggered something, two guards dashed into the area.

***

"*What?*" Satiah was asking. Tabre was piloting the escape pod, Kelvin watching over him as he did while Satiah pulled on a spacesuit.

"It's an old story from a long time ago but here's the important part. *That* space station is going to detonate, so get out now!" Reed implored, levelly.

"We were just leaving. It seems the weapon could be on Earth…" she began.

"*We?*" Reed clarified, seriously.

"Yes… I have a prisoner," she told him, eyeing Tabre. He pulled a face, a rather genial one, back at her.

"*Professor Sam?*" guessed Reed, interested.

"No…" she said, casually. "Tabre."

***

Ruby collapsed as they reached the edge of the forest. She was not an athlete of any sort and her lungs were in agony, as were her legs. Carlos and Deva, breathing hard but still irritatingly fresh stumbled to a halt, as did Ash. Ruby tried to speak but she literally was incapable of anything other than breathing. Ash picked her up and started running again. Through the trees they went, although now it was twilight and hard to see. Deva had the pod's regular signal on her homing device so there was no question of getting lost. Ash knew the way in any case.

"*Will you kindly explain...!?*" Ruby was asking.

"I will," Ash replied, vaguely. Then he stopped dead, nearly causing Deva to crash into the back of him. She had to physically forward roll to avoid him.

"*Ash!*" she hissed, furious. "What..." Looking forward, the reason for his instant halting became apparent. The pods were not there. She adjusted the tracker, which clearly indicated that the beacon was still transmitting and still coming from that exact area.

"Obviously this place is not as dead as a lot of people think," Carlos growled, training his rifle on the surround. There was still no sign of anyone. Ash allowed Ruby to slip to the ground.

"Reed," Deva called, on her communicator. "We have a problem here." No response. "Respond please?" Ruby gulped.

"What could have happened?" she asked, uneasy. "Malfunction?" Deva was already taking the device apart to check but it was apparent that if there was a fault it was not at their end.

"There's a trail, whoever moved it dragged the pod away," Ash stated, pointing. Advancing cautiously, they found the deep furrows in the ground. The craft that Carlos had borrowed for the occasion was also missing.

"Then why is the signal still coming from...?" Deva began, when she realised. She saw the small silver disc on the ground. Someone must have removed it.

"So whoever moved it is smart enough to understand homing devices but not capable of getting inside," Carlos theorised.

"All of this is reliant on certain assumptions, the primary one being..." Ash trailed off, suddenly looking up at the sky.

"*What?*" Ruby asked, tense. "What can you sense?"

"That we are in the correct dimension," Ash concluded, in a very quiet tone.

"Why would we have switched dimension?" growled Deva, a little irritated. "Don't you need a special ship to do that?"

"Not if you're close to a barrier or a gateway," Ash replied. "It would explain why your device is working but you can't reach anyone on it..."

"Yes but not *how we got here*!" Carlos argued. "The ships *were physically here*! You can *see* they were..."

"That could have been decades ago..." Ash argued.

"Oh so we travelled in time now as well as space?" Deva cut in, equally obstinate. "I'm *pretty sure* we would have *noticed* if that had happened."

"Perhaps a lapse or shift then..." Ash trailed off, deep in thought. Temporal theory was not a subject taught to most Phantoms and Carlos wondered if Ash was deliberately trying to confuse them. Trying to blind them with science for some reason. But why? What did he have to gain? Indeed he seemed just as muddled as they were. All of this came to an end when a loud voice called to them.

"Phantom Carlos!" called a man, on a loudspeaker system. Everyone dived to the ground seeking cover, Carlos included. Ash and Ruby peered up to see about six men, standing on a ridge several hundred metres away, overlooking them. They were armed but they had not opened fire. They were in the direction that the furrows in the ground led. It seemed likely that these men were responsible for the absence of the pods.

"Who the hell are *they*?" Deva asked, aiming. Carlos was doing the same when he saw something. They were wearing black armbands, with the number sixteen on them. That was when he realised who they might be.

"You must be Division Sixteen?" he shouted. The men began to scramble down the hill towards them. Carlos and Deva stood together. If these men had meant to kill them, they'd already had ample opportunity to do so. Tentatively, Ash and Ruby followed their example.

Captain Berry reached them, and saluted. Carlos did not return the gesture. He, like Satiah and Randal, was not a fan of the rival organisation. Instead he gave a rather curt nod.

"Were these two pods here yours?" Berry asked, eyeing him.

"Yes," he growled, a little annoyed.

"Follow us, you need to get back to Reed. We have brought another ship for him as he requested," Berry went on, turning.

"You work for *Reed?*" Deva asked in a circumspect manner.

"Not all of us but my unit has been ordered to do so," Berry replied. They all began to follow him back up the hill. After the mad dash earlier, the hill seemed to go on forever. Ruby struggled the most and had to be helped.

They reached the top and stared down at the ships in the next ravine. There, resting silently as if awaiting their arrival, was a brand-new Covert-Class Phantom fighter. Carlos couldn't stop himself smiling eagerly at it. It was just like *Vulture* had been. Reed *must* have some contacts.

"Reed requests you bring this ship to him and Satiah," Berry explained, waving at it.

"...So *where* are the pods?" Ruby panted, wanting to know.

"We have removed them," Berry answered. "Reed told me you wouldn't need them if you had this."

"He was right," Carlos stated, a little more politely. It was never good to annoy anyone without a good reason. "My compliments to you, Captain Berry. We'd better get on with it." Berry nodded and went back to talk to his men who were looking on.

"*Typical Reed,*" grumbled Ash, a little irritated. All the wild ideas that had come to him and all that had actually happened was that Reed had juggled the transport and not told anyone.

"Just get in," growled Deva, as she motioning to him and Ruby. Carlos was the last to get inside and the two of them took the pilots' chairs. It was a wonderful thing to control a ship like that. Especially after the previous one. No more balancing power fluctuations or being unable to scan anything bigger than an escape pod.

"Cloaks on?" he asked, seriously. This ship, although it only needed one, had three cloaking devices. It was one of the many reasons it was a *Covert*-Class ship.

"Check," Deva nodded. "*I shall not be sorry to leave this planet.* How are we going to find Reed if he's not answering?"

"Knowing him, he will find us," Carlos smirked, confidently. She grinned.

***

"She's on Vugarna Four!" Jenjex exploded, excitedly. Wester sat up in bed, alarmed at the sudden intrusion.

"What?" he asked, bleary and confused.

"Ro Tammer is on Vugarna Four," Jenjex repeated, still animated. "Look, we just had this report arrive!" Wester sighed, and stood slowly to take the correspondence from her. It was a list of speakers at a public announcement on the Colonial capital world... *in three days' time*! He grinned, all weariness and confusion gone.

"We've got her."

***

The pod lurched to an abrupt halt and Satiah almost lost her balance because of the rapid deceleration.

"*Tabre!*" she barked, angrily suspecting the worst. "I *said* no tricks...!"

"Not me!" he stated, folding his arms. A knowing smile was on his face to accompany his annoying calm demeanour and she didn't like it. A new voice spoke over the communicator.

"Satiah, I know it's you." It was Alex's voice. She had been waiting and tracking Tabre's movements until she was ready to perform a rescue. "Let Tabre go or I will be forced to cripple the ship."

"And she will, have no doubt," Tabre stated, shrugging.

"...*She works for you*," Satiah guessed, annoyed. She *should* have anticipated this! Why else would he have come so quietly? He had been planning on this interception from the moment they'd met in the cell most likely. "What's to stop me killing you right now?"

"You wouldn't shoot an unarmed prisoner and even if you would it would solve nothing. Alex would blast you to pieces in this thing. I'm the only thing keeping you alive," Tabre argued.

"True. But it works just as well in reverse. *If we hand you over there will be nothing to stop her blowing us up anyway*," Satiah pointed out, her tone turning techy.

"*I* could persuade her not to," Tabre offered, with far too much sincerity.

"I'm sure you *could* but why would you?" Satiah scoffed, mockingly.

"We *both* want this weapon, albeit for different purposes and *my offer* still stands. We stand a better chance of finding it if we search and work together," Tabre explained, trying not to sound too patronising. It had been a day and Satiah's head was still throbbing from the blow she had received just before her capture. He understood that her bad temper was due to the pain she was enduring rather than the situation itself.

"Which brings us right back to what happens when we *do* find it," Satiah bit back. He grinned at her, genuinely amused.

"Do what you like but right now…" he began.

"You've got ten seconds," Alex's voice interrupted him. He chuckled.

"That girl does not mess around," he stated, trying to contain the laughter.

"I'm listening!" Satiah replied, addressing Alex. "State your terms." She was playing for time, trying to keep the other woman talking. The pain was making thinking straight harder by the second.

"You will release Tabre immediately and surrender yourself to him, he will take it from there," she instructed. Tabre obligingly held out his hand for her gun. Satiah glared at him, although she admired his cool headedness.

"And if I don't?" Satiah asked, still trying to draw out the conversation. If that space station exploded, which now seemed inevitable, they may be able to slip away in the confusion. Or Reed might perform one of his unexpected interventions.

"Then I cripple your pod, call for back up and then you will eventually be killed," Alex spelt out. "If I were you I wouldn't do anything stupid." Tabre chuckled at that but his eyes never left Satiah.

"I'm going to need some time to think about it," Satiah stated, as anyone would.

"No time, no deals, I know you're playing for time," Alex stated. "Five seconds." Satiah winked discreetly at Kelvin.

"Four…"

"Strap yourself into the chair," Satiah ordered Tabre. He pulled an unwilling face.

"What are you…?" he began to object. Was this the 'anything stupid' that she had been told not to try?

"Shut up and do it!" she hissed, seriously.

"Three…"

Satiah made sure her suit was ready. All she had to do was clip her helmet on.

"Two…"

She made as if she was going to hand over her pistol to Tabre. Knowing she was up to something, Tabre did not move to take it. They made eye contact.

"Don't you like my gun. Tabre?" she asked, a grin on her lips.

"Less than I like you," he answered, tense.

"One…"

"Code 443!" Satiah bellowed, at Kelvin. She withdrew the offered gun and yanked her helmet on in the same second. Kelvin promptly blasted out the forward viewing screen with his repeating laser, causing instant depressurisation. Satiah and Kelvin were sucked out into space in less than a second and Tabre fought to get his own helmet back on. He was strapped down and so did not leave the ship.

"*Don't do it!*" he screamed, at Alex. Alex opened fire but missed… it had been a warning shot. For a moment he thought he was dead. Then that instant passed and he was quick to regain his composure.

"What just happened?" Alex's confused voice answered. She would have detected the damage that Kelvin had done but would have known she hadn't done it.

"Tabre? *Are you there?*"

"She got away," he growled, shaking his head. It had been a

desperate move and one of last resort but it had worked. He had known she was up to something but he'd been unable to decide precisely what it was.

"I'm detecting her, shall I...?" Alex began, seeking permission to kill her. She would be drifting outside somewhere.

"*No*, we need her alive to find the weapon, *she will know where to look*," he argued. His face became harder. "Besides... if *anyone* is going to kill her... *it will be myself.*"

***

"I'm going to do what has to be done this time," Lara whispered, to herself. "When we know death has come to kill us, it's strange what goes through your mind. For some it all slows down, for others they see their whole lives in flashbacks and for me... I only see the future. It is also said that you will regret the things you didn't do more than the things you did. I wonder whether that would be true for you... I don't know if you can hear me... part of me believes you must and part of me doesn't want you to. I know you will be frantically trying to step in, to prevent this... But you know it must be done. KZ15 must be removed from human history. And I'm going to be the one to do it, with a little inadvertent help from the humans, I might add. It's been... a wonderful journey! Full of life and miracles! Something I will never regret for one second is asking to go with you. Please don't mourn me; it's just my body that's gone. My spirit will stay with you for as long as you want. I love you, goodbye."

As if bolstered, somehow re-energised or reinforced by the spiritual power she felt inside her, Lara rose to her feet to confront the guards. An unwavering, almost trance-like state of calm enveloped her, like she was somehow divorced from the situation completely. Just because she knew she was about to die, she wasn't going to make it easy! Pushing the rifle to the side, she open-palmed the man in the sternum, halting his advance and driving the air from his lungs. Snatching the rifle from his grip she was quick to turn it on them both, dropping them instantly. More people were rushing in, some guards and others patients. Lara never hesitated, her sole objective to keep them away from the controls of the reactor. She had lied to Satiah. She'd told her that she intended to cool it down. In reality, she'd returned there to ensure that it melted down.

For that had been her mission and she'd known since before it even began that it would be her last. Her steady and accurate blasts cut down anyone who got close. Something ignited, she wasn't sure what but flames were everywhere. She dashed over to the controls, closing the door and sealing the flames out. She could hear the screams of those trapped beyond. It was too late for them all for multiple reasons; nevertheless it was unpleasant to witness or to consider. She scrambled back into the control area, surveying it all in a slow circle. It was time and she looked up. She didn't know what she expected to see. A bright white light? The sounds began to fade first; she didn't even hear the rifle land as she dropped it.

Memory is all, as without it it's impossible to know anything. It affects your ability to reason but more than that it's what gives you your personality. That's all there is: urge and reason. As the fires spread, the alarms wailed and the people screamed, Lara remained a statue, staring up. Her mind reached out, across space, time, all of it… Was the sacrifice a gift to the person who makes it? She wasn't sorry, she wasn't! Pride, certainty and fortitude swelled within her. Her body, a little emaciated and weak stood firm for the last time. A red glow took over all as the reactor flashed out its closing, fatal message of impending collapse.

"Smile when you think about me and don't forget!" she bellowed, over the din. A white mist descended on her, obscuring her from sight.

Critical point reached. The reaction was beyond the engineering tolerances of the reactor to contain or control. From the bowels of the diabolical machine, it happened. The flash of the explosion came a fraction before the noise of the ignition, as light beats sound. The place erupted with the white, yellow and red of destruction. Then came the blast force, shattering everything in its path and unleashing a wave of pure devastation. The Orion Observatory, a place as shrouded in mystery as it had been death, detonated with scarcely conceivable potency. So powerful was the wave of energy it began a chain reaction of explosions on the neighbouring stations that just seemed to go on and on.

***

Carlos saw the aftermath of the explosion as it lit up the sky on Durrith. Deva let out a gasp as she swore under her breath. Ruby too looked on, slack jawed. Carlos set the ship to hover mode, guessing what would happen next. Only Ash looked on, shaking his head slowly. He didn't know the circumstances but he assumed Satiah was to blame for the destruction of the station. The first came into view in seconds. A piece of debris, almost a mile across was descending through the atmosphere, burning as it went, and speeding towards them. Carlos instantly set them on an evasive course to avoid the deadly wreckage. But there was more and more. One thousand and eleven space stations had been caught up in that and while they couldn't all have been destroyed, those that were would be numerous enough to cripple the planet they orbited.

Deva hurriedly sent a message out on all channels urging everyone to either leave the planet or take cover without delay. More and more detritus came down, from several directions at once. They swung the ship this way and then that to avoid them. The distant booms of impacts could be heard even in the ship as the debris slammed into the surface of the planet, throwing up most things into the sky.

"*God!*" Ruby uttered, fearfully. This, to her, looked like a scene from an apocalypse. Carlos remained focussed on dodging anything that came their way but inside he was worried. Had Satiah survived that? Had Reed even survived it? He'd grown in ability and confidence but he didn't feel he could finish the mission without them. Another ship, presumably Captain Berry's, shot past them and away into the distance.

"He's not hanging around," Deva noted, her tone subdued.

"I don't blame him," Carlos said, finally producing a smile. He reached across and squeezed her hand. "*It's okay.*" She grinned.

"Let's hope it was *the right station*," she joked, starting to feel a little more normal. A message came through, weak and scratchy. White noise threatened to drown the robot out. It was Kelvin.

"Carlos? Can you hear me?" he asked. Carlos scowled, expecting that it would be Reed or Satiah calling him.

"Reading you," he answered, wondering if the big robot would hear him.

"I'm sending you coordinates," he said. "You will need to rescue us, the ship has been critically damaged and life support has failed. The hull is breached. Reed and Satiah are unconscious but alive."

Carlos locked onto the signal as Deva's eyes widened. Ash too was genuinely surprised. If they had been caught up in it, maybe it hadn't been them. The orbit zone was now a graveyard of space stations and ships. Even though they were close, it took Carlos nearly half an hour to get to them. Using a gravitational beam, Carlos towed the ruined ship free of the orbit zone and out into deeper space. Finally, Kelvin, dragging two people with him, space walked across and into the airlock. Deva headed down with some medical equipment.

Ruby took her chance and whispered to Ash.

"What was that thing you hid in your cloak?" she asked, inquisitive. Ash glanced at her, polite enquiry in his expression.

"What...?" he began. She squeezed his hand hard

"*Ash*," she warned, cautioning him not to evade her this time. He smiled apologetically and handed her a golden disk-like thing. She turned it over in her hands, trying to figure out what it was.

"What is it?" she asked, perplexed. He took it back, ran his finger along it and it reformed into a throwing star.

"Just a late birthday present from Mum, nothing to worry about," he replied, smoothly. She smiled and sighed.

"I have been meaning to tell you this for a while now. When Satiah and I were investigating the stations, I found this *silver bauble thing*..."

***

Without knowing exactly when but knowing it would explode, Reed knew he was caught up in, as Princess Callisto would say, a hang-fire situation. He'd therefore taken a number of precautions. The ship had been overstretched as it was; there was no chance of activating shields or being able to outrun the blast. So, he'd fetched a spacesuit, suited up and strapped himself into the pilot's chair. He didn't know if the ship would survive the effects of the coming explosion so he had to ensure that even if it didn't, he did. Next he debated the pros and cons of deactivating the cloaking device. Arguably he didn't need it anymore and it would free up the ship's power for the shields or engines. Then, after detecting *two* departures for the space station, he'd contacted Satiah.

It was quickly apparent that Satiah had commandeered one but the other was a mystery. Perhaps it was just station personnel abandoning ship before the reactor went up. Perhaps not. Reed was quick to ensure that all data about the ship was recorded as it vanished very quickly, heading away from all of them. Satiah had been moving away from the station too when suddenly her ship had been trapped by another vessel. One that until now had been cloaked. Unsure what to do, Reed had waited for a sign. It had come in the form of an explosion; the hull of the pod had been breached by an explosion from within.

Useless they might have been but his scanners *could* detect a human drifting in space. Reed had taken the decision to rush in and pick her up. If the station blew up while she was drifting there she would stand no chance. She and Kelvin had made it on board and Reed had been trying to put some distance between them and the station when it had happened. He'd managed to get at least two stations between them and it but the power of the blast was still too strong. The wave of destruction had practically shredded the ship completely. Strapped down as they were, both Reed and Satiah had been knocked out during this process. Luckily Kelvin had remained operational. He had got both bodies free of the ship and had instantly contacted Carlos.

Reed opened his eyes. Satiah was staring down at him; blood stained her face but she seemed ok.

"Morning," he smiled, quietly.

"My contacts are working on Sethryn Ring right now *and* on that other ship you saw evacuate the station alongside us," she said, by way of greeting. She thrust a drink at him. "Drink this. You will feel better." He hoped he'd got enough of the second escaping ship for Satiah to track it down.

"Discreetly, I assume?" Reed growled, as he sat up. He took the drink.

"Naturally," she said, crossing her arms and leaning against the bed next to his. He sighed heavily after a few gulps and looked down.

"What a mess," he murmured, to himself.

"I have more bad news," she stated. "That silver sphere... we haven't recovered it." He looked up sharply.

"Why not?" he asked, concerned.

"During the explosion, while you and I were out of it, the crate it was stored in seems to have fallen out into space," Satiah answered, although she did not sound sure. "Whatever, we can't find it."

"…Maybe it's for the best," he grumbled. She sniggered.

"Wow, *you* must be in pain," she teased. He glared at her sternly but Satiah was never easily intimidated.

"What's the situation?" he asked, letting it drop.

"Well, Carlos and Deva are getting some well-earned rest, as is Ruby. Kelvin is piloting us back to Earth, where we think Sethryn Ring is, and Ash is waiting for you," she stated.

"And Tabre?" Reed enquired, not sure he wanted to know.

"Following us," Satiah said, starting to look a little more troubled herself. Reed nodded slowly, it was only to be expected. "Now Ro Tammer knows about the weapon, it changes things. Debatably she has *good reason* now to start a war with the Coalition."

"And we still don't know how it really works nor what Sethryn Ring intends to do with it," Reed muttered.

"Or what Ash was playing at," Satiah stated, grimacing. "Carlos and Deva were not really equipped to handle him, after all. Next time I think I should do it."

"I sense you weary of him," Reed noted.

"I am tired of his interference," Satiah admitted, her temper flaring. "His disruption almost cost us dearly this time and I'm not just talking about Carlos and Deva. *Because of him* we could have lost the trail."

"Agreed," concurred Reed, darkly. "What of Lara Clement?"

"Vanished as mysteriously as she appeared. She told me she was going to try to stop the reactor… it is clear that she failed and most likely paid for it with her life. She knew more about the weapon than she said but… dead end," Satiah admitted.

"That could be for the best too," Reed said, nodding slowly.

"Her presence here is unexplained but it indicates to me that this weapon is certainly not as secret as it used to be. Someone might have let something slip," she stated.

"Ash?" he asked, expecting her to accuse him.

"I point no fingers, only guns," she remarked, scowling. "But we have two days before we get to Earth and I need to get some rest. I just wanted to catch up with you before I went."

"*Appreciated*," Reed smiled, warmly. He grunted slightly as he stood and rubbed his lower back. It had been jarred painfully during the explosion. Of course it was nothing compared with what Satiah had endured so he did his best to hide the pain.

"Kelvin could help you with that," Satiah stated, seeing the injury.

"Really? He's very impressive," Reed complimented.

"I'll get him to look at it."

***

Tabre didn't need to follow her; he knew where she was going. But he wanted her to see him, he wanted her to know he was still after her and to get into her head. Alex was asleep, exhausted after almost fifteen hours' work. And so the chase continued. As on Ionar 12 she'd slipped through his fingers again but he felt he was getting closer. As in symmetry, the lines of life had to intersect at some point… and when they did… He checked his gun, ready and waiting as always. As so the game of cat and mouse across the galaxy continued. He smiled; he was good at that game, and the endgame was drawing near.

***

Finch hadn't seen the explosion but he knew it had happened. He'd received no word from Professor Sam and that meant the insane man had probably not made it out. Finch adjusted his suit and thought for a few moments. He had been right about Lara not working alone. And Sam's refusal to believe him had led to the destruction of the Orion Observatory and the loss of their entire supply of KZ15. Ever since that incident on Station Denepler preluding its scheduled demolition, he'd suspected *someone* was onto them. His team had never returned from their assignment to kill the last of the Jaylite Industry workers and retrieve the information. The station had been destroyed though so, *at the time* he had felt that he had nothing to worry about. Then *Lara* had turned up, claiming to be a consultant sent by Sethryn and had endeavoured to get Professor Sam to end his experiments.

Finch had secured the amount of KZ15 they needed on board his ship before escaping but there would now only be enough for once. He was bringing it back to Earth himself as he had originally planned. Yet his subconscious nagged at him… As a successful mercenary a certain paranoia always dominated his mind. When he looked around at the people close to him, his first question was persistently the same. Who would betray him first? Sethryn Ring was also one of those people and, knowing what had happened to his previous head of security, Finch was expecting the backstab. He activated the communicator.

"Yes," answered a woman.

"*Lilith*, how are you?" he smiled, officially. "It's Finch, I need to speak to Sethryn, is he around?"

"I'm fine, thank you," she replied, and then she called to her husband.

PART FIVE

Loose Ends

"Sethryn Ring," Rainbow read aloud. "Well-known tycoon, major bondholder, market coordinator and frequent high-risk investor. Key shareholder for Jaylite Industries, he owns 35% of that company. Married, two children. He does have some previous history though, Vourne had him investigated under asset manipulation. All that was about six years ago and no further action was taken." Satiah was sitting in her cabin, listening to him patiently through the communicator.

"As he is still alive, I'd agree with that," Satiah remarked.

"You think he funded this whole thing?" Rainbow asked, curious. "I should tell you to exercise caution in regard to him. He is a powerful individual with many friends in high places and can cause the government problems."

"I have heard at least two people directly incriminate him. His own former security chief and one of his other cronies," she replied. "Besides... I'll kill anyone I have to regardless of who they are or what they are capable of."

"Will they testify?" Rainbow asked again. He was referring to those people who had implicated him. A silence. "Okay, is there any way you can make this *legal* or official?"

"...No," she replied, honestly.

"So, you and Reed are just going to take it from here?" Rainbows asked, a little unnerved. "*Seriously*, this guy is tough."

"So was Vourne and we all know *that* story," she shrugged, dismissively. She knew they didn't really... only *she knew* the end of that story... the correct end anyway. That she had defended him and hidden him only to murder him herself.

"Are you sure you can handle this?" Rainbow persisted. "Randal could help you..."

"What else do you have on him?" Satiah interrupted, trying to contain her discomfort.

"Gives generously to charity..."

"*What villain doesn't?*" she mocked, quietly. Rainbow chuckled. In her experience the corrupt businessmen always donated the most to charity. Whether they did this to compensate for their own behaviour or donated to help create a false impression she was not sure. A little of both, she suspected...

"Indeed. He's a shrewd businessman who has considerable influence. If you take him out there will be *repercussions*," he warned.

"I can't promise a clean kill," Satiah admitted, not caring. She was cleaning her suppressor as she spoke. A device used to effectively silence a gunshot and conceal the flash. Hers, like her pistol itself, was personalised. It was fine-tuned to the point at which it no longer *even resembled* standard issue. Kelvin loomed silently behind her as she worked.

"Do you still not know what he intends to do with the weapon?"

"It's still not known if he has a working prototype," Satiah admitted. "I am just assuming the worst case scenario."

"Sensible."

"Even if he hasn't built it, he has certainly masterminded the deaths of thousands of people. Innocent or not, there is still a price to pay for that," Satiah muttered.

"Yes..." Another silence. This one she knew was the prelude to something else, a new and perhaps more painful subject.

"She's pleading innocent, you know," he told her. Her eyes glazed over a little as her gaze shifted to the middle-distance.

"...She would," Satiah shrugged, at last. "And, *if you look at it a certain way*, perhaps she is."

"What are you going to do?" he asked, inevitably. She sighed, pushed her red hair away from her face and leaned back in the chair. Rainbow had already informed her that the trial was starting, back when she'd been infiltrating the Orion Observatory before Tabre destroyed it.

"I don't know yet," she confessed, a little woodenly.

"Why are you troubling yourself with this? It was all such a long time ago, I'm not sure digging all this up again is... *healthy*," he stated, his voice expressing genuine concern and care.

"Fifty-four years, seven months and twelve days," she told him, a little bluntly.

"...You've not forgotten about it then?" he asked, trying to be funny. It worked and she relaxed into a smile.

"It's kind of hard to forget your own mother trying to kill you and in the process is then killed by your sister," she stated, still with a smile.

"This is why I don't understand your hatred *of* your sister, *she saved your life*," Rainbow stated.

"And how many people have died *because* I am alive? How many people have I killed? *How many will I still kill?* I'm not saying it was my sister's fault that I have done all these things. I'm just saying that *saving me* might have been a mistake legally... she too is now a murderer... only her crime was in self-defence. And, as a Phantom, we are supposed to support the law," she said, a little weariness creeping into her tone. She of all people knew that Phantoms only helped the enforcement of law and order when it suited them to do so.

It all reminded her of how twisted she was, how twisted she had become over the years. Who could she have been? Was Satiah's resentment towards her sister born out of a reluctance to admit *she* had been the one who should have fought back and didn't? Too young, too scared, too... *weak*. A *jealousy*! A reaction to a perceived failure. She didn't want to help her sister because her sister had proven stronger than her when it had counted. At least that was how she looked at it. It should have been *Satiah*, not her sister, who had killed the deranged parent! And now she was allowing her sister's life to collapse as some kind of warped punishment over five decades later?! Now she felt that old fear welling up inside of her, only now, instead of the face of her mother, the dark figure coming to kill her, wore Tabre's face. Inwardly she was starting to believe she was too weak to kill him too.

A family shattered by an act of brutality. A crime. It had broken the mind of a young girl and turned her into one of the most efficient killers there was. But had it not also broken another girl's mind too? Had it not hurt her sister as badly her? More so even, as it had been her who had done the deed? She didn't know: they had never really spoken about it without others present. Though her sister, again proving stronger, had succeeded in finding something more stable than Satiah. As the black sheep, Satiah roamed the galaxy killing on command and her sister... She had her own children now. A husband. A family. And that tore at Satiah also... reinforcing the old jealousy. Why should she be happy when she was the one who'd murdered? Did she just want the same love that her sister already had?

She thought of Tabre again and a single idea came to her. She had to end this. *End it now.* It had gone on far too long already. Her thoughts found Carl next... it was never too late.

"You haven't spoken to her for twenty years," Rainbow stated, truthfully. "*Maybe*... it's time you thought about concluding this self-imposed exile?" Rainbow knew her well, probably better than anyone else alive. He knew how her mind worked and his seemed to be following a similar path to hers in terms of reasoning.

"...Maybe," she answered, evasively. She was still far too badass to admit how close he was of course. Literally standing outside the door to her heart of hearts, kicking the litter around, as if waiting for opening time. Talking about one's feelings was something she despised. Never could she show weakness, never could she say how she felt. The silence was now becoming agonising.

"...Well, whatever," he said, understandingly. "Is there anything else?"

"Of course," she grinned, pleased to change the subject. "I want everything you have on his wife and children too." She glanced across at her half-written mission report. Operation Orion. She'd not touched it since the journey from Ionar 12 to Durrith. And so much had happened...

"Will do," he said, disconnecting. Immediately another call came through.

"*Satiah*, long time no speak," Randal said, by way of greeting. He didn't even bother to wait for her reply. "I've been told by Reed that the focus of your investigation has shifted to the entrepreneur Sethryn Ring."

"It has," she allowed, guardedly.

"There's a seminar occurring soon, a meeting of sorts between him and several of his known associates. More than a few of these *are* known offenders or people with links to unsavoury occupations. There *are* more but we have no further details yet. I can only presume that he will be planning something," Randal went on.

Satiah had to agree.

"You want me to go, don't you?" she guessed.

"It's technically Reed's investigation now so my authority over you is limited. I just wanted you to know what I think," he stated, seriously. Tactically it was sensible, maybe even crucial. Even if it wasn't her, someone would have to go or at least have ears there. His tone lowered as he gave her the final instruction, the one she had sort of expected.

"I give you full authority to use whatever means you deem necessary, Satiah... *regardless* of Reed... *regardless* of fallout... *you have my backing*." That was his way of telling her that he, at last, trusted her.

"Send me the details and I will take it from there," she replied, tense. "And thank you."

"Good luck," he said, ending his transmission.

She adjusted her pistol noisily, slammed it into her holster and turned in her chair to face Kelvin. His red eyes focussed on her brown ones. Before she could do anything else an urgent knocking on her cabin door occurred.

"Satiah, it's Ruby!" called Ruby, awkwardly. "Ash and Reed are at it again; can you play the role of peacekeeper? I don't have a gun." Satiah rolled her eyes and elicited a tiny growl of frustration.

"*Fine.*"

***

Everything sounded different underwater. Distorted, far away and haunting to the ears. Only the screaming of the lungs seemed audible to the mind despite never making a sound. Sethryn broke the surface, inhaling deeply as he did. He swam strongly forwards from one side of the pool to the other with minimal splashing. In an odd way it felt to him vaguely like pacing up and down inside a prison cell. Back and forth endlessly, nowhere to go, possessed only by a burning purpose that prevented stillness. Lilith, his wife, was lounging on a sofa, overlooking the pool. She was browsing through a clothing hologram. He looked around and noticed that two men had entered since he had last looked. Finch, his new head of security, was one of them. Sethryn rose to his feet and began to wade out of the pool towards them. They in turn advanced towards him.

"Is everything ready for tonight?" Sethryn asked, confidently. Regular updates reached him all the time, as if somehow constantly telling him how things were progressing actually helped. He never read them. He considered updates a wasteful exercise as his only real interest was in the outcome. The result was all that mattered. How it was reached or other matters were what he considered beyond relevance to him. There were always the costs, of course, but when you were as rich as Sethryn Ring, even those rarely bothered him. For, like most of the super wealthy, he understood that once you had the money, getting more was almost effortless.

"It is but..." Finch began, seriously. He had... *reservations*.

"Why is there always *a but* with you?" Sethryn snapped, irritably. Finch always appeared ludicrously cautious to the point of paranoia, Sethryn put this down to the criminal mentality.

"I still think we should call the whole thing off," Finch stated. He was not reacting out of fear. For Finch, it was just not sensible.

After the destruction of the Orion facility, Finch had been

reminded that *people* knew their business. *Dangerous* people. He couldn't know if any had escaped like he had but years of mistrustful thinking told him to just assume that they had. Sethryn, however, didn't seem in the least bothered by such possibilities. The only thing he cared about was money. Normally this was one of the qualities that Finch appreciated but now... his survival instincts were telling him that this was not a good time. All right, there was never a good time for this kind of thing, it was true. But he thought they should *lie low* and wait for at least a few months. His gut felt that way and his mind always agreed with his gut's instincts.

"We know that someone, somewhere is trying to get at us," he concluded.

"You said yourself, every space station orbiting that rock was blasted into oblivion and that no one aboard any of them would have survived," Sethryn reminded him. It was factual, he had said that back when he was trying to make things sound better for Sethryn. But he had no way of knowing if everyone had been on the stations when they blew.

At the time he'd been trying to avoid making Sethryn angry... he seemed to become increasingly unstable when angry. Erratic. Unpredictable, even murderous. His predecessor had found that out the hard way when he'd refused to drop his scruples and had ended up becoming just another specimen in the Orion facility. Now though, Finch was regretting not telling him everything. He knew about Lara and the death of Sam, naturally, but... *the others* had been a detail he'd failed to give.

At first he'd almost talked himself into believing that they too had died in the explosion. But no... Lara had been weak and compassionate. A crusader for justice who'd been trying to make a martyr of herself, she had never been a real threat. The other two were of a very different mentality... a mentality that spoke of a casual indifference to suffering. Their own or other people's. He still didn't know who they were, never mind who they worked for. That alone unsettled him, he liked to know who he was dealing with and everything about them. His position normally allowed him to bypass the usual no-questions-asked policies that many in their business employed. The low creepy chuckle of the woman, still deeply engrained in his memory, never failed to make him shudder. And her eyes... the eyes of a born killer. Worse... a huntress and a predator. *Go and die* had been her only words to them. He faced Sethryn, the buffoon, in front of him again.

"I did," Finch agreed, tersely. "*Nevertheless* I maintain we should exercise restraint. Perhaps the infiltration was organised directly by one of *your* rivals. One of them that will be present here tonight... *They will want to steal it from you.*"

"Agreed, which is why I'm paying *you* to keep it and me safe," Sethryn argued, levelly. "When I hired you, your previous employer told me that you think of everything. She *didn't* tell me that you think too much. *You're paranoid.* Everything will go as planned."

"...As you say," Finch stated, in defeat. Sethryn did have a point. From the start, they all knew how risky this scheme was. And several hundred people had paid the price. The prize was now due... as was the debt *in theory*. Sam's death had been unfortunate. If, for whatever reason, there was a problem with the weapon, they now had to find someone new to fix it. It was guarded night and day by androids because only androids could be exposed to the KZ15 without dying.

"How much will you sell it for?" Finch asked, genuinely curious. Sethryn hadn't actually decided yet but he'd made up his mind that he didn't want to let it go for anything less than three billion Essps. It would be a bidding war and in this case it was hard to predict how high anyone would be prepared to go, yet he was optimistic. Why wouldn't he be? He had what everyone wanted and stood to profit no matter who won. What did concern him, however...

"Have you installed *the insurance?*" Sethryn asked, quietly. Insurance was a euphemism. Sethryn, despite not caring *who* would win the bidding war, was prudent enough to ensure that the weapon could never be used against him. So, he had ordered the installation of an explosive charge within the weapon itself so that, if he felt threatened, he could destroy it. Finch had been the one who had thought up the idea of a bomb. The risk would be the discovery and removal of the explosive but he had hidden it well.

"It's done," Finch told him. Finch had disguised the device as a secondary safety valve. Sethryn seemed visibly relieved.

"Excellent," he smiled, in the exact same way villains had done since time immemorial. "It would be ironic to supply your own murderer with his weapon." Finch had to concur with that much.

"Who is coming?" asked Finch, seriously. Running the security for the evening, Finch had been asking for weeks.

"Moly Wiles, Victor, Tonqui and... *Ro Tammer,*" he smiled, a devious gleam in his eyes. In that list was a fellow business man, a pirate gang leader and *a boast*! He was proud of himself for knowing these people of wealth and substance.

"*The leader of the Colonial Federation?*" confirmed Finch, unable to hide his astonishment.

"Word reached my ears that she is struggling to maintain her leadership and... with this weapon, she could do it... if she can find the Essps," Sethryn grinned, in apparent triumph. "There will be a few others no doubt, a few that have heard something and want to learn more. I will refuse none of them..." Finch knew that if anyone would try to take the weapon by force either during or after the auction, it would be Ro Tammer.

"As five million Essps is the entry fee, they will have to be rich to even get in... I will check everyone for weapons or surveillance equipment personally," Finch told him. "And the guards will also be restricted in what they can carry... just in case *any of them* chose to betray us." That last part actually impressed Sethryn, he always expected a betrayal but he often forgot about the people supposedly working for him. With Finch backing him up, it meant he could concentrate fully on those in front of him.

"Naturally we will not be holding the auction here," Sethryn stated. Finch, who had already arranged this, let the comment pass - but would not forget it. "Is the location on Vugarna Four ready?"

"The Palace of Glass is up to standard," Finch replied. It was. He had personally checked it three times. It was a truly unique facility. Previously a solar power plant, it had become a Galaxy class executive hotel of some repute before being bought by Sethryn a few years previously. At first he had wanted it to be his third home but its location was not ideal despite its state-of-the-art facilities.

It was out a fair way into neutral space, between the Coalition boundary and that of the Nebular Union. Its position there had been deliberate as it meant elite guests from any one of the three superpowers could visit without the multiple security checks. It was also where he was storing the weapon… in orbit around Vugarna Four… where his guests could see it but not touch it. The three men stopped and fell silent as Lilith wandered by.

"Darling," she addressed Sethryn. Her voice had a grating, lilting quality that could set one's teeth on edge when she let loose one of her shrieks of laughter. "What are you doing? You *know* we have guests for lunch today! The Mawlells! Do you never listen?"

"I hadn't forgotten, cuckookins," he smiled, pleasantly. "I'm on my way to change right now. Finch and I were merely discussing a business deal." Lilith turned up her nose, as if such a topic of discussion was beneath her.

"Ten minutes," she stated, crossing her thin arms disapprovingly. For one moment Finch thought she was going to start tapping her foot or something. He'd never understood why Sethryn and Lilith were even together as the only thing they had in common was their mutual love of luxury. When he'd first met her he'd almost dismissed her as a snobbish airhead but there was something about her that worried him. The way she would openly question him about anything and everything. She seemed increasingly capable of seeing through his evasions.

"Feel free to show them around," Sethryn smiled, still outwardly pleasant despite the frustration Finch knew he had to be feeling. Lilith smiled but her body posture remained the same.

"Don't be too long, darling," she said, her tone unwavering. He nodded courteously and motioned to Finch and the other guard to follow him. Lilith began to march away in the opposite direction but as they exited, she turned to watch. Her eyes were narrow, crafty and one eyebrow was slightly raised. Finch saw this curious display out of the corner of his eye. What was she thinking?

***

Raised voices meant that Ruby was right and the argument had once again escalated. Satiah was getting sick of this.

"How can we work together if you constantly hide things from me?" demanded Reed, fury in his tone.

"Like you would have done anything different," Ash retorted, angrily. Their argument had reverted back to their usual one about who could trust who. The Silver Sphere, or rather lack of Silver Sphere, had obviously kicked it off again. Despite no one really knowing what it was, it was causing a major argument. As immortal technology, Ash had wanted to know all about it after Ruby made the mistake of telling him. Reed though, as usual, refused to tell him anything.

Satiah burst into the control room, Ruby on her heels. She smiled chillingly, recognising the words but maintaining a poker face. Time to remove the velvet glove from the iron fist and maybe force them to eat it a few times.

"It's time," Satiah said, a firmness in her tone. "Time *this* ended." There was a pregnant pause as everyone tried to understand exactly what she was referring to. Ruby shuffled nervously and got a look from Ash. He guessed she'd brought Satiah in to interfere.

"And by this you of course *mean...*?" Reed asked, still impatient. "Could you elucidate further?"

"I have some information, data that gives us our next move. If you and Ash intend to be part of it I suggest you listen. *Ruby*?" Satiah asked, turning to the younger woman. She nodded, expecting to be told to get lost. "Fetch Carlos and Deva, I have a job for them," she instructed, her tone grim. Ruby, relieved, fled for the door. Satiah sighed as she reached the table and stood between Reed and Ash. She placed her gun onto the table, then leaned forward onto her fists as if forced down by some great burden. Her voice became low and menacing.

"I *also* suggest we wait until this is over before we start fighting *each other*," she advocated, in a tone that broke no argument. She'd become very exasperated about Ash and Reed recently. Their constant sniping and wrangling. She secretly had indulged in a fantasy where she tied them both to chairs and electrocuted them whenever they spoke. This had presented a good deal of escapism and a small amount of satisfaction to her.

They both remained silent. Neither had a shred of emotion on their faces, though. Ruby returned with the teenagers in tow.

"Now there are two things we need to discuss. And Ash, when I say *discuss*, I mean you and Ruby had no say in this whatsoever. I would appreciate it if you *didn't* interrupt. The first is the next step and the second is the mission report. I will begin with the next step," Satiah stated, her tone commanding.

Eager, Carlos and Deva sat next to each other, both sets of eyes never leaving Satiah. Despite her loathing for the young and their boundless enthusiasm, Satiah was glad of their unquestioning obedience. Unlike their elders and *supposed* betters they at least knew when to shut up and listen!

"The weapon *exists* and has enough KZ15 to be used at least once. Now that it has been built it remains hidden but it is for sale. I have been informed that Sethryn Ring intends to hold an auction, the purpose gives us our reaction," Satiah explained, relaying Randal's tip-off. Carlos nodded, remembering one of the first lessons she'd ever taught him. *Objective dictates action* just as *purpose dictates reaction*. Satiah had said it to him time and again and despite this he understood that it was more than necessity. It was a stable foundation of principle that could support many others. The target was taking the action, in doing so he gave them theirs too. The reaction.

"*Well, well,*" murmured Reed, deep in thought. Satiah glanced around. For once they were all listening and not arguing.

"There will be a meeting tomorrow in which the deal will be discussed in detail and..." She paused, with significance. "Carlos and Deva, I want you to be at that meeting."

Their faces were a picture. A mixture of emotions. Excitement, fear, and pleasure at being trusted and chosen. In secret Carlos had guessed this was coming but it was still a shock to hear the words. This was big in two main ways. First it meant that at last Satiah was investing real trust in him and also it demonstrated that she felt he was ready to step out into the dark on his own. He felt a surge of pride inside but fought to ignore it and concentrate on the job. "Naturally you will not be going there as yourself but as a pair of mercenaries who have an interest in buying the weapon. I will go into that more later with you *personally*," Satiah went on.

"You're sending *them*?" Ash asked, incredulity in his tone. Satiah almost flinched as she controlled her rage at the interruption, her fingers aching to snatch her pistol and fire a round or two into something or someone. What had she just *specifically* said? Reed stepped in.

"She cannot go *herself* as her face may be known to them and no one trusts you enough to go instead," Reed stated, smugly. "Besides, I have *every* confidence that Carlos and Deva can manage." Ash went to say something to that but a stern look from Satiah prevented him. He crossed his arms and made a show of very deliberately restraining himself. Ruby also gave him a look that implored him to remain quiet. There was absolutely no need to rock the boat now. No point in making things difficult. He had to trust in the humans getting it done by themselves.

To their credit, the teenagers, despite the slight against them, remained quiet, although Satiah suspected they were now holding hands under the table. She knew they would understand the gesture on her part to them.

"As Reed says, *I* may be known to them," Satiah continued, having a sip of water. Kelvin took the glass from her obligingly. "But I wanted to put you in the firing line, give you a real bite of undercover work. Myself and Kelvin will be acting as your backup and emergency evacuation team. You will most likely be searched but all you have to do is provide a believable deposit and listen carefully to anything about the weapon."

"I also have Captain Berry and his squad from Division Sixteen standing by should you need any additional assistance," Reed added, very politely and very quietly.

"Your job will be twofold," Satiah stated, to Carlos and Deva. "*First*, place a bid in for the weapon and operate as mercenaries would, I have your background histories prepared for you. *Second*, find out all you can about the weapon itself and all those out to buy it. I'm looking for technical data that may expose a weakness in its design. Or something that can counter its effect."

Carlos and Deva nodded in unison, their eyes gleaming with intense concentration born of devotion to duty..

"Naturally I would like you to embellish your roles with whatever personality traits you like but remember not to overdo it. And when you meet anyone, never forget that this could be your *first time* meeting them. You *don't know* their names, or anything about them. Too many people have died through forgetting to act as though they are strangers meeting for the first time," Satiah instructed. Again the nods of silent compliance. "I'm sure mercenaries must court one another from time to time so do not be afraid to inject a little sexual chemistry into your act, it's called the mirror technique. When your character's traits reflect your own. It makes acting a lot easier when the person you are playing is a lot like you. Also it can be used as a distraction at important times." She didn't add that injecting *that* would not be hard for *them*.

The pair were young and did look it, Deva especially but with the right disguise that wouldn't be a problem. Their main problem would be deflecting any suspicion. Assuming they made it in, she had a fair assurance that they could hold their own. It would test them, certainly, which of course was partly the idea. Reed gave her a meaningful look. He was pleased so far but he wanted to know more. Explicitly, he wished to focus in on her role. This was where it got complicated as Satiah wasn't sure what she was going to do. Of course she would break in and try to uncover all the technical information she could along with information relating to other potential buyers. There would also be the task of protecting Carlos and Deva but... Satiah knew there would be much more for her to worry about.

"Once in, Kelvin and I will provide an easy escape option for you and I will do my best to record as much of the proceedings as possible," she explained. "Also if the weapon's location becomes apparent, I will destroy it."

"The weapon *won't be on Earth*," Reed stated, with conviction. "What if there was an accident? There are too many people and too much chance of accidental exposure. The risks would be too great."

"Then we will find out where it is and destroy it," Satiah amended, swiftly.

"Assuming you find and successfully destroy it. Then comes the question about what to do with Mr Ring and all the others," Reed went on. "They may somehow gain the ability to restart the process in some way."

"All I can do is destroy it as quickly as possible," Satiah shrugged. She knew he was right and that was a danger but there was little she could do to counter it. Sethryn would no doubt try to keep the design secret, if for nothing else than to protect himself, but that didn't mean someone else couldn't find out.

"Now, the second matter, *Reed*?" she asked, nodding to him with significance. He rose and they went outside into the corridor.

"What do you think about the report?" she asked, without waiting. Not being able to finish something she had started always bothered her and this was important. It was certainly important to Randal. Satiah often found bureaucracy and the associated documentation unthinkably boring but she recognised it had a purpose.

"It's going to be one of those where we have to be as careful about what we don't say as what we do." They both grinned at the mildly nonsensical sentence even though they both knew it was true.

"I have had a look at what you've created so far and I have to say I was impressed. Operation Orion, very poetic," Reed stated, not being serious. She raised a piqued eyebrow. "The details are all about as good as we're going to get I think, naturally it is not complete yet."

"I'm going to see Randal shortly, I will tell him we are in the process of organising the report but that will not hold him for long," Satiah stated, in complete honesty.

"Well, sometimes you just have to tell the truth," Reed said, looking into the middle-distance briefly. "It's *really* not ready for him to see it, so I would just tell him so. And I think you know as well as I do what the full truth would lead to." He gave her a look that was almost sharp, almost accusatory. Satiah made eye contact and wondered for a moment if he knew about Vourne. No, that wasn't possible, how could he know?

"...*Yes*," Satiah stated, leaving it at that. An overly elaborate lie wouldn't help anyone... not in either case.

"And we cannot finish it until it is over," Reed went on, seeming to let it go too. "Until that weapon is destroyed, *along with any methods of rebuilding it*, the mission continues."

"Agreed," she said. There was nothing else she could say to that.

***

Wester's eyes narrowed. They were there.

"Maintain radio silence and cloaking," he ordered, his voice low. The low hum of the command deck was oddly soothing and matched his tone almost exactly. There was no chance anyone could hear him outside of his ship, of course, but nevertheless… Jenjex touched her hat to him as she reached him and he nodded to her. She stepped in close and lowered her voice to a husky whisper.

"Sir, what will you do?" she asked, directly.

"For now… *nothing*," he replied, honestly. "Watch and wait." They both turned to regard the distant sight of Vugarna Four. An unremarkable place at first glance but home to the Glass Palace. It hung there in the mysterious silence of deep space. The distant sunlight revealed the Glass Palace as a tiny glimmer.

"I will order the usual battery of scans," she said, turning to go.

He stopped her, by holding out his hand. It was like a static electrical change detonated between them and their eyes instantly found each other. That awkward, tense pause happened again. How could he ever allow her to put herself in danger now? Not when he felt this way about her. Not when he loved her.

"…Will you join me for dinner tonight?" he asked, seriously. Her expression contorted into one of intense concentration. She was seeking the purpose or the meaning in his intention and he was sure she could see right through him.

"…Yes sir," she replied, a little uncertain.

"Sorry, carry on," he said, releasing her. Wester felt so close, he was wondering if he was starting to crack up. Just the sight of planet seemed to make him feel like death was standing right behind him. Captains Keane and Clarissa were nearby, each cloaked and each taking up a different position. Jenjex had already provided a report on the planet itself and the Glass Palace.

Its shields would be no match for three destroyers' converging firepower. At least they *shouldn't* be… Egill insisted that as the facility was now privately owned, it was likely that such data that they had would now be incorrect. There would likely have been upgrades, alterations and possibly replacements. Also Egill had highlighted that there seemed to be no reason to explain Ro Tammer's presence here in the first place. There was also an orbiting satellite that should not be there to take into account. It was impossible to work out what it was but it seemed too small to be any sort of habitation. Its orbit was regular, governed only by gravity and not by engines. There were no detectable life signs. There was a good deal of residual energy readings. Wester couldn't be sure as to what any of that meant, he had to assume they were part of the new defences. Perhaps an additional shield generator that was currently inactive? But the residual power level had been a lot higher than a shield generator would usually emit. Okay it could be faulty but...

Jenjex returned with a pocket projector, showing him the scan results.

"It looks like a tourist resort, sir," she explained, not bothering to hide her concern. She was worried that their intelligence was wrong. And indeed, they still had no idea *why* Ro Tammer would ever come here. Their source remained adamant, though, that this was where she was going to be. Wester knew not to remind her that appearances could be deceptive. Besides, according to the scans, she was right. Everything was on standby mode and nothing seemed to have changed for some time. Inside his heart, though, something told him that Ro Tammer would be there.

"Permission to take a shuttle and investigate more closely, sir?" she asked, eager to learn more. Wester would normally have agreed but that same something told him that staying hidden would serve them better. And he would never send *her*...

"Later," he allowed, a thoughtful expression on his face. "For now I want us to just wait and watch. I have no doubt that doing a shuttle run would reveal much useful information but... I don't want to chance disturbing anything yet." She nodded, understanding at once. She didn't seem to realise that he was protecting her against her wishes. She'd made it clear that regardless of their feelings, they had a duty to perform.

"You don't think she's arrived yet, do you?" she whispered, neglecting the sir. A token of their new intimacy.

"I don't think anyone has yet, the place looks and feels deserted," he concurred. "We have to trust that they have not yet arrived but are en route."

"But without knowing where they are coming from..." She trailed off. It was impossible to accurately predict when they would get there without more data.

"Do the usual, save as much power as possible," Wester

instructed. "In any case, as we are still lying low, this is as suitable a place to lurk as any."

"Clock?" she asked, touching her hat. Wester paused as he had begun to turn away.

"...Forty-eight hours," he said, after a moment's consideration. She nodded and spun on her heel to obey. Wester slowly wandered back to his cabin, deep in thought. Why was Ro Tammer, while in the middle of the biggest constitution crisis, taking the time to come all the way out here? It had to be important! Crucial, even? Egill had a few theories but speculation would not help them. He reached his room and sighed heavily as he sat down. He felt weary yet taut. Like a forgotten mine, all tired-looking but still ready to explode. He leaned back, forcing himself to relax. This was going to be a long forty-eight hours.

***

"Look, Tabre, I appreciate that but I'm out of options," Ro sighed, heavily. Tabre glowered silently and Alex concentrated hard on the space ahead of them as it whizzed by.

"Sethryn is putting the weapon up for auction and I'm going to buy it," she went on.

"I can still get it," Tabre insisted, levelly. "I *know* where it is." He didn't actually know but he was confident that Satiah did. And he would follow her.

"Even *I* know where it is going to be soon enough," Ro argued, starting to get intolerant. "*With this weapon I can solve all my problems at once*. I can *crush* Wester's rebellion; I can flatten the Coalition completely..." Alex went red and glanced across at Tabre. If there had been any doubts left about Ro Tammer's sanity in her mind, they'd just been blown away.

"You still do not know how it works," Tabre tried to explain.

"And neither do you!" she yelled, over him.

Tabre's voice became low and dangerous.

"Ro, what if you cannot outbid your competition?" he asked, reasonably. "What if the weapon is *not* all Sethryn says it is? What if...?" Tabre was really starting to regret his decision to inform her of the thing's existence.

"*Tabre!*" she cut in, her tone one of frustration. "Money will not be an issue, President Raykur has given me full access to the central banking system." Alex's eyes widened. Tabre didn't pause for long though he decided to end the quarrel.

"Outstanding," he said, pretending to be pleased. He forced a smile. "In *that* case I will continue to track it, should they try to switch it for a dud. A switch is always a backup plan if nothing else."

"Yes… and eliminate *anyone* who tries to outbid me or interfere with the transaction in any other way," she amended, as she disconnected.

A long silence ensued as Tabre sat there, his head in his hands. Alex stared at him, awaiting his prognosis. She'd never seen him look so… pressurised? She didn't know how he was feeling really but, despite initially hating him, she had begun to empathise. Okay, so he had been right about Ro Tammer being insane. She'd never doubt him again. After a few more moments he sat up with a swift exhalation and poured himself a large glass of Homely Deputy. He caught her watching then cordially offered Alex another glass. She accepted gratefully. Still not a word, as he took a deep swig and she sipped carefully. It was strong for her and she flushed even redder, coughed and gasped.

"Alex, this is a very problematic situation," Tabre stated, without looking at her. She nodded; the alcohol seemed to have burned her voice box away temporarily. She managed a soft growl in response.

"Can you guess how it will end?" he asked, eyeing her.

She shook her head, not daring to say anything. He looked angrier than anyone she'd ever seen before. She knew it wasn't aimed at her; indeed he had been very complimentary of her rescue and everything. Nonetheless she'd learned to fear his temper. It was rare that it ever showed but when it did, no one was safe.

"Badly," he stated, with a cold conviction. "Very, very badly." He downed the rest of his drink and poured another. The second one, though, he did not throw back like the first; he stared into it, as if studying an intelligence report.

"…I'm *sorry* I didn't believe you," she managed, at last getting her voice back. "About Ro, I mean."

"Not your fault, you were lied to," he replied, with a crooked grin. "*Funny, isn't it?* You know what most people, most people in all existence are looking for? Across all the cosmos and all species… you know what they all are looking for?"

She shook her head, wondering if he was cracking up as well as Ro.

"Truth," he told her, his voice quietening. "They *all* want answers of some sort." She nodded earnestly, wondering where he was going with this. He sighed and looked right into her eyes.

"You know what?" he growled, much more gently. "I forgot what my question was. We have the answers and no one wants to hear them. *Nothing matters really.*" Okay, she realised that he was brooding. Tabre, the master of hiding his emotions, was openly brooding in front of her. Why did it scare her even more? She found it terrifying, what was making him be like this? Someone who openly feared so little, unfazed by even death itself. Was it Satiah? She couldn't think of one word to say to him but she couldn't stand the silence either.

"I'm seriously considering pulling out," he admitted, waving his hand around. "This isn't the kind of job I enjoy."

"But… You're the best," she uttered, almost inaudibly. He shot her a wry smile.

"Right now I feel like a bird lost in a cyclone, like it's all starting to get out of control," he explained, with some obvious difficulty. Evidently he was not used to talking to anyone about his feelings. Alex, equally troubled by the conversation, reached across and squeezed his arm tentatively.

"Don't worry, I'm sure it will be okay," she chanced, although she clearly had to work on her acting skills. He glanced at her and then burst out laughing. She winced, a little hurt.

"*Alex*," he said, more normally. "You're going to have to sound a lot more convincing than that." He continued to laugh and Alex began to laugh as well. He wasn't mocking her, in an odd way her failed attempt to raise his spirits had cheered him up… ironically.

***

Earth, the planet in the centre of everything, or at least that was how the slogan had it. Geography would disagree strongly, as would Satiah but for different reasons. Culturally and politically it did dictate everything that went on in the Coalition, though, that was beyond dispute. The cityscape of structures which openly challenged the laws of physics were as much an attraction as they were a necessity. People have to live somewhere, right? Satiah preferred the view after nightfall. All the lights and colours had a strange, calming effect on her. Familiarity. Or, at least, they normally did. Last time she'd made this journey she'd been returning to Randal with the wordless mute from Jaylite Industries. This time, arriving in the twilight of early evening, there were more than enough lights to please her eyes. Annoyingly they reminded her of Carl.

"Phantom Satiah," came a familiar monotone, on the computer. She actually jumped in her seat, tensing instantly, despite expecting the traditional call.

"Reporting in," she replied, tying not to sound too weary.

"Hatch sixty-three," he replied, and cut off. Carlos eyed her and grinned. She glared across at him playfully.

"What?" she asked, expecting a joke.

"A little tense, aren't we?" he smiled, without any real sting in his tone. "Did you not finish our mission report?" He'd sent her his document several hours ago and clearly he wanted her opinion on it. He'd been a little too accurate, a little too truthful for her liking but she'd not worded her evaluation of his report yet in her mind. She forced herself to relax.

"I have been busy," she evaded, deftly. He chuckled but did not pursue her further.

Reed and Ash entered.

"Will Randal want to see all of us?" Reed asked, casually. Satiah found herself tensing up again. She had to make an effort to relax her hand's grip on the controls. Maybe she should have let Carlos bring them in after all.

"No," she replied, shortly. She didn't know if that was true but she didn't want Reed or Ash around when she interacted with Randal directly. Especially Ash as technically he shouldn't even be there!

They would just make things harder for her. Reed eyed Carlos who merely shrugged enigmatically. Satiah caught the exchange in her peripheral vision and felt a surge of pride in regard to Carlos. She'd done a good job, much better than she thought she would, of his training. He would be a worthy Phantom... if he survived the next part of the operation.

Bringing the ship into land, Satiah sighed as she stood and slipped into her grey Phantom cloak. She gave a nod to Kelvin to get him to follow her and began her exit. The last time she'd done this she'd been thinking about Vourne and whether Randal would guess at her involvement in the conspiracy. In retrospect, perhaps she had been paranoid. Now she had plenty of other things to worry about. So much to remember, not to mention. She didn't have to find his office this time, he was waiting for her. She pushed her hood back as she reached him.

"I want an update, I am aware you have little time," he said, curtly.

"We will be moving in tonight, infiltration that I myself will be coordinating. We will stake a claim on the weapon while trying to learn its current location and detailed technical plans. Once those have been determined, I will take it from there," Satiah outlined.

"You can handle it alone?" Randal asked, some doubt evident in his tone. It was a reasonable point and Satiah didn't take umbrage.

"I'm the backup, Carlos will be playing the part," she explained. This was it. The tricky part. What if Randal objected?

"You... think he's ready?" Randal asked, tentative.

"Absolutely," she answered, without hesitation. He nodded.

"Good," Randal said, leaving it at that. "Now we all know it is real, do you know when they intend to use it? Or *who* they intend to use it against?"

"Several of the buyers will have motivations other than selling it on. I was wondering if any of them had Neo-remnantist leanings," Satiah replied. He nodded.

"It's likely," he stated, with conviction. He was right. They reached the end of a maintenance walkway and watched as the robots washed down the ship's bodywork. A thin layer of steam rose into the air.

"This Division Sixteen thing, did you mean what you said?" Randal asked, making eye contact. Satiah found herself momentarily caught out. She'd not expected him to bring that up.

"They could be useful, I have found them to be useful and Reed seems pretty determined to integrate them but I would suggest you make it work like a pool where they are never working with the same people for too long," she said. Satiah, despite having no love for the circumstances, had devoted a lengthy duration to think about the merger. If Reed didn't back down, which seemed increasingly likely, then it would be very much down to the terms they could work out.

"Like the PLF," he noted, the edge of something in his tone. Acceptance? Reluctance? "I was thinking along those lines too. It's technically true that you can never have too many people. Not in this line of work in any case. Arguably they could be considered more trustworthy than the PLC due to their openly patriotic stances."

Satiah grunted, unconvinced. In her experience patriotism never equated to loyalty or even reliability. Indeed, in her mind, it was little different in many ways to an anarchist. Yet she was unwilling to argue the point either way, it made very little difference to her. She would work with, kill or ignore anyone, their background made little impression on her. Randal began talking again.

"I still haven't had a written update from you or Reed as to how things are going. I know I don't need it but others might," he said.

"We have been working on it," Satiah dismissed, awkwardly. "I do have some equipment I need for the next stage."

"Of course," he nodded, apparently deciding to let the matter drop. Satiah could get used to this; Randal was much easier to work with than Vourne had ever been.

"What are you going to do about your sister?" The question made her freeze in shock, only her hand was moving and it took an act of will to stop herself from pulling her gun on him. How did he know about that? Rainbow would never have told him! Outwardly Satiah gave no sign of this inner panic.

"What are you talking about?" she asked, her voice nonchalant.

"Satiah…" he sighed, a wry grin curving his lips. "As Phantom Leader I have access to almost any file ever written. When I took over I took the time to study the backgrounds of my remaining agents. You were just one of many but I reread it recently when I saw some news channel about her trial. As a Phantom you have the right to veto the trial and prevent your sister from going through any more. Apparently the lawyer in charge of her defence, Dohead Rens I think his name is, has run into difficulties of a legal nature... which is essentially the media's way of saying serious trouble," Randal explained. Satiah wasn't at all pleased that one of her most private matters was now common knowledge. She knew why he was talking to her about it though. He was concerned that the additional strain, if it could be perceived as a strain, might affect her ability to do her job. This was his way of covering his own arse.

"I'm not up to date with the trial's progression and I never believe anything I see or hear from the CNC," Satiah replied, a little defensively.

"Satiah please," he smiled, waving an apologetic hand at her. "Perhaps if there is something personal between you, you would prefer someone else to intervene?" The idea had never occurred to her that anyone else would halt the proceedings on her behalf.

"That's very considerate of you but I've not really decided yet," she admitted, almost cringing. He frowned as he stared at her. She knew how callous that sounded, as did he but they both knew it was a reflexive answer, not an honest one. He should not have surprised her but then how could that be avoided if he intended to bring it up?

"Does it affect your judgement?" he asked, outright. Clearly he was enjoying this conversation about as much as she was. She paused, giving it some real thought.

"...No," she stated, her voice bleak. He watched her eyes and face closely, trying to work her out. He understood that many of those who worked as Phantoms lacked in, what some might call, compassion. Her face remained unreadable but her eyes stayed challenging.

"Had to check," he said, shrugging.

"Who else knows about this?" Satiah asked, genuinely curious.

"Only me and you," he replied. He gave her a hurt look. "I wouldn't go around chatting about you to anyone, not if I wanted to live."

"Your discretion is appreciated," she shrugged, as if no harm had been done. If he'd checked her out, he might have discovered something about Vourne as well. Satiah was obsessive about covering her tracks but the idea that she had missed something was ever present. She supposed it was her own twisted version of a guilty conscience. Mensa didn't know the truth but she might still be implicated in Dasss' murder. She shook herself inwardly, this was nonsense. Ancient history as far as they were concerned now. She was the only one keeping it alive by constantly fretting over potential backlashes.

"I thought when you told me that you were allowing Carlos to do the undercover part that it was to shield yourself," he confessed, without shame. Now Satiah saw it how Randal did, she could see why he'd been wondering.

"Sometimes a coincidence is just a coincidence," she smiled, deftly. That last comment brought a cold smile to his face. They both shared a meaningful laugh. There was no such thing as happenstance. Too many years of cynical thinking and treachery had confirmed it. Betrayal and corruption were ever present like twin vultures on each shoulder supported by the chips. Their bloody talons clenching the rotten beef and their red eyes gazing vengefully down. Were there no tears in their gimlet eyes? Were they not as tired of the never-ending cycle as Satiah was?

"Good," he said. "Remember, the weapon must be destroyed along with all evidence of its invention. We don't need anyone else trying it."

"Sir," she nodded, crisp.

"And be careful," he warned, seriously. "I need you back to help with other things soon."

"I will interview the Jaylite Industries employee now, although it will be pointless, we're way past that stage now," Satiah went on. "I will probably release him." Randal nodded.

"We need every cell we can get."

***

Anarchy. That was what it was. Just mindless chaos. And Ro had been close to creating order and peace! Wester had ruined everything!

The navy was divided, the people were undecided and constantly trying to reorganise everything. President Raykur was showing signs that his condition was improving. She was running out of time and options. All she had wanted was order. Uniformity. Control! And it seemed that everyone was against her. Did they want to be ruled by the Coalition? Did they want to be constantly divided and unable to agree on anything? The weapon would give her the power to stop it all. She could control the Federation and prevent a civil war breaking out while also guarding them against the imperialistic Coalition. It wasn't how she had planned it or even how she had wanted it but it would have to suffice.

At last Sethryn answered the call. It pained her to have to negotiate with a Coalition business man/criminal in this fashion but she'd convinced herself that it was a necessary evil.

"Ah, Ro Tammer," he said, with false warmth and joviality in his tone. She could see straight through his act, not that he was trying hard to hide his true self from her. Her mind hardly registered the shiny outer coating and focussed intently on the monster within. "At last, I was wondering when I would hear from you."

"You must understand that I cannot possibly chance coming to Earth for the meeting later," she stated, getting straight to the point. She didn't bother with trivialities unless she felt she had to. Leaving aside how busy she was, she didn't wish to prolong any interaction with this man, however distant.

"Naturally," he nodded, taking it in stride. Had he expected this? She wondered.

"I will be present in audio form," she went on. "I assume this will be done anonymously?"

"Ah no, of course not," he chuckled, his voice sounding sinister. "Everyone present at the auction will have to be informed who else is there, it will affect their decisions. It is only fair to let them know *who* they are up against." She growled softly to herself, she'd thought this might happen but there was nothing she could do to effectively counter it. She was confident she could outbid anyone but she didn't want to bankrupt the Federation doing it. He failed to hear her growl because of his own put on jolly laugher.

"I don't see why fairness should come into it," she stated, her voice as clipped as it was menacing. Again more laughter of the same ilk was his immediate reaction.

"Of course *you* would say that," he quipped. Ro didn't know why but that jibe really stung her. She thought she was fair and reasonable. It was an accusation that many had flung at her over the years and somehow it never failed to hurt, it never failed to make her want to lash out. She contained it this time though.

"No one can outbid the whole Federation," she stated, genuinely believing that.

"*Really*?" he replied, sarcastically. "That military build-up you have been conducting must have been cheaper than it looked. Besides, who am I to deny anyone the chance of trying?" She knew the question was rhetorical but she answered anyway.

"*You're* running the auction, Mr Ring, *you decide everything*," she stated, inflexibly. She'd run out of patience.

"Indeed and therefore, knowing that that is so, you should respect my methods," he replied, thinking he'd won the argument.

Ro badly wanted to just pull out and refuse to deal with him again but she needed that weapon! Everything hinged on it. She toyed with the idea of using it on him when she acquired it, just to punish his impudence! She ached to wipe that smarmy, arrogant smile from his wretched face. It offended her, as did his cavalier attitude towards her! She was the leader in all but name of the Colonial Federation! He was merely an overgrown parasite by comparison. But he had something she desperately needed…

"Very well," she restricted herself to utter, playing along. Maybe Tabre would kill him for her.

"So we are agreed?" he clarified, still infuriatingly cheerful.

"Yes," she replied, through her teeth. Once she'd disconnected she placed another call to Tabre… Even though she wasn't going to be there that did not mean she couldn't be represented.

***

Quadlink Towers was a conformist structure in its own right, just like any other. Dark blue, shiny and cylindrical, it was situated among many titanic structures. Built less than one hundred years previously, it was a luxurious pad for the outrageously rich and powerful to play hard in. Each floor operated as a private function area for parties and meetings alike. Finch had been over the layout extensively. It was familiar territory in that he had held several events on the premises. Tonight's opening gambit would settle the matter of who took part in the real auction to be held in the Glass Palace on Vugarna Four. Nearly one hundred individuals had expressed interest and were going to descend on that place later to hear Sethryn's presentation.

The speech would not last long, maybe ten minutes. Then the real thing would start. The entry biddings and then the vying bidders would attempt to outpace one another. Financially this was playing right into Sethryn's hands but… Finch knew there would be trouble. He had a sixty-strong team working as security so he was confident that he had the numbers to take out everyone being as none of them would be armed. He'd checked every floor of the adjacent structure for any snipers. It was clean, as he had expected. He hadn't spotted the craft hovering approximately sixty miles above the towers. It lurked just below the Karman Line, like a silent bird of prey.

Cloaked, Satiah stared at the screen in front of her, displaying the roof of the towers. Originally she had planned to enter the building via the maintenance facility but had disregarded that. A detailed government plan of the establishment, laid out the two hundred and forty floors logically.

"There," Kelvin stated, in his usual monotone. Using his appendage he pointed to a hatch on the roof.

"Looks like part of the cooling vent system," she replied, eyeing it. "It's easily big enough for us. Did you get the stuff?" He held up the small bag of equipment. The only real difficulty would be getting in without anyone realising. She plotted the course through the ducts to the toilets. While it was clear that there was a vent there it didn't specify the exact size or location in the room. Satiah sighed. Nothing was easy.

"We have forty-nine minutes and twelve seconds before the meeting starts," Kelvin prompted. Satiah strapped the bag to her and then pulled the mask over her face. She hated freefalling but it was the easiest way to get on top of the building minus being detected. Kelvin would be going with her just in case. Memories of her last freefall besieged her momentarily but she shook them away. The pod began a swift descent and started to break up as it did around them. Satiah checked her things for the last time and then jumped out. Kelvin followed. Winds instantly buffeted her and her chest leapt painfully as the sensation of falling made her cringe. She flipped over a few times and then stabilised, facing the rapidly approaching buildings.

Her own breathing was very noisy in her mask and she tried to make out the countdown displayed on the device on her wrist. T minus four minutes. Wind continued to howl all around her, any unsecured fabric flapped madly. She tried to think only about the countdown. She hated falling. Twenty seconds. Twenty. She glanced quickly around, spied Kelvin, some way ahead of her. Ten seconds. Five. On zero she hit the switch. Tiny thrusters on her hands and knees fired into action, cutting her speed and making her change her posture. The system was used when any form of sail technology may betray your being there to anyone. This method was much more expensive but almost undetectable. The four thrusters, preprogrammed with her body weight and meteorological conditions instantly adjusted. Her descent slowed more and more.

She was less than a few hundred metres from the roof now. The thrusters were winding down, starting to increase her speed again. She unfastened her grapple gun and aimed. She couldn't see the hatch at all but she knew it had to be there. She fired. The cable struck the pinnacle of the nearest tower and she flew straight down, past it. She braced herself and almost cried out as she was yanked to a halt. She swung in against the flat metallic wall of the tower. Gripping the pistol with both hands she activated the pull and she began to rise slowly. She allowed it to drag up back up to the spire area. Kelvin was already there.

"The vent is here," he explained, pointing down. Using his magnets he had fixed himself to the side of the building so she could use him to climb on. She did.

From her boot she slid out a long silver cutting device.

"Anyone see us?" she asked, as she leaned forward to find the seal.

"No," he replied. She found the slightest of creases in the otherwise sheet smooth metal of the room and probed it with the device. There was no give… clearly it was only opened by the inside automatics. She withdrew the prong and pulled out a square module from her pocket. She held it over the seal and began to move it along as she scanned for anything useful.

"Thirty-nine minutes, fifty-nine seconds…" Kelvin began, reminding her yet again when the meeting was due to start.

"*I know!*" she hissed, irritated.

A bleep sounded. "*J* config system," she pondered, aloud. "Interesting." Normally that kind of lock was used for safes, not cooling vents. "We are quite sure this is a cooling system we are breaking into?" she asked.

"We reviewed the same design," he answered, his red eyes watching her.

"…In other news, it isn't alarmed," she went on. She pulled a strained face as she tried to force another device into the lock. A loud click occurred and she froze.

"Got it," she said, wondering if any backdrafts might occur when she opened it. She yanked. The hatch, surprisingly thin and light, rose as she pulled and a residue of pale gas whooshed out past them and away.

"We're in."

***

Carlos and Deva made their way up the steps towards the entrance of Quadlink Towers with several others. Both were armed with rifles and both wore typical mercenary garb. Deva had dyed her black hair golden and had an ill-fitting beret on her head. Her brown eyes peered out from under it. Carlos wore a hip-cape and had a carefully prepared false moustache. Both had taken the time to ensure their costumes were riddled with authentic-looking damage marks. Burns, rips, and wear. No one would believe that two mercs would have completely fresh clothes for anything. They were trying to make it obvious that they were forcing themselves to remain calm, as a mercenary would in such an environment. Ironically it was how they needed to work anyway.

"*That* does not suit you," Deva stated, for the sixth time. She didn't like facial hair and had made that abundantly clear on plenty of occasions. He was just glad it didn't chafe.

"Mercs aren't known for their style," he replied, eyeing the security at the door. "Remember to be extremely bothered when they ask you to hand over your rifle."

"Like so much of my act tonight, that will not be hard to fake," she muttered. The swell of people increased when they came to the bottleneck that was the entrance. Security was scanning everyone and a large pile of guns, blades and other assorted personal weaponry lay nearby. Carlos glanced upwards into the sky briefly. He knew Satiah was up there even though he knew he probably wouldn't be able to see her.

"Remember what Reed said," Carlos joked, running his hand up her back. They both looked at one another.

"If you can fake sincerity, you can fake anything," they mumbled, in unison. They reached the first guard. In one hand he held a remote scanner and in the other he was holding a security baton.

"Put those rifles on the pile and anything else that may be a weapon, be turned into a weapon or could in theory be used as a weapon," he drawled, at them.

"I prefer to keep my rifle within reach," Deva stated, her tone obstinate. Carlos too, adopted the posture of unwillingness. The guard just sighed and rolled his eyes. He'd heard that so many times already it didn't even faze him anymore.

"Then I cannot permit your entry," he replied, equally obstinate. "And you will have wasted your entry fee." Deva glanced at Carlos as if seeking his permission. He gave a reluctant shrug and then a nod. With unnecessary volume she dumped her rifle heavily onto the rickety pile. She stooped, pulled a knife from the inside of her right boot and chucked that onto the pile as well. Lastly, she removed a thin whip-like wire from around her middle and surrendered that too. She then put her hands on her hips, a sulky expression on her face.

"Thank you," the guard said, as he ran the scanner over her body. He was also checking for any technology used for recording or transmitting, not just weapons. A gentle bleep sounded as the results made themselves known.

"You're clean," the guard grunted. Then he faced Carlos. "Same goes for you, pal." Without a word, as Deva entered the building, Carlos disarmed himself. Deva entered a foyer or lobby type of area, Deva wasn't sure what the difference was exactly, where everyone else still milled around. She concentrated on the other people, seeking potential threats or agents of Sethryn Ring. Carlos found her quickly. The guard had not scanned the ring on his finger which was fortunate because that was where the homing device Satiah had provided was concealed.

"Did you clock the balcony?" he asked, softly. She hadn't and quickly noticed a lone figure overseeing the area. At first she wondered if it was Satiah but quickly realised it was a man.

"I can't be sure at this distance but, working from her description, he looks a lot like the man who tried to interrogate Satiah on the Orion Observatory," he informed. Deva squinted without making it too obvious.

"Yes… it could be him," she agreed, levelly. "It makes sense that he would be here if he survived the station's destruction."

"*Refreshments!*" called a waitress, startling them both.

"Water please," Carlos requested, recovering quickly. Deva managed a smile and nodded to indicate she wanted some too. Her Colonial accent shouldn't be too much of a problem, nevertheless she didn't intend to talk too much. Carlos peered back at the entrance, still several people had yet to be allowed in.

"Ten minutes," he estimated, wondering if Satiah was already on the roof.

"I hope we are high up," Deva said, a bored expression plastered on her face. It had been a potential problem that Satiah herself had brought up. What if the meeting was to take place on the lower levels or even the basement? It wasn't unheard of.

Her plan had been to access the building from the roof rather than chancing the security below. But this would make it difficult for her to get close to Carlos should the meeting take place too far down. And regardless of where it was, she still had to somehow find *them*. She had Kelvin but even so, it was still a calculated risk.

"I wonder how much it will go for in the end, assuming it does get sold," Deva pondered aloud.

"Whatever it is, it won't be worth it," Carlos smiled, coldly. She sniggered.

"True." Carlos found this very different to how he was expecting. Being undercover he'd imagined it to be very tense and he'd be fighting the temptation to keep glancing over his shoulder. Instead he found he was more worried about Satiah than he was about himself.

Not every look was significant. When someone openly stared, it didn't mean you were exposed at all. In this scenario everyone was staring at everyone. This only worked to Carlos's advantage. Finally, the last of the people were allowed in and the entrance closed.

"Please can all guests make their way to floor two hundred and eleven please," announced someone. Carlos glanced up, correctly deducing who it was that had given that instruction. The man on the balcony. A gradual process began as all eight lifts were utilised. The lifts were fast and spacious so despite the number of people, the move only took twenty minutes. Carlos and Deva pressed in close to each other as they were brought up in the lift.

"Sexual chemistry," she whispered, grinning.

"They need bigger lifts," Carlos growled back.

Floor two hundred and eleven had clearly originally been designed as an adaption of the open office variety. Desks, consoles, folders and documents were everywhere. Carlos found empty offices eerie. All silent and still after a day of swarm-like activity as if waiting for something. The chatter had become more hushed now as the crowd were led through this deserted office area. It was well lit even though the lights were out so there was no question of falling over anything. Also, the conversations that were occurring were now all about last-minute financial matters or negotiation techniques. Carlos could guess though, that hardly anyone here would be rich enough to even get a look in.

Reed had worked extensively on Carlos's financial background. For him to be placing that amount of money, it had to be plausible. So Reed had made him a highly successful criminal who, despite being wanted in several galaxies for various crimes, had recently stolen a fortune from an obscure tribe of primitives. That would go at least some way to explain how he could afford this kind of thing. And then of course there had been motive. What interest would he have in such a weapon? Well, leaving aside the obvious of either selling it or the technology it had, Reed had invented a story. A rival gang of pirates that Carlos was meant to be in a supposed blood-feud with. The idea being, that when Sethryn looked into his background, which he or someone working for him inevitably would, they would discover all this. Deva would be an unknown quantity, a mystery mercenary girl from Colonial space, someone out to make a quick Essp, or something like that.

There was a hall at the end, set out for a presentation and there, standing on the stage, all suited and booted, was Sethryn Ring.

"Come in, come in," he beamed professionally, at them all. Once they were all inside and seated, he began his act. Carlos noticed that though the guards remained by the doors, the doors remained open. Upon entry, Carlos had activated his homing device. It took several moments for everyone to be seated.

"My friends," Sethryn smiled, deviously. *"Today's* business is always about *driving up* efficiencies and profits while *pushing down* costs and reducing resources. We, all of us here, know all about today's business. I brought you here to talk about tomorrow. *Our tomorrow!"* He paused for effect. Despite what they were doing, Carlos and Deva both felt a yawn coming on. "Now I know that most of us here, working as we do with *such pressures and problems*, would want tomorrow to bring with it some solutions." He clasped his hands and nodded in that irritating body language business people adopted throughout all existence. The kind of exaggerated gesticulation and overemphasis of certain words as they spoke. He did it well.

Having followed the homing signal Carlos had activated, Satiah had made her way to the level everyone else was on. Luckily it had not been too far down. Kelvin waited upstairs, while Satiah followed the sounds of voices along the deserted office. Cloaked and hooded, she was a grey shadow among grey shadows. Easily eluding the guard's sight, she entered a small storage room to the left, a room with a wall that also acted as the wall of the hall. She attached her suppressor to the end of her pistol before setting the power to the lowest level. Carefully she burned a small hole in the wall at waist height. She could now hear everything Sethryn said. Pulling up a chair, Satiah settled herself down, crossed her legs and began to record everything. While recording she readjusted her pistol to kill mode and then just sat there listening.

"Beings! I have here a *solution* that you may wish to purchase," Sethryn announced. With a dramatic wave of his hand, Finch activated the holographic projector. Besides Sethryn, a representation of the weapon flickered into life. Several people leaned forward in their seats. As they did, Carlos glanced across the gap and saw the next figure along whom, like him, had not leaned forwards. Tabre was sat there... staring right at Carlos. Oblivious to this, Sethryn carried on talking.

"This instrument, originally financed by none other than Balan Orion himself, is a specialised weapon. I will go into the technical details in just a moment. First I have to tell you all that the weapon is not here, nor in this system. Rightfully it should not even exist. But thanks to one or two keen enthusiasts, it does." Deva couldn't help raising an eyebrow at that. Professor Sam, an enthusiast? That certainly would be one way of looking at it. Raving sociopath was another.

Carlos nudged her and she glanced over at him, he wasn't looking at her and she followed his gaze. She too saw Tabre.

"What do we do?" she whispered, maintaining a show of casualness.

"Nothing we can do, keep listening," Carlos replied, in a similar tone. Both teenagers stared rigidly forwards at the hologram. Tabre couldn't help but smile. If Carlos and Deva were there, that meant Satiah would be nearby. He had no interest in any of them though, at that moment. He was there only to stake Ro's claim to the weapon, nothing else. Naturally they would never believe that. That was why he smiled as he imagined what they must be theorising right at that instant. He readied himself mentally for a firefight. It was in none of their interests to start one but that didn't mean it wouldn't happen.

"Within a certain range of exposure, this device can completely prevent any sleep, effectively killing those exposed even for a moment. The longer they are exposed, the quicker they die. The best part of this is that the substance is completely new so it will have the benefit of not being easily detected. It has a large range, large enough to affect about ninety percent of the largest planet's surface. Now, *I'm* not going to give you *any ideas*," Sethryn went on, making a joke. A ripple of callous laughter went through the audience. Carlos felt sick inside, how could anyone joke about it like that? He was talking about murdering billions of people! He glanced across at Tabre. Tabre was not laughing either but he was facing Sethryn now rather than them.

"But with such a weapon you could extort a superpower," Sethryn continued. "Imagine the Essps they would pay you just to persuade you not to use it." Tabre raised his hand.

"A question?" Sethryn asked, rather pointlessly. A silence descended as Tabre stood slowly and adjusted his sleeves. He smiled broadly, a killer's grin. Carlos and Deva tensed. Satiah leaned a little closer to the circular opening in the wall.

"A thought occurred to me as you were explaining the possibilities. *Why are you selling it?*" Tabre asked. As he asked, he shrugged nonchalantly, as if he were discussing heavy traffic. He had done that for two reasons, the first was obvious to everyone. He was trying to imply there was something wrong with it and pointing it out to discourage others from trying to buy it. The second, far less obvious reason was to *say hello* to Satiah. To let her know he was there as part of their mind game. Even though Tabre was sure she was not in the room, he knew she had to be listening in from somewhere. It's what he would do. Satiah, upon hearing Tabre's voice, sat bolt upright, pistol already in her hand.

Sethryn had an answer prepared for that.

"Now that would be telling," he joked, again. Then he became more serious in attitude and demeanour. Again displaying the corporate playacting he used so well. "The truth is I don't need it but I do need the money it can get me. I don't have the time or inclination to start a war to make a profit for myself but I know for some of you... *well, it's different.* I never ask why, I only sell and buy." More cynical laughter. Tabre retook his seat, his face impassive. Carlos raised his hand and Deva's eyes widened.

"Another question?" Sethryn asked, still the very soul of cordiality. Carlos, as Tabre had done, waited for silence before he began. Deva was unsure where to look other than away. What did he think he was doing?

"This is a weapon," Carlos stated, grim. "And you're not

concerned at all that giving it away might put yourself in danger?" Now it was Finch's turn to tense. Tabre raised an eyebrow. Satiah was as surprised as Deva but saw immediately what he was doing.

"It's a *fair* question," Sethryn replied, taking it in stride. He had prepared for it on the off chance but he'd never expected anyone to ask him so publicly. "Naturally we are all familiar with the concept of betrayal. I'm confident no one here has anything against me." Carlos sat back down, inwardly amazed by his own action.

It had been spontaneous but he'd realised he had a chance to destabilise the enemy a little. If they could make Sethryn look over his own shoulder a bit it was all to the good.

"What was that about?" Deva growled, shocked. "We're supposed to be keeping a low profile here."

"Tell you later," he answered, quickly. Sethryn began his talk on the more technical aspects of the weapon and, for the first time, Carlos and Deva got a true understanding of the thing they had been hunting all this time. KZ15. The ratio of time exposure and numerous other things. How to use the weapon. It seemed that it was less like a bomb and more like a molecular weapon. Soon they also learned that despite his limited supply of KZ15, the weapon *could* be used time and again because the particles could be retrieved by the weapon after being used. Carlos couldn't be sure if that was the truth or just a selling strategy that Sethryn had employed to hide the drawback but he didn't want to take a chance on it.

In short, it reloaded itself, if you believed what you heard. It disbursed, waited and then reclaimed the KZ15 using specialised magnets. They had not known that KZ15 was magnetic. Again, no way to be sure if he was telling the truth. Question was, how could knowing that help them? After a few moments of various questions and deliberation... the choice came. In or out? Who wanted this thing and who didn't? About half the people decided, probably because they knew they couldn't afford it, to leave. And, with some guards escorting them out they left. Deva was watching Tabre, convinced he was going to move in on them, but Carlos was pretty confident that he wouldn't. There were many times he could have killed them already and he hadn't. Sethryn waited until the guards had returned and then told everyone that he had no intention of selling anyone anything without them seeing it first.

Those who remained would take part in the sale, but the actual auction would not be held here on Earth. It would be held in the Glass Palace. Away from prying eyes. Or at least that was the idea. Satiah's mind raced, like her heartbeat. Tabre would be there for Ro Tammer and there was no way that she could allow Ro to get her claws on it. But when it came down to the bidding... Carlos had Phantom Squad backing him but she wasn't sure that it could compete with the entire Federation financially. The weapon would have to be destroyed either before or during the auction. And they still had no idea where it was! Naturally they would be told soon but... She listened in again and realised there was someone rummaging around in the room next to hers on the other side. She rose silently, gently laid the chair on its side and then crouched in the corner, shrouding herself in the shadows.

A guard entered, glanced around in a cursory search before backing out again and heading away. Satiah returned and sat down again.

"I will send you all the details of where to go for the auction. They will be in code but you will find the correct way of deciphering it under your seats. Attach the device to your communications unit and it will translate it automatically. Naturally there will be time for frivolities at this exquisite resort," Sethryn was telling them all. Satiah glanced down at her pistol with a grim smile. Oh yes, there would be *frivolities* all right. En masse, everyone got up and began to head for the exit. Each was given a communicator; presumably that was how they were going to tell everyone where to go. Satiah couldn't decide if she should leave now or stay. Presumably she could learn more if she remained. She once again placed the chair on the floor and hid herself as everyone moved away.

Then last two to leave were Sethryn himself and Finch. She followed them cautiously as they paused to chat in one of the many aisles.

"I think that went well," Sethryn said, visibly relieved that the presentation was over. He was less worried about his performance than he was of possible assassination.

"There are more people interested than I thought there would be," allowed Finch, ever pessimistic. Satiah stood nearby, hidden from view by a vertical support beam.

"I think Ro wants to cut down her competition," Sethryn smirked.

"They all want to do that."

"She's going to personally be there at the Glass Palace," boasted Sethryn, showing off. Finch remained cold and unmoved.

"That merc guy almost guessed about our little insurance policy," Finch grumbled.

"*What?* He was just guessing and trying to knock me off balance. He was copying Ro's representative," Sethryn argued, dismissively. "Do you see menace in *everything?*"

"Yes," Finch answered, levelly. Satiah listening in intently. Insurance policy? What had they done? "If anyone of them learns…"

"They *won't!*" cried Sethryn, incredulous.

"Speaking of Ro's representative, I've seen him before," Finch cut in. He'd recognised Tabre from the Orion Observatory. And Tabre had recognised him. Finch knew instantly that this meant there was a change coming his way.

"*Tabre?*" Sethryn clarified, a little caught out by the change of subject.

"Is that his name?" Finch asked, rather pointlessly. Satiah listened in harder. Sethryn grunted to the affirmative as Finch leaned in close to talk more quietly.

"*He* was one of the infiltrators that we caught shortly before the destruction of the space station," Finch explained, shaken. "Sam believed he was one of those working with Lara." Sethryn, for once, was stunned into silence. Satiah held her breath. This could ruin everything!

"So… *they were all* working for Ro Tammer the entire time?" Sethryn concluded, still a little shell-shocked. He had been expecting betrayal from her of course but he never considered that she knew about the Orion Observatory and had presumably tried to steal the weapon once already.

"…It's a possibility," Finch confined himself to saying. He didn't add that he had never been convinced, as Sam had been, that the infiltrators had been working together at all. Tabre and the woman possibly as they were more like… Lara didn't fit in with them.

It had been the final confirmation to Finch that he had been right to assume the survival of those people after the destruction of the space station. Tabre was certainly alive and clearly still active. That probably meant Lara and the other one were also amid the living. So where were they now? And who the hell were they working for? Sethryn, like Sam, was quick to lump them all together but Finch had been living his life too long to be so quick to jump to a conclusion like that.

"Did Tabre have *anyone* with him tonight?" Finch asked, casually. "A woman perhaps?"

"I did see him talking with a few people," Sethryn replied, thinking back to the introductions. "What did they look like?"

"Average height, long red hair, brown eyes," Finch answered. Her image was indelibly in his mind after her strong resistance to the torture. Sethryn paused, trying to remember. Satiah knew instantly that Finch was describing her and realised that this might not be such a bad thing after all. It was no secret *to her* that Ro Tammer wanted the weapon even though Randal didn't know yet and she wasn't even sure that Ash knew. Reed knew, of course.

The idea that Finch and Sethryn would automatically think she and Tabre were *working together* amused her, as she knew it would amuse Tabre when he found out. It also meant she might be able to chance openly appearing in their environment so long as she stuck close to Tabre. It was a very dangerous move but bold too. It would really unsettle Tabre, she was sure, and that made her smile.

"No," Sethryn said at last, shaking his head. "Why?"

"I will review the security footage," Finch replied, thinking ahead. "I think that the woman from the station, the one who I thought may have died, is working with him. She may even be his partner and could be useful to put pressure on him if we need to."

Satiah almost laughed out loud at the thought. Tabre wanted to kill her himself, he'd never tried to hide that. She wasn't sure how he would react if someone else tried to kill her while he was there. Would he let it happen? Use it to discover more about her fighting skills? Or would he even kill them in case they deprived him of his... obsession? She couldn't really call it a vendetta. It was strange in that it was at once *completely personal* while also being *nothing to do with her.*

Contest perhaps was a better word. Tabre wanted to be the best to prove to everyone, and maybe even himself, that he was the best killer that lived. As long as Satiah lived he was challenged and he had to be the one to kill her to prove he was the best… therefore…

"You think Lara Clement and Tabre…" Sethryn began, a little confused.

"No, *not Lara*, the one with no name," Finch clarified, flustered. Sethryn made a noise of annoyance and Satiah again had to fight to contain her mirth. This was what she loved to hear! She loved to hear her targets rattled, confused and floundering in speculation and potentials. Trying so desperately to figure out what was going on. They were so close to the point of panic now. The point where they couldn't decide which shoulder to look over first. She yearned to burst from cover and see their faces as she gunned them down but… she couldn't. Not until she knew for sure where the weapon was and maybe not even then.

"This is *ridiculous*," Sethryn spat out. "None of this matters really. What *they* want to do with it, who *they* really are or who *they* are really working for… *I care about none of it!* Just think of *the money!*" Finch didn't react immediately; he was too deep in thought. "Activate the Glass Palace," Sethryn ordered, as he marched off.

Satiah stayed a seamless statue as Sethryn departed. Finch remained, standing there by himself, apparently cogitating the conversion. She listened intently, pondering herself. It was nearly five minutes before Finch finally sighed and pulled out his communicator.

"Activate," he mumbled, his tone conveying nothing. A noncommittal rumble, betraying no emotion. Then he too departed, leaving Satiah alone in the dark. She crept back to the little room she had used to observe the meeting from and returned to the seat. What was the Glass Palace? And what was this mystery insurance policy?

"Satiah?" Kelvin's voice came from her earpiece. He'd heard everything of course, as she had done.

"We wait until they all leave and then we slip out, join me here," she instructed, seriously. "Did Carlos and Deva make it out okay?" She'd heard nothing so she presumed that they had.

"They have reached the agreed upon neutral location and are awaiting instructions," he said, in his usual monotone.

"Good, tell them to return to Reed and give him their report while it's still fresh in their minds," she mused, standing and stretching. She turned and almost walked right into a surprised looking guard. He tried to pull his gun on her but she was faster. She intercepted his arm with her own, pushing away and broke his nose with her elbow. He cried out and fell back, blood dripping down his lips. She lashed out with a powerful high kick that sent him clattering to the floor. Lastly she finished him with an efficient double tap of her trigger, both shots to the head. Sighing in relief that he'd failed to alert anyone else, Satiah relaxed. She told Kelvin to hide the body when he got there.

She wandered into the conference area where Sethryn had given his presentation less than half an hour previously. There was little chance he would have left anything behind, especially with someone as cautious as Finch overseeing things, but it never hurt to check. She quickly found the crushed data cube that had probably been the one that Sethryn had used. He would have removed it from the reader and then most likely stepped on it to destroy it. She picked it up and pocketed it. Maybe Rainbow and his *techno buddies* could make something with it. Kelvin entered silently behind her as she continued to search. The body was concealed. Discarded half-finished drinks, the odd article of clothing left behind and absolutely nothing of any use to her!

She stood still, feeling a distant deep vibration run through the floor as a large ship passed underneath the building. The twilight had faded completely now into the night. She stared out of a viewport at the city. Kelvin joined her.

"Search your memory for anything called the Glass Palace," she instructed, her voice soft and thoughtful. He did.

"One hundred and seven findings, how would you like them listed?" he asked, his red eyes focussing on her.

"I have no preference," she said, her voice remaining the same. Her eyes never left the city. Her mind was thinking about her sister. She could not see the place where the trial was being held, nor could she remember exactly where her sister lived but... just being on the same planet suddenly jolted her. She'd told Randal it didn't bother her, well didn't affect her ability to do her job. Did it?

Two weeks ago it wouldn't have but she realised she had changed. Kelvin began talking but she wasn't listening. Her mind was replaying that horrible day when she was still a child... the day her own mother tried to murder her. The day her sister had saved her life by killing their insane mother. The blood... so much blood. It had been a hot day, a real scorcher. Sweat made everything slippery. More than fifty times, the planet had circled the sun since that day and still the pain remained. Drowned, burned, crushed and ignored but still it clung to her soul. Too young to understand insanity, her mother's eyes burned into hers with what a child could only understand as anger. The knife coming at her, straight at her face.

A lone tear braved the journey down Satiah's cheek. She let it. Kelvin stopped talking.

"Why couldn't I kill her, Kelvin?" she whispered. "If I had, everything would be correct."

"You were a child and a child never expects to be attacked by a parent," Kelvin stated.

"So was my sister..." Satiah reminded him.

"She was older," he said.

"I am stronger than she could ever be..." she trailed off.

That moment of weakness, *that one time she had failed to react*, to which the only living witness was now going to possibly lose her freedom. All because Satiah couldn't let go of the shame. Shame was normally a consequence of doing something bad, she had it the opposite way around. Shame for failing to do something. A failure to kill someone.

"It's not about strength," Kelvin answered, in his usual monotone. "It's about forgiveness. It will benefit your mental health if you mediate. In a way it would be akin to making you even at last." She saw his reasoning of course. Her sister had saved Satiah's life and now Satiah could secure her freedom... and they would be even.

She'd not seen her sister for so long that... she could hardly remember what she even looked like. They had had different fathers and therefore didn't look as alike as some sisters did. Technically they were only half-sisters. But until that day... they had been best friends. She could remember playing hide and seek. *It was all gone.* Could

Satiah forgive her for shaming her? Two weeks ago she would have never even considered it. Now... She groaned out loud. This was worse than she feared; she'd started to develop a conscience. She'd have to safeguard against that in the future. She shook herself, trying to bury herself back into her mission.

"It's time we returned," she announced, her voice both bleak and blunt.

***

Carlos nudged Deva as the coordinates arrived. Probably sent out in some complicated and secretive version of a blanket message, the coordinates to the Glass Palace had been disseminated. The device that Sethryn had provided everyone with *was* a code breaker and *did* indeed translate codes correctly but that wasn't *all* it did. Suspicious, Carlos had scanned the instrument thoroughly and had discovered it had another more sinister purpose. It concealed a homing beacon. Sethryn obviously wanted to keep a track of whoever was coming for their entire journey. Presumably if any of them deviated from a straight route to the destination he would be instantly aware and would be expecting treachery. Smart, the kind of thing Carlos realised that he would have done. He had informed Satiah who had been impressed with his find although strangely preoccupied.

Deva patted Satiah's shoulder. She was busy at a mobile terminal and she turned to see in response.

"That must be it," Satiah growled, pointing to the controls of the ship. "Kelvin, cross reference that with the results of your databank search."

"Vugarna Four, item two," Kelvin stated and passed a report to Satiah. Everyone crowded around as she inserted the data cube. They needed all the information they could get about this remote place.

"Get Randal," Satiah said, to Reed. His hands flew across the controls with a practised ease.

"Channel three," Reed stated, alert and excited.

"Anything from that cube I found?" Satiah asked, while she waited the report to load fully.

"You hit a gold seam, Satiah," Randal answered. He sounded pleased. Satiah didn't think there was any chance of data recovery but obviously she had been wrong. Rainbow was a genius! It just went to show that it was a mistake to throw anything away without making sure it was rendered completely useless beforehand. Everyone forgot the rubbish... everyone except her. They could hear talking in the background between Randal's words.

"*Everything* is on here, the designs and everything," Randal told them.

Carlos and Deva whooped and slapped each other's palms together in celebration. Reed took a deep and rewarding swig of fruit beer. Satiah allowed herself a small smile of pleasure before becoming serious again.

"Based on the audio I sent you: is everything Sethryn *said* correct and accurate? *Does it reload itself?*" she asked, levelly. A short conversation that was not intelligible occurred before Randal came back to her. Glances were exchanged.

"If the information on here *is genuine*, then yes, *everything he said is true*," Randal answered, grimly.

All joy faded.

"We are prepared to leave now," Satiah said, giving Kelvin the nod. "Vugarna Four is our destination. The Glass Palace, I need everything you have on it *and the planet*, Randal!" She glanced over at Reed who held up one finger to her. "We *should* get there in a day," she added, remembering to give herself a variable. More conversation in the background as Randal conferred. A low hum began as the engines powered up. Dutifully silent, Ash and Ruby sat together, listening in. Ruby was visibly animated and completely enthralled. Ash looked wary but controlled. Deva did a safety check before raising her eyebrows expectantly at Satiah.

"Get us in orbit," murmured Satiah, to her. Deva nodded and they quickly accelerated away.

"*Here we go*," Randal stated. "Neutral space, between the Coalition frontier and that of the Nebular Union maybe three hours to the boundary of the nearest one..."

"Which is?" Satiah asked, abruptly. A short delay.

"Federation," he answered. Carlos swore and Deva grinned at him. Satiah rolled her eyes, *it would be wouldn't it?*

"Go on."

"Its position there was intentional because it once catered to customers from any of the three superpowers. Sethryn has owned it for a few years now and get this: it was where *Balan Orion* himself often stayed."

"*As private property we will need to be aware of customised security*," Kelvin warned, in an undertone. Satiah nodded.

"Recent scans reveal a new satellite orbiting..." Randal continued.

"That's it, *that's the weapon*," Satiah, with conviction. "*It has to be.* It's the only safe place to keep it, it must be there."

"All *we* can see is an *inactive body in orbit*," Randal stated, hoping she was right. At that distance the only thing they could know for sure was that *something was there*.

"Keep going," Satiah urged, annoyed at her own interruption. Deva turned, eyebrows raised again, they were in orbit. They were in a rush as the longer they delayed departure the more suspicious it looked. Also they may lose their chance of getting access to the weapon if someone else swept in and took it by force. Ro Tammer, perhaps...

"It's called the Glass Palace because of the unusual light refraction. It interferes with most lasers so your weapons may not work inside," Randal warned. *Sblood!* Satiah dumped her pistol heavily on the table in regret.

"Is it dangerous to the *eyes?*" Reed asked, curious. He had been wondering *if as the KZ15 affected the human mind in terms of preventing it from resting*, the light, may *also* have a role to play in the matter.

"No... it *will* look bizarre though, I imagine. We're trying to get an image but, it *seems*, most cameras automatically filter it out – only the naked eye or special cameras can see it." Carlos scowled, not liking the sound of that. He pondered the role of specialised goggles and wondered what advantages they may give the wearer.

"What the hell is this place again?" Carlos muttered, a little disbelieving.

"What else?" persisted Satiah, conscious of every second that slipped past.

"Long tracer probes are detecting an unusual amount of static build-up in the nearby area," Randal answered.

"*Cloaked ships*, I bet Sethryn's got his own private army too," Satiah growled, annoyed. She knew it couldn't be Tabre as he'd not had enough time to get there. Granted it might not be down to Sethryn but it seemed likely.

"It *could* be natural," suggested Carlos, although he didn't even believe it himself.

"That's it, Satiah, *you know everything we know*," Randal told her. "Good luck." He disconnected.

"Good thing he warned us about that lack of laser gun thing," Ruby said, still awestruck. Satiah gave Deva the nod and she initiated the acceleration.

***

On board Tabre's ship, in the control room, Tabre was relaying the coordinates to Ro Tammer.

"Coordinates are here, sending them on to you," Tabre stated, nodding to Alex. She was already powering up the thrusters. She had stayed on board while on Earth. She wanted to see the planet but not enough to chance getting into a fight. The population, despite acting tolerant, were naturally wary of anyone from the Federation. How deep did that tribal awareness go? She looked as a normal human would look but her accent was a dead giveaway. She stretched again, the long period of inactivity making her fidget more than usual.

"At last," Ro stated, sounding more relieved than ungrateful. "Vugarna Four?"

"That's the place," Tabre concurred, checking the chart. The ideal place for a clandestine deal to be made, miles away from anywhere, and not overlooked by anything. A bleep made him look around and focus on the communications device.

"*What?*" Alex asked, concerned. His eyes narrowed deviously and he tilted his head to the side. A look of understanding then took over. Alex waited, holding her breath without realising.

"What is it?" Ro demanded, edgy. He seemed to relax at the sound of her voice.

"It's nothing, I'll let you know when we arrive," Tabre answered, trying his best to sound normal.

Ro disconnected and Tabre slowly picked up the decoding device. Alex watched, uncertainty in her expression.

"Homing device," Tabre explained, regarding it thoughtfully. "Its own signal betrayed it to my computer."

"Wow, they *really* don't trust anyone do they?" Alex replied, a little relieved. For one moment she thought he was going to tell her it was a bomb or something.

"Question is... Keep it or not?" Tabre pondered aloud. Alex shrugged. The ship shot away from Earth, aware that a few others were also heading in their general direction too. Tabre grinned. If they were using the beacons to track everyone, not just him, they would not know who Ro was when she arrived. She was coming in her own ship, not his. That could be interesting. They might even try to shoot her down.

"Destroy it," Alex suggested, a little unsettled. She stood and pointed over her shoulder with the thumb. "We *don't* need Satiah to figure out where..."

"She doesn't need to figure out where we are because she already knows *where we are going*," he interrupted, with a sigh. "It's not her I was worried about. *Finch* will be worried about *me*, and he will most likely have told Sethryn that I was on the Orion Observatory *with* Satiah *and* Lara."

"...So?" she asked, a little bewildered. Why would that matter now? Surely, if at all, it would have mattered *before* the meeting?

"They *may* even think we are still working together, it is certainly a probable possibility, *so they will think*..." he carried on. Alex frowned as she set the ship on auto before turning to face him.

"But you *weren't*," she stated, confused.

"I know but we didn't tell them that. Besides... *in a way* we *were* working together in order to escape the station," he corrected. "Albeit it briefly."

"*Again, so what?* Ro *knows* you work for her and I do as well so anything Sethryn says to her is..." Alex began again, thinking she understood what he was worried about. Alex presumed that Finch or Sethryn would damage his reputation in regards to Ro Tammer, which given her recent behaviour, could be fatal. Tabre, though, had a good record with Ro for many years and frankly the whole idea that he might be turning against her sounded more like a destabilising strategy of Sethryn's invention than it did a genuine tip-off. But alas, Alex had missed the point. Tabre wasn't at all concerned about what Ro did or didn't believe about him. He never had been.

"If *I* have realised this... *Satiah* will realise it too and she could try to use it," Tabre stated, waving her to silence. "That is going to be where the trouble is." Alex sat back down properly, dumbfounded.

"You got all that from a *hidden homing device?*" she clarified, pointing at it. He shrugged.

"That and about forty years of experience," he muttered, smirking.

"But... but..." she stuttered, confused. "How could she make that work exactly?"

"That's the worst part of this... I have no idea what she may try," he said. But he didn't sound scared or uncertain. He expressed... excitement. Then Alex realised... he was enjoying this.

"You're mad," she stated, simpering slightly. "You and her."

"*Brilliant*," he corrected, grinning. "We're both brilliant, not mad... *but who is the best?*" She shrugged.

"I'm not sure I want to know," she admitted, a little worried.

"It will be decided soon, one way or another," he said, with absolute conviction.

"You said it would end badly," she reminded him, with a slight shrug.

***

Satiah disassembled her pistol in regret. She eyed her collection of hypodermics and needles. With the amount of people she may have to take down, being without a gun was not going to help. A knock came on the door.

"Satiah, *it's me again*," Ruby's voice came. Satiah opened the door and Ruby scuttled in nervously. Satiah stared right at her without a word. Ruby was scared of Satiah and only sought her out when something else scared her more. Or… persuaded her to.

"…Yes?" Satiah asked, coldly.

"I was wondering… *if you can't use your gun*, what will you do?" Ruby asked, hesitantly. She was avoiding Satiah's penetrating stare and looked very shifty. Granted Ruby always looked shifty but she was looking even more suspicious than usual.

"Did Ash send you in here?" Satiah asked, perceptively. A flash of red on Ruby's face gave away the truth but Ruby shook her head and replied.

"No, why would he do that?" Satiah smiled tightly.

"You can tell him you didn't find anything out from me," Satiah told her, as she returned to the equipment on the table. Ruby followed her over, a little crestfallen.

"I'm going to ask you something and you have to promise not to get angry…" Ruby stated, more seriously. Satiah picked up a nearby syringe and tilted her head to the side as she regarded Ruby with apparent intent. Ruby swallowed but held her ground.

"You're not going to allow Randal to rebuild the weapon with those designs he has, are you?" Ruby asked, tentative.

Satiah didn't move. That idea had never actually occurred to her. Ruby took the silence as refusal.

"You mustn't or Ash thinks this could start all over again," she urged, emotionally.

"…Randal would not be stupid enough to rebuild it," Satiah stated, placing the needle back in its place.

"How can you know that? Ash thinks that once this mission is over Randal might have you killed in order to hide the fact he now has the designs, *you, Reed and Carlos* are the only witnesses," Ruby warned, seeming to genuinely believe this. Satiah had to admit that Randal now did have more on her than he had ever had before. Okay he still didn't know about Vourne but he'd discovered more than enough about her methods…

"This thing that you're doing," Satiah stated, a little harshly. "Ash should *know* how dangerous distrust can be… especially when it is not warranted. The trouble it can cause… *Or* is that his intention?"

Ruby froze, unsure what to say. Satiah made eye contact and Ruby quailed slightly.

"I don't think he cares about you at all," Satiah said, cutting loose. "I think he's using you. He claims to want the best for humans yet refuses to intervene directly *when it suits him*! Instead he sends you in here to try to start something between me and Randal!" Satiah took a sudden and aggressive pace toward Ruby. Ruby tripped over herself trying to back away and ended up on the floor with a groan. "I should have gone with my first instinct and arrested you on the spot!"

"*Wait!*" Ruby cried, frightened. "It's just a theory…!"

"Definitely one you shouldn't bring up," Satiah interrupted, seizing her arm and dragging her to her feet. "Get out." Terrified, Ruby fled. The door closed and Satiah slowly sat in her chair, her mind chewing on the new possibility.

Except it wasn't new, was it? Not *really*. Hadn't Randal moved her prisoner without telling her? Rainbow had told her it was due to refurbishment and it probably was but… She sighed. This was why Ash and the immortals were so dangerous. They knew that humanity's worst enemy was itself. And they knew just where to poke the stick to get the right reaction. She took out her communicator.

"Reed," she called, casually. "I'm in my cabin, could you come here for a moment? Thanks." She cut off before he actually answered. She knew it was likely Ash would have heard that but… he would soon know what had happened when Ruby told him anyway. Less than thirty seconds later Reed entered looking… his usual self. He didn't say anything as he surveyed the room, seeking a place to sit. He found one and stared across at her aloofly.

"Was there *anything specific* you wished to talk about?" Reed asked, indicating that time was passing at its usual speed and might be used better. Had he been working on the mission report without telling her? He'd not actually done that yet but she was afraid he would.

"Do you think the designs of the weapon are safe with Randal?" Satiah asked, directly. Reed paused, a crafty grin emerging on his face. Satiah suspected the idea must have already occurred to him.

"You know, *that's* just what *Ash* asked me," he chuckled. Satiah's eyes narrowed… Ash was deliberately trying to manipulate them.

Were he a mere human, she'd shoot him. "Did Randal give you a reason to assume they might not be?"

"No," she replied, shortly.

"Have you uncovered something…?" he began.

"No."

A silence.

"He doesn't give up easily," Reed smiled, casually. He was talking about Ash.

"Yes well, that last effort nearly cost Ruby her life so he'd better *watch it*," Satiah grumbled, irritated that Ash had managed to cause yet more anxiety. Reed lifted an eyebrow, concerned. He chose to temporise.

"*Just a little longer*, that's all this is going to take and then you can say goodbye to both of them," Reed said, patiently. She relaxed noticeably in her chair. In her mind though… the resentment remained.

"*Can't wait*," she limited herself to saying. Reed chuckled again.

"I think the feeling is mutual."

"You know what else is mutual?" Satiah asked, her tone surly and sour together. "Distrust. I'm asking your permission to arrest them."

"On what charge?" Reed asked, even though he knew it was a stupid question.

"On any blasted charge I please! There are plenty to choose from," Satiah raged back, seriously. "Interfering in an investigation, treason, resisting arrest… Take your pick!"

"Satiah… *No*, just let them go," Reed ordered, placidly. Just hours ago, he and Ash had been yelling at one another and now… Satiah did not understand Reed, not at all.

"What's going on?" Satiah asked, reading between the lines. "Why are you defending them?"

"*I'd rather the galaxy not know that the son of Dreda lurks among us*," Reed answered, darkly. "Besides you know that if you threaten either him or Ruby it will not get you far. Personally I've just settled for letting him watch but not taking part."

"Dreda died ages ago; no one remembers who she even was…" Satiah snapped, irritably. She stopped herself quickly though, knowing it was not true. People did remember Dreda. Not always with much accuracy but her name still brought fear and admiration in equal percentages. The fact that hardly anyone knew she even had a son didn't really matter.

"Precisely," Reed said, almost as though reading her mind.

"Well, Ash is *really* agitating… only this time he's doing it differently. Instead of directly confronting things, he's planting seeds of doubt, that kind of stuff. *I want it to stop*," she complained. "I don't need it. I have to be thinking about that weapon, Tabre, Ro Tammer and anything Sethryn might throw my way or Carlos' way… I don't need to be keeping an eye on Ash and Ruby as well."

"Leave it to me," smiled Reed, cooperatively. "I'll make sure they stay out of your way from now on." Once again Satiah found herself struggling to deal with someone so reasonable.

Satiah drew out a thin blade from a shelf and shoved it into a slot on the inside of her boot lining. It was impossible for anyone to see and hard to find unless you knew where to look. What once was, didn't have to control the future. Today didn't have to be what it used to be. It always felt good to have a blade within reach. The present is the only reality. The trouble was, from day one a lot of people are taught to think about their futures to the extent that they forget all about today. The sands were constantly running but for someone like Satiah there only ever was today. The future was as good as a void-like oblivion. A land of hypotheticals and maybes that might as well not even be thought about. For her, the past was an ever-expanding reference manual, a glossary of experiences. The easiest way Satiah felt that she could connect to the actual present was to listen to her own heartbeat and concentrate on slowing it down. There was some sanctuary to be found in stillness.

She was already going into her pre-battle meditation. A state of mind where a deep calm swept through her. Preparing herself in every way for the next fight. Next were two silver bracelets that were built about nine years ago when she'd been sent to the Caves of Ormoana. She'd got lost in the tunnels and had spent nearly forty hours roaming in complete blackness. If nothing else worked, a violent struggle for survival would help keep you in mind of the present. In those tunnels she'd known that guns did not work due to the energy-sapping qualities of the crystalline rock faces. So she'd build these miniature needle launchers. They each held one hundred tiny darts. Every single projectile was loaded with one of her own chemical mixtures. Twenty for sedation and the rest to kill. On her belt she attached five new compact mines. Each looked like a metal stud but would blow apart a metal door easily.

Reed looked on interested as she meticulously checked, rechecked and got everything together. Her breathing was slow and deep, her muscles and posture completely relaxed now. Oddly, Reed felt like he was intruding in some deeply private moment. Since working with Satiah he'd got to know her ways very well but even so he wasn't entirely sure what she was going to do when they arrived at the Glass Palace. He knew she had a plan; she always had a plan much like himself. Ash was a problem and Reed wasn't wholly sure what to do about him either but he had a few ideas. Quietly he rose and sighed heavily.

"I will promise to do my best to prevent Ash from interfering any further," he said, honestly.

***

Roxanna pulled on her uniform and then smoothed down her sleep-tousled hair. Her communicator was bleeping. Bleeping for the seventh time in three days. For her, that was a lot. Stuck out there, in the Glass Palace skeleton security crew, she wasn't exactly in the middle of things. She already knew it would be Finch as she answered.

"Yes," she answered, a little grumpily. She'd got used to lying in as there literally was no good reason to leave her bed these days. She'd done the bare minimum to maintain her fitness level but she'd be the first to admit, stuck out there, there was little reason to do anything. Even the daily patrol checks she was supposed to supervise seemed faintly pointless. No one stayed here anymore, no one even wandered in by mistake because they were lost or... *anything!*

"We are about an hour out," Finch's voice came. That got her attention. She'd guessed that a visit might occur at some point; nonetheless this seemed like a bolt out of the blue. The last time he'd been here was a few weeks previously but only to install that new satellite. And he still hadn't told her what it was for but as she didn't have to patrol or maintain it she didn't particularly care. That was another thing that had almost deserted her in this mind-numbing, monotonous job... curiosity.

"*We?*" she asked, picking up on the strange choice of word.

"Is everything ready?" he asked, sounding unduly concerned.

"Yes," she almost snapped, defensively. "They have been ready for weeks."

"Good, power everything up, you have guests coming," he stated, coldly.

"How many?" she asked, immediately. Guests?! That hadn't had guests for years!

"Maybe a hundred, certainly no more than that," he replied, as if it was nothing. Roxanna swore violently.

"Why the hell didn't you warn me *earlier*!?" she demanded, furious. "We don't even have *one* chef..."

"*Relax*, we're providing the catering," he replied, as if it was nothing. Providing. Providing! He couldn't do that! They might not be certified! Roxanna didn't know what to think. Somehow she managed to condense all the frustration, confusion and no small amount of outrage into a one-word response.

"Fine."

As soon as the call was over she'd hit the general alarm and the fifty or so people who still worked there actually had to get up on time. Spot checks were completed, systems were activated. Long disused areas were opened up again, filtered, cleaned and readied. The hundreds of rooms designed for customers to stay in were all set up and all lighting systems were activated. The metal glass shields were raised and that was when the eerie green-yellow light took over. It was bright enough to see by and even read with but Roxanna had never liked it. It gave the whole building a bit of a haunted, murky feel. Calming music was played quietly in an effort to counter the creepy feel. That when combined with the sounds of gentle waterfalls was enough to make the place seem much friendlier.

Finally there was just the conference centre to set up and... all the old uniforms to put on. Nostalgia hit Roxanna, all those grand parties of the super-rich she had been lucky enough to work at? In fact Roxanna loathed the super-rich. The *so-called* elite classes. Their arrogance, wealth and self-righteousness made Roxanna want to spit with bile. But... a job was a job. She practised her very convincing yet still *utterly false* welcoming smile before practising the old greeting.

"Welcome to the Glass Palace, my name is Roxanna, have you stayed with us before?" It sounded mildly stupid as she was fairly sure that no one would have been there before. Nevertheless, Sethryn had never bothered to amend their script so that was all she had to work with.

***

Entangled together, naked in his bed, Wester and Jenjex lay there in the darkness. It hadn't meant to happen. They had agreed that they would only do anything about their feelings in better times. Trouble was, there was no way of knowing when, or indeed if, better times would ever reach them. And it had been a bit of an accident. Despite being fully awake neither of them trusted themselves to say anything. It had been a tense but uneventful eight-hour watch. Nothing had happened, nothing had moved. Then they had had dinner and... one thing had led to another.

"...Sorry," he said, at last. Wester felt he had instigated it by inviting her into his cabin in the first place.

"I love you," she told him, ignoring the apology. They stole another deep kiss and were about to go in for seconds when the door bleeped.

"Admiral," came a woman's voice from outside. "There's been a development." Jenjex hissed in amusement, annoyance and mild fright all at once. Wester tensed and sat up abruptly.

"Very well, I will be there directly, return to your station, thank you," he stated, on autopilot.

"Very good," she replied, as the speaker fell silent. Rapidly, Wester and Jenjex hurried to get dressed. This took a little longer than usual as Jenjex was unable to find one of her boots at first.

"Stay here, wait three minutes, then head to the bridge," Wester instructed, seriously. She nodded, backing into the shadows. No one could know they were sharing a bed; leaving aside it being against regulations, it would also be rather embarrassing. She made up her mind to at least try to appear on the bridge from a different entrance too, to try and enforce the idea that they had come from different places.

Wester reached the bridge, breathing hard. A flight officer touched his hat to him.

"Sir, a power reading is registering, coming from the planet surface, sir," he stated, pointing. Jenjex stumbled onto the bridge from another direction and forced herself to stop in attention posture.

"Very good," Wester said, and motioning for her to approach. "Power reading," he began to explain to her, pointlessly. They both stared at the reading. It was clearly rising.

"Power levels are increasing all over it." Orange readings were replacing yellow ones all over the screen.

"*It's a facility*," Wester stated, as much to himself as to anyone.

"Coded message from Captain Keane, sir," said someone. Keane wanted to know if any change in orders was coming.

"Tell him we maintain vigilance and nothing else," Wester stated, trying not to stare at Jenjex.

Jenjex was agitated and rechecking something. Lights were beginning to flash.

"What is it, Lieutenant?" Wester asked, uneasy. She spun to face him, touching her hat as she did. Luckily the news was of an urgent enough danger to distract her from focussing in on the tell-tale smudges on his lips from her lipstick.

"Sir, we have an influx of approaching craft. Maybe sixty ships," she told him, obviously concerned. An alarm started and that meant the crews would all ready by rushing out to their fighters should they be called into action.

"*Not yet!*" Wester ordered, seriously. "Tell everyone to stay where they are and do nothing… we watch and we learn."

"It seems our tip-off was accurate after all," Egill stated, casually.

"Scans," Wester said, to Jenjex. She obliged and began to run them as a large group of flashes appeared in the distance. Many craft were indeed arriving. They were small, most were personal transports. Wester stared out at them, his eyes narrowing. What was going on?

"Sir, it's squadron leader for you, wants to know if you want to launch or not?" the flight officer said, touching his hat.

"Tell him to stand down," Wester stated, hardly thinking about it. His mind was going through other possibilities. Was Ro Tammer on one of those ships? Even now was she flying right past him? But he would stay hidden and watch, there was a reason all these craft were here and he wanted to know what that reason was. Jenjex returned to him, excited.

"Sir," she said, touching her hat.

"Report," he stated, his tone urgent.

"Sixty-three ships approaching the Glass Palace, sir, some with as many as seven on board but none of those ships are heavily armed," she explained. "They are beaming coded signals at the Glass Palace."

"Record everything, I want listings, and then get the techs on it," he instructed.

"Already done," she smiled, her eyes finding his. He had to fight not to laugh.

"Very good."

***

"Here we are," Carlos stated, into the microphone. They were about to arrive at Vugarna Four, he and Deva were still in their mercenary disguises. They were meant to be the only two aboard. Yet Reed, Ash and Ruby were concealed in a storage area, in a makeshift control room. Satiah and Kelvin were literally hiding in the ceiling. They all heard Carlos' warning. He shot Deva an evaluative stare. She grinned.

"How bad can it be?" she asked, sarcastically. He smiled back as he cut the engines back, slowing them to a regular pace. The small planet loomed into view, as did several other vessels at once.

"Good not to be alone," he remarked, pointing to them. He activated their entry signal and waited.

"This is the Glass Palace, you are cleared to approach," came a woman's crisp voice.

"*Welcome to you too*," Carlos joked, as he disconnected. Deva sniggered as she adjusted her gun. They knew that guns wouldn't work there but they had to act as if they didn't. Following the coordinates, they had just been sent, they joined a queue of other craft. Deva stared out, her eyes seeking threats. There seemed to be no security at all... certainly no craft on patrol. Granted they could be cloaked but...

"Very lax," Deva stated, in disapproval.

"Wouldn't want to scare the money away," Carlos shrugged, not really knowing what to make of it either.

"What would've happened if we had no clearance?" she asked, a little incredulous.

"Maybe we would have been politely asked to leave," he murmured, also curious.

A docking bay was opening for them and Carlos adeptly swung the craft inside, parking so that they faced the exit. Unstrapping himself from his seat, he stood, stretched and glanced down at Deva. She remained in her seat, staring ahead almost blankly.

"What's wrong?" he asked, uneasy. Then he noticed. As the hangar shield came down, all the lighting changed. A yellow green tinge, making everything look murky and strange. A shadowy slow-motion whirling sort of spin that was constant. And it was like the light itself was shining through water, giving it an almost marine like feel... tranquil yet mildly disorientating. Deva eyed her gun meaningfully. Carlos nodded and let out a breath.

"Come on." The ramp went down automatically as they disembarked. Carlos was last to leave and, when he did, he struck the hull of the ship twice very hard and then followed Deva.

Satiah heard the metallic thuds, their signal, and rolled off of her back onto her side.

"They are out," she stated, to Kelvin. "Start the countdown." A timer was already running silently, counting down. They waited and Satiah slid the panel aside so she could look down into the corridor below. No one was searching the ship as she had expected they would.

"*Sloppy*," she condemned, seriously. Scans were never enough on their own, to find contraband or anything else a physical search was always recommended. They had no doubt been scanned the instant they had arrived but they had the beacon's signal, the fact that they were among many other ships, and that the ship could basically thwart any scanner. The scan would only have revealed Carlos and Deva, everything else was shielded. Speaking of scans...

"How are you reading Carlos?" she asked, to Kelvin. "Is the link okay?"

"Data building... the facility is a standard layout with one or two minor alterations," Kelvin answered. "Ten minutes." She nodded.

Much like when visiting the Pune home world, Carlos was feeding data back to Kelvin so that he could create a map of the structure. Unwilling to risk using communicators yet, Satiah tapped on a nearby pipe a couple of times. Reed began tapping back. All was fine. She tapped again, informing him that they would soon be moving on. He acknowledged her with more tapping. Once they left the ship they encountered the odd lighting for the first time and Satiah sighed heavily. From this point on they would be forced to use communicators for further interaction. And this lighting was going to make concealment an interesting problem. She caught Kelvin staring at her.

"What?" she demanded at him, almost hostile.

"Your hair looks terrible," he stated, in his usual monotone.

"Shut up," she muttered, irritated.

***

"Do you want me to go with you?" Alex asked, seriously. Tabre paused on the threshold. They had just landed in a hangar area of the Glass Palace. She was scared but she was also sick of just sitting around in the ship on her own.

"Do you know how to use a gun?" he asked, interested.

"I was in the Colonial *Navy*," she stated, a little haughty. He noticed she had used the word *was* without realising when she probably should have said *am* but he stood there, unmoved.

"Does that mean you know how to use a gun?" he asked,

deadpan. She stretched before simpering.

"Probably not. I was a fighter pilot, not a trooper or officer," she admitted, giggling sheepishly. "I thought you said guns *don't work here* anyway?"

"I never believe what I read," he replied, motioning for her to follow him. "Besides, that's not meant to be common knowledge." She noted that he was not carrying his usual gun though, he was carrying something else. "*An intelligent being can always adapt.*"

Together they walked out into the hangar area and Alex gasped at the peculiar lighting. Tabre found it irritated him more than anything. This was the sort of lighting that could make targeting a real nightmare. He'd seen nightclubs that had similar systems although this was apparently natural in origin. He found it necessary, in order to hit the target, to just go left of the target in order to ensure he hit them. He wondered what he would have to do this time.

"No one to come and show us in," Alex stated, a little pointlessly. "In the Federation it's against the law to run accommodation without conducting a mandatory safety tour of the premises…"

"If you're just going to prattle endlessly, you can stay in the ship," he told her, playfully grumpy. She pulled a face at his back but said nothing to that. Another ship was just coming in to land; close enough to them to make them pause with uncertainty. Tabre recognised the ship and knew who was aboard.

Ro Tammer, led by a contingent of her most loyal guards, came down. Alex stood to attention reflexively but started to wish she'd stayed in the ship after all. Tabre made no move other than a curt nod.

"Tabre," she smiled, formally. "What an outlandish spectrum show they have here."

"How did you land without a signal?" Tabre asked, interested. She tolerated impertinence only from him and it was not an unreasonable inquiry.

"…I am the leader of the Federation, Tabre, I can land anywhere I like," she stated, arrogantly. "It's not like they would dare shoot their richest customer down, is it? Besides, I was scanned intensely." She had a point there, Tabre had to agree. As if summoned by some secret means, Finch appeared in the entrance way.

"Sethryn sends his greetings," he stated, his tone also one of formality.

"*How thrilling,*" Tabre murmured, rudely. He gave a commanding gesture with his head to Alex to get her to follow them.

"I hope Sethryn *appreciates* how much of a disturbance this all is to me, I have an empire to run," Ro complained. They were all walking down a long corridor now, still in the strange watery light of yellow and green. *An empire to restrain from tearing itself to shreds,* Tabre thought.

"I know he is aware of how valuable your time is," Finch allowed. They passed Roxanna, who stood to one side, all prim and proper.

"How long is all this going to take?" Ro asked, although she didn't seriously expect a real answer. She was an impatient person and there was a real urgency for her to return with the weapon and sort out everything.

"No longer than it needs to," Finch replied, making Tabre smile.

"It needn't take any time at all if Sethryn would just sell it to me," Ro stated, with some venom in her tone. "There is no need for any of this." The background sounds of light music and fountains that was meant to be soothing just made Tabre tense up, expecting an attack.

"We will begin as soon as we can. Drink?" Finch deflected, adeptly. If there was one thing Finch was good at, it was maintaining a humble disinterest. Inwardly, however, he was sorely wishing that he could just shoot her.

"Yes, immediately," she stated, as if it were obvious. Finch gave Roxanna a nod and she darted away to fetch one.

"Don't we get one?" whispered Alex, to Tabre. Tabre almost laughed.

"There's a bar area over there, please feel free," he suggested, backhanding her on her backside. She glowered but then grinned, pleased that she could escape Ro Tammer's company. Ro was watching their odd exchange and couldn't resist commenting.

"Well, well Tabre, I never pictured you as *ever* having someone," she remarked, dryly. "Wouldn't that be what you *and others like you* consider a weakness?"

"And I never pictured you as doing anything so stupid as this so I guess we're both deluding ourselves," he stated, harshly. *Touché,* Ro mused. He was the only man alive who would dare talk to her like that, without fear of instant death.

"*I* can handle this," he went on. "You're exposing yourself unnecessarily."

"Perhaps," she allowed. A beat of silence occurred between them. "But what with everything happening back home, I may actually be safer out here. The people are getting restless, *I am getting restless.*"

"Admiral Wester getting too good at stalking and countering your every move, is he?" Tabre enquired, casually.

"*Acting Captain* Wester," she corrected, with no small amount of hatred. "He is *only a minor issue* currently and when I get this weapon he will cease to be an issue *of any kind.*"

"He's crippled your navy, divided your followers and remains somewhere out there ready to deal out more," Tabre pointed out. "You're lying to *yourself* now *as well as your people.* Great skill in a leader, *self-deception.*"

"It's no lie that this weapon could solve all my problems in one," she argued, in a low voice.

"Or it could backfire and multiply them," he warned. He still wasn't convinced that the weapon was all that Ro thought it was. If it was, surely Sethryn would never consider selling it.

"...Your drink," Finch smiled, politely. He took it from Roxanna and passed it to Ro. Ro went to drink it but Tabre stopped her. He raised his eyebrows.

"Have you *even* checked it for poison?" he asked, chidingly. She huffed and moved away from him with her guards. Tabre smirked and advanced over to Alex who was perched at the bar, looking on. A woman as openly poisonous as Ro Tammer would need a particularly formidable dose to finish her off.

"*Amateur,*" he muttered, referring to Ro.

Alex took one look at him and said, "Oh, this is going to be fun."

"Do they have any Homely Deputy here?" he asked, dumping his communicator on the surface of the bar noisily. Alex shook her head.

OPERATION ORION

"This place just gets better and better, doesn't it?" She giggled, then swung around in her chair so that she was facing him and he realised she was already rather drunk. He felt it as she gently pushed her knees against his hips, squeezing with just enough insistence to let him know what she had in mind. Clearly she'd rethought her technique on how to cheer him up and he approved of this new strategy.

"Try *this*," she mused, handing him a glass of something. "Could be your last, if you're not careful." He did, knowing she could easily be right about that. It was a little tangy... certainly no match for his favourite. She ran a hand down his face softly and pulled a regretful face. He made eye contact with her. She was too drunk to be quailed by any look from him now though.

"You look awful," she purred, sympathetic. That made him chuckle.

"Are you trying to mother me?"

"Would you shoot me if I was?"

***

The muffled noises of the dark dusty vent shaft, unvisited for so many decades, were drowned out by the deafening blasting noise of a powerful burning unit. A square hole was cut into the metal with impressive speed, sparks rupturing like a miniature fireworks display. Satiah kicked it open when the cutting was done before scrambling in; Kelvin followed and started soldering the metal back together.

"How goes it?" asked Reed, in her ear.

"We are in the vent system," Satiah told him, mindful of the fumes. She distanced herself slightly from Kelvin. "I'm going to mine the primary *and* secondary power generators before I do anything else. Without guns, everything's going to be a little awkward so I would like to be able to cut the cable if I need to." *A little awkward?* Who was she trying to kid?

"And then what?" he asked.

"Then we have a straight choice between *destroying the weapon* or *buying it*," Satiah spelt out, wincing as a stray spark flew past her.

"I think you mean buying it or not, we are going to destroy it either way?" he replied, his tone revealing nothing. Satiah was crawling forwards, breathing hard.

"Yes," she replied, between her teeth. It was hard work, even for her, to stay ahead of Kelvin.

"How do you plan to destroy it exactly?" Reed asked, astutely. "When you can't gain access to it and even if you could, you would die?"

"A well-placed missile should do the job," she grunted, with certainty.

"And you have a missile lodged up your top as well do you?" he asked, doubtfully. She almost laughed.

"Why do you think I can't run properly?" she joked, checking her wrist launchers.

"...Let me know if you need help," he said, trusting her.

"I assure you, you'll be the first to know," she replied, nearly choking on the dust.

***

Roxanna was watching over the guests as they mingled and socialised with each other. An unusual collection of beings she thought. Her communicator went off.

"Yes?" she asked.

"Sorry, we've got a vibration in the ventilation system," said a man. She rolled her eyes. Not vermin again! It was always the way, you get rid of one infestation only to discover another. They can *sense* the food!

"*Where is it?*" she asked, exasperated. This would happen now!

"Generator area, just going into it now," replied the man.

"I'll take care of it," she sighed. She picked up an electric stunner, a long pole-like implement with an electrical current that flowed at one end, and made her way out.

***

Carlos and Deva were standing by themselves but in the middle of the crowd, awaiting the bidding to begin. Where was Sethryn? Surely he should have been the first to arrive being as this was his show!

OPERATION ORION

"This delay is making me nervous," Deva confided.

"I don't think it's doing much for *anyone* in here," Carlos smiled, trying to make light of it.

"He did say this would take a few days most likely," Deva stated, trying to reassure herself. "That being so, I'm surprised he's not started already."

"Maybe he's been arrested," Carlos suggested, humorously. He wasn't looking for Sethryn though, he was looking for Finch. Deva turned and paused in shock.

"*Ro Tammer*," she said, simply.

"In person," Carlos added, without missing a beat. "Any doubts I had about that weapon not really working have just evaporated."

"*She's* here so... *where* is Tabre?" Deva asked, inquisitive. Carlos was about to reply when he spotted Finch. Finch was setting up a speaker system, looking balefully around for someone. Carlos wondered at the cause of his apparent foul mood but could only lament at the broad playing field of likelihoods.

"Here we go," Carlos said, nodding towards Finch. Deva followed his gaze, noting that none of the guards were carrying guns but they did have crowd control batons. From behind them a familiar voice boomed out.

"Welcome," Sethryn announced, loudly. A chorus of replies sounded. "We will begin in a few moments!" Then he was mingling with the crowd but making his way slowly towards Finch. In the strange lighting, the whole place and all the beings looked very strange. Greens, yellows mixing with the blacks and whites into a bizarre tableau. Carlos did a quick calculation and realised that Satiah would have started her business a while ago. No alarms or explosions yet... All to the good, they would continue playing their parts. But for how long? How far would they be forced to go with Ro Tammer as an opponent?

"How far are we allowed to go again?" Deva asked, thinking about the auction to come.

"As far as it takes," he grinned back. She did have a point, how much money would it actually take?

525

***

Roxanna entered the musty generator area; it was quite loud in there because of the constant rumbling of the heating system, the rattling of the life support and the drone of the actual generator itself. She poked around in the corners, with the stun stick, seeking whatever vermin had managed to survive the previous months purge. There was no sign of anything. Maybe it had just been a powerful air current. She frowned and then noticed something. The generator was dusty, as was mostly everything in there... but attached to one of the main power cables was a brand new bit of shiny metal that Roxanna could have sworn that she'd never seen before. It was clean and therefore couldn't have been there long. She reached out to touch it when something hit her hand. A tiny needle like vial. She gasped and then went down, as the chemical did its work, unconscious. Satiah emerged from behind the generator, staring coldly at Roxanna.

***

Tabre, while adjusting his sleeves, turned to regard Alex's naked, sleeping form. She lay on her front, partially wrapped in the sheets. His lower lip felt like it still had her teeth marks in it and it pleased him. He ran his hand softly along her smooth calf and she stirred a little but did not awake. Then, after allowing the flash of smile to appear on his face, he turned and slipped away. He reached the main room where everyone else was and noted the positions of Carlos, Ro and Finch. Still no Satiah... He thought about it and then smiled. She was there... he knew it, he just couldn't see her. She must be trying to steal the weapon. She would have a distraction planned. Perhaps a way of forcing the place to be evacuated...

A large holographic projector was showing a live image of the weapon as it orbited the planet. Many people were gazing at it. Sethryn was explaining how the auction would be shepherded. In a large hall, usually used for parties, small booths had been set up. Each would act as a display for both the progress of the auction as well as a way for the computer to keep track of both the offers and the totals. Some of the prospective buyers were already making their way towards them. Anxious to waste no time, Ro had already taken one. She was in the process of setting it up. He wandered over to join her and her guards.

"Everything... all right?" he asked, although he could see that it was.

"I wish they would just get on with it," she muttered, irritated. Tabre was starting to agree with her, this was taking too long.

Carlos and Deva, still disguised as mercenaries were at a booth on the other side of the hall and, feeling adventurous, he ambled towards them. They saw him coming of course, however, they had to act like they didn't know him even though he knew they both did. He reached them and he could tell they were both on edge, ready to react at the first hint of danger.

"Hello," he smiled, with false cheer. "Who are you here representing?"

"What business is that of yours?" Carlos shrugged, much as Tabre had expected he would. Deva was very still and pale and remained mute for that part of the exchange.

"No harm in checking out the competition," Tabre shrugged, amiably. "Where is Satiah?"

"Does it matter?" Carlos asked, letting the act slide as it was rather pointless.

"If she still intends to steal or destroy the weapon, *which your being here tells me she does*, she will have to make her move soon before Ro buys it," Tabre drawled, as if the whole thing bored him rigid. "I don't expect you to tell me her plan, partly because I know you wouldn't but mainly because I'm guessing she probably hasn't told you anyway. I want you to send a message to her for me."

"Why?" Deva asked, at last breaking her silence. He smiled deviously.

"*Does it matter?*" Tabre echoed, rather mockingly.

"What's the message?" Carlos asked, seriously.

"Tell her that I know that she's here and why she is here and I will stop her, just that and nothing else," he replied, bluntly.

"Yeah whatever," Deva muttered, returning her gaze to the computer screen. Tabre raised an eyebrow but then smiled pleasantly and returned to Ro's booth.

***

Satiah was busy dragging Roxanna's body along the floor when she got the next call from Reed.

"Tabre knows you're here," Reed warned, and then gave her his message.

"*Brilliant,*" she spat, sarcastically. That was all she needed, although she knew it was inevitable he would challenge her again. She'd placed her mines in specific areas. Two on the main supply cables to stop the energy flow. And two more inside the actual generators. That was to enable her to effectively destroy them twice; once would be easily repairable and the second time would be the crippling blasts. She kept the fifth mine for the weapon itself. They had studied the weapon and she'd quickly identified a good place for it. But... *how* to get close enough to plant the mine without dying from exposure to KZ15?

It was clear that the weapon was being watched by almost everyone in the building which presented the other main problem. Kelvin emerged from the darkness.

"Scan complete, no alarms raised yet," he explained. She handed him the mine and her grapple gun. There was a short silence.

"You know what to do?" she clarified, worthlessly. Of course he knew, she'd told him at least twice and he often guessed what she was thinking without her saying a word anyway.

"Get to the weapon, place explosive device and then return to the ship," Kelvin repeated. She nodded, her brown eyes making contact with his big red ones.

"Don't get destroyed, *you are very expensive,*" she advised, hiding her emotional attachment behind humour.

"Don't die, *you are unique,*" he responded, in his usual monotone. With a final nod, they separated. Kelvin would be heading for an exit to the Palace. Satiah would operate as a distraction for him... the *one* distraction she *knew* Tabre would fall for... herself moving to *assassinate* Ro Tammer.

***

Erica Moxin's voice sounded as deep and Colonial as ever as her message reached Wester, Jenjex and Egill.

"Ro Tammer is inside the Glass Palace, Randal has a few agents present that have confirmed her being there but you have to hold back, there is another operation taking place *that must happen,*" Erica explained.

"*What* operation?" Wester asked, immediately.

"Randal can't say," Erica answered. Jenjex eyed Egill.

"Even if I knew I wouldn't have permission to tell you," he responded, guessing what she was asking.

"How long will this operation take? How will we know *when* to move?" Wester asked, agitated.

"Do *those agents* know *we* are here?" Jenjex asked, concerned.

"Randal doesn't know but he doubts they do," Erica said.

"Well, now we *know* for sure that she is there we can at least set the trap," Wester stated, frustrated. "Lieutenant, send my orders to Captains Keane and Clarissa. Tell them to move to the encirclement coordinates, power up their systems and maintain amber alert. We attack on my command."

Jenjex touched her hat in acknowledgment of the order and left the conference room to go back to the bridge.

"What about the others?" Erica asked. She was talking about the Coalition agents that Randal had referred to.

"…I don't know," Wester answered, sad and uncertain. "If Ro capitulates then they should be fine, *however*…" He didn't need to say any more.

"The Phantom agents will be informed of your presence," Erica stated. "I know it's a risk but now you've surrounded the place, Ro won't be getting out, not without help."

"Please convey our thanks to Randal," Wester said, formal again. The link was closed and he rose to stand next to Egill.

"How will you decide when to move in?" Egill asked, curious.

"I will use my own judgement," Wester stated, a little pompously. He clasped his hands behind his back and began to pace towards the bridge, Egill in tow.

"Most likely there will be a moment when whatever is meant to happen, happens. And that moment will be my signal to act," Wester explained. "I just have no idea what form this signal will take."

"Whatever this mission is it must be *absolutely crucial* for Randal to try to get us to work around it," Egill sighed, pondering. He'd heard nothing much from Phantom Command since being stationed on Wester's flagship.

They returned to the command deck and watched as, disciplined and tense, the crew went about the gradual shift in coordinates to the new, much closer position. Keane and Clarissa, invisible to everyone, even each other, would be doing the same. Soon they would have Glass Palace in the centre of a deadly triangle of fire. Earlier in the conversation, it was established that although the light rays would interfere with the laser fire from hand-to-hand guns, interplanetary power guns wouldn't be affected, they were literally too strong. Scans taken showed the maximum power of the shield protecting the Palace. It was negligible and concentrated fire from all three ships would be more an enough to overwhelm it. The structure itself was in no shape to repel any sort of spatial attack.

When it was in business, it did have a fleet looking after it but obviously that was long gone. Wester had already prepared his ultimatum for Ro. Surrender or die, basically. Not particularly elegant or memorable but it would make the point and hopefully do the job. Of course he had no idea how Ro would react, the virtue of surprise had been a blessing for him more than once in the recent past. He hoped it would remain so.

"We are in position," Jenjex said, breaking into his reverie. She touched her hat.

"It won't be long, make sure the fighters are standing by," he said, trying to think of everything.

"Sir…" She turned to go but then came back. Something was bothering her. "I know this is not the time or the place but shouldn't we talk about…?" She trailed off. It took him a moment to figure out what she was talking about… then he realised.

"Yes, I think we should," he agreed, darting a quick sideways glance over his shoulder.

"I think it's a good idea we don't…. Well, we don't… *No one can know*," she stated, falteringly. She wanted to keep their affair a secret, wisely. It was against naval regulations and it wouldn't do morale any good either.

"Yes," he managed, a mixture of feelings assaulting him. Was she

OPERATION ORION

really going to end it already?

"We will need to develop *a code*," she stated, completely serious. "And a way of ensuring *no one discovers what we're doing*." He smiled in relief.

"Agreed. We can discuss it later," he said, nodding. She stood to attention, touched her hat again and then hurried away to check on the fighters.

"All ships in position."

"On my command…"

***

Satiah didn't think getting so close to Ro Tammer would be so easy. Having carried out many assassinations over the years, Satiah knew what to expect and was pleasantly surprised. She blended in so well with the crowd in the odd lighting that, she realised, had she actually thought about it, taking out Ro Tammer would have been easy. The idea lingered for a little longer than it probably should have. Killing Ro Tammer would not solve anything though. Besides… she had nothing to do with the mission. Carlos may have spotted Satiah; she couldn't be sure but as he was not looking her way in a very definite way told her he may have. Then Satiah clocked Ro, at her booth and began an almost leisurely approach, wondering how long it would take before *anyone* saw her. There was Tabre… looking all around. His sixth sense was telling him something was going on. Satiah tried to ignore him and kept coming.

Completely openly, she continued her straight-line approach and managed to get within twenty yards of Ro before Tabre spied her. Pulling out the automatic pistol, loaded with bullets, he fired a shot. Sometimes, the dim and distant past offered a tiny advantage in the far future. The bullets weren't at all affected by the strange light. His aim apparently was not immune to the lights, though. The bullet ended up in the belly of one of the guards nearly three metres from Satiah. She dived to the left, between several confused people who were also trying to get out of the way. Forward rolling, even closer, Satiah sent one of her tiny needles flying at Ro Tammer's face. Unfortunately it slammed into a thin glass barrier that Satiah had not seen in the light. The glass cracked from the force of impact, for a moment seeming to cut Ro's astonished face in half. Then Ro was gone, forced down by one of her bodyguards.

Tabre was rushing to try to get another shot in and guards were scrambling over towards her as others fought to get away from her. Downing three of them with killer chemicals, Satiah found a way out just as another bullet screamed over her head and bounced off the wall. Sprinting as fast as she could, Satiah made it out into the corridor and continued flat out along the next. She just got around the corner in time to avoid the next bullet. The ricochet gashed her forearm but she kept going. Alarms were blaring now and shouting was also audible. She reached a ladder, climbed up it and then dived over the guard railing to land on top of a large container. Tabre would have carried on running past had he not heard her land and looked up. He'd never expected her to react so aggressively this time. He was impressed by her brazenness.

A needle bounced off of the ladder rung he was about to grab hold of and he let go, falling painfully to the bottom. Satiah waited at the top, wrist launchers aimed for the top of the ladder. A noise from behind her gave away the guard trying to sneak up on her. She brought him down and then activated the first two mines. The rumble of the blast could be heard and the alarms fell silent as the power was cut off from everything except basic life support. Finch was trying to understand just who was attacking who. Ro and Sethryn remained, with Carlos and Deva and a few of the other braver people, in the auction, but a mass exodus of people were trying to get to the ships. Finch was about to activate the lockdown when all the power was suddenly cut and the control room was plunged into darkness.

"Backup generator!" Finch shouted, over the startled chorus of voices.

"Not working, sir!" replied someone. It took Finch less than a second to put the escaped vermin location and the site of the explosion together. It had been a viable tactic and Finch realised even he had been naive about this whole thing. Phantom agents were trained in many secret things but one thing was known. They were very difficult to kill. Finch should have got out before this stage. The fight was not over yet though.

"She's *mined* the generator," he hissed, angrily. He tried to put in a call to Sethryn but he wasn't answering. *Typical!* If he could forget the blasted auction for one minute…! A maintenance robot had made it into the generator area.

"Only the cables are damaged, replacing now," came its voice. Finch frowned. Cables only? Why would she only blow the cables away? That made no sense *unless*...

"Check the area for any more mines," he instructed, as lights began to flicker on again.

Tabre had gone after the woman; therefore they were not working together after all, not unless this was some weird type of bluff. The only one who'd been targeted was Ro Tammer, the woman hadn't even looked at *Sethryn*. Finch couldn't even begin to guess what that was all about.

"Close the door, cut each section off and trap her," Finch commanded, trying to be logical. "She will either try to kill Ro again or try to run."

"Sir, several craft are demanding to leave...!" said someone.

"Don't let *anyone* leave, not until we know where she is!" demanded Finch, struggling to hold onto his temper. She could be planning to escape via any one of those craft. Where the hell was Roxanna?

***

Satiah lurked in the darkness, listening as the footsteps crept nearer. The flicker of a shadow caught her eye and then she leapt out. The man didn't have time to react as she pushed his baton away with a blow to his wrists and then killed him with a powerful jab to the throat. Snatching up the baton from the metal floor, Satiah hurled it end over end at the next incoming woman. She dodged but in doing so fell from the walkway with a terrified shriek. The shriek came to a crunchy end as she hit the floor below. Flooring another guard with one of her needles, Satiah launched herself into a third guard. Her momentum took them both to the ground. Seizing his baton, she pinned and then bludgeoned him. Rolling to the side, slowing her own breathing into silence by force, she crouched, waiting for Tabre.

Yet Tabre made no move and the sound of the doors, heavy doors, began as they slid downwards. They were trying to seal her inside! Racing, she ran as fast as she could and skidded underneath it, just making it through before it crashed shut. Two guards tried to pounce on her but they were undisciplined enough to get in each other's way. The scuffle was brief but long enough for Satiah to regain control of the fight. She shot them both with her wrist launchers. Another sound made her spin to look. Nothing. Rolling for cover, Satiah expected another bullet to come her way at that moment. She pulled out her controller and tried to set off the next set of mines but… silence. They had to have been found and disarmed. She swore under her breath and then began to stealthily crawl along. She had to ensure that everyone's attention remained on *her* so that Kelvin could infiltrate the weapon without anyone seeing.

***

Seventeen million Essps. That was how high things had got in the time since Satiah's clumsy attack. Carlos only called it clumsy as he presumed Satiah had meant to be blunderbuss for a reason. A distraction for something else. Carlos and Deva, unsure what the plan was, could only continue on with their covers. At least Tabre had been drawn off. Ro Tammer, though, was really going for it, no matter how high things went she never hesitated in going higher. The attack had even helped her in a way as *now* there were less people to bid against. Carlos always waited, making sure he took as long as he could before going higher himself. The power failure had abetted and suspended the process for a while but only for about five minutes. That was when Ro finally lost patience completely.

She rose to her feet, pulling a gun on Carlos and Deva.

"There is no possible way that two *mercenaries* could have *that much capital*, I don't care where they are from," she stated, lividly. "Whatever I say you just keep adding *one extra Essp every time!*" Had they not been at gunpoint Deva would have giggled, as that had been exactly what they had done since the start. Carlos didn't have time to say anything in their defence or otherwise, as Sethryn intervened.

"*Now, now, Ro* you *know* the rules," he stated, warningly. "We had an *agreement* and part of that agreement was that you didn't antagonise anyone!" She whirled on him.

"*That weapon is mine!*" she screamed, waving the gun around wildly. Carlos's eyes narrowed with concern. Laser guns didn't work but shouldn't she already know that?

"I cannot *believe* she is the leader of the Colonial Federation,"

Deva murmured, shaking her head. "I just cannot."

"Right now, it is mine!" Sethryn argued, still with a maddening smile across his features.

"Dead people don't own anything!" Ro snapped and pulled the trigger, aiming right at his chest. A purple pulse of intermittent energy fizzled away from the nozzle of the gun. Ro stared at it, baffled and then tried again. Sethryn laughed.

"Did you imagine I would be insane enough to stand unarmed before *you* unless I knew it was safe to do so?" Sethryn asked, as Ro fumed. "Did you really believe that I was that stupid?" For a moment Ro was lost for words. Then she gestured at one of her guards who, carrying a blade, advanced towards Sethryn.

Carlos watched breathlessly as Sethryn just stood there, completely unmoved. Was this a bluff? He looked all around, seeking some other action that this was meant to conceal from him. That was when he saw Finch. Finch was aiming a very strange-looking pistol at the guard's back. No one else had seen him, transfixed by the drama unfolding in front of them. Sethryn, probably because he already knew Finch was there, held his ground, even raised a challenging eyebrow at the guard. A final warning: do and die! The guard did and was shot in the head by Finch. As he collapsed, everyone turned to face Finch. Sethryn though, continued to face Ro.

"Are you done?" he asked, coldly. Now, she looked scared. As Finch approached, she knew she only had one option… play Sethryn's game. She slumped down in the chair again, glowering up at him.

Sethryn then turned to Carlos.

"My apologies for your rival's brief loss of temper," he stated, pleasantly. Carlos managed a shrug.

"Losers often react that way," Deva said, in a stuffy tone. Ro glared at her but had the sense to refrain from any further violence. She did note Deva's accent though and couldn't help but wonder… Sethryn gave a little grin at that.

"This contest is not yet over," he reminded them, casually. "Finch?" The two men put some distance between them and the others as the auction continued mutely.

"Tabre's gone after the woman," Finch stated, without preamble.

"How did *she* get on board? She wasn't at the meeting," Sethryn demanded, seriously.

"All I can tell you is that every ship was scanned and every ship had a beacon bar one…" Finch told him, and pointed at Ro. "She was the only ship that was not scanned but she was *the target* of the assassin."

"I suppose it was inevitable that someone would find out about this," Sethryn sighed.

"It's impossible to know if they understand what is going on here or if they are here only to assassinate Ro," Finch explained, even though he knew that was not quite accurate. He had no idea why the woman from the space station had gone after Ro instead of the weapon and it seemed unlikely, as Tabre had gone after her, that he would ever find out.

"I think we should pull out," Finch suggested, though he knew Sethryn wouldn't stop now.

"We're *so* close now," Sethryn argued. "We only need a few more hours and then we can leave."

"…Okay," Finch said, trying to inwardly tell himself that a few hours was not that long.

Several people entered the room and made a beeline for them.

"What's going on? Why won't you let us leave?" demanded one, furious. All the craft had been forced to remain inside the hangars.

"Either return to your craft and await clearance or re-enter the bidding war," Sethryn instructed, maintaining a show of good humour. "Those are your only options." Guards were moving in to ensure a fight didn't start. Finch had his gun on them. He'd adapted it especially for use in the light waves, a precaution that had been well worth implementing.

"This is a set-up!" someone shouted.

"No, it is an auction," corrected Sethryn, patiently. He gestured with his hands and gave a laugh. "Please, there is no reason to panic."

There was a flash from the screens as the satellite detonated. The satellite, the weapon, had just been destroyed utterly in front of everyone. There was a stunned silence. Carlos and Deva, despite being the only two who'd known it would happen, also froze for a few seconds. There had been no signs of anything untoward, not from there leastways. Sethryn looked like he'd seen a ghost and Ro's incredulous face was a picture too. Finch stared out at the wreckage in the way an engineer would look at a malfunctioning computer. What had gone wrong?

"Now what?" Deva whispered, to Carlos. He was thinking frantically. It was Ro who came out of her trance first.

"What just happened?" she asked, her voice hard. "Where is the weapon?" No one, not even Sethryn or Finch, could answer her.

***

When the satellite blew, Wester had decided to take that as his signal to reveal that he was there to Ro.

"Initiate," he ordered, loudly. A chorus of responses and gestures were made as all silence ended and the three destroyers launched fighters. Egill was looking on, unsure. Wester stood there, communicator to his lips, for the first time in everyone's eyes did he truly look like an Admiral.

"Ro Tammer, this is Admiral Wester of the Colonial Federation. You have twenty minutes to surrender yourself to us for trial. If you do not hand yourself over within that time, we will obliterate the Glass Palace and everyone in it," Wester said, his voice firm and fortified. Jenjex felt a rush of pride and glory at once. For the first time they were facing their real enemy.

***

Ro was gobsmacked! How had he found her? *How*? Had Sethryn done this? She heard Wester's message, just as everyone did, and saw a countdown begin. She could see the three destroyers, surrounding her, hemming her in. She had one destroyer waiting nearby but, even with surprise on its side there was no way it could hope to make a real difference. She had to think of something... and the weapon! Had Wester known about that too? Had *he* destroyed it? She could try to talk to Wester... maybe bluff him into backing down. Where was Tabre? He'd know what to do! Everyone else had heard it and everyone was looking around in confusion. Finch looked at Ro and began to genuinely believe that she was behind all the problems. Her ship hadn't been scanned, the assassin had most likely been working for her to act as a reason for her to distrust Sethryn.

"*Friends of yours?*" Sethryn asked, to Ro. They were obviously Federation destroyers. That association was easy so work out or *so the crowd thought...* Ro was still slumped in her chair, a panicked expression on her face.

"How did he know where to find us? *How?*" The last word was uttered in the form of an angry bellow from her.

"*Now the weapon is gone, I think we should make our excuses,*" Carlos muttered, to Deva. She nodded, in full agreement.

"I didn't tell him!" Ro stated, in complete honesty. "How could I when *I didn't know?* One of your people must have let it slip somehow..."

"Seventeen minutes, Ro, you're going to have to talk to him, *at least stall for more time,*" Finch implored, not entirely sure why he was trying to help her. He wanted to live certainly but he wasn't sure if Ro's negotiating skills would help with that goal in mind. She burst into hysterical laughter and everyone but Finch found it intimidating.

"*Great idea!*" she cackled insanely. "How exactly am I supposed to do that?"

"Do you have *anything* he might want *other than your own skin?*" Sethryn asked, seriously. "Can he *be bought?* Now the weapon is gone, all that money *which you should give me in compensation* could be used to bribe him into..." Ro couldn't believe that even now Sethryn was thinking only about the money! Worse still he was as good as blaming her for this whole scenario!

"That was *not* my fault!" she screeched, lividly. "I *needed* that weapon and *you know it!* Why the hell should I want it destroyed?" Finch had to intervene or they would run out of time before they even figured out what to do.

"Everyone has a price or a breaking point," Finch stated, cutting through the argument coolly. "You can at least buy more time as you attempt to negotiate while we think of something else."

"...Fine," she agreed, seeing that she had little choice if she wanted to live. Besides, time was certainly something they all needed. "Get me a line to him." That was the last thing Carlos heard as he closed the door and locked it. Deva smashed the control, effectively trapping them inside. They grinned mischievously at one another as a panicked pummelling began on the other side, before fleeing back towards the ship.

***

"It's gone!" Reed announced. Satiah could tell he was smiling and that the weapon had been destroyed. She'd heard nothing from Kelvin though and that bothered her more than she knew it should. Yet she was in no position to do anything much about it now. Tabre was stalking her somewhere nearby, as were several guards.

"*Get Carlos and Deva out,*" Satiah whispered back, urgently. They had done enough, no reason to leave them in danger now. "No point in trying to buy something that doesn't exist anymore."

"They are *already* out; I've been chatting to Randal and apparently there is some kind of situ…"

Satiah didn't hear the rest as a concussion charge went off very close to her. She was shielded by the crate she was crouching behind but she was still knocked to the floor. Her earpiece fell out, vanishing somewhere in the peculiar lighting and she had no time left to search.

She started sprinting, making for a set of steps leading down. As she got to them Tabre burst from cover, firing the rest of his rounds at her. She forward rolled down the steps painfully, as bullets struck practically everything but her. She felt one skim her thigh. She hit the floor hard, rolling behind the next wall. Tabre, reloading hurriedly, dashed after her. A guard stepped out to interpose but Tabre shot him before he could. Satiah had to fight the guards too and Tabre wanted this fight to be as even as possible. Satiah got to her feet and, with the agility of a gymnast, she leapt up, grabbed the guard railing and hauled herself up onto the next floor. She rolled onto her side and lay still. Tabre ran past underneath her. She tried to get an angle on Tabre but the angle wasn't doable in her position. She sat up slowly; and made sure she was temporarily safe where she was, before slumping back down again to recover some energy.

***

Finch and the others were trying to force the door, there was now less than ten minutes before those destroyers would open fire. Ro had sent out a call for her reinforcements although she knew they would be hopelessly outnumbered. She was in deep regret at the loss of the weapon. Sethryn, too, was bitterly disappointed. *All that money*! The whole scheme was collapsing around him, at least it seemed that way. Finch had no sympathy for either of them and was giving serious consideration to letting everyone go while trying to slip away himself in the pandemonium. If he was realistic with himself though, he knew that there was little chance anyone would escape three destroyers. Especially when they were under the direct command of Admiral Wester.

"How can I talk to him when we cannot leave this room?" asked Ro, pointlessly.

"We're working on that," Sethryn said, thinking things through. Wester may speak to him, as he was owner of the Palace. Ro was bound to make a mess of things so perhaps…

"Use the manual override!" yelled Finch, giving up on brute force.

"*It's smashed too*! Why do you think we hadn't done it already?" shouted someone else, angrily.

"Maintenance!" Finch shouted, into his communicator. "Door 4432 is jammed shut, amend please."

"Can we not use your communicator to talk to Wester?" Ro asked, sensibly.

"No, it's the facility communicator, only for the *local systems*," Sethryn sighed, having already thought of it. Finch, however, still holding it, paused. Conceivably…

"Perhaps, *now that maintenance is on the way*, we can adapt it," he said, thinking fast. Ro and Sethryn watched as Finch adeptly disassembled the communicator and replaced two components. He was sweating and it was a conscious effort to keep his hands from shaking from the strain he was under but somehow he did it.

"You should be able to get him on that," Finch stated, holding it out. There was a slight scuffle as both Sethryn and Ro tried to grab it. Less than two minutes! Finch would have laughed had he not been so angry with them! With all of this coming down around them they were still fighting one another.

"*You* want to talk to him?" Ro asked, to Sethryn. She looked disconcerted. She didn't know his motives but her paranoid mind was already creating theories.

"As *owner* of this property *I surely have the right*," Sethryn began, carefully. "I *may* be able to stall him."

"He doesn't give a damn about you or this place, it's *me* he wants," argued Ro, snatching it from him.

She activated and then realised she would actually have to call Wester an Admiral if she seriously expected him to answer. She almost choked on the word. *Acting Captain*... deserter! *Traitor*!

"A-Admiral Wester, this is Ro Tammer," she stated, her voice regaining some of its former superiority. The countdown stopped at fifty seconds. An audible sigh of relief passed through the room.

"Yes," Wester answered, his voice giving nothing away.

"How do I know that you won't kill me the second I'm out in the open?" she asked, trying to sound distrustful.

"Why bother when I can destroy you *where you are now*? I would like to take you back for trial; I would *like* you to expose your own lies but... *I'll do it all on my own if I have to*," he responded, coldly. "I've made it this far without you."

"Maybe we could come to some kind of understanding?" she offered, thinking on her feet.

"I *really* don't think so," he replied, as if it was nothing important.

"I have the entire central banking system of the Colonial Federation at my disposal, I could make you *and your crew* all *very* rich," she stated, tensely. "Life can't have been easy, hiding out there all this time."

"We'd all be dead in less than a month," Wester answered, putting an end to any possibility of bribes. "No deals Ro, *you surrender or you die*, it's up to you."

"This is *treason*!" she exploded, tears in her eyes.

"No, this is *justice*," he corrected. Ro opened her mouth but no words came out. Her destroyer was less than five minutes away.

"Let me, let me," Sethryn said, taking the communicator away from her. "Admiral Wester, my name is Sethryn Ring, I *own* this Palace. Is there a reward for Ro's capture?" Ro stared at him, her mouth slack. How dare…

"Perhaps… do you consider *survival* a reward?" was Wester's taciturn reply.

"There are *a lot* of people trapped in this place, you should already know that. If you destroy us, Ro will not be the only one you have murdered," Sethryn said, warming to his own new plan. Finch looked on. He had thought of that himself but betraying Ro was probably not a brilliant strategy, particularly when locked in a room with her and her guards. Finch was sure to let them all know he had them in his sights.

"Pirates and other criminal scum most likely," Wester replied. Sethryn twitched with displeasure at being labelled like that. Ro had to admit Wester had got that right. "Ro is there so… Can't be many civilised people in her company." Ro bridled this time but also held her tongue. Three minutes until her destroyer arrived.

"Admiral," Sethryn began again, his eye twitching now. "Do you know *why* we are here?" Ro started shaking her head, guessing his idea. Of all the nonsensical notions!

"*No, no, no,*" she mouthed frantically, at him. Threatening Wester would be a stupid thing to do, especially now they didn't even have anything to threaten him with, even she knew that.

"Not a clue," Wester freely admitted, some carelessness creeping into his voice now. "If you hand her over to me then naturally I will not eradicate your Palace, however, I *doubt* you can deliver."

"We are here because we have been developing a *new weapon*," Sethryn told him, taking the plunge. "And if you continue to threaten us, we *will* use it!" Ro held her head in her hands. There was a silence. Then a blast of fire came from two of the three destroyers and the whole place shook. Ro shrieked and looked all around, expecting the building to break up.

"*…There go the shields,*" murmured Finch, through his teeth. One more blast like that and they'd be frazzled to crisps.

"Do you *think* you will have *the time* to use said weapon in time to *prevent your destruction?*" Wester asked, sounding angry now.

Ro swore as she ripped the communicator out of Sethryn's hand. There was a struggle as they tried to take it from each other. Ro won.

She belted him across the face so hard, she drew blood. He stared at her stunned, her nail marks on his cheek red and bleeding.

"You *idiot!*" she screeched at him.

"It *could* have worked," he stated, shaking with rage.

"*Another mistake* and we will be reduced to a pile of rubble!" she shrieked, lividly. "Everyone get ready to run for their ships!"

"*Why?*" asked Finch, suspiciously. "Even if we get to them *before* he destroys this place we will only get shot down!"

"Trust me!" she yelled over him. "Help is on the way. It will not be enough to overwhelm Wester but it may provide a long enough distraction for us to escape." Finch could tell straight away that she was gambling.

"*What help?*" he growled, distrusting.

"Wester," Ro began, addressing him again. "If you kill me, the people *will believe you to be a barbarous pirate* and a civil war *will* start as power factions vie for control! Do you *want that* to happen to the Federation?" She was desperately playing for time now, trying to use his love of the Federation, as they all edged their way out into the corridor. The robot had at last got the door open and mostly everyone else had fled.

"That is by no means certain," he retorted, bluntly. "Even if it were, *your removal* can only help matters."

"I want the best for the Federation, *I always have!*" she declared, starting to pick up her pace. "I want to make it strong enough to defend itself against the Coalition or any other hostile force."

"You want more than that, way more," Wester argued, his anger rising again. "And how can you make something stronger when you keep killing parts of it? When you order the mass murder of an entire department for one simple mistake…"

"Thanks to you and your *rebellion*, I'm not in the position to get more now!" Ro shouted back. "*You* have crippled the whole Federation! *You* have made us the punchline of every joke being told in the Coalition! *You*…!"

"*Enough!*" bellowed Wester, over her. "Surrender now or I will open fire regardless of whatever else is there!" Ro and her guards reached her ship but the hangar doors were still closed. Alex, sitting inside Tabre's ship, observed Ro and her guards panicking, unseen. She had gone back to the ship the moment she'd realised things were going wrong as Tabre had told her to. All systems were powered up and ready to go. She knew she could blast her way out of the hangar if she had to but she would wait for Tabre as long as she could.

Ro's ship, although armed, would struggle to smash its way out. If it sustained damage... Alex turned back to the scanner and watched as the destroyers were joined by another. This new ship, however, immediately began to attack one of the other destroyers. Ro must have called in her backup but it was hopelessly outgunned. Within moments of arrival, it began to turn and retreat. Ro was clearly aware of what was going on too as she had begun raging about the ship's Captain's betrayal. *Screaming* about how he was effectively *leaving her to die* and the dereliction of his duty *this* and the summary execution *that!* Anyone sane, though, would know *exactly why* he had pulled back. *It was three on one.* There was nothing he could do other than get himself and his crew killed. What self-respecting Captain would do that? Next Ro was raging at how the hangar doors had prevented her using her distraction to escape. Rage! Rage! Rage! Did she *never stop*? Alex continued to watch, almost starting to laugh at Ro, intensely interested in what she would try next.

***

"So where is she?" Carlos asked Reed. Having locked everyone up in the auction area, Carlos and Deva had safely returned to the ship where Reed and the others were waiting. Satiah, though, was conspicuous due to her absence...

"*Somewhere* on the lower levels. I fear she and Tabre are re-enacting their duel again," Reed told him, looking taut.

"*We have to help her*, this place could be destroyed any second," Deva replied, referring to Wester's fleet.

"We, until the hangar doors are opened, *can't* leave," Reed said, tilting his head to the side. "I did try to tell her that but we got cut off."

"Give me an earpiece," Ash sighed, standing abruptly. "I'll get the hangar doors open..."

"Not *all* of them, just ours!" Carlos stated, instantly. "We *don't* want Ro escaping..."

"*Why not?* She's nothing to do with *our* job," Ruby asked, confused. "Now the weapon's gone, we just need to extract Satiah and Kelvin and then go home…"

"Don't you *see* what a great prospect we have now?" Carlos asked, seriously.

"I do," Reed admitted. "The removal of Ro Tammer as a Federation leader *is* an attractive proposition. However, we would be operating outside the boundaries of what could be construed as *plausible priority*." He was implying that such an action could be considered illegal regardless of the political implications. Ro's assassination could not, in any way, be worked into their mission as a *necessary action* now. Even before, when she would be the potential new owner of the weapon, it had been dangerously presumptuous territory. Understandably Satiah had only attacked *her* to draw out Tabre and distract everyone from what Kelvin had done.

"Whatever happens we need to ensure that *we can leave*," Ash stated, his tone dogmatic. He was right of course and Carlos realised that Ash had deliberately said no more.

Yes, whatever happened they had to get out and of course in order to do that… *anything* could happen. And *of course* if Ash had any more of his little secret errands to run… now probably seemed like a great time to him. Reed, though, ended any chance. He didn't want Carlos and Deva returning to tell him that Ro's death had been some kind of *accident*! And he certainly didn't want Ash out of his sight!

"I'm officially ordering you all to remain here with me. We can shoot our way out if we have to but we cannot interfere with Satiah's job," Reed stated. Of course Ruby was the first to voice her disapproval of his apparent hypocrisy.

"Okay, so when Ash *doesn't want to interfere* you tell him *he must* and now he's happy to help you and Satiah *you prevent him* saying the very same thing he always says?" she demanded, a little incredulous. Carlos too, was stumped by this reaction. None of them were aware of Reed's promise to Satiah regarding Ash.

Reed, ever the agile lawyer, was quick to dig in.

"We are here for a *very specific purpose*, this purpose is now fulfilled. We await only the return of Satiah and Kelvin. Going out looking for them might only make things worse, indeed I'm sure it would," he rattled off, dismissively. "Anything else that happens here is not within the considerations of plausible priority! Besides, Satiah knows what she is doing and may not appreciate *any* deviation from the plan. Carlos and Deva, prepare the ship, we may have to run at any time. Ash, there is *no need* for you to concern yourself this time."

Plausible priority and *necessary action* were legal terms. Explicitly *Phantom agent language* used for allocating events or courses of action in both mission reports and plans. Plausible priorities were *events or courses of action* that clearly had to be taken, *with premeditation*, in order to accomplish a mission goal *or* mitigate collateral damage. Necessary actions were events or courses of action that had to be taken either to accomplish a mission goal, prevent mission failure or conceivably to reduce collateral damage *without premeditation*. That was the crucial difference between the two, one was premeditated and the other was not. Now the whole *legal definition* of premeditation was something subject to often *heated* debate since trials were originally thought up. This always offered a certain degree of legitimate flexibility.

Reed considered their suggested course of action. The dispatching of Ro Tammer would certainly be a blow for universal peace, he was certain of that much. However, that course of action could not easily be legally defined as either plausible priority or necessary action and thus could only be illegal. The assassination of Ro Tammer was *not* a plausible priority of the mission and could not be considered to be so in any way. Neither could she be considered a necessary action for similar reasons. Therefore, no matter which way you tried to play it, her death, *were it of course proven that you had taken the action*, would be illegal. This was the argument he'd been forced to hurl out at them all because Satiah didn't want Ash to try anything funny.

"So *what?*" Deva was saying, as she and Carlos went to the control room.

"I do not understand you!" Ruby exploded, at Reed. "We are *trying* to help you and Satiah! *We have no agenda!*" Ash was remaining silent but ever watchful. He knew Reed had his reasons but was busy pondering what they could be.

"You do not have to understand a command to obey it," Reed remarked, almost careless. Then he pulled a face to himself as he realised how stupid that sounded. All right, maybe not but it *really* helped a lot if you did understand it. The hangar door was what bothered him now. It was true they could shoot their way out but that could take too long. And if all the doors were opened, Ro Tammer would escape. He put a call in to Randal.

"Yes," Randal answered, within seconds.

"Am I correct in presuming that it is *the illustrious Admiral Wester* that has blockaded Vugarna Four with the *sole purpose* of killing Ro Tammer?" Reed asked, casually.

"That's what we think yes. Killing *if necessary*, it is my understanding that he wants her alive," Randal stated, on guard at once.

"*Did he tell his gunners?*" Reed quipped, raising his eyebrows. "*Here's the situation.* We are trapped inside his main target and we cannot get out. Is there any way you can get him to hold fire for a moment?"

"*What?*" Randal asked, in disbelief. Reed asked again. "No! Is Ro Tammer still there?"

"I presume so but typically she's not giving herself up so *I imagine* that means Wester will move onto plan B which is understandably *obliteration of the whole Palace*. I do not wish my team to become a part of the slaughter."

"Understandably," Randal echoed, without trying to be funny. "I cannot stop him though, he's in *neutral space*, and he has a *valid* enemy. Politically I cannot possibly look as if I'm trying to *help her*, I would be thrown to the dogs for that."

"Very well, try to get him to hold in any case, I'm going to try something," Reed replied, cutting off. Ruby and Ash exchanged uneasy glances as they watched Reed.

He placed a call and waited.

"Who is this?" demanded a very overexcited sounding man.

"My name is Reed and as you probably already know I'm calling from inside the Glass Palace. Is there *any* chance that I could speak with the Admiral or one of his officers? It's rather urgent!" Reed asked. "Tell him that we have a mutual friend, *Phantom Leader Randal.*" There was a silence. Red hated namedropping but in this case he felt it was warranted.

"What if he won't speak to you?" Ash asked, calmly. Reed whirred on him.

"Then it *won't work* obviously!" he snapped, irately. Ruby flinched away from his hostility.

"This is Admiral Wester," came Wester's voice. Reed closed his eyes and exhaled hard in respite.

"You want Ro Tammer alive?" Reed asked, his voice changing. It became more feral and bitter, as if he was pretending to be someone else entirely. Ash's eyes narrowed.

"Alive if possible, *why?*" Wester asked, his voice clipped and sharp.

"If you give us some time, we could get her for you," Reed offered. "We are Coalition agents, here on other business but we would like to live and *helping you get her* seems like a good way of allowing *both of us to achieve our objectives*." There was a pause as Wester weighed the options.

He knew Reed was who he said he was thanks to Reed mentioning Randal's name. But Wester would be concerned that Reed might be there to *kill* Ro Tammer. She *was* an enemy of the Coalition and Reed had never actually stated what their so called other business was. On the other hand, Ro dead was better than Ro escaped.

"Very well... you have two hours," Wester stated. He disconnected and Reed raised his eyebrows again, this time in triumph at Ash and Ruby. Ash said nothing but Reed could tell he wasn't enjoying himself particularly.

"Carlos! Deva! I have a new task for you!"

***

"You have to get the hangar doors open!" screamed Ro. Tabre, sweaty and breathing hard, had answered the call when he had realised he'd lost Satiah. She had to have somehow doubled back or hidden and waited for him to move on. He knew she had no interest in killing Ro Tammer but he hadn't known about Wester's unexpected appearance.

"How did he find out you were here?" Tabre asked, seriously.

"Right now that doesn't matter!" Ro shouted, clearly losing all semblance of control now. Tabre was ignoring her nonetheless as his mind raced. He was still seeking Satiah, trying to figure out *how* she'd slipped away. He hadn't known that the weapon had been destroyed either, thus proving what he had suspected from the beginning. Satiah's attempt on Ro's life had only ever been a ploy. A distraction, a hoodwink. A way for her to trick him into focussing on her but... as he only actually wanted to focus on her it hadn't really bothered him.

"Get Sethryn to open the hangar doors, this is *his* base! Where is he?" Tabre demanded, keeping his voice down.

"*I don't know where he is!*" she howled back. "I don't know how long Wester will hold fire..."

"What about Finch?" asked Tabre, casually.

"Did you not hear me...?" she began. Tabre threw himself to one side as Satiah popped up from behind a crate about twelve metres away. The needle embedded itself deeply into the floor, exactly where he had been standing. He peered cautiously in her direction from behind cover. She'd disappeared again. Hit or run? Hit or run? He noticed a support beam, corroded and not being used, propped up against a crate near Satiah's last known position.

He fired at it. The bullet was meant to rebound around the corner but, in the bad lighting, it was slightly too far to the left and went the other way. What it also did, however, was send the beam sliding down right on top of Satiah. She tried to roll away but the beam still half landed on her. Had she not been wearing her bracelets she would have broken both her arms when she blocked the beam from her head. It had cost her both of her dart launchers but she was unscathed. Tabre now had the advantage. Perhaps she should have slipped away when he had gone past her... but she had promised herself that this had to end. Now he was between her and her escape, he was armed and he knew where she was. She crept over to a stairway leading down and climbed up carefully onto the pile of crates next to it. There she waited, trying to stay calm. Like a darker shade among the shadows Tabre moved in, quickly discovering that she was no longer near the fallen beam and... she'd lost her weapons.

She watched as he loomed closer, covering the stairway and advancing warily towards her. He thought she would have gone down to the next level. He kept scanning from left to right, as she would do. She waited until he was just past her before moving in. Yet it was a trick, Tabre had known where she was and spun, gun raised, to strike her with the handle. Her reflexes were fast enough to react in time, however. Her boot planted itself hard into his chest, sending him flying backwards down the steps. The gun went off as he landed with a grunt into a clumsy roll that prevented serious injury. She leapt down after him; her only chance of survival lay in getting the gun off him. She succeeded in getting her hands on it, pushing it up and away. It span off into the air, away from their grasping hands.

Tabre's fist struck her ribs and chest hard and all the air left her lungs in an agonised whoosh. The gun clattered as it landed somewhere and Satiah fought to block the torrent of attacks Tabre threw at her. Left, left again, right, knee block. A blow struck her across the jaw, almost spinning her around with the force. She kicked off of the wall, throwing herself into him shoulder first. They both smashed through the glass of an internal window and landed heavily on a triangular pile of metal prongs. They collapsed the pile as they landed on it, sending some rolling away noisily. Both were on their feet again within a second and carried on oblivious of the shards of glass everywhere. Satiah clocked the gun on the floor nearby. Then Tabre somehow got in close, grabbing her top in a cross-armed grip. He ran forwards, squashing her against the wall painfully.

Her head snapped backwards into the wall from the momentum and she almost collapsed as Tabre dragged her forwards again and went to repeat the move on the opposing wall. He was trying to daze her or knock her out. She punched wildly at anything, striking his chest, face and eye. He threw her instead, letting go. She hit the wall but was able to roll and avert any fatal wounds. She reached the gun and rose, aiming it at him. He paused in mid-step. Everything was still and silent but for heavy breathing.

"It's over," she breathed, and pulled the trigger. It clicked but nothing happened. Tabre held up a magazine and waved it at her mockingly. It wasn't loaded, he'd just pretended it was and because she was unfamiliar with his type of pistol she hadn't noticed the incorrect weight until it was too late...

Next thing she knew the magazine was coming at her face, as he hurled it at her before running straight at her like a mad bull. She ducked away, dodging the charge at the same time, trying to make note of where the magazine had ended up. The gun was left on the floor, abandoned. They circled one another, each adopting a posture of defence. Searching for an opening, trying to find *that one weakness*. A brief exchange occurred in a flurry of open palms as hands intercepted hands and elbows deflected elbows. Satiah managed to trap Tabre's arm in a lock and slammed him, face first, into the wall. He stumbled away and fell forward into Satiah's knee. He slumped back, momentarily off balance. Satiah snatched up the magazine and tried to load the gun. She'd just got it ready when he crashed into her.

***

Wester and Jenjex paced up and down the bridge. Ro's *attempted-rescue* destroyer had been chased off by Captain Keane. Everyone was still trapped inside the Palace, presumably planning to all escape at the same time in an effort to reduce the chances of being captured. Trouble with that plan was, Wester knew *every ship* that was there because he'd seen them all arrive. He had three destroyers and every squadron of fighters out and about, surrounding them. They had even made a few pre-bombing runs on the facility. And now, he had a team of Coalition agents supposedly working *for him* on the inside.

"I could tell that she was scared," Jenjex stated, talking about Ro. "I could *hear it in her voice*. You did really well, not losing your temper, sir. I nearly lost mine and she wasn't even talking to me." He smiled.

"My only worry is that she might be right about the civil war if she dies," he admitted. "But… in a way it's sort of out of my hands."

"News travels fast," she went on, encouragingly. "President Raykur is apparently feeling *a lot better* suddenly. So suddenly it makes you *wonder* how sick he *actually was… He wants to speak to you.*"

"*He* knows what's going on *here*?" Wester asked, puzzled. "How?" She shrugged.

"Maybe Moxin said something to him or Simmons… who knows?" she offered, thinking about it.

"Possibly," he said. As he glanced out of the viewport, he almost expected to see journalists turning up. None did, though. The CNC would have a field day if they knew what was going on out here.

"Sir, what do we do with the others?" she asked, referring to all the other people currently trapped in the Palace. They didn't know exactly how many but they estimated about three hundred individuals had been alive there before the destruction of the satellite.

"And we still don't know who did that," Wester murmured, thinking about the detonation. Jenjex eyed the spot where it had happened.

"There were no life readings, either *before* or after the explosion. It's possible that it could have been a malfunction," she answered, although she didn't believe it. The type of explosion indicated intention rather than accident.

"Egill never did tell us exactly who his source was when it came to finding Ro, did he?" Wester asked, his tone curious.

"Not a word, assuming it *was* his source, *could have been anyone's*," she said. "If we take them *all* prisoner, it will not exceed our capacity but..." She trailed off sagely.

"But we would rather not," Wester finished for her. He nodded and she sighed.

"Do you think what Sethryn said about that weapon was true? Do you think that that was why Ro was there... and why the Coalition agents are there?" she asked, giving voice to her own theory. Wester surreptitiously glanced around for Egill but the Phantom had evidently gone back to his cabin.

"It seems depressingly likely," he replied. "Whatever it was, I think it's safe to say they are unable to use it or they would have already done so."

"*Must have been that satellite*," Jenjex said, considering. Wester didn't need to ask her who she thought had destroyed it. After Reed's call it was pretty self-evident now.

"It *wouldn't* have killed them to let us know what we were running into," Jenjex noted, a little annoyed.

"For the sake of future peace with the Coalition, I think we're going to have to forgive a lot," Wester smiled. He glanced at the countdown. Less than an hour and a half to go, still nothing from Reed.

***

"This is going to be fun," grumbled Deva, mordantly. "Trying to kill Ro Tammer was one thing but capture her alive, *without guns* sounds like a complication too many to me."

"I'm starting to wish I'd never thought of it but it has bought everyone here more time at least," he replied, thinking about the same thing. The corridors were empty now; everyone was waiting in their ships. Everyone, with the notable exception of Satiah and Tabre of course. Carlos paused.

"Do you remember the number of our hangar bay?" he asked, in a low tone.

"Forty-nine," she stated, casually. That sounded right. Carlos lifted his communicator.

"Reed," he said, calmly. "We're going to go to the control centre to find out which hangar Ro's ship is in. While there I'm going to open *your* hangar bay door if I can."

There was a strangled noise in response.

"Ah, err… well; I'm not sure that's *advisable*. I know it's sensible and everything but if we open the hangar bay door, Admiral Wester might decide to raid the place using our hangar as a way in, that's the thing."

"I'm sure you can persuade him not to," Carlos argued, stubborn.

"I may," he conceded, reluctance in his voice. "I don't want him to decide that everything I said before was lies and this is some sort of strange escape attempt *or a trap*."

"If time runs out and for whatever reason we are *unable* to get Ro back to you, you're not going to be able to get out in time if you have to blast your way out first," Carlos countered.

"Leave it with me," Reed grunted, opening a new channel. "Wester, you still there?"

"Where else?" came the response.

"One of the hangar doors might open soon; number forty-nine. When it does no one is coming out, not yet anyway. Can I rely on you not to send anyone in? It would be pointless in any case as laser guns do not work in this light," Reed stated, warningly.

"…Why is it going to open?" Wester asked, wary.

"So that when we *do* come out, we won't have to shoot our way out," Reed answered. "It is merely a matter of convenience. Nonetheless, I thought I'd better *explain* what was going on in case you *thought...*" He didn't have to explain further.

"Thanks for the warning," Wester said.

"Pleasure," Reed said, reconnecting with Carlos. "All right, Carlos you can open the doors now, it should be fine." By now Carlos and Deva had located the control room. Deserted now as all the personnel had fled some time ago, it was aglow with flashing red lights. Alarms and warnings of all sorts. Deva took the time to ensure nothing catastrophic was about to happen. There were multiple incident reports, damage reports and system malfunctions but all were minor in scale. *Individually* they were *minor enough* anyway; all at once, however, was another story. Again nothing fatal looked likely, not yet anyway, but many of the systems were malfunctioning. Lighting, doors, heating and numerous other things were badly disrupted.

"He agreed?" Carlos asked, surprised by the rapid success. He knew nothing about Wester other than what had been said in the news and that was never accurate. But he was certainly young and young people often resorted to aggression faster than necessary. "No... *problems?*"

"Not yet," Reed answered, a little hurt in his tone. Deva grinned. She was busy checking all the camera screens. One or two were completely black but most of them were still working. In a few moments she'd spotted Ro, pacing up and down with her communicator looking frantic and stressed. She pointed in silence for Carlos to see. They both made a mental note of the hangar number.

"Any sign of Satiah?" Carlos asked, trying to spot her himself. Deva had already started looking.

"No... nor Tabre," she replied, uneasy.

"Right, let's get Ro," Carlos said, grit in his voice.

"*And how would you like us to do that?*" Deva asked, a little sarcastically.

"I did have *one idea,*" he smiled, deviously. "It could work." She scowled at him. "We ask her to escape *with us.*" She crossed her arms thinking it through.

"It could work…" she said, unconvinced. "If we tell her we've got our hangar doors open, but how will you get her to trust us?"

"Naturally we will have to somehow trick her," he said, confidently. Deva couldn't understand his sudden poise. He must know something she didn't.

"*What don't I know?*" she asked, crossing her arms.

"Ro came all this way for *one reason, to get the weapon*," Carlos stated, seriously. "If we could make her believe that it was never destroyed but was in fact *stolen shortly before the explosion…*"

"But she *saw* the designs, *we all saw them*, she won't buy it…" Deva scoffed.

"Of course but *what if Sethryn lied* about those designs?" Carlos asked. "Even *we* didn't believe they were accurate for a long time. It would only be natural for Ro *to suspect the same thing*. And *this time* Sethryn will not be there to answer any questions." Deva tilted her head to the side.

"And you plan to convince her that you have *stolen it* and now want to sell it to her?" Deva guessed. He shrugged.

"It's a *suggestion*," he replied, with false modesty.

"Why don't we just go in, knock her out and drag her back to the ship?" Deva sighed, dismally. "I think this could be one step too far. What if she tries to steal this fictional weapon from us to threaten Wester?"

"Well now, that does sound *a lot simpler* but I don't fancy dragging her body halfway around the Palace," Carlos replied, influentially.

"If we mess this up it will be *our* bodies being dragged around," she muttered, uncertainly.

"I never said it would be easy," he shrugged. "Do you trust me?"

"You know I do," she nodded, in defeat.

"It will work," he said. "The difficult bit will be what to do with her *if* we successfully lure her back. She has at least two guards with her and they will have bladed weapons."

"Let's go get her before we decide that," Deva said, heading out.

***

Reed and the others looked on as the hangar door slid slowly open. Without warning, while they were still opening, a drone shot in and vanished down the corridor.

"*What the hell?*" Ruby cried, in anger. "He said he wouldn't…"

"It's just a drone," Reed sighed, seriously. Inwardly he'd expected Wester to do something no matter what he said. He had a crew to impress and sending in a drone was frankly a lot better than what he could have done.

"*I love it when humans try to work together*," Ash muttered, nonplussed. Reed raised an irritated eyebrow but couldn't argue with him on that point. He was just glad Ash was sticking to his quiet cynicism rather than trying to force any issues.

***

Satiah rubbed the blood off of her lips with the back of her hand. They were on the lowest level now, literally the foundations of the building. Tabre was still out there, stalking her. They had lost the gun and had been reduced to knocking the stuffing out of one another. Satiah had come off worse in their last exchange. Her head was killing her and at least one of her ribs was cracked. She could feel it grinding as she moved. Tabre was still in relatively good shape. Cut and bruised but nothing debilitating. Satiah knew she had to kill him quickly now, she knew she probably wouldn't survive another full-on clash. Not without a weapon. She'd even lost her communicator! Forcing her frustration away, as she knew it would not help her, she thought calmly about how she was going to live through this.

Glancing around, she noticed heavy coolant storage vessels. The coolant was for the reactor, should it overheat. She quickly limped over to the nearest one to examine its housing. Held in place by two metal beams, locked in place by safety caps. Expertly and quietly, she unclamped the first one, expecting a shift in weight. Nothing. She frowned in confusion… there had to be another crossbeam somewhere. Cautiously she ducked under the railing and moved across to the next cross passage. Then she froze… Tabre was there, standing directly under her. He was poised, ready and alert. He was listening for any sound. She held her breath… if she could get the vessel to fall on him… Wincing as she stepped up onto the railing to get to the top of the vessel, her injured rib grinding painfully, she found what she was looking for. The third beam.

It was capped in, just like the other two. She reached across, hardly daring to breathe. She glanced down; Tabre was still there, now facing the other way... listening. Don't look up, don't look up! A droplet of her own blood fell from the end of her chin but she managed to catch it with her boot before it hit the floor. To her the patting sound it made was loud but Tabre didn't seem to hear it. The cap came free, almost making her lose her balance. Gently she placed it next to the beam before beginning to slid the beam out of its supportive position. It was tougher than the last one as more weight was on it. Grinding her teeth, sweat pouring now, she silently eased it out. She felt rather than heard the shift in weight this time as the railing she was perched on lowered fractionally. She gingerly positioned the redundant beam next to the cap before regarding Tabre again. He was creeping forward, moving away very slowly. Aching all over from the exertion, Satiah fought to silence her breathing.

One more beam. She bent her knees, lowering herself silently to get closer to the railing. If she jumped, he'd hear her. And she could only climb with her left side as her ribs hurt too much for her right. Taking each move as a separate task, she made her way back to the second beam. It was already bending under the strain now. Still keeping one eye on Tabre she began to work on the furthest safety cap, delicately twisting it around and around to loosen it. It made the slightest popping noise as she removed it and Tabre tensed. Satiah too stopped all movement, just watched him. Sweat leaked into her eyes, forcing her to blink the tears away. Tabre moved in a slow circle, checking everything. There was no way out of this place other than the way they had entered and he knew it. That was why he remained where he was... in sight of her only exit.

Fatigue almost got her, as a fresh wave of exhaustion made her want to collapse. She clung on grimly, refusing to give in. She concentrated on the last beam... if she could only remove it and the whole lot would crash down onto him. Making sure her grip was firm, she pulled. It didn't budge, with all the weight holding it there and the beam forced out of shape by that same weight, it was effectively jammed. That left her with a final option. She had to increase the weight further somehow in order to physically break the beam. And… there was only one way she could think of. Slowly she edged around to the opposite side of the vessel and began to climb back up to where the crossbeam had been. Instead of staying off of the vessel, like last time, she carefully scrambled on top of it. She stood, very slowly, to touch the ceiling. She could still see Tabre waiting for her to give herself away. Then she shoved against the ceiling as hard as she could.

***

"I'm leaving you."

"*What?*" barked Sethryn, unable to believe what he was hearing. Lilith was talking to him as he had called her to try and involve his contacts, such as they were, in the Federation. It had been a last-ditch attempt to get Wester to back off. Finch was looking on, listening in and Sethryn felt like he was enjoying it.

"You think I didn't *know* what you were up to *you pretentious little snake?* You think I was blind to all of your pathetic schemes? If you had included me from the start this wouldn't have happened but you convinced yourself that I was somehow *unworthy*. Well… *that was when I chose to tip them off*," she explained, in spiteful glee. Finch felt a wash of understanding… he had been right about her all along. And she had betrayed them as he had felt she had the potential to.

Sethryn, as usual, had never seen betrayal coming. Not from his own wife leastways. But then, why shouldn't he have seen it coming? They had no love for each other; if they ever had it had died a long time ago. And she had always been snooping on their dealings; it could even be described as inevitable. Blindsided twice in one day, Sethryn could only stand there mutely like a dummy.

"*Who* did you tip off?" Finch asked, as clearly Sethryn was incapable of speech.

"By way of several others… Admiral *Wester*. I understand he and Ro don't get on and *I thought…*" she trailed off, proudly.

"*Very clever of you*," growled Finch, dangerously. The derision was palpable.

"Like I said before, *if* you have thought to include *me* in the profits, I wouldn't have had to do this, but Sethryn was holding me back," she stated, as if she'd done nothing wrong at all. She seemed to think they would just accept it. Even understand it.

Finch understood just as he understood what he would do to her if he ever escaped this situation. He glanced back at the scanner. No change. What he couldn't understand was why Wester had not blown the whole place yet. Ro must have somehow succeeded in delaying it. That didn't change Finch's plan, though. When the base was destroyed around them, they would just drift away with the debris, and wait until everyone else had been mopped up. They would wait until the destroyers left and then *they* would reactivate all systems and leave. It was risky but Finch predicted a better than half chance of survival. And... while here, now that he had more time to think about it... why couldn't *they*, as in him and Sethryn, just become *him*?

"You're dead," Finch growled, at her. He eyed Sethryn who was still agape. "*As are you*," Finch continued, and shot him in the back. Sethryn collapsed, the wound smoking slightly. Lilith saw and gasped in dawning fear before she disconnected. Finch went about deactivating all systems, including life support and communications unit. He was glad of the chance to show Lilith just what to expect. He slowly dressed in a bodysuit, taking care to check the air supply. It would be a long wait but he'd had to endure long waits before. He eyed Sethryn's body and made up his mind never to work for anyone so stupid again. It made working security look like a good career move, sure there was plenty of money in this line but if you could never get to it...

***

Ro couldn't understand why Wester was refusing to talk to her! She paced back and forth constantly, her steps jerky and uneven. The two remaining guards looked on. There had been three but one had volunteered to guard the corridor outside and had not been seen since. Alex, who was still in Tabre's ship, had grown bored of watching Ro's panicky outbursts. Her eyes noticed movement near the door and stared as Carlos and Deva appeared there, also watching. Alex had seen pictures of both of them before, nonetheless it took her a moment to penetrate their disguises.

"Two guards," Carlos sighed, uneasy. There may be more concealed in the ship too but that was an unknown. "I honestly figured they would all have left her to it by now."

"Not *everyone* deserts," Deva sighed, a little shamefully.

"Not everyone is smart enough," he smiled at her. "Follow my lead." They entered openly, making no effort to hide. The guards split up, standing between them and Ro defensively. Ro turned at the movement and stared at them in surprise.

"Seventeen million!" called Carlos, as a greeting. That had been the amount that the auction had reached before it had been interrupted.

"What?" Ro asked, wondering if they had come in some crazed attempt to rob her.

"That's the sum with which you intended to purchase Sethryn's weapon, seventeen million," Carlos reminded her, staying in character. Shouting a random yet high figure of money often ensured people listened.

"It is," she concurred, suspiciously. "What of it?"

"Do you still have the money?" he asked, shrugging. Her eyes narrowed.

"Maybe," she responded, unwillingly.

"Do you still want the weapon?" he asked, deadpan.

That last question caught her off-guard. An odd question for a potential robber...

"It was destroyed," she stated, flatly. "How...?"

"The *satellite* was destroyed to cover up *the theft*," Carlos interrupted, as if he was discussing the weather. "It's still out there, still in orbit, only cloaked to hide it from Admiral Wester and his mob." Ro was inwardly elated! *Not destroyed!* It was not destroyed; it was still out there and within her grasp!

"We want to get out of here but your friend Wester doesn't seem to be in the mood to negotiate so... we came to you," Carlos went on, bluntly.

"He is *not* my friend," she corrected, tetchy. "And, if *you* have the weapon, *why don't you use it on him?*"

"Because I can't use it," Carlos said, thinking on his feet. "Sethryn, the treacherous swindler, saw to that." Deva eyed him carefully. Ro frowned.

"What happened?" Ro asked, curious. This was most interesting, had Sethryn planned to deceive her or just whoever bought it? She had suspected that something would go wrong. Tabre had hinted at potential sabotage.

"Let's just say he *added his own insurance*," Carlos explained, remembering Satiah's words. "He's worked it so that only he can use it. Well, him… *and you*."

"*Me?*" she asked, in confusion. "Why would he do that?" Carlos shrugged.

"That's what he said right before he died and he had no reason to lie," Carlos told her, with an evil grin. Now she understood. Sethryn had known it was highly likely she'd be able to afford more than anyone else and therefore must have introduced some kind of failsafe in the weapon that only he and she could overcome. It was practical and sensible but…

"Why didn't you just force him to use it against Wester?" she asked, wary.

"We tried, *by God* did we *try*," he laughed, as if recalling something. Deva had to admit it, he was so convincing. "At first he tried to play dumb and pretended to deny it still existed. In the end he was *surprising* loyal and refused to betray his *ally*." Ally? Ro's eyes went wide! Sethryn and Wester, working together? *No* they couldn't… Yet Wester had been lying in wait *right here*, he'd known where to find her and when to strike. And hadn't Sethryn tried to use *her life* in an attempt to supposedly save his own? Maybe that had been his game! Pretending to be only trying to save himself when really he and Wester were working together just to get her to surrender. And… although she hated to admit it, it had almost paid off. Wait… why would Sethryn have worked it so that the weapon only worked for him *and her*? That made no sense *unless* he was expecting Wester to double-cross him…

Carlos and Deva waited for nearly thirty seconds for a reply.

"Sethryn and Wester were working together from the start?" Ro asked, shell-shocked still. Carlos played it cool and shrugged again.

"Who can know who was *really* working for whom or when?" he asked, a cruel smile on his lips. "All I know is, *that weapon* is my only way to get out of this alive. And that *you* are the only person that can get it to work. So... I would appreciate it if *you came with us*." There was a threat now in his tone, one that escaped no one and Deva realised *she* was almost starting to believe him too. Nothing was more convincing than someone behaving as if they wanted to live. Ro's mind was still going through the possibilities, now considering that maybe Sethryn had been trying to play her and Wester against one another just for his own profit. He may even have engineered Wester from the start... She'd never discovered who else within the fleet had helped the young man.

She heard Carlos's threat despite the multiple theories on her mind and that brought her out of her thoughts.

"What happens when and if we *succeed* in escaping?" she asked, prudently. She guessed he had decided that he might not be able to force her to do it as otherwise he would most likely have already tried. Therefore she could still negotiate.

"I'm willing to be... *generous*," he replied, reticent. Deva checked the countdown. Less than forty minutes now, this was cutting it fine. Reed may be able to buy more time. But what if he couldn't?

Alex could hear every word and was bamboozled by all these apparent revelations. She knew they were most likely lies but they all made rather good sense in a twisty turning kind of way. Just as she knew the best way to appeal to a paranoid mind was to replicate the mentality. If someone distrusts you, then you distrust them. Carlos was playing on psychology very well indeed. Before she'd met Tabre she would have ran out and interfered, maybe tried to kill Carlos and Deva. But, now she knew what Ro *was really like*, and she knew guns didn't work, she decided that no matter the outcome she'd just sit tight.

"How do I know that you won't just kill me once you have disposed of Wester?" Ro asked.

"I give you my word. Besides, as long as I intend to use the weapon I need you *alive*... at least until I figure out a way to bypass the safeguard," Carlos said, showing his very real impatience. Ro didn't take much longer. If she stayed where she was, she was pretty sure she would end up dead and if she went with the mercenaries...

there was still a chance.

"*And the weapon?*" she asked, finally. "I'm assuming, as you brought up the money again *you* now intend to sell it to me?"

"We'll survive first and discuss that later," Carlos replied, turning to go. Ro almost ran after him and Deva as they left. The guards followed, their faces hidden behind white armoured masks that hid their expressions. Alex sat there in deep thought. Why was Carlos trying to get Ro to go with *him*? Their mission had been to destroy a weapon and she knew they had succeeded. *So why?*

***

The beam sprang apart in the middle with a screeching metallic wail that would have set Satiah's teeth on edge were she not shrieking as she fell. All the vessels of coolant, now being dragged down, began to fall. Tabre, turning, saw what was coming at him and started to run. A mad explosion of freezing water sprayed everywhere as the room began to fill up. Tabre was ripped off of his feet by the wave and swept along uncontrollably. Satiah emerged gasping from cold shock. Fortunately, landing in the water had softened the fall considerably. She stood shakily, the coolant already up to her thighs. Tabre emerged and began to wade towards her. She screamed impudently at him, despairing because of the failure of her plan and started to back away. Her foot caught on something under the surface she hadn't seen. She fell over backwards with a splash. Tabre saw his chance and leapt forward.

Satiah tried to stand again when Tabre's hands found her neck. She was forced backwards again into the water as Tabre tried to pin her hips, hold her down and drown her. The coolant level was rising. Satiah struggled but he was too heavy and she was too tired. Desperate, she tried every method she knew of freeing herself but Tabre countered them all. She knew that even playing dead would fail as he would predict it. A terror she had experienced so many times rose in her. Tabre gritted his teeth, holding her down with difficulty. He could sense her weakening, her body softening and her will to live ebbing from her. He was going to win, he was going to win!

Satiah didn't have it in her to give up and though her thoughts were frantic there was one thing that formed into certainty. She wanted to see Carl again! She needed to live! A thought... her blade.

She slipped her hand, now almost numb with cold into her boot and pulled the knife free. It felt odd in her grip but Tabre couldn't possibly see it through the foam and water. Then, despite her ribs grinding agonisingly, her lungs desperately screaming for air, she thrust it upwards with one final rush of strength. Tabre froze as the blade slammed up into his heart, ice cold and hard. His hands fell away from Satiah's throat, suddenly limp. Blood was now everywhere and Satiah erupted from the water, gasping and coughing. Tabre just stood, watching her, one hand on the handle of her dagger.

She shakily stood once again, the water now higher still. They stared into each other's eyes. The water around them was red and slightly warmer with Tabre's blood. He gave her a strange smile, almost rueful. She pushed aside her wet hair from her eyes and face reflexively.

"*Good one*," he said, to her. She was panting and shivering with cold but she didn't move away, just listened. "It... was a pleasure..." he uttered, struggling to stay with her. He extended his hand and she took it in hers. It was a strange deathly handshake. She was briefly taken back to when they had first met, on that peculiar Pune world so far away.

"Honoured," she hissed, her teeth chattering. She then yanked her blade free of his body with her other hand and let go of him. Tabre pitched over backwards and floated slowly away. Satiah stood for a moment longer, watching, as if in shock.

The water was now almost to her neck and she knew she would still die if she didn't get warmth soon. Slipping the knife back into her boot, she knew it was time to get out. She swam painfully out of the exit just before the water rose above it and then was dragged along towards the stairs. Each stroke hurt as her ribs moved. She reached the steps and began to stride as quickly as she could, finally escaping the rising water and hastening upwards. She reached a landing and was shocked to encounter two guards, holding batons. They seemed as surprised as she was momentarily.

"Freeze!" ordered one, as astounded as he was angry.

"Too late," she joked, with a cough. Without warning flames engulfed the two men and both tumbled off of the walkway screaming. Satiah watched in relief as Kelvin's familiar bulk emerged from a side room, his red eyes burning. Of course his flamethrower would work in any light.

"Target destroyed," he said, in his normal voice. His red eyes surveyed her. "You have several injuries," he began.

"*You think?*" she uttered, still shaking excruciatingly. "Hold me," she ordered. She wrapped herself around him, feeling the heat as Kelvin deactivated his cooling systems and allowed the heat from his power core to permeate his metallic body. Satiah groaned in relief. It was very hot, almost uncomfortable now, but she clung on anyway.

"We need to leave," he said, his head swivelling to survey their surround.

"I know," she replied, softly. "What's happened to the others?"

"Reed mentioned Admiral Wester, a countdown and the possibility of using Ro Tammer to enable us to escape destruction," Kelvin told her. Satiah filled in the gaps. She groaned as one of his hands stabbed her with needles, injecting painkillers into her blood.

"We need to leave," he repeated, without sympathy.

***

"You never mentioned any *drones!*" Ro complained. All five of them were concealed in a room, as the drone Wester had sent in, slowly floated along the corridor. Carlos hadn't known about the drone but even if he had he wouldn't have mentioned it. He wondered if it could detect their heat signatures.

"It's of Federation manufacture," Deva stated, grimly. "Wester must have sent it in to look for *you*." Ro had to agree that that seemed likely and for the first time, maybe because of her accent, she noticed Deva again. A Colonial girl... a *vaguely familiar Colonial girl*. Wester would know that guns did not work inside the Palace so flooding it with troops seemed a bit pointless, as a result he'd sent in a drone.

"*How could it have got in?* All the hangar doors are closed," Ro pondered aloud.

"*All but one*, we got ours open shortly before we came to look for you," Carlos stated, seeing no danger in saying that. She would see it for herself soon enough. "It must have entered right after we left."

"Or followed you," Ro suggested, seriously.

"It's possible," he allowed. "Though if it had, surely we would have encountered someone trying to arrest you by now?" Ro had no answer for that.

After a few mysterious bleeps, the drone moved on and they moved back out into the corridor. On they went, stepping over bodies and trying not to get lost. The odd lighting added more difficulty to this task. Shouting could be heard as some people still battled to get their hangar doors opened. Some people may have thought to do what Carlos and Deva had done and gone to control to try and open the doors from there. Before they left the control room, however, Deva had changed the passwords. The staff had left the system in operation without restarting the security system, luckily. They reached the hangar.

Approaching the ship, Carlos started talking again.

"How do you want to do this? Speak to Wester, maybe get him to back off?" Carlos asked. He knew full well she'd probably already tried that. Deva remained at the ramp into the ship, as if checking the surround. Carlos made sure he was a good three paces ahead of Ro and the others. He didn't know exactly what they planned but... A shooting sound came from behind him and he spun to see Ro and her two guards lying on the floor unconscious. Kelvin marched out from concealment to drag the bodies away. The bodies all had darts embedded in their skin.

"Four hours," Kelvin said, telling Carlos how long they would be unconscious for.

"Well done," smiled Reed, genuinely impressed. "Someone else wants to see you... and we still have ten minutes to spare."

***

Carlos entered Satiah's cabin. She lay, semi naked on her bed, bruised and bloodied but alive. She smiled and grimaced as she sat up. Those painkillers were strong but they took a while to kick in. Her body was aching worse than she could recall.

"I heard what you did," she croaked, wearily. "I'm going to have to watch my back with you around now." He was so shocked by her look that he could only cough. "It's nothing," she explained, guessing why he was struggling for words.

"*Tabre?*" he asked, seriously.

"...Done," she breathed, openly pleased. Carlos smiled and squeezed her hand. He let go though as she winced again. Did everything hurt?

"You look like crap," he said, bluntly.

"Looks are *always* deceptive," she simpered. "You did well; I will mention your role in my mission report."

"Actually, are you *sure* that's for the best?" he asked, thinking ahead. "Ro Tammer's capture wasn't technically a part of our mission... I suppose it *could* be described as a necessary action."

"*Essential* action," she replied, coyly.

"Nah... I think it's got to be considered a *plausible* priority," he said, after thinking again. "If we had died the mission could be considered a failure based on the lack of survival."

"Can't it be both?" she murmured, softly. "*You did the whole galaxy a service today Carlos*, handing Ro to Wester. I *know* without conflict *we are out of work* but in this case... It's a shame no one but us will remember it but... somehow I don't think you care much about fame or gratitude, do you Carlos?" Her smile became both cold and comradely.

"No, Satiah," he replied, gritty pride in his tone. "I did my job, just like you and that is all."

"Good. Now get lost, I need to heal," she smiled, pleasantly.

***

Ash entered the room and Reed looked up expectantly.

"Yes?" he asked.

"About that Silver Sphere," Ash began, seriously. Reed groaned inwardly, he'd seen this coming. "What happened exactly?"

"We lost it," Reed stated, simply. "During the explosion *it was lost*." Ash regarded him intensely for a few moments before seeming to relent.

"Pity," he allowed, quietly. "Perhaps if you encounter another...?" He trailed off and awaited Reed's reaction.

"I'll certainly remember," Reed smiled, pleasantly.

***

Ro opened her eyes, slowly looking around at her surroundings. She felt woozy, almost hung over. Her limbs were heavy and unwilling. Grey ceiling, grey wall… where was she? She sat up abruptly, at last her body starting to feel more normal, unable to figure out where she was. It looked unpleasantly like a prison cell. She stood and realised she was wearing a convict's uniform. It *was* a cell! That could mean only one thing! No! How had that happened? She had to get out, she had to get out before Wester blew the whole place away. She rushed at the door.

"Hey!" she screamed, and began pounding the locked door with her fists. There was still time, there was still time! "*Hey, let me out!*" She presumed that Deva was somehow behind this, she now recognised her as the girl who had deserted on that first mission long before she'd even known about the weapon.

"Ro Tammer," came Wester's voice, from speakers in the ceiling.

"*Wester!*" she hissed, spinning around and actually looking up as if she expected to see him.

"I trust you are well rested?" he asked, cordially.

"You can't…" She stopped herself. Now she knew… they had all been in on it. All of them! *It was a conspiracy!*

"Yes," he argued, lightly. "We are taking you back for trial *and sentence*. President Raykur is most anxious that justice be done."

"*I'll bet he is*," she growled. She looked up but there was no defeat in her eyes. "Wester, I've been kicked to the side-lines before; I always come back, *always*. The people *will tire* of the cowardly moderates and I will rise again!" No response came.

"It's only a matter of time and you know it! *I'm the Federation's only hope!* My followers will rescue me from this outrage! And when I get back what is rightfully mine, you will suffer!" Still no response. "Wester!" she screamed. "*Wester!*"

Wester and Jenjex looked at one another as they listened to her rants and threats. Jenjex finally turned it off and eyed Wester.

"I hope she's not right," Jenjex sighed, thinking of how easily the masses lost their minds.

"The darkness comes only to remind us what the light looks like," Wester answered, staring out into the stars.

She followed his gaze, leaning against him and resting her head against his shoulder. They were going home. Home as heroes. Lucky to be alive, lucky to have won and lucky to have each other. Jenjex never used to believe in luck. His arms slipped around her and gently held her there.

"The best part of all of this has been finding you," he said, softly. "Makes me want to just run away with you again, creep around the stars together." Then he smiled. "Now it's all official. I think it kind of loses something…"

"How does it feel? Being a *proper* Admiral?" she asked, her eyes shining.

"*Sir?*" he reminded, pointedly. She raised an eyebrow but neglected to correct herself.

"When I was a boy I, all of us actually, we were all taught to look to Captain as our career target should we enter the Colonial Navy," he explained.

"Us too," she agreed, sighing. "Although after all this I'm not sure I would want to be one after all."

"I still don't think this is real. Part of me doesn't believe I'm a real Admiral," Wester said, smiling. He shook his head.

"You deserve to be," she said, proudly. "The moment you chose to follow Tristram's example. You earned the rank of Admiral, you won their loyalty of your crew… and you stole my heart."

"…That's very a very poetic way of saying I *made it up as I went along*," he chuckled. She smiled too.

"With a little help from your friends," she amended.

***

(UE) OPERATION ORION (UE) REPORT: Dated at end. Designation (TS): Top Secret. Status: COMPLETE. Satiah Reports… Initial intel correct, see reference pack one. Space Station Denepher identified at coordinates 6648-2458. Station suggested as possible storage site for information concerning a

secret weapon of undisclosed type or classification of the Balan Administration. Site to be demolished on third rim, second cycle.

Infiltration taken in 20 minute window. 1 subject found, male human, see attached file one. Three unidentified beings attempted to prevent extraction. They failed. Male returned to Earth for interrogation, there were... medical issues. See attached file two containing details and computer diagnosis. Interrogation was conducted, for methodology and results see attached file three and generic anatomy reference pack 2.

New task assigned, while rescued man recovers, second interrogation deferred. Refer to mission file Serial number: 95577784166. See attached file four. Diplomatic endeavour on Yavaicha, security duties allocated. Refer to file four for mission methodology and results. While operating there information fell into my possession by way of research into Phantom files. Linked into Term Search on Denepher for data sifting. Operation Burning Bridge, see attached file five.

Encountered aggressive force on Ionar 12 while refuelling. Colonial Federation agent Tabre was clearly targeting Reed and myself. It is unknown if he had or later gained any knowledge of the weapon during this operation. Multiple confrontations occurred, eventually leading to Federation troops being called in. Intervention from Division 16 occurred; I refer you to Captain Berry's report. Once space ship was acquired, using information from the source we reverted back to initial mission goal. Previous task reassigned.

ITP6/Orion Observatory located at: 0000-0002. Infiltration taken in 8 hour window. KZ15 identified and later confirmed from stolen information. See attached file six. Existence of weapon confirmed. Owner, Sethryn Ring, confirmed. Medical experimentation was occurring regarding the KZ15 exposure ratio, see attached file six. Infiltration compromised, Orion Observatory destroyed by Tabre after he sabotaged the reactor. All aboard presumed dead, excluding Tabre and Finch.

Sethryn Ring researched, see attached file seven. Meeting tip-off received and returned to Earth. Location of weapon confirmed, technical data of weapon confirmed, and purpose identified. See attached files six and eight. Weapon located orbiting Vugarna Four: 3779-9945, enemy base located at Glass Palace. Infiltration taken in 6 hour window. Auction began shortly after infiltration.

Weapon confirmed destroyed. Intervention from cloaked Federation fleet led by Admiral Wester occurred, effective lockdown introduced. After intense negotiation involving the capture and exchange of Ro Tammer by Phantom trainee Carlos, Wester agreed to allow us to leave. The place was then searched thoroughly by Federation troops under Wester's command. It is unknown if they had or later gained any knowledge of the weapon during this operation.

To summarise: weapon destroyed. Plans confiscated and will be archived accordingly, see attached file nine, serial number: 125773744761. Deva defected to Coalition. Conrad deceased. Tabre deceased. Professor Sam deceased. Sethryn Ring deceased. Ro Tammer arrested, see Egill's report. Wester departed for Federation space, see Egill's report. Alex unaccounted for. Finch unaccounted for. Carlos recommended for distinction. Dated. Report ends.

Randal continued to read in a frosty silence, while Satiah and Reed sat opposite him. They had finally completed the mission report and submitted it to Randal. He was now evaluating it. Randal let out a sigh. Satiah and Reed sneaked a sideways glance at one another. What did that sigh indicate? Doubt? Disbelief? Anger? Or just that he was that he'd missed breakfast again? Satiah and Reed were making every effort not to look at one another or behave in a way that Randal may interpret as suspicious. Twenty minutes had gone by while he studied their report before Randal finally looked up. Sethryn was shot in the back... odd way to commit suicide... well that was down to Egill to explain. Satiah suppressed the last question she felt still mattered to the mission. Did Randal have a personal interest in the weapon?

She composed herself and remembered the hundreds of times she had gone through this process before. Until recently it had been Vourne, not Randal, who would have debriefed or interviewed her. All those missions over the best part of a forty-year career as a Phantom. It made her think back to that feeling she'd felt when she had been much younger. The feeling she got when she knew that she could change the course of history. Perhaps even literally. It had been stronger when she was younger and more innocent but even now, despite the cynicism, she could still feel it. She was just one of thousands of agents, one of thousands of missions... there was no reason to think that Randal would be doubtful of her report. And there was no reason to believe that he wanted the weapon for himself. With the KZ15 destroyed... it would be near impossible to reconstruct a working model in any case.

"Catchy name," Randal had said upon seeing what Satiah had called the mission. He hadn't got a response to that comment but Satiah began concentrating fully again.

"It's a shame that Tabre destroyed the Orion Observatory... much could have been learned from the on-board computers," Randal stated, sounding a touch put out.

"*I don't think so*," Reed said, a little severely. "Only more evil could have come from that place." Randal nodded slowly.

"Yes, I suppose you're right about that," he replied, appearing to think very hard about it. Another silence as Randal's sharp eyes stole another quick review of the report.

"Why were you on Ionar 12 in the first place?" he asked, confused.

"We were being chased, it was convenient," Satiah shrugged. *All of that* was just to avoid bringing up anything to do with Ash, Ruby, the Sisterhood, the soil sample, or any of that odd business on Durrith. In a way Tabre had been a godsend, in retrospect of course, anything awkward they could just blame on him.

"The computer diagnosis seems to have missed *a trick* with your prisoner," Randal noted, checking that too.

"*Computers have no imagination*," Reed murmured, in a disinterested tone. Satiah said nothing, going for ignorance.

"I was wondering if maybe Satiah had left out one or two illegal methods of *chemical torture*," Randal said, eyeing her.

"No," she denied, flatly. Randal didn't give her a second look; instead he pointed at the screen where he was reading.

"This whole business at the end though, with *Ro Tammer*... I know you weren't looking for it, Satiah, but this puts you in line for medals you know? She could have caused us all a lot of trouble later down the line, with *or* without the weapon."

"What the hell would *I* want with medals? *They would just slow me down,*" Satiah responded, as if deeply insulted. Reed snorted. "Besides, Carlos did the hard work there, he deserves the recognition."

"Maybe the medals could deflect a shot were anyone lucky enough to hit you," Randal suggested, dryly. "I see from your additional notes that Carlos has made phenomenal progress. Satiah, do you think Carlos is ready to become a Phantom?"

"… Not yet, he did excellently, much better than I thought he would but… After two more missions of that kind of complexity, *if he survives*, he *will* be ready," Satiah said, glad to put in a word for him.

"And Deva? Trustworthy, is she?" Randal asked, casually. Satiah almost smiled; at the time she'd been ready to shoot her.

"Yes," she replied, leaving it at that. A defector could surely never really be considered *completely* dependable. But she was young enough for it to be overlooked.

"Any ideas about Finch?" he asked, a little more seriously.

"No," she replied, bluntly. He sighed and began to scan the report again, seeking the words between words.

"…Are we done here, sir?" Satiah asked, impatiently. "I have a few things I really need to take care of."

"You have *already* released your prisoner," Randal stated, confused.

"*Other* things," she clarified, coldly. She stood decisively.

"Reed, at least will *you* join me for a celebratory drink?" Randal asked, standing.

"Normally *I would be delighted* but unfortunately I have somewhere else to be as well," he replied, evasively. "*Besides we would only get into a barney about Division Sixteen.*"

Randal frowned at them both as they left and called after Satiah.

"Your next assignment is awaiting your attention!" No reply came and the door swished shut. Randal grinned to himself. He'd give her a week to recover, although he suspected she would return quicker than that.

***

Once safely in the transporter, Satiah slumped against the controls briefly, her mind still swirling. They had been lucky, Randal was thorough. To get away with only a few cursory enquiries seemed, to Satiah, *too good* to be true. Reed had been right about doing the report together, each had complimented the other perfectly, seeing flaws and correcting when it counted. And Randal had focussed exactly where Reed intended him to. That had been tense but she'd got away with it again. Somehow. She sat up abruptly, just managing to stop herself going for her gun as Reed got in. He rubbed his hands together, cheerful and off-the-cuff in manner. Like a man expecting some kind of feast. He said nothing to her though. There was a beat of hush.

"*Yes?*" she asked, a little vexed. What did he want *now?* She had nothing against Reed but she was hoping to have a moment to think without being observed by anyone. For a second she wondered if Randal had guessed the truth and he was assembling a team to arrest her.

"I need a lift," he told her, casually. He looked all around briefly as if perplexed. "Have you seen my other shoes?"

"*You don't even know where I'm going,*" she pointed out, a little affronted by his unexpected intrusion.

"You're going to veto your sister's trial," he stated, flatly. She stared at him, shocked and silent inside, but giving nothing away for free.

"How did I know?" he asked rhetorically, grinning a little. "I know your sister's lawyer, a man named Dohead Rens. He's run into difficulties so I thought I might pop along and see if I could help." Satiah forced herself to relax, she supposed with all the secrets she had, this was of the least danger. Nevertheless it was unnerving now that apparently everyone knew it. And, most annoyingly of all, it was forcing her to confront it head-on.

"...I hadn't actually *decided*..." Satiah began, tense. She still didn't know if she would intervene or not! She had been rather preoccupied lately!

"Well, you can decide on the way," he smiled, motioning for her to drive. "Come on, *citius in melius!*"

"What?" she scowled, her hackles rising.

"The sooner the... Look, *just hurry up, will you?*" Reed muttered, apparently getting agitated.

"*Fine*," she growled, hitting the accelerator. They flew amongst the thousands of ships until they reached their destination. It was a short and silent journey, as she concentrated on piloting and he just stared out of the viewport in lofty disinterest. Reed got them into the craft parking zone, close to the entrance. He got out when they stopped but Satiah made no move to follow him. Even after she'd powered everything down, she just sat there as if paralysed. He turned and frowned.

"Come on," he implored, enthusiastic.

"...I've not seen her *in years*, Reed, we were never *friends...*" Satiah explained, woodenly. With a sigh, Reed slumped back down next to her.

He rubbed his face with his hand, pondering what to say to her. Satiah just stared ahead, looking vaguely robotic.

"Have you ever imagined what you would want if this were the other way around? That it was *you* on trial in there for *saving your sister's life* and *she* refused to help you?" he asked, a little irately.

"Actually yes," she replied, seriously.

"Ah," Reed said, as if in triumph. Then he frowned as if he'd only just realised what she had said. "*Are you sure?*"

She turned to face him properly, incredulity in her eyes.

"Reed, *I'm a Phantom agent*, I'm not trained to be *particularly empathic*," she stated, as if that should be obvious.

"I understand that but then *why come at all?*" Reed countered, shrugging as if it all meant nothing. That made Satiah look away again if only for a second.

"*She did what I couldn't*," she admitted, looking ashamed. "She has what I don't... *I'm jealous.*"

Reed could only assume what Satiah looked like when she felt shame, as he'd never seen that expression on her face before. But she looked ashamed. And he'd certainly never expected her to admit any of that so easily. Slowly he reached out and patted her forearm softly.

"She loves you," he stated. She almost whirled on him.

"She doesn't even *know* me and how could you know that anyway?" she demanded, angry.

"*Just take it from me!*" he said, unexpected power in his voice. "She does."

"...If she knew me she wouldn't love me, no one would," she argued, more gently.

"That's up for debate," Reed replied, thinking of Elle and Venelka. "I'm begging you, Satiah… Please help. *Please.*"

She let out another long sigh before giving a curt nod. She got out, pulled her cloak on and hid her face behind the hood. Together they marched into the building. They found the correct courtroom but did not enter. Satiah made her way to a small computer room at the back of the hall area. Every trial was recorded and broadcast, it had been so for centuries. In that little room, it was possible to see and hear everything and yet be completely invisible to everyone else in there. It must be quite a good job, Satiah decided absently. To overlook hundreds of cases for free. Granted they weren't allowed to talk to anyone about it and the place was protected but it wasn't like it was enforced outside much. Then again, if the trial was being broadcast anyway, there was little they could know that would be a proper secret.

They entered and a guard looked up in astonishment. It was a normal reaction as the odds of anyone entering such a place other than the guard himself were very low. She eyed his half-eaten food and a steaming beverage of some sort.

"Phantom Satiah," she growled at him. Her cloak made her instantly recognisable though. He nodded.

"Ma'am," he said, puzzled. "Please, don't mind me." She'd already forgotten he was even there. She advanced over to the window and looked out at the proceedings. There she was. A woman, long dark hair, pale skin… looking scared. Exhibiting a naked sort of fear. Her defence council was noticeably late. She would be worried that

Dohead Rens, *wherever he was*, wouldn't turn up at all. Satiah moved over to the controls and slid her hand onto the palm reader.

Reed smiled as everyone looked around in confusion. A rarely heard automatic announcer began speaking.

"This legal proceeding is now closed with no further action authorised by order of Phantom 48882627, councils and audience will disperse in an orderly fashion please," it said. The guards, as astonished as the people, began to ferry everyone out. Satiah let her own arm drop to her side again. Her sister, maybe out of some kind of sixth sense, stared over in Satiah's direction. There was no way she could see through the screen but the expression on her face was one of puzzlement. Satiah stared into those brown eyes, so similar to her own for a long moment before bowing her head to break the moment. Slowly, her sister was led away to be released.

Satiah did not look up again, just stood there, very still and very quiet. Her sister was free, she could go home and be happy... and be loved. Why didn't this make Satiah feel any better? A new pain suddenly made itself known to her, in her heart... where it can hurt the most.

"How do you feel?" Reed asked, softly. He was still behind her but she didn't jump... she felt too numb to jump.

"...Alone," she replied, in a similar tone. He raised his eyebrows, he knew that feeling well. Soon the room was empty and the cleaning robots began their sweep. Reed left too, talking on his communicator. Satiah just continued to stare at the empty room, her mind roaming free.

***

It had only been a week, maybe eight days since Alex was last there. She'd gone back to barracks. Tabre was dead and, after this had been discovered, she had decided to simply return to where she was supposed to be. She'd brought his body back with her in the hope of returning it to his family only to realise she had no idea if he even had any. She wondered if he had a lover... She wished she'd asked him more questions. But... she'd gone back to discover, of course, that there was no such thing as going back. Not really. She'd even met Admiral Wester... He was a lot younger than she had expected and she wasn't sure why but that bothered her. He had proved himself, of course, but nevertheless her personal doubts remained. Still, he had let her go without question which was decent of him, she supposed.

She'd never left the Colonial navy although she'd given it serious consideration. She examined her fighter craft, unchanged since she'd last been there. She watched all of her squadron buddies milling around, chatting… doing what they always did when they had nothing particular to do. Not so long ago she would have joined in the gossip and probably believed most of it. From now on, now that she knew at least some of the truth, she was no longer interested in military propaganda. Instead she took her craft out for a training flight. It would clear her mind and help her decide… what to do with her life. She would miss Tabre, she knew, but she also knew a man like him could never love her. Not really.

On her own then, dancing between clouds, soaring further and further upwards back into space. There seemed to be such a long way to go in more ways than one. She wondered what would happen to the Federation now. President Raykur was back in control, much to a lot of people's relief. Yet, a lot of people still believed Ro's lies. Alex knew they always would. Her targets were ahead, one moving and the other stationary. She began a swooping approach. Going fast always felt good. She opened fire, watching the bright blue lasers fly in a lightning-like display of destruction. Just knowing that people like Tabre were out there, gave her hope that the masses would not destroy themselves.

***

Finch had been surprised when the Palace was not destroyed at all. Indeed it was most likely still there now for all he knew. Everywhere had been searched by Wester's men. Well, everywhere except where Finch had been hiding. They had taken Sethryn's body away, he wasn't sure why. He quickly realised Ro Tammer had been captured and that realisation made him feel oddly pleased. If anyone had deserved it: she did. He had waited for a long time but eventually Wester had left and the whole place went silent. He'd then taken a ship, not Sethryn's, to leave in. He would get his revenge on Lilith for her betrayal but that could wait. He knew he would be on a few lists to say the least and he would have to remain hidden, possibly for years. But Finch was good at hiding. He would wait in the shadows until it was safe to move.

***

Mensa and Jess, his 'assistants', were sitting there calmly, as Randal entered.

"Ah, you made it, brilliant," Randal said, casually. He didn't know Jess but he understood many Phantoms had long-term accomplices so he let her being there slide. Mensa said nothing, his face hidden in his hood. Randal sat at his desk and sighed heavily. Jess was staring at him, her body language already defensive. This could turn nasty and he would find no joy in it but he had to ask.

"Mensa, how well do you know Satiah?" he asked, seriously. Jess seemed to relax a little.

"I don't," Mensa answered, with a cruel smile. Randal tried again.

"How close were she and Vourne?" asked Randal, still solemn. "That *was* an official question."

"About as close as I was in the end," Mensa remarked, after a moment's thought. "So... not that close at all."

"I was reviewing your mission statement, *badly worded and disappointingly vague as it is*, and I couldn't help but wonder... You said that Vourne had killed himself and we have his body so I know that to be true. Yet *Dasss'* body was never recovered and *he* was the one who was working on Operation Burning Bridge," Randal stated. "He was also one of the last known Phantoms openly allied with Vourne. You said you killed him but that Satiah helped you. So my question is... what was she doing there if she wasn't *with you* and she wasn't *with Vourne?*"

"That sounds like a question *for her*," Mensa shrugged, after thinking about it. "Personally I think she was going after Vourne but never told anyone in case he somehow returned to power. I don't think she believed he'd committed suicide, I know I didn't, *not right at once.*"

"All three of us found Vourne's body together," Jess added. "That *is* a fact. She was with us when he did it, so it is unlikely she was involved."

"But Dasss was killed by...?" Randal asked, curious.

"By someone *opposed* to Vourne," Mensa answered. "There was a lot of shooting in that place at the time, I thought I hit him, maybe I didn't but the fact remains he was dead and I was firing in his direction."

"He wrote the mission report that Satiah *found*. There were only two ways she could have *known about it*, which would be if *she and Dasss* had spoken about it, or *her and Vourne* had discussed it," Randal said, apprehensive.

"I *don't know* about the missions you're referring to," Mensa evaded, adeptly. "The only one who can answer your questions is Satiah herself. As far as I know, she's not involved in the Vourne conspiracy and even if she was it would not be the role of a *major player*. Vourne worked with *a lot of people* and finding links between all of us *isn't hard*. Don't waste a good Phantom *for nothing*."

There was some truth there certainly and Randal leaned back in his chair, in defeat. If there was anything buried there, it was buried well and digging it up again would only cause pain. Perhaps his own… and he knew he trusted Satiah to get the job done. Perhaps it would be better to leave this buried.

"Thank, you've been very helpful, you may go," Randal said, dismissing them. Mensa and Jess left the room without a word. Randal stared at the painfully thin file on his desk. A file he'd been building, a file about Satiah. After all she had done… It just didn't seem right to implicate her in the Vourne conspiracy. And it wasn't that he had any hard evidence of anything criminal. Just a few circumstantial details that looked odd. He set fire to the file and watched it slowly burn on his desk.

He was low on good Phantoms as it was and he needed her. Regardless of what she had done before she had proved herself to him. Too many people had been lost because of that whole affair, some rightly and some wrongly. In the end, like most enquiries, it had just left a bad taste in his mouth. He swigged a glass of his favourite beverage before checking on a new file. This one a little thicker than the last and this file was also meant for Satiah when she came back. Carlos was reassigned to another active Phantom as part of his training and Deva was going with him. This meant Satiah was free again for Randal to assign someone else to. Her next mission was already in that file, as was her new pupil's details. He smiled as he imagined her face when he told her that he felt she could become a permanent teacher. Perhaps that would be punishment enough.

**

Ash and Ruby waited in silence as Reed emerged. He and a much taller man were laughing together and clearly in the midst of a fond farewell. Ash sighed impatiently but Ruby was too tense to be impatient. Reed had gone in there nearly an hour and a half ago to discuss her case with one of his *colleagues*. The other man went one way, away from Ash and Ruby, and Reed approached them with seemingly intentional slowness.

"*Well?*" demanded Ruby, standing. "What did he say?" Ash looked up, curious.

"It seems *a lot* has happened since you ran away," Reed answered, looking perplexed. "We didn't know because we were looking at other things. It seems *your father confessed everything*... You lost your job but no legal action will be taken against you." Ruby was very relieved but did her best, which wasn't very good by Reed's standards, to hide it.

"Oh really?" she asked, trying to act normal. "That's decent news. I thought that would most likely happen but as you know I had to be sure…"

"For *you* certainly," Reed stated, understanding why she'd not asked after her father's fate. She still blamed him. She still held her father accountable.

"I should go and see them… let them know I'm alive," she said, her eyes becoming watery. "I'll be back soon."

"How deep is that love buried?" The question came from Ash and Reed turned to face him. He was still studying her, still learning about humans. Reed shrugged.

"I find your interest interesting," he replied, a little sarcastically. "Be careful, Ash." Ash turned to regard him properly, the very picture of innocence.

"*Me?*" he asked, as if in confusion. "I'm always careful."

"Well, there are only two of us here and your name *is* Ash," Reed specified, irate. "Humanity is *always* on the edge… *Don't* push it off."

With that, Reed strode away, leaving Ash behind. Ash watched him go, his expression thoughtful. It was a pity that the Silver Sphere had been lost and that Satiah hadn't taken steps to effectively neutralise Randal. Yet, Ash was satisfied at the outcome. He knew as fact that the designs of the weapon would only be joining a huge pile of similar things acquired of decades of missions. He had been meaning to head off again, just disappear and continue his odyssey. He hadn't intended to wait for Ruby. Nonetheless here he was, waiting for her.

***

After living in a desert for so long, Carl was having trouble adapting to the icy plateau he was now forced to call home. He had fled the fiasco on Ionar 12. Who wouldn't? Not knowing if they would realise he was involved or not, he'd decided to play it safe and flee before they started looking. He'd thought about using a contact he knew but in the end, fearing he could be traced, he'd just decided to start again. Wrapped in several coats and a cloak, he staggered along through the snow. He had sold most of his ships now and had enough Essps to live comfortably but, unable to do nothing, he'd got himself a job. A guide at a local museum. Secretly he reviled museums, he had nothing against them in principle, he just found them dull, but a job was a job and it paid a fair amount considering. He staggered up the wooden steps to his new home, a giant tin carton of a house with an innate *inability* to remain warm.

Clouds of vapour betraying his heavy breathing vanished into the dark sky as he fumbled for his entry card. In the millions of pockets he had, he knew it had to be there somewhere. He found it at last and entered. Gasping as he tugged off his outer layer of thick skins, he activated the light and closed the door. He locked the door and staggered into the living space beyond. Approaching the stove, he breathed out onto his hands before rubbing them to together to try to warm up a little. He opened the storage area and frowned as he remembered their lack of variety. Hot, thick, veggie stew and... even more of the same type of stew. He sighed, muttering to himself, as he snatched one and activated it. It took thirty seconds to sort itself out into an edible substance.

In fairness it was very nutritious, tasty and filling. Nevertheless, it lacked something. He brewed a hot drink while he waited. As he turned slowly and yawned, he noticed something. He was sure he'd left the place in a much worse state than this in the morning. His boots, for a start, had been all over the place yet now they were lined up neatly in a row. He frowned and blamed it on his bad memory as the food pinged to indicate readiness. He just allowed his other coat to fall to the floor as he moved over to the chair and sat down to eat. This was without question the best part of the day and possibly the warmest. He was so engrossed in his thoughts; he didn't noticed Satiah slip out of the bedroom. She picked up his coat, hung it up, turned and then returned to the bedroom without a sound, not even glancing in his direction.

He sipped his drink as he tried to find a station to listen in to. White noise, then crackles, then some faint music of some kind. Carl was not a music lover by any means but it was nice to have something on… to hide the buffeting windy noises. He continued to eat slowly, glancing down at a book in front of him. He was certain he'd closed it before he left that morning but no, he must be forgetting things again, as clearly it was still open. He downed the last of the drink, enjoying the warmth now in his stomach before placing the empty container behind him on a shelf. Then he focussed on the stew. Satiah re-emerged, took the container swiftly and deposited it into the automatic washing machine. Then, grinning mischievously at his back, she went back into the darkness of the bedroom.

A few minutes later, when he'd finished, Carl stood slowly to stretch. Then he grabbed the empty stew container and turned to get the cup he'd been using to drink out of. It was gone! He crouched to see if it had fallen and maybe rolled away somewhere. There was no sign of it. Mumbling grumpily he moved to the automatic washing machine to place the food container in it, only to find the cup already inside. He opened and closed his eyes a few times before shaking his head and yawning again. He must be more tired than he thought. Then he noticed his coat was on the hanger and stared at it in shock. How the hell? He closed the cleaning unit, activated it and shuffled off into the bathroom, disregarding the matter.

Here too there seemed to be a few subtle differences. Things had changed from when he'd left it this morning. The mat had been straightened. His stuff had been rearranged into tidy squares. He was sure this place had been a tip that morning. He began to undress, deciding that he was too tired to figure out what he may or may not have done in the frozen blackness of the morning. Then he entered the showering unit. Satiah came in, squirreled his clothes away, put fresh sleeping clothes down in their place and departed, making no sound. After washing, Carl was automatically blasted dry by the machine and came back out. He stared in outrage at the clothes waiting for him. Okay, he must be nearing the point of physical collapse.

He dressed again and eyed himself in the mirror.

"*You look rough tonight,*" he growled, at himself. He went out and turned off the light. Now the worst part, that cold, clammy bed. It was supposed to sort itself out automatically when he left each day but then why was it always so cold? He entered the bedroom and tried to turn the light on. Oddly it didn't seem to be working. He swore. Typical! He'd only replaced it two days ago! This was beyond the pale! Knowing he could do nothing more about it until morning he felt his way over to the bed and got in. It seemed abnormally warm. Maybe it had repaired itself or something. He turned onto his side and shrieked in fright. Satiah was lying there, naked on her side, staring at him.

"*Hello Carl,*" she purred, grabbing him before he tried to run. She clamped his mouth shut with her other hand. "I bet you thought I'd forgotten you, hadn't you? *Come here.*" Suddenly he didn't feel tired anymore.

Printed in Great Britain
by Amazon